COLTER'S RUN

BY

STEPHEN T. GOUGH

Colter's Run

By
Stephen Gough

Copyright 2008 by Stephen Gough

Library of Congress Control Number: 2008931869

ISBN 1-931291-71-3

Published in the United States of America

COVER PAINTING BY MARK STEWART

Interior Illustration by Gale Gough

ALL RIGHTS RESERVED
No part of this publication may be reproduced, stored in a retrieval system, or transmitted in any form or by any means without the prior written permission of the copyright owner or the publisher.

STONEYDALE PRESS PUBLISHING COMPANY
523 Main Street • P.O. Box 188
Stevensville, Montana 59870
Phone: 406-777-2729
Email: stoneydale@montana.com

PROLOGUE

THE LIFE AND TIMES OF JOHN COLTER

If the story of the American West and in particular the opening of exploration begins with the Lewis and Clark Expedition then surely its first hero must be John Colter.

Backwoodsman, hunter, guide, explorer, trapper and patriot, John Colter forswore the comfort and security of civilization and even the companionship of a single comrade, striding through a vast unexplored wilderness like a giant of legend. His footsteps left an indelible impression on early American western lore and the intrepid mountain men who followed in his wake. Yet his claims of geological wonderment would lead to outright skepticism if not rejection among his peers, and his finds would not be verified, much less acknowledged, for more than two decades. His audacious episodes and dramatic escapes from the warlike Piegans, the southern clans of the Blackfeet Nation, were a harbinger of the relationships that would set the tone between the white man and the red for generations to come.

Colter left this world barely a footnote in American history. But of those who knew him, General Thomas James best summed up his character. Many years later after a compelling experience with Colter in the headwaters region of the Missouri River, James wrote in his autobiography <u>Three Years among the Indians and Mexicans:</u>

"Danger had for him a kind of fascination... Nature had formed him... for hardy endurance of fatigue, privations and perils... His veracity was never questioned among us, and his character was that of a true American backwoodsman."

Towards the latter part of the nineteenth century, General Hiram M. Chittenden, writing in his <u>The American Fur Trade of the West</u>, elevates Colter... "to stand with the greatest of American explorers."

According to William Ghent's <u>Unpublished Biography of John Colter</u> (1926)... "Of undaunted courage and incredible endurance, his whole career, as far as we know it, was filled with perilous adventure, and his exploits might pass for fairy tales were they not substantiated by the most-reliable evidence."

"Simple, fearless and trustworthy." This is how the late Judge Walter H. Douglas of the Missouri Historical Society sums up John Colter and describes the legendary mountain man as a "typical example of the pioneer Virginian-Kentuckian-Missourian."

Who was John Colter? What did he look like and what of his life before and after the Corps of Discovery and his subsequent adventures in the Rocky Mountains? These are questions that have perplexed historians and interested parties for the better part of the last century and a half. Little is known of the life of John Colter. Virtually no paper trail exists for us to witness or examine. Colter was mentioned several dozen times in the journals of both Captains Meriwether Lewis and William Clark, as well as Corps Sgt.'s John Ordway and Patrick Gass and Private Joseph Whitehouse. And all we have are but three lean accounts of his adventures in the nearly four years spent in the Rocky Mountains after his departure from the homeward bound Lewis and Clark Expedition…

H. M. Brackenridge retells secondhand from Manuel Lisa of Colter's 1807/08 winter trek of discovery and his subsequent fight alongside the Flatheads/Salish against the Blackfeet (_Views of Louisiana and Journal of a Voyage up the Missouri_).

English botanist John Bradbury, who accompanied the Hunt Expedition in 1811, interviewed Colter near his farm in Missouri and wrote of Colter's adventures with the Blackfeet (_Travels in the Interior of America in the Years 1809, 1810, and 1811_).

Writing in 1846, General Thomas James would recall in his _Three Years Among the Indians and Mexicans_ his experiences with the legendary scout in the ill-fated Menard/Henry Expedition of 1809/10. As well as Colter's own personal recounting of his three previous episodes with the Blackfeet (spring, summer/fall and winter of 1808/09). Thanks to James, we have a physical description of John Colter in which he described him as…

"*About thirty-five years of age, five feet ten inches in height and wore an open, ingenious and pleasing countenance of the Daniel Boone stamp. Nature had formed him, like Boone, for hardy endurance of fatigue, privation and perils. Colter had to a supreme degree that instantaneous coordination which was always possessed by those pioneers who lived to die with their boots off and in their own bed.*"

William Ghent, in his _Unpublished Biography of John Colter_ (1926), gives us the only known anecdote of Colter's early years. The story apparently came down through family tradition and in all probability was John Colter's first brush with death…

"*The family was preparing to move, and in the hurry of clearing the house of its contents, some witless assistant wrapped the infant, John, in a feather mattress, tying it securely with a quilt, and rolled the package down the stairway. His mother, Ellen, learning a moment later what had happened, rushed downstairs and tore open the package just in time to save her unconscious offspring from suffocation.*"

We know that Colter was literate. Members of his family in Virginia were well-known local professionals: a judge, doctor and landowners. Research by Colter descendant Ruth Frick has found Colter's signature on a note to a John G. Comegys dated December 12, 1810, several documents – receipt of payments dated May 28, 1811, and a note to William Clark on February 24, 1812. The list of assets in Colter's estate included three history books. However, there is no known record of Colter having kept a journal or any personal letters or correspondence.

What were Colter's qualifications to join the Corps of Discovery? Family tradition states that Colter along with two cousins, the Ray brothers, journeyed to Maysville, Kentucky, on the Ohio River where Colter subsequently enlisted in the Lewis and Clark Expedition. There were persistent legends of Colter's outstanding feats of woodsmanship in the Stuarts Draft, Virginia, area of his birth. He was renowned as a swift runner (a talent that would serve him well). And the journals of Lewis and Clark and Sgt. Ordway made numerous mention of the game Colter supplied throughout the Expedition. Undoubtedly, he was a great marksman as were other members of the Corps of Discovery.

Meriwether Lewis was descending the Ohio River in a keelboat on his way to join Clark in St. Louis when he enlisted Colter in the Expedition on October 15, 1803, in Maysville, Kentucky. Lewis, who was otherwise meticulous about the entries in his journals, had a curious lapse between September 18th to November 11th (Burton Harris – <u>John Colter– His Years in the Rocky Mountains</u>). For whatever the reason, it has been history's loss as to Lewis' thoughts on Colter's qualities and background. However, months before, Lewis, in a letter to William Clark dated June 19, 1803, had already summed up the qualities he was looking for and set the standards for recruitment as... "Good hunters, stout, healthy, unmarried men, accustomed to the woods and capable of bearing bodily fatigue in a pretty considerable degree."

Rich men's sons seeking adventure were specifically excluded by the realistic leaders, as they chose the civilians and soldiers who made up the roster from the frontier settlements and army posts along the Ohio River (Burton Harris). John Colter was such a man.

The captains were faithful to their journals, instructing the sergeants to be likewise. They even encouraged the enlisted men to keep them. From each entry in the journals citing Colter a pattern begins to emerge of increasing responsibility. From the backbreaking work of rowing, poling and cordelling the large fifty-five foot keelboat against the Missouri's inexorable current that seems to be his lot in the beginning of the expedition, more and more the journal entries attest to Colter's prowess as a marksman and a skilled hunter. His name appears thirty-two times in hunting episodes. More and more the assignments given him by his commanders express a certain confidence in his ability to get the job done.

July 7, 1804, Private Joseph Whitehouse enters in his brief journal... *"Towards evening a man espy'd a wolf lying a sleep with the noise of oars racing he awoke stood to know what was a coming captn Lewis shot at him wounded the animal, Colter like ways killed him it was thought he was mad when the first bawl struck him he snap'd at his hind part Roed 15 miles."*

Sgt. John Ordway, September 6, 1804, listed the game that was found drying on a scaffold left by Colter us... *"One buffelow, one elk, 3 deer one wolf 5 turkies and one goose one beaver also."*

Tuesday June 24, 1806... *"Colter joined us this morning haveing killed a Bear."*

Sgt. Ordway, while descending the Missouri River to Great Falls... *"Colter killed a panther and a deer and a rattlesnake."*

Increasingly, the entries mentioning Colter add to the legend of outstanding endurance and vigor. During periods of hunger, when the men were exhausted and unable to go on, only Colter and Drouillard (Drewyer), the half-Shawnee, were relied on to hunt. And not once was Colter listed on the sick rolls.

Burton Harris, in his <u>John Colter – His Years in the Rocky Mountains</u>, cites one episode during the expedition of Colter's stamina, strength and instincts...

"During one difficult passage over the Bitter Roots, Colter's horse fell with him while crossing a creek; both horse and rider were rolled down stream among the rocks for a considerable distance by the rushing, icy water. Fortunately, Colter suffered no serious injury, although, his blanket was carried away by the current. Demonstrating the practical, instantaneous judgment that characterized him, Colter held on to his rifle rather than the blanket. At this stage, a gun was of far more value that a blanket, even though it was early spring in the mountains."

That he was not killed may have been a minor miracle. However, he was soon spending the good part of the afternoon that very same day with George Gibson fishing for salmon.

Hardship, privation and deadly perils were the lot of all the members of the expedition. That they handled these experiences with a certain aplomb was characteristic. Every member was expected to carry his own weight and, with very few exceptions, all performed with outstanding behavior. Colter, no doubt, grew in confidence and ability and in the esteem of his comrades and leaders; the Expedition proving for him the great training ground for his ordeals to come.

On August 12, 1806, as the expedition was nearing the end of its roundtrip journey, an event of great significance affected the life of Colter forever and sent him back into the Rocky Mountains. Descending the Missouri River, Meriwether Lewis came upon the camp of two trappers, Joseph Dickson and Forrest Handcock. The two men were not exactly strangers to some of the members of the expedition and may have visited the Corps at Camp Dubois (Camp Woods) in 1803 prior to the Expedition embarking on its historical odyssey. Handcock probably knew some of the men and in particular John Colter. Joseph Dickson is said to have rescued one of the Lewis and Clark men from a fight in a Cahokia tavern.

Handcock and Dickson had met one another in Missouri in the spring of 1803. Later they formed a trapping expedition, leaving the same year as the Corps of Discovery and traveling up the Missouri River (*John Colter: His Past Rediscovered* Ruth C. Frick and Shirley A. Winkelhoch 1988).

The two men accompanied the Expedition on its descent to the Mandan villages, talking continuously to the enlisted members (Burton Harris). Handcock and Dickson "played up" the success of their beaver trapping, emphasizing the pelts they had cached, but curiously down-playing a narrow escape and loss of property from the Teton Sioux. Handcock and Dickson were low on supplies, lead and powder and must have reasoned that adding at least a third member, one who was familiar with the Yellowstone country, would greatly enhance their chances for success.

By then, Colter had already seen and experienced the rich beaver country of the upper Missouri and its tributaries. He had taken many beaver skins during the course of the Expedition, accumulating a small amount of furs. Sgt. John Ordway's journal contains many entries itemizing Colter's "bag of game and beaver."

He had made up his mind, however, and in the words of Sgt. Ordway… "Colter and his two companions were determined to stay up the river at least two years 'until they make a fortune'."

Colter advised Captain Clark that he had decided to "throw in" with Handcock and Dickson and requested permission to leave the Expedition. Like every other enlisted personnel of the Corps of Discovery, he had signed on for the duration and up to then there had been no exceptions.

Captain Clark did make an exception, and in the entry dated August 15, 1806, wrote… "Colter one of our men expressed a desire to join some trappers (the two Illinois men we met, and who now came down to us) who offered to become shearers with him and furnish traps etc. the offer was a very advantagious one, to him, his services could be dispensed with from this down and as we were disposed to be of service to anyone of our party who had performed their duty as well as Colter had done, we agreed to allow him the privilage provided no one of the party would ask or expect a similar permission to which they all agreed that they wished Colter every suckcess and that as we did not wish any of them to separate untill we should arrive at St. Louis they would not apply or expect it etc....we gave Jo Colter Some Small articles which we did not want and some powder and lead. the party also gave him several articles which will be useful to him on his expedition."

(Aug. 16.) ... we Settled with and discharged colter. (sic)

(Aug 17.)... at 2 oClock we left our encampment after takeing leave of Colter who also Set out up the river in company with Messrs. Dickson & Handcock.

August 17th, 1806, was also the day when Sacagawea, her infant son Pompey, and husband, Toussaint Charbonneau, along with Colter, Handcock and Dickson, bade the expedition farewell. From here Colter fades away temporarily from history into the valley of the Yellowstone and the massive Absaroka/Beartooth Mountains with the two trappers from Illinois. There has been much speculation as to his experiences during the course of the next seven to ten months and his partnership with the two men. But, of the several interviews with him in later years, no mention was made of this particular time in his life.

Nearly ten months later, probably late in June 1807, (Ghent), history finds Colter paddling down the bloated Missouri River, still treacherous with melting spring run-off, in a dugout canoe bound for civilization and St. Louis. At the confluence of the Platte River, regarded as the boundary line between the Upper and Lower Missouri, Colter unexpectedly met the Yellowstone-bound Missouri Fur Trade Company expedition led by the infamous Manuel Lisa. Here he reunites with three of his Corps of Discovery mates; John Potts, Peter Wiser and George Drouillard, all now employed by Lisa.

Manuel Lisa, a Spanish-born Creole from New Orleans and then of St. Louis, had made for himself a formidable reputation among all associated at that time with the fur trade. Writes Chittenden...

"In boldness of enterprise, persistency of purpose, and in restless energy, he was a fair representative of the Spaniard of the days of Cortez. He was a man of great ability, a masterly judge of men, thoroughly experienced in the Indian trade and native customs, intensely active in his work, yet a perfect enigma of character which his contemporaries were never able to solve. His conflicts, as well as the accusations heaped upon him, were all due to his rivals' jealousy of his success as a trader. If, as was charged, he did unscrupulous things, the only difference between him and his detractors is that he was too sharp for them and succeeded where they failed. Like the others, he practiced the code of the wilderness; he practiced it, moreover, with 'unflinching severity,' and his superior skill was chiefly what aroused the ire of his less expert rivals."

Ensign Nathaniel Pryor (late of the Corps of Discovery), in his report of the first phase of the 1807 Lisa expedition, implies that Lisa was… "Treacherous and treasonable."

And General Thomas James, who was particularly vehement in his denunciation of Lisa many years later in his <u>Three Years Among the Indians and Mexicans </u>(1846), writes… "Lisa we thoroughly detested and despised, both for his acts and his reputation."

History has left us without a hint of any inducements made by Lisa to Colter. But whatever the offer, it was enough for him to turn about and accompany this new expedition as an employee. His coming was definitely Lisa's gain. "Here was a man," says Brackenridge, "whose knowledge of the country and the nations (Indian) rendered him an acquisition."

Colter accompanied Lisa's expedition to the Yellowstone, arriving at its confluence with the Big Horn or La Corne as Lisa called it (Harris) in late October/November, 1807. Camp was set up on the south side of the Yellowstone and the east bank of the Big Horn.

Construction began immediately on what was to become the first permanent building in the state of Montana (Harris). The trading post, a log cabin with two rooms and a loft with a later added log palisade, was named by Lisa in honor of his son, Fort Remon (Raymond), but throughout its history it was more familiarly known to the trappers as Manuel's Fort.

Trapping operations were immediately sent out into the neighboring vicinity. But Lisa gave Colter a more critical assignment… to contact the Crows and certain other tribes, presumably the Shoshone and Salish (Flatheads) and inform them of the purpose and location of the trading post and to bring them in to trade. It was on this assignment, a solitary journey through the worst months of Rocky Mountain winter, through deep snow and frozen creeks, forbidding cold and in a totally unfamiliar territory, that began the Colter legend.

Of Colter's trek in the winter of 1807/08, Chittenden in his <u>American Fur Trade of the Far West</u>, wrote… "This very remarkable achievement– remarkable in the courage and hardihood of this lone adventurer and remarkable in its unexpected results in geographical discovery deserves to be classified among the most celebrated performances in the history of American exploration. Colter had now accomplished enough to entitle him to lasting distinction in the cause of geographical exploration."

Brackenridge writes…"He (Lisa) shortly after dispatched Coulter, the hunter before mentioned, to bring some of the Indian nations to trade. This man, with a pack of thirty pounds of weight, his gun and some ammunition, went upwards of five hundred miles to the Crow nation; gave them information, and proceeded from thence to several other tribes. On his return, a party of Indians, in whose company he happened to be, was attacked, and he was lamed by a severe wound in the leg; notwithstanding which, he returned to the establishment, entirely alone and without assistance, several hundred miles."

Nearly three years later and back in St. Louis in conference with William Clark, Colter retraced his movements with Clark who penned on his own map… "Colter's route in 1807." The map and "Colter's Route" which appeared in the Biddle-Allen 1814 edition of "_Lewis, Meriwether, and Clark, William. History of the Expedition, 1804-5-6,_" led William Ghent to conclude that… "Colter had of course no means of determining latitude and longitude, and Clark's maps shows strange distortions. Yet, the location of Jackson Lake is not far wrong (less than a degree too far west, and somewhat more that a degree too far south); while the relation, both as to direction and as to distance, of Lake Eustis (now Yellowstone Lake) to Jackson Lake is shown with astonishing accuracy."

Washington Irving would later write in his _Captain Bonneville_… "A volcanic tract is found on the Stinking River (Shoshone), one of the tributaries of the Big Horn, which takes its unhappy name from the odor derived from sulphorous springs and streams. This last mentioned place was first discovered by Colter, a hunter belonging to the Lewis and Clark's exploring party, who came upon it in the course of his lonely wanderings, and gave such an account of its gloomy terrors, its hidden fires, smoking pits, noxious streams, and the all pervading 'smell of brimstone', that it received, and has ever since retained among the trappers, the name of 'Colter's Hell'."

William Ghent in his unpublished biography on John Colter more than a century later would conclude… "In the years following there grew up on the frontier the legend of Colter's marvelous discoveries. How much he told of what he had seen we cannot know. But doubtless he found, as (Jim) Bridger a generation or more later also found, that it was not discrete to talk much about the incredible things he had seen. Perhaps he hesitated to tell even Bradbury, who makes no mention of these wonders; and what he told Lisa/Brackenridge has to do more with credible things– the mountain ranges, the passes which could be easily traversed, the Indian tribes he had met. Nevertheless, the word traveled from man to man that this Colter had seen an inferno in some mysterious region of the west, an inferno in which no other white man had seen. A place, as Washington Irving described, 'of gloomy terrors, hidden fires, smoking pits, noxious streams, and the all pervading smell of brimstone'."

Contemptuous of danger, John Colter had set out into the unknown, and had safely returned. It is at the conclusion of this unexampled journey that our story begins.

"Hear now, oh Sun, listen all above persons. We have built a sweatlodge as you directed. It is round. Inside the ground is flat, above us the lodge arches from all directions, thus do we represent the world, your own, as you long ago directed; and as you further-in the long ago-said should be done, we now purify our bodies for we ask you something. Let us live! Let us survive the perils!

"Even as you sink behind the mountain tops, your children here gathered will depart for war. They will seek to be revenged on our enemies. They will fight our enemies who live in the south. Now hear our prayer. They will leave their relations and friends to make war with our enemies. Pity them these relatives that they sit not with covered heads in their lodges mourning. Let them go about and say, our young men have gone to make war, and they will soon return with scalps and many horses.

"Hi-yu, oh Sun, look down upon us. Let there be high growing sagebrush to conceal our warriors from the enemy. Teach them to travel like the coyote through tall grass and bushes and in the low places that they be not discovered by the enemy. Now we have built a sweatlodge, as you directed, and here we give you presents-even parts of our body-as a sacrifice. Pity us. Let us live. Let us survive."

Blackfoot medicine man's prayer

PART ONE

"Something hidden. Go and find it.
Go and look behind the Ranges.
Something lost behind the Ranges.
Lost and waiting for you. Go."

Rudyard Kipling: The Explorer

CHAPTER ONE

Spring labored in the high-up mountains of the *Absaroka* and in the valley of the *As-to-pah-oan-zhah*, the Elk River. The long wait was almost over. Warmth was coming. Dreary months of sunless days, of long nights bitterly cold gradually, stubbornly, almost reluctantly giving way, and, yet, it was as it had always been. Seasons come and seasons go, changing little in the life of the nomadic red man in the twelve millennia since his distant ancestors first crossed over to the New World and the last vestiges of the ice age receded to the far north. The culture of the *Absaroka*, known far and wide as the Crow, never reckoned the progress of time by the white man's calendar, but by the vicissitudes of nature and its four seasons, fickle, capricious and unforgiving daily influencing their very existence. And this particular winter-past would not soon be forgotten in the buffalo-skin lodges of the *Absaroka*. A new conflict inevitably ending their way of life was also coming with scant warning to these "*children of the big-beaked bird*," and to all the native peoples of the West. They did not recognize its approach nor heed the ominous signs.

Far to the east across the vastness of the great arid plains to the very banks of the Father of Waters, a different people were also emerging from a long winter's icy grip. They were a race of a fairer hue, equally proud, but profoundly ambitious, possessed of energy and resources hitherto unrealized by the horse-loving nomads of the West. They called themselves Americans, many of whom were looking west, coveting the land of the Crow and their neighbors. They too acknowledged the four seasons coursing their life's annual paths. Unlike their red brethren, though, the land, in fact nature itself, was to be conquered, controlled, harnessed to their advantage and behest, all too often heedless of those who rightfully claimed dominion. To these Americans the *As-to-pah-oan-zhah* was Yellowstone country, the great watershed of the upper Missouri, claimed by international purchase and commercial rights and to hell bedamned the red skinned savages who just happened to reside therein.

The year was 1808. Thirty-two winters have passed since the Colonies, those rebellious thirteen of my father's time, declared their inalienable rights and sovereign independence from the English Crown. The author of their declaration, the Honorable Thomas Jefferson, was still the President of the United States and his lifelong vision of the young republic, "the rising nation, spread over a wide and fruitful land," was slowly, inexorably, coming to pass.

The time of conflict has already arrived, two summers removed since Captains Meriwether Lewis and William Clark and the men of the Corps of Discovery returned from the western lands in triumph to St. Louis on the

Mississippi. With their return, that sleepy little riverport was transformed into a hotbed of economic exploration and adventure, the point of origin for the first fur trapping expeditions to challenge the wilds of the Yellowstone and the upper Missouri River territory, the extreme range of the Louisiana Purchase. The word was soon out across the land setting in motion a national movement unmatched since its inception. It was an optimistic time, rife with expectation, fueled by unbridled exuberance, and of such vital importance to the young Republic bulging at its seams to grow, to achieve, to manifest its destiny. An age replete with audacious, resourceful, courageous men, independent, strong-willed, capable frontiersmen, men who would lead the way west, endure loneliness and hardship, privation and fatigue and for many, ultimately, an ignoble death. All the while tapping its riches, bringing commerce and trade, planting the seeds of an ever expanding American culture.

The first entrepreneur of note and boldest challenger thus far was that most infamous of all the colorful characters to ever sail, paddle or pole the western waterways of the American frontier, the half Spaniard, half Creole, New Orleans born Senor Manuel Lisa. Organizing the Missouri Fur Company, the first American trading enterprise to vie for the beaver riches of the Northwest, Lisa gathered a small armada of keelboats and wooden pirogues, manning them with seasoned crews of salty, veteran French Canadian rivermen, those sturdy *engages* of wilderness riverway lore. And with his trusty *engages*, the irascible Spaniard enjoined a ragtag command of long-rifle toting American backwoodsmen and set sail and pole and oar for the fabled *la Roche Jaune*, the Yellowstone, soon after the Corps of Discovery's return.

By the fall of '07, Lisa had pushed fifty of his backwoods argonauts all the way to the confluence of the Yellowstone and the Big Horn River, *le Gros Corne*, establishing a rough-hewn log stockade, the farthest continental reach of American civilization. He called his cottonwood redoubt Fort Remon.

Fort Remon was the loneliest of lonely, high-walled, honed-log outposts, in a land so remote, so unfriendly, so adverse to the comforts of even the simplest of backwoodsmen. This fort, this wilderness hovel of logs and mud, for all its coarseness, was christened and named with sublime-affection by the Spaniard for his pampered young son, Remon. Yet, to the rawboned men who held no such affectations for Lisa or his blood offspring would forever know this crude trapper's enclosure, derisively, as Manuel's Fort. From this most distant of all outposts, American trappers, the first of the "mountain men" set their metal traps for beaver in the nearby waters of the Big Horn and the Yellowstone in the heart of the land of the *Absaroka*, the proud, the ever-vigilant Crow Nation.

From Manuel's Fort, little noticed by man, civilized or primitive, a lone horseman rode west with the Yellowstone as his guide towards the far-off river valley of the headwaters of the Missouri River. Near mythical, known to the red man and the white alike, was the fabled Three Forks, *the many-come-together* country. This game-filled river valley was fed by three merging mountain-bred streams to create the greater river. It lay secluded, this upper Missouri "Garden of Eden," some two hundred miles from Lisa's stockade, deep within the realm of the feared *Piegans*, the southern-most clans of the warlike Blackfeet Nation. It was from here that our solitary wanderer dared to leap into Western lore.

Yet, he was not the first white man to pass this way. Twice before, albeit briefly, the valley, and for that matter all of the Shining Mountains, had witnessed the fair skin of white European men and heard the sudden, jolting pop of their deadly fire-sticks, their long-rifles, momentarily splitting the serenity of the air. These white-eyes, like wispy clouds casting fleeting shadows upon the land, were just passing through. Yet, they had stayed long enough to marvel and record in their individual journals of wildlife so plentiful, so diverse and so easy to dispatch. Marked in their collective memories the valley's three rivers and innumerable cool, clear running creeks teeming with fat, industrious, luxuriantly-coated beaver, so numerous, so prolific and tantalizingly so, whetting the white men's appetites for the riches from back east that their furs would bring.

The chief of the expedition, a tall dignified looking man known as Captain Meriwether Lewis, gazing-out from high atop a scarred, limestone crag overlooking the valley and its rivers, had dubbed the three waters thusly, duly entering in his journal:

Sunday July 28th 1805… Both Capt. C. and myself corrisponded in opinon with rispect to the impropriety of calling either of these streams the Missouri and accordingly agreed to name them after the President of the United States and the Secretaries of the Treasury and state having previously named one river in honour of the Secretaries of War and Navy. In pursuance of this resolution we called the S.W. fork, that which we meant to ascend, Jefferson's River in honor of that illustrious personage Thomas Jefferson. (The author of our enterprise.) the Middle fork we called Madison's River in honor of James Madison, and the S.E. Fork we called Gallitin's River in honor of Albert Gallitin (Gallatin)

Rested after two or three idyllic days of hunting, of soaking tired and blistered feet, of mending worn buckskin clothing, fashioning new moccasins and leggin's, they packed their dugout canoes with their bags of "possibles," their personal belongings, and proceeded on. With backs straining away, gripping smooth, hand-polished wooden oars, they paddled westward against the stubborn current of the Jefferson fork towards the distant sunset and the faraway, great salt waters of the Pacific Ocean, leaving the valley behind.

Yet, this buckskin-clad band of white men could not stay away. Not when the valley and the great river were their nexus between the East and the West. So they returned the following summer on their way home towards the rising sun from whence they came. These strange "white-eyes" with their pale, ruddy skin were never to be seen again in the *Piegan* people's *Ahkoto waktai Sakum*...their *many-come-together* country.

Never! Never? That is, until that lone rider from Manuel's Fort with that same fair skin was to be seen invading the valley of the three rivers once-again. He was a strangely clad man, aboard a small Crow paint, a piebald mustang, all of thirteen hands high. And he rode that tough, compact pony, sitting tall upon a finely tanned *apishamore*, the red man's saddle blanket of soft buffalo-calf skin that made the rigors of long days on horseback more comfortable, endurable, warming him on cold, chilly nights when his saddle blanket became his bed-roll. Surely, he was not an aboriginal Indian man, not an indigenous native of the high-plains country or the mountains of the Northwest. Yet by every outward appearance, he was aptly suited for this wild, untamed land. A well-setup man, strong of arm, broad of back and thick of shoulder, with piercing pale-blue eyes, wind and snow and cold and sun burnt face and hands, all the while sporting an instinctive countenance that told of one who never stopped looking, listening, sensing all about him. Yes, he was undeniably a white man, yet, with a look and manner of one entirely at ease in the uncivilized West.

Who was this stranger, what kind of man was he to dare trespass in the land of the *Siksika*, the *Blood* and the *Piegan*? Surely, the Great Spirit must know. Was not the divinity, *Api-stoh-toh-ki*, the Creator, the knower of all things? So, why was he here? What sacred quest allowed our curious buckskin-clad paladin to travel so boldly alone in a land of perpetual internecine strife, devoid of friend, ally and favor, risking life and limb, sanity and scalp so far from kin and home? Did he not fear the wrath of the red man? Two centuries of deceit and distrust and bloodshed between the white man and the red demands explanation here and now, or surely our stranger's tale will be short-lived and not so sweet. If only he would talk and tell us his story, let us understand the mystery of his journey unfolding before our eyes.

Voila! Behold, he chances to speak, to shed anonymity before the passage of time and the winds of discord erase all trace of his memory and deeds. For you see I was that man, that solitary wanderer, that lone rider, that buckskin-clad stranger passing through the valley, fording those very same river forks for the third time in as many years. My name, John Colter and my story has no precedence on the Western frontier. I was a veteran of the Corps of Discovery for Northwestern Exploration, the Lewis and Clark Expedition, raised in the Blue Ridge and the Shenandoah, the Valley of Virginia, by Presbyterian

Dissenters of good Scots-Irish stock. And, yes, I was, most certainly, a long way from home, in a time and in a land that had yet to feel the will and the plow of the white race. But, I was no stranger to the wilderness or the red man; life had prepared me well for what I sought to undertake. I was a careful, thoughtful, deliberate man. A man who took calculated chances, relying on the good sense and instincts that the Almighty had given me. *Aux aliments du pays*… I lived off the land, respecting nature, its critters and the wild primitive people who inhabited its uncharted domain. Yet, I could be audacious, bold, venturing forth where none of my kind dared venture before. I was the ol' curly wolf of the high plains and the western prairies, the cock of the walk of the Yellowstone, the king of the Shining Mountains. I could run with a horse, wrestle with a bear, swim with a beaver, and out-cuss, out-wit, out-hunt and out-injun any man, white or red, on the whole wide frontier.

Thickly soled buffalo-hump-hide moccasins, with tanned deerskin leggings and a fringed hunting shirt covered all five-foot-ten of me from head to toe. Along with a monstrously heavy buffalo coat to withstand the cruelest, coldest, bitterest of winters, I wore skins of the wolf and the river otter, along with a most oddly peculiar snarling badger-head contraption perched atop my sandy blond mane in the most menacing of ways. For sure I was a sight to behold, for even the wisest, the most curious of beasts could only gawk and stare in disbelief.

Straddling my lap, carefully perched, was a sleek shooting iron, my Kentucky rifle. 'Twas not a flimsy *fusee*, an English manufactured trade-musket of inferior quality, to be traded to liquored-up red savages of the Canadian wilds so cheaply for skins of any number of God's furry critters. No, my weapon was a work of love. Shaped and balanced by a skilled craftsman, a master armorer, and carried by a man of the frontier with a keen shooting eye and a respect for what he knew this piece was made to do.

Warily, as one should be in a land where one does not belong, I deliberately threaded my way towards the West along that same meandering Jefferson fork as it snaked its way diagonally across the valley of the forks. Horse and rider hugged the cottonwood giants that blanketed its forested banks, taking advantage of the shade and cover and concealment afforded, avoiding the open country of the prickly pear plains and almost certain discovery. Until, just like the Corps nearly three years before, I bared my backside to the Three Forks, disappearing into the northern reaches of the distant foothills of the Tobacco Roots range.

Once beyond the valley I breathed a little easier, sat a little straighter, a little taller. I was feeling something I had not felt in many a month, lightening my mind and my heart's load. The strangle-hold-grip on the thin, hand-polished neck of my long-rifle eased ever so noticeably, loosening taut and callused fingers. My brow, even the palms of my hands stopped sweating altogether, for injun sign had been scarcer than hen's teeth. The trail was clear, no skulking hostiles to contend with, nothing to warn of pursuit from behind or deception ahead. Relief surged, numbing my nerves in the subtlest of ways. I was dropping my guard. I hardly cared. Why not, I was only human. The mind, the senses have to rest sometime. Fatigue, hunger, fear, a man could only take so much before his thinking becomes a mite-too-addled, imagining things that weren't exactly there. Before he knows it the edges of a once sound mind begin to fray, unravel, like the cuffs of an old worn homespun shirt.

Watch yourself, Johnboy! Just where in tarnation do you think you are? Take a good gander around. Smell the air. Taste the wind. Do you feel those tiny hairs on the back of your neck a crawling and a talking? If so, what are they trying to tell you? Go on, ask yourself, what do they know? All right, then, how do they know? Humph! Got you all confused do they? Instincts, boy! You had better listen to those lil hairs. Pronto! Cause things have been a mite-too quiet of late. Something does not exactly smell right. Smell? So, what do you smell? Yeah, that's it, take a good look and a whiff around. Now you got it! You don't have to see a skunk to recognize the offending odor. Injuns on the warpath are just like skunks, you know. Remember you've only your own wits guarding your own ass. No one is covering your backsides. The Corps has dispersed and is long gone. No whining, mind you, cause that is the way you wanted it. Just you and that mangy excuse of an injun hoss you are setting on. Oh, lest you forget, there's that little ol' matter of a thousand scalp-hungry *Piegan* and *Gros Ventre* bucks itching to take your measure the moment you give them cause. So, quit playing the pilgrim. Keep your eyes peeled, your nose and ears to the ground… lest you wind-up a scalpless gutpile fit only for varmints and the like.

SAVVY?

Lord of Mercy, I do. I surely do.

The lonely life has a way of creeping up on a fella and I was no different in that respect to most any other man I had ever known. So far I'd been lucky, my own brand of discipline and instincts watching over me, keeping me alive, one step ahead of the savages and an early unmarked grave. Good fortune continued to be on my side. But, the doubt, the questions never failed to keep pestering away. Why exactly was I here? Remember? Think hard, has it been worth it? Sometimes! Sometimes… I did not rightly know. Often times I was too lonesome to tell, having not been home in five long years and missing loved ones more than I was ever willing to admit.

Maybe I have been out here too long. Maybe it is time to cut my losses and move on while I still have my hair. Maybe, maybe… oh hell, son, you're fixin' to maybe yourself to death. Face it Johnboy this is what you know and what you chose. Nobody held a gun to your head. You know you love this life, these mountain valleys, to go where you want, do what you please, with no one to report to, no towns or nosey neighbors fencing you in, breathing down your neck, knowing your business. No, this was the life for me. I was as free as a man could be. Besides, I promised myself I would stay until I made my fortune. So why the constant doubt, what exactly is worrying you? Can't say? I thought so. Maybe you just like the sound of your voice… or any voice for that matter. Come on man, spit it out if you can or hold your tongue, cause I am sick of listening to it.

How many times have I put myself through this very same thing? Too many I reckoned, ever since I left Manuel's and entered the mountains of the Bear Tooth last fall. It'd been a long, hard winter of looking and searching that I'd put myself through, a journey of questionable merit from the start. But, back then, I never did see it that way. Nothing was too hard or too daunting for me to wrestle. And I sure wasn't about to let others think that John Colter had bitten off more than he could chew. I had my pride and more headstrong cussiveness than any two men ever had a right to be; besides, I'd given my word, made my brags. My name and reputation were riding on it. I wasn't about to turn-tail the moment things got a little hairy or uncomfortable without giving a good account of myself. I'm not blowing my horn, mind you, thats just the way I was, I stood by my word, come what may.

I'd spent the past six months mostly trying to stay warm, fed and alive. Not an easy thing to do, not in the high-up mountain country of the *Absaroka* and the Bear Tooth, unless one chose to sit it out, to hunker down in a warm Crow lodge with a winter-long supply of pemmican to see him through. And maybe, just maybe to cozy-on-up to a tenderhearted, raven-haired young injun gal to cavort and wile away the freezing time of year. But that was a conjugal luxury not to be savored by me this winter past. No, a grander, loftier purpose awaited John Colter, preordained by a chance meeting with a certain Senor Manuel Lisa and his company of hirsute adventurenauts near the Platte River in the early summer of '07.

The broad waters of the Platte loomed large in the minds of the men who paddled by its mouth and knew of its geographic significance to commerce and trade. The Platte was a visible dividing line, demarcation between the furthest reaches of European civilization, a thousand miles to the southeast, slowly spreading upriver from St. Louis towards the Northwest, the high plains and the Rocky Mountains. A point of no return, once crossed, daring those who would to take up the challenge of the upper Missouri wilds.

'Til Captains Lewis and Clark, few whites penetrated past the Platte. *Le Hivernants*, the experienced French Canadian trappers and traders representing the Hudson Bay and the Northwest Company had made deep forays for more then two decades from Canadian strongholds into lands now recently claimed by the young United States. Trading with the *Mandans*, the *Hidatsa* and *Arikara* and even the feared *Lakota*, the *Teton Sioux*, they were a shrewd, conniving, opportunistic bunch as far as the Indian trade went, making life for the newly arrived Americans along the upper Missouri untenable, whenever, wherever the chance presented itself. To be sure, the Northwest Company was a particularly ambitious outfit, aiming for hegemony of the northwestern beaver trade on both sides of the border. In Western Canada, they established Manchester House in 1786 deep in the heart of Saskatchewan and the land of the *Siksika*, the Blackfeet proper. They kept moving farther west, into Alberta, and, by the late 1790's, began establishing a whole slue of trading posts along the North Saskatchewan River: Rocky Mountain House on the Clearwater, Fort Vermilion on the Vermilion River, Forts Edmonton, Augustus, George and Buckingham House. The men who ran these posts, like young Alexander Henry, held few scruples when it came to dealing with competitors. As they looked south towards the upper Missouri greedily eying the Yellowstone country, they were not above conspiring with the *Siksika*, *Bloods* and *Piegans*, liquoring them up with fire-water, arming those savages with factory-made *fusees*, trade muskets, and steel-headed tomahawks. And, as many unsavory events would later reveal, not above turning a blind eye to outright murder and grand theft, bedeviling future American trapping efforts in the region of the Three Forks. Into this hostile mix came Manuel Lisa with his Missouri Fur Company, hellbent on making the Yellowstone his own private beaver preserve.

 I had been heading home, leaving the mountains and the valley of the Yellowstone behind me, with nigh on ten-months of trapping under my belt. I had wandered up and down the high *Absarokas*, strung trap-lines on dozens of nameless streams, and gotten my fill of solitude and near-frozen toes and jerked meat. Yet, I accomplished what I had set out to do; it was time to head home and count my blessings and enjoy my earnings. Three years and then some away from civilization was enough for any man, I told myself. With a whole season's worth of tightly baled packs of prime peltry sitting in my dugout, the last thing on my mind was yet another winter in the Rockies. No sir, corn whiskey and kicking-up-my-heels with flaxen-haired young gals were what were on my mind, and nothing else seemed to matter. Until I ran smack-dab into Manuel Lisa's flotilla bivouacked near the Platte. Lord of mercy, what in hell… Where in tarnation were all these men and boats coming from? And where in the devil were they heading? Something or someone had to of stirred-up an awful hornet's nest back downriver. Something and someone had… the return of the Corps and the story they had to tell. I should have known.

There were friends aboard that little river-borne fleet. Trusted companions from my days with the Corps, men whom I had spent three whole years and more in the most trying of ways. Men whom I thought I would never see again.

No sooner had I begun to paddle towards shore…

"Colter! John Colter!" Someone amidst a crowd of hard-faced, gawking bearded men had called out my name. His voice was familiar, the accent stern, decidedly Germanic. I knew to whom it belonged, right off.

"Humph! Well, I'll be," I said quietly to myself. A coonskin-fleet and now a friend named Pete. I shook my head, "What next?" The day was sure shaping up to be full of surprises.

"Yep!" I replied rather calmly. "That's the name I go by."

The afternoon sun glare was intense, the men, the scene ashore indistinct to my reddened, waterweary eyes. Casually, I looked up and down until I could focus. Then I saw him standing by the rivers-edge, nodding his head and wearing a great big glad-to-see-ya smile.

"Howdy Pete! Sure good to see your ugly face." God, I was smiling, inside and out, and it sure felt good.

"My, oh my, lookee what der 'big muddy' brings down river. Johnny Colter, himself back from der dead and still sportin' that fine mane of his'n. It is you, Johnny, ain't it? Tell me I ain't a seein' things. Tell me you ain't no ghost or river devil of some kind."

"It's me, alright, Pete, in the flesh."

"Ya-hooo! Ya hear that, boys? Help der man out. Help der man out. Drag that log of his'n ashore. Git us a jug, boys, we got some reason to celebrate. Ya-hooo! Wait'll brother Potts gets a load of dis," Pete chortled. "We all have been wunderin' 'bout you ever since ya left us at the Knife."

"Pete, you son of a gun. You sure are a sight for sore eyes. And Potts, too? I might've known you two would be joined at the hip. Where's Potts, I can't wait to see his sorry hide."

"Sorry hide? What do ya mean, sorry hide?" Another familiar voice arose from further aback, a testy voice, brash, impertinent, now heard pushing its way through a growing throng by the river's edge. Men were stepping aside, some smiling, some puzzled, some silent, some whispering, all interested.

"Pete, which one's the polecat with the shit eatin' mouth soilin' my name? C'mon, fetch him out."

Pete smirked, carefully hiding a most mischievous little smile as he turned away.

"Humph! Yer no help ya dumb Lutheran son of a bitch." Potts then turned to my dugout. "Are you the one? You, you in the canoe speak up if you got the balls. That mouth of yourn is trespassin' on dangerous waters, my friend."

I sat motionless, not a word out of my mouth.

"I thought so. Chickenshit, huh! From under what gutpile did ya crawl from? Speak up, stranger. I dunno take kindly to anyone runnin' their yaps and thrownin' my name around like they wuz my friend or kin or some such. So speak up… or shut up or I'll…"

Potts stopped abruptly and stared hard. Something about the man in the dugout canoe was beginning to bestir memories. "Say, who are ya? Great day in the mornin', my eyes must be playin' tricks on me. Can it be? Great jumping Jehosaphat, George Rogers Clark and Dan'l Boone, is that who I think it is? No! Can't be? Yeah! Got to be! My, oh my, John Colter, man of mystery, wild injun lover gone to the mountains, swallered up like ol' Jonah without a trace. Wait! Let me get a closer look. Sure looks like him, but I got to be certain."

Potts makes a big to do sniffing the air in mock earnest. "Ugh, what a stink! Phew! That does it! Hell, got to be… nothin' reeks worse than a pig farmin' hokie from Blue Ridge country."

Potts could continue his charade no longer… a wide grin breaking out over his face like rosy dawn on the prairie. "Damn if this don't beat all. Pete, stop yer foolin', I know yer holdin' out. Can ya believe yer eyes!"

"I do!" said a still smiling Pete Wiser. "Recognized him right off."

"Yep, it's me, all right, Johnny, none t'other, man of mystery no more," I piped in.

"Well, I'll be a son of bitch," said Potts shaking his head. The joy in his eyes soon spilled over, his face radiating aglow. "God damn it's good to see ya!"

It was a happy reunion that breezy day by the Platte and Mizzou, the backslapping, handshaking, bear hugging kind of affection that only the best of old long lost friends could share. We spent half the day laughing and talking, jacking our jaws, reminiscing about old times and ol' friends, the Captains and the men, the adventures we shared and the word on the River. I had an awful lot of catching up to do. And then the attention gradually shifted solely to me. I figured it would, sooner or later, the tanned skins in my canoe being the object of many wandering eyes from the moment I pulled ashore.

"Nice furs you've got thar, John, mighty nice," noted Pete Wiser, of a sudden, casually indicating the peltry sitting conspicuously in my dugout. Pete was nodding his head, looking at me in a way that implied more than just mere casual interest.

I liked Pete. He was a careful man, accustomed to quiet talk and deliberation, frugal with words and most always direct to the point. You could bet your poke Pete wouldn't miss a thing.

"Yeah, they sure are," piped in Potts, jabbing a stiff finger towards the contents of my canoe, all the while counting every single tanned hide therein. "Damn, you did good. You've been right busy since we seen you last, must be a small fortune tied-up in those packs." He kept staring at my peltry, all the while you could see his mind doing the calculating, adding up silver and gold. "Hope to God," he added rather testily, "you left some for the rest of us backwoods paupers?"

Johnny's gaze turned from my canoe and came to rest squarely upon my eyes. He was prodding me with his stare, impatient for an immediate answer. He had that way about him, nettlesome like a tick or a chigger, sucking the patience right out of a man. What he wanted right then was readily apparent, and he wasn't about to be put off by any fanciful smokescreen I could conjure up. And then he broke the silence, asking, or should I say, demanding, "Where'd ya git 'em, Johnboy? Don't be holdin' back none on yer old pard, this is Johnny Potts yer talkin' to."

Listen to him, will you? Up to his old tricks, as dogged as ever. He won't give me a momen't rest. Might as well spill… "I was wonderin' when you'd get around to it, Johnny P. I guess you two boys have me over a barrel. Just keep yer buckskins on, there's a whole lot more beaver to go around where those skins come from."

Well, why not, I told myself, you've had your fun, you've trapped enough beaver to be comfortable for a month of Sundays; those skins sitting in that canoe of yours are worth a tidy sum. So share the wealth. You've known all along that you couldn't keep the Yellowstone to yourself. Look at those two pards of yours itching for you to open up. They're rarin' to go. They want the same chances you wanted. You can't blame 'em; you wanted to make your own mark, too. Remember? So what's the rub? You're heading home, right? You've had enough, right? Oh, I see, you just didn't think it would come so soon, did you? Well, it has, so you'd best get use to it. You might as well admit it; your days roaming the Yellowstone country free and clear have come and gone. These boys and the next wave and the next will overrun the Northwest before you know it. You might as well tell 'em what you got to tell 'em and be done with it.

So I lit right into it, all the while a growing crowd of bewhiskered trappers gathered around me as thick as fleas on a hound's behind. They were a slackjawed bunch to be sure with a wandering curiosity to boot. One thing only was on their minds, the skins in my canoe and the waters from where they were fetched. I had their ear, all right, but it didn't really matter for all the evidence they needed sat before them, and nothing talked louder and clearer about a trapping man than the skins he had to trade. And in those days the hide of the beaver was the surest way to fame and fortune on the

Western frontier.

While I talked a certain diminutive man of obvious, Latin extraction listened quietly off to the side. Unbeknownst to me he studied my face, my eyes, my gestures and expressions. Listened with keen interest, intuitively sensing confidence in my voice, the veracity of my words and the strength of my spirit. He was a man who knew men well. Knew hot air and smoke and deception when he heard it. And he had heard it all before, from one end of the territory to the other. Just as certainly, he knew when a man was speaking with a straight tongue. He liked what he was hearing, unobstrusively nodding his head appreciatively. He knew of the various places I spoke of, studied them from sporadic injun and trapper accounts for years from afar. His face fairly lit right up with a smile with each familiar telling. This is it, he told himself. This was what he had wanted to hear, apparently from the man he had waited to hear it from. You see, he knew exactly where he was going and what he aimed to do. And all along he'd been searching for a man to guide him there. *Voila!* I appeared at the River Platte like an answer to his prayers, a man he could depend on, a Corps veteran, reliable and resourceful. A man who'd been there, survived its many dangers, knew the land and the Indians that roamed and ruled it. A man regarded with trust and confidence by the "highest of the high" on the River, Captain William Clark, himself. And what's more, a man who wasn't afraid to go it alone. He admired grit and spunk, having a gutful of it himself. He was comfortable around an equal, a man whose wit and courage and resourcefulness he could relate to and respect. Finally, hearing enough, it was his turn to do the asking. He was not a large man, and standing behind the mostly taller, broadshouldered trappers he had gone unnoticed by me. When he stepped forward, all other voices were suddenly quieted. It was a moment I did not fail to notice.

"Mssr. Jean Colter, I have not had the pleasure," he said, offering his hand in greeting.

"Nor I," I replied, somewhat startled. "You, sir, have me at a disadvantage."

Pete Wiser stood right up, immediately stepping forward and introducing the two of us. My old friend was never a man to shirk his duty or his manners or fail to recognize an event in the making. "John, this here's Senor Manuel Lisa. He's der boss, honcho of dis here trappin' concern. And der man responsible for puttin' this whole dang shebang together."

I sensed the sudden gravity in Pete's voice, emphasizing the Spaniard's obvious standing. The look in Pete's eyes said it all, he was hoping the two of us would hit if off. But, why, what mischief was he up to? I smelled a rat right then, albeit a friendly one. Pete, are you trying to keep me from heading on south or what? Whaddiya got up your sleeve, ol' buddy? All right, I'll call you...

"Pleased to make your acquaintance, Mr. Lisa," I said, reaching out and grasping the Spaniard's hand. He was not a big man, shorter than most, about five foot four or five I'd say. His fingers were slight, his hand almost delicate, belying a firm, callused grip, no doubt accrued from years of working riverboats and Mississippi wharves and the manual business of the trade. Small in stature, but that's where any importance of size ended. I could sense an unusual energy radiating from him, instantly realizing that this little man was a veritable wildcat not to be trifled with. And putting together an enterprise such as the one he now commanded meant he was a man to be reckoned with, a man with a giant vision and a wit to go along with it.

"I have heard a great deal about Mssr. Jean Colter from my good friend, Mssr. Capitan Clark."

Lisa was looking at me straight in the eye, sizing me up, all the while I was doing the same. Kind of tickled me, like a duel between two old scratch and claw fighters staring each other down, looking for an edge, a sign of a weakness or strength, to take advantage of or to stay shy of. It took a moment to break our eye to eye embrace, but there he was, returning my smile, seemingly pleased at the kind of man he had just met.

"Cap'n Clark's a good man," I responded, "none better that I know of." And then I added as a gesture to smooth the way. "A friend of his... is a friend of mine."

"Ahhh, *certainement*! But of course, I like that, straight to the point, no misunderstanding. Better for business. Better for me. Capitan Clark said you are a man of your word. He speaks of you and your mutual experiences with admiration and fondness. He says you are a man whose judgment on the trail is to be trusted and believed."

Lisa was not a loud or a loquacious man. He spoke softly, deliberately weighing his words. I sensed he was not a man to jawbone, to speak idly or engage in small talk with lesser beings. He was a man of purpose, of clarity, grasping intuitively exactly what he was searching for and recognizing it the instant it appeared. It was soon apparent to me that this Mssr. Jean Colter had that certain something he was seeking. So I decided to test the waters and see where they led.

"I'm flattered that Captain Will still remembers my name. That's the kind of man he is, I reckon. He speaks with a straight tongue. Every man this side of Charlottesville, includin' President Tom Jefferson knows it to be so. His word can be trusted. As for me, well, what I've done don't exactly 'mount to too much. Least not as I see it."

"Oh, *mon ami*," Lisa responded, chuckling, "you are *tres modeste*. I was told to expect this of you. That your deeds speak louder than you are willing to admit… that even the impossible somehow trifles when placed in your capable hands. This humility you wear fits well. A wise man knows his limitations as well as his strengths. It is a quality rare among your boisterous countrymen. But, others have also spoken astutely of you. Your words carry weight and your sojourn to the Yellowstone has quietly drifted down the river, even when you thought yourself anonymous. It takes a bold man to do what you have done. I would like to hear more of these *aventures* of yours. And then maybe we can talk of the kind of business that concerns us both."

"Huh!" Was all I could manage to say, but, I was thinking quietly under my breath… whoa, Johnnyboy, this little senor is moving way too fast for an ol' backwoods knothead like yourself. He has something up his fancy sleeves. You had better keep your cards close.

Indeed, I must have looked somewhat taken aback. It was hard to imagine reputable people of substance talking about John Colter or Jean Colter, as Lisa put it. Hell, I was just a lowly buck private, never looking to make a fancy, highfalutin name for myself. I was beyond that kind of self-foolery. For the most part I enjoyed my solitude, though I did miss my family and some of my old friends and, God knows, a good woman to have around would have certainly taken the edge off of a lonely life. And if people wanted to know about my business, well, they could keep it to themselves for all I cared. Now, people talking about John Colter. Hah! That'll be the day.

"*Oui, exactemente,*" Lisa said, as if reading my mind. "You don't believe it, do you? Well, *mon ami*, your name is the-talk-of-the-river, though most, I'm sad to say, believe that *malheur*, misfortune, has befallen you. Unfortunately, with the good news coming down river, also comes the bad. Ahhh, but in your case, I'm so glad to see those fears have been proven false by your most timely appearance today. You have shown *audace*, a great boldness challenging the wilderness by yourself. Few men have the *cajones* or the wherewithal to pull it off. No, Jean Colter, this alone says you are *le grand homme*, a man to be reckoned with. And little that occurs on the Missouri escapes my attention. Providence, Mssr., and the River have delivered you to me. Believe it! I have, no… our enterprise has need of you, of your knowledge and experience of the Yellowstone country and the savages. I would like to put that *savvy* of yours to good use," Lisa suddenly paused, letting his words sink in, and then adding quite succinctly, "to both our benefit. If you agree, then let us sit down and discuss our *mutuel petit ami… le beaver* and how we intend to acquire them."

My head bobbed like a canoe in troubled water, the Spaniard gave me much to think about, all of which was coming on way too fast. After all, we had just met up. I hardly had time to catch my breath. I'd been deadset on cashing in my furs and drinking my way downriver to St. Louie and beyond. Hell, as far as I was concerned, I was long overdue for a little sinning. Besides,

I had friends to look up, renumeration from the Corps to be collected and just maybe to find me a fine looking young gal to spark and court. The last thing on my mind was turning around and heading back upriver to the Yellowstone. And Lisa, apparently, had more in store for John Colter than running traplines and nursemaiding a company of tanglefoots. My mind spun like a top. Now, damn, why did I have to go and meet up with his crew? What to do? I wasn't quite so sure now. And the Spaniard knew it, too. In fact all the boys did and they weren't about to let me say no. The whole dang bunch of 'em was staring me down, awaiting my reply. What else could I say or do?

"Go on, I'm listenin'," was all I could manage to say.

By early October, we reached the mouth of the Big Horn.

"Johnny Colter!" The voice was Pete Wiser's.

It was a fair autumn morning, one day removed from our arrival. Sunrise revealed clear blue skies as the rosy light of dawn fell on bustle and commotion. Men were early at work, felling cottonwoods, digging trench-lines and laying out the stockade's perimeter, unloading the boats, stacking supplies. Hunters went out ranging for miles about seeking game and bringing in fresh meat. Firewood was gathered. Fresh water lugged to the new site. Months of tedious river travel and outright boredom were at an end. Idle days on end dreaming of setting traps and making fortunes were about to be put to the test. Manuel and his fort were fixin' to open for business.

I'd roused myself long before sunup, itching to get going, to get my legs back into my walk, to get the months of stiff crick from boat travel out of my back, shoulders and arms. Toting my rifle, I had climbed the bluffs to enjoy the morning view and get my bearings.

"Yo, Pete!" I called back. "C'mon up and join me."

"Can't, too much to do and no time fer lollygaggin'." And then his tone changed a-mite, adding a cup of urgency to his morning brew.

"Manuel wants to see ya right now down by der river. Pronto fast! Says it's time fer ya to earn yer keep."

"On the way." I took one last long look and headed on down.

Lisa wasted little time. Up before first light he set the camp in motion, cracking the whip so to speak. He was an easy man to find among all those burly engages and bewhiskered trappers. Fastidious to a fault, refined even in the wilderness, he held none of the rough and tumble characteristics of the profession he chose to master. As for attire, he never did cotton to sporting buckskinwear as the rest of us humble backwoods souls. But he tended towards a prediliction to finely tailored linen coats, weather permitting, ruffled-collared blouses and the like and knee high black leather boots… gentleman's riding boots. But, that was about as far as his genteel side allowed him to go.

Dealing with the hired help, his acerbic tongue could instantly lash-out and cut even the stoutest, saltiest of his men. His reputation of rigid discipline and punishment on the Missouri and the Mississippi had benumbed more than a few hardbitten toughs. This morning proved to be no different. I heard his distinctive Latin-whine long before I saw him by the riverbanks supervising the unloading of supplies and barking his displeasure at a particularly inept *engage*.

"*Sacre bleu… Pendejo! Une telle insouciance!* You careless Cahokian idiot. It'll take six months to replace those instruments if you break them. You'll pay for the damages out of your thick Gallic hide."

Flogging was the usual sentence of the day and no one doubted Lisa's will or capacity to carry it out. I had seen the effects administered by the lash a time or two coming up river. It was never pleasant, always morale crippling and maybe even repugnant to a young Virginian's righteous sense of justice and fair play. And just this moment I sensed the chill, the fear in that *engage's* eyes as he redoubled his efforts to please his master.

I stood by quietly for several moments watching the diminutive Spaniard, seeing another side of him, one that left me rather cold. And then he noticed me, his demeanor suddenly changing from crass to charm, instantly beckoning me forward.

"Come, come… Jean Colter! We must discuss your journey." With an upturned palm he motioned me to join him by a row of stacked wooden crates. "*Veuillez vous asseoir.*" Momentarily dismissing the clumsy engage, Manuel was his pleasingly cordial self once again, exuding a certain refinement… a New Orleans-bred gentility, I presumed, characteristic of the few fops that I had occasion to observe downriver in my younger days. Dandies, they were, sophisticated, outwardly courteous and seemingly dignified, conscientious in dress and habits. I was not taken-in by it, though. I'd been around long enough to recognize that a snake could inhabit fancy duds and wear phony airs. Hell, wasn't that what I just saw moments before? Then Manuel turned his back to me for a split second. I chanced to see a wicked little dagger stuck in the rear of his cummerbund, a wide crimson waistband near blood red. That blade wasn't exactly some kind of fancy letter opener, handy for accounting and bookwork purposes. No, uh uh! That waterfront shiv was for much nastier, bloodletting work. Humph! No doubt he knows how to use it. I thought to myself, the lil' senor conceals a sharp blade to backup that bark of his with bite, steel bite, all right. Well, I shrugged, fingering the hefty head of my own tomahawk, out here he'd be a fool not to.

But, now it was time to talk and the Spaniard went right to it. "The Snakes, the "bird woman," Sacajawea's people… you say you can find them? That they will talk with you?"

"Done it before, reckon I can do it again. Trick is findin' 'em. The Crow say they winter southwest of here a couple of hundred miles or so. They make it sound easy to get there… but somehow I doubt it. A lot of tall mountains 'tween here and yonder, I reckon. If not, I can always loop back and pick up the Corps' trail from '05. A might longer way to go, but I figure I can find it easy enough. As for the Shoshone, I suspect they might be willin' to trade, judgin' by the way they eyed our 'possibles' and such. Not much to worry about, Snakes are friendly enough. Of course, one never really knows what an injun is thinkin'. Still, I like my chances. I can do it."

"Bon! This country to the southwest, what do you know of it?"

"Nóthin'!" I replied. "Nothin' at all! I'm goin' strictly by Crow say-so. I'm hopin' their way's a shortcut, especially with winter comin' on. If not, like I said, I've got my options."

"Be wary, *mon ami, le savages*, even the Crow are not to be trusted fully."

"No doubt!" No surprise there, just about everything an injun has to say, especially when it came to time or distance or location, is to be taken with a grain of salt. They tend to look at things differently than the white man. It's a fact, half my life spent running around on the frontier had taught me just that. Lisa, also, knew it all too well. A man lived to trust his instincts and his rifle and little else. Still, I listened to what the Crow had to say, put it in my memory's book of possibilities. It was always a gamble; you could never be quite sure. Take the Mandans back at the Knife. They'd told us about the Great Falls and we found them, more or less where they said we would. They also said how easy it was to cross the Bitterroots, a simple one or two or three-day hike, with little difficulty. Bullshit! Those mountains wore us down to a frazzle, the whole lot of us near to starving the whole danged way. It was a bitter pill to swallow and a hard lesson to learn. A man learns if he is lucky, lives to stay alive another day. Like I said, trust your instincts and your rifle and little else.

"It's worth a try," I said, finally. "Besides, there's more than one way to skin a coon. If nothin' else, I can get a good look at the lay of the land. Won't hurt to know what's on the otherside of these mountains. Might be prime beaver country. Who knows?"

Lisa listened, impassively watching my face, quietly taking in what I had to say. "*Bon! Bon!* Of course, you are right. I am sure you will succeed. But, in any case, do not limit your search to the Snakes, solely. Le Flatheads! Le Cho-punnish… Le Nez Perce! I understand they are of considerable means and lands… rich in beaver. Rich in beaver, Jean Colter, le Capitan Clark recommends them with ardor."

"Yep! Big Red's got good reason to. They're plenty smart as injuns go.

Well heeled with more ponies then you can shake a stick at. And those mountain streams of theirs are loaded with beaver. Yeah, be a good trick to get 'em in here. But, I'll find 'em, work a little magic, God willin'. Make no mistake, those people are natural born swappers… can talk the bark right off a tree."

"Bon! Time, *mon ami*, time is of the essence. I have not forgotten your cache of beaver back at le Platte. Beautiful furs! Exquisite! That is *exactamente* what I want from these savages. Beaver. You must make it plainly clear to them that I will not accept inferior summer skins, only the richest of pelts, thick, luxurious from the coolest times of the year, well able to command the best prices on the Continent. *Comprendre*, Jean Colter?"

"Gotcha, clear as mountain water," I said, nodding my head. "That about do it, Manuel?"

The Spaniard paused for a moment, twisting the end of his thin moustachios, deep in thought. His breaths, his heaving little chest more pronounced and a mite heavier than a moment before. "Le Blackfeet. What say you about those savages, Jean Colter? Do we risk it? Do you think they're worth the trouble? Or perhaps they're more trouble then they're worth?"

"Whew!" I sighed aloud letting out a voluminous whoosh of stale air. "Hell, I don't rightly know. I've been kinda dreadin' them injuns the whole dang time I've been here. Figured I was lucky. Sooner or later, luck runs out. Sooner or later we'll find out, I reckon."

I sat rubbing my chin whiskers for several long minutes contemplating Manuel's last probing questions. Now pondering those particular red devils gave a man something to think about. From all that I'd gathered, the Blackfeet were just too unpredictable a race, not to be trusted, but avoided and given a lot of room if at all possible. Yet, smack dab in the middle of their land lay some of the richest beaver country in the whole dang United States of America. The temptation to work it would be overwhelming, but like Manuel was now implying… maybe more trouble then it was worth. I thought about it awhile longer. Looking ahead down the road, I sensed that conflict might prove inevitable as far as those savages were concerned. Sooner or later it was an issue that would have to be resolved. But for now…

"Like I said, I don't rightly know. I think it's got to be one way or the other. If I take up with the Snakes or the Flatheads, I don't rightly see how I can countenance approaching the Blackfeet. There's too much hate between 'em from all that I've heard. The Crow have told me as much. And the Mandan downriver warned us to 'watch 'em' long before we ever got up here. You could see the fear and the hate in their eyes just at mention of their name. Besides, Cap Lewis has already spilt first blood and started the feud a rollin'. You know the story. And you know they're still smartin' from it? You can bet your hide they'll take it out on the first white man they get their hands on. I'd hate to be that unlucky son of a bitch."

Shuddering at the thought, I added shortly, "Besides, all that I've been hearin' from here-abouts is that the Blackfeet do business solely up in Canada with the English traders. Knowin' the Hudson Bay and that other redcoat outfit, they won't cotton to any newcomers from the States coming in and stirring up what they consider to be their pot."

What I had to say seemed to be sinking in. I continued rubbing my chin whiskers right down to bare skin. Lisa waited patiently, quietly watching me, all the while unconsciously rubbing his own little stubby chin. It wasn't hard to see that he was hoping I would change my mind. He was looking to trade with every tribe he could and the Blackfeet surely had the potential to help him corner the trade. But, there were just some things you couldn't do and some people you couldn't do it with, no matter how hard you wanted it to come about. I hoped he saw it, that greed wouldn't cloud his judgment. He was too smart a man for that. Still, I didn't want to close the door all the way.

"I don't know," I said again. "Risky business at best. I guess I could see how this thing plays out. I mean, you never know how things are gonna go with any injuns." Then I added. "Tell you what… I'm game 'til events prove otherwise. If I can find a way to approach 'em without gettin' my fool scalp lifted, I will. That's about the best I can do for you for now."

That seemed to please him. "*Bon!* Fair enough. I cannot ask for more. We shall trust your instincts… just like le Capitan Clark suggested. But, remember… time, time is of the essence. You must convince them. Bring some small trade goods to entice the savages, some colorful trinkets for their squaws, mirrors, beads and such. Show the men your tomahawk and your skinning knife… they are fine weapons we can furnish them for a fair trade. I will make sure that you have plenty of powder and lead for your journey. Pick out one of the little Crow ponies that Mssr. Rose brought in and make ready to leave on the morrow. Winter will soon be upon us… we've wasted enough time already. We shall be ready for business upon your return, all the business you can bring in. So make the most of it, *mon ami.*"

We stood up, with Lisa looking at me squarely in the eyes. He offered his hand and I took it. His face was devoid of expression, but the tone in his next utterance left little doubt as to what he expected me to accomplish… "I trust you will not let me down?"

I returned his look directly, nodding my head. "I'll get it done, one way or t'other."

"*Bon!* Then we are agreed." There was nothing else to be said. He had heard what he had wanted to hear. "*Au revoir, Jean Colter! Que Dieu soit avec toi...* May God be with you."

Lisa had left little doubt of what he expected of me. His parting words, "I trust that you will not disappoint me," weighed heavily on my mind. Failure was not suffered easily by the Spaniard, results were what he was paying me for, and injun trade was what he wanted. He was a hard driving, whip cracking sort of man, used to getting his way. He didn't seem particularly concerned about launching a one-man search for injuns who didn't particularly want to be found, at least not while holed-up in their remote winter camps. His was a tall order no matter how I looked at it. But, I was used to tall orders. Besides, parlaying with the Shoshone and the Flatheads rather intrigued me. I liked those injuns; they were simple, easy folks to get along with. I began to look forward to meeting up with them once again, enjoying their hospitality and maybe even renewing an old acquaintance or two. Shades of the Corps, by now I had convinced myself that the trail ahead had the look and feel of an adventure with my name on it, doing what I do best.

I rode away the following morning with the season's first falling snow. Change was in the air. September had been stifling, the air hot and dry and unrelenting. Early October had been no bargain to be sure, offering little respite until this the very morning of my departure. Cooling weather came on of a sudden that day as welcome as a newborn babe. Nature was smiling on me and nothing else mattered... or so it seemed.

Little had I foreseen what lay ahead to daunt my task for the fall in the Rockies and the northern latitudes proved short-lived that year, and winter deigned to be long and hard and cold. I rode forward, undiscouraged, to a land no white man had ever stepped foot in before; a mountainous, snowbound, frozen world, seemingly devoid of life, abandoned by all, save the hardiest of creatures. Week after numbing week I kept to an unfamiliar trail, duration and distance inexorably adding up to months of mounting frustration and hope-denied. And through it all not one sign lit the horizon, not a single track or vestige of man was to be found.

At some point I began to lose track of time, each day passing as gloomily, as unrewarding as the next and the next. Tiny cracks appeared in my veneer questioning my resolve. I was slowly weakening, and I knew it. Like I've said, I'm only human. I could feel the letdown coming. The path, the task I chose was not an easy thing to do. I had to remain strong, keep my head and keep moving. I urged myself to "stay the course," don't be discouraged, the Snakes are out there, you will find them. You'll see, give it time. You are John Colter, you know. Lisa, the mission, the journey have challenged your sacred reputation. Don't get soft on me now... damn it. Show your stuff, man. That a way, Johnny, I knew you had it in you.

There's something about being alone in the wilderness, getting to know yourself in a way that you never would have otherwise. It tests your mettle, challenges your determination and ingenuity and yanks oh so subtly on every fiber of your mental and emotional well being in every conceivable way.

But, I was really little different from most other men. I, too, needed an occasional positive sign to keep me going when everything about me said otherwise. Yeah, a man has got to know his limitations and when to cut his losses. And how often had I heard that before? For nothing that whole winter-long trek seemed to go right. The trail, the way ahead, the search for the Shoshone had gone awry from the start. But, one thing had remained constant since I first entered the mountains, the incessant cold. It had made little difference whether I was walking alongside my mount leading him by the reins or riding atop his narrow back, sitting on a warm blanket, bundled up in every kind of animal skin imaginable. Steadily, the chilblains had worked their way through the thickest of my furs, penetrating my own hide, through my bones right to the heart of the marrow. There was just no escaping it. It was there to stay 'til spring and well I knew it. Fortunately, it came as no surprise. I'd weather it, I knew I would as long as I used and kept my head. It was an uncomfortable annoyance best ignored. Rigid discipline and sound practices would overcome; travel slowly, take my time, be methodical, waste little energy, avoid getting wet whenever possible, stay out of the wind, find good shelter, get plenty of rest and eat meat, plenty of meat to fuel the internal fire.

Then one particularly gray day I sensed a sudden change in the air and the land, something I couldn't quite put my finger on. I had come out of the mountains finding myself on a more or less flat, arid, sterile stretch of ground. Off to my left paralleled a rather swift-moving stream coursing through a narrow canyon. To my right arose a strange, almost heart-shape mountain, standing eerily alone. There was a deathly silence to the place that was not quite quiet at all. My every instinct stood on edge, warning me to go around, to avoid this place and find another way. And yet, my curiosity was great, I continued on. Ahead to the west, rising up from the ground, I could see a large bank of low-lying clouds that I took to be morning mist, the cold air meeting warmer river water, giving rise to a wintry fog, not an unusual sight, not at thirty below. But, the steam, the vapor, the foggy mists were everywhere to be seen to the front of me, a frigid veil hanging eerily low to the ground, drifting across the entire broad flat plain, enshrouding as if consuming the whole of the countryside. But the fog wasn't just solely arising from the river. No, there was more to it than that. I scanned long and hard searching for clues. Maybe there were a whole passel of little springs and streams working their way down from that mountain adding to the mix. Nah! That doesn't make any sense. It's too dang cold. Little cricks and rivulets would be frozen for sure. I must be missing something. There must be some other explanation. Maybe my imagination was getting the better of me. What else could it possibly be?

I rode forward, eyes alert, every sense of my being straining, studying the terrain with a jaundiced eye, wondering all along just what it was that I was getting myself into. I wasn't the only being noticing the change, my pony had too. He seemed to have more energy that day; maybe it was his curiosity along with a little measure of fear that had sparked his pace. Hell, we were both more than just a little disconcerted. And who could blame us?

Then, rather oddly, I noticed I was no longer quite so cold. And yes, the air was warmer, with a hint of a foul odor reeking like so many rotten eggs wafting across the open plain. The soil was thin and cracked, brittle. Fissures abounded, the very ground itself seemed to have grown nigh on hot the closer I neared. And then, I realized it all too late. I was right in the middle of it or should I say… it was everywhere around me.

I pinched myself. I knew I was tired… by rights near the end of my rope. But, I wasn't that bad. And I wasn't dreaming. The place was real, all right; my mind and senses were still to be trusted. It was time to quit wondering, use my brains and start asking the right questions. I began to see some sense, some reason to this place, though I little understood it. I had entered a strange volcanic tract of ground, an eerie region of noxious vapors, of steam and fire and brimstone. I gawked and gazed utterly amazed; every sense of my ordered mind was beset by what unfolded around me. Nothing in all my born days had prepared me for such a place as this. My nerves, my mettle, my whole being wavered like quaking aspens in a storm; the unknown, the uncertainty knocked at my knees. I struggled to make sense of the place. I fought to keep my grip, to steady myself. I held my nerves with a tightened rein, holding our course straight and true, all the while gently soothing that anxious piebald pony, as well as my own shakey-self. I talked with a soft gentle voice, issuing words of calm encouragement. "Steady, boy, nothing here can hurt us. We'll be out of here in no time at all. Steady! Steady!"

What kind of nightmarish hell had I wandered into? We had never been warned that such a place existed. The Corps had had no inkling or a wisp of rumor or injun myth and yet we had passed so relatively close by. The Crow should have known, but they had said nothing to me. Bad medicine to the primitive mind, I thought, how strange not even to talk of it. There must be a reasonable explanation for all this earthly madness. Yes, there must. The questioning helped to settle my mind. I recalled all the strange places in the world that I had heard of. I remembered the accounts of ancient Pompeii and Herculaneum and the volcano that had buried them both. The world was full of wonder, mystery, and upheaval. I could only guess that this was such an unfortunate place. I began to sense and construct the unfinished strife of this unsettled land. Mother Earth after untold eons was still not through announcing her displeasure, and she hissed-on like so many cornered rattlers, belching her contempt, shaking the very ground beneath our feet, everything within visual range portraying havoc, utterly and completely. From below, the noxious bile of her discontent spewed forth steadily from a thousand earthly pores leaving the very air about me thick and acrid, fetid and foul, despoiling the senses.

To know and to understand is to conquer one's own fears. Yet, warily, mustang and man continued to tread knee-deep in trepidation, stepping gingerly about on thin, brittle, yellowish sulfuric laden soil, avoiding open pits of seething, molten mud, stopping and staring entranced at alluring pools of boiling waters, enchanting liquid mirrors hot and clear, aquamarine hues of unsurpassed visual beauty.

How does one explain away the unexplainable, convince the mind that lay unconvinced? Why was this earthly hell here? What exactly was this place, its purpose for existence? Had I stumbled or trespassed onto sacred, forbidden ground? Were its spirits now this very moment investing my mind and soul? I could only conject. The answers were not forthcoming, my simple backwoods intellect's capacity and limitations were not up to any such scholarly or mystic interpretation.

I thought of heaven and hell and all that I had been taught. My folks had believed in the Good Book and what it had to say. Back home at Tinkling Springs Presbyterian, our pastor, the Rev. John McCue, warned the god-fearing among us that just such a place existed to punish the sinners, the wicked and the evil. We used to laugh at such foolishness, snickering in the rear pews, the Ray brothers and me, that is. Words for the meek and the timid, we use to giggle and smirk and say. Yeah, we boys were pretty dang smart in those days, "know-it-alls," if the truth were known. Now, I wasn't so sure. Maybe meek ol' Parson John wasn't so dumb after all.

As suddenly as I had come upon it, I left it behind, though the foul stench stayed embedded in my buckskins for days to come. An all too noxious reminder, I had dreamt it not. Nightmare, no! Nightmarish, yes! An explainable phenomenon to be hailed one day by others of credible foundation, more scientifically astute than myself? Certainly! Repeatable to my fellow trappers… not hardly, if I esteemed my reputation and my friends. Anyway, who would believe it though it all true? Should I even dare recount it to some? Tough to say. Maybe to Lisa, he should know. He had said that my word was to be believed, trusted. Yet, I would have to think on it long and hard. In the meantime, best to put it in my memory book of places to avoid without giving it another thought.

I moved on pushing ever-deeper through unknown country, skirting high, forbidding ranges, crossing more valleys, chancing many a treacherous ice-bound stream and frozen crick. Gazed in wonder upon craggy mountain peaks most glorious, picked my way through dense woods of pine and fir and walked the shorelines of pristine alpine lakes wide and deep and nigh on frozen. I persevered, each new day wearing on my mind and my body, testing my resolve like never before. Weeks passed, little changed, including my luck. By rights by now I should have found some Shoshone sign, something to hang my hat on. What should I do? Go on? A wise man once observed that there was no combination worse than being stubborn and stupid, that reasonable men must know when to admit their mistakes, when to cut their losses. That when was now and none too late for me. I had gone about as far as I was going to go. I was not going to find Cameawaite's people, not the way I was going about it.

"C'mon, boy," I said, gently nudging the piebald, "there's got to be a better way."

So we left the bitter cold and the grim loneliness of those mountains behind, backtracking to the Yellowstone from whence we came. Which brings me right up to now, to the far side of the Tobacco Roots a few weeks hence.

I can't say exactly what it was that roused my attention, but I yanked hard on the reins, snapping my pony's head rudely back, while bringing that piebald mount to an abrupt stop. We had grown comfortable together these past few months, depending on each other for companionship as well as survival. Right then, survival was on his mind. He too sensed an unexplainable presence and settled down right away.

Now whatever it was that was bothering us was of no minor concern. Maybe it was an old grizzly bear, just emerging from a winter den, lean and hungry and on the prowl. Maybe it was a hunting party out looking for buffalo or young bucks on the prod for scalps and ponies.

There was nothing, however, I could see, hear or smell. Something, though, was itching my craw. Whatever or whoever it was, was not coming from anywhere near the river on my right or the Tobacco Roots to my left. I was certain of that. Whatever or whoever it was lay directly to my front and was apparently heading my way. I sat, watched, and listened, patiently biding time.

The wind out of the southwest had calmed down to a gentle breeze. Stillness prevailed. Nothing moved save for beads of perspiration forming on my brow and slowly trickling down my face. Even the incessant chattering of birds came to a sudden swift halt; they, too, must have sensed it. But, what or who was it? What had caused both horse and man to come to such a sudden jolting stop? Intuitively, I knew. Thank God, I did. Instinct, that undeniable mysterious sixth sense cautioning, divining… warning of peril ahead. Skullduggery! Ambush! Something untoward! Fear suddenly gripped me, running unabated until the bloody specter of painted savages formed a hard dry lump in the middle of my throat I could not void. Yet, I dare not move. I stayed put, continuing my quiet vigil, all the while resisting the rising surge of angst building within me. I began to feel that old familiar itch rising on the back of my neck. Those hackles had always been there when the unavoidable, the undetectable, indefinable were about to appear. How long had the itch been with me, I couldn't say, though it was tried and true, saving my bacon more times than I cared to recall.

Sweat trickled down the back of my neck, diving under my hunting shirt, working its way towards the small of my back. I was breathing heavier than normal, barely even noticing it, until I realized it was the only sound I was hearing. That and my own inner ear now pounding steadily to the tune of a worried, rising beat.

"Whoa!" I whispered. "Get a hold, Johnboy. Get a hold of yourself."

I waited a few moments longer, waiting, watching and then, "C'mon!" I spoke gently to the mustang and quickly pulled him farther back into the shaded shadows of the cottonwoods. The pony needed no convincing, obliging me right off. The trees, the thick underbrush and the darkness of the forest shade quickly gobbled us up. We stood there as quiet, as still as stone. Again, nothing moved save for the ever-present breezes gently ruffling and swaying limbs, branches, leaves, and the tops of the cottonwoods in an undulating rhythmical dance.

The piebald's soft hairy ears craned forward, straining to catch the slightest of sounds of movement. His eyes bulged, his nostrils flared sniffing the air for sign. A nervous rumble echoed from deep within his throat and then blew long and heavy right out his nose. He was agitated and growing more so by the minute.

I reached forward and rubbed his neck again, "Easy does it, fella," I whispered. "Easy does it."

My mouth and throat were bone dry. My lips parched and cracked. I strained to swallow, all the while wishing I had a mouthful of cool water to drink.

"Damn poor time to think of that, you knothead," I mumbled.

I squirmed uneasily in my saddle blanket, scrunching shoulders and neck muscles made taut by the steadily growing anticipation and tension welling within me. I was becoming more uncomfortable, edgier by the second.

I watched the pony's ears continue to flicker and strain to catch even the slightest, imperceptible of sounds. I could feel his body beneath me quiver and shake in an unexplainable spasm. He knew. And just as assuredly, I respected those instincts, he was too wild a critter to miss a trick.

That hoss felt it again. Ah, Gotcha! I caught it. Slight as it was… I felt, no I sensed it, too, right along with him. That something was there, all right, growing steadily. And while we waited, this unseen disturbance began to groan on and on, growing louder and louder, stronger and stronger reverberating through the very ground itself upon which we stood. Its presence, still unseen, soon became inescapable; growling, rumbling like an impending earthquake of cataclysmic proportions or…

A herd of hundreds or thousands of shaggy buff' on the move and coming our way? It had to be for what else could produce such a rolling thunder upon the land? It was the only answer possible. Yes, it had to be.

I stayed put, continuing to watch and wait. Tender thoughts of juicy, buffalo hump steaks, sizzling over a cooking fire, tantilized my senses. I began to taste a supper of what possibly lay ahead, relishing every succulent, delicious morsel. Strange what a man can think of during the oddest of times. But, the mustang, though, wasn't seeing it my way. No, his thoughts of dinner were interrupted by what he couldn't divine. And it worried him. That little pony began to paw the ground nervously as if wanting to dig a deep, deep dark hole to hide himself in. I snapped right out of my trance, instantly. Once again I could feel the anxiety coursing through his veins, disturbing his delicate equilibrium. Continually, I stroked his neck, steadily reassuring him, all the while struggling to contain my own rising angst. My heart beat louder, faster. My dry mouth grew dryer.

Unconsciously, I regripped the thin neck of my long rifle, squeezing the smooth hand-polished wood tightly. Sweat began to stream steadily off my brow. The chill I had felt out on the open prairie was gone now, replaced by a different chill, less tangible, of fear and foreboding.

The crescendo rose unabated. It came on not as an onrush or stampede, but more of that of a large host, slowly, inexorably pushing forward, as irresistible as the incoming tide. Soon, a thin veil of dust, growing expedientially to form clouds of dirt and grit, announced its presence from out of the southwest, a wall of dust kicked-up no doubt by thousands of hooves, unshod hooves and something else… moccasins?

I was completely taken aback, refusing to believe my own eyes at first. It was as if I hadn't expelled a single breath that whole suspenseful wait. Finally, I could hold it no longer, letting out a voluminous discharge of stale, liberated air in one giant pent-up whoosh, draining me completely. I sucked in air by the barrel-full and when I finally caught my wind, I stared and gawked in disbelief at what now appeared out on the naked grass prairie… people, many, many people.

As the dust trailed away, hundreds of figures emerged coming my way. It was now quite clear that that ponderous, head-throbbing crescendo was not caused by a vast herd, at least not of shaggy buffalo moving to new feeding grounds. No, it was the din of a nation on the move, an Indian nation, with hundreds, maybe thousands of fine ponies driven by young herd-tenders. Camp dogs pulling loaded sleds of wooden poles and stretched animal skins, travois, packed with lodge-hold and family belongings. Women, children, old folks, walking with purpose, like Moses and the children of Israel heading for the Promised Land. Never had I known such movement as what now unfolded before me. Inexplicably, I was overwhelmed, somehow in the process feeling irrelevant, insignificant, whether or not they would prove be friend or foe. I remained, watching and waiting, keeping my presence unknown.

Hundreds of mounted warriors rode on the flanks and in the vanguard of the march, alert, watchful in a most disciplined, martial way. Even from afar, I could sense their proud bearing, sitting atop their elegant mountain-bred ponies, like mythological centaurs of old… their near-naked magnificence easy to discern even from the distance that still separated us: lithe, lean bodied, sinewy and strong. I recognized them instantly. They were friends. These were the people of the mountains who befriended the Corps just three years before on our western trek. They were the tribes of the Bitterroots, the Salish, so often called Flatheads, and the people whom Manuel Lisa was intent on making allies. I was so sure that I readied to risk my life on it. Confidently, I nudged my pony with a heel to the ribs, prodding him forward away from the shadows.

Two sharp-eyed scouts riding point saw us the moment we emerged from the shadows. They stopped dead in their tracks, never for an instant taking their eyes away. Their gaze was intense, burning a hole right through me from less than a half a mile away. And while they stopped and stared, their whole nation, still to the rear, seemed to sense their trepidation and concern. My sudden appearance to the scouts was nigh on pandemic… Blackfeet land did that to these people, I was to learn. It didn't take much to cause a stir and my presence was doing just that.

I could see and sense a ripple of alarm racing back through the length of their entire column. The whole damn caboodle came to a stop, hundreds and hundreds of faces were riveted my way. All those dark eyes fixed on me. I could sense the heat, their anxiety and fear.

I felt an electrified charge of excitement shoot back through my pony's body like a current gone awry. His body recoiled, tensing beneath me. His ears flickered and twitched and stretched forward to hear; his nostrils, his sharp sense of smell strained to recognize the scents along with the sounds of the mounted cavalcade of hundreds, maybe thousands of his kind. He whinnied, again and again.

I gently reined-back on the thin rawhide strip wound around his lower jaw, Shoshone style. My pony came to an abrupt stop.

"Good boy," I said softly and leaned forward, patting him several times on the neck to soothe his heightened anxiety.

He started to rear, his nerves still unconvinced, his excitement almost more than he could contain.

"Whoaaa, boy!" I cautioned. "I know they're eyein' us. Question is, what are they goin' to do about it?" I was thinking out loud, talking to my horse, as if half expecting a reply. My voice seemed to calm him down and eventually it did. We each waited motionlessly, sensing the unabated curiosity and wariness that our presence had stirred.

From the flanks, four more riders came racing forward, careening to a dust-flying halt at the side of the two point scouts. They talked excitedly, loudly and even angrily as if in heated debate. Arms gesturing, flailing, pointing my way, stabbing the air with balled fists and stiffened trigger fingers. They looked all about, nervously, wondering where the rest of the enemy lay concealed.

Even at this great distance the guttural brogue of the Salish tongue was easily recognizable. A few words I thought I remembered. I strained to pick them out. It was most futile. Then, a slightly built warrior, obviously older than the rest for his long hair was streaked with gray, raised his hand. The others were stilled. He talked for a few moments and then signaled by sign to the rest of the tribe to his rear.

From far to the rear, a squad of horsemen charged forward to take the scouts' places covering the van of their nation. Words of instruction were quickly passed between them, tension arising with each passing breath and utterance. And just as quickly their conversation ended. Their plan was formed. With that the first six riders strung their bows, turned in my direction and came forward at a measured walk.

On they came, never for an instant taking their eyes off of me, each face a blank mask, grim, resolute, revealing nothing save determination. And each warrior armed with a stone-headed arrow notched in his bow and prepared to let fly. The closer they neared the more distinct their faces and features became, all were young save one. But, it was exactly that older one with the gray hair who held my gaze. I found myself transfixed on him, obviously an older warrior of distinction, the way he had quieted the others earlier had proven that. What was it about that old warrior that seemed so familiar? I couldn't shake him off, yet I couldn't recall his face or what it was about him that had me so perplexed. He was still too far away, I'd have to get closer to find out.

Again I rubbed my horse's neck.

"Here we go, fella," I said. "Better start saying your prayers."

We rode a little further and then stopped. I took one last long breath, reinforcing my nerve, and then, I dismounted, slowly taking my reins and letting them fall to the ground.

The riders kept coming, watching my every move. They would not miss a trick, no Indian in their situation ever would.

I continued to wait, watching their approach, steeling myself for what lay ahead, hoping all the while they would recognize me as a friend and not a foe.

Casually, I reached up, unstrapped and took hold of my belongings from the pony's back. Deliberately, I made a big "to do," untying my blanket and rolling it out. Stepping away from the horse, I spread my blanket out on the ground, smoothed out the creases and laid my long-rifle down. I stood up and deliberately moved a few feet away and waited with my arms held out from my sides, unarmed, unthreatening, peaceful-like. A white-eyed stranger near-prostrated before them, a stranger, nevertheless... confident, unafraid and ready to talk. I was set to palaver and issued my invitation, plains-Indian style.

Those Flathead boys pulled-up short and for several minutes eyed me real wary-like. Hell, I could tell they didn't know what to think. I could see their lips moving, no longer excited or yelling, talking to each other in low, careful voices. Their talk didn't carry, but their intent surely did. Those Indians were checking me up and down and scanning the surrounding countryside as suspicious as an ol' coon dog smelling a fox near his master's hen house. Excepting, it was a two-legged varmint and not a fox that concerned them right about now.

I would have felt the same way had I been in their moccasins. I appreciated their caution, wouldn't have expected otherwise. But, I soon tired of the standoff and began to make gestures of peace and parley in the "language of sign" known to every Indian nation of the Northwest and the high plains. I called out what little of the Flathead brogue I knew and even added some other tribes' lingo thrown in.

Nothing seemed to be doing the trick, until I yelled out...

"*Mokoman, Gitchi Mokoman!*"

Now I think that was Shawnee or some such, kinda more of an eastern injun language as least as I recall. That's what all the Indians called George Rogers Clark back in the old days of the Revolution when he took Cahokia and Kaskaskia and Vincennes in the Wabash country. His name and that handle had spread far and wide in those days. I was hoping and praying and reaching.

Well, I'll be. The Shawnee talk seemed to be doing the trick. Got their attention, yes, sir. Those Indians were talking up a storm, now, especially the old one. Yeah, he knows it all right. That ol' boy has been around. Good, let's see if he remembers.

The gray-haired one was doing the talking. They took another hard look, all of 'em. Something about me, the way I looked, the words I spoke, resonated with ol' gray-hair. Something familiar, I knew it right then, things were about to work out. I strained to get a better look at the old man. He appeared to me to be of a different cut than the rest of those Indians. I'd bet on it. Maybe he was not a Flathead after all. His pony wasn't that's for sure. Scrawny, like it was missing too many a meal. I could see the difference plain out.

Hold on! Movement! All six of 'em are heading right towards me. Slowly, cautiously they fan out into a defensive arc. They are taking no chances.

The sweat streams down my face, flowing over dry parched lips. I taste the salty dew, as if savoring each drop. My tongue nervously laps away like a pony's tale swishing, swatting away pesky, annoying flies.

Look at 'em, will ya! Their eyes are burning holes in me, and each one of 'em with an arrow notched in their bows, ready to let fly. The two in the center, one being the old man, never took their eyes off of me. The rest covered every conceivable hiding place on the prairie. They were still taking no chances. White man or not, this was dangerously close to Blackfeet country and those devils were never to be trusted.

I calculated my chances right then and there. One dumb move and they would ride me down and riddle me like a porcupine with half-a-dozen arcing shafts. I winced. "Hooo! Take it easy, Johnboy. Stay cool. Stay cool."

They kept coming, drawing nearer, closer, closer. Until, I could make out the details of each of their faces, the lean, lithe, sculpted bronze of sun and wind-worn bodies. I studied them intently, poured over every change in expression. Yet, there is no change. They are in fact expressionless. Doubt uncertainty creeps in. God, have I made a mistake coming here? What are they thinking? What are they going to do? I just could not tell. Each appeared cool, steady, determined... like wolves coming in for the kill.

Wait! The old man, I cannot shake that little old man. God, if he doesn't have a familiar look and gait to him. Now, wait just a minute. The ancient one's face was perplexing the hell out of me. "What on earth... wait a minute," I yelled aloud. I know him. Damned if I don't know him.

"God Almighty," I shouted in disbelief. "That old boy don't belong with those 'Flats'. He ain't one of 'em, no sirree. By God, that injun's a Snake."

The old Indian wasn't a Flathead, not at all like I remembered them. No, he was from a different tribe, a Shoshone for sure, by his look and get-up. I took a further look, this time eyeing his mount. His pony iced the cake for me. A little Snake pony, tired, worn-out and damn near as old as the wizened man riding him. Right then my brain found its trigger and squeezed off, firing one memory after another. Lord of Mercy, I know that old Snake, you dang straight I do. I could suppress the joy building up within me no longer. And out it came gushing like a spring torrent.

"Toby!" I called to him as loud as I could. "Hey, Toby, you ol' rickety Snake son of a bitch, lookee here, lookee here. That's right! That's right! Get a good look." Again, I yelled to the old man at the top of my lungs, all the while unable to hold down a belly-busting laugh at the sheer coincidence and luck of it all. "*Tab-ba-bone. Tab-ba-bone. Gitchi Mokoman*... God dang yer hide. Toby, look at me, will ya."

I was rattling off all the injun lingo I knew: Snake, Salish and Shawnee, Crow, Mandan, every injun word in my frontier lexicon. Desperately I was trying to pull the trigger to the old man's memory. Hell, I even threw in a few choice cuss words of my own to boot. And if that didn't do the trick, I'd use sign, I'd find a way. He'd remember, that old Snake would remember.

"Can you believe it?" I gushed, unable to contain the sheer relief built up within me ever since leaving Manuels on the Big Horn. Month after long month, cold and lonely, looking, searching, never finding a hint of sign. And now...

"Toby. Toby." Again, I rattled-off the name the Corps had dubbed him on the trail to the Bitterroots. He'd remember. He'd get it. That old man would recollect those who had christened him so. He could never forget us in ten lifetimes, no sir, not a chance in hell.

My mind shot back to the summer of '05, barely three years before. By then, we had seen the last of the Missouri, at least until our return the following year. Tremendous mountains lay before us. What lay beyond, how far we had to go we did not know. Months more of fatigue and travel remained our fare until we would finally reach the Pacific Ocean and build our winter home, Fort Klatsop. Yet, that summer held in store for us such an exciting, momentous time, a grand, joyous reunion for little Janey and her people. Many, many faces flashed before my mind's eye, Indian and white. And this old man approaching me this very moment was one of those I remembered best. Toby, what had his people called him? Think! Yeah, I remember it now, a big bird, an eagle. Yeah, that's it, *Swooping Eagle*. *Swooping Eagle*, our Toby was a Northern Shoshone, a Lemhi of Cameahwait and Sacagawea's tribe. With his young son, he had helped guide us in early September '05 to the Bitterroots and over the south part of the Bitterroot Mountains into the land of the Salish, the people some called the Flatheads. In the few short weeks that he spent with the Corps, he had become a trusted companion and a keen observer of our ways. It was going on three years since I had seen him last, a virtual lifetime in the Rockies. Today, right now it seemed like yesterday.

Not a one of the six, including Toby, was making a move. They just stared at me with the most dumbfounded of looks. I swear one of them was even scratching his head.

Inside I was laughing, Good Jesus, what in hell is it going to take?

"C'mon, you dumb bunch of shits," I swore under my breath.

Again, I cried out to the old warrior, "Toby, take a good look at me… it's Colter, John Colter. Goddang it, man, think back, will ya… John Col-ter. Col-ter." I said it loud. I said it slowly, damn near spelling it out.

The fading embers of the old man's dimming memory finally glowed bright. The white man, *tab-ba-bone*, the voice and the name he called out had a certain ring, a certain familiarity. He had not been hailed by that name, that way since the white men had departed the mountains nearly three years before.

"Ugh!" he grunted, finally, turning to his companions and they each nodded, realizing the old Snake had recognized a friend. All eyes watched him as he boldly strode towards me. There was no fear, no hesitancy in his approach, just outright curiosity. A sparkle gleamed in the old Indian's eyes and with it a broad-toothed smile spanning his leathery face. Recognition had finally come and with it that wiry little Snake lit up like an Independence Day celebration back home. He unnotched his arrow and deftly replaced the stone-headed missile back in its quiver, his bow dropping unthreateningly to his side. Any sign of fear, of caution was now completely gone.

And then he howled in delight. "Ah-hi-e. Ah-hi-e… Col-Ter… Col-Ter… Goddang! Goddang!"

That did it. The old man finally figured out who the hairy white man calling his name was. He rushed forward as if he had found a long lost brother… me. He grabbed my arm and shook it violently. He hugged me. He slapped me on the back repeatedly, and then lifted me clear off my feet. That wiry little Snake man was strong as a small grizzly, damn near taking the wind right out of me in the crush of his exhilaration.

All I could do was stand there and smile and gush. And those Flathead warriors standing back yonder watching, well, they could hardly believe what they were seeing. I mean their scrawny, little Snake friend hugging this big, hairy white man like a long lost brother. What in the hell would happen next? They were all eyes, staring, looking back and forth to each other, mumbling, pointing, all in confusion, wondering just what in tarnation was going on and just who or what exactly was this strange-ass looking white man.

Old Toby stopped for a moment to catch his breath. And when he did, he turned and shouted to the Flats, "John Col-Ter… goddang. *Gitchi Mokoman*… big knife, big knife." That and a whole other slue of Salish and

Snake lingo to boot.

That broke the ice. It all made sense now to those savages. A collective sigh was released and the five warriors instantly raced forward on their ponies, whooping and hollering.

Toby lit up. "Goddang, goddang," he sang over and over, as happy as a pig in slop.

"Ah-hi-e, ah-hi-e. Col-ter. Col-ter. Col-ter. *Gitchi Mokoman! Gitchi Mokoman!* Goddang! Goddang!"

The Flatheads picked up Toby's refrain and wouldn't let go. Soon the epithet rang over the prairie till it was picked up and repeated by their whole nation. And while their excitement continued all about us, Toby suddenly had looked at me standing alone and grew somewhat solemn…

"You, John Col-ter, where Big Red? Merree-wether, no read stars? No Cru-zzatte, no play fiddle? Black York? Where your big warriors?" Toby had stopped smiling long enough to ask in earnest, wondering why I was traveling alone.

"Home," I said, pointing to the east. "The captains, all the boys went home, to their lodges, to be with their people, two winters ago."

"Col-ter… goddang… you stay here? No go home? No squaw?" He stared at me kind of quizzical like.

I knew he wouldn't understand. Hell, sometimes even I didn't understand. And I knew I couldn't explain it to him. The white man's ways were often strange to the red man's way of thinking. Hell, half the time of late I had found myself starting to question my ownself.

It had seemed so easy a decision back in '06. We were a month out from St. Louis, near the end of the Expedition's trail. The boys were all anxious to get home. It had been the great adventure. We all swelled with pride at the Corps accomplishments, knowing the whole civilized world waited to hear what we had seen and done. And we knew we had done something to be proud of, each man sharing in it equally for nigh on twenty-eight hard months.

Yet, I was not ready for the adventure to end. I was not ready to call it quits while a fortune in beaver skins was to be made. And it beckoned to me, lying in wait back in the Yellowstone country, ready to be trapped and skinned and tanned and brought back to be sold to an eastern and European society hungry for the fashion that could not do without the soft, rich fur of the beaver. And at that time nothing else would do.

I had no loved-ones waiting for my return. My ma and pa had both passed away. No sweetheart pined for me to come home, no estate for me to inherit, nor lands to farm, stock to breed and raise. I had little to call my own, save for the pack on my back, a long-rifle over my shoulder and the desire to see the wilderness and what lay over the next mountain and the next... and the nerve, the gravel in my gizzard to see it through.

And yet, there were nagging, pestering questions. When would the day come when I'd be ready to settle down? To find a woman, raise a family and give up my independent, wandering rambler's life? No, I had never really thought about it until now. And realizing that I had never really thought about it, I began to slowly consider it earnest.

To Toby and the Flatheads' ways of thinking all the beaver skins in the world wouldn't stack up to a bucket of spit if they didn't have a squaw or two, a mess of children and a village of kinfolk to share it with. These Indians were naturally communal, unselfish people. They shared hardship and misery as equally as they did bounty. White-man's ways were something to shake their heads at in disbelief, rarely at times to be understood. Seeing me here alone only confirmed it.

"There ain't no home, at least not right now," I said rather forlornly.

After a moment Toby nodded his ancient gray head. He understood. There was a look of melancholy, of sadness about him. Bowing his head he said ever so softly, "Home...good medicine!"

While we enjoyed our reunion on the far side of the Tobacco Roots, two suns travel to the northeast another Indian nation was also on the move, a nation not anything at all like the friendly Flatheads. Ever vigilant and wary they erected this night hundreds of their buffalo-skin lodges, colorfully painted conical tipis they called *Nii-to-yi*, the-only-peoples-home. Set in their own peculiar defensive pattern, they bedded down, weary after a long days travel.

Not all slept, some stayed awake, for important issues were at hand. Deep in the midst of their encampment, a swarthy looking savage with the demeanor and carriage of a leader of his people stared into the blazing logs and glowing embers of a roaring campfire. He was not a particularly large man, though he was still lean and athletic looking with wide shoulders and a broad backside, and supple, well-defined arms. Strong arms, backed up, apparently, by an equally strong will.

Many of the men of his tribe stood about him wearing heavy coarse brown robes of tanned buffalo hide, taken from their sacred *enee*. And others, yet, wore the warm, thick, white Hudson Bay woolen blankets, trade gifts from their English friends in Alberta and Saskatchewan, wrapped around their bronzed torsos to keep out the late evening chill. The mood was somber, quiet, subdued. Until one warrior, a wide-shouldered youth, he of the long, raven-colored hair flowing loosely over the swales and ripples of a muscular back, could no longer contain the brashness of emerging manhood and stepped forward to speak to the war chief.

"*Kootenae Appe*," he said with a fire in his voice.

The older man, responding to his name, barely turned a dark eye to acknowledge the youth's presence. Arms folded tightly, fingers massaging warmth into his arms he appeared not to acknowledge the youngster for several long moments. And then…

"Speak, *Maa-koyou-mah'-kaa*… Running Wolf," he commanded in a low almost inaudible tone.

"*Ap-pe-ki-yiks! Napikwan ap-pe-ki-yiks*… white men skunks. They come like the English have warned… maybe six, seven suns from where we stand. I've seen them with my own eyes, smelled their treachery." The young warrior spat a mouthful of spit and scorn into the flames. A defiant scowl appeared on his face as if nothing in the world could be as despicable as the words he had just uttered.

There was an immediate murmur from the crowd to be heard. Thinly veiled smiles and nods of approval surfaced on the proud faces of *Maa-koyou-mah'-kaa's* retinue. They were all young braves, drawn from several different hunting bands out of mutual respect and ambition and bloodline. There flowed in their veins the blood of Piegan manhood past, the progenitors of eons of Blackfeet warrior societies. These were the emerging leaders of their nation, the newest warrior society of the *Piegan* peoples, all eager to be recognized by their elders and just as eager for their acclaim. And in honor of the sacred *enee* and those massive male guardians of the herds, they called themselves the Buffalo Bulls.

Kootenae Appe, the war chief of the southern branch of the Blackfeet Nation, the *Piegans*, turned slowly as if he hadn't heard the young warrior correctly. The whites of his eyes appeared to swell with near-disbelief, staring hard at the young warrior.

"*Napikwan?* You have seen white men? Where?"

The older man no longer spoke softly. Anger, even hatred was felt and heard in the temper of his voice. A stern, hard, dark look came over face, one that forebode violent claps of thunder and bolts of lightning. The muscles in his jaws became more pronounced, passionately raised by the very thought of the ever-encroaching white man. He had sworn vengeance on the *napikwan* just two summers before, after the murder of two fine young Piegan warriors at Two Medicine River and Badger Creek by white strangers. The lamentations were especially loud and long in his lodge, his *nii-to-yis*… for one of the slain was dear to his and his family's heart. *He-that-looks-at-the-Calf*, was his nephew, the bold young son of his little sister, and she was beside herself with grief, flaying her own flesh bloody and raw, demanding revenge, satisfaction for her great loss. Never, not for one single day would she let him forget this gravest of reproach. The *napikwan* had spilled first blood, and now, they were back.

"We were in the land of the Crow dogs to steal their *ponokamitas*, their fine ponies, by the river they call the *As-to-pah-oan-zhah*, the Elk River... near the waters of the Wind."

Maa-koyou-mah'-kaa spoke proudly, confidently. His unfettered daring and brash exploits raiding their traditional enemies were already becoming legend with the *Piegan* people. And nothing spoke louder and higher to the Blackfeet than stealing their enemies' elk dogs, their *ponokamitas*, their swift ponies, and dispatching their enemies.

The old chief stared intensely into the youngster's eyes and face, searching for greater revelation, silently commanding the youth to go on. *Maa-koyou-mah'-kaa* was emboldened and continued with his hero's tale. Those around the fire crowded closer to listen. All eyes and ears were trained on this young warrior. It was a big moment in his young life; one that he hoped would elevate his esteem in the minds and hearts and paeans of his people.

"There are many whites, many. These *napikwans* have built a great wooden lodge of *ah-uo-nis-tsest*... lodge poles like the English traders in the lands of our northern brothers, the Siksika and the Bloods. They have cut many lodge poles to sink into the ground, side by side, to cower behind like cowards. Dogs."

His vehemence, his tone, his passion was laced with the virulent poison of outright hatred. His hostility for the newcomers was more than he could contain. *Maa-koyou-mah'-kaa*, this Running Wolf, took a moment to regain his composure before continuing. "These walls they build... are as tall as the lodge poles of our tipis. The eagle and the hawk would nest atop them if it were not for the *napikwan's* fire-sticks. There is more. They trade with our enemies the Crow for their ponies. They hunt our game, walk our land, going as they please, without fear. Their boldness mocks us. I have seen all of this... and it is as I have said."

He stopped and waited for the chief's reaction. Several of his young companions nodded their heads in agreement, looking to the others for acknowledgment. Again there was a loud murmur to be heard from around the campfire gathering.

Another, taller, even more strapping youngster stepped forward. He appeared cut out of the same chiseled mold as *Maa-koyou-mah'-kaa*, his bronzed countenance and easy gait remarkably like that of his vaunted friend. However, the long narrow lock of his bangs, traditionally cut squarely over the bridge of a warrior's nose, could not conceal the evidence of battle-past. It was a nasty horizontal scar, emblazoned across his right cheek, completey covering the bridge of his nose, a vivid reminder of his first youthful raid for

Absaroka ponies and Blackfeet glory. But such disfiguration was not to be scorned among the *Piegans*. No, on the contrary it was his badge of courage, worn with honor.

Ak-o-tash-iks... Many Horses was his name and he spoke without hesitation, his voice, his words were unbroken, firm. "It is as my brother *Maa-koyou-mah'-kaa* says. He speaks with a straight tongue, the *napikwans* are there... and their presence does mock us."

Ak-o-tash-iks reached out with two stiffened fingers of his right hand and made the sweeping gesture of the sign talk that left no doubt that his friend spoke straight and true.

No one else spoke. All eyes returned to the war-chief, awaiting his response. The fire continued to roar and crackle and pop and the northern breezes whistled through the opened flaps of their lodges. There was consternation here tonight in their village. They had been warned that the white man would come. The English traders talked of little else.

"They have many fire-sticks?" the chief asked, returning his gaze to *Maa-koyou-mah'-kaa*.

"Many, as numerous as the sharp quills of the porcupine. Every *napikwan* is armed with a fire-stick," assured *Maa-koyou-mah'-kaa*, looking to the faces of his companions again for verification. They all nodded grimly in agreement.

It was not necessary. *Kootenae Appe* was convinced of this young leader's veracity. He never doubted him for an instant. His was the Blackfeet way, the straight path of his ancestors. And the Buffalo Bulls were rapidly becoming a society to be reckoned with.

"*As-to-pah-oan-zhah?*" The old man suddenly asked, he was thinking of his Crow enemies trading with the *napikwans* ... and trade possibly meant trade muskets.

Maa-koyou-mah'-kaa spoke again, barely concealing his disdain for what he perceived as the white man's ways. "They hunt the *ksis-tuk-ki*... the tree-biter... what the English traders call beaver. They are like squaws hunting rabbits, setting snares in the waters to catch them. They barely eat the flesh; all they want are the skins. They are crazed for their skins, like their white brothers to the north. We have watched them, hoping to lift their hair and take their fire-sticks. These dogs, these *napikwan* stick close to their fort, but sooner or later they will stray farther and farther away and..."

"Were you seen?" The chief interrupted the young warrior before he could finish.

"No. Not even the Crow knew we were there. Of this I am sure." A smirk appeared on his face. He wore it proudly with confidence. His friend, *Ak-o-tash-iks*, Many Horses, smiled right along with him. Not even the wily Crow knew. His stealth, his bold courage was to be admired. His name, his deeds would spread, borne on the winds of talk by his people. Until all the Blackfeet: the Piegan, the Siksika, the Bloods and even the Atsina, the big hearts of the plains, knew and sang of *Maa-koyou-mah'-kaa's*, Running Wolf's daring.

"Good!" Kootenae Appe nodded and turned back to face the flames. Silence fell over the campfire, until he was heard to say, "These *napikwan* are dangerous. We will keep an eye on them and their fort."

The Flathead scouts waved their *apishamores*, their saddle blankets high over their heads, signaling the rest of their people that all was well, summoning them forth. And then, while Toby and I talked, the scouts raced their swift ponies around and around us, raising the dirt and the dust and the sod of the plains and whooping it up in grand, spirited fashion.

I smiled that day for the first time in many months. It was good to be alive, good to be with honest, friendly people. It had been way too long since I enjoyed the company of such folk. It was as if a tremendous burden of doubt and loneliness was lifted from my shoulders. Suddenly, I longed for home, for companionship, for the love of a good woman.

Mounted warriors charged across the plains, kicking up clouds of dust and sod and an ocean of celebration. The hooting and the hollering began. The fun, the excitement kept on, continuing well into the late afternoon; by then the rest of their people had arrived and joined in the merriment. They came forward, crowding around me, engulfing me in a sea of hands and arms and outright curiosity, to touch, to speak, to see if I was indeed of real, human flesh and bone. The warriors, young and old, the proud, the curious hanging by my side, gawking at my long rifle, measuring my strength, my mettle, in awe of the white man's medicine. The young squaws, their maidens, soon handsomely decked out in their finest tanned deerskin finery, smiled and giggled and flirted and made me squirm and blush. The young un's stared bug-eyed, running amuck like kids everywhere will do. I caught bits and pieces of their talk as they peppered me incessantly with a thousand inquiries. Their language was strange, guttural, like a primitive Celtic brogue. Yet, it made me feel strangely at home. I laughed. I listened and tried to answer their many questions. My head spun like a top, dizzy from the excitement, the attention of a whole nation, all starkly contrasted when compared to a winter of solitude.

They remembered Big Red as they liked to call Captain Clark, the bone-breaking strength of York, his giant black slave, and the stories told by Sacagawea, the demure Shoshone girl with her infant little Pomp. But mostly, they talked of the men of the Corps, of their many remembered kindnesses, their boldness, bravery and big medicine. They spoke fondly, with respect of the tall white captains and their white warriors, the *Gitchi Mokoman*... the big knives.

The recollections that surfaced brought back more than a little melancholy for me. Somehow I had let the memories of my friends in the Corps slip away to some hidden corner of my mind as I went on with my life. The hardships, the camaraderie, the years we spent together, all seemed so long ago. I had become so absorbed in my own loneliness and isolation that I had forgotten all those who had been close to me. Now, with the curious questions of these Indian people, faces of the men I knew and liked and respected flashed across my mind, questioning my very reason for being here, chastising my solitude, the emptiness in my heart I continued to endure.

The excitement of the afternoon wore on into the late evening without respite. With Toby happily by my side, we whiled the night away, smoking their *kinnikinick* and talking up a storm. It seemed like their whole nation, warriors and chiefs, women, young 'uns and the old folk, all crowded around that big blazing campfire to see and listen to the *tab-ba-bone*.

The squaws brought out *parfleches* filled with dried cakes laced with chokecherries and serviceberries, along with pemmican, jerked meat, the winter staple of the high plains. We ate and laughed and burped and farted unrestrained. Toby and his friends told many funny stories, all the while pointing my way, eversmiling, their faces loaded with mischief and delight. They found great amusement in me, the way I looked: my long, scraggily beard and unkempt hair, that odd-looking, snarling badger's head, covering the top of my own pate like some bygone ancient warrior's war-helmet. They saw and heard me talking to my horse as if half-expecting some equinal response. They liked my smile, sensed my warmth, nodded approvingly at the easy way I walked among them. I was something to marvel at, all right, a strange warrior so unlike them and from such a faraway, magical, distant land. And they loved to laugh, to bust a gut at my expense... good naturedly, of course. There was no slight, no reproach intended. And I was not offended. On the contrary, I, too, liked their warmth, their humor and innocence. They were simple people without guile or pretensions. There just wasn't an unfriendly face in that whole dang tribe. And from all I could see, it meant my acceptance.

I smiled and nodded and took it all in, but I could tell from many an emaciated look that the cakes and the little bit of pemmican we ate were all that the tribe had to offer. Their larder was about empty. All those people, all those mouths to feed and so little food left in their *parfleches*. It made me wonder.

I looked up to a clear, cloudless nighttime sky, to the thousands of glittering stars shining brightly above, and then to the east to the snowcapped granite peaks of the nearby Tobacco Root Mountains. It was a big land with a big sky and these people were a long way from home.

I turned to my Shoshone friend. There were questions that begged to be answered.

"Toby, why are the Salish people so far from their Bitterroot Mountains? And why are you here with 'em? Where is your son and your people?"

The smile disappeared from the old man's face. He sat still for several long moments in quietude. And then he pulled back on an imaginary bow and let fly an invisible arrow.

"Hunt buffalo."

"Buffalo? Where?" I asked

"One sun from here. Near place where waters come together."

He stared off into the distance of the night for a moment.

"Old place... *pishkun*... falling off place. Shoshone peoples hunt there for many, many winters, from the time of my grandfather's grandfathers' grandfathers. Before ponies traded to my people by the Utes." Toby pointed to the south and then he added, "Before Pahkees come with fire-sticks." And the old Snake pointed to the north, his face grimly set.

"Humph! Well, I'll be," was all I could manage to say.

But, hell, wasn't I the lucky one. They were heading to the Three Forks, and, with a little more luck and a little convincing, heading with me to Manuel's Fort on the Big Horne.

Late into the night, the Flatheads gathered around a large, blazing campfire, as it lit the stark prairie night. I sat cross-legged, Indian-style on tanned skins, sharing and passing around to Toby and the respected men of the tribe, the people's ceremonial peace pipe, smoking *kinnikinik*, the bark of the ever-present red willow and a tobacco-like plant that grew in the nearby mountains that got its name. Each of the Flatheads in their turn raised and pointed the sacred medicine pipe of soft catlinite to the four sacred directions: to the east, south, west and north. To most Indians, damn near everything in nature holds spiritual meaning and is sacred to them and that includes the four directions.

To the east, *pe-nap-ohts,* the sacred pipe was held to the rising sun to symbolize the Creator, *Api-stoh-toh-ki,* and his power through the sun to begin each day.

And then the pipe was held to the south, *am-skap-ohts,* which symbolizes youth and where all things are made to grow. And when the sun on its daily journey passes by, the plants, as if by magic, turn towards its direction for life giving energy.

To the west, *ah-met-ohts,* from where the clouds and storms come from and with them the sacred waters of rain and its life giving nourishment a gift from the Creator.

And finally, in respect to life's renewal, to the north, *ap-put-os-ohts*, which signifies the venerated generations of their ancestors and old age and wisdom and the rebirth of life that follows the bitterness of long cold winters to be reborn again with the coming of spring.

I watched silently as the people prayed for the safety and health of their women and children and for the success of their upcoming buffalo hunt. It was no different listening to their prayers than being back home at Tinkling Springs Presbyterian Church with my folks and our Christian congregation at prayer meeting on a quiet Sunday morn'. It was a homey feeling, comforting, one more and more I was beginning to long for and miss.

The Flatheads had come together to hunt buffalo near the valley of the Three Forks to feed their nation, to help carry them through another long, hard Bitterroot winter. And they were here in force… five, six hundred warriors strong to guarantee their people's survival. From what I gathered, they half-expected the *Nimpau*, the *Nee Mee Poo*, the people of the Camas Prairie we called Nez Perce, to join them for the hunt. So far there was no sign of the Nez Perce and that seemed to worry my friend Toby. The Shoshone, the Flatheads, the Nez Perce… they all feared the Blackfeet. And those three nations often banded together to hunt in strength for their mutual protection, especially when they dare encroach the Three Forks.

Toby didn't miss a trick. He watched me looking around, counting braves, ponies and the few flimsy-looking ancient trade muskets they possessed. He knew right off why that curious, doubting expression was spreading over my face like a dark rain cloud, a look that need not be questioned to know what my mind was thinking and my eyes were asking.

He looked at me rather gravely. "*Pahkees!* Blackfeet! Too many warriors… too many fire-sticks. Bad medicine! Good Indian… no chance."

When Toby uttered the word *Pahkee* he got an immediate reaction from the Flatheads. Many a head turned our way. The rising murmur of concern was like an unmistakable crescendo that spelled fear and hatred.

A gray-haired man, old and wizened and wrinkled beyond his years, spoke to the little Snake. That old fella was obviously a respected leader of the people. You could see by the way the whole bunch of them hushed right up and stepped back, giving him room and command to speak. The very plains itself was stilled, only the crackling, hissing embers of our campfire and the whistling nighttime breezes dared to interrupt this venerable Salish sage. He spoke softly in a low, near whispered tone, barely perceptible to my ears. I strained to pick out his words, the intent of his ancient guttural brogue. I could make out the word *Pahkee*, Salish for their bitter enemies the Blackfeet. All else escaped me. I looked around the blazing fireside at the warriors, the old folk, the squaws and young'uns. Everyone listened in rapt attention. Several were nodding their heads. All wore the same fearful, passionate countenance as far as the mention of the Pahkees was concerned. When he stopped, there was a loud, agreeable murmur rumbling throughout the throng.

"What did the old one say?" I asked Toby.

Toby turned towards me, his face was grim, sober. The old chief and those around us stared directly into my eyes, looking for a sign of strength or weakness, testing my reaction, seeing where I would stand and what I would say.

"He, C`e~ll sq'qeymi...Three Eagle. He, chief of Salish people. He say, 'The heart of the *Pahkee* is a lie and his tongue is a trap. If he says peace it is to deceive; he comes to us as a brother; he smokes his pipe with us, but when he sees us weak, and off our guard, he will slay and steal. We will have no such peace; let there be war'."

I would never forget Three Eagle's words, spoken by the leader of a people whose very existence often hung by the slim hairs of Blackfeet deceit and treachery. These were people who had reason to hate. That fear and hatred sparked by constant internecine warfare and raids. And with the depredations came utter contempt and loathing for a nation of outright bullies that preyed on all the friendly Indians, driving them away from the buffalo lands to the distant mountain ranges, to near hunger and starvation.

The *Pahkees* were like the Huns in olden days, invading the Roman Empire; sacking, raping, killing, enslaving, driving all before them into complete submission. I had read about these ancient peoples in my pa's history books when I was growing up. Everyplace, every era of man seems to have suffered from these same kinds of people. And the Northwest, here and now was no different. I knew the story. The Mandans and the Hidatsa down on the Knife had told us about them years ago. They, too, spoke with contempt of the way the Piegans and their kin the Bloods and the Siksika and their allies the Gros Ventre had come by trade-muskets and rot gut whiskey, the white man's water from the English traders in Canada. The Blackfeet overpowered and brutalized all the peaceful Indian nations who stood in their way, constantly harassing the weak tribes to the north like the Kutenai and the Pend d' Oreille, lying in wait for the Salish and Nez Perce to venture forth from their western mountains. They pushed the Snakes out of their ancient hunting grounds, hunting them down, enslaving their women, their kids and marauding the high plains and the mountain valleys, even taking on the proud *Absaroka* their mortal enemies, in their valley of the *As-to-pah-oan-zhah*.

I understood their concern. I was amazed at their courage, their willingness to brave potential confrontation and disaster, just to hunt where their ancestors did.

I nodded to Toby and then to the chief.

"Tell C`e~ll sq'qeymi…Three Eagle," I said to Toby, "I know of these *Pahkees*. Tell him that Captain Meriwether had a fight and killed two of their young warriors to the north of here just two years ago. He took first blood."

Toby turned to the old man relaying what I had said. The wizened one nodded, and uttered a response.

That wily old cuss shot a questioning glance right back at me, demanding directly, "Col-Ter, Three Eagle say… why you here?"

I smiled right back. I'd been waiting to answer that very same question all day long. "Why, looking for you folks, why else?"

The Snake looked at me quizzically like, as if he couldn't believe his ears.

I smoothed the ground before us, snapped off a twig from a nearby willow and began to sketch a map right there on the prairie sod.

Toby drew closer, the Flats and their old chief, likewise. They all gathered around, wondering just what was I up to.

"We got us a Fort… a tradin' post. See… right here." And I drew a long line to the east, bisecting it with another.

"*As-to-pah-oan-zhah,* the Yellowstone. And this one here is '*la Corne*', the Big Horn."

"Ahhh! The Waters of the Wind!" said Toby, turning and speaking in the Flathead brogue he relayed my words.

"Exactly!" I replied with a smile. "We're makin' headway, boys."

They nodded in turn. They knew the place… right in the middle of their allies, the *Absaroka*. There was a distinct murmur just then coming from many of those who stood looking over my shoulder. It was all such wonderment to these simple folk; big doin's as far as they were concerned. The movement, the activity of men, strange men so close their own country was always a cause of interest and concern.

"Why, here… by the Wind?" asked Toby pointing to my map.

"Safer, I suspect. Didn't want to bite off more than we could chew. Especially, since we weren't too sure how the Blackfeet would take to us. In any case that's where Mr. Lisa decided to hang his hat."

Leave it to an Indian to start asking the right questions. Toby had given me my opening. I arose and went directly to my kit and unrolled a skin I had packed for just this moment.

"Beaver," I said displaying the tanned pelt for all to see. "To trade for beaver. All you can fetch."

I rubbed the fur's fine hair, caressing its softness and then handed the skin to Toby.

"Ahh," Toby grunted and turned, uttering several words to Three Eagle.

The old man said nothing... his face remained unreadable. He continued to stare at me. All his people did. They were waiting for more. Beaver meant little to them, though they respected all of nature's critters.

"Hold on," I said, as I unpacked and spread out on my blanket the trade goods I had brought.

"We got mirrors, beads, all kinds of fancy stuff to trade for." I took my tomahawk and skinning knife from my belt and casually handed them to Toby to pass around.

"Get a close look at these blades... you'll see they're fine quality. There's plenty of these and much more at the Fort," adding, "Tell 'em, Toby, tell 'em everythin' I said."

The old Snake thought for a moment and muttered to the ancient Salish chief. Three Eagle's comments were short and obviously terse, to the point. Toby turned back to me. His face appeared to have a somber bent to it, grave, if not outright sullen. There was silence where I thought there should be excitement. What now, I thought to myself? I knew injuns drove a hard bargain, but my bag of tricks had run dry, I showed them all I had to offer.

"Fire-sticks?" He said. "White-man-Fort trade fire-sticks for skins?"

He looked at me right straight in the eye. They all did. It was a most uncomfortable feeling. His gaze could've burnt a hole right through me. It was a question I should have been ready to answer. But, I wasn't, Manuel had never broached the subject and I had never brought it up... medals and trinkets and such were all that I had ever dealt in. Three Eagle wanted more, much more.

"I... I don't know," I said hesitatingly.

"*Pahkees...*" his tone, the vehemence virtually spat to the ground with all the hate he could muster, "have many fire-sticks from the white-English trading fort."

Toby was rather matter of fact, pointing to the north with a stiffened finger poised like an arrow in flight. The crowd turned with him in that direction, grunting as one. And they were unanamous to a man. They left me that moment with little doubt of what they expected Lisa to provide.

I wondered... could the Missouri Fur Company do no less for these peaceful Flatheads? Especially, if we wanted their trade and their fight allied alongside us against the Blackfeet. That was the unasked question and a mighty big one at that. Even a bonehead like me could see the unbalanced odds. The far more numerous Blackfeet had gotten a deadly advantage from their trade with the Canucks and the Brits, allowing their red hordes to run roughshod over the Northwest, dominating the lesser, the peaceful Indian nations. These Flatheads weren't shirkers like some might have thought. Hell, Joe Whitehouse said it best in his journal, "the likelyest and honestst

Savages we have ever yet Seen." No, they were as brave as a people could be and they sorely wanted a fighting chance. They were looking to me right then to help them even-up the odds.

I found myself nodding my head, taking a big hard swallow to clear the voice- ways. "I won't lie to you, cause I just don't know. The best that I can do is to tell y'all that we'll have to wait and see what Mr. Lisa has to say."

That was all I could think to say. Somehow I didn't think that that would set right with these folks. But I didn't want to lie, not to them or to any man. They wouldn't respect that in me nor did they deserve to hear it. I wasn't about to trample on the one thing that meant something to men of honor out on the frontier, a man's word. No matter what Lisa told me to do or say.

Toby grunted, turned away and went off talking with his friends.

I wasn't sure he was convinced either, but he was the best bet I had to get these people to come to Manuel's. If Toby and these Flatheads wouldn't buy in, then neither would his Shoshones. The Nez Perce would probably follow suit. My mission would fail, there would be nothing left for me to do. It was beginning to be every bit as cold as the mountains I had just left behind. I was feeling a mite low right then, that ol' hangdog feeling.

Later that evening, Toby finally got around to talking about his boy, his pride, Runs with Horses. Tears welled in the old man's eyes, his whole frame sagged, that seemingly undaunted spirit seemed to wilt right out of him. He had lost his son in an accident of somekind and in remorse wandered away from his people, the Snakes and by sheer coincidence found himself with the Flatheads in time for their annual hunt.

I put my arm around the old man's shoulders and hugged him. What could I say to ease his pain? Life is hard, especially in the West. The wilderness is neither merciful, nor empathetic. There is only life and death. One keeps living 'til it's his turn to die. After two years of tracking, trapping and living on a lonely trail of wandering solitude, I was sure glad to meet up with this good man. We were fast developing a friendship that I dearly wanted to keep, with or without their trade.

Toby had palavered with all the chiefs for quite a spell, talking far into the night. I sat off by myself a ways away watching the debate. The tone was sober, the content obviously forthright with few wasted words. Indians always spoke straight to the point, never beating around the bush. And they expected you to do the same. Being glib was not especially one of their traits, but being astute definitely was. Not a smile cracked a single face that night. Nothing to reveal or give away their hand. These were cool people, sharp witted, hard bargaining people. They had to be, life out here was too demanding. Several times those Flats would listen to Toby and then stare long and hard at me. I could feel those questioning glances burning a hole right through me. It was downright discomforting, I twitched nervously more than a few times, but I held my poise, my composure. Win, lose or draw... I'd ride out of here with my head held high. Maybe those old boys were trying to figure if my words spoke with a straight tongue or if my heart was true. All the while calculating in their own way just what kind of man this so called *tab-ba-bone* be.

I made no move or gesture to influence them. I just sat patiently, listening, letting old Toby do my talking for me. When the moon had drifted high in the night sky, the conversation came to an abrupt end. Several nodded to the Snake and then watched him walk towards me.

I looked up anxiously, unable to hide the strain of anticipation, whispering everso softly under my breath, "Uh, oh! Here it comes."

Arising to greet my friend, we looked at each other over a moment of silence. The worn features of his face were as unreadable as mine were so blatantly clear.

Then abruptly Toby gave me Three Eagle's decision. "Col-Ter, tomorrow scouts look for buffalo. People go too." He paused, then... "Three Eagle say, you come hunt buffalo with his people."

"Fine by me, ol' friend," I replied nodding my head, my face suddenly aglow. Buffalo meat sounded awfully good right then. What's more it would put us a lot closer to Manuel's, giving me time to work on them. Stupid me, little did I know that their minds were way ahead of mine.

The little Snake gently touched my arm. He was staring straight into my eyes, probing deeply. I think they all were. It was somewhat discomforting, my mouth and lips going bone dry. There was something else. I waited. Life was too short in these wilds to take anything for granted especially, a white stranger with no discernable purpose... at least to their way of thinking. They had to be sure. Indians have a way of delving into a man's eyes right to the core of his soul, as if reading his mind, divining character and intent. I should have known. They might be a superstitious lot, primitive and savage and all, but nobody reads the trail of a man's worth better. They had just read mine and apparently trusted what they had found.

"After hunt... Three Eagle say, Toby go with Col-Ter to the *As-to-pah-oan-zhah*, to white trader's lodge. Three Eagle come too with warriors." Then my little Snake friend added rather wryly, "Three Eagle talk trade... talk *Tushepah* beaver skins for white man fire-sticks."

"Whoa! Now you're talkin'!"

How about them apples, I could hardly believe my ears. This was it, then, what I was waiting to hear and sent to do. What more could I ask for? I would bring them to Manuel's just as the Spaniard wanted. From there on out it would be all up to him. It dawned on me right then and there the whole long miserable winter trek was worth it just to hear Toby's words.

"Toby, ol' friend," rubbing my stomach I replied with a wide smile, "my belly's primed, tomorrow will be a good day… to hunt."

CHAPTER TWO

As the Nation prepared to move earlier that morning hours before sunrise scouts ranged well to the east in search of the buffalo herds. By midmorning two had reached their sought out destination, bypassing entering the valley of the forks altogether. Approaching from the southwest and paralleling the valley from the bluffs beyond to the south, they had crossed the rolling short-grass country completely undetected. Halting, they found themselves looking down upon the swift cool stream their friends the *Absaroka* called the Straight, just a few short miles from where the three rivers come together. To their relief, they were alone or so it seemed.

They were young, yet patient and cautious as befit their natural mien... carefully scanning the river below and its tree-lined banks. They looked beyond to the short grass plains stretching towards a long elevated front of sandstone cliffs, two, three miles distant to the east. A family of swift, graceful pronghorns, wind-eaters they called them, could be seen peacefully browsing unperturbed. A lone red-tail hawk glided idly above the flat plains on routine gopher-patrol. The air was still, the land, the day looked plenty peaceful.

They gazed longingly, almost affectionately at the unbroken line of sandstone cliffs where rested the *pishkun*, the buffalo-jump-place, the sacred site used by "the people" since before their grandfathers' grandfathers' time. It was an ancient place, ancestral in line, filled with the spirits of those who had hunted, lived and died there in the dim, remote past, harkening back to the earliest days of their forefathers memories and beyond.

Bones were there at the base of the *pishkun*... the accumulated bones of buffalo carcasses piled higher than the tallest of lodge poles from centuries upon centuries of deadly, suicidal plunges and mass butchery. *Tipi* rings were also there, the *tipi* rings of smooth, polished, stream-bed stones... stones that marked and held down the edges of their animal skin lodges for eons against the ravages of incessant winds and inclement weather.

Now, the lodges were long gone, but the spirits that inhabited the ancient site were still there. You could feel their very presence, catch their fleeting shadows and hear their long ago silenced voices still very much alive... borne as well by whistling winds as by subtle evening breezes.

We heard of this phenomenon, these buffalo jumps, many times since the Corps first met up with the Mandan and the Hidatsa and learned the ways of the red man of the high plains and the mountains of the Northwest. To the red man, the buffalo and all it had to offer sustained their way of life, their culture. The rich meat, the skin, the bones, the hooves and sinews and organs meant survival, food, shelter and tools. Before the arrival from the arid south of the horse, the sacred *ponokamita*, the red man hunted the herds afoot. Never haphazardly, but in carefully orchestrated moves, the ancient ones funneled the frightened beasts from higher ground, thru ever-narrowing lanes of piled stone-cairns, driving them off the precipices of the steep cliffs to meet a violent crashing death below. And, so, it was here for the ancestors of the Shoshone and the Salish, the Crow and even the Blackfeet. The *pishkun* by the Madison had witnessed this same annual ritual for thousands of years. But now, the horse had changed the way of the hunt forever.

Below the scouts, the banks of the clear running river were thick with rows of red willow and tall stands of broad limbed cottonwoods. Beaver, otter, muskrat all called this riverine place home. High above the river, an osprey soared on a solitary hunt; her hungry little ones perched a few miles downriver nesting atop an old dead tree, screeching with hunger, demanding their due.

To the scouts the river crossing appeared peaceful enough, calm, devoid of human presence, the way they hoped it would be. And, yet, they hesitated, eyeing patiently the darting movements of a pair of cedar waxwings flitting through the trees and willowy underbrush, watching for sudden interruption, unerring flight inexplicably veering away. Danger was deceitful, particularly the two-legged kind, often lurking undetected amidst such idyllic splendor. Thus was the life of the red man in hostile country. Thus, it was he lived with a wary eye.

The cedar waxwings flew undisturbed. No panicked alarm ensued. No painted *Pahkee* nightmares awaited in ambush... of this they were certain. The two braves smiled, breathing relief with their good fortune. *Pahkees* were treacherous, cunning, never to be trusted, but not the equal of the Tushepaws of the Flathead nation in individual combat or valor. Why else did the Blackfeet avoid their Bitterroots?

They looked at one another, each doing his best to conceal more than a few tics of unsteady nerves. They were both young and eager, excited at the prospect to be the first to bring back word of the great herds. The sacred buffalo waited, browsing on spring grass a short ride across the valley, an easy climb to the top of the far cliffs and beyond to the verdant bluffs. They would be there, surely. They had always been there. Our two scouts could see in the distance the faint buffalo trails leading down from the high bluffs to riverwater. They both smiled and rubbed their bellies in circular motions. Then they laughed, happily, smug, relieved, nodding their heads, completely, irrevocably satisfied. Today would be a good day to hunt.

Down to the water's edge they rode. Quietly, carefully, they forded the shallow river; their unshod mountain ponies gingerly negotiating the slippery, smooth stone-strewn bed, until they reached the opposite shore, climbed its grassy banks and entered the riverside woods beyond.

Swallowed by the shadows of the riparian copse, the two scouts again waited in the near darkness of the woods and surveyed the plains before them. Nothing had changed. Satisfied, they looked at one another, each nodding approval. Off they rode at a spirited gallop, covering the span of grasslands between the river-line and the high cliff ground to the east quickly without a single enemy the wiser.

Reaching the base, they steadily worked their way up the wind-eroded sandstone palisades, following a worn, winding buffalo trail, until they topped out beyond the edge of the cliff. Again they watched and listened, every instinct straining to detect. With a soft heel kick, they nudged their pony's slats and moved forward, threading their way through a network of dry coulee bottoms, working their way farther and farther into the interior of the rolling bluff uplands. They continued to advance at a measured walk, slow and deliberate. Eyes and ears, every sense and intuition, pony and man primed and alert.

Little moved, save for waves upon waves of lush spring grasses undulating to the gentle rhythm of the southwestern breezes… mesmerizing, enchanting, nigh on fixating our two Bitterroot riders. It was all they could ever hope to find in this land of annual promise. Each brave smiling inwardly, sated by the beauty and the rapture of spring amuck, all the while visions of massive herds of shaggy beasts danced in their minds. Tonight promised a feast to satiate all their hungers. Oh, their people would be pleased.

Suddenly, inexplicably, one of the scouts stopped and sniffed the air. He did it again and then again.

"What are you doing?" His partner asked, irritated. "Have you gone mad?"

"Quiet!" his partner snapped, and he sniffed the air again. "Can't you smell them?" he finally whispered. "They're close."

"Smell… what?" The look was incredulous, shaking his head at his friend as if to say that his quiver was missing more than a few arrows.

"Buffalo… I tell you I can smell them." Again, he sniffed, breathing in hard, closing his eyes for maximum concentration. His countenance said as much, he was convinced beyond doubt.

"You fool, no one can smell buffalo… they don't stink, everyone knows that."

"I can… I'll show you. Follow me… and keep your magpie's tongue silenced"

They turned up from the coulee bottom and ascended until they topped out on a wind-blown, rock-crowned knoll. The search was over. The two scouts need ride no further for off to the east were hundreds, perhaps thousands of the great humped-back-beasts spread out over the rolling grasslands for miles, grazing placidly.

The agnostic, the non-believer could not believe his eyes. Indeed, he was silent. His jaundiced-tongue rebuked, words neither forming nor escaping his lips. His companion sat quietly upon his pony, smiling, gloating, vindicated, all the while taking in the magnificence of what lay before him. "The people" were blessed, again, and so near the "old ones" *pishkuns*. It had always been this way. The spirits of their ancestors were indeed favoring "the people" as they always had. What else could it possibly be?

The first buck, the breeze-sniffer turned to his friend and beamed. "Told you I smelled 'em."

"Ah hah!" the two warriors laughed in unison.

Yet, even as they congratulated themselves, caution returned, and instincts prevailed, wariness to the red man being as natural to their survival as eating and drinking. They turned their ponies and immediately headed back down into the coulee bottom from whence they came. Dismounting, the two scouts loosely tied their ponies to a pair of gnarly, deep-rooted sage. They waited for several moments listening, smelling, almost divining, relying on every instinct, every sense, bodily and otherwise, that the Great Creator had given them. As I have said before, to an Indian caution is a way of life. Without it a man, any man would be as naked and unarmed as any "babe in the woods."

Satisfied, they crept back up from the bottom of their dry ravine to the top of that rock and shrub crowned outcropping. The breeze had subtly changed, now solely wafting in from the direction of the herd. Even the non-believer could smell them... a scent ancient to tribal memory and hungry senses. The two young braves smiled, again, quietly congratulating themselves on arriving downwind.

They now turned their intention to watching the herd and counting, separating bulls, culling cows and calves. While not quite a *fait acompli* their eagerness for the hunt swelled, anticipation was almost more than their empty bellies could bear. It all seemed so perfectly clear and simple. Flathead hunters on their fleet mountain ponies would swoop down on the unsuspecting herds driving them to the far reaches of the grassy plateau, slaying hundreds of the sacred beasts en route. Today's reckoning would bring tonight's feasting warming their stomachs and memories for many a moon to come. Yes, indeed, today was a good day... to hunt.

The scouts had seen enough. It was time to alert "the people" and bring them on. The great animals would continue to munch away undisturbed. They would do so all day long. Plenty of time to backtrack across the short grass plains and …

A sudden movement from below inexplicably caught the eye of one of our scouts freezing him in place as solidly as the lichen dressed stone by which he lay. What had he seen? What could it have been? Whatever it was, it did not belong. An out of place hue, a brief flash of color, appearing from behind a narrow finger of land. And then it was gone. Somehow, he deigned it of human origin. Yet, he must be sure, maybe his eyes, his mind was playing tricks on him. He rubbed his eyes repeatedly, clearing away the dust the grit of the trail, the glare of the sun. He stared hard anew…

There it was again. Whatever or whoever that something was, does not belong… not there… not like that. He held his breath, scrunched his eyes and refocused.

There… there it was again. This time the scout was certain… movement in a coulee bottom between two fingers of land, close enough to smell and see. It was human to be sure, and not of his Nation. Are they friendly? Can they possibly be Crow who so often hunted hereabouts? He was not so sure. Uncertainty welled within him. He felt a dry lump stuck in his throat and desperately tried to disgorge it… to no avail, kicking himself for want of water, but more so for lack of sand and nerve.

He nudged his partner, pointing to the coulee below.

His friend nodded, he too caught the movement.

They lay still, petrified limbs waiting quietly, utterly silent. Patience paid off, as the movement below edged forward, again, exposing themselves in full view. Now, they could make out ponies and saddled ones at that emerging from the coulee bottom. At least two of the saddled ponies had high pommels and cantles of rawhide covered wooden frames, Piegan saddles to be sure, distinctly those used by young squaws that often accompanyied the hunting bands. These would be the herd-tenders, the skinners and butchers. They would do the bloody work when the killing was done.

They kept watching, now counting a different kind of critter. They could see ponies trailing empty travois and tallied many painted *parfleches*, brightly decorated sacks of tanned animal hide to carry butchered meat, hanging from the squaws saddle horns. Several more saddled ponies appeared. The two scouts gawked, staring hard. Hair halters! Hair halters and padded buffalo-hide saddles… that of the ever-daring *Pahkee* buffalo hunter.

Pahkees! How close they had come to blundering into a hunting party. They hugged the ground where they lay, their heads, their bodies becoming as one with the grassy knoll. Did the *Pahkees* know? Had they been seen, their trail, their ponies' prints found? They thought not, yet, could they be sure? Barely a breath escaped between them as they remained deadly still. An electric jolt of realization streaked throughout their nervous systems of just how close they were to discovery and certain death… or worse.

Deftly one scout carefully touched the other's arm and with an empty hand motioned him forward while the long finger of his other touched his lips to command silence and discretion.

His companion nodded solemnly, the look in his eyes, his countenance effacing all trace of recent joy.

They crept forward at a slow crawl, slithering on their bellies, human snakes inching ahead, to come to a sudden rest a few feet shy of the top of the knoll. They had used every form of concealment at hand, every trick in the red man's book of stealth. Fear and excitement the blood of adrenaline alternately pumping, flowing, electrifying their minds and their bodies as they lay prone atop the summit, scanning the hunting fields ahead. They must stay a little while longer. They must wait and watch and see. They must find out how many *Pahkee* hunters were nearby.

"Count their ponies."

"I don't like this. We must go. We must warn the people, now."

"Shhhh! Be still. Be patient. We will… as soon as we are sure."

Tense minutes pass. Before long, they could see several packhorses being led by squaws and young boys in their early teens. The ravine was more crowded than they at first imagined. They counted between them many ponies, belying twenty, thirty hunters… maybe more.

The sudden appearance of the *Pahkee* hunting party had rattled our two scouts beyond any grip of trepidation they had ever known. Surprisingly they had remained calm despite their youth, their inexperience. Duty, responsibility now dictated a new course of action. Their mission was to find the herds, but that quest no longer took precedence. Peaceful pursuit no longer was possible. Disaster loomed. A different stealth, cunning, instinct now prevailed and our two scouts knew it instantly, from that first moment of detection, that first realization that they were not alone.

Time moved ever so slowly, just then. Our two scouts waited, exercising all the patience their bodies and minds could muster. And still no sign of the hunters. They began to get edgy slowly searching, scanning the rest of the landscape for sign of the two dozen or more hunters sure to be about. Two dozen, even three dozen *Pahkee* fighters, our warriors could easily handle. Our two braves were confident, proud. But, how many *Pahkees* were nearby the three-rivers-valley or within a short day's ride? Where was the rest of their vaunted nation? How many bands had moved down from winter encampments in their northern mountain valleys? That was the real, unanswered worry. Their enemies traditionally hunted the Forks later in the warmer summer months, unwittingly leaving their own people a short gap in the hunting season. So why the change?

It was all so very tenuous, nerve-wracking. They could hear each other's breathing, the incessant pounding of equally racing hearts, see and sense the concern and anxiety in one another's face. They remained muted, though, neither of them uttering a sound. No word was needed, not when they could read in each other's eyes and thoughts what their tribal training and instincts told them must be done. By noon, their people would have crossed the waters of the Straight unaware of the looming predicament, venturing out onto the plains between the river and the *pishkun* cliffs, completely exposed. Time was fleeting; they must warn "the people," soon.

But, was it already too late? Indecision dominated them. What were their people to do? They couldn't give up the hunt. Not now! Not when they were so close and so tired and hungry. But, everything before them told otherwise. The portent of conflict-to-come hung imminently and ominously overhead in the bright blue sky as if pre-ordained. And the questions remained. How strong were the *Pahkee* and how close were their legions? Was this *Pahkee* band a long way from home on a solitary hunt or was their nation nearby?

The younger of the two braves suddenly had a change of heart and now waxed daring-do. He whispered to his companion, boldly, albeit foolishly. Courage, he thought, demanded action, even if foolhardy.

"Come, let us work our way behind the coulee, dash in and steal their ponies. The *Pahkees* will be too surprised. Think of the honor... think of the songs our people will sing. We'll be heroes."

"Fool... and have the whole *Pahkee* nation swoop down on our people. Be patient, you son of a marmot's crap. Wait and watch their hunt, we shall learn more, count their strength, their numbers. Besides, once their hunt begins we will be able to pull-back unnoticed."

It was well that prudence and maturity prevailed. Suddenly, from out of the coulee bottom two files of mounted hunters on swift buffalo-runners burst out at a dead run. They were a sight-to-behold. Of magnificent bearing, longhaired mounted *Pahkee* bowmen, naked, sinewy and sun-bronzed becoming as one with their sleek ponies as they raced toward the startled herds. The land began to shake and rumble as if locked in the spasm of a tremendous earthquake. Blood curdling, aboriginal screams rent the air in a strangely exhilarating knell, panicking the timid, placid, hapless animals.

The air, the ground suddenly exploded with the incessant pounding of thousands of hooves as the massive creatures bolted and plunged, running amuck, hither and yon, seemingly without purpose or poise. The rolling green prairie grassland literally turned into a sea of brown, frothing, bulging-eyed critters. An irresistible tide swept across the land. An ocean of buffalo kicked up great divots of sod, uncontrollably, crashing, caroming into one another leaving the peaceful plateau and the calm of the noontime day in ruin and chaos in their wake. They drove on, bawling, bellowing and screaming in fear... and soon for so many, taking their last gasps, their final death throes, here and there, dotting the land like so many scattered stones and fallen leaves.

"Look, look!" One of our scouts cried, barely able to contain his ownself.

"I see, I see, you idiot," replied his partner.

The thrill of the chase inspired the two hidden scouts to a brashness they had never known. Unconsciously, certainly without thought or caution, they half-arose for a better view, highlining themselves atop the stony knoll.

The two files of *Pahkee* hunters charged on unaware of enemy presence, as they splintered left and right, adroitly, precisely as if on silent command. Left-handed bowmen rode to the left and the right-handed bowmen rode to the right of the herd, funneling the crazed beasts on a frenetic collision course at a dead run. On they came, the swift buffalo-runners dashing by the slower, heavier bulls, passing them by in a deliberate pursuit of the choicer delicacies that were the cows and the young calves. Why settle for a tough old male when plenty of delectable and tender veal was in their path and so easy to bring down?

With recklessness that knew no bounds, with wanton abandon and insatiable zeal, the mounted-bowman veered their racing ponies perilously near their thundering foe. Ancient skills born to the Plains tribes let fly notched arrows from near point blank range, releasing stoneheaded-missles-of-death into the tender vital spots behind the cows and calves vulnerable forelegs with near-pinpoint results and fatal accuracy.

The great, shaggy animals felt the sharp, piercing pangs invading their sacred bodies with terrific impact, causing instant disruption to their internal organs. Those dumb beasts could not be expected to know what was causing such great pain, robbing them inexorably of all their strength. Their adrenaline was pumping at too massive a rate and their fear of the mounted hunters was way too great. They just kept fleeing, fast as they could towards the distant horizon. With every stride, their exertions became greater, their breaths harder to come by, their vision narrower and narrower, until one by one they could go on no further. With the last beats of their enormous hearts, each dying *enee's* knees would finally buckle and they would collapse to the very prairie grasses that nurtured their lives from their very first days to await their final gasps of life.

The swift runners then veered away in a narrow arc, returning for another close-in shot in a deliberate attempt to finish off their quarry. Their method was all the same, tested by a hundred years of the mounted hunt and repeated until each one of their targets succumbed to weakness or death and came to a crashing halt. The *Pahkee* hunters were relentless as wolfpacks, spellbound by bloodlust, undeviating in their pursuit to the end. As each victim dropped, individual hunters continued the chase pursuing another choice target and repeating the process over and over until their insatiable lust was satisfied and the herd eventually outdistanced them, disappearing over the easternrise. Such was the mad reckoning of the buffalo hunt, practiced by every horse culture on the plains and today's pursuit would be no different.

The disciplined files of bowmen off now on solo hunts left the prairie strewn with the carcasses of their fallen prey as the mad flight of the buffalo herd broke into a chaotic escape headlong into the farthest reaches of the rolling grasslands. Disorder reigned, every beast for himself, age-old instincts of survival and herd integrity now dissolved into mass turmoil, propelling each of the furry giants to the limits of their stamina and nervous endurance. Wild-eyed and bawling, sweat and blood, saliva and dirt stained their fur and hide. Their massive hearts continued to race and pump beyond control. Their lungs gasped and sucked and burned inside starving for want of more fresh air.

Out of the defiles that hid their presence, squaws and young boys alike ventured forward, bright-eyed, beaming with excitement, cheering their hunters on with screams, exhortations of encouragement to… "Kill, kill, kill the sacred *enee*."

The smiles and glee that lit their faces with the fall of each wounded calf or cow signaled their role in the hunt was now beginning. It befell to them the bloody task; to gut, to bleed, to disembowel, to skin and quarter and butcher, to pack and load every ounce and inch of the life nourishing *enee*.

Our two Flathead scouts were both caught up in the excitement of the chase, vicariously joining the enemy band in the sheer enjoyment and exhilaration of buffalo hunting, Plains Indian style. But their enthusiasm led them to abandon the last vestige of caution as they each arose side by side to their full height to watch the chase and follow its thrilling pursuit.

A young squaw was inexplicably drawn to their presence atop the outcropping, immediately spotting the two *Salish* scouts. She could hardly believe her eyes, rubbing them over and over to get a second, clearer look. Could it be, she asked herself disbelievingly? Yes, yes… it must be so. What were they doing here? Were there more to be found? Was this a *Salish* trap, the treacherous dogs? The questions came to her young mind at an accelerated pace. But, she didn't panic, she of good *Piegan* stock. She knew what she was seeing, instantly feeling the fear, the loathing that was now spreading throughout her veins. She did the only thing she could do. She gave a startled cry… quickly sounding the alarm to her fellow herd tenders, those youngsters who were yet to reach their manhood. They were the young boys of her tribe, scions of glory-past, heirs to infamy, warriors-in-waiting. They looked towards the knoll, the rocky outcrop, all eyes intent, straining and when they saw the two spies standing exposed on their flanks, they grew bold, notching their arrows, walking forward menacingly to confront the enemy interlopers.

Unnoticed by the Salish still spellbound by the chase, the squaw quickly mounted a saddled pony and raced from the coulee bottom to alert the far-flung hunting band. She had almost reached the tail end of the speeding bowmen when our scouts first realized they had been spotted. Fear instantly took hold, the realization of discovery by the hated *Pahkees* quickly sinking-in. Their stupidity and carelessness, their inexcuseable guilt being more than they could endure, the two were ashamed beyond anything they had ever known. Guilt, shame, dishonor… exposure, realization, fear, all coming together simultaneously, merging in their souls and minds, instantly holding them captive. Their breath was taken away, for one long, lone beat their hearts had stopped altogether, time stood still… that excruiating moment would live forever in their minds.

By then, the squaw was directing the attention of one hunter after another. Blood-splattered bowmen were soon looking back, scanning the top of the outcropping where our two immobilized scouts yet stood. The affront of their presence drove each of the *Piegans* to outright rage. One by one, they dropped their hunt. *Pahkees* converged on the knoll from every corner of the killing fields.

Finally, our scouts snapped out of their trance. Even the bravest of the brave knows the peril of a moment's hesitation.

"Ride!" screamed one of the scouts, exhortng the other. "Ride like the wind."

Off they went, turning and fleeing down the rock and sage covered knoll. They leaped atop their ponies, speeding away as fast as their mountain-bred carriers would take them. Trailing winds kicked at their backsides, carrying fading *Pahkee* cries and spurring the two scouts on, faster and faster and faster to breakneck speed. They rode with grim determination, confident of their Bitterroot chargers' bottom and speed. Their steeds were more than equal to any Plains bred horses: stamina and heart were their breed's trademarks. They quirted their ponies bare hinds furiously. With every lash of rawhide, they strained their mounts to greater and greater effort to distance themselves from certain pursuit. They dug in their heels, their lean, sinewy thighs pressing in ever so tightly. Gripping their ponies sweating flanks with legs-of-steel they raced northward, across the rolling hills, away from the River Straight. The last thing they wanted to do was to return by the same trail from whence they came, leading the *Pahkees* down upon their unsuspecting people. Down through the ravines, dips and gullies to conceal their flight. Onward they fled towards the distant waters of the Cherry, the Gallatin, to throw off the wily *Pahkee*. Instantly, betweeen them they had drawn a plan-on-the-run, and it all hinged on deception. Keep to the north, eventually, break free of the high bluffs with its rolling lands. Then, abruptly, turn west and cut back south to the line of cliffs overlooking the plains, holding-close, until, they could make a timely dash across the grassy plains to the Straight and warn their people.

It was in the end a good, expedient plan, the only real choice they had. Their deception was momentarily complete, and a slight advantage of time and distance gained. But, the day was still young and much could still happen. And their people, ohh, their people…

As the two scouts fled, a tall, broad shouldered young *Piegan* rallied his dispersed hunters about him. There was something altogether distinctive about this particular brave; his bearing, the way he stood and spoke and carried himself befit the look of one in command; cool, decisive, unwavering in resolve. Charisma was not a word bandied about by the Piegan, least not the members of the elite Buffalo Bulls society. In theory, they were equals. Yet, if any warrior that day exuded such magnetic-appeal he alone possessed it. He was tall, yet others were just as tall. In fact they all carried the same muscular frames, lean, hard, lithe. Little separated him from his companions, save for the internal fire burning from deep within an undaunted spirit, barely fettered, smoldering like a runaway prairie conflagration threatening all in its path. The Buffalo Bulls heard white-hot-rage when he spoke, his voice bristling authority and determination. Even more cutting than his bark's bite, were his eyes; cold, black, penetrating orbs, demanding hegemony over their wills.

He spoke softly to the squaw that alerted them to the presence of the foreigners, for she was dear to him. "Little sister, you saw only two?"

"Just two," she nodded. "No more, I am certain."

"We shall see," he said to no one in particular. Then…"Go, little sister. Warn Kootenai appe. Tell him *Salish* dogs are about. Tell him to come, not worry, the Buffalo Bulls will hunt down them down. Be wary, though, my little sister. Treachery may be about."

"Yes, my brother," was all she could manage to say.

Quickly, the young girl and the herd-tenders gathered the spare ponies and were off, racing west towards the valley of the three rivers. She, of the shiny, raven hair, could not have known at that precise moment how timely her alarm would be. Two enemy scouts were not cause for major concern, certainly not panic. Yet, *Piegan* land, her land had been invaded, a grave, unforgivable affront committed. But were there really only two? Such *audace*! Not possible! Never would they be so daring, so bold, so foolish as to come alone so far from their mountain aeries. Yet, the fresh meat of the sacred *enee* was a powerful lure, too strong for their hungry mountain dwelling neighbors to resist. Yet, they had done so before, many times before. Yes, that was it.

They were here to hunt the herds, *Piegan* herds. And they would come in strength. Yes, there must be more, but how many more? Nothing else made any sense.

Running Wolf's gaze grew grim as he looked in the direction of the Cherry and the fleeing spies. His dark, swarthy face bore an evil scowl, emboldened with hate as he watched and waited for the rest of his band to arrive. When they all returned, gathering about him with their hands, arms, bare torsos soaked with the sticky blood of the *enee*, they eagerly looked to him.

"*Maa-koyou-mah'-kaa...* we are ready. The dogs of the Bitterroot run away fast, but they will not get far if we hurry. Give the word, our knives are crying to be fed."

The voice was familiar to his ears beyond all others, belonging to his best friend, the trusted *Ak-o-tash-iks*... Many Horses, a strapping youngster with a vicious telltale scar emblazoned across his cheek. Many Horses looked upon Running Wolf as if in adulation. Boyhood friends, they hunted together even before they could string their first bows. Barely out of puberty, they raided the lands of the Crow, the Cree and the Assinibone, stealing many ponies, harvesting scalps like the Mandan husked corn, all the while adding to both their fame and their tribe's fortune. A recent raid caused his friend, Running Wolf to redub him. Honoring his daring and guile and the great battle scar that now graced his face, the new sobriquet, Many Horses, had stuck, becoming known among the *Siksika* and the *Gros Ventre*. Right now, though, Many Horses was chomping with impatience. The Buffalo Bulls were eager to prove their prowess again. This time, though, they were not thinking of *Salish ponokamitas*, soley, they were thinking of scalps... *Salish* scalps.

Running Wolf stared at his friend. His face remained expressionless, and then he spoke what they all wished to hear.

"Hear me my brothers. Let them run and tire their ponies. Let them lead us to their brothers... We go."

"*A-eeee-ah! A-eeee-ah!*" The Buffalo Bulls shrieked their delight, the very land itself trembled with the reverberation of their cacophonous din.

They raced to their ponies, leaping effortlessly aboard their mustang chargers. The dreaded *Piegans* were off, racing on their wingless steeds as fast as their speedy mounts could carry them. The excitement of the hunt was all but forgotten, saved for another day. There was now a different current running through the blood of their veins. Age-old hatred and hostility from innumerable tribal wars and raids and skirmishes now transformed these buffalo hunters into the savage *Piegan* warrior brotherhood of the Blackfeet Nation.

These were proud, defiant people, distinctly different from the many tribes who tried to share the bounty of the Three Forks. A people of great physical prowess and beauty; tall, muscular and lithe, with large, dark eyes, black and piercing, and long, straight, raven-colored hair, freely flowing with the wind. All in all this rabid, unfettered countenance, their warlike bent made them the fiercest visage in all of the Northwest and high plains to behold in the face of mortal combat. No mercy, no compassion to be reckoned with… for those unfortunates who dare enter their land were subject to immediate torture, humiliation and death… death at the hands of the Spartans of the Northwest.

Piegan reputation was well deserved, their infamy known far and wide across the breadth of the red man's lands. They lived for war and not much else, every day of their manhood spent preparing for it. They were the hoplites of the New World, the warriors that comprised the southern clans of the Blackfeet Nation, duly armed and befitting of their warrior class. Their personal arsenals were a primitive armoire of death and mayhem… blades of stone and metal honed to a skin and scalp ripping sharpness; heavy trade tomahawks from the English trading posts to the north and stoned-headed war clubs to pound and mash and pulverize. Coup sticks to attest individual valor and their sacred war honor… *namachkani.* Short sinew-backed bows and otter-skin quivers full of lethal stone-headed arrows. For those who had increasingly obtained them, trade muskets, British "fusees" with lead shot and black powder. Yet, no single weapon in their war-chest spoke louder than the unfettered tenacity of their fighting spirit.

The chase was now on with two distinct races. So quickly had the hunter become the warrior, springing after the fleeing spies like a wolf pack of rabid lobos running down their prey. The two scouts, the interlopers, racing to warn off the rest of their nation. The *Pahkee, Piegan* war band in hot pursuit… and lastly, their women and young boys to rouse the rest of the tribe… which would ultimately add an additional, deadlier race.

Who could have foreseen such a sinister convergence? Certainly not the Flatheads… all they wanted was to feed their people, to get in and get out with meat to last the coming winter and their scalps intact. The ever-warprone *Piegans*, arrogant, blustering… who would dare challenge their hegemony, certainly not the simple folks of the Bitterroots. What hellish mischief, what unknown evil conspired to bring this reproachment, this turmoil about? Had my presence somehow insured it, a harbinger of white, red conflict ahead? Was it preordained? None of these thoughts had entered my mind that day, certainly not when the morning ride had been so peaceful, with thoughts of the impending buffalo hunt so inviting. No, these questions were to be asked by me at a later, another time, a time to reflect, to wonder why, to rue the day ever happening.

I had ridden ahead with Toby and a small party of warriors early that morning after the scouts had left. The sky was clear, the sun rose bright and warm. The air crisp, clean with a hint of breeze, again blowing in from the southwest. We traveled over rolling grasslands to the south and west of the valley of the Three Forks. It was a bare ground kind of country of dips and swells and dry coulees and rolling hills and not much else. It was a lonely, windblown land, yet to feel the plow of civilized man and home only to badgers and hawks, mice and rabbits and not much else.

The Flathead hunters were young braves, eager for the chase and barely able to contain their youthful exuberance... nor the spirited steeds they rode. I, too, knew the sensation, the excitement and anticipation of the hunt; that tremendous rush of nervous energy, that irresistible surge of adrenaline coursing through my own spirited veins. It was man's age old instinct... a heritage, a right of passage passed down through blood since the human ape first dropped from a tree and hurled his first stone weapon. Out West it was the way of all plains and Rocky Mountain Indians. It was the way of survival and nothing else these people did seemed to stack up so magnificently as a buffalo hunt.

We rode at a steady gait, lathering our little ponies to a good sweat as they kicked up the prairie sod, eating up the miles from the far side of the Tobacco Roots to the valley of the Three Forks. Those Flatheads were having fun, laughing, and talking... full of spirit and hope. They were an intelligent, friendly people... quick to crack a smile, quick to learn. Watched my movements, the things I did, the way I responded to their people, their customs and fears. They were particularly keen on my rifle, unable to keep their eyes off of my piece the night before while I cleaned that weapon from butt to muzzle. They watched with great interest, especially when I checked my powder and my load and sighted down the length of the barrel, taking an imaginary bead. They cooed their "ahhhs" like expecting squaws as if I treated that piece like a wee bairn. Big-eyed they were, fascinated, all the while watching me, not missing a trick, learning, occasionally nodding to each other as if in mock approval. They thought alike, plain to see.

Truth was, I watched my hosts every bit as interested in them as they were in me. I didn't miss their keen interests in my weapon, either. I just kept it to myself as I went about my business. That flintlock was big medicine to those folks. Oh, they owned a few, worn-out, old trade muskets, picked up along the way... though nothing, according to my astonished companions like the *Pahkee* arsenal. Lead shot and gunpowder was hard to come by, used sparingly, and like all things hard to come by, quickly becoming a most cherished possession. But my long-rifle was no trade musket and they knew it. No sir, to these savages that long barreled Kentuck' piece-of-work was the fire-stick-from-hell. They weren't above envy or speculating, either… many a discerning eye looked my way, sizing ol' John Colter up, pairing rifle and white man together just to see what the two could do. I just hoped that I would never have to disappoint them.

Now, that old Snake, Toby, was something else altogether. He had spent a few weeks a couple of years back in the summer of '05 guiding the Corps. He and his boy, Runs With Horses, had lived with us, hunted with us, rode with us and led the whole kit and caboodle of us to the Bitterroots. As far as the Flatheads were concerned, Toby was a walking almanac on the white man. I liked that old Indian, trusted him and valued his judgment of injun ways. Truth was I was mighty glad to have his company right about then. I had been alone too long, all alone with just my memories and my little Crow piebald to keep me company. I was long overdue for something and someone to shout, smile and laugh about and with. Toby knew, recognized it right off. He felt the loneliness in my heart. He had felt the same way since losing his boy. Overnight we had become kindred spirits, brothers of self-imposed solitude. But, now with the hunt so near, with the work and its rewards soon to be undertaken, we looked forward to the chase, the exhilaration and excitement. Fresh life was about to be breathed into two melancholy spirits.

By late-morning we reached the Madison. Looking down upon the river and out across the grass plains beyond, nothing stirred, not even the vaguest sign of the scouts that preceded us earlier that day.

In the distance stood the sandstone cliffs of the pishkun. One after another, the Flatheads grunted their guttural brogue, each pointing to the sacred place, each face solemn in awe as if paying homage to their ancestry. Even their mounts were strangely quiet, save for an occasional tail swatting at some pesky fly.

"Col-Ter," Toby broke his silence, "*Pishkun*… buffalo-jump-place."

I nodded, equally enrapt. So, this is the place, what all the hullabaloo's about. "I'd like to see it," I said.

The old Indian looked at me and nodded.

Shortly, we forded the river and advanced out onto the plains. As far as the eye could see there was not a hint of impending storm… human or otherwise. The sun hung high overhead by then, warm and bright. The sky was clear without so much as a single threatening cloud. Even the daytime breezes were slight, barely noticeable, a perfect day to hunt buffalo.

Toby was the first to see our two scouts racing across the open plains, trailing a cloud of dust behind them They were flat-out moving, far too fast for any peaceful purpose. Even from a distance, we could see that their ponies were lathered in sweat, straining with every fiber of their being. Foam spewed from open mouths and nostrils, their two riders forcing every last ounce of exertion from their exhausted bodies.

Flathead agitation grew with each approaching stride. I sensed fear. A murmur of discontent steadily rumbled throughout the ranks, an ominous crescendo of unchecked angst rising from deep within hundreds of parched throats. Hundreds of pairs of dark eyes concentrated on the returning scouts, straining to hear their emerging cries.

The scouts were screaming. At this distance, even a fool could see they were sounding the alarm. As they drew nearer, we could see terror in their faces, feel their urgency, their desperation. But it was the words that finally discerned their fearful pace.

"*Pahkees! Pahkees!*"

CHAPTER THREE

Bedlam broke out amongst the ranks; alarm instantly sounded, quickly passing to the rear, soon encompassing the entire Flathead nation. Warriors raced forward, converging on the front of the column, spurred forward by the dreaded word. Up and down the line, the word of the hated *Pahkees* spread like a dry prairie wildfire consuming all in its path. And with it pandemonium and pathos, those twins of dire emotion soon took hold.

The scouts were upon us, sliding to a hard, punishing halt... dirt, sod, a shower of dust and grass and gravel kicking-up in our faces, adding to the confusion and uncertainty that their sudden return had created. They leapt from their mounts, sweat pouring from every pore. The grit of the prairie, the anxiety, the sheer apprehension of the message they carried was etched soul-deep in both their faces.

Their ponies were near-exhausted from their great effort... lungs afire, nigh on bursting, their massive chests heaving, pulsating with every painful throb, their bodies quivering, a foamy saliva frothing from their nostrils in an unending stream. They had raced with every ounce of spirit they had to give and now were paying-the-piper for unswerving loyalty.

Quickly, the Flatheads thronged around the two scouts. At first, too exhausted to speak, they gradually regained control, struggling to tell the gathered clans of their desperate flight and near fatal encounter.

The look on every Flathead's face was the same... stunned, horrified, right down to the marrow of their bones. Families, kin, all their women and children suddenly and irrevocably at the mercy of their worst nightmare. Fear took hold, shouting, yelling, all in confusion. Some urged immediate flight. The more foolhardy, the untested cried for combat... here and now, from right where they stood. It was a brief moment of indecision and panic: everyone was talking at the top of their lungs. Few seemed to be listening. But, time was not to be uselessly wasted on such uncertainty, not with sure calamity at hand.

For a moment, I was not sure if anyone was leading this command. No one stepped forward. No one seemed to want to. They were like a wagon with a team of runaway horses and no one holding the reins or yanking on the brake. I was beginning to wonder just what I got myself into. I thought of my two captains and the men of the Corps, our discipline, the way we handled each crisis with a certain amount of aplomb and cool. Damn, we sure needed some of that spine right about now. I was fixing to step forward, myself, when...

Toby nudged me with a bony elbow right square in my gut, stopping me in my tracks. He was staring at Three Eagle. The chief was stirring. He had heard and had enough. Standing like an old oak, wrinkled and wizened by time and test, he raised a withered arm for all to see. Suddenly, immediately, silence. All those squawking injuns just shut right up.

Gray and white streaked his long scraggly mane. And as he began to speak, his voice cracked with the fatigue of a long and hard life. Yet, there was a certain quality to the man; the way he spoke, calmly, but with command, reassuring, thoughtful and direct, and inexplicably, a raw inner strength that shone through as bright as the noon day sun. His composure, albeit humble, was one of wisdom and courage incarnate.

It was time for all the others to listen. No one disputed his right to speak or questioned what he had to say. All ears, all hearts, all minds were at rapt attention. His face, his unwavering voice spoke volumes of the gravity of the situation they now faced. He addressed the warriors and sub-chiefs of his nation in a calm, deliberate manner. His orders, his strategy, were simple and terse and final. His people hung on his every word, realizing the grim import of his edict. His instructions were as lucid as the clear waters of the Madison, no one misunderstood, for the fate of their people hung in the balance.

Toby and I stood side by side. He whispered to me out of the corner of his mouth, "Col-Ter. Chief say, no run and fight. Say we must stay and fight... there is no other way."

"Yep!" I bobbed my head. I understood.

Toby turned, the look on his face was grim, askance. "You fight *Pahkees*... with Toby?"

"Dang right, I will. Wouldn't miss this shit for nothin'," I said with a reassuring smile, placing my hand on his naked shoulder.

A wry, barely perceptible smile lit the old Snake's face. I swore I saw a twinkle in his eye as he nodded his approval. "Good... *Tab-ba-bone*. Col-ter, good friend, *tab-ba-bone*."

"Likewise, pard," I said.

The old chief finally finished dictating his battleplan. He had taken a firm grip on a bad deal, restoring calm, and order and purpose. Now his Salish minions exploded into action. The noncombatants, the women, children and the old folks headed back across the river to begin the retreat home. With them, the pony herds, the wealth of their nation, guarded by the herd-tenders and all those fit enough to lend a hand. No goodbyes! No farewells! Time and desperation would not allow it. Urgency drove them every step of the way.

Warriors raced out onto the plains to prepare themselves for battle. Weapons readied to repel the expected enemy onslaught. The few ancient trade muskets loaded and primed. Bows unsheaved and strung. Tomahawks and warclubs loosened in their belts. Weapons, food, water... everything was in readiness. I took it all in. The captains, I thought, should see these people now.

For a brief moment, I felt like the proverbial "fish out of water." All I could do was prepare my own kit and try to fit right in. But, fit, I did. This is more like it, I thought. I should have known. These poor people have had to put up with the likes of these *Pahkees* for a dang long time. They hadn't survived for all these years without learning a thing or two about war and tactics and such. But, what kind of strength would we be facing, would our side be strong enough? Damn, what in the hell are we facing? Uncertainty gripped me. I was not alone.

Toby and me as honored guests sat in on a hastily assembled war council as chiefs and sub chiefs and respected warriors finalized their battle-plans. The Flatheads by nature were not war-like, never went riding for trouble like their bitter, bloodthirsty neighbors. But in their high-up mountain valleys, where the spirit of the grizzly is king, they had grown accustomed to life the hard way. They knew what to expect from the *Pahkees* and, likewise, knew what every man of their nation expected from each other. And now, grim, silent, martial business was at hand as each warrior prepared himself for the trial ahead in his own special way.

The wait was not long, a few short anxiety-ridden minutes. Hundreds looked askance back across the plains towards the distant Gallatin, straining the limits of visual perception. Never, had I known such powerful dread. I sensed it intuitively in each warrior, saw it in their faces, their reflexes and the way they gripped their weapons… all the while chanting quietly their sacred songs, preparing for the ultimate sacrifice… if need be.

Even their mounts fidgeted nervously, pawing the sod, pacing, whinnying to one another. Eyes alert, watching the plains. Nostrils flared, sniffing the air. Uneasiness settled over the Flathead's war ponies, jarring their ancient primordial instincts. It was as if they too sensed an approaching conflict. They couldn't help but feel the anxiety coursing their masters' veins. Animals are sensitive that way, reading a man's emotions sometimes better than we read them ourselves.

"Steady, boy," I reassured ol' piebald, rubbing his neck, never for an instant taking my eyes off the plains before us.

Faint clouds of dust, the first sign of approach from across the grassy plains heralded their arrival. Pounding hooves building to a crescendo, growing louder and… nearer. Until…

"*A-eeee-ah! A-eeee-ah!*" Forward positions raised the alarm.

"*Pahkees! Pahkees!*" And with their guttural hue and cry a loud, wary grumble arose, racing across our battle-lines, sending adrenaline fever-high.

Pahkees were now seen bearing-down, coming-on fast and furious, whipping their mounts with rawhide quirts, closing the span that separated them from their despised enemies. Reckless, yet, heedless, seemingly ignorant of the superior host they were about to engage, their pace never slackening. Surely, this was sucidal. Such was the blind fury of the Buffalo Bulls.

Squads of Flathead cavalry, one hundred strong, took the challenge, leaping forward with their own spirited charge. Each side now bound on a collision course on the plains between the Straight and the Cherry... the Madison and the Gallatin.

Back by the Madison, we were transfixed in awe of the spectacle unfolding before us. No one spoke. Every warrior holding his breath, clenching his fist.

Realization finally set in. Surprise was now on the Flathead side. Running Wolf reined in, stopping his band just in time to avoid a humiliating if not decisive defeat. This was no small band trespassing covertly on Blackfeet hunting grounds. No, this was an outright invasion, completely undetected. The Bitterroot dogs were almost upon him with overwhelming strength. "Flee. Flee," he screamed. "Back to the Cherry."

Salish bowmen let loose a salvo of stoneheaded arrows, whistling through the air, arcing their way towards the bare bronzed backs of the fleeing *Pahkees*. Death rained upon the fleeing Buffalo Bulls, felling several of their numbers. Astonishment, confusion suddenly was the order of the *Pahkee* day.

As quick as the confrontation had come about it was short-lived. The *Pahkees* offered no further fight, they were just too busy fleeing the way they had come. The Salish reining in to release their deadly barrage now watched the retreat, reluctant to pursue. Several youngsters exhort their leaders, "Give chase. Give chase. After the *Pahkees*! They're getting away." They implored. Yet, to those who knew, *Pahkee* treachery was never to be underestimated nor ignored if one relished life and scalp. They were masters of the game of deception, of bait and trap. Who knew what devilry lay ahead just out of visual range? Yes, a wise man lived to fight another day. "The people" needed protection, not foolish battle glory.

When the last of the *Pahkee* horsemen disappeared from view, the Salish nudged their ponies and turned back towards the Madison.

"No fight? No chase?" I asked Toby, wondering at the sudden halt. "Why'd they stop? Why don't they git after 'em and finish the job?"

Stupid! Keep your mouth shut before you embarrass yourself. As soon as I asked, I realized the answer. Continued pursuit might just be more than they bargained for. Either way, this thing was not over. Better to make a united stand then spread yourself too thin. From what I could see, these people knew what they were doing.

Toby kept watching. "More come... soon," said the old man.

The way he said it left me with a chill. More coming, soon, I thought to myself. I turned and looked at Toby, hoping for once that he was wrong.

Toby had a habit of being right. The *Pahkees* did not stay gone for long. Within minutes they regrouped and were soon filtering back, the more daring edging within musketball range of the Salish lines. They had been surprised, even routed. They had taken their licks. But, theirs was a warrior society, not easily dissuaded. No, defeat emboldened them. Their pride would not let them have it any other way. This time, no surprises, no matter the uneven odds, no matter how much outnumbered. This time the Buffalo Bulls knew the score and prepared to give a different accounting of themselves. Running Wolf decided to play a new type of game… a delaying game, harassing the Salish lines just beyond his enemy's reach. A tactic meant to keep the Salish at bay, until help arrived. Their return, however, did not go unnoticed.

A report, strangely sounding somehow crisper, sharper than that of their own fusees, rang out from behind the enemy's lines. That shot struck paydirt and down went a *Piegan* warrior with a horrible hole in his belly. He was gutshot, and he was not long for the world. All who could see knew it. They were aghast. The distance the shot had travelled was greater than they thought possible.

Running Wolf stared long and hard across the plains at his enemy's lines. At first he had not believed his eyes. He knew he had seen something, something extraordinary. So extraordinary, he had to look again, to pinch himself to be sure.

He had first seen them at the white mans' wooden-fort by the Waters of the Wind. Yet, surely, none of them had dared venture this way. It was too far and they were much too timid. Now he wasn't so sure. Could it be, he asked? A *Napikwan* fighting alongside his enemies. He looked again to be very sure.

Yes…yes!

"Napikwan!" he yelled out, pointing across the plains. *Ak-o-tash-iks…* Many Horses, look, look," he called to his trusted friend.

"I see him. I see him." The big scarfaced warrior responded excitedly. He too pointed across the field of battle, directing the other warriors to the presence of the white man in the *Salish* ranks.

Running Wolf's blood began to boil, vividly recalling the incident from two years before on the plains by Two Medicine River. He remembered the squaws' mournful cries, the lament in his kinfolks' lodges at the death of two young *Piegan* warriors. He remembered the sacred vow they had all taken to punish one day all the *napikwan* trespassers. And now, here was a *napikwan* with their hated enemy scorning his people by his very presence and… slaying his warriors with an accursed fire-stick.

Somehow, despite the presense on the battlefield of the host of Salish warriors, Running Wolf deigned the *napikwan* to be his sole personal vendetta, his life's quest if need be. Nothing, save this white man's death and humiliation would deter him from revenging his kin and people forever. His would be first white man's scalp to dangle on his family's lodge pole. *Siksika*, *Blood* and *Sarsi* would all come from many suns away to see his trophy scalp, sing his praise.

Racing west, Wind in Her Hair and the other squaws and the young boys, the herd tenders, met up with a second *Piegan* hunting party, on the fringes of the Cherry. They, too, had enjoyed a successful hunt and they, too, were covered with the blood of the sacred *enee*. Coincidently, they thought they had heard a far off shot and were on their way to investigate. And now, Running Wolf's little sister strained with her every excited breath to give them the word.

"Hurry!" she exhorted them. "My brother needs your help."

And the word was quickly passed to astonished ears. The shock was momentary. The hunt quickly forgotten. The changing situation appraised with typical *Piegan* aplomb... or lack there of.

Worry not, little sister," one had said.

"*A-eeee-ah!*" rose the cry from several warriors' lips like the chilling moonlight howl of the great gray wolves they so revered, reverberating from mountain peak to peak in the dead of many a dark gloomy night.

It was as if they too could already smell the blood of the lowly Salish dripping from their scalping knives, lances and war clubs. The newcomers whipped themselves into an instant frenzy, speeding off toward the distant *pishkun* plains to join Running Wolf's band. Whooping and hollering, their war cries rent the placid air of this warm spring day in a most unsettling way. Soon, they would double the number of warriors in pursuit of the enemy scouts. They too would partake in the fun, the hunt. They too would vie for scalps. The *enee* dead left lying on the new green grass by the waters of the Cherry would wait for their return. Squaws could be dispatched to take care of that gory business. There was a different business at hand, war business. If only the Buffalo Bulls would leave some scalps for them.

The squaws and young boys resumed the race with Wind in Her Hair, the little sister, in the lead, lashing away at her pony's rump. It was such a large responsibility for one so young. Wind in Her Hair, she the sister of the bold, defiant Running Wolf, had looked upon her big brother adoringly ever since she left her mother's bosom and watched her older sibling grow strong and tall. Though a half dozen summers separated them in years, Running Wolf had seemed to her forever bound for glory. She reveled in his youthful exploits, his prowess in the hunt, his daring adventures in the lands of the Crow and the *Kutenai* and the lowly *Pend d' Oreilles*. She spoke with pride of his bravery, his strength and growing importance in the council of elders and chiefs. Now, her hero-brother had entrusted her, a young girl, a most critical role… to warn their people of the intruders. Now, Wind in Her Hair was emboldened by the prospect of another glorious victory by her sibling. Never had she felt such exhilaration, such adrenaline pumping through her veins.

Oh, to be a *Piegan* warrior; to count coup on your enemies, to have their blood-dripping scalps dangling from your family's lodge pole, to snatch their fire-sticks and steal their ponies, to be the envy of kin, clan and Nation. What *namachkani* her brother possessed. She was filled anew with lofty thoughts of grand exultation, and the adrenaline that her pride pumped through her veins drove her on, pushing her little band to keep up with a lung busting effort.

Approaching the wetlands where the rivers come together, Wind in Her Hair chanced a look over her left shoulder. To the south, she could make out clouds of dust… clouds of dust made by ponies, hundreds of ponies. What was this? These were not her peoples' ponies. She continued to watch. Literally, hundreds and hundreds of ponies were descending the steep slopes to the waters of the Straight from the grassy bluffs above. But, wait… there were people, she could see people, too, hundreds and hundreds of people spilling from the prairie over the bluffs' edge, down towards the river, driving the ponies. Who were they? But, she already knew. Running Wolf, she cried aloud evoking her brother's name. Tears instantly welled in her eyes. All she could think of was Running Wolf charging blindly ahead right into the whole Salish Nation. The realization was instantly sickening, a wave of shock and stunned disbelief taking hold, immobilizing the young girl. This was not the treacherous movement of a slinking, skulking pair of spies nor a war party bent on taking scalps or stealing her peoples' precious *ponokamitas*, their elk dogs. No, this was a whole filthy nation trespassing, defiling their land, coming to hunt and take their sacred *enee*, brazenly in full view of the Piegan people.

Wind in Her Hair had heard of great affronts such as this happening before, never believing for an instant in her proud mind that the lowly Salish, those despicable Flatheads of the western mountains or their southern neighbors, the equally despicable slithering Snakes, would dare risk her people's wrath.

She and the rest of her troop careened to a sudden, jarring halt. They all stared in horror, no one dare uttering a sound or word. The scenario unfolding on the plains between the Straight and the Cherry needed no interpretation. An impending clash was all too evident and the balance was weighed heavily against her brother's band, unless she could reach and warn her people in time to avert a sure massacre. Oh Running Wolf, she moaned. She was struck with a sudden pang of revulsion and terror, feeling faint, weak, a lump as big as a frog growing large in her throat. A short cry escaped her lips as she envisioned her beloved brother's peril. He'll charge right into that huge host of enemy warriors and be driven down to the ground, pummeled, killed. The dog's will butcher him, humiliate him. He and the Buffalo Bulls won't stand a chance.

She suddenly screamed, frightening the young and the ponies in her care alike. Instantly, she was off, laying a hard slap across her ponies rump, quirting the tired beast again and again and again. The rest followed, close on her tail. There was a new, even greater desperation to her mission as the spirited band of young Piegans strained to consume the miles between the forks where the rivers came together, and then, onward, straight across the plains to the swift, muddy Horse, the Jefferson. And just beyond, hidden in a protected canyon, lay the great tribal village of the Piegans, the southern clans of the great Blackfeet nation. There, in the serenity of that narrow canyon, her people camped in peace, protected by high sandstone walls and the feared reputation of their warrior societies. Safe and secure… at least they thought they were. For there, laid out in an age-old fashion, according to the various Piegan bands and societies, was a vast circular defensive pattern of hundreds of painted buffalo skin lodges, their *Nii-to-yis*, housing the gathered thousands of their tribe. What nation in all the high plains and Shining Mountains would dare approach the fifteen hundred strong brotherhood of warriors of the Piegan people? It was unthinkable to this young maiden and yet, she had just seen the enemy defying all reason.

Wind in Her Hair's approach was seen from miles away by alert camp lookouts stationed atop a high promonotory to watch for just such commotions. They could sense the frenetic pace. The ponies were plainly empty, carrying no sides or quarters of fresh killed meat. Nothing to indicate a successful hunt. No hunters accompanied them. And the squaws and the youngsters were slapping their mounts like hellfire was burning their tails.

Signals were immediately sent to the huge encampment below. The alarm was passed from lodge to lodge, from one band to another, until all had heard the word. The whole village responded like ants repelling invaders and soon the 'people' gathered by the hundreds to see what was causing such a stir.

One man stood out from the rest, a swarthy, hard looking warrior with piercing black eyes and distinguished bearing. He was the warrior chief that his nation looked up to and his leadership though often tried remained uncontested.

Wind in Her Hair and her band had crossed the river called the Horse, followed a dry rocky stream-bed up through a sparsely-wooded canyon of pine and sage, riding right into the center of the Piegan village. She leapt from her pony as agile as a deer. Long, wonderfully luxurious, black hair flowed to the small of her back as she strode boldly and directly to the awaiting war-chief. There were lines of worry and beads of sweat streaming off her brow. Her breaths came hard and fast. Her face was a strained mask of desperation and urgency.

"What is it, girl? Why do you ride like the wind and stir up the dust on our people? Have you no respect?"

"Kootenae Appe," her words came amidst great gasps for air. "Invaders…"

A hundred gasps arose from around her, many cupping their mouths to hide their astonishment and their fear. The chief was instantly taken aback. And then he grabbed the young girl's arm, squeezing ever so gently. He knew the girl, admiring her from afar. Knew she bore the same spunk that marked her brother. She would make a good wife… one day; that is if she didn't get her fool self killed.

"Go on, my little Wind in Her Hair," the great man's tone softened.

The chief turned to several squaws standing-by and ordered, "Bring water, quickly."

Turning back… "Speak, girl… tell me about these trespassers? How many have you seen? And where are they?"

"My brother, Maa-koyou-mah'-kaa and his band… we were hunting beyond the pishkun… we were watched by two cowardly Flathead spies. I swear we saw them. They ran like scared dogs when we caught sight of them and warned my brother."

The chief looked to the still panting young herd-tenders. They all nodded in agreement. He knew they would, but still, it was smart not to show too much deference to one so young.

"Go on, girl. Quickly."

"Maa-koyou-mah'-kaa," finally catching her breath. "He is after them, but…"

"Only two?" the chief interrupted her, chuckling with disbelief. "Your brother is not a man to cower before two Flatheads nor twenty-two. The Buffalo Bulls have nothing to fear."

"Wait, wait…" she cried, "when we reached the place where the rivers come together, I saw hundreds of them pouring down to the river from the bluffs. There *ponakamitas* were like blades of grass on the plains, as great in number as our own herds."

The young squaw paused, gathering herself, pleading. "Maa-koyou-mah'-kaa will not stand a chance, there are too many for him to fight. We must save him."

The war-chief stood motionless for several moments, his mind racing with unanswered questions. A furrowed look creased his brow.

The Salish, those Flathead dogs... by the hundreds, he thought, could only mean that they once again were defying Siksika edict, challenging Blackfoot hegemony over their own land. Once again, the mountain people of the Bitterroot had banded together in strength and invaded the valley where the rivers come together to hunt their '*enee.*'

The fools would pay for their affront. He would see to it. Today will mark the last time his valley is invaded by these treacherous dogs. They must be taught a lesson. There will be many scalps and ponies to take today. Salish blood will run red across the plains of the pishkun, the river Straight will flow with their blood. Their squaws and children captured by the hundred-fold. The death songs, the lamentations in their lodges will be loud and painful for many moons to come... if any survive to mourn.

He turned to Wind in Her Hair. "Maa-koyou-mah'-kaa will not die... not today."

Kootenae Appe turned to the gathered throng and issued his battle instructions, spitting out his orders in rapid fashion like the staccato rap of the woodpecker.

Spare ponies were ordered up from surrounding pastures. Parfleches to be packed with pemmican. The call was given out for all the sub-chiefs and warriors of the gathered bands to come in all haste, armed and painted for war. Scouts were hurriedly sent out to bring in the remaining scattered bands hunting in the far reaches of the valley and beyond to join Kootenae Appe en-route. For today, the people would give great battle to the despised interlopers. The Piegan lived for war... nothing else in their brief harsh life mattered quite as much.

In their eagerness to chase down the two Flathead spies, Running Wolf's band had been unprepared for the massed strength awaiting them. The rash, bold young warrior leader had charged recklessly across the plains towards the Straight, plunging headlong into the numerically superior ranks of the mountain dogs. His band had no strategy, no plan of attack, just brutal one-on-one hand-to-hand combat... brief and decisive. But, circumstance, unfortunately, had rapidly dictated otherwise.

In his rabid haste, Running Wolf had not even allowed his band the spiritual protection that the donning of sacred 'war-paint' and the unwrapping of their special individual war medicine would certainly bestow. Their fire-sticks were still sheaved and their arrows remained in their quivers, as they rushed in to count coup with their coup sticks and bash skulls with their heavy stone-headed war clubs.

The enemy response at first confused him. Their charge was bold, audacious, seemingly without fear. The devastating hail of arrows confronting his ranks could have meant disaster. As it was they had left several wounded behind on the field, exposed to the heat of the midday sun. And their they waited, moaning and… for some, dying. And there was shame in the Buffalo Bulls' ranks. Their fellow warriors must be avenged, but, how? The enemy's cavalry charge was too tenacious, too overwhelming, their warriors far outnumbering his beleaguered band. A few steps more and Running Wolf and his warriors would have been overrun… cut to pieces.

Where did they all come from? He knew the answer, the mountains of the bitterroots. And it was all a matter of timing. For the first time in many years the Piegan had come here in the early spring. They should have known. But, that was not what was vexing him. It was that damned *napikwan*. Who was that damn *napikwan*? Why was he with them and were there more whites about? Did he bring those Salish dogs gifts of fire-sticks? He hoped not. He didn't recall any shooting during the charge. In fact, there was none. But, that didn't mean they had no fire-sticks.

Running Wolf had wisely broken charge, retreating to a safe distance a short ways away once he realized the Salish were not in pursuit. But, in the disorder of it all they had left behind several of their band lying prostrate on the short-grass sod midway to the Flathead lines. The virulent moans and cries for help from his wounded and dying friends drifted across the battlefield, sending worried looks throughout the Piegan band. There was nothing they could do. A rescue attempt would only expose them to more arrows and that damned fire-stick with the deadly-aim. He would need time to figure this enemy out, to count their strength; their warriors and fire-weapons and divine their intentions. He had noticed the dust clouds to the southwest arising from the bluffs beyond the Straight. It could only mean they and their pony herds were fleeing to the West to their Bitterroots. What a prize, he thought. Never had the Piegans beheld such an opportunity. But not to worry for soon the rest of his people would spill over the plains and join him in battle. In the meantime he must keep these Bitterroot dogs from slipping away from the lands of the three rivers and escaping to their western mountains. And then and only then would the *napikwan* be his.

Kootenae Appe, the able general of the high plains, war-chief of the Piegan people, ordered a single band of his youngest fighters to stay behind and protect the village and tribe's great pony herds, their precious *ponokamitas*. He now rode at a spirited gallop at the head of nearly one thousand warriors, grim-faces painted for battle. Soon hundreds more would join en-route to the plains of the pishkun. With such strength his confidence knew no bounds. They had never suffered defeat by these lowly western dogs, and certainly today would be no different.

In short order the massive cavalcade of Piegan cavalry forded the river Horse and made a straight line across the prickly pear plains towards the Straight five miles distant. As he rode his mind wandered across the plains, spanning the day and the conflict that lay ahead. He was already relishing victory, an undeniable victory. It would be a day such as his people rarely knew. A day remembered with pride for many seasons to come. And with Piegan victory his leadership would be ensured far into the foreseeable future.

A smile appeared on his face, a hard, evil smile…one that portended bad-tidings for the invaders. His black, narrow-set eyes squinted hard, straining to cover the distant Straight and what lay beyond, trying to visualize the Salish position, the lay of the land, their possible strength, their intent. He had faced these Bitterroot people before, many times during the course of a long life fraught with internecine warfare. Raiding, horse stealing, riding roughshod wherever, whenever they pleased. These little mountain people had proven wily, resilient, tough fighters… so much so that the Blackfeet often avoided their mountains. Strategy would have to wait until he reached the scene of the battle and received Running Wolf's report. But, it mattered not. Today could only have one conclusion. And while Kootenae Appe rode in the van of his warrior nation, he began to contemplate with fiendish delight the ultimate fate of his despised enemy.

We stood with our backs to the Madison. The people, the young, the old folks, the women and their great pony herds had already disappeared from view, moving fast across that very same prairie bluff country from whence they had arrived. I could sense, I could feel, almost hear a murmur, an angst-filling tremor arising from each and every Flathead warrior. I needed not to understand the guttural brogue of the Salish people to know that every man by my side prayed that their delaying action would shield their people's flight and create time to distance their loved ones from sure Pahkee retribution. And with that grim realization I waited with them. The white-man, the *gitchi mokoman* their guest alongside his host, the warriors of the Bitterroot watching silently, never taking away our gaze from across the plains to the enemies' ranks.

We could hear the shrieks and war cries coming from the Pahkee's skirmish line as another large Blackfeet hunting band raced across the plains from the Gallatin to join Running Wolf, arriving with much noisy hullabaloo. They made quite a show of it, whooping it up, mostly for our benefit.

There was hardly a murmur coming from our side, nothing to show anything but passive concern. Those young Bitterroot warriors just stared back, stoically, as cool as stone, not a whimper or a peep out of any of 'em.

Those boys weren't about to show fear, not with their whole brotherhood waiting there together, side by side, ready to give a good account. Not when the whole tribes' life depended on them. I looked up and down our lines, to Toby, to the old wizened chief, Three Eagle, and all their fine young men. These Flatheads were as steady as oak.

Suddenly, I felt proud to be with them, reassured by their quiet strength, their loyalty and steadfastness to one another. I had known such men before, men whom I had felt equally proud to be counted amongst.

I glanced to Toby. "Hell, there still ain't enough of 'em to give us a good fight."

"No fight now," the old Snake said soberly. "Pahkees wait… they want warriors to stay. More come… Col-ter see."

He was as calm as stone. Nothing seemed to disturb my ancient friend. A lifetime of hardship and danger seemed to inure him to battle and death and misfortune. Hardship was all he ever knew. It was his way of life and he accepted it. But, he was no different that day than the hundreds that stood beside us.

So that was the way it was. Manuel's Fort and trading beaverskin with the injuns seemed like a long forgotten dream. Bringing in the peaceful tribes to Lisa's would never see the 'light of day'. I became resigned to it. My skin was now the only skin I was concerned with. I was in the wrong place siding with the wrong injuns. My hide wouldn't be worth a mouthful of spit. Those Piegan would see to that. And that was the size of it. We couldn't run and we had to fight. If we had fled, they would've hunted us down for sure. Caught the whole Flathead Nation out in the open in broad daylight on the bare-ass prairie with no place to hide or redoubt to defend. It was our backs to the river or annihilation or slavery or both. The young'uns, the old folk, their women and all their fine ponies would have been at the mercy of the Pahkee… and they would have shown none for sure. These good Indian folks knew it and bet on it. They had known Blackfeet treachery way too many times before to let themselves be fooled ever again.

The Blackfeet knew it too, feeling pretty cocksure right about now of their chances. Sure as shootin', those savages knew they had us run up a tree with no way off. And while they waited, they took the time to make their battle preparations that their previous haste had denied. They weren't in any hurry now. They had an ace up their sleeve, loving the hand they were dealt and biding their time to suit their bidding.

I watched them closely, fascinated as they stripped right down to bare-nothing, save for a little deerskin patch of a loincloth covering their privates. They were utterly shameless, as devoid of Christian dignity and propriety as any heathen pagan in history.

They commenced to daub their faces, shoulders, chest and arms with ocher and blacks and yellows as shamelessly as a houseful of whores of fancy French tarts. It was a most curious spectacle and they acted the part to the hilt, preening like a bunch of two legged peacocks doing their version of the pishkun-plains-promenade.

While I stared, an older warrior, with the scarred countenance of many a close encounter, was standing near me and uttered several words of Salish brogue. I looked at him, wondering what he had said. Several of his companions mumbled, seemingly in agreement. I gave Toby a queried look. The old Shoshone grunted and with the fingers of his right hand made sweeping motions across his forehead and down both cheeks.

"War paint. Pahkee make ready to die," the old man said and went back to watching.

Now you might think that these savages paint their faces and bodies to scare and intimidate their enemies. But, it just isn't so. And they sure in hell don't do it because of some death wish. No, Sir... it's all for spiritual reasons. They paint themselves up for battle in their own special, individual way, according to their own vision and design... and that's to look good for their Creator in case their vaunted war medicine fails to protect them. They just want to make sure that the old man above could identify each and everyone of them if they come knocking on his pearly gates.

My grandpa Joe once told me that the Indians were called redskins because of the red ochre that they painted on their skin to identify themselves as people of the Great Spirit's earth. I guess they were worried the Almighty wouldn't recognize 'em and let 'em in the door.

War medicine was also unique to each warrior. Some wore a single feather, others had bunches of 'em in their hair. Still others had their war medicine attached to their weapons or to their rawhide shields... oval shields of special magic made of the stretched thick hide of the buffalo bulls' neck. And these they painted in red, blue, green, black and yellow pigments of the sacred symbols of the sun, moon and stars and especially of *enee* the buffalo. These were the symbols of their war medicine that would protect them from the gunshots and arrows and blades and the stone-headed death of their enemies. This they believed and this they dare-not go into battle without.

The day wore on, hot and dry and dusty. The sun moved slowly westward on its daily journey and now hung high in the sky directly overhead. That ol' blue ether was cloudless, casting not a single shadow to darken the battlefield, or give shade from the heat or from prying eyes. Lips became parched, throats and mouths dry. Men and horses sweated. Pesky flies tormented them equally alike.

One mile, maybe two, to the east, rose the sandstone cliffs of the pishkun and the rolling prairies beyond. Between where we stood and those bluffs, there was nary a tree, a rock, nor dip or swell of land to use or hide behind. Just behind our lines, a long thin row of red willow and cottonwoods was all that stood between our backsides and the clear, swift flowing Madison. Both battle lines were set, each side starkly exposed.

Periodically, puffs of burnt black powder and the telltale pop of gunpowder ignition heralded musket rounds whistling through the air as we sniped back and forth at each other occasionally finding the mark. The moans, the pitiful wail of the wounded and their death cries haunted the field of battle. Insults, taunts and threats were repeatedly hurled back and forth from both sides.

It was an age-old ritual and the Blackfeet were masters at it. They vowed with their every breath to wipe out the Flathead warrior bands, to enslave their women and offspring, to destroy, to leave destitute their old ones. Vows of mutilation, hacking of limbs, disemboweling, scalping, and decapitation. Of promenading body parts and embedding severed heads with their stone lances, parading their enemies' remains around their great tribal village in victorious celebration and savage pomposity. They poured it on without let-up.

I was sick of listening to them. Somebody had to shut them up. I had had it with their blustering and their sniping and their prancing around like a bunch of painted dandies. And at the range that separated us, I knew it was solely up to me.

"Lets see how you like my lead, you red-hided sons of bitches," I cursed aloud.

Old Toby glanced my way as I shouldered my rifle and settled my aim on one brazen Pahkee warrior, dancing in front of the Blackfeet line just out of trade-musket range and doing his best imitation of an Irish jig. Toby motioned to several Flathead warriors near-by. Soon they were all staring.

It became a point of honor… honor and morale. I knew I couldn't let them down, not after all of Toby's bragging about my shooting and the white man's big medicine.

So, I took my time, staring down the length of my rifle's long, thin barrel. I wiped sweat from my eyes. I licked my lips. I took a careful bead. I took one, two last breaths, then squeezed, ever so gently, ever so tightly.

My rifle fairly leaped in my hands with the ignition of black powder and flint, its result near instantaneous. A hot ball of lead hit smack dab in the middle of that warrior's exposed belly, his meat bag, blowing a major hole right out his backsides. The poor devil never knew what hit him, never thinking for an instant that this would be his last day. He was thrown to the ground, flopping about uncontrollably like a fish out water, all the while screaming in pain and shock as his insides spilt out onto the prairie sod in a mess of blood and guts.

Death is not a pretty sight… it never is, especially if it's you or one of your own that's doing the dying. There was an uncharacteristic silence, a stunned-hush if you will, coming from the Pahkee side. My rifle had talked and now they were all listening, except for that poor youngster convulsing on the ground, singing his death song.

The Flatheads roared their approval. Up and down our lines our boys were whooping it up, shaking their fist. Even old Toby had a smile for me. He was as proud as proud could be. His *tab-ba-bone* had brought his big medicine to bear.

The Pahkees had just learned the hard way. They knew right off that that my shooting piece of mine was not a trade musket, at least one that they had ever heard before. No, that big bang of mine was something else entirely.

And then they saw me. Both the Pahkee bands spotted me sticking out amongst all those red Indians from the Bitterroot Mountains. Something didn't sit right with them. It took a moment or two for them to realize it. But, once they did, they just glared straight at me. I could feel their hatred and loathing and it was white hot. The Flatheads invading Blackfeet country was one transgression hard enough to swallow, but, me, a white man, fighting side by side with their enemy was something else entirely. They were mad as hell, all right. Of course it didn't help much that all the Flathead warriors in the world were standing around me, patting me on the back. Being white and all, I just naturally stood right out.

One lone Pahkee, a tall, wide-shouldered youth was staring a hole right through me. There was something about him, somehow different from the others, more intense, bitter, plainly obvious to my way of thinking. His companions seemed to dwell on him as if looking up to him for leadership. And then he screamed across the battlefield. Or should I say he issued his challenge. One word was unmistakable amidst his chilling tirade. A word I had never heard before and he repeated it over and over.

"*Napikwan! Napikwan!*"

Another tall warrior arose and joined him. And he was a big brute, broader of shoulder and from where I was standing, ugly to boot. Now they were both pointing, screaming their vile Pahkee epithets. Soon all the Pahkees were up and screaming at the *napikwan*, me that is.

The whole complexion was about to change. I suddenly felt as if the Blackfeet and one warrior in particular were now solely interested in old John Colter, and the Flatheads be-damned. It was not a good feeling to be so singled-out, kinda gave me the shivers, making me a little edgier than a moment before.

Toby turned to me, his face expressionless. He sensed my concern. "He,

Maa-koyou-mah'-kaa... Running Wolf. Him bad medicine. Say he kill the *napikwan*, you, John Col-ter, *napikwan*."

"He don't say. Well, lets give him something to think about."

I wasn't about to cave-in to Pahkee threats. Not while I had my rifle and my nerve primed and ready to go. So I picked out a nice, comfortable piece of sod to lie down upon and propped that Kentucky long of mine for easy shooting. At this distance with barely a breeze blowing and the terrain table-flat... I couldn't miss and I wasn't about to.

Toby had bragged a blue streak about his white friends, told the Flatheads that all the *Gitchi Mokoman* could shoot and fight with the best of 'em. And now he had his proof. Those Indian boys watched me reload and prime my weapon and pick out another target, all the while a smiling and a nodding their heads and congratulating my little Snake friend.

As for my little Snake friend, why that old rascal just stood behind me with that scrawny chest of his all puffed-out proud-like, arms folded and smiling like the cat that just ate the mouse.

I cranked off another belly shot, this time hitting a young brave doing his damnedest not to be seen. Soon there were two Blackfeet to be heard singing their songs of death, a regular death scene lament duet.

"Hey, Running Wolf. Stick that in your craw, you son of bitch." I stood up, raising my rifle over my head and yelled across the plains as loud as I could.

We both stood glaring as if locked in each other's gaze, neither one of us flinching or backing down. I knew I wouldn't, never had, never would, and that Running Wolf fella looked like the kind of man who had no backup in his vocabulary. Both sides sensed a deep, personal confrontation developing between the two of us. Everyone seemed to step back in awe, giving us our due; respecting courage in battle above all other manly virtues. Suddenly, the pishkun plains battlefield was quiet, all taunts and shrieks and war cries coming to an abrupt end. The moaning, the death chants of their wounded were growing weaker, their end was drawing near.

That's two who won't be takin' scalps anymore, I thought to myself as I poured powder for another go at 'em. By then those Piegans had had enough of my big medicine fire-stick and wisely moved back, well out of my rifle's range. Their retreat only served to incense their leader even more. Running Wolf was easy to recognize, even at a distance. He was making no effort to find cover. On the contrary, he just stood right out, bold and brazen, clenching his war-club with an iron grip and glaring in defiance. Didn't take any genius on my part to see he was seething. I could feel his hatred all the way across the flat, empty plains. He never seemed to take his eyes off of me, not for a second. Got to be where I knew this fight sooner or later would come right down between the two of us. He was boiling for revenge, all right. I had taken the stuffing out of his cocky band, right in his own neck of the woods and with their enemies watching the whole shebang and loving every minute of it. Running Wolf's warriors would never live the humiliation down, this insult to their national pride and honor. And no people on God's green earth could hate like these savages.

It became a game of watch and wait, of cat and mice to see who would make the next move. We settled down, both sides eyeing each other and no one blinking. The minutes dragged on. Soon, an hour or more had passed. The standoff wore on everyone's nerves, most of all on Running Wolf. What held him back from charging right across the open plains and challenging me to a duel to the death, I'll never know. That's how bad that youngster wanted a piece of my hide and scalp.

Here and there, a daring Pahkee sniper would crawl forward on his belly and risk a shot with a trade musket, never doing any damage. A puff of black powder, a delayed report punching the air with an occasional errant lead ball kicking up sod in front of our lines or zinging away off into void, was all they got for their efforts.

When they'd really get their nerve up, one or more brave souls would standup and bare a bronzed backside, naked ass and all. They'd hoot and holler and keep up the taunts, all the while the Flat's around me would shake their heads and return the favor.

We were both stalling for time, burning what daylight was left. Hoping we could out last and out wait them until nightfall and then pull-away, sneak off into the darkness of the night and skedaddle out of their accursed lands as fast as we could. And all the while we waited buying time, the women and old folk, their young'uns and their great pony herds were making tracks back to from where they came, each and every one of them sporting an empty, growling, unfed belly, bone tired, scared, dreading the trail ahead. But, nevertheless, a people alive to hunt another day.

I had this real queasy feeling deep down in my gut. It was a sickening feeling. I had all I could do to hold it down and keep from puking up my innards. I was scared, all right. More scared than I'd ever been in my whole life. But I was doing my best not to show it. I looked around at Toby and our companions. I could see the strain in their faces, the worry in their eyes. The way they stared intently across the empty plains at the Pahkees. Periodically, the old chief, Three Eagle, would turn around and look at the fading dust clouds made by his people high-tailing it out of the Three Forks to safety. Soon, all traces vanished and the old man would turn to stare once again at his enemies.

Strange what you can think of in moments like this. The Pahkees had quieted down, tending as best as they could to their wounded. During the lull my mind began to wander. I guess I wasn't any different than my Indian friends. They were worrying about their kin, their survival and maybe even dreaming about happier times in their high Bitterroot valleys.

I, too, thought about my family back home in ol' Virginny. About what my grandpa Joe and my pa John would've said and thought about my predicament. They were educated men. Set store by book learning and had a high regard for standing-up against what wasn't right. We Colters had always been that way.

But it was my ma, Ellen, whom I was really missing. Always worrying about me every time I was off hunting in the woods, always fussing over me like a mother hen. Standing over my shoulders on many a candlelit night making sure I did my book lessons and wrote my A, B, Cs. Drilling me, testing me, never being quite satisfied enough. Instilling in me a sense of pride and accomplishment. Setting the course for a lifetime of interest, of curiosity of the ways and minds of man and nature. It was because of that wonderful lady that I learned to read and write and think things out and I'm a better man for her efforts.

The truth of it is I loved to read and needed no encouragement from anyone. The family read Virgil and Homer, Mallory and Thomas Paine and I grew up dreaming about heroes and knights and the rights of man. My folks believed in the nobility of man and the right to self-determination. And when word reached Staunton of those patriots at Concord and Lexington rallying to battle and dog the trail of the fleeing redcoats, the men folk in my family, naturally, were the first to volunteer for the county levy, fighting with General Washington himself throughout the course of the war.

We were Scots-Irish, proud and patriotic, simple and humble, honest and bright. Never would we abide by deceit or arrogance nor bow and scrape to the high and mighty of a faraway English society. "By your leave"… to hell I say. Not on our honor and certainly not on the honor of freemen. That's how I was raised and that's what I believe and I guess you might say that's why I was proud to be standing side by side with my friend Toby and these simple Flathead people.

Now, you take these Indian folks. Back east they'd be thought of as ignorant savages and not worthy of the white man's respect. But they're good people, honest and neighborly. They love their kin and have good relations with the other tribes that allow them to do so. They aren't greedy or warlike and will often band together with different tribes and hunt out here in the valley of the Three Forks with everybody getting their fair shake. They love their mountain valleys and probably just as soon would never leave them. But their way of life doesn't leave them much choice as far as fresh meat goes and feeding their Nation during a long, cold winter and that's where the rub is.

Now the Blackfeet feel the same way about their people and are quite spiritual about it. Nigh on everything in nature is sacred to them: the sun, the moon, the stars and the land, mountains, and the rivers. The birds that fly and the animals they eat. But when it comes to this land, their land and any trespassers there upon, that's where the difference lies. They have a lot of folks to feed and clothe and aren't about to share the bounty with anyone else. From what I've seen, they're mean and cruel and spiteful without mercy. Diplomacy and relationships with their neighbors is one of cheat and deceit, steal and kill. They live for war and pity the man or tribe that gets in their way.

As I looked around at the worried faces of old Toby and our friends their plight called me back to the immortal words of the Greek Simonides in praise of the slain Leonidas and his three hundred men at the narrow pass they called Thermopylae in ancient Greek times.

"Go, tell the Spartans, thou who passest by, That here obedient to their laws we lie."

More than two millennia and a half a world away the fate of a nation again hung on the brave and resolute few. I thought that I was in pretty distinguished company if I had to meet my maker.

The tangled strands of a man's life can be so twisted, so contorted, the irony of which I couldn't get it out of my mind. Here I was, a sandy-headed boy from the woods of Stuart's Draft, Virginia, two thousand miles or more up river from St. Louis. Two hundred miles of Indian infested country to get to Manuel's Fort and no one even knows where I was nor probably even gave a dang. And before this long day is over, I'd probably be a gut pile along with a thousand Flathead and Piegans fighters and no white man ever the wiser.

"Hell," I mused, "I won't even get a cairn of rocks, a headstone or anything else to be remembered by."

Mine was a pretty discouraging future to look forward to that day. And then I thought of my hair and began to conjure up the vision of a bloody scalp dangling from some savage's lodge pole... my scalp, that is. It was a lonely, forlorn feeling coursing my veins 'til Blackfoot daring brought me back to reality.

Running Wolf could wait no longer. The two combined bands he now led had made their final preparations. Their war medicine emboldened them to face the odds and my stinging fire-stick. He was gambling, throwing caution to the wind.

The whole bunch of 'em crawled forward on their bellies, slithering like snakes across the plains 'til they easily had us within their muskets' range.

They began shooting, opening up with more firepower then the whole Flathead nation possessed. Lead came whizzing by, landing all around me. It was as if each Pahkee *fusee* was aimed directly at me.

The Flatheads responded with their few ancient irons, accompanied by dark flights of their stone-headed arrows. The battle had commenced in earnest and I played my part. I raced to return fire; loading, aiming, firing; loading, aiming, firing, over and over. Somehow my aim was not entirely true. I was becoming frustrated, angered. The Piegan presented themselves as too flat, too indistinct with the surrounding land, too easily a 'hit and miss' for all our weapons, as they lay prone on the short-grass sod, firing away. They had wised-up, making themselves as small a target as possible. Yet, their own aim was proving pretty good, their lead coming closer and closer, all the while their firepower was growing heavier and heavier, directed entirely my way.

And then, it happened… A hot, fiery stab of pain sliced through the upper part of my right thigh throwing me hard to the ground. A sickening, numbing sensation began to spread throughout my body as I realized that there was now a bloody furrow in my leg, sown by a Pahkee musket's lead ball. It was deep… deep enough to plant a row of summer corn and spilling more blood than I dared to lose.

Seeing me shot down Running Wolf's band was ecstatic at my misfortune. Whooping up and down like a bunch of mad fighting roosters, they began to pour it on even more. I winced and jerked every time a ball of lead whistled closely by.

All the while blood poured out of my leg, uncontrollably. I began to panic, to lose my nerve. For once, the steely bands of backwoods' courage were wavering with each drop of lost blood.

"Get a hold of yourself," I commanded myself.

Toby had reacted right off. With a worried look on his face, he and a young sprig of a warrior grabbed me by the arms and quickly dragged me back into the dense thicket of red willows behind our lines. Out of sight, the fire directed my way began to fade.

Toby saved my bacon right then. That old Snake saw what needed to be done and went right to work. He was fast, that old man, slitting my leggings into thin strips, bandaged my wound neat and tidy and fashioning a tourniquet to cut the flow of blood with the speed and skill of a medical doctor. And all without so much as a… 'How do you do or a thank you, mam?'

I must have made quite a sight lying amidst the willows, half-naked, growing as pale as a ghost and all the while bleeding like a stuck pig. My wound was deep, but not fatal, the old Indian's bandaging seemed to be doing the trick.

Meanwhile the battle raged on without us. The reports, the screams of the injured and dying, their ponies rearing in fright and falling as mortally wounded as their masters, brought me quickly back to it all. My strength began to return, slowly building, taking its time. I was not whole, I was not ready to stand up and be accounted for. Yet, I had to do my part. My rifle had to speak once again and unerringly so.

"Leave me here," I said to Toby, the tone in my voice leaving no doubts.

The old Snake grunted, "Col-Ter... you fight good." He left me there, quickly returning to join the Flatheads.

With my rifle as a crutch I pulled myself up on my one good leg. The throbbing, the pain, the ache were still there. The emptiness I felt from loss of blood had left me weakened, struggling to suck in enough air to breathe and concentrate. But, I was fired up, pissed off and just mad enough and scared enough to send half the Blackfeet Nation to Kingdom Come.

I primed and loaded that iron once again and picked-out my targets with care. There were plenty to choose from, the Pahkees had grown brazen once again, rising up, seemingly indifferent to Flathead muskets and arrows. They had all but forgotten the wounded white man, the *napikwan*. His 'big medicine,' his fire-stick was silenced once and for all. Or so they thought. They moved foolishly closer, well within my range. Several were less than a hundred yards away, and their bronzed bodies stood out starkly in contrast to the greening plains.

Stupid... I thought. They'll pay for this. Taking advantage of the concealment that the willows provided, I took aim anew. Suddenly, somehow, I was able to forget my wound, my discomfort and fear.

By then the people of the mountains had had enough of the withering barrage and audacity of their enemies and mounted their own charge. Hundreds of Flatheads rushed their foe with a tenacity and savagery that was a glory to behold. Running Wolf and his band quickly fell back to their ponies, mounted up and raced rearward. In short order, the Flatheads had swept the field, and now the pursuit of the hated Pahkees was on in earnest. This time they would not fall short. This time the Pahkees would pay. This time the Flatheads would clear the field of battle, once and for all.

As the rest of us watched, a loud rumble began to fill the air and shake apart the very ground upon where we stood. A growing cacophony swelled in our ears and filled us with fear anew. Hooves, thousands of hooves, were pounding the plains like the chaotic rush of a gigantic herd of stampeding buffalo. The dust clouds announcing their approach grew voluminous, all-encompassing as if this new arrival's disruption of the land would soon block-out the sun and the sky.

"What the hell?" I said as I stared and listened in wonder. "What now?"

I didn't wonder for long. Soon our hearts began to sink ever so deeper in despair. The brave riders of the Bitterroots returned, recrossing the 'pishkun' plains in complete disorder. Their faces, their fearful screams echoing once again that hated cry. Yea, so close to victory, death raced back on their tails like an evil wind.

The dreaded word rang out again and again. *"Pahkees... Pahkees!"*

Now, we could see fanning out onto the plains from the direction of the Gallatin, that the very ground itself was bronzed with Blackfeet, a thousand strong or more. And as they approached, ever so nearer, grim faces painted for war came into view. The tide, the odds had now changed irrevocably. What had been feared all along was now coming to pass. The Piegans were here in force, their whole Nation.

"Holy shit!" I waned feebly.

The approaching Pahkee horde had heard sporadic sniper fire as they drew closer to the pishkun plains battlefield. The reports were few and far between, hardly revealing the amassed numbers of warriors by the Straight, the Madison River.

Was Running Wolf and his warriors already decimated by the interlopers? Did the young squaw, Wind in Her Hair, exaggerate the strength of the Salish invasion? Or did their enemies escape leaving only a small rear guard to defend their fleeing Bitterroot peoples? Was the Piegan warrior brotherhood to be cheated, denied their battle glory?

Kootenae Appe could only guess what lie ahead. But, as the musket fire reports increased, his pace quickened and his adrenaline pumped all that much more. He knew well the vibrant currents running through his warriors' veins. Sensed their animal-like tenacity primed to burst upon the lowly dogs from the western mountains.

As quick as their speeding mounts could take them, the Piegans passed through the wetlands of the rivers-that-come-together and emerged onto the flat, short grass plains between the Cherry and the Straight. The unfolding scene before them answered all doubts. The narrow valley was alive with warfare. Running Wolf and the two Piegan bands had been overwhelmed by the massed charge of the Salish dogs and were this very moment fleeing the onslaught, all the while drawing their enemy into a web they could not hope to escape. The clever young Piegan warrior had divined his people's approach and was now leading the enemy right into their grasp, squeezing them into a fight they could not win and a trap they could not escape.

Blackfoot impatience could no longer be contained. The long, hot, dusty ride, their eagerness to punish, to annihilate their lifelong adversaries was in the end too great to bridle. Unrestrained, the swelling ranks of the rabid Piegan divisions broke discipline and raced forward in a wild, unruly charge sweeping across the plains towards the hapless Salish, routing their foes into a mad dash for their own lines.

A hideous, bellowing, gut wrenching Pahkee war cry, the pent-up fury of the nation, split the air, and sent its shock waves careening across the plains shattering all Flathead resolve. As one, the on coming red-tide roared their challenge in an explosion of their wrath as deafening as a thunder clap, raining down mercilessly on the inferior numbers with their backs to the river, fraying the already fragile edges of their nerves beyond raw.

I was stunned by the sudden turn of events, shocked utterly and completely at how swiftly the tide of battle and the odds had changed. How peacefully the day had begun... what hope the hunt had promised. How quickly life in the wilderness could evolve into a deadly struggle for survival. Not at all too different from the sylvan scene of a family of white tails grazing in a quiet glade, suddenly, ruthlessly shattered by the terror of the wolf pack, of stalking, ravenous canines hell-bent on feasting on their tender flesh. The ultimate horror of our fix was now sinking in.

I held little doubt. Blackfeet victory was as sure to follow as the sun would rise tomorrow. My Indian friends were brave and stout, but the overwhelming numbers of their bitterest enemy seemed to wither even the strongest of their men. But, I for one, meant to give them a good fight and take with me as many as I could.

I found myself yelling to Toby, exhorting him and his mountain friends. Sign was passed back and forth between us, furiously. Resolve was slowly returning to the hearts of everyone around me. And not a moment too soon. Their chiefs, their ablest warriors saw my example, what I was encouraging them to do and took up the cheer, rallying their brethren to regroup, to reunite, to defend their honor, to fight for the lives and future of their loved ones.

Up and down the lines, I sensed and knew their pleas. "Think of our women and children, our families and friends. Do you want them to be Pahkee slaves? Our fathers and mothers limbs hacked and dismembered, their spirits to wander in darkness forever?"

Flatheads, rallying together in unison, now once again, became fierce and resolute. Pride and determination and the will to live as free men resonated throughout their ranks as the six hundred awaited with a determined reception to counter the Pahkee onslaught to seal the fate of their nation.

The plains thundered with the incessant onslaught of thousands of pounding hooves, reverberating, echoing off those very sandstone cliffs of the sacred 'pishkun' itself. Never had this ground witnessed such human tragedy. Never had the two peoples in all their collective ancient memory recalled such an effort, such a monumental clash of arms. Never had the combined might of two great Nations of the Northwest come so perilously close to an Armageddon and the utter destruction of a people.

Kootenae Appe was caught up by the very ferocity of his own warriors' attack, that sudden explosive surge of human passion literally propelling his legions across the battlefield on a collision course; unstoppable, irrevocable, beyond recall.

And as he raced at the head of his minions, he exhorted, he commanded, he fanned the fire and roused the anger and hatred of his people and drove his Blackfoot fighters onward and onward to deeds of tenacious savagery, heroism, sacrifice... vengeance.

Halfway across the plains Kootenae Appe was met by Running Wolf. The young warrior strained to incite the new arrivals to an even greater pitch. His countenance now one of a yelling, screaming, frothing apparition gone berserk with vengeance on the fleeing Salish enemy... and on the unspeakable, the '*napikwan*', the white devil with the deadly fire-stick, in a land he did belong.

"Napikwan. Napikwan," he screamed to Kootenae Appe. His eyes were ablaze in fury. Every sinew of his body was taut, the invisible cords that connected his rawest emotions were gripped by one thought and one thought only... to kill the white man.

Napikwan... here, now? Kootenae Appe was completely taken aback. This day was becoming more amazing with each passing second. Now, an even greater treachery was being perpetrated on his people by the hated white-eyes.

The news was quickly passed to his whole devilish throng, racing throughout the ranks of charging warriors even as they surged forward 'til soon they all knew of my presence.

We watched and waited in grim silence. The Pahkee horde surged forward, unwieldy, a red army amuck, high plains paladins of savagery, not like the disciplined formations of a well-formed phalanx of Greek hoplites, but of chaos and disorder, wild and unrestrained, hell-bent on butchery and individual battle glory... *Namachkani! Namachkani!*

Their howling din, their shrieking war cries grew closer and closer, louder and louder, fiercer and fiercer, shaking the wellspring of Flathead bravery and resolve.

The noble men of the Bitterroot Mountains stood their ground, steadfast they would be to the bitter end. Lord knows what was going through their minds, but it was no mystery to see they were scared right down to the thin soles of their moccasins. I could see it in their faces and quivering limbs. Heard the low chant of their death songs, their final chorus, wafting through our lines.

I turned briefly from the oncoming charge to look at my Snake friend. He looked back at me, thoughtfully, as if to say ... "so long old friend."

I reached out and we both clasped each other's hand in one last farewell. One last appreciation of what had and could have been. One old Shoshone man and a young white buck fighting side by side like brothers in a land where neither belonged.

Toby knew it too, but stoically accepted our fate as he had our all too short friendship. And while I sat by my old friend, partially hidden by the willow thickets, I propped my wounded leg, rechecked my rifle's load and waited for the Blackfeet.

I must've done a good job concealing my own fear, for the truth beknown I was as scared as the rest of those braves. My mouth had gone dry, sweat filled the palms of my hands and streamed off my forehead. That feeling in the pit of my gut had long since gone, but I couldn't stop my fingers and hands from shaking like aspens in a storm.

I swore inwardly at my fear, ashamed of my own human frailty. I began to pray, silently, fervently, mumbling my own Christian death song, asking the Almighty to give me the courage to die like a man. And in the end, if it be his wish, to lift me to his heavenly confines.

Bows were held at the ready and musketman were spaced apart to concentrate on the lead warriors. As the Pahkee enemy neared their lines, the little men from the Bitterroots held their aim, calmly awaiting the signal that would erupt from their whole nation a barrage of lead shot and stone arrows. They knew well that their first volley might be their last, the Pahkees en-masse were coming-on way too fast. Their first salvo must be true and deadly to blunt the Piegan charge and spirit if they were to have any kind of chance.

Then it came. The pent-up fury and fear of the Bitterroot brotherhood let loose with a tremendous burst. Muskets fired and hundreds of bowmen let fly clouds of whistling arrows as they arced their way with deadly accuracy across the narrowing expanse into the bared flesh of men and beasts alike.

Vaunted Pahkee war-medicine failed to protect the front ranks of the charging host indiscriminately. Few were spared, many fell, the youth the pride of their nation, never again to see the light of day. Dozens lay prostrate, horse and man, blood and guts and broken limbs. Their agony, their pathetic wails, the bawls of their wounded beasts drowned out, swallowed up in an instant by the mass of thundering hooves and war cries of those that followed directly behind them.

The fragile discipline of the Flatheads now gave way. The Pahkees were on them like stinging hornets and the clash now became warrior against warrior, war clubs and tomahawk, vicious and fatal. The Piegans had them by at least two to one, but the brave people from the Bitterroots fought with a desperation and fervor they'd never known before.

Literally hundreds of individual combats broke out simultaneously... hacking, stabbing, thrusting back and forth along the whole battlefront; a collage of death, a panoply of hand to hand combat, gory, maiming, repulsive. Blood and innards splattered the ground from arena's end to end a veritable human deluge of misery and suffering.

Whack, whack... the ominous thud of primitive stone-headed clubs crashing, cracking, splintering exposed skulls. The telltale thump of an arrow piercing, invading, defiling naked flesh. The incessant swinging, hacking of a viciously swung tomahawk on its merciless journey. The rip, the tear, the deathly screams as scalp and flesh are torn and rent from body and skull. The equine shrieks of dozens of terrified ponies gone mad in stark raving fear. On and on the onslaught continued without respite.

From inside the thicket of red willow, I was forced to change my position constantly to avoid a withering fire directed my way. Musket lead chewed and shattered and shredded limbs and leaves, bows and twigs all about me.

My rifle though was a different story and it spoke with deadly words of lead. And I aimed and squeezed and fired... over and over, one painted savage after another feeling its wrath, slammed ever so rudely to the plains' sod below. The look on each ashen face the same... one of sheer, utter horror, masks of death, confused beyond all reckoning, unable to comprehend the hideous pile of guts protruding from their soft, exposed bellies or the sickening, helpless, numbing feeling overtaking their whole being.

I had little time to gloat or dwell. I just kept firing... again and again, praying all the while that my lead and powder would hold out. Amidst the confusion and din of battle, a half dozen Blackfeet were struck by my long-rifle, never again to see the light of day. A half dozen down amidst hundreds of fighting, wounded, dying men.

Sweat continued to pour off of me. Sweat and blood seeping from my bandaged wound. I gritted my teeth, ignoring the pain, the revulsion and nausea. My hands, my fingers ran wet and slippery with perspiration. My face was caked in dirt and grime and black powder, I tasted it and smelled it. It watered my eyes, blurred my vision. I fumbled with my powder horn time after time spilling, wasting its precious contents. My haste, my nervousness dropped many a lead ball to the grassy sod where I lay. Over and over I shoved that ramrod home, pulled it free and fired anew. I cursed, I swore, I reloaded again. I kept on firing like a man possessed, in a fumbling, frantic, frenetic fight to the finish... kill or be killed, on the plains of the Madison.

Through the mist and din and cloud of strife, the Pahkees finally found me... first by one, then another and another. The word was screamed over the length and breadth of the entire battlefield almost instantaneously. And that word to me now was... infamy incarnate.

"*Napikwan! Napikwan!*"

A hundred heads, a thousand heads turned my way. The battle seemed to stop for a brief moment of hesitation. It was as if everything and everyone stood still.

Realization was instantaneous that very moment. And that realization jolted me with a fear like I had never felt before. To be the object of such unforgiving, unremitting hatred was far beyond any emotion, any feeling I had ever known.

They rushed me with mouths agape and sinews straining, with fire and death in their eyes.

This is it, I thought, the end of my rope. There was no escape for ol' John Colter, not now, not this time. Quickly, I looked about. There was nowhere to turn to, no place to hide. I couldn't run. I could barely stand. I had used up all my nine lives and bag of tricks. I half-arose, slumping to one side, holding on for dear-life the barrel-end of my empty shootin' iron, ready to swing at the first heathen in reach and to hell with what came to follow.

Just when they had me within their reach, when I thought for sure my goose was cooked, that wily old Snake, Toby, and a roiling rush of Flatheads swept in front of me in a blur of hacking, chopping, stabbing. Such ferocity I had never known. The warriors of the Bitterroots piled their hated enemies in a heap of bloody gore, stacking them like human cordwood. The affair, my rescue was short and deadly. The tenacious Flats fell on the Pahkees, driving them back with nary a loss.

I wanted to thank them, every one of them, especially my Shoshone friend. He turned and looked and smiled. It was a close call and the battle still raged on. I nodded amidst gasps for air. I had hardly a moment to catch my breath, to regain my composure, when, right in front of my eyes, a sudden blur of color raced by, a bronzed warrior darting past too quick to catch or stop. The words of warning never had a chance to leave my lips.

The assault was swift, brutal, fatal. An avenging angel of the Pahkee brotherhood swung and drove his tomahawk down in a vicious arc, crashing into the exposed, unprotected skull of my little Snake friend with a hideous, bone-crunching thud.

The little man fell to the ground. Just crumpled to a lifeless heap. His head was rent horribly open, a cavernous ravine appeared, spilling out brains and precious life fluids. I was aghast, numbed… helpless to prevent or to avenge.

Several Flathead warriors quickly fell on the guilty Pahkee, pummeling his tender melon of a skull blood red, dispatching Toby's murderer in a rain of stone-headed blows.

It all happened so fast. I screamed, I bellowed, I roared. Tears flowed from my eyes. My grief, even in the midst of a battle for my own life, was far too great. I looked down upon Toby's countenance, his death mask. His thin, wiry limbs and torso wrinkled and battered and worn by a lifetime of living the Shoshone way. His great shock of gray and white and raven mane now lying lifelessly on the plains never again to flow in the wind. Sadly, I knew that I would never again grasp his hand in friendship, nor smoke kinnikinnick on a dark night by a blazing campfire. Death had robbed me of one true friend.

The battle raged on. The scale of victory and defeat heavily balanced towards the side with the greatest strength, the greatest array of martial power inexorably overwhelming their numerically inferior foes.

I shook myself from my grief, my anguish. Contemptuously, I ignored the throbbing pain in my leg temporarily forgotten in the adrenaline pumped fight for life. I reloaded and fired, reloaded and fired, reloaded and fired, over and over in a dire effort to shoot every Pahkee within my sights.

Everywhere throughout the battlefield blood flowed like water from hundreds of bursting human dams. Sweat poured from two thousand straining bodies. The screams of pain and fear, the wails and laments of death echoed the battle arena of the 'pishkun' plains from hundreds of wounded and dying warriors: Flathead, Piegan and ponies alike. The butchery, the carnage, the death songs raged on unabated without respite.

Trade muskets were silenced. Combat was too close, too personal. The lines too tightly drawn, too enmeshed. A writhing, grappling mass of human beings in its most debased, primeval form; Pahkee and Flathead, Salish and Piegan, an enigmatic jumble of Indian warriors, striking, kicking, swinging their deadly war clubs and tomahawks. The hum of a thousand arrows whistling through the air, striking bare, unprotected flesh of men and ponies alike. Death indiscriminate on an epic scale, uncaring, ruthlessly, hopelessly final in its pronouncement.

Up and down the field of battle the overpowering superiority of the Blackfeet Nation came into play. The Flatheads willingly made the ultimate sacrifice for the survival of the rest of their nation. They fought with a valor and spirit little seen since the days of Leonidas and his Spartans at the pass they called Thermopylae. Yet, even as great as their valor was the enemy host was too great. No give, no quarter, no mercy to be had. The dead, the wounded piled atop one another. The battlefield was literally blanketed in manslaughter, the ground mired in human waste, slippery with the carnage, the gore, the spilt guts and innards, and the torn scalps of hundreds of intended victims and their haplessly faithful, steadfast steeds.

As Blackfeet superiority began to show, they grew in confidence and boldness, depleting the thinning ranks of their enemy alarmingly so. Defeat and decimation was now a foregone conclusion, boiling down to a matter of time and numbers.

God, help us! The prayer raced through my mind.

At the most critical juncture of the battle, when the Piegan army was surely bound to sweep the field in complete victory and utter annihilation of the Flathead warrior brotherhood, a horrific rush of humankind poured out onto the plains from out of the east. Three hundred Mountain Crow slammed into the exposed flanks and rear of the Piegan-horde with tremendous impact. They just suddenly appeared on the "pishkun plains" without warning as if God himself had ordained a timely rescue.

The Crow, the Absaroka of the Mountains, also, hunted where the rivers-come-together. The Crow, also, were sworn enemies of the Blackfeet. And now, their timely arrival had instantly thrown an assured victory into bedlam... bedlam, panic and rout. And on they came, the graceful, high-pompadoured Absaroka, the people of the *As-to-pah-oan-zhah*, swarming over their backsides, attacking the Blackfeet with a zeal that they could only have for their worst enemies.

With victory so close the abrupt arrival of the Crow threw the whole Pahkee side into an uncontrollable panic. Confusion reigned throughout their ranks. Once again, their vaunted war medicine had failed them, and without it, they fled the field in abject horror... their discipline and courage quickly disintegrating into a wild defenseless flight.

Crow and Flathead together fell upon the fleeing Pahkee with savage delight, a feast of blood, of vengeance beyond all measure. What had been certain defeat, sure annihilation, turned to sudden triumph and overwhelming victory.

This day's battle would long be remembered in the lodges of the Flatheads and Pahkees alike. Its outcome, its echoes would reverberate among all the nations of the high plains and mountains and even reach far into the wilds of Canada.

The battlefield was desolation incarnate. The dead, the dying, the wounded a specter so grim I prayed to God to erase it from my mind forever.

The Blackfeet had indeed fled, but they would fight another day. They would not give up so easily their hegemony over the 'rivers that come together' land.

My friends with their Crow allies wandered about the battleground, tending to their wounded and dead, grieving, crying. Their wails of lament riveted the pishkun plains with an eerie, haunting melody.

Occasionally, a distraught warrior would bend over a fallen foe and rip his scalp from his skull with an odious rent. Some even maimed and desecrated the departed, resorting to the lowest of human depravations. Who could blame them? Who could deny their vengeance? Yet, there were no more cheers, no more exhortations to continue the violence, the mutilations. The warriors were all too tired, too worn out, too disgustingly sick of it all.

I watched with little empathy, numbed beforehand by the mindless, senseless cruelty of the Blackfeet. The sons of bitches had it coming. And yet, I closed my eyes in a vain attempt to shut out the horror, the misery. The pleasant memory of last night's campfire, smoking kinnikinick, eating chokecherry cakes with warm friendly, innocent people, seemed a thousand years ago in another world. The recollection of my friend, Toby, bandaging my leg in the heat of battle, saving my life and rushing to give his, flashed over and over in my mind. It tormented me with an unrelenting, nightmarish anguish that would be borne by my heart, my soul and memory for the rest of my days.

The Pyrrhic victory we enjoyed at such heavy cost held little satisfaction to the Flathead nation as they mourned the loss of so many loved ones. That they would be eternally grateful to the timely arrival of their Crow friends would not be soon forgotten. But this place, this battle, this loss would forever haunt their national memory.

The Blackfeet would not go away, this they knew all too well. Never again would Kootenae Appe be caught so easily, so unprepared. He and his minions, especially the young warrior leader, Running Wolf, would stew and seethe and boil. Their lodges would sing their death songs, mourn their fallen, until finally no power on earth could stop them from exacting revenge.

The old Flathead chief, Three Eagle, knew that his people's enemies would lick their wounds and come back with a vengeance. The Piegan host was still a mighty force and his people were a long way from home. He knew it would be some time before his people would dare venture again into the land of the rivers-that-come-together. His Bitterroot mountain valleys looked real good right now, a safe haven they had better stick close to for a time to come.

I figured my own luck was about used up, especially with the way those Piegan came after me, the way they screamed for my blood; death to the *napikwan*. And me standing side by side with their enemies, gut shooting the pride of their people, killing all those fine young warriors with my fire-stick.

I shuddered at the nightmare of being caught by those merciless brigands, unconsciously flinching at the visages of that old Piegan war chief and his rabid young warrior bands. They weren't the caliber of men to forget or let it ride. My face, my fire-stick would haunt them to the end of their days.

This land was big, big enough for all the Indian nations here to get along. But I wondered... wondered if it was big enough for me never to cross paths with the Blackfeet again. I pondered the thought awhile and then put the idea in the back of my mind.

The Flatheads hoped to make tracks and be long gone, safely back in their Bitterroots haven, before the Pahkees could mount another offensive. It would be many years before they would dare to venture forth to visit the Three Forks again. And if they did you could bet they'd be sure to scout the valley where the rivers come together long before they risk another such deadly confrontation.

I sat for awhile paying my respects to the lifeless body of my dead Shoshone friend. Toby, as sure as Damon did for Pythias, sacrificed his life for mine. A truer friend never was.

My tears had stopped flowing, my grief now grown muted, reserved and inward. Several Salish and Absaroka warriors gathered about me, standing quietly in respect, all sensing my anquish and my loss.

A tall Crow brave stepped forward and gesturing towards old Toby, asked, "*Isaahke*... old man, friend?"

I looked up at him and replied from parched lips, a gravelly... "Yep!"

I thought a moment longer and with a yet unswallowable lump stuck in my throat, added with all the grit I could muster, "And a mighty good one at that."

The warrior nodded his head, he understood. For several moments he stood by and waited patiently, almost reverently. Then, he let out with a grunt and pointed towards the fading dust clouds of the fleeing Blackfeet.

"*Pahkees*... come back."

His words, tersely delivered, stung like a hornet. That Crow warrior had a stern, hard look to him. A look that said he knew the Blackfeet and their ways, all too well. Life to his people held no delusions as far as their enemy, the Piegans and their northern cousins were concerned. They'd always been on the warpath agin each other; no truce, no parlay, no respite for any amount of time. Kill or be killed... as simple as that. It had been that way for as long as the Absaroka could remember. He'd taken his share of Blackfeet scalps today. His Crow brethren had reaped the whirlwind, dishing out their brand of mayhem on the confused, fleeing ranks of Blackfeet in the most horrific of ways. But, now was not the time to gloat. Vengeance held long memories for both sides. It was time to leave; only fools would languish on a battlefield so close to a still very dangerous foe. The Crow would gather up their own dead and wounded and depart immediately. Enroute, they would paint their faces black and return home to their villages by the Big Horn to celebrate the "scalp dance" while their victory remained fresh and the Blackfeet in retreat.

I nodded, I knew.

And then he added, with a sense of urgency. "Soon… plenty soon."

Sadly, the Flatheads left many of their dead on the battlefield where they lay. It was a tough thing to do, hurting them deeply. But, the battle that day on the "pishkun plains" had devastated their ranks, threatening their very survival. They could not mourn and care for those they lost the way they wanted to do. Ritual and tradition had to be put aside. The closeness of the *Pahkee* horde left them but little choice; they had to flee, put time and distance between them and their enemies. I'd said my final goodbyes, clasping the arm of the old chief, Three Eagle. We stood facing each other, gazing into one another's mind and soul and heart. In barely a day's time an undeniable bond had developed between us… one built on trust and friendship, forged by battle and blood. He and his people I'd come to respect and admire. For the rest of my days I would remember them thusly. And while we stood there those few short moments, I swore I saw tears well in that tough old man's eyes.

"Col-Ter, *Tab-ba-bone*."

"C'e~ll sq'qeymi, *tab-ba-bone*, my good friend," I replied. My voice choked-up, I could hardly get the words out. There was nothing else we could do, save to move on and live for tomorrow. And with much regret and sorrow, I bade his nation a final farewell.

I didn't look back as I rode away across the "pishkun plains" in the company of the Absaroka. My heart was heavy; it just wouldn't let go of the pain. The din of battle raged on ringing in my ears, investing my mind's eye like a black plague gone wild, infecting every part of my being, physically and spiritually. There was no respite the rest of that day, nor the next and the next. Even the Crow were silent, rueing their own losses as sadly as I did mine. One persistent thought would not go away, dominating all others… the murder of my little Snake friend, ol' Toby. He was a kind, simple, gentle soul. No threat to the stinkin' Pahkees or any other injuns for that matter. What injustice, as if there was any justice in this god-forsaken wilderness to be had. What cruel mockery, I had made a friend when I most needed one, only to be taken away less than a day later. Why? I looked to the heavens for an answer, but there would be none, just life and death, I knew. So be it, you sonsofbitches. You can't take away the memories. I got them right here in my ol' melon; his smiling face and wispy gray hair, the way he rode that pony of his, so natural-like and the way he walked the land.

I'd much to ponder. I thought of all that had taken place... a nation saving battle by primitive man of epic, even heroic proportions. Who would believe it? Who would even care? And what of me, a lone white man, thousands of miles from home, fighting side by side with the Flatheads against the most feared savages of the high plains? What would my countrymen, what would history think of me? Would I be thought touched, crazy in the head, the biggest liar in the West? So what, they could all go to blue blazes for all I care. I'd done my duty. I'd tell Lisa, he had the right to know. And his men, they'd better develop a healthy respect for these savages... and pronto, regardless, whether they believed me or not.

The Crow had no delusions as far as their northern neighbors were concerned. They couldn't, their very survival was at stake. And staying alive meant keeping a step ahead of your enemies, of being utterly ruthless... no quarter given or taken, brutality matched by brutality. It was a never-ending saga of these warring peoples. The battle of the "pishkun plains" was just one of many such, a constant struggle against Blackfoot treachery and deceit that wasn't about to go away anytime soon. And now I'd fought by their side, becoming for at least that day one of them. I could sense their respect and their acceptance as we rode east. Somehow that made the trip a little easier. As for the rest of the world, well, maybe I'd be smart to keep it to myself. I'd just have to wait and see how it played out.

My leg festered, throbbing the whole week-long ride back to the Big Horn. The pain at times was excruciating, jolting me right off my apishamore half-a-hundred times. I was weak, worn out and sick of the trail, tired of living on horseback and eating meager fare. The long winter, my trek through the mountains had aged me more than I could say. I missed the friendships I'd made with the Corps. I'd been alone far too long, meeting up with ol' Toby had made me realize just that.

For the first time in my life I was not so sure of myself. Those Pahkees had scared the daylights out of me, chilling me right down to my bones. And now I shook at the thought of them. Their tenacity, the way they charged across the plains, the recklessness and abandon of their attack, their ferocity, their sheer hatred for me was nigh on unnerving. But, there was no shame in being scared. The stoutest of hearts would've been daunted, even the most battle-tested of history's warriors would've had to think twice before crossing blades with the likes of those bronzed demons. Hell, I was no cherry. I've had my fair share of bloody scrapes and armed set-tos. I wasn't naïve to the ways of neither the red man nor the hard life they lived. The wilderness of the American frontier was not an easy place to grow up and injun trouble was as regular as the sun in the morning and the stars at night. A man always had his rifle primed and loaded within handy reach and ready to use, for keeping one's hair was a never-ending concern. Neighbors along the fringes of civilization stuck together, just naturally counting on one another for mutual protection and survival. It's the way it is… fight or perish. There is no other way. I'd seen men and women and even little children suffer and die, seen them scalped and mangled and mutilated and charred beyond recognition right in their own homes and fields. I thought I'd seen it all. But, the killing, the sheer magnitude of slaughter and mayhem on the plains by the Madison beat everything I'd ever known. It was not going to be an easy thing to forget. Maybe it never would. I'd been lucky, even Lisa would have to admit to that, no matter how much he wanted the injun trade. As for me returning empty-handed, he'd have to accept it. There was no shame in leaving empty-handed and I wasn't really running away. The Three Forks wasn't a place for a white man to be caught dead in, at least not while the Pahkees were on the warpath. And that's about the size of it. No need to give it a second thought. I've done my duty, made contact with the friendly injuns, like I said I would and fought as well as any man could've expected to do under the circumstances.

Uh huh! Sure you have! Tell me now, why do I detect something unpalatable sticking in your craw? C'mon, fess-up, spit it out. I know you too dang well; you can't hide it from me. Get it off your chest before you crush your fool-self to death.

So, that's it! Why, you jackass! You just don't want to give it up, do you? I might've known. I swear I smell some harebrained scheme cooking-up inside that thick head of yourn and you won't let it rest till it kills you. Will you?

That's it, you're right. I do know myself too dang well. You're wasting time, Johnboy. Might as well take a look back yonder while you can. You're dying to, ain't you? Admit it! Yeah, I am. Funny how a feller can be so damn predictable… even when he swears to himself that he ain't. All right, what the hell, no harm in taking one last little look.

"Whoa, hoss!" I commanded abruptly, reining in. Slowly, I turned, twisting to take in the valley. I could feel my *apishamore* sliding somewhat loosely beneath me, bunching up as if in quiet protest. Both my hands left the reins to shade my eyes from the glare of the late afternoon western sun. I sat for several minutes taking my bearings, staring long and hard, all the while my mind wandering in conjecture. The dust clouds of fleeing horsemen by then had settled down. The Pahkees and the Salish had had enough of the Three Forks today, tomorrow and maybe even for the foreseeable future. I'd bet my poke on it. Soon, not a living soul would be there to be seen or heard, just the spirits of the battlefield-dead whose silent wails and appeals for a proper injun burial would go unheeded. All those dead… and hundreds and hundreds of stinking, feted breathed buzzards and crows and magpies, all joining the fray, circling ever so nearer, descending like airborne wolfpacks, hellbent on eating decaying human flesh. The gutpile feast would last for days to come; till the varmints picked every carcass clean, till scant remained save wind and sun-bleached bones and skulls.

I turned away, shuddering, repulsed by this most unholy, sacrilegious of nightmarish visions. This was not a place that would rest easily, not a place for a lone white man to be wandering about, no matter what the reason, no matter what the reward, no matter how careful and deliberate. Yes, even a fool could see that. But, I was also seeing something else… something a little less chaotic than what portended today. Maybe, just maybe… Hmmph! Don't you ever give up? Why you ol' curly wolf, you've got some nerve, Johnboy, even for you. Yeah, I know… dumb, just plain dumb, but, why not? The Pahkees won't be expecting me to come back, not with a hole in my leg and the fear of God in my guts. Besides, they've got enough troubles of their own. The place is like poison to them right now. They can't even properly take care of their dead. No, they'll head north and lick their wounds. And that will take some time. They've got a long winter ahead of them. They'll stew and plan some kind of reprisal on the Salish to be sure. But, they won't want to hang around the Forks with the stench of their own dead in the air.

Don't be so sure. Are you ready to stake your life on it? You know injuns will fool you everytime. Hold on, I didn't say I'm coming back for sure. It's just something to fool with, to mull over while the hullabaloo simmers down. But, why not, what if I did? There's beaver aplenty to be had, money to be made? That's what's kept me out here for the better part of the last two years. And better me than those fools back at Manuel's. The Lord helps those who help themselves. Remember? That's what the Good Book says. Hell and tarnation, I'm all for that. Now the least I can do is come up with a plan while I'm waiting to decide. There's little harm in that. Thinking is good exercise for the brain… and for the soul. And that's the way I'm seeing it. Maybe wait 'til the end of summer, beginning of fall, when the chill comes on… fur will be primed by then, ready for the taking and the tanning. Don't get too greedy. Get in and get out, quiet as a church mouse with no hostiles the wiser. Just keep it to your self. And come alone. You hear me? Come alone, no wet nursing, no tanglefoots. Depend on you own instincts, your own guile just like pa taught you.

Hmmph, what a mouthful I'd given myself to chew on. In the meantime I'd let my leg heal up, collect my kit, my traps and possibles and bide my time. By rights I'd no business contemplating what I was thinking to do, it was a leap in the dark even for me. I was playing with hellfire and I knew it. But, that's what made it so damn enticing. Do the impossible, the unexpected. Playing it safe was for other men. I didn't have the time or the inclination for that sentiment; otherwise, I might as well pack up and head on home. Yet, every instinct I had, every shred of sense cried caution and warned of madness. Though I continued to listen, I still kept at it, formulating the beginnings of a plan despite all I knew and feared. Oh, I was still shaken badly; Toby's death and Salish sacrifices tormented me in ways I'd never known before. Nor did I underestimate Piegan guile or determination or treachery. Those injuns were enough to scare the daylights out of any man. But, I wasn't just any man. At least that's what I use to tell myself back then. I hadn't lost my nerve; in fact what I was affixing to do was bold beyond anything I'd ever conceived of, slowly turning a questionable idea into outright resolve. All I needed to do was to get back to Manuels in one piece and set it all in motion.

PART TWO

"Of undaunted courage and incredible endurance, his whole career, as far as we know it, was filled with perilous adventure, and his exploits might pass for fairy tales were they not substantiated by the most-reliable evidence."

William Ghent ... *Unpublished Biography of John Colter*

CHAPTER FOUR

Manuel's Fort was quiet, too quiet for broad daylight. Not a sound or a sign of life stirred from within to reveal the company of armed trappers that should've been waiting behind its barred gate and high honed-log walls.

Funny, maybe the sentry is catnappin'. I'll wake his sorry hide up. "Hello the Fort," I bellowed with all the voice my withered constitution could muster.

Silence. No response, it was as if the stockade had been completely abandoned. "Humph! Now this is a fine how-do-ya-do." I was talking tough, but I wasn't buying what I wasn't seeing. The walls looked perfectly stout, even impregnable by frontier standards. Lisa's engages had done well. The savages would have played hell attacking such a fortified redoubt. Yet, there were no signs that injuns had even been around, certainly nothing to reveal a conflict had taken place. So where was everyone? Surely, Lisa would have posted a sentry, maybe even two. No man worth his salts trusted anything to chance while in injun country... and Manuel Lisa was no fool.

I called out a second time, louder, more forceful. "Hello the Fort... white-man comin' in with injun friendlies." Again, I went unchallenged. "What in blue blazes is goin' on?" I grumbled aloud to no one but myself, knowing full well a skunk when I smelled one. I shifted uncomfortably in the saddle, all the while warily eyeing the fort as if its silence was a prelude to deception or treachery. I knew we were being watched, but by who, whites or hostiles? And where were they, what were they up to? For once I had no answers, just questions begging explanation. I liked it not. Suddenly, my mouth and throat went dry. Sweat beaded on my brow, streams of salty dew trickled down the back of my neck. After all I'd been through, I wasn't prepared for this. What to do, backoff out of range or keep walking in towards the fort like nothing was wrong? I wavered. I wasn't alone in my suspicions. Even my pony was holding back, his ears reaching forward straining for a hint of movement, disturbing, guttural rumblings of hesitation emerging from deep within his own gut instincts... instincts, I had learned to trust. And right then he was as nervous as I was. "That's all right, fella, I don't like it none too much myself." I reached down gently rubbing his neck. "Steady, boy, steady." Then I looked up to see something I hadn't noticed a moment before. What the hell, looks like Manuel's has taken on some strange new growth. I put both heels in my mount's flanks and edged forward. The closer I neared, the more obvious the long, smooth, leafless branches protruding over the top of the palisaded walls were not tree limbs at all, but the barrel-end of long rifles, every one of which was trained on a human target... including yours truly. "Whoa! Hold up, fella." I gently pulled back on the reins, my pony coming to an abrupt halt.

"Nice reception," I mumbled acrimoniously, not liking my welcome reception one dang bit. Liking it or not, those rifles meant business and whoever were holding them at the ready were not buying my story, yet. "Steady, Johnboy, don't get hasty, now."

I raised my hand halting my Crow companions. Now, those Absaroka braves hadn't missed a trick, eyeing the stockade every bit as warily as I had, readying to bolt and run and scatter with the wind at the first sign of trouble. Once more I nudged the piebald forward towards Manuel's front gate, watching those quivering rifles every step of the way, 'til I was right under their very noses. I sat in the saddle for several minutes in silence waiting to be challenged or acknowledged. It was a standoff in the making, nobody on either side making a sound or a move. To top it off, my leg was acting up again and my gut was getting queasy. Fact of it is I was hanging on, barely, taking every ounce of strength I had left in my worn out body just to sit on my hoss without keeling over and falling to the ground like a sack of spuds. But, I wasn't about to right then. I was too stubborn, too ornery, and getting more pissed by the minute. I'd held out for nigh on two hundred miles and I was in no mood to put up with any further aggravation or trapper shenanigans. Yet, the boys in the fort were giving me no other choice.

"Damn," I swore softly, "if this don't beat all. Wait a minute..." Movement up above. Yeah, that's it, come on, here I am, it's me, all right. Men were chancing a look, their curiosity being more than they could bear. There were hairy heads behind the hammers of those rifles, with eyes that looked at me like I was their worst dream. Plain and simple, those boys didn't know what to make of me.

I wet my lips and took a long swallow, clearing my throat. Affecting my best Virginia drawl I called out. "Ease off those triggers, boys, y'all wouldn't want to shoot ol' John Colter... would ya?"

Silence, still. Damn, not again. I was mighty exasperated by then, my patience and my tact at an end. "What's it gonna take to get one of you idiots to talk to me?" I yelled rather disgustedly. That seemed to do it, I could hear whispering... and it sounded American to me. "Well, what do you know, somebody has got some balls after all. C'mon, take a good look, it's me, all right, dyed in the wool and in the flesh, here to tell ya, I'm back."

Several bearded scruffs stood up on their tippy-toes. To a man they stared at me with the most dumbfounded of looks, several even rubbing their eyes in disbelief.

I shook my head. "Yeah, it's me all right. Open up the dang gate, will ya, 'afore I kick the dang thing in."

"Hold on right thar, mister, don't git in such an all fire hurry… and keep that firin' piece of yourn pointin' to the ground. We ain't a trustin' no kind of man ridin' up with no war party of painted injuns… friendly or not. So back off a ways so's we can see ya, cause ya sure 'n hell don't look like no John Colter to me?" His tone was testy, hard-edged, spoiling for a fight, yet that voice of his was unmistakably familiar to my ears. It had a western Pennsylvania bent to it, like from around ol' Fort Pitt and it was one that I knew all too well. "In fact, now that I see ya clearly, ya look more like some kind of a hairy injun to me… and a butt ugly one at that." With that he began chuckling, no longer able to keep a straight face or a civil tongue. Yeah, he was having a right good time at my expense, putting on a show and amusing his companions standing right alongside him. And he wasn't alone in his fun. More then a few guffaws were to be heard egging him on.

"Pour it on, Johnny," a snicker arose from the ramparts.

I smiled at the unveiled insult, perfectly assured by now as to whom was the guilty offender. So, he wants to play, act the big man. All right, let's see how he fares. I lifted my nose in the air, immediately recoiling with distaste as if catching some repugnant, foul odious scent. "Phewww, what a stink. I smell a polecat here, boys… a two-leggedy skunk to be sure." It was my turn, now, time to return the favor and I layed it on, thick and heavy. "Potts, that is you, ain' it, little girlish voice and all? Just how in the hell have you managed to keep your cherry with all those horny trappers fawnin' all over you?"

Stunned silence. You could've cut the air with a wave of a feather. Guffaws. Then more guffaws, rumbling unabated for several minutes. Johnny Potts was struck silent; unable to mount even the simplest of ripostes without tripping over his own tangled tongue. He had stuck his foot in his mouth and I was content to let it stay there awhile longer.

I continued my repartee, pouring it on as mercilessly as I could. "Potts, ain't you learned yet, you know better than to duel wits with me? As for bein' butt ugly, looks whose paintin' the kettle black. Why, I've taken better lookin' craps than you. Hell, just a few rods back yonder on the trail, we came upon a great big greasy pile of bear scat I swore was momma Potts' little boygirl catching some winks."

That did it. General pandemonium broke out, laughter, mirth contagious, epidemic. Men began to stand up, no longer afraid to reveal themselves. And as they arose they eased forward their weapons' heavy hammers, withdrawing their shootin' irons from the ready and standing down.

And me… why, I breathed a little easier. Even the nervous Crow behind me knew that all was now well.

Redfaced and all, Potts called down to the inner stockade floor below. "It's Colter, all right, no one else has the balls. Open the gates 'n let him in 'afore he shames me to death."

I moved on in. They were all there to greet me: Johnny and Pete Wiser and Manuel Lisa, himself, and none of them were believing their eyes. Of course, it didn't help matters much what with me riding up with a mess of fierce looking *Kee-kat-sa* painted for trouble, fresh scalps hanging from their shields and lances and acting just as squirrely as the trappers themselves. There was still uneasiness surrounding the men of Manuel's Fort. Very few whites trusted any injuns, including the Crow. It was mutual, the red man feeling no differently towards the white. A lifetime of mistrust and treachery by both sides had seen to that. Trigger fingers were always nervous with savages about and today was no different. But, what the hell, there were always trade goods, powder and lead to be had for the price of a few measly pelts of the beaver. The red man could never understand what all the fuss was about with the skin of the beaver. Especially, since they were everywhere and in such abundance. But, if that's all the white man wanted...

And here I was a mess of an excuse for a man. My pa's hounds used to drag in more respectable-looking varmint carcasses. My hair and beard had grown long and scraggly, completely masking any resemblance to the man who'd left Manuel's Fort half a year before. My blood stained leggings, my fringed hunting shirt, what was left of it, were torn and shredded rags. A makeshift bandage, a soiled compress of animal skin still covered that nasty musket ball wound in my leg, barely concealing the festering sac of pus that just wouldn't quit oozing. I had a ragged, unkempt, hungry look... a look that warned that I had missed many a meal and wasn't in any mood to be jerked around. And besides all of that, they hadn't heard from me in a month of Sundays, quite rightly concluding that ol' John Colter had met his end, bleached bones and all scattered on some distant prairie... dead and gone forever.

I was feeling as bad as I looked right then; the pain, the infection and fever it wrought, the days in the saddle when I should have been bundled up in a warm buffalo robe by an even warmer fire. I was spent... worn to a frazzle. Too many hard winter months in the mountains and the battle with the Pahkees had aged me more then I cared to admit. And nobody, but nobody was welcoming me back, 'til now. I could've tumbled from my hoss before I cleared the stockade's gate. I was that tired, that weak. But a pair of strong arms held me up and wouldn't let me go. And then another familiar voice, a friendly voice was talking to me, reassuring, soothing.

"Hang on, John, just a little bit more... what the? Holy shit!" A startled cry, the voice was Pete Wiser's, and he was helping me down. "John, you sure look like you've been dragged through a briar patch by a passel of pissed-off wild cats."

"I wasssss..." I managed weakly, looking up to my friend. Pete wasn't far off, though right about then a briar patch didn't seem quite as prickly as the "pishkun plains" had been.

"Give me a hand with him, Johnny. I don't know what's holdin' him up, cuz he look's just about done in."

"Pete?" I said feebly, "Is that really you? Why you ol' son of a bitchhh…" That was it for me, all I could handle. Instantly, I became light-headed, darkness suddenly coming over me without warning, stars began twinkling and careening about in my mind's eye. In and out of consciousness I roamed, helpless, everything about me spinning dizzily around 'til I could stand no more. And then my legs seemed to give-out, my knees buckled, I went limp, collapsing to the ground.

"Steady, John, I gotcha. It's me, all right, yer ol' buddy Pete, none tother."

Funny, I could barely hear him, like he was whispering from afar… and I knew he wasn't.

Pete stepped back, aghast… "John, what in the hell has happened to you?"

He finally saw the festering musketball-wound in my thigh, gawking in disbelief for the longest of seconds. His face suddenly became ashen, revulsion and realization setting in. Now, Pete was no pilgrim and gunshot wounds were a fact of life on the American frontier, especially when deep within injun country. And he had doctored a fair-share of bloody wounds himself in his day. I guess we all had. But, this was different, it was his friend whose blood he was seeing and somehow my wound and condition struck him deep down and personal.

"My God, man! Johnny, get a look at Colter's laig. Sure as shootin' he's taken a musketball right in der thigh."

Potts saw it for the first time. The realization hit him hard and fast. Bravado seemed to drain out of him right then and there. His face suddenly turned green like a slab of rancid bacon. A most unsettling look coming over him, like he wanted to puke his guts out or bolt and run. For once the loquacious youth didn't utter a single word. If I hadn't felt so lousy, I might have enjoyed the moment for it was a rare one as far as Johnny Potts was concerned.

"Get a hold of yourself, Johnny. I need your help, now." Pete wasn't about to let Potts get off so easily. "We need to take care of his laig… and mighty quickly or he'll lose it fer sure." And then Pete turned back to me. "You gonna make it, boy?"

"Yeahhh!" I waned. "It'll take more than one little ol' lead ball to slow this curly wolf down."

"Uh huh! Keep thinkin' that way," he said, shaking his head, but obviously glad I still had some sand left in my veins.

"No need to fret, Pete… us Colters are fast healers." I made a piss-poor attempt at a smile, but I wasn't convincing to anyone, including myself. I was drunk from pain and exhaustion and that one big, bad, dark memory that wouldn't go away. But, I still had my pride. I could still muster a little spunk. I was glad to be back, glad to be with friends once again. And then a fit of giddiness took hold of me. I giggled and laughed, uncontrollably. I couldn't seem to stop. From where I got the strength, I'll never know.

"I suspect you are that," Pete responded, shaking his head and frowning. "Colter, nuthin' you do ever surprises me."

It took a spell, but I recovered, thanks to Pete and Johnny. They were my mother hens; feeding me three squares a day, daily dressing my wound, nursing me right back to health, and all the while, nightly enduring my fitful sleeps and ramblings, my feverish recollections of the chaos of battle and the death and loss of ol' Toby. Unable to keep quiet my delirium from the rest of the Fort, trapper gossip spread like wildfire, infecting the whole command. By the time I was up and about every trapper within hailing distance of the fort knew of it; John Colter had been through hell. And none of them knew what to think.

"Ahh, Jean Colter, *entre parle vous*… *s'asseoir*… please, sit down, we are long overdue for a talk, *mon ami*. You look well, but I must tell you that I have been concerned. Your friend, Mssr. Wiser, tells me you talk uncomfortably while you sleep. It worries him greatly. He says your dreams, *vous-reve*, are heavy with pain and sadness and regret."

"I'll get over it."

"But, of course you will, I would expect no less. Danger is a *risque* peculiar to our trade, is it not? And you've undoubtedly seen more than your share. In the meantime, please, we must discuss your journey and *aventures*."

Lisa had finally gotten around to hearing my report, though I suspected he'd all ready gotten an earful from the Crow through his Osage half-breed confidante, Ed Rose. That was all right by me, they'd only verify what I had to say. Besides, coming from their mouths added gravity to the danger of confronting the Blackfeet where we didn't belong.

I watched his face for sign, studying the man as best as I could. Lisa was a hard read, but not that hard. He wasn't much on sympathy… at least for another man's troubles, regardless of his clever attempt to allay my mind otherwise. But, this was about doing business… a business in a wild, untamed land that could be cold, hard and ruthless, mastered by men who had the sand and smarts to make it work for them. Everything about him and his reputation said he was such a man, a man not to be put off easily, regardless of those very *risques* he so deferentially addressed moments before. So, I told him. I told him every dang thing from the day I left 'til the day I returned. And he listened in silence, occasionally twisting the ends of his thin moustachios, twirling the delicate black hairs to a fine, sharp needle-like point. Otherwise, he remained impassive, as stoic as the cold granite pinnacles of the Absaroka and the Beartooth I'd grown to know and respect. As I talked, reliving frustration amidst so much wonder, his mind seemed to roam as if riding by my side, accompanying me in my own wanderings. Occasionally, he evinced a startled look, a raised eyebrow or two at something extraordinary to his ears. Why not, I'd seen things even I couldn't believe or explain? But, he remained silent for the most part, letting me ramble on uninterrupted. He did keep a log, though, jotting down a few sentences from time to time, mostly, from what I could tell, about the fight at the "pishkun plains." But, was it the fight? I wasn't certain, for any mention of the headwaters seemed to get the man stirred right up. I could see it in his eyes as those dark orbs literally sparkled and danced. His fingers in accompaniment, tapping away to some lively tune known only to him. Now that little clue I didn't miss. And I had my answer; it wasn't about injuns battling to the death or hardship or perils; it was about the beaver, always the beaver.

"*Fantastique!* Truly, *fantastique! Les places du etrange, mon ami,* I do not know what else to say," Lisa blurted out, breaking his silence.

But, I was finished, taking nearly the whole morning long to complete my report. Talking has never been my strong suit and being long-winded was the last thing I'd expect out of myself. But, that's exactly what I'd been. I was bone dry, near worn out from the effort. Yeah, I came back empty-handed, but not for wont of trying. I'd nothing to be ashamed of. I'd done my best, even if my best wasn't good enough. Question was, what did Lisa think? I'd given him much to chew on, packing more territory and imponderables in the last couple of hours than he had any reasonable right to expect. My encounter with the Salish and the Piegans should have stopped the man's plans of trading with those injuns, cold. But, like I've said, he was not the sort of man to be put off easily.

"Volcanoes and irregularities of nature, unfortunately, at this time do not interest me. Maybe, one day we can sit down and talk of these places and things. I am not of so singular a mind as not to appreciate that which I do not understand, but, not now. Mon ami, I am here for beaver. Nothing else satisfies my hunger and your recent misfortunes have even put a damper on that stubborn appetite. So you will forgive me if I seem not so enthusiastic about your results. They are a disappointment, but… maybe only a temporary one. These *le trois fourches* may yet prove fruitful in time, *certainmente,* the place is worth considering. In the meantime, continue your convalescence; visit with your friends, do a little trapping, make some money… it will be good for your soul. Shortly, I will return to St. Louie to attend to business. When I return, I may have further use of your talents. In any case, Jean Colter… *au revoir*."

That was the end of our conversation. One whole winter, five hundred miles deep into country no white man had ever been before… and my efforts, my odyssey were dismissed with a wave of a greasy hand. I left him and his little two-room cabin feeling as low as a mangy mutt with his tail between his legs only to run smack-dab into Wiser and Potts. The two had been hanging around, anxiously waiting for me, and the devil was in their eyes. Whatever it was, their curiosity, their eagerness to lay it on me was nigh on getting the best of them.

"What mischief are you two up to?" I asked.

"What'd the greaser have to say?" demanded Johnny impatiently, a smile breaking out over his face, a nervous foot tapping away on the stockade's dirt floor.

"Greaser? Oh, is that what you call the Spaniard?" I chuckled. "Not much, I doubt he heard a word I said."

"The prick," retorted Potts, "the little prick. He only hears what he wants to hear. I swear… he's a no good son of a bitch."

"There's talk goin' around," said Pete, cautiously. "Ain't no secret 'bout what you've said since you've been back. We've tried to keep it quiet, but the walls have ears. You know what sorry-excuses some of these backwoods bummers are; they just luv to live it up with other's misfortunes. Some of 'em are fit to be tied and mighty loose and insultin' with their lips. I don't much like what they're sayin' about ya. Johnny and me have been talkin' 'bout bustin' some skulls."

"Huh?" I groused. "Hell, don't bother, let 'em have their laugh. Lisa's already told me as much. Damn, I knew all along I'd be in for it, but, a man's gotta do what he's gotta do."

"Well, are ya gonna tell us, your ol' pards, about yer talk with the greaser?" asked Potts trying to worm his way into my confidence. I knew he was sneaking up on me, itching to know everything that was said. Johnny was the type of man not to be denied, the more you hid… the deeper he dug.

"Nawww! I'd best leave it be, Johnny. I can only put up with so much snickerin' behind my back. But, I will tell you this…one-day another poor fool will stumble into what I saw. Sooner or later the whole world will know and somebody will figure the place out. I know what I saw and heard and smelt and felt.' And that's all I'm gonna say…"

"John Colter, I declare… you are a strange one," said Pete. "I mean goin' out yonder to those high mountains all by yerself with winter comin' on, and then returnin' a half a year later all shot up, with a festerin' hole in your leg, accompanied by a swarm of injuns with fresh scalps danglin' from every place imagineable. I gotta know, what in der hell fer, what's out thar that's so all fired important? Are ya holdin' out on us? What is it ya got up yer sleeve? C'mon, we're yer friends, we gotta right to know."

I looked at the two of them and decided for the moment to let it lie. I had a lot to think about and I didn't need my mind muddled by Pete Wiser and garrulous Johnny Potts, even if they were the only friends I had.

I shook my head, no. "Not now, Pete, I got some powerful thinkin' to do."

Pete nodded his head, knowing I meant what I said. And then… "Say, how'd Lisa look to you?"

Now Pete's question struck me as strange. He was angling, adroitly changing the subject. Why, I didn't know. But, come to think of it, Lisa did look a little yellow around the gills. I thought about his face, the way he avoided my stare, looking off to the side the whole conversation. It never occurred to me that he might be hiding something. But, I was to find out, something, indeed, had happened and the boys were dying to tell me.

"I don't rightly know, though, come to think of it, he did look like a man that was nursin' a beatin'. Why, what did I miss? What are you two rascals up to?"

They both looked at each other and then at me and chuckled, both squirming with giddiness.

"We ain't up to nothin'," Potts grinned. "But, while you were off with them Flatheads, you really missed somethin' special… the greaser's comeuppance." Potts continued chuckling. Pete just smiled.

"I can see you're rarin' to tell me about it. Might as well go ahead, I've got nuthin' else to do."

Johnny was itching, all right. He could barely contain himself. Seems, there had been a fight and it involved two of his least favorite people, Manuel Lisa and Edward Rose… an Osage half breed with a none too favorable reputation or disposition. Rose was a loner, a bully, a man who never seemed to fit in with any of us white backwoodsmen. But he did like injuns, their customs and ways, forever singing their praises. He was a hard man, though, make no mistake about it. Sooner or later where Rose was concerned trouble was bound to follow.

Wiser and Potts kept grinning, both fit to be tied. If they didn't tell their story pretty soon, I swear one of 'em would explode. Pete nodded to Johnny to go ahead and the youngster commenced with relish.

Potts still acted like a kid. He just couldn't help himself. His five years out West did absolutely nothing to dampen his youthful spirit or tame the brashness that marked just about everything he did or said. He had a cocky swagger with a red-hot temper to match. More than once he'd fly off the handle at some purported affront or another, occasionally biting off more of a man then he could possibly chew. There was no 'backup' in Potts, his sense of manhood never allowing it. Most men on the frontier had that quality, guts being a requisite, preferably right along side with a good dose of savvy. That last notion, though, was sometimes in question as far as Johnny Potts went. It was a likeable part about him, one I appreciated, but at the same time it was a side of his character that was bound for trouble one day. You could see it coming, the odds were all in its favor. I should have realized it right then, but I never did catch on, until it was way too late.

"It wuz last fall... just after ya left," he began on a somber note. "That mornin' had all the earmarks of trouble ahead. You remember... it started snowin' and it didn't let up the whole dang winterlong. We watched ya go, headin' west all by yer lonesome, nobody givin' ya much of a chance to see yer mission thru... or to keep yer scalp. Everybody wuz feelin' a little gloomy those first few days, what with the walls only half up and plenty of sign of injuns skulkin' around the post, spoilin' for mischief. Who knows what those heathens were up to, hard to tell what goes thru their minds? We kept our rifles close at hand, nobody wantin' to find out. One of our half-breeds swore they were the Atsina, the Gros Ventre of the plains. And that had us worried. The Crow swore-up and down that they weren't their people. No body believin' their lying shit anyways. We were all actin' a mite touchy. Pete and me even thought about headin' back downriver come the first opportunity. But, we didn't, as ya can see... not when our ol' pard was unaccounted fer."

"I'm beholdin'," I said with a smile.

"Tou-che!" saluted Potts.

Pete nodded, giving me the ol' thumbs up.

"Well, no sooner had ya cleared the gates and disappeared upriver, when Lisa calls in that skunk half-breed Ed Rose. They had their parlay, the upshod being the Spaniard completey outfits ol' Osage Rose with most of our trade goods and sends him off to swap for beaver with those horse thievin' Kee-kat-sah, the Mountain Crow. No one missed the disparity of that fact... that Lisa sent you off to the west with only a blanketful of trinkets and Rose the kit and the kaboodle. Seems like he didn't put much faith in yer endeavor.

Ya shouldn't have trusted him, I tell ya."

"I knew what I was doin'," I replied, testily.

"Cut to it, Johnny," said Pete, all of a sudden. "You'll bore poor Colter here to death."

"Awright, awright… Long story short… none of us liked Rose to begin with. And fer sure he didn't like us. What's more… he's a liar, convinced Manuel from the start that he wuz his man as far as tradin' with the Crow were concerned. Hah, hah, hah! What a crock, Rose wuz full of shit, we all knew it. And what's more he knew we knew. That's why he avoided us. But, ya couldn't convince Manuel, no, sir, thought his injun lover wuz the 'second comin'…"

Pete smiled, revealing several missing teeth. He'd heard it all before. But, he never seemed to get tired of listing to his younger friend. And Johnny's retelling got better with time and age.

"The boy's got a gift for der gab, don't he?" Pete said, looking to me.

I shook my head. And Johnny, with a face full of dimples, couldn't help but chuckle and beam.

"Off he went traipsin' into the mountains like he wuz General Washington, himself, crossin' the Delaware on the Fourth of July."

Pete and me both looked at him kinda queer like. The kid had his history a bit askew. Didn't matter, Potts was laying it on thick. He liked to talk, to be the center of attention and the more he did, the more loquacious he became.

"Der meat… get to der goddamn meat!" Wiser snapped at his younger partner.

"Oh, right… Well, long about a week or two before your return, his 'lordship' Rose comes sneakin' back in here as quiet as a church mouse. Came back empty handed… all the trade goods gone and not a single skin to show fer the trouble. The word wuz out and soon the whole lot of us trickled back to the Fort… curiosity being more then we could stand. One of our frog friends from down St. Genevieve way, ol' Sebastian Picon, went with Rose, reluctantly, I might add. Seb hates the breed. Said he was mighty carefree with the Company's trade goods, giving 'em out to the Crows like hard candy and gittin' nothin' back in return."

"Humph!" I said. "I bet that didn't set well with Manuel."

"Damn right it didn't," said Pete, "he was fit to be tied."

"Yeah, he sure wuz. Let me go on… the shit wuz about to commence. Ya knew it had to. Lisa could stand only so much, his reputation and pride wuz takin' a serious rebuke. Of course we didn't help matters much… giggling, smirking, embarrassin' the livin' shit outta the greaser. I tell ya the pot wuz boilin' and we wuz doin' the stirrin'.

You knew Lisa wuz furious, he'd been buzzin' around the compound like an angry hornet, lookin' fer someone or something to sting. The scene wuz set, we all marched into the countin' cabin to watch the fireworks begin. There they be, the two of 'em, facin' each other off, all the while the whole lot of us standin' all around 'em, givin' 'em no breathin' room a'tall. Manuel's gloves were off, demandin' an immediate explanation from the breed.

Rose stammered', red as a beet, unable to come up with anything other than a feeble tale to cover his sorry hide. Lisa knew it, we all did. He didn't buy a word the breed said, launchin' himself into a terrible tirade of cussin', words I ain't never heard before: French, Mexican, American and probably a few choice injun ones to boot. Revilement poured like water out of his twisted black face and he cut that dumb son of a bitch Rose to the quick. Hell, if words were like steel the breed would've bled to death. Rose was no match for Lisa when it comes to repartee.

Potts laughed so hard he snorted up a noseful of snot. It took a minute for him to regain his composure well enough to continue his story.

"Sorry, John, Pete," he said, apologizing for his crudeness, all the while struggling to control runaway mirth.

"It wuz too funny. Ya had to been there. Right, Pete?"

Wiser smiled again and nodded. "Had to been."

Pete stood up, turned around and began scratching my pony's nose, as it stuck its curious head over the top pole of the corral. Pete had heard it before and now was quite bored with the latest Pott's rendition. I watched him for a moment, noticing that several grizzled trappers were also listening to Johnny's tale. Soon we had a crowd of buckskinners gathered around us. They were all nodding and smiling, evidently pleased at what had happened and dying to relive it again. Amusements were few in Manuel's stockade, a roaring tale at someone else's expense was much in demand and life was what you made of it.

Me, I was ready to leave, soon as my leg was healed and my kit ready to go.

Johnny didn't miss the crowd gathering. His chest was pumped up, proud as a strutting barnyard rooster.

"Now, the breed ain't an intelligent man, being crude, uneducated and all. And like I said… he wuz no match for Manuel when it came to words.. But I'll give him this, there ain't no backup in the man, he's got gravel in his gizzard and the more Lisa lit into him the more we could see the scrape a comin'.

The two of 'em are too much alike, burst from the same seed, they did: arrogant, unsociable with the likes of us, distrustin' of everyone around 'em. Downright vicious, too… backstabbers, through and through. Contemptuous to a fault, like they wuz better than everyone else. Hell, everybody here hates both their guts and equally so.

When the 'git to' finally got a goin', we all just stepped back out of the way and let 'em have at it. None of us said a word. We just kinda looked at each other with that same pleased look. And that look said, 'they both deserved whatever they had a comin'… and rightly so."

"Smells like the pot done boiled over," I said to Johnny. "I'm rather glad I missed it."

Ol' Pete nodded, a smile on his face. "It did and I'm glad I missed it, too."

"Lucky you," snapped back Potts. "You always seem to miss the shit."

"And you always manage to step right in it…" retorted Wiser with a scowl, shaking his head. Pete was slow to rile, but once he reached his limit, he was more than a match for Potts.

"All right… all right!" I said. "No need to get testy with each other. Let's get back to Rose and Lisa before I fall asleep."

I had seen the beef a brewing and nipped it in the bud. Even the best of friends can get irritable with each other after a while. And these two were no different. Poor Potts was always starting something he couldn't finish. It was probably the one thing he did well and on a consistent basis.

Johnny calmed down. Rubbed his chin for a spell and finally shrugged his shoulders.

"Sorry, boys…"

Well, ol' Rose wuz worn down right to the frayed end of his short ass rope. Whupped liked a dog in front of the whole durn company. That breed's pride had been insulted one too many times by the Spaniard and in front of all our men… and it smarted. He just shook right in front of us, shook so hard we thought he would fall apart. Clenched his fist. Spread his legs. Eyes got reallll big. He wuz ready to blow. He just couldn't take Lisa's barbs one second longer.

Johnny began to laugh again. "Especially with all of us idjits a standin' thar grinnin' 'n gigglin' 'n snortin' like fools and all the while eggin' him on to beat the devil.

"Yeah… we wuz real baddd that day.

"You know that big ugly scar on his forehead? Like he had been branded by a red hot iron."

I nodded. I remembered the scar. Who could forget it? It was an unusual birthmark, and it stood right out, purple in color and uglier than sin. You couldn't miss it with your eyes closed.

Johnny went on… "Ya could see it glow bright purple-like the madder he got. He'd get that way anytime agitation set in, and with him that wuz more times than naught. It wuz his way of warnin', like a skunk's tail risin' up afore it sprays its stink or a rattler coilin' and shakin' them rattles when its gittin' ready to spring and snap and sink them fangs deep in yer hide.

"When ya see it, you'd better git, 'cause it sure won't give ya much time to do anythin' else. Exceptin' to prepare for the worse and that's what Lisa wuz about to get.

Lisa saw it comin,' whippin' out that wicked little waterfront dagger of his that he always keeps tucked away in his belt. Nasty little blade it is... razor sharp and needle-thin. Gives me the shivers thinkin' 'bout it.

Should've left it in his belt, 'cause Rose wuz too quick fer the greaser. Knocked it right out of his hand with one swift kick. Usin' that 'la savat', that kickin' shit those 'frogs' are always braggin' about.

The dang thing flew past my head and stuck right in the wall. Quivered for the longest time. We all just stared at it 'til it stopped a shakin'. Scared the livin' daylights outta me.

Now, Lisa had no knife... no nothin'. No one wuz liftin' a finger to help him and there wuz nothin' within easy reach to defend himself with... just his mouth and his fists. What a joke, ya should've seen the look on Manuel's face when the breed grabbed him by the throat. Those little beady black eyes of his'n ready to pop right out of his gourd. He was chokin', coughin' and gaspin' for air. His face done turned blue. His feet were completely off the floor. Arms flailin'. Legs kickin'. What a sight... Lord a mercy!

Rose wuz squeezin' the begeezous out of his windpipe with one hand and beatin' on his head with the other. Poundin' away with those big paws of his and enjoyin' every bit of it.

Lisa tried his best to let out a scream, carryin' on like he wuz bound for the bottom end of the Promised Land. But, not a word wuz able to escape those thin, sneaky lips of his. That's 'cause Rose would just let up long enough for the Mexican to catch a breath... which wuz all of maybe once or twice.

Hell, the man couldn't put up a decent fight, not that the little weasel had any chance a'tall. Damnedest thing ya ever saw. Yes, sir, quite a sight thoroughly enjoyed by all.

No one wuz makin' any move to stop it. Like I said, we all figured they both had it comin'. I don't know right then what got into me. I mean, I figured the way the breed seemed to be plumb out of his head, he might kill Lisa and then no one would have a thing to show from this whole miserable expedition. I just sort of jumped right into the thick of it and tried to pull Rose off before he did Manuel in for good.

Humph? I guess I must have felt to Rose like I wuz somekind of flea or pesky fly. He shucked me as easily as ya would doff yer hat, throwin' me to the floor like a sack of shit. I really pissed him off. He commenced to whuppin' and stompin' on me even harder than he did the Mexican.

Ya should have seen the look in Rose's black eyes. I'm tellin' ya the man wuz in a foul mood. I wuz scared... right down to the soles of my feet and wouldn't have given ya a plug fer my chances or my life. Lucky fer me, the others woke up… and just in time, too. Hell, but by then, Rose had already put me down and knocked my lights out.

Anyway, while I'm gettin' whupped, that coward Lisa picks himself off the floor and sneaks out of the countin' cabin without anyone a noticin'. Just leaves me thar to take his beatin'. He slips down to the boat. Doesn't tell the 'frogs' what's goin' on, and orders the Frenchies to cast off right then and thar. That son of a bitch…"

Potts was knee deep in his story, caught up in the fury of it all. He shook with each new revelation, sweat pouring from his brow. The look on his face was intense as he relived every second, every detail and every painful blow of it.

"Whoa, Johnny," I broke in, giving the lad a chance to calm down and catch his breath. "And leavin' you to take his whuppin'. Spineless-bastard," I said, adding, "I never did like Rose, couldn't stomach more than a day or two of him, I knew all along the man was poison. Damn! It sure sounds from the look of it… ya shouldn't have butted in."

Pete Wiser was standing off from the rest of us not making any attempt to hide his pleasure nor stifle his laughter. "I told Johnny to butt out of Lisa's affairs, but ya know he never listens."

"Hang on," Potts snapped back, "that ain't the end to this thing… it gets richer."

"Go ahead," I said reluctantly, shaking my head.

"The breed must've had three or four of the boys on his back, holdin' him down. He wuz really pissed off. But, he's such a powerful bastard. Fought like a cornered wild cat, finally throwin' the boys off of him. He tore out of that cabin just in time to see the Spaniard on the keelboat pushin' off and catchin' the current.

Lisa wuz sure smug, grinnin' from dawn to dusk, all the while thinkin' he wuz safely on his way back to St. Louie. He just stood thar on the deck of that boat belittlin' the breed and makin' no attempt to hide it. He even had the gall to wave good-bye… with a big smile to boot.

"Ta, ta," the greaser said. No shit, we all could hear him.

What nerve! But, all he managed to do wuz piss off Rose even more… if that wuz possible. Maybe Lisa should've waited a little while longer, 'til he was farther downriver, 'cause the breed wuzn't through with his brand of talkin' and got in the final word."

"How's that, Johnny?" I asked.

"You'll see," said Pete, smiling and nodding, "just listen."

"Swivel gun, the one we brought upriver with us." Potts was smiling, broadly. "Someone finally found a use for it," He chortled.

"You don't say? But, why can I believe it?" Lordy, I could see what was a coming. Amazing, I thought to myself, absolutely amazing… the things that men will do.

Johnny stood up, his feet spreading wide apart. He was flailing his hands and arms with a flourish. This part of his story really tickled the kid and he became more lively, more spirited and more animated, if that was at all possible, building his crescendo towards the finale… a real piece of work, his opus 'de la Roche Jaune.'

"Lisa himself had that gun mounted. Placed it so's it was aimed in the direction of whar the rivers came together. He wuz right proud of that little cannon; made him feel like a big man, a regular Creole Napoleon he wuz. Gave him a sense of power. You saw it yerself, always puffed up like a peacock when he wuz around it. Hell, it wuz just a toy to him. No one took the dang thing serious and fer sure no one took care of it properly. Just left it there, primed and loaded… through rain and snow and all the shit that Heaven crapped on us. Just sat there ever since the *frogs* finished their work and opened the Fort for business.

All that time. Imagine that, rust, wet gunpowder and all?"

"I can," I said shaking my head. "Nothin' out here, anymore, surprises me."

"Humph!" Pete grunted. "And it shouldn't… not if yer smart."

"Yer right, Pete," responded Johnny, his face, deadpan, "it shouldn't. But there it wuz, nevertheless… and ya know it true.

"The breed wuz quick as lightnin', saw that cannon sittin' thar right off. An ugly smirk came on his face and he started to laugh… an evil laugh.

"An engage wuz standin' right in the way… between Rose and that gun, smokin' a pipe and watchin' the whole dang show.

"The breed rushed him. Snatched that lit pipe right from that startled Frenchie's mouth. Spun him around, kicked him in the seat of his pants and sent him sprawlin'. The frog didn't know what hit him.

"We all came runnin' out just as the Frenchman hit the ground. But, we wuz too late.

"All I could see wuz Rose aimin' the swivel gun towards Lisa and his boat and firin' the fuse with that hot pipe… all the while laughin' his ass off.

"The fuse took and that powder went off with a god-awful blast. We watched the whole thing. Ya could almost follow that ball's trail all the way to the river and the boat. Lisa saw it comin', too. He froze to the deck, like he wuz stuck in mud. He couldn't believe it… nor could we.

"Hell, I still can't.

"Helluva shot it was. Struck square on that boat, crashin' right smack dead-on the cargo box, blowin' it to smithereens. Everyone on deck was knocked flat on their asses. Wood splinters, dust, whatnot and confusion rainin' everywhere.

"We wuz all dumbfounded. What a sight! No wonder we can't get any injuns in here to trade... they must think were all plumb crazy."

Johnny chuckled at his own wit. Spontaneity erupted... first from me, then Pete, then every trapper within hearing distance. We were all rolling on the ground, kicking up a dust storm. Even my pony got excited, whinning and snorting and kicking up his rear legs, and commenced to running around that little corral faster than lickedy-split.

It took a while for us to settle down. Johnny was wearing a wide smile and kept on a talking.

"The crew wuz mighty lucky. When the smoke and fallin' debris finally cleared the deck... nary a one wuz hit by flyin' splinters or such. They wuz all shook up, though, eardrums a hurtin', god-awful ringin' in their ears, their heads ready to pop. All of 'em wuz screamin', swearin', not knowin' what the hell had happened... whether they were under attack or whatnot. Hell none of 'em knew what wuz a goin' on.

"Lisa did, though. El grande pindejo jumped right up from the deck like he wuz shot from that swivel. He kicked those Frenchies in their rears. Screamed at 'em. Got 'em movin' and up. All the while, he kept glancin' back to the Fort at Rose, scared out of his tree.

"Rose didn't care who got kilt, 'cause just when he had fired that cannon, a long-leggedy 'frog' of a Frenchman walked unknowingly right in front of the muzzle, completely oblivious. Near as we can tell by our calculations the shot must've gone right between his legs. Blew the 'frog' a dozen feet away. Landed right on his back. Clothes torn to rags. Dirt, grass, sage hangin' all over him, stickin' out of his hair, his mouth... hell he wuz eatin' that shit. He wuz covered in blackpowder from *tete d'orteil*... head to toe. Damnedest sight ya ever saw. Hollerin' and screamin' like he wuz blown to hell. Must've thought he died and went to heaven, but thar wuzn't a scratch on him.

"Can ya believe it?

"He's still shook up. Walks around here mumblin' to hisself all day long. No one'll talk to him anymore... pathetic frog.

"God Almighty, if the breed didn't try to reload that gun for another go at the Spaniard. By then we all had come to our senses. The whole Fort piled on top of Rose, pinnin' him to the ground. Oh, he fought like before. This time, though, it wuz a different story. Everyone had had enough of his shit and shut him right-up fer good.

"I wuz pissed, I tell ya, more so then I'd ever been before. I hurt everywhere from his punches and kicks. My clothes were torn. I wuz bleedin' from my head, my nose, my lips. The prick had bit my ear, stomped on my hands and kicked me square in my balls.

"Dirty, rotten, son of a bitch. It wuz payback time. I grabbed me a rope and while the boys held the 'breed' down I hogtied him good. He struggled and cursed and swore he'd kill me. I got tired of listenin' to him and shoved someone's ol' smelly loincloth right in his mouth, just so's I didn't have to listen to 'em. I bet he didn't like that. Tough! Then for good measure, I returned the favor and planted my toe right in his balls, good and hard, buryin' my moccasin all the way up and out his asshole. Rose liked to explode, what with that rag in his mouth, and no where for his scream to go. Uh uh! Yes sir, he wuz shut up fer good."

"Whoooo! That must've hurt," I said, wincing myself, groping my own privates rather defensively. "Where's Rose now... not that I care?"

"The hell with him," Johnny spat on the ground. His face, his mouth was twisted, sneering with contempt. "We kept him tied up for hours. He got the message. By then Lisa wuz long gone, caught the current and headin' to St. Louie, or so we thought, not that we could blame him.

"The boys grabbed their rifles while some of us untied him. A few words were said, he knew we meant business. He stuck around here for a couple of days, broodin' like a wounded grizz'. We watched him like a hawk, waitin' if need be to give it to him again. Nobody wantin' nothin'to do with him. He got the hint and packed up his kit. Said he wuz headin' back to his Absarokee friends.

"He no sooner got outside the gate, looked around, and called-out my name. The breed swore at the top of his lungs that he'd be comin' back to get me.

"Good riddance, I say. And that's about the end of it."

"We got word downriver to Manuel," said Pete. "He hadn't gone far. He was back here in no time… in a foul mood. Stayed in that dang cabin of his, hidin' his face, 'til you came back with der heathen Crow.

"Humph! That's some story. Now I know why you boys were actin' so strangely, especially with me ridin' up with a passel of Crow and lookin' none too friendly, myself. Had you worried, huh?"

"Yeah, John, sorry. I guess we wuz overdoin' it a bit. We all half-expected to see him back with a bunch of his Crow friends. I suspect they're smarter than that. As fer Rose, probably ain't the last we've heard from him."

"Best keep an ear to der ground," cautioned Pete Wiser, "that man is bad medicine."

I had a lot of thinking to do. The streams about the 'Big Horn' were fast becoming trapped-out by Manuel's men and it was no place for me to be. It had been five years since I had last been home. Lewis and Clark and the whole Corps had returned to the East to hero's welcomes... received land, money and acclaim. Many of the boys for the most part started new lives.

And me, I had stayed out here to make my fortune. So far I'd done a pretty poor job of it with little to show for my troubles. It gave me plenty to think about. I brooded for weeks, never for a moment forgetting the miles of beaver sign in the valley of the forks and beyond. Why, the Jefferson fairly crawled with beaver, living in bliss, virtually owning the river and its tributaries, never knowing, never feeling the terrifying crunch of sprung steel from the whiteman's metal traps, crushing their tender limbs, drowning them in their own ponds and waters. They were ripe for picking and I knew it.

The problem was… my hair, and in particular… keeping it. I mulled the dilemma over and over. It hadn't changed one bit since leaving the Forks the day Toby died. If I could just sneak in there, set my traps, make my hit and light out with no one the wiser. Don't get greedy, careless. Work the smaller streams away from the valley. Cache my skins where no injuns could find them, amass a fortune, enough for me anyways… 'til it was time to light a shuck and skedaddle. And then be smart about it, don't dawdle or tarry, assholes and elbows as quick as you please, straight to St. Louis without stoppin' to so much as take a shit. Yeah, it was starting to sound like a plan. Ride in, the end of summer, early fall. That would do it. The Piegans would have moved north to winter in their mountain valleys. When they'd think no man, white or otherwise, in his right mind would have the nerve, the audacity and the stomach to dare risk their wrath.

The more I thought about it, the more I became convinced. I thought of little else as the summer wore on at Manuel's Fort. I had no problem keeping it to myself. I liked to work alone and everyone knew it. Besides, the horror of the "pishkun plains" fight was enough for any sane man to stay shy of the Headwaters country. The Blackfeet had most everyone buffaloed, even the boldest, guttiest of trappers. But, there is always someone who can't be convinced. Someone with a devil may care streak in his spine. Someone who never thinks that it could be he who would be caught and vanquished. And that someone knew me at that particular time like no other man, at a time when the first cool breezes of autumn announced its coming. When the days became a little shorter, the hair on my horse's back a little longer, shaggier.

"You're a going back… ain't ya?" Potts put it right to me one day, months after my return.

I could tell by the look in his eye and the tone of his voice that Johnny had been studying me for quite awhile, maybe even the whole summer, reading my mind, slowly gathering my traps and kit. He had watched me for weeks. Sensed the distance in my mind. Knew how I thought, felt. And when the time was right, worked his way right into my plans.

"Going back, where?" I tried to be convincing, but it was soon a losing proposition.

"Don't give me that horseshit, Colter. I know you better than that. And you know it." Potts wasn't about to be thrown off the trail.

"Don't be foolish," I responded. "I've told you what those injuns are like. They're like no other savages you've ever seen. They're worse then any nightmare you can ever imagine. Trust me, you think this hole in my leg is some made up tale?"

"Uh, huh! So what? That ain't goin' to stop ya. I know ya... yer one, crazy son of a bitch. Not all the stinkin' savages in the world can keep ya from those beaver. Hell... yer just as broke as I am and twice as crazy. Even Pete thinks yer goin' back."

He was sure testy, crawling right under my skin like a bloodsucking tick. Trying to reason with Johnny Potts was like pissing in the wind.

"Ain't no way the Blackfeet are goin' to tolerate us trappin' the Three Forks."

"Just the same, yer goin' back. I know ya too well, Colter. Yer shifty and crazy, but yer crazy smart. In fact, yer worse then Drouillard. But, I like that. Makes chances for survival a heap alot better."

"I'm stubborn, all right," I snapped back, "but not stupid. And look at whose doin' the talkin'. You ain't exactly the sharpest arrow in the quiver."

There was a hint of anger in my voice that I didn't think Potts was used to hearing. I could feel the tightening in my jaw. I didn't like the comparison to George, but Johnny was right and I knew it. What's more I knew that my two friends deserved an explanation.

"Awright," I said. "Look, Johnny, I've always done better by myself. That's just the way I am."

"Yeah, we noticed," Potts said with more than a hint of irritation, pointing to my leg.

I shook my head. "That was unavoidable... a risk of the trade, you both know it. Listen, you two remember when I lit out with those two Illinois trappers, Dickson and Handcock?"

"Yep!" Potts replied rather sarcastically. "How could we forget?"

"Everybody, including the Captains, thought it was because of them two and all the rosy-talk of trappin' and gettin' rich quick that I stayed behind. Curious how those two fellas never had any skins to show for all their supposed success. I never missed that fact. Hell, I didn't need 'em. Truth is they came along at the right time. I wasn't ready for the Expedition to end, at least I wasn't ready to get back home just then. Not by a 'long-shot.' I had nothin' and no one to go home to. Hell, by then there was no home left, just the memories. I was itchin' to stay out here and trap and make some money.

Trouble is, we had that rule that every man had to stay on to the finish. So when Hancock and Dickson talked big, I went along with it, hoping the captains would see fit to let me go.

"So we left y'all at the Mandans, headed back upriver 'til we reached the Yellowstone. We worked the streams comin' off the Absarokas all that winter, but our partnership just didn't work out. Stuck up in the mountains, I had had enough of those two and parted company last spring when the weather broke. I suppose it was mutual, I know I ain't an easy man to get along with. So, they went their way. I went mine. I trapped some more. Had some pretty good success and then, come early summer I lit out for St. Louie just in time to run into y'all at the Platte.

"What I'm trying to say is that all my life I've tended to bein' a loner. It ain't you, fellas. It's me. You know how much I think of you two, and for that matter all the men of the Corps. Johnny, you're as good as any man I've ever known. And I'd 'ride the river' with you anytime, anyplace. I'm just so use to workin' and livin' by myself. It ain't nothing personal. It's just the way I am."

Potts looked at Wiser, who nodded. And then he turned to me.

"Hell, John, we all wondered about those two from the start. Not one of us cared a hoot for either of 'em. It was plain to see they wuz a lot of fast-talkin', smoke and hot air. And yer right, not one of us missed the fact that the two of 'em had barely a skin between 'em for all their supposed success. Fact is they needed you a lot more than you needed them. All along, though, it wuz you we wuz concerned with. All the boys thought right much of you and didn't want to stand in your way. Even Cap'n Lewis and 'Big Red' felt that a way. We knew that if anyone could handle this here wilderness alone and make it pay-off, it'd be you. Even Drouillard, wouldn't begrudge you that. Fact is he wuz probably a little envious."

"Drouillard?" I said, disbelievingly. "He can't stand me, never could."

Potts turned to Wiser and said, "Pete?"

"That's a fact, John," said Wiser. "All der boys thought a lot of you… yeah, even George, too. And dat took some doin' for him to admit it. We all wished ya well. But, ya know, no one would ever think of sayin' it to ya. Ya ain't exactly a man who takes to any kinda butterin' up. You are rather a stubborn mule, you know."

"I, I don't know what to say. Exceptin', I'm mighty grateful to you boys. I never rightly gave it much thought. I guess I should've," I said rather sheepishly.

"But!" Potts said rather indignantly, "I resent like hell you lumpin' me in with the likes of those two former partners of yourn."

I signed deeply. Potts was not going to be put off by me… or anyone. He smelled beaver and beaver meant money. A lot of money if you played it just right. Besides, he trusted me. That was all he needed to know.

"I'm goin' with ya," he said matter of factly. "And you might as well get use to the idea, 'cause I made up my mind."

"Oh, you have, have you? Damn it Johnny! If you ain't the most stubborn man I've ever known," I swore.

"Swear all ye want," he shot back. "I owe the greaser a pile of money fer my upkeep. You know the only chance I got to clean his books is to go with you. So you might as well git use to the idea."

Damn, the kid was pushy. I looked directly to Wiser. "Pete, he'll listen to you. Say something to that partner of yours. Talk some sense into him, will ya."

"Waste of time," he replied, shaking his head. "You know it as well as I do." And then Pete added, shaking his head. "You both need to unlock yer horns a mite. I swear you two are der orneriest cusses I've ever known."

I sighed once again and stared off at the clouds. Damn, tell me this isn't happening, I demanded of myself to know. But, Johnny was one resolute, determined son of a bitch. He wouldn't be put off and I'd play every bit as much hell trying to talk him out of it as I would to change the course of the Yellowstone or stop the morning sun from rising in the East. Once that boy got a notion in his head it was there to stay. And I knew it then all too well. I wondered… just what in the devil was Johnny Potts getting me into? Hell, what was I allowing myself to be dragged into?

Oh, what's the use, I said to myself? And I gave in like he knew I would.

"All right, suit yourself. It's your funeral. But, just you and me and keep it to yourself. Do I make myself clear?"

He returned my gaze, stare for stare, looking at me straight in the eye, deadpan for long unanswered seconds as if thoughtfully weighing my decision. But he was fooling no one… this was what he waited for all along to hear. What a devilish imp he could be and it soon showed. He began to smile, slowly abandoning that serious, sober bent his face was wearing but moments before.

And then relief flowed, "Yeah… hell, yeah! You and me, Potts and Colter bound for the Promised Land. Hallelujah! Hallelujah!"

He chuckled and laughed. Soon he was busting out of his skin like the kid he still certainly was, slapping his thighs, dancing a jig, kicking up dust and crud as happy as a hog in slop.

As for me, I was shaking my head in disbelief. The worry in my gut, the look on my face said it all. What had I done? What kind of mess had I just let myself be talked into?

CHAPTER FIVE

"See yah, Pete. With any luck, we'll be back in a few months, so keep a fire goin'."

I reached down from the saddle and shook Wiser's hand. He had a strong grip, one that was used to swinging an ax, pushing a plow and more than a time or two, wielding a heavy hammer, pounding on an anvil and working a forge. Although German born, he was like many a backwoodsman I had known from my time on the frontier west of the Blue Ridge. Pete was a stubborn, independent thinker, relying on his own wit, his own honed wilderness skills, slow to boil, yet once committed not a inch of backup in his spine. And like the rest of the men that made up our Corps he was patriotic to the bone.

"Just a minute, you two, ol' Pete's got somethin' fer ya." Wiser handed me a couple of small phials he'd been saving for this very moment. "This ought to see ya through der winter and attract all der beaver yer traps can handle."

I opened one of the phials. It was castor, the castoreum glands of the beaver. I knew it right off. I took a short whiff. "Whew, smell the nutmeg," I said, rather pleased… a grateful smile gracing my face.

"Prepared it myself," replied Pete with a pleased smile and a noticeable wink. "My own special brew."

We both chuckled.

Pete's recipe was no secret at all. They say the injuns of the Northeast were the first to put together this enticing brew, adding spices and whatnot to the beaver's glands and mashing them all together into a paste-like consistency that was bound to guarantee devastating results. Smear a little daub of the pungent salve on a willow-switch, place it directly above the submerged pan of a metal beaver trap during the breeding season, and… *voila*. It was an irresistible draw whose aroma no self-respecting beaver could resist. And when those horny critters leaned to close to sniff the enticing bait, stepping hard on your trap's trigger-pan… wham! Up springs the heavy trap, clamping down hard on tender feet and legs.

"Jesus, Pete… dang fine of you," I said.

He nodded, a sober look replacing his smile. "Yeah, it's fer good luck, as much as anythin', Colter. I wanted to contribute a little somethin' to y'alls success."

And then he added, "Mind yer hair 'n keep yer powder dry, you two. And Johnny, listen to der man."

His voice faltered, sounding sadly melancholic. Certainly, his heart wasn't into it... lacking the usual vitality and grit I had become accustomed to. I suspect Pete held little hope of us returning alive.

I found myself looking down at my friend, wondering what was really going on in his mind. Right now he was a hard man to read. I liked Pete, I always had. He was a rangy fellow, tall, broad shouldered, long of limbs with a hard, no nonsense demeanor about himself. He was a good man to have around, especially when things got a little hairy. A man who possessed more than his share of ice water nerves, and when it came to shootin'... steady hands and a steadier aim. I knew him well, knew he was apt to make few mistakes. I trusted his judgment, his reliability and instincts in the wilds. We thought alike in so many ways. Maybe that's why I didn't try too hard to talk him into going to the Three Forks... and just maybe that's why his outright refusal had me more than a little concerned.

"Damn yer thick German-hide, Pete... ya can still come with us," Potts pleaded with his friend one last time.

He didn't admit it, but he didn't have to. We all knew it... Johnny liked and respected Pete Wiser more than any other man alive. The days and weeks leading up to our departure Potts worked hard on him to change his mind. They were the best of friends, took to each other from their first days at Camp Dubois on the Mississippi late in '03. Hunted together, palled around and caroused and got drunk together in riverside grog shops from St. Louie to St. Charles. Trapped together on the 'Big Horn,' the Yellowstone and dozens of unnamed streams. They had become inseparable, 'til I came back from the Three Forks with a tale to tell.

But, Pete Wiser was way too attached to his scalp to part with it on some harebrained scheme to trap in the middle of Blackfeet country. He wouldn't hear of it from the first nor the last and Johnny Potts and their friendship be-damned.

Pete saw us off at the gate with a casual stroke of his hand. The lack of spirit in his voice, the uncertainty, the reluctance in his final "good bye" was too unsettling a farewell as far as I was concerned. I looked back over my shoulder to return the wave and caught Pete's eye for the last time. He was smiling, trying to keep a front up for Johnny and me. Even in the darkness of that moonless night's parting, I could see the sullen graveness in his face. The cheerful countenance he tried to wear couldn't mask what he really felt. No, it all came out, like a grim, foreboding omen, leaving me with a sudden case of uncertainty.

Johnny never caught it. At least he never let on he did. Probably wouldn't have bothered him even if he had. All he could see was trapping beaver and making a pile of money. Making money, paying off his debts to Lisa and returning home with the trappings of a successful man. He dreamed of it, talked of it, lived it from dawn to dusk... day-in and day-out. Nothing was going to stand in his way. Nothing, as far as the limitations his mind's-eye could see.

And so we left that warm September night, pushing west from Manuel's Fort. We stuck close to the river, mostly traveling by night, resting by day. The days were still warm. The nights were somewhat cool and getting cooler. The land was dry, the ground caked as if slaked for want of a single drop of rain. Pesky, biting, nipping blue bottlenosed flies ruled the day, blood sucking mosquitoes the night.

We watched the weather: the clouds, the winds, the rise and drop of temperature, the change of season, the intrinsic transformation of a wilderness universe we had so boldly invaded. All of nature; the critters, the bunch grasses, the flowers, the trees, the changing leaves became our barometer, our window to winter's approach. The wariness of elk and mule and whitetail deer as they grazed on rich bottomland grass. Beaver gnawing and falling cottonwoods and quakies, preparing their dams, their ponds, their homes, storing limbs and boughs to carry them through a long winter. Flight after noisy flight of honkers heading south. An occasional 'griz' sow and her young cubs gorging themselves on army cutworm moths under the shattered rock of talus slopes, on beetles and grubs and ants, on elk carrion and skunk cabbage, chokecherries and huckleberries and white bark pine. Putting on the fat thick before digging their cozy dens for the long winter sleep.

And we watched constantly for sign, injun sign. The faintest of white smoke trails billowing to the sky. The distant glow of a campfire lighting the night. A brief glint, of brilliance, of the midday sun in all its glory reflecting off an exposed metal tomahawk or the polished glass of a trade mirror. An unshod pony track, a moccasin print in soft mud at a stream crossing or treading a worn game trail. An unexplained flight of a herd of antelope speeding off in the distance or a sudden snap of a dry twig or branch ruffled by an unseen hoof or pad or... human foot.

We watched our horses, their ears, their flaring nostrils, trusting their ancient primeval instincts for survival. They were our eyes, our ears, our four footed equine sentinels ever alert.

There was another instinct I relied on... an intangible, invisible twitch that lay dormant in the blood of my veins. Unexplainable, inexplicable, an ancient vigilance lying just beneath the surface of the hairs on the back of my neck. Asleep, dormant, awaiting to rise up like a black tail prairie dog on sentry duty to sound the alarm at the first nefarious approach of the red-man.

That itch never arose once for the whole trip to the Three Forks. There was just nothing there to cause concern... not a sign, not a vestige of the

Piegan, not a whiff of his presence to foul the air.

And although, just a few short months before, thousands had raced and fought and hundreds died on the 'pishkun' plains nearby. It was a strange, almost unnerving, inescapable feeling to ride so near this heroic field of sacrifice and infamy, to know and remember and relive in one's mind all those many horrid events. And here I was doing exactly that… accompanied by a good friend and companion, yet so terribly alone was I in thought and remembrance.

Bleached bones picked clean, prostrated on the plains like rows of fallen human-corn, still lying where they fell, a grim reminder to all who dare pass by; grotesque masks of death, vivid, haunting. Twisted, cruelly misshapen faces of dread and horror in their final death throes, caught forever as if etched in stone, affixed for all eternity. Ironically, these the only reminder, the only discernible link to a human presence on this ancient land. The savage hordes, the pounding hooves, the blare of war cries and the screams of the vanquished had almost vanished without a trace as if swallowed up and damned to eternal hell for all their evil doing.

I had every reason to believe the land would be abandoned. I hoped it would be this way. Planned that the headwaters country would be vacated… deserted by the Piegan clans for their northern valleys. Prayed that in biding my time patiently I had waited long enough. That Blackfeet vengeance would be put off for another season, another year. At least until I got in and got out with enough tanned skins to take me home for good.

Yet, in the midst of all this evidence, I still remained skeptical, like the 'doubting Thomas.' The hair-trigger nerves of my angst still lay unconvinced, fearful, waiting to ignite. Uncertainty accompanied every step the deeper we rode into the Headwaters land. I never could leave life to chance, not out here. And so far caution and instincts had kept me alive.

Potts saw it differently.

"Well, looks like them red-hided 'peee-gun' boys heard ya were a comin' back and lit a shuck," chuckled Johnny as we descended into the valley of the three rivers.

"Yer a baddddd man, John Colter," he chortled. "Yes, sir, a baddddd man."

The kid was happy, seemingly not a care in the world. Smiled all the time, whistled, hummed, sang the same French tune over and over, 'til I got sick of hearing it.

"Alouette, gentile alouette

"Alouette, Je te plumerais,

"Je te plumerais le coup,

"Et le coup, et le coup, et le coup.

"Alouette, gentile alouette."

He'd catch me eyeing him out of the side of my eye with more than a little irritation rubbing me raw and just keep on chuckling away.

"Yer gonna get a crick in your neck fer sure... if ya don't stop twisting in that thar saddle," he'd say with a little devilish smirk.

That boy could get under my skin like a tick and suck my patience dry. And it pleased him to no end to do so.

Me, I was of a different mind. I liked the sounds of nature and life in the wilderness. I could listen for hours on end to the undulating rhythm of the wind fluttering, waving the tops of a forest of cottonwoods or the babbling, gurgling echoes of a swift mountain bred stream. And silence at times was the best music of all.

I liked the feel of the wind blowing in my face, the pungent smells of sage and lilac and pine. The sweet, refreshing taste that cupped hands brimming with cold water from a clear running stream brought to parched and thirsty lips; deliciously clean, cool and invigorating.

I never appreciated the idle talk of my fellow man. Unless, it was from a thoughtful, intelligent conversation or that of plain good company, the kind that would warm your heart or make a curious mind to ponder the ways and the whys of man and the world he lived in.

I was a loner, always have been. Tended to mind my own business and avoided that of others. I guess Johnny and me were of a different sort, 'cause peace of mind nor survival never seemed to concern him the way it did me. I didn't like taking any unnecessary chances, especially with Potts along. I had to have eyes a plenty for the two of us and that's what worried me most. Maybe I'd been out here in this God forsaken wilderness too long. One too-many shaves with a dull knife. And what for I asked? Was all this worry worth it? I asked myself that question many a day and many a time. My nerves were wearing thin and it was beginning to show. I had that itchy feeling about the Pahkees; like they never did leave, just hung around hoping I'd be foolish enough to comeback. The feeling persisted. It just wouldn't go away. I had become downright jumpy. And the more I thought about it, the worse I got.

The way I looked at it, the Pahkees wouldn't winter in the Forks. No Indians did that I could see. It was too damn cold and too damn windy. No, the Three Forks was a place for the Blackfeet to summer and, sometimes, their friends the Atsina, the Gros Ventre of the Plains. It was their prime place to hunt buffalo, jerk meat and store up a mess of pemmican for the winter. For some it was the time to pick wildflowers. And for others, the wilder ones, a time to go on the prowl, reek trouble and raid their neighbors; count coup, steal ponies and capture all the young squaws they could to satisfy their lust for everything that didn't belong to them, including other folks' scalps.

Come fall or the first signs of winter, those Pahkees would light a shuck and head up yonder to the north and hold up in some secluded mountain valleys. Warm and protected, they'd sit out the cold. Smoke kinnikinick. Swap stories and squaws. Get a little fat, a little lazy. Come next spring they'd start the process all over again.

Indians weren't fools. Only a fool like me would be out here with the dead of winter coming on. But, I liked it that way. Less chance for trouble, less chance to be surprised, more beaver for me, for Johnny and it all made sense.

Too much was going through my mind. I couldn't concentrate on the trail ahead. It got so that I was sick of hearing myself talk and think. And it sure in hell didn't help that I was riding right back into this valley where all the Piegan in the world might be holding out, waiting for the *napikwan* and his fire-stick to return. Try as I might, I couldn't forget the way the Blackfeet looked at me by the Madison that past spring; utter surprise, astonishment, a '*napikwan*' in their land. Taking sides and fighting agin them on the side of despised and hated enemies. Picking off their young warriors with that deadly fire-stick, his 'big medicine' gun killing their best, stacking 'em dead one atop another. Writhing, moaning, dying gut-piles of human misery left to the mercy of the Crows and the Flatheads and the bone picking scavengers of the critter world. It was for them a bitter defeat, much too humiliating for their national pride to swallow.

What bitter hatred seethed within them, what unfettered loathing was in their eyes and in the way they recklessly charged my position, racing to be the first to slay the '*napikwan*'. The elation they showed when I went down with lead in my leg. The way they whooped and hollered... and all for me. Those warriors would have rather captured me than kill a hundred Crow or Flathead.

The realization of just how important vengeance might mean to those savages made me wince from time to time. I was glad to disappoint them, occasionally becoming smug, almost cocky. And that could be dangerous. And so the fear persisted. The question begged to be answered. How could they forget me, the *napikwan*? Not with that much hatred to be avenged.

And Manuel's Fort, surely the savages were watching that pile of logs and mud on the 'Big Horn.' My God, they could have followed us all the way here, right back to where it all started. They could've hung onto our trail and us never being the wiser.

I looked about constantly, taking in every bit of land where man could hide: every dip and swell, far and near, high point and river-bottom, wooded copse and bare prairie. I doubled my efforts. If possible I became warier. Watched like I never watched before.

They might not go into the Bitterroots after the Flatheads, not into those high, rugged crags far away from their safe, friendly high-plains country. No, they wouldn't take that kind of chance. But they would look for me. Dog my trail. Swear the oath of vengeance and blood 'til I was in their clutches or kilt for sure. Then and there I convinced myself I was a marked man. It was only a matter of time.

"Get a hold of yourself, you fool," I cried aloud, momentarily betraying all caution, defying the very mettle that had stood me so well. My hands shook, my lips quivered, for the briefest of moments I was naked with fear. It was as if a yellow streak of cowardice was doing its damnedest to take a hold of me.

"Ya all right, Colter?" Potts shot the question at me with a nervous edge to his voice. He had reined in with my first outburst, startled by the abrupt, unwarranted change in my demeanor, my sudden, inexplicable loss of composure. Johnny didn't miss the beads of sweat percolating from my brow nor the decided crack in my voice. He sensed my torment, that nightmarish ordeal I was undoubtedly putting myself through. And it shook him deeply, shook his ever-present confidence and his trust in me. His perpetual swagger, his cock of the walk attitude was suddenly not there. That incessant broad, grinning smile deserted his face, replaced by uncertainty, doubt and maybe even his own measure of fear.

"Ya better take it easy on yerself. Thar's no injuns within a hundred miles of this place," he warned, though not convincingly, and shook his head as if to reassure his own fractured nerves.

"I'm fine," I replied, swallowing a hard lump in my throat. Damn fool. I cursed under my breath. I was irritated with myself for talking aloud, letting my thoughts, my fears get the best of me.

Potts kept staring at me, unconvinced, afraid to move on, afraid not to.

"It's over with, Johnny. No need to fret any more. I just had to get something out of my head."

I meant it, too. I had had enough of sleepless, restless nights, of 'cold sweats' drenched in fear, dream after nightmarish dream. And they came like clockwork, unwelcome and uninvited, vivid, daunting, scowling, flailing apparitions of painted red-men, clutching their cruel scalping knives and war clubs, stained red, dripping with blood, hovering over me in fiendish delight. The horror, the death and senselessness of all I had witnessed came at me without respite.

I purged and spat the foul bile of those black memories, casting their evil spell from my mind and my soul. I had to or it would have continued to eat away at me everyday. It was time for me to emotionally move on, to lay Toby to rest along with all the hundreds of Flathead and Piegan warriors who died that fateful day.

We passed on through the valley and followed the Jefferson until sundown. There deep within a tall stand of cottonwoods by the river's edge we made our camp, setting our first traps the following morning.

It was a pleasant time of the year, the passing of one season to the next. The leaves of the aspen were yellowing, brilliantly, with every passing sun. Tall, stately cottonwoods quivered and shook in the crisp autumn winds, shedding, shaking loose their leafy mantle to flutter, to drift quietly to the riparian carpet below. A hint of chill nipped the air announcing the approach of fall weather. Change was happening, graduating daily and with it we moved with a sense of urgency.

Daily the beaver were adding fat, getting plumper, their fur becoming thicker, warmer, shining luxuriously as the cool of fall set in. The innocent, the unsuspecting critters of the streams and wetlands and rivers and ponds, had never seen the white man's traps before. Never felt the bone crunching snap of heavy metal clamping down on their unprotected legs; crushing their limbs, sapping their strength, their lives and robbing them of the last breaths of freedom.

It was easy, way too easy. We set our traplines, taking their measure one lazy stream, one small pond after another. Mornings checking and resetting traps. Days spent skinning and graining hides, scraping, clearing excess flesh, fat and hair away. Stretching plews on willow hoops. Stacking tanned skins and locating hidden caches, safe and dry. And then move-on downstream or cross over the divide, to the next watershed and start all over again. There wasn't much more to it, except that a man had to be resigned to being cold and wet on a near daily basis… fall, winter and spring being the prime fur bearing season. And making a home in the wild might be little more than a lean-to of boughs and branches, a willow clearing campsite or cuddling up behind a rocky ledge to keep out the wind, the snow and all kinds of prying eyes. You could count on it being a touch lonely if solitude was your way. But if your traps clamped down on some curious beaver's leg there would always be plenty of tail to boil or smoke or roast.

And Johnny and me… why, we were having more than our fair share. Those final days of September of '08 were unlike any we'd ever known before, halcyon days of trapping beaver in a land of abundance. Warm, sunny days and quiet campfire nights so serene, so peaceful we wished they would go on forever.

And Potts, for once his mouth wasn't running perpetually at full gallop. He was happier than a lovesick sailor with a fist full of silver and a tankard of ale… caressing the soft curves of a harem of lusty whores… 'cept those whores weren't women at all, but rich pelts of skinned fur, warm and soft to the touch. And they would have to do.

And me, well, I had my whole kit here with me, my 'possibles,' all I possessed, all the good traps I'd managed to accumulate since I left the Corps in '06, by the Mandans. This was it for me, my last go around in the western mountains. One last time to bag me a fortune in skins and, come hell or highwater, I made up my mind, I was heading on home.

I wasn't so much homesick. I really had nothing to go back to. My family, my kin in Virginia had all grown old. Passed on or moved on, leaving me with nary a soul to write to or care for. Life as I had known it growing up in the Old Dominion might as well have been a million miles and years away. But, the Missouri country was another story. It was a new land, full of energy, excitement. People were moving in, farms springing up. The land was feeling the plow. Folks were there to stay, bringing civilization to the wilderness. And life on the frontier, as it had been known, was slowly fading away.

I was lonely, though, lonely for a woman to have around, to make a life together, raise a family with plenty of young ones running amuck. Plant roots like my pa and grandpa had done, work the ground, plowing and seeding and reaping life's bounty. Breeding fine horses and fat cows and healthy, strong little Colters. And at night, after the sun had gone down and the kids were tucked away, enjoy the warmth of the woman I would love. That was it, I wanting to start life… all over again.

On many a night, Johnny and me would sit and think and talk idly, occasionally telling a yarn, an old memory, or for him, to pine aloud for the girl he left behind. One night the memory was so strong he finally let it go.

"I had this gal back home," Potts said out of the blue. "Rebeccah Lee Wilson wuz her name. Sweet as buttermilk pie, she wuz. Her folks were our closest neighbors, just a hoot and a holler away."

Potts had a dreamy, far away look in his eyes. Nary a hint of a smile creased his face. He was as lost in his boyhood past as I had been in the mountains of the Absaroka the winter before.

"Pretty?" I asked, knowing the kid had grown more than lonesome these past few weeks.

Neither of us had been home for more than five years and on him the loneliness was beginning to show. Tears welled in his eyes. He stared at the glowing coals of our campfire, refusing to look away.

Melancholy sapped his energy, his vitality that night. The mood would pass, I knew. He'd snapped out of it shortly. But, this time the boy felt compelled to speak his heart. Sure, he was full of bravado, spunk and grit, fun loving, full of life and forever pulling my leg for a chuckle. He never was malicious, though. But, he sure could be impish, attention driven more then anything else. There was a part of him that never belonged out here in the wilderness. I sensed it right off a long time before. But, now, it was way too late to make a change. We just had to play this hand the way it was dealt. Until the game was over, for better or worse.

"She wuz, all right... prettier than a rainbow," Johnny said, answering me after a long moment.

His eyes still searched the void of those bygone days. The girl's vision must have been pleasing to Johnny for he was now smiling. His pale blue orbs fairly sparkled with the memory of his long lost sweetheart. He sat up tall. His voice, his being becoming animated, lively, full of life, just like his old self. A startling transformation as he fairly lit up a moonless night.

"She had hair like corn silk, soft as a baby's belly, flowing like a waterfall all the way to the small of her back." He reached around his own back as if to show me.

"She wuz a real beauty. She had a way about herself, always flirtin' and teasin', coy as can be. Every knucklehead within a hoot and a holler came a sparkin' around Bethlehem Baptist every damn Sunday just to see her all gussied up in her best go to meetin' clothes and glowing like the moon.

"Use to piss me off to no end, the way they looked at her. Didn't do those fellers any good at all... Becky Lee only had eyes for me." Johnny nearly choked saying it.

I sat open-mouthed, not knowing whether to feel bad or good for the kid.

Johnny continued to stare deeply into the glowing embers of our fire. He was lost in time, in another place, thousands of miles from where we camped. His sweetheart's vision, her face, her youthful beauty, vivid, compelling. To him, their unfulfilled love was a powerful magnet drawing him back home. After all these years, he now seemed to regret ever leaving. Though, I doubt he'd ever admit it. He had too much pride. And joining the Corps had been the proudest moment of his life. Nevertheless, loneliness can be a powerful struggle and having a sweetheart to ease the solitude goes a long way towards lifting that burden.

"Don't fret none. She'll still be thar awaitin' for you?" I remarked confidently looking into the blueness of his eyes, hoping to cheer my friend up.

He waited for a moment as if ignoring what I said.

"Nawww... she won't."

A hint of anger crept into his voice. Johnny's resentment soon came out.

"She up and married the preacher's son soon as she found out I signed on with the Corps. Didn't even wait to congratulate me. Just flat out did it."

"Oh!" I responded regretfully, realizing the depth of how deeply her loss affected him. It was his pride that was busted more than anything, and for a young fellow that can be pretty hard to take.

"That's all right. She ain't the only bitch in the woods."

"Now, you're learning," I said.

We sat a little while longer, Potts pondering what could have been. I could see he was missing that gal's company. But, she wasn't afterall the only fair damsel for our young knight to swoon over with regret. There was another fine creature that apparently had captured his heart. One unlikely lass whom he had a deep, unabiding soft spot for. As it turns out, a fair, comely two-legged fawn of a female who we all likewise held in respect and admiration... tacitly, if not secretly. And she was an injun squaw we all knew.

He had kept his secret to himself for these many, many months. It was little Janey. Janey was the nickname the boys and Cap'n Clark gave to Sacagawea, the young Snake girl that helped guide the Corps to her brother's people, Cameawait's Lemhi Shoshone.

Young as she was, that squaw had sand, gravel in her gizzard, as we used to say. I mean she kept up with the men, bearing the hardship, the hard road, often doing more than her fair share. Never complaining and all the while carrying that little infant strapped to her bosom. Every time one of us would whine or gripe, whether from work or hunger, exhaustion or fear, one look at that little injun girl quietly carrying her load would shame them right up. She had that way about herself, a real calming influence. It was almost magical the way those lonely men would buck right up when she was about. One that brought all of us back home to clean clothes, darned socks and maybe the wonderful smell of a hot blackberry pie right from the hearth, cooling on your ma's window sill.

She was smart, awright. 'Big Red' thought so and we all knew he set store by her and her little boy, Pomp. Clark was sweet on Janey and made no attempt to hide it. More than once, he was itching to bust up that no good husband of hers, Charbonneau. The 'Cap' watched him like a hawk. Made him watch hisself, all the while that surly 'frog' could see that Janey was treated like one of us, respected like any white woman would be and growing on us lonely backwoodsmen as welcome as a warm summer day.

One day, on the way to the Forks, Johnny and I rode up to a sandstone butte overlooking the Yellowstone. We called the place Pompey's Pillar, named by Captain Clark after little 'Pomp', Janey's baby boy… and the name stuck. The place brought back the memories, especially of Clark and ol' York, the captain's 'man-servant.' York was a black slave, though none of us ever thought of him that a way. But it was that little kid, that half-breed Indian kid of Janey's, the boy we called Pomp and his young ma that set us both to wondering.

We stopped and rested our mounts, each of us staring at that high, flat tower of rock and sandstone so prominently stuck-out in the middle of nowhere. It was as if God, himself, had dropped it from heaven in an unaccountable fit of creativity. It had an eerie feel to it, haunting, sacred. The ancient ones had thought so. Indians had been coming here for centuries, leaving their marks, their primitive drawings and etching in the sandstone walls an historical record stretching back long ago into the earliest sands of time of the red-man's memory.

"Wanna take a look?" I asked Potts.

"Yeah, I do." Solemnly said, Johnny quickly dismounted and headed directly to the butte's base.

It was a sentimental moment, the two of us briefly trying to fetch from the past. After a short climb, we reached the spot where Cap'n Clark had carved his initials. There his signature was, etched in sandstone, as clear as the day he left it. We gawked for the longest of time, breathless, nigh overcome with emotion.

'W. Clark July 25, 1806'

We sat for a spell, lost once again in our own thoughts. The vision, the memories, the people recalled by Big Red's name and that wonderfully sanquine time was more than my young partner could bear.

Tears began to run down his cheeks. He arose and turned away from me, quietly mourning the loss of those better days, his old folks and long gone friends. It was taking a heavy, heavy toll on him.

I understood his feelings, the compassion, the longing he held for those so dear. I let him cry. There was absolutely nothing wrong with it as far as I could see. Hell, more then a few times during the course of my last half dozen years, I caught myself feeling the same way. It isn't always easy being alone. Sometimes the solitude can be downright depressing, especially if you miss the company of friends or womenfolk.

Pott's stood gazing out from atop Pomp's butte, though I doubt he saw anything but the past that was flashing through his mind. His tears had stopped flowing, his memories were about to be placed into words.

"Ya know, John, just a few weeks before the Cap'n carved his initials on this here wall, we wuz back yonder in the mountains."

"I remember," I said, "it wasn't all that long ago, you know."

Johnny looked at me, nodding in agreement.

"Yeah, it wuzn't."

"Do you remember how cold it wuz, even though spring wuz just about over? How everythin' wuz pretty much still locked in ice. Well, one day, I wuz chippin' away with my knife at a frozen beaver dam that wuz as hard as a rock. I kept at it, trying my damnedest to bust a hole right through it.

"Don't ask me why, 'cause I don't have a good reason, 'ceptin' I wuz bored and had nothing better to do, I reckon.

"Well, the more I chipped, the harder it seemed to become. It wuz frustratin' the hell out of me... pissin' me off to no end. I whacked away at it over and over, cussin' the whole dang time like I wuz the town drunk.

"Then I did it. Like a damned fool, my knife slipped on that ice once too many times and careened into my leg with a sickenin' thud.

"It happened so almighty fast. My own knife sliced me a terrible wound, cuttin' me right to the bone. Must've hit an artery for sure, 'cause blood poured out of me like a broken dam.

"I panicked. I admit it. I wuz scared to death. All I could see wuz me bleedin' to death right then and thar and I couldn't do a damn thing to stop it.

"Lord have mercy."

Johnny stood rubbing his hands tightly over and over. His brow became furrowed with fret, his face grew pale, ashen, as if reliving the memory would kill him for sure. He soon regained his composure with a long sigh, exhaling deeply and went on telling his tale.

"Lucky for me, Cap'n Clark wuz nearby and heard me scream. Yeah... I wuz screamin', all right. I've never been that scared in all my life. Ol' Billy Clark wuz faster then greased lightnin'. Otherwise, I would have been a gutpile of skin and bones, drownin' in a pool of my own freezin' blood.

"I thought I wuz a goner fer sure. I can't begin to tell ya the helpless feelin' I had watchin' my blood, my life drain right out of me. I knew I wuz beyond salvation and savin'. I was scared, scared right out of my tree, convinced thar wuz absolutely nothin' I could do, but sit thar 'til my blood ran dry and die like a man.

"Pretty pathetic, huh?

"But, the Captain got to me in time to stop the flow. I wuz pretty close to bein' a goner for the next few days afterwards. I wuz awfully weak, helpless. Had all I could do just to lay thar and keep from dying. And death wuz that close.

"I have two people to thank fer savin' my life. Big Red and lil' Janey. They both took turns a watchin' me, tendin' my wounds, feedin' me elk and onion broth and giving me Janey's herb teas to sip. Big Red kept a talkin' to me, a keepin' my spirits up. And I got strong, I healed-up.

"And Janey... Janey sometimes a hummin' some injun tune gently in my ear. Caressin' my hair, holdin' my hand. Soothin' she wuz and downright wonderful. Weren't a squaw, as far as I wuz concerned, but as good a nurse as any white lady back home.

"I still can see her every day preparin' those injun herbs and a dressin' my wound, with a tenderness that warmed my heart and set me at ease.

"John, I tell ya, I wuz pure butter in her hands."

Johnny paused for a moment, the memory of the young Indian girl bringing sweet, tender thoughts. His face seemed to glow as he spoke.

"And that smile of hers, those deep dark eyes, her soft, velvet like, long black hair a trailin' behind her, almost touchin' the ground. What a pretty sight she wuz, what a comely gal.

"Ohhh! The way she moved, light as a fawn, her moccasins a skimmin' atop the ground, like skatin' on ice. Lord a mercy, she wuz a plum beautiful creature."

Johnny fairly screamed his last sentence. That's how excited he was. He paused again and sighed. He trembled and swallowed hard the lump that had developed in his throat.

And then he added, "Ya know fer a while I didn't care if I ever got better, 'cause I sure enjoyed her lookin' after me... didn't want it to ever stop. I think I wuz as close to heaven as I'll ever get. Hell, I know I wuz the envy of all the guys.

"Ya know John, I really liked Janey."

"I know you did, Johnny. I think we all did. Likewise, I think we all hated that bastard Charbonneau all the more for it. I know 'Big Red' would just as soon have put a lead ball right between his eyes and be done with him. It would have been a sight easier on her and her little boy, Pomp."

"Yeah, little Pomp," said Potts with another long stare.

"Do you remember when we wuz portagin' around those Great Falls on the Missouri? I mean the time when Janey came down sick."

"Can't hardly forget it," I had said matter-of-factly. "Never thought we'd ever get around 'em and on top of all that, the little 'Bird Woman' got sicker 'n a dog. Didn't look like she was going to make it for awhile. That was a tough time."

"Yer damn right, it wuz," Potts agreed. "We wuz all mighty scared."

"Huh! Thar wuz sure a bunch of long faces droopin' around that campsite. Amazin' how much the boys cared for her, like she wuz everyone's favorite lil' sister and all. But, I think the worse thing wuz watchin' Cap'n Lewis bleed that poor girl with them damned lancets of his.

"Ugh!" Potts grimaced, making an ugly distorted face.

"Still gives me the chills thinkin' about it." He flinched anew in discomfort.

I stood up and scanned the full panorama we had from atop our lonely sandstone tower. It was breath taking to behold. The land, the great river, the distant mountains beckoned to us. The Yellowstone fairly shimmered below on its long voyage to the Missouri.

"Hey!" I snapped back. "Why do you think I never got sick on that expedition? No way was I gonna let Lewis bleed me with those lil' medical prickers of his, no way. I never did cotton to blood lettin' anyway.

"Hah, medicinal, my ass. It's medieval, it is. I'll take my chances any day with an ol' injun medicine man than a white quack like Meriwether Lewis."

Potts broke out giggling and laughing.

"More like torture. I saw some of the boys on sick watch ailin' in the worst way; fevers, sores, down with the 'trots.' Here comes ol' Meriwether with Dr. Rush's pills, them damn 'thunder bolts' and his medicine chest of sharp little lancets. If he didn't bleed ya to death, those 'thunder bolts' would shit to death. If one remedy of his didn't get ya, the other one would fer sure."

We had a good laugh at the memory of Lewis' medicine bag of tricks.

"Suddenly, miraculously the boys wuz all cured and off to the woods like their tails wuz on fire, when they heard ol' doc Meriwether wuz on his way. Hellfire, after the injuns watched him a doin' that to some of their little ones back at Fort Mandan, they thought we wuz the bloodthirsty savages."

I cracked up and bust out a laughing anew. Johnny hit it right on the head as far as Cap'n Lewis' medical practice. Hell, the men feared him and his little bag of lancets a helluva lot more then they ever did the Blackfeet, Sioux or an army of grizzly bears.

"Can you imagine if Janey died? What wuz we gonna do with her little Pomp?" Potts suddenly was somber. "That 'frog' husband of hers, Charbono couldn't take care of him."

"Nor wouldn't if he could," I reflected with an anger boiling in my veins at the memory of Toussaint Charbonneau the Corps interpreter.

"No good lazy *frog*."

"Big Red woulda worked it out, sure as shootin'," Potts interrupted 'fore I could get out my last thought on the despised Frenchman.

"I can still see Clark bouncin' that papoose up and down on his knees like he wuz his own. He sure loved that little kid."

"Seems to me that I can recollect quite a few of us bouncing Pomp on our knees," I responded with certainty.

"Yeah," said Potts letting out a long sigh. "Those wuz happy times, all right. Ya know, more than once I saw her watching the rest of us, kinda lovingly, if ya know what I mean. Yep, no two ways about it, in her own way she loved the lot of us… like one big family with the little injun gal bein' our mother hen. Ya know, in a way it's too bad it all had to come to an end."

"Wonder what happened to 'em? I mean Janey, Pomp and the 'frog'," I said after a moment or two.

Potts looked at me like he didn't believe that I was asking.

"You should know as well as me. The three of 'em left the Corps on the Missouri the same day as you and those trappers from Illinois country, Handcock and Dickson. Far as I know, no one has heard a word since. But, ya know it seems to me before they parted, 'Big Red' offered to raise and educate lil Pomp in St. Louie. Maybe Charbono and Sacagawea took him up on it."

"Well, I'll be, don't that beat all? I never knew."

Potts stared at me for the longest of time and finally asked, "What about you, John? I ain't never heard you talk about a sweetheart or any woman to be exact."

"No, you haven't," I said, not answering him right away. "I've known a few gals in my time, mostly around Maysville. But, I never seemed to find the time to do much sparkin', always on the go and all. I guess I just never found the right one. But, believe me, when I get back East, I will."

Womanfolk was a subject that I found myself thinking of more and more. Pott's pining for the gals was near contagious. The more he talked of it the more I became infected. And there was little else to talk of in the quiet of a hidden campsite. There wasn't much time for idle talk, when there was so much to do. Beavering is tedious, wet work, often downright dangerous. Felling a couple of good-sized cottonwoods, hacking, carving a pair of dugouts was demanding, time consuming. Setting traps, snagging beaver was the easy part of our business. The laborious work, the crucial work came next. Cutting, laying in a substantial supply of willow boughs to the right lengths, bending them carefully into place, forming hoops to stretch hides. Scraping flesh clean from the inner hide, attaching the hides to the hoops, carefully as to not damage any of the precious cargo. Tanning, stretching, curing all took care, all took time. Patience was demanded if what you were looking for was fine thick fur to sell to the markets of the world. And then when satisfied of what we had done, stack and tie them into neatly compressed bundles, periodically hiding them in dry, well-concealed caches free from the damage that nature and weather would surely wraught or the greedy, clutching hands of any number of thieving competitors… white or red.

It was all silent, quiet work. It was hard, lonely work done in the wettest and coldest months of the year. And that's why we chose to be here now. The beginning of cold weather, with winter preparing to set in was the time of year the beaver's skin came into its primest condition. That's when it needed the protection of thick fur and that's when the little critter's hide became rich and most luxurious. That's the skin that Manuel Lisa craved. That's what the millinery-shops, the fine hat makers of the western world demanded. And that's what we were getting in our traps. Nothing but the finest skin was worth our while, at least while we were in a place of such abundance. And all the while every sense of our being forewarned caution, commanding that nothing escape our attention. There were just too many forces, human and otherwise, that could quickly turn our days and nights into something more than we bargained for.

And yet, our patience, our diligence, all our hard work began to pay off and show signs that we were realizing all that we had hoped for. By our account, we'd done quite well, accumulating a tidy fortune in skins… enough for both of us to get a good start back in civilization. Some people though never seem to be satisfied.

At times I couldn't believe what I was seeing myself. Nothing I had experienced my whole time trapping the Yellowstone country had prepared me for the kind of success we were now enjoying. Oh, I had some good luck trapping the Yellowstone when I first hooked-up with Handcock and Dickson, compiling enough skins to fill my cottonwood dugout, enough of a cache to turn men's heads back in St. Louie. In fact when I was heading back down the Missouri I had felt right good about the whole venture. I hadn't even given it a second thought about returning to the Northwest.

The Crow knew we were there that whole long winter, but we got along fine with those thievin' redskins. Mainly, I guess because we didn't have any horses to steal. They coveted our shooting irons, all right. But, that was one item that never left my sight. They had no need for metal traps, being basically a lazy people. The men especially never cottoned to any kind of hard work, work of any kind being their squaws' jobs. There was never the sense of trepidation like I felt in Blackfeet country.

My partner had a different reaction. He never felt the same fear of the Blackfeet that I had. He simply never had a reason to. And no amount I told him of the horrors of the "pishkun plains" and ol' Toby's death seemed to faze that kid. All he cared about was returning to Manuel's Fort with a pile of furs and a smile on his face. Johnny Potts was having the time of his life.

"All those months that Pete and me trapped the Yellowstone didn't bring us nothin' like these," marvelled Johnny late one afternoon after we'd been at it for several weeks straight.

"I mean these skins are really prime. I've never seen their like. Hellfire, John, we'll be rich. Thar's sixty skins alone in that first pack, maybe a good hundred pounds worth. We'll have another just like it in no time at all. Why, do you know how much money they'll bring down in St. Louie? We got more plews here than Manuel Lisa's whole outfit put together back on the 'Big Horn'."

And then he added with more than a hint of acrimony, "Pretty soon I'll have seen the last of that skunk."

"Don't like the little senor, do ya?" I said.

"Nope!" Potts replied. He was caressing his cheek with the soft fur as tenderly as he would a newborn babe. "I don't cotton to the way he does business."

"You know, Johnnie," I interrupted, trying to change the subject, "a thought came to me, one I'd been holding ever since that day we stopped at Pompey's Pillar. Little Janie, Sacagawea, talked about this very place."

Potts looked up at the mention of little Janey. "She did? I don't recollect the conversation."

"Yeah, I was there to hear about it. She told Big Red and Meriwether that this was the place where she was taken hostage, when she was a little kid. Her people use to summer hereabouts. The Hidatsa of the Knife, those sneakin' Minn-a-tareeees, swooped down on her band one summer, chased 'em across the 'prickly pear plains' right into the woods of the Jefferson, just about to where we're settin' now."

"Huh!" said Johnny. "What happened?"

"Minn-a-tareeees took her as a slave along with some other young squaws from her band. They killed everybody else… men, women, boys. Hauled their take all the way back to the Missouri and the Knife. I guess those injuns make a habit of raidin' her people, though they never let on when we were there."

"I'll be. I never heard that story. I didn't recollect the Snakes being here in this part of the country. Thought they were yonder to the southwest." Johnny began looking around a little nervously.

"That's the point," I said. "This here's a peaceful place. I could stay here for the rest of my days. But, don't let if fool ya. It can sour real fast. And some of these injuns can make life real hard on others."

He looked up, staring me in the face. "I'm sorry about Janey. But, everythin' worked out 'bout right for her. She's better off now, even if it is with that 'frog' Charbono, at least better off then she'd be a grubbin' and a scroungin' with them Snakes."

He went back to caressing the beaver pelt, remembering why he was here. "Besides, I don't intend to be caught by no redskins… Uh uh! Gonna be rich, by God, once we're shed of injun country." He was smiling just then with an odd, distant look on his face, a dreamy faraway stare.

I looked at him, shaking my head. Potts never listened. He never got the point. Oh, what's the use, I thought, frowning at the kid's stubborness.

"Not bad for a half dozen traps and a few of weeks of steady work. I've never had a run like this. Thought I might be a mite rusty. I haven't been doin' much beaverin' lately. But, these hides should bring us some good money. Johnny, I gotta admit, it looks like you've brought me some good luck."

"Not bad? Not bad you say. You are the sly one. Colter, my hat's off to you. And as for me bringin' you good luck, that's a laugh. I knew you were some kinda frontier man and all, but never did I believe that you could work such magic with a mess of beaver skins like these here plews. I swear, I can't wait for Pete to see what we bring back. He'll have wished fer sure that he would've come along. I know he will."

"Speakin' of Pete, Johnny… we need to be thinkin' of headin' back pretty soon."

"Now? Why? Were doin' too dang good to quit now."

"Why… cause we've enough skins to carry back and these parts will soon be played out the way we're goin' at it. That second pack of plews just about equals the first, more than enough for us to handle gettin' back to Manuels. They both add up to a right good pile of money. I don't want to stay here any longer than I have to and I don't unnecessarily want to start caching skins, because that means we gotta come back. We've been pretty smart so far and we've still got our scalps… Savvy?"

I could see that this wasn't sitting well with my partner. That stubborn look came over his face and I could sense the argument coming. So I decided to head it off.

"Look, Johnny, I told you 'afore we left that we weren't goin' to get greedy. And gettin' too greedy is a sure 'hellfire' way to gettin' waylaid by the injuns. You agreed, right?"

"Right, I did," he said. "And I'll do what I said I would. But, I got a hankerin' before we leave to see how fat those critters are down the Jeff' closer to the Forks, just a day or two worth, enough to fill up that second pack… how about it? And then we'll head out and I'll never look back."

"Just leave everythin' here?" I asked.

"Oh, hell, Colter," he said. "We got these two dugouts settin' here, doin' nuthin'. Let's put 'em to use, load up our traps come mornin', a couple more days of eatin' beaver ain't goin' to kill us. Paddle towards the Forks, set our traps, get what we can and skedaddle right back here without losing more than a day or two. The ponies won't wander far, not while there's plenty of grass and water right here to suit 'em. No 'pee-guns' are gonna find this campsite, we've hid too well. Those red, dumb sons of bitches will never be the wiser.

"Whadda you say?"

"Huh! You make it sound really easy. All right, I guess we can do that," I said it, not believing for the rest of my days that I did.

I should've realized that things had gone far too good far too long. Get in and get out, I had said. Don't be greedy, don't get careless… so far, so good. I know when to quit, at least I thought I did. But, it was hard to keep Johnny down. The better we did the more pelts he wanted. With every fresh skin we stretched and stacked, you could see his mind a turning and the gold adding up.

The thought never occurred to Potts that by returning to the Forks so soon after my recent trouble was a foolish and dangerous gamble. The jagged scar that creased my thigh, the hundreds of scavenged carcasses picked clean, lying prostrate on the "pishkun plains," bleaching in the sun, didn't seem to bother him the moment after we left. I wondered what if anything would?

With each passing day bringing us closer and closer to winter, I knew our chances of running into the Blackfeet or Gros Ventre or any other hostiles were less likely to happen. We hadn't seen a single injun sign since we first stepped foot. They'd be wintering up north most likely. Maybe the fight at the "pishkun plains" had knocked the stuffin' out of 'em, after all. Good! Couldn't be better to my liking.

We shoved off early the next morning catching the lazy current of the Jeff", dipping a paddle here and there, rarely straining, watching the banks, the treelines, the baldies roosts high up in their cottonwood aeries, gliding above the peaceful river without a care in the world. Johnny was in high spirits. Hell, he always was. Me, I tended to be a bit more reserved, this was not the time to play. Let him have his fun, I'd watch for the two of us. It was nothing new, I'd been doing it that way since the day we left Manuels. And he knew it, too, always getting a kick out of it, rarely letting up on me, ribbing me, teasing me, forever the constant pain in the ass that he was.

It was a quiet morning on the river. The air was still… the wind had yet to show-up. The current was even slower, lazier this time of the year, not at all like the swift stream I had known a time or two in the past, when its mountain bred waters surged and boiled and ran amok, bloated by spring melt. We paddled on, unconcerned, time, distance, the lay of the land passing with hardly a notice, the splash of an occasional oar, the perpetual lap of the river slapping the shore, the wind in the trees the only sounds to be heard. The river curved, snaking its way across the valley from south to north, sheltered by groves of tall, stately cottonwoods, alder and birch and the ever-present willow. Dense stands of old growth shrouded the meandering Jefferson in a cloak of anonymity, hiding river-life from the view of the rest of the valley that surrounded it.

We were in another world; a riparian world, remote, alone, far removed from the rich bunch grass plains that lay just a short distance away beyond the trees. Hidden, that is, until a high, rugged palisade of steep, rocky promontories rose abruptly from the river's edge on the northern side of the valley, towering above the Jefferson with an eagle's eye view.

I didn't like it. We were far too exposed for my blood. Maybe I was too edgy. But, I just couldn't help it. My hair was standing up on the back of my neck. My pulse for some unexplainable reason started to sprint. I began to get that itch all over… that same alarming tic that never failed me before.

"Johnny," I yelled, "look at those high cliffs in front of us. We're sticking out like sore thumbs."

"So what?" Potts grew irritated, his voice, his demeanor, testy.

"Don't be a fool," I warned. "Start watching the banks and keep an eye on those rises."

Potts turned around in his canoe, a big smile spreading across his face. He was laughing at me, shaking his head and chuckling once again. There was a light-hearted contempt in his voice and he made no attempt to hide it.

"What are ya, some kind of mother hen? Cluck. Cluck… Cluck, cluck, cluck."

I reached the point of exasperation. I didn't mind him having a little fun at my expense, didn't even care about the occasional barb thrown my way. But I did care about my scalp and he was showing absolutely no caution or care or good sense. He just didn't give a damn, paddling downstream with that infernal clucking of his, happier than a pig in shit, riding high without a care in the world.

I stared at his backside as he drifted away. God, I was mad. Mad enough to turn back and get my skins, my possibles and head-on home. Leave him there alone in the wilderness to survive on his own. I should have listened to Pete. Now, I knew why he wouldn't come. He was smarter than me, knew Johnny as well as he did his own brother, all the while knowing that Johnny sooner or later would bring on trouble. And Pete evidently had had enough of Johnny's kind of trouble, friend or no friend.

Up ahead there was a clearing, a break in the cottonwood forest on the river's bank on the starboard side, with the plains of the valley floor suddenly emerging into view. It happened so swiftly, before I could react or pull up. And Johnny, the kid just kept on moving closer and closer obliviously.

A low rumble was resonating from the plains. The rumble of thunder… four-footed, hooved thunder pounding the ground in a rising crescendo.

I froze, listening intently, unable to move or think. Every facet of my being was alarmed, every instinct warned me "to get the hell out of here."

Immediately, I yelled to Johnny, "Get away from the banks. Get out in the middle of the river and get back here. Do it, now."

I started to pull at my oars and turn hard around, to fight the current, to head back up the river and lose myself in its forested domain.

But, Johnny held me back by refusing to listen.

"What fer? It's just buffalo on the move," he hollered, shaking his head in disgust.

"Jesus Christ, Colter, we've been hearin' 'em fer days."

He turned and continued paddling down river right in the direction of the approaching din.

I stared incredulously. Nothing I could say or do seemed to matter. What arrogant, pompous, jackass stupidity I fumed. Desperation, fear, anger, all converged within me. Wasn't there anything that would turn him around?

"Johnny, turn back while you can. Hurry up, damn it, I don't like the sound of this," I pleaded with him.

We were now drifting further and further apart, literally and figuratively. I had never been as baffled or as frustrated in all my life.

"Christsakes, Colter, they're just thirsty. You go on back if that suits ya. Ain't no damn critter gonna hold me back. Besides, what's wrong with a little fresh buffalo tongue?"

Potts continued to shake his head all the while drawing nearer to the clearing. The staccatoed thunder of hooves grew louder, closer. The din, the clamor became deafening, frightening. It was as if a herd of hundreds, thousands of shaggy, humped beasts were bearing down, funneling their wild charge across the plains to the Jefferson on a collision course with the river.

The surging mass abruptly changed its direction, veering straight towards the clearing at the water's edge to where we bobbed like two corks adrift. We both saw instantly that it was too late. The approaching horde was not thirsty buffalo on the move, but hundreds of painted ponies mounted by those very same injuns I swore to avoid.

They crowded right up to the river's bank, the dust settling to reveal a long, martial line of Indian cavalry, lancers of the plains, wearing grim, silent, painted faces.

Painted? I thought. War, with whom? Here? Why?

Suddenly, I knew why. Their faces, their get up was all too familiar. They were Pahkees all right, Piegans of the Blackfeet Nation. Sure as shootin', they'd known about us being here for some time. Everything I feared was coming true. What a fool I had been, a stubborn, single minded, blinded fool of a horse's ass and now I was going to pay for it. Damn it, I swore, looking about, there was absolutely no place for us to run to or hide. We gambled and we lost.

We both sat motionlessly in our dugouts staring across the few yards of river that separated us from the unwavering ranks of mounted Piegans. Every bronzed countenance was staring our way; taut, strained, as if ominously biding their time, awaiting their leisure to burst forward with all the pent up energy that their loss from the battle of the 'pishkun' plains had wrought. Each unflinching gaze was intense, bitterly poignant, burning a hole through the two of us as sure as if we were shot by flaming missiles. No one moved on either side, save for a nervous fidgeting of fingers on notched arrows and strung bows and the yellow streak working its way up my spine.

"Holy shit!" A jolt, like a bolt of lightning, raced to the very ends of my limbs, jerking my toes, my fingers taut with fear. My mouth, my throat ran bone dry. My inner ears rang and peeled like a church bell. My head began to pound and pound, beaten senselessly by a heavy unyielding, invisible hammer striking my gourd from deep within. Nowhere could I see escape or freedom as my mind raced for answers. All my cunning, my instincts were dumbfounded, checkmated by the Pahkees at every possible move.

I looked down, forlorn, to my precious traps lying on the bottom of my canoe. For a brief moment I thought of all those fine furs cached back at our campsite, everything I had worked for since leaving the Corps. Our hopes, our plans, our whole venture had come to naught. A sudden streak of defiance bolted through me as I casually reached down and grabbed a trap. Deftly, one by one, I slipped them over the portside gunnel of my dugout, dropping them unseen into the waters of the Jeff to sink to the shallow rocky bottom below.

No one seemed to catch it, not even Johnny. I couldn't believe my luck. They got me, but I'll be damned if they are gonna get my traps, I cussed under my breath.

The brief standoff soon came to an abrupt close.

"Who are they?" yelled Potts, his face an ashen mask of steadily growing terror. His words, his tenor cracking the air like a rawhide whip.

"Colter, I'm talkin' to ya. Who are they? What do they want?" His voice was quivering, urgent, demanding. Uncertainty had now taken hold.

I looked ahead to where he sat adrift. He was no longer brash or confident. His last chuckles and chicken clucks were left a hundred yards back down the river and a lifetime away.

He was petrified, pitifully so. The strain showed in his face, in the faltering stutter that suddenly controlled his every utterance and negated his every move, chipping away at what mettle he had left. No longer smug, confident, brash, but a man whose strands of courage were unraveling, thread by vital thread, at an alarming rate. An uncontrollable twitch jerked his head spasmodically like that of an old enfeebled man on his last legs as he eyed the long phalanx of Piegan warriors lined abreast on the riverbank. Johnny's composure, his last remaining mettle completely and utterly abandoning him.

I continued to return the Piegans' stare. Not a one of them flinched nor varied their steely gaze. They were like a pack of ravenous wolves appraising their prey, licking their chops, and patiently biding their time to strike when it suited them best.

What are they waiting for? I asked myself.

And then, I glanced at Johnny. I could see in his eyes, his face, he was about to act. He was unnerved by the amassed lines of painted warriors staring directly at him, desperate to escape, to bolt and flee for freedom.

I had to reach him, reach the one last vestige of sanity… the good sense I prayed remained within him.

"Don't move, Johnny. Just sit real still. Do you hear me?"

He didn't say a word, though the flailing, spasmodic twitch had abated. His eyes even at the distance between us appeared glassy, their lids unblinking. His limbs, his torso appeared frozen, lifeless, every bit like a marble statue.

Again, I urged, "Johnny, nod if you understand me."

The tightness in his face seemed to ease up, to relax as if he understood.

"Good. Don't do anything stupid. Just sit real still."

The developing drama between Johnny and me and the Piegans somehow became more intense, both sides locked in stares, no one making a move. But, they held all the cards, the whole deck to shuffle as they saw fit. They meant business, evil business… a hand only a cruel savage could deal. It was as plain as the paint on their faces and the dried scalps hanging from their shields and lances.

Potts appeared to loosen up. Maybe he had gotten a hold of himself. I had to try something to break the stalemate. We were both in this together, but, somehow, I felt it my fault, my own doing. After all, I didn't have to to agree to his coming, I didn't have to come back to the Forks. Somehow I must barter my freedom for his. It was the last decent thing I could do.

I knew these Piegan wanted me. Realized the butchery they intended, the humiliation and finality of it all. I held no illusions, no hope of escape. I just prayed I could somehow make it quick, painlessly if possible.

"Johnny, I know these redskins. I recognize some of their faces from the Madison... and they sure seem to know me."

There was no doubt, no question in my mind. Hope had drained right out of me the instant I saw their faces and realized their intent. Somehow, though, I had to hang in there tough. How I did, I'll never know.

I now knew the depths of their hatred, sensed the fury that burned within them, envisioned the horrors they intended. They sat calmly, astride their ponies; barely flexing their taut, sinewy, sun bronzed muscles. They all wore the same look; a furrowed brow, a frozen scowl as if set in stone. Black and red ochre stripes lined each of their foreheads, the bridges of their long aquiline noses, their cheeks, their bared shoulders, their smooth chests. All the while, their hands itched to pull the gut strings of their bows and squeeze the rusty triggers of their "fusil' trade muskets.

Their ponies, their precious ponokamitas, all likewise painted for war, pawed the ground incessantly with unshod hooves, kicking up shoreline dirt and sod and smoothed river-pebbles. Their shortcropped tails twitched and flicked at bothersome, nettlesome flies. They literally breathed the tension their masters felt.

"Lord have mercy," I whispered softly. All I could think of was 'shit creek' and no paddles.

These Blackfeet had been so awfully patient. Indians naturally tend to be that way, more so than the white man could ever hope to be. I knew I should've listened to all those nagging little voices of intstinct warning me to go it alone, to say no to Johnny, and to keep out of a land where I didn't belong. But, I didn't listen. Johnny didn't either and now somewhere, probably still at Manuel's Fort, a friend's ears, Pete Wiser's ears, were burning red.

"Sorry, Pete," I whispered softly. "I let you down."

As the time ticked away, the seconds seemed like minutes, soon a lifetime. My mind wandered, racing to all its far corners. The questions came, the answers fired back with lightning speed in a vain attempt to counter each and every expected Pahkee move. They must've left scouts in the valley to look for my sign or maybe they had spies waiting by Manuels or between there and here. Maybe they saw the glowing embers of our campfire one night or caught a glimpse of us riding across the bunch grass prairie or heard us hacking away, carving out cottonwood dugouts. Who knows? What difference does it make now, I'd never find out?

But, somehow, someway they found out, spotted the two of us and raced back home with the news. Now, they had us by the short hairs. The Pahkees had won, it was their game to play and they made all the rules. I could imagine the excitement, the furor, the lust for vengeance when they arrived at their village, especially when they gathered their most aggrieved, the kin of the many warriors slain by the *napikwan's* fire stick, his big medicine that spoke death that fatal day on the "pishkun plains."

I continued to stare at my accusers, transfixed by an overwhelming anticipation of doom. The wait, the mounting tension all calculated with purpose, excellently crafted by masters of intimidation. And while I watched and waited, I couldn't help but admire their little ponies, up and down the line, silently waiting, as well trained and as disciplined a steed as any cavalry mount on the European continent. Nor did I fail to notice the respect engendered by their riders' presence. They were taller than most Indians I had come across, lean like wolves, athletic… a warrior race seldom seen save for the magic of myth and folklore… and everything about them exuded it.

Damn, I should've known, I chided myself anew, what a fool I've been. But, it was too late for me to start throwing the blame; too late for anything save steeling myself for what was bound to come.

"What's he want?" screamed Potts, no longer able to conceal the unsteadiness and fear quaking in his voice, now grown as fragile as a dying aspen in a mountain storm.

"Colter, wake-up, man… dang it. That older injun is talkin' to ya, and he sure looks like he knows ya."

Johnny's voice snapped me back, all right. I looked ashore and saw whom he meant. That old Indian, I thought, was a hard looking man. And Johnny was right, the Indian did know me, I had seen him before on the plains by the Madison whooping up his boys. And then our eyes met and locked. We just naturally returned each other's stares, cooly and direct. No use trying to fool him that I wasn't his man. He wouldn't respect that in me and I wasn't about to disappoint him. Injuns just naturally set store by courage and grit and disdained the man without it.

"Yeah, we know each other, though we haven't formally met," I said quite casually, trying my best to throw-in a little humor.

There was hardly a quiver in my voice to betray what I was really feeling right about then. I was scared, scared right down to the bottoms of my moccasins. But I knew the last thing I should do was show fear. If those Blackfeet felt it or heard it, I wouldn't give a plug for our chances. They had nothing but contempt for cowards. Guts was what they set store by. So I just kept a good hold of myself and continued to talk to Johnny as calmly as I could.

"The Flatheads and the Absaroka know the 'old coot' as Kootenae Appe. That ol' boy is the big whoopdeedoo leader of the Pahkees, and he badly wants my hide. I'm afraid, Johnny, the two of us are in for it. I tried to warn you all along. I wish the hell you would have listened."

"He's motionin' us to come ashore," cried Potts. "I ain't goin', John. They're thieving bastards. They're not takin' my skins and traps. They're not takin' 'em."

"Forget the traps, they ain't worth our lives. We don't have a choice, Johnny. There's no way we can get away. You've got to stay steady 'til we can figure a way out of this mess."

It was the only advice I could give him. Indians like to see nerve in a man. You lose it and they'll play hell with you for sure.

"Stay put," I yelled. "It's me they really want. I'm headin' in."

And then I hesitated, compelled to leave my friend with one last goodbye and piece of advice.

"If they do me in, Johnny, it's been nice knowin' you. And you'd better be ready to swaller your gun."

That was a hard farewell I gave my friend. But we couldn't run and couldn't fight and I was resigned to it. What a hell of a mess, I thought to myself as I dragged my dugout in towards the bank and up onto the gravelly shore where they waited.

I found myself staring once again at angry, painted faces… faces and shoulders and arms and chest daubed with yellow and red ochre and glossy black. Red-skinned warriors with painted circles and stripes and dots around dark, penetrating eyes, across the bridges of their noses, over their chins and down their cheeks, across their bare shoulders and chest and long, lithe, smoothly muscled thighs.

Many wore a single feather of accomplishment in their hair. Others had bunches tied to their long, raven manes, hanging loosely draped around their sinewy necks and broad backs. Locks of hair, symbol of Blackfeet manhood, fell over their brows and the bridge of their long, aquiline noses. They all wore the fiercest of visages, meant to send fear into the hearts of all those who dared encounter them. And it worked, it worked on me and it definitely was working on Johnny Potts.

Yet, even with all that was happening, I didn't miss a trick, desperately trying to keep my wits about me. My mind, my every sense was primed and firing in the quest to somehow save at least one of our lives.

It seemed a hopeless task. The Blackfeet were not about to show any mercy. Fair play, chivalry meant nothing to them. They would not dare give an enemy the chance to fight another day. They had already learned that lesson. If anything the heat of their hatred burned even hotter and deeper within their eyes, their souls. The entire band was strangely silent, intent on me like nothing else in the whole world mattered. Not at all like the frantic whooping and screaming savages I remembered from the nearby 'pishkun' plains.

"Maybe it's just the calm before the risin' storm," I whispered under my breath, chuckling to myself in a thin attempt to reinforce my dwindling nerve.

I stood by my canoe on that narrow, gravelly beach and faced the dark-eyed Kootenae Appe. The ol' injun grunted and pointed out to Potts sitting in his dugout. His fingers motioned, commanding me to have Johnny come ashore.

I didn't hesitate, stalling for time would have been futile… and risky.

"Potts, come on in. The ol' boy could've had us riddled a hundred times over if he wanted to."

"Shit… yer crazy," Johnny responded acidly, the bite of his tongue hot with indignation.

"Yeah, I am, but we're still alive. Come on in before they get more pissed off than they already are."

Potts trembled like a leaf in a storm. His fear permanently fixed to his face, his eyelids unblinking. As he sat there in his dugout, near immobilized, betwixt paddling in or fleeing, I fought to keep him from doing anything sudden or rash and getting us both killed.

He started to paddle forward hesitantly, his heart not in it. Every instinct in his being warning, "this is stupid, this is fatal."

I knew the feeling, but what else could we do.

As Johnny's canoe pulled in close to shore, several warriors dismounted. One injun, a big, broad shouldered, fierce looking young Pahkee entered the water with a powerful, determined stride, wading right up to Johnny's canoe and just reached out and grabbed the prow, giving it a vicious yank. He was arrogant, scornful, the wrong man to dare Johnny. I could see the confrontation coming.

Like I've said before, Johnny Potts didn't cotton to being pushed around by anyone, injun or otherwise. And sound judgment never seemed to be his strong suit, at least not in a situation as heated as this. I knew poor Johnny would be unable to restrain himself. And I... I was as helpless to stop him as I would be to stop the tide or to piss out a wind borne prairie wildfire on a dry, windy summer day.

And yet, that big Indian was the first to make the next move. He reached into Potts' canoe and grabbed Johnny's prized U.S. Army '03 issue. It had been Johnny's pride, issued to him by Cap'n Meriwether Lewis, himself, way back down on the Ohio River in that very same year. The boy had kept that piece spotless from the day he got it. That '03, all the way from Harper's Ferry Arsenal, back and forth across the country, now resting in the hands of a redhide savage of the Blackfeet Nation on the banks of the Jefferson. It was never meant to be that way, and for sure, it didn't sit well at all with Johnny Potts.

"Shit!" I swore.

That dumb Pahkee had done it. I knew right then and there, it'd be too much for the kid to stand. I could tell by the angry, frustrating look a growing on his face as he instantly sat up tall in his canoe. His fists clinched tightly, with every fiber in his being now taut, rigid and ready to fire. I saw the muscles in his face constrict, stand out like bands of steel, as if readying Johnny to spring to action... and take his weapon back.

"*Namachkani! Namachkani!*" The injun screamed over and over and he waved Johnny's short barreled piece over his head, shrieking triumphantly.

That word he yelled again and again I had never heard before. But I knew what he meant all the same. Taking Johnny's rifle was a big deal, big medicine for that warrior.

"*Namachkani!*" His Piegan brethren instantly came alive, roaring back their approval.

Their war cries split the air with a deafening response, nigh on shattering what little composure was left between the two of us.

It was my moment of decision. Maybe the biggest I ever had. I knew I couldn't stand there like a whipped dog, like they'd expected me to be. No sir, the sons of bitches needed to come down from their high horses, right then and there. And I needed to do it now, before Johnny blew his cork... while I still had the advantage.

I honestly don't know where the guts came from. I just stepped right up. I faced that grinning savage, staring him down with the hardest look I could muster.

He looked at me kind of dumbfounded. His arms went slack, holding Johnny's rifle with both hands right in front of his chest at port-arms like a soldierboy on parade. In that brief moment the Pahkee's nerve faltered, his jaws dropping all the way to his balls. If we weren't in such a serious predicament, it would have been downright comical.

"Hell, you dumb red-skin... give me that gun." I just reached out and took hold and with a good yank wrenched Johnny's rifle right out of his hands. I surprised the living shit out of that Indian. For that matter I surprised the rest of his howling band, including ol' Kootenae Appe, himself.

That whole Blackfoot cavalcade suddenly went quiet. They couldn't believe their eyes or my sand. I bared my backside to the whole shooting match, calmly walking over to Potts' canoe and handing Johnny his weapon.

"Colter, yer crazy," said Potts.

Even he refused to believe what I'd just done. His face was twisted, the look, the expression all askew. His eyes bulged so fast, so big they could have literally burst right out of their sockets. The cords in his neck began pulsating, throbbing. His adrenaline pumped beyond his control. Every bit of sense and nerve abandoning him right at the time he needed it most. And with that rifle of his now safely back in his canoe, Johnny started to paddle back towards the middle of the river.

"Do what ya want," he said, "I'm gettin' the hell outta here."

"Johnny, no," I pleaded. " Jesus Christ, don't."

But it was too late. Nothing in this world could have turned him around or brought him back.

Kootenae Appe was the first to return to his senses. His eyes were ablaze, his voice angry, intense as his words literally exploded from his lips. Instantly a half dozen warriors sprang from their ponies, raced into the river and grabbed me like I was a raggedy doll.

A vicious thud slammed into the back of my head. I reeled with pain and nausea. For a moment the lights were going out in my head as I fought to stave off the darkness and the quickly fading, tiny flickering twinkles of light racing across my mind's eye.

I was dragged back onto the bank and thrown rudely to the gravel covered shore. I could feel warm blood streaming down the back of my neck from where I was struck as I struggled to regain consciousness.

Without command, every stitch of my clothing was torn from my body, right down to my bare feet. There they left me, naked as a jay, exposed to ridicule and shame. I had never been so humiliated, so helpless in all my born days. But that was the least of my worries.

No signal was observed, no order heard. But, a single shot rang out from ashore, slamming into with a decided impact and knocking Potts flat on his back to the bottom of his canoe. I could hear him moaning in pain as he struggled to right himself.

I managed to get up onto one elbow and cry out to him, "Johnny, are hit? Are you hurt? Talk to me."

"I'm hit... Uhhhh! The stinkin' savage got me in the leg and smashed my hip. I'm bleedin' all over the place. The filthy bast..."

He never finished his sentence... the shock beginning to take hold. But, he wasn't giving up. He would be game to the end.

"Colter... I told ya they aren't gettin' my traps and now I'm all busted up. I can't even move."

God, help him. I heard his lament, his struggle. I pleaded with him. "Hang on... hang on."

His voice was weakening. I could see his body writhing in agony from the ball of lead that tore through his upper leg and shattered his hip. He began weeping, the sobs barely audible above the lapping waves of the Jeff. His plight was pitiful. He had no where to turn to: no hope for salvation or mercy or rescue. It was the end of his road and he knew it and faced it. I'm here to tell you that... Johnny Potts was tough. I'll give him that. Without much 'adieu' he sat up using every ounce of strength he could muster. And then he cried out...

"I'll kill ya... ya dirty son of a bitch."

And with that Johnny Potts deliberately shouldered his '03 and in an act of supreme defiance, took quick aim, and fired right, square into the belly of the one who had laid him low. That Indian was flung to the ground in a prostrated heap, never again to see the light of day. It was Johnny's last act... desperate, courageous and final.

Instantly, the Piegan throng responded with shot and bow and launched a hundred balls of lead and stone-headed missiles his way. Johnny was riddled like a porcupine. The last look on his face was one of surprise, almost as in disbelief. Death kindly followed instantly.

"Oh, my God!" I was mortified beyond all I had ever endured or suffered or knew. Tears welled in my eyes, rolling steadily down my cheeks in an unending stream. I gulped and swallowed hard, my mouth, my lips and my throat were slaked and dried. A numbing helpless feeling soon overwhelmed me, robbing me of my strength, my spirit and my will to go on.

Death, apparently, was not near enough to satisfy Piegan blood lust. They leapt from their ponies, horrifying shrieks of grief and vengeance simultaneously filling the air as they raced to the now lifeless body of Johnny Potts. His carcass was wrenched from the canoe by a dozen strong hands and flung to the shore in utter disdain.

Quietly, I watched in abject horror as I realized what the murdering savages were about to do. I saw their cruel bloodsport many times on that spring day and shuddered at the savage butchery now being performed on my dead friend. I steeled myself to remain strong and resolute. If I had to go, it would not be as a whimpering coward in front of these spineless savages. And yet inside, in the sanctuary of own mind and soul, I cried and I cried and I cried.

With tomahawk and knives and warclubs they hacked, they maimed. They savagely ripped open his still warm torso and tore out every vital organ of John Potts' young body: his lungs, his heart, his liver and intestines. Nothing was sacred; no part was spared. They cut off his head, slamming it with glee onto a stoneheaded lance, promenading about this river bank scene with sardonic cheers of derision and delight.

The butchery, their blood orgy of degradation did not let up. His feet, his legs and arms and penis were all severed, disdainfully ripped from his body. His member, his privates were shoved into his mouth as his cruel, vile tormentors roared in delight. Oh, the shame, the humiliation went on and on.

Throughout this barbaric carnage I stood by helplessly, stunned by the horror of their fiendish acts of inhuman reprisal and reproach.

They raced with their prized trophies to the ground where I stood, laughing insidiously, screaming humiliation after humiliation. Taunt after taunt was flung at me in their savage Algonquian tongue.

They whipped and flogged me over and over with every torn piece and severed limb of my dear friend's remains. Again and again and mercilessly again, my face was slapped. I was pummeled incessantly, over and over, hard, bitterly hard, chafed raw by flesh and sinew and organ and limb alike, until every single square inch of my naked hide and head was painted red with pulp and bloody stain. The nightmare kept up for intolerably long minutes. And when their fury was sated, when their own limbs grew weary from the effort, they discarded Johnny's flesh, flinging away what little remnants of his bodily past remained intact… grim pickings for the scavengers. They stood back, momentarily revelling in their fiendish artistic design.

Yet, even then their fiendish appetites were still not satisfied. They surged forward anew, circling me, chanting, laughing, from hand to hand, warrior to warrior, passing around that accursed stone-headed lance where rested impaled Johnny's severed head, thrusting his death mask in my face… taunting me, jeering me. I thought their madness would never end.

CHAPTER SIX

Hopeless, benumbed by despair, awaiting the same cruel fate that befell my friend, Johnny Potts, scant moments before.

Amidst bestial celebration, my nearest tormentor suddenly stops his revelry, his victory dance. He stares at me long and hard, hooking his eyes on my nakedness, seeing something they've all missed. Why they haven't noticed 'til now, I do not know. Maybe it was in their great haste to capture us. Maybe the confrontation with Johnny P had caused them to somehow dismiss me… and the threat I could no longer offer. After all, many moons have passed since our first encounter. I was no longer the hirsute creature trespassing on the plains by the Madison in the company of enemy hunters, meting out death by the fire-stick from hell, dispatching so many of their Piegan warriors to the not-so-happy hunting grounds. I'd shorn my long locks and shaved my beard while recuperating at Manuel's Fort. New duds have replaced worn-out, bullet-torn, bloodstained buckskins. I have the look and feel of a different man. It matters not, for now my duplicity faces exposure by this one alert warrior whose eyes are transfixed on the musket-ball scar, the wound that furrowed my leg a half a year before by a well-aimed Piegan fusee.

"Ah-eeee-ah, ah-eeee-ah!" A startled cry burst forth from deep within his bowels, punching the air like a midsummer thunderclap as he frantically points to my leg, to the long jagged purple memory coursing my upper right thigh. "*Napikwan, napikwan,*" he screams over and over.

The savage frenzy by the banks of the Jefferson abates as abruptly as it had begun. The word is passed quickly through their ranks, something extraordinary has been seen. One by one, hundreds of curious warriors come to see, to gawk and stare at my leg and what that purplish scar surely must mean to every man in their tribe. Each brave nods his head in turn towards another and then another and another until they've all seen and most assuredly now come to believe.

Pathetically, I stand alone; stripped naked, ringed by a host of the hated Piegans and they in turn are riveted by that accursed scar. If they need any further evidence to prove me the one, the slayer of so many young braves on the "pishkun plains," then they need look no further. Somewhat surprisingly, I remain as calm as stone, my gaze firmly locked ahead, seemingly oblivious to the tragedy and furor at hand. Steady, Johnboy, no whimpering. Don't give 'em the satisfaction of seeing you crawl and beg. Whatever they dish out, you've got to take. Otherwise, you're in for hell no matter how you look at it. The Blackfeet detest weakness in a man, though strength and courage,

I know, doesn't necessarily insure a quick, clean death. Sarcasm flows from within as the curious peer deep into my eyes. Yeah, get a good look. It's me, all right; you dumb sons of bitches. So what're you waiting for? Come on, get it over with, I'm ready. Do your stinking butchery and let me die. Yeah, right! Who am I fooling? Wishful thinking, boy, you aren't that lucky. These savages won't be content with just the spilling of your blood, especially with an enemy who has vexed them so. No, they need more than merely to commit simple murder. They demand me humbled before their very eyes. They want their sport. They want me cowering before them, begging for mercy or quick dispatch. Nothing less will suffice for my utter humiliation will be their national pleasure and revenge, cleansing the shame and dishonor of the pishkun plains defeat forever.

Words never leave my lips, yet I scream every vile expletive I know, cursing our luck, reviling my own stupidity. Damn you, Johnny P, I silently fume. And damn me for bringing you here. I should've never listened to you. I should've never taken you along. Hell and damnation, why didn't I come alone? Heed my own instincts? Why didn't I listen to Pete Wiser's sound advice? He told me not to do it. Lord God, we should've returned to Manuel's while we still had the chance. Yeah, right! Now look at the scrape you're in. It's way too late to be expecting any miracles. So save your breath, cut the pussyfooting. Your chances are all used up and you'd better get use to it. Johnny's gone. You're next.

My insides roil, a tumult of shame and guilt and fear and loss. Remorse rules inside me beyond my capacity to reason or control. My guts churn away, sloshing over like a swollen dam ready to burst in one gigantic cataclysmic deluge of emotional anguish and raw puke. Get a hold of yourself, right now, inwardly I command myself. But, I can't. And I know it. Too much wrong has happened; I can no longer bear the responsibility. Tears have yet to flow, but I cry just the same at the despicable tragedy that just ended my friend's life. I'm not even thinking of myself. How can I when Johnny's bloody remains are splattered and caked all over my own face and hide? Woe! Woe! And then the floodgates open in earnest. Try as I might, I can't prevent the inevitable, weeping uncontrollably. In all my days I've never suffered such loss, such grief nor bore such a heavy heart. All the horrid accounts of frontier depradations by the red man I was weened on have now come home to roost in vivid fashion.

Bewildered and spent, my mind soon wanders aimlessly, adrift in an ocean of denial. Oblivious to the savages festering about me, I recall a nighttime discussion at Manuel's Fort just a few weeks before when I had cautioned a seasoned group of trappers who thought they'd nothing to fear from entering Blackfeet country.

"So, y'all want to go beaverin' in the Three Forks?" I had shaken my head in disbelief that night at the thought of a bunch of noisy, stinkin' trappers rooting around the Three Forks like a herd of wallowing hogs.

"Downright dumb, boys, I'm here to tell you. Hell, every injun within two hundred miles will smell you comin' the instant you step foot out of the Fort and head up the Yellowstone. Injuns out here are that way. Little gets by 'em. You won't be able to hide it. Sooner or later you'll get tripped up. But, if you think you can sneak in there a couple at a time and make your mark then good luck, I'm all for it. If not and you're still hankerin' to risk your scalps, then go in force armed to the teeth. Hell, pack a cannon if you can handle it. And all the powder and lead you can carry. If you're strong enough, maybe they'll leave you be. But, if not, you'd better stay out of sight. Do your business at night. Stay low, hide out during the day. Burn dry, smokeless fires, if you must. Keep quiet, watch your every step and above all don't underestimate 'em; I'm here to tell you, these injuns will fool you every dang time."

I should've listened to the words coming out of my own mouth. And Johnny P, bless his soul, he never heard a word of warning I had to say. He pestered me relentlessly, to the point I couldn't take his infernal nagging one-day longer. I gave in. He knew I would. Kicked myself a hundred times since. It was the worst decision of my life. Potts' fate was sealed forever without so much as a headstone or a cairn of river rocks to mark his passing. As for me, well, all I can do is wait and pray and…

What's this? Yeah, that's right, I'm looking, if you can call it looking. Watch yourself! Uh huh! Slowly I begin to look about. But, I'm not seeing much. Blurring my vision, blood and sweat and tears and the trauma of it all conspire to wreak and present before me an unclear, confusing picture. I can barely make out the shapes of dozens of savages milling about me, their faces and individual features swarthy by nature, now entirely indistinct. I rub my eyes and still I cannot see clearly. Damn it! I want to scream my utter frustration. Yet, I dare not. What does it matter anyway? Maybe it's better this way, better to not see what's coming or who's bringing it on.

The wait is not long. Soon a hushed commotion settles over the hunting band like an early morning mist. My tormentors are suddenly quiet, looking to the gravelly beach near where I stand. The slain warrior, the recipient of Johnny's last defiant act, is solemnly placed over the back of his pony and led through the cottonwoods out onto the plains, no doubt heading to his kin's distant lodges. No sooner has the funeral procession faded from view, than the savages' grief returns, boiling over anew, sheer hatred twisting the emotions of the distraught heathens into a furious rage.

Wails and lamentations run its course, inevitably replaced by discordant grumblings, growling louder and louder, rising to a crescendo, a veritable fever's pitch, until a multitide of cries demanding revenge fill the air, sending shock waves rippling throughout my whole being. I waver momentarily, trying to remain strong. It's no use. It is a futile endeavor. A grim, forlorn malaise takes hold. I can't shake it. I flutter like a leaf in a storm, trembling in the wind beyond control.

They're coming. I can hear them angrily shoving aside other warriors, pushing their way through the crowded gauntlet that hems me in. The aggrieved kin of the slain warrior surge forward, weapons in hand. They crowd me closer and closer, leaving me with little room to squirm or breathe. The air about me becomes thick, almost suffocating. Slamming into my face, their every breath is fetid, acrid with the taste of hatred coating their tongues. Their bodies exude an abominable, unwashed stench so repugnant to my senses that I've all I can do to hold my last meal down. My knees rattle and knock, buckling under the strain, my vaunted mettle quickly deserts me. I fight to resist the trembling quakes defying my nerves, wracking my whole emotional being. I jerk. I flinch. I blink and quiver uncontrollably. Never have I known such fear, felt such desperation. I can't believe what's happening to me, the very heart and soul of my manhood. I'm no longer the John Colter I've always known. All that I've ever been and stood for flees in panic before their approach. At the very instance of emotional collapse an old man steps forward and takes control.

Yes, an old man, oddly familiar, the only one in the whole tribe who can. No one else holds such power and sway or commands such unanimous respect. No one else can blunt the inevitable thrust of Piegan retribution. Kootenae Appe, the able injun general of the pishkun plains, stops his braves at the height of their frenzy and saves my hide, momentarily prolonging fate.

I gaze through veiled eyes in disbelief, so complete is my astonishment. I shake my head, barely able to believe it true. It's as if the hand of Moses had parted the Red Sea of the Piegan Nation and waved me through.

Kootenae Appe speaks as much with his hands and his glaring eyes as he does with his words. He points to me, then to the east across the plains, directing my attention to the recently departed funerary cortege. Grim faced, he shakes his head almost sympathetically and looks down upon the shredded remains of my dear friend John Potts, now but a scattered mass of gore and pulp, decapitated limbs and head-impaled. He turns and faces in the direction of the "pishkun plains," and points with a stiff, almost accusatory finger. Anger steels his voice. Fury is etched ever so deeply in the steep canyons that furrow his brow, bespeaking volumes of unrequited vengeance. His fists punch the air casting imaginary lightning bolts hurtling my way. He knows that I'm the one, the white man whose "big medicine" firestick rained death on his warriors. He glares at me, eyeball to eyeball, challenging me to deny complicity, if I can.

I cannot. He knows I can't. So what's this all about? I've no clue what he's getting at. Surely, he isn't about to let me go free. He has no love for me or any other white man for that matter. So why, pray tell, has he stepped in?

I hear others talking. Near as I can figure, they must be the kin of the warrior Johnny slew. Their voices are filled with anger unassuaged. The dialogue between them and the old Indian is brief, heated and obviously demanding in tone.

"Ni-Kso-Ko-Wa! Ni-Kso-Ko-Wa!"

Over and over the same phrase is repeated in earnest. Whatever it means must be powerfully big to them. I strain to make out what few words of the Piegan dialect I know. Some I think I recognize. Most I do not. I'm certain that several warriors are near tears, barely able to contain their grief. While others amongst them are white hot, scowling in derision, their cries rage with passion and loathing. I can't help but tremble at the outright hatred looming my way, this unfettered desire demanding vengeance and reckoning. The charges arrayed against me are hurled furiously in my direction. I know not what they say, yet I have little doubt of their meaning. Only torture and death will do.

"Get on with it, you sons of bitches," I mumble rather defiantly, drunk with despair, resigned to my fate. Yet, I have to hand it to Kootenae Appe; he's doing a pretty good job of keeping his warriors reined in, but why? What's he waiting for? God damned injuns!

The chief suddenly turns and points again in the direction of the ancient pishkuns, to the sandstone cliffs beyond the Madison. I can make out the Piegan words for their Flathead enemies and the *Kee-kat-sah*, the Crow, as he recalls that bitter day. There's not a word of dispute from any of his warriors. He has them spellbound. And he isn't through. He points to the other bands besides just the kin, the *Ni-Kso-Ko-Wa* and rambles on until he includes damn near every injun there. His intent has become painfully obvious, even to my enfeebled brain.

So that's it. Even a fool like me can see that the old boy is struggling to decide how he's going to divide me up fair and square between them all. Oh, great! The bloody bastard is divvying me up so every one of his stinking savages can get their fair slice of Colter pie. I bow my head, cringing at the thought of what they hold in store and pray, beseeching my God for a swift deliverance. What else can I hope for? The old man has got me convinced, for soon every danged one of 'em is looking my way and nodding in agreement. I turn my head aside to avoid the hundreds of dark, penetrating eyes glaring my way, hungrily licking their chops. I want to shrink right down to the size of a river pebble and hide myself in beach gravel to escape their fiendish glares. Whom am I kidding? There's no escape. There's just time dwindling away, what little I've of it. My God, what a pathetic sight I must be to them, cowering, tail between my legs like a whipped dog, all the while awash in Johnny's guts and gore.

While Kootenae Appe and the Ni-Kso-Ko-Wa argue my fate, I sense that my time is nearing, one way or another. Of a sudden I'm feeling defiant. Are you going to take this lying down? What would Pa or Uncle John say? The Captains would expect a helluva lot better from one of their own men. Don't shame them or yourself. You'd better come up with something, boy, and mighty fast. C'Mon, Johnboy, think. There's got to be a way out of this mess. Think! Think! Use that noggin of yours. Addled, as I might be, my mind starts to work again, slowly taking in the woods, the river and what little I can see of the surrounding lay of the land. It is a most awkward, desperate quest. My eyes continue to burn; everything about me is still hazy. Tears well and run down my cheeks, stream over my lips. My tongue flickers, gathering in the salty dew and rolls what little moisture there is around the inside of my mouth. I lick my lips back and forth, the taste of tears almost satisfying. My struggle continues; my eyelids and lashes are near to becoming caked shut by Potts' drying blood. I've got to try it again. I must be able to see. I have to know what lies ahead for John Colter. My face contorts, twisting and straining, the exertion eventually forces lashes and lids to respond. I dare not move a hand to wipe the scum away. Too obvious, the guards are too damn close by. Watch it! Don't let 'em see you. Don't antagonize 'em. They like whupping you way too much. It's too easy for 'em to reach over and whack you good with a stone-headed warclub or jab you with the butt end of a spear. Fist and feet you can handle, those crude weapons are another-matter all together. Yes, I fear 'em, all right. I've plenty of reason to. And, yet, I don't. My Scotch/Irish is way too stubborn. I hate their guts, everything they stand for. I won't give 'em the satisfaction. Besides, what's a little pain compared to losing a lifetime of self-respect? Guile and the will to live keep me thinking and plotting. Somehow, someway, I must resist, yet play a most convincing game. Be the possum, act it out, string 'em along, but keep my cool, control mounting frustration and... fight, repress with every ounce of strength I have the hopelessness that wants to consume and overwhelm the last morsels of my resolve.

Without warning, I sense the presence of two, tall sinewy young warriors standing by me. Reptilian glances watch my every move. I can feel the very heat their loathing generates. Barely able to control their unchecked fury, when the mood suits them, the two braves take turns striking, pummeling me with their clubs and their fists. They beat me down to the ground, and still that's not enough to satisfy a most wanton bent to chastise, to punish me. They kick me incessantly in the ribs, guts and head. Indefensible plight arouses a deep malignant hatred within them, goading them to thrash me again and again. They can't seem to get enough; the more they hit me, the more they want to. They continue unabated, insidious laughter highlighting their glee.

Common sense warns me to stay still, act the conquered lamb and lay prostrate at their feet. But, I'm way too stubborn now; my pride is too great to stifle. I refuse to concede the last vestiges of dignity so easily to such wretched cowards. To hell with 'em, I say, death awaits me, but I'll spit in their eyes. I don't have to take their shit without a fight. I have my own sense of *namachkani*; my own war honor, and my two zealous tormentors are about to witness a double ration of Colter mettle. I straighten like a bent tree to weather their arrogant Piegan wind, defiant 'til the last breath and thought in my body and soul. I literally confound my ownself. Something is happening to me inside. A surge of anger anew, grief replaced by enmity and the will to live, to fight-on another day. It isn't courage solely that compels me. No, what they had done to Johnny P they meant to do to me. I hold no delusions; surely my fate is soon to be sealed. My life's last minutes are nearing to a final conclusion. And I know it. So what's giving rise to such sudden defiance? What brings me back from the depths of despair and hopelessness? I'll tell you. It's the disdain they hold for Johnny and me and everyone else in the wilderness for that matter. The irreverence and irrelevance they hold for the dignity of human life outside of the three tribes that constitute the Blackfeet Nation. Their contempt for all other men makes me mad. And in so realizing it my anger swells, soon giving rise to hatred, giving further rise to an uncommon renewal of strength, slowly but surely begetting the steely resolve I've always known. I'm coming back, come hell or high water, consequences be-damned.

Kootenae Appe watches me stand up. The old Indian steps forward, pushing the young guards aside. He stares directly in my face, taking my measure, curious as to what kind of man I truly am. He looks me over from head to toe. Locks into my eyes, trying to understand what I'm seeing and thinking and doing.

Yeah, have a good look, injun. You'll never see my like again. Will you look at him? He's amazed. He doesn't know what to think. He just can't figure me out. Uh oh, here come the rest of 'em.

Now they're all curious, edging forward to get a closer, better look. I stand before them with a blank vacant stare, as far away as my mind's gaze can reach, revealing nothing for them to see or read. I remain mute. I don't waver or flinch or wink. I've gathered-up all the self-control I can muster. I know I'm playing with hell. Yet, I have to keep it up. It's a deadly game I've chosen, the longer I play, the longer I live. But, it's also a double edged blade.

Kootenae Appe is speaking to me. I'm befuddled, recognizing little of what he has to say. I continue the addled state. My silence frustrates him. He wants answers. He wants to see fear and respect. Again, he tries talking to me, this time haltingly in the language of the Crow. Several times he repeats. "*Napikwan, Ahkoto waktai Sakum. Ahkoto waktai Sakum.*"

I vaguely remember hearing that phrase before. Toby had mentioned it once on the way to the hunt. Spoke of it in wary tones as if it should be avoided. I had almost forgotten it in the maelstrom of events. I shake my head replying somewhat feebly in the language of the Absaroka, "Me no understand."

The old injun's about to lose his patience. He repeats rather forcefully, "*Napikwan.... Ahkoto waktai Sakum.*" As he speaks, he spreads his hands and arms out cutting a wide swath as if to encompass the whole mountain-rimmed valley-floor where we now stand.

His last gesture finally sinks in. I understand what he wants to say, "many-come-together country." That's it, the three rivers coming together.

"Ahhh! Now I know what your tryin' to say, chief. *Ahkoto waktai Sakum*, you mean the Three Forks. Hell, chief, why didn't you say so?" I nod my head, a small smile appears, pleased that we finally find something we can agree on.

The war chief's face suddenly waxes grim, brooding storm clouds darkening an already swarthy pallor. Gritting his teeth his jaws clench and tighten like a steel beaver trap, his dark beady orbs narrowly focusing on my own reddened, weary eyes. And in the Crow dialect we both seemed to agree on, the old man avows in no uncertain terms, "*Ahkoto waktai Sakum*... belongs to Piegan peoples."

I want to say we come in peace, we mean no harm, but it's way too late for that, and the thought never has a chance to form the words nor pass my lips. The last thing I remember is the tremendous thud of a heavy warclub slamming down hard on the back of my skull. Darkness and the twinkling stars of a heavenly night fall over my eyes before I hit the ground.

How much time has passed, I do not know, but the sun has risen to its full height and several hours for sure have elapsed since Johnny's death. I'm slowly coming out of the fog of unconsciousness. I begin to stir, finding myself wallowing about the pebbled beach, awash in blood and gore, river rock and sand. My head hurts, incessantly, sharp violent jolts wrack my skull, both my orbs recede, fleeing deeper and deeper into their sockets. There's no escape from the pain. But I'm still alive, though; I can barely believe it. Best not to move, John. Better to lay still, see what if anything has changed.

But, I can't. The tiniest of critters won't let me. Gnats, hordes of swarming pesky, unrelenting gnats buzz about me, covering my head in a dense black cloud, crawling in my ears, up my nose, in my eyes. What a nightmare! Lord God…

Ooomph! A violent kick to the ribs, followed immediately by several harder thrusts variously delivered to my belly and backside, painfully deep and punishing. All the breath in my body seems to gush right out of me. I moan. I hack in fits of spasm coughing up gobs of blood-laden phlegm. The pummeling stops, leaving me flopping about like the proverbial fish out of water. Several minutes pass. Slowly my breathing returns to a more recognizable pace, though each agonizing gasp stabs me anew with pain. Respite, however, is brief.

Barely unintelligible grunts gather in my ear. I can't seem to respond. I hear them again, louder more forceful. I look up to see the dim outline of a tall, swarthy Blackfeet warrior standing straddled over me. His hand is moving, motioning me to stand. I move ever so slowly, arising unassisted to all fours. I feel weak, lifeless. The effort takes all my strength. Without warning he delivers another swift, violent kick to my flanks.

"Ooomph!" The wind rushes right out of me again and sends me sprawling back to the ground.

I hear myself moaning. It's the only sound to hear. All else is drowned out. Gingerly touching my side, I probe tender ribs, searching for damage. It should hurt, but it doesn't. I won't let it. Beat to hell, but not broken, I'm damn near immune to their cruelty by now. But, I can't show it. Got to keep the ruse going. C'mon, Colter, play it out, give 'em what they want to see. C'mon, groan, louder, let 'em hear you.

They howl in delight, hundreds of rollicking savages beside themselves in glee. What sport, what Lilliputian fun they're having at my expense. A second warrior steps up. The two of them grab an arm and jerk me to my feet. I'm left to wobble unassisted, teetering on unsteady legs, trying to regain my balance and what little composure I have left within to fortify me.

Kootenae Appe is arguing once again. A verbal duel with his warriors careens back and forth in heated debate. They're all shouting. The infuriated family members, the *Ni-Kso-Ko-Wa*, are still here, enraged at the delay. But, new arrivals have joined the fray.

I listen, straining to hear and to see, struggling to open still blood-caked eyelids. I concentrate for the longest of seconds. Vaguely, I recognize some of these newcomers. No, how can I? Come on, John get a hold of yourself, you're seeing things. These injuns are all the same. And yet there is a familiarity to this band of recent arrivals. My mind, my memory can't seem to shake them. Yes, they must be the ones. It just wasn't that long ago. They're still vivid in my mind; that first hunting band that had charged so recklessly into the entrenched ranks of the Flatheads; the bold, defiant ones who bared their backsides and rumps daring me to shoot. Somehow they stand taller, prouder then the others. Yes, it's them, all right. I'm sure of it. And then the thought, the recognition leaves me completely. I shake my head, scrunch my eyes. My mind slips in and out of the fog, confused and disoriented. I'm having a devil of a time concentrating. There's too much going on. Give it up, Colter. What difference does it make now, they're all the same.

I listen as they continue to debate my fate. The horror of the battle by the "pishkun plains" comes racing back to my mind. Hell, I'm hardly an hour's ride away. Inexplicably, I feel the long musket-ball scar on my thigh tingling anew, drawing me to it in the strangest of ways. And I wonder, searching amidst the throng of savages mulling about me, which of these red hided skunks put the lead in my leg? If I can only get a hold of my rifle, but I put the thought instantly out of my head. You fool – you go too far. I resist a chuckle, concealing the tiniest, wriest of smirks. I've got to watch myself, but at least I know I'm not losing my mind. I'm still holding on strong. I'm getting testy, though. And, I don't know how much more of this I can take. My constitution grows noticeably weaker. My thirst unbelievably great. I lick my lips with a dry desiccated tongue, looking longingly towards the friggin' Jefferson River all but a few yards away. My belly growls like a hungry bear, yet breakfast was but six hour ago. Smoked beaver tail, damn, it was delicious. Johnny loved it, once he got used to it. That Potts, I picture him earlier this morning before we took to the river, so full of life. Damn rascal, always finding something to laugh about, always pulling my leg. Now look at him. Somebody has got to pay. Those dirty stinking polecats I fume barely able to hide the rage. My rancor is now every bit as strong as my fear. But will I have the chance to prove which one the greater? I grit my teeth and continue to stare. Hold on, John. Hold on.

The ol' eyes are coming around. The fog is clearing up. Thank you, Lord. For once I can see the ongoing debate without obstruction. Look at 'em arguing over me like they're swapping for trade goods. Hey, I want to yell at 'em, there's no fur on my hide. I'm not worth a dang thing. Do you hear me you dumb savages? Yeah, right! Quit wasting your breath, Colter. They're not interested in swapping. It's your hide and scalp they want, boy; every last injun here wants a piece of you. You'd better get use to it. Hummph! Yeah, right, fat chance. There's far too dang many to please, and too little of me to go around. As I watch the warchief cajole his braves, I conjure up a little more sarcasm, just barely muttering over my breath.

"Oh, he's so durn fair, a regular Rocky Mountain's Solomon, right out of the Good Book. Hey, heathen, wish to hell you'd make up your dang mind and get this thing a goin' before I freeze to death."

An unstoppable chortle busts right out of my gut. Thank God, nobody's paying attention to me. I'm irrelevant, who cares what I think or say. Just shut up and wait like a good white man to meet your maker.

That dull throbbing ache in my head is still there, along with midday heat and the arrival of a lone bluenose fly looking for someone to aggravate. My eyes leave the chief, wandering elsewhere now, slowly getting my bearings. I'm thinking gamble, risk it all. The Jefferson's right behind me, not a stone's-throw away. I glance left, watch the river curve towards high sandstone crags maybe a half a mile to the north. Picture the shallow bedded river-course as it sweeps eastbound towards its junction with the Madison and Gallatin to form the great muddy river. I know the spot well, camped there twice in more agreeable times with the Corps. Forded the wetlands just weeks before on the way here. Is that the way to go? My mind wonders on painting the rest of the valley, due east across the plains to the Madison. How far away is it? If I cut straight for it, four, five, maybe six miles, over treeless terrain, with no place to hide or turn to. Just flat-out run as fast as I can with all the Blackfeet in the world on my ass, if they give me the chance. And that's a mighty big undecided if. Both choices are maddening. I can't make up my mind. Don't be stupid. Patience, think this thing out. Use what little time you've left. You haven't lived this long to go throwing your life away on a foolish gamble. Something will come up, but what? I look back once again. The Jefferson, close as it is, will do me no good. They'll head me off long before I can reach it and chop me up like they did poor Johnny, raw meat for the wild critters. No, I won't have a chance that a way. Once again I start to look to the East, reconsidering. Unaccountably, silence snaps me back.

The debate is over. The talking has ceased. Instantly I'm drawn to the old injun chief striding directly towards me. Kootenae Appe's face, dark and worn as it is, is now decidedly clear and resolute. His warriors' eyes trail his approach, shifting to lock right in on the two of us. Momentarily there is a strange, almost unexplainable silence, blocking out even the wind and the river, the din of the entire valley. My heart pounds away at my eardrums and won't stop its incessant beat.

Uh oh! This is it. The wait's over. Looks like the old injun is making up my mind for me. Humph, 'bout time, thank God, the dang wait's killing me, them, too, for that matter. I can sense the anxiety and tension in the hundreds of warriors crowding around me. Smiles, sinister, sneering, evil smiles form on their faces before my very eyes. I jerk, anticipating renewed whipping. I can't help it. I'm damn near unnerved. Look at 'em. Look at their faces, they're all smiling, so friggin' full of confidence. The sons of bitches are not to be denied or disappointed, or so they think.

"*Napikwan.*" Kootenae Appe scowls in my face. There is scorn and derision in his voice. He's no longer arbitrating disputes. He's fixing to settle a score. His glare is unwavering, filled with contempt.

Whoa! Listen to him now, will you, proud as the devil? He barks out commands like ol' Sgt. Ordway, swaggering like a peacock on Blackfoot parade. I hear and smell an assurance in his voice not evident before. I can only surmise that the great national dilemma is over. The venerable sage of the Piegan people is vexated no longer; he's found a just solution for all his savage heathens to agree upon. Pshaw!

God, forgive me, I want to smash his face in and cringe in fear all at once. I feel an incredible sense of trepidation and anger. I swallow hard, there's nothing there; my mouth and throat are as dry as bleached bone. I tremble, barely noticeable to all but me. The anticipation is more than I can bear. Silently, I command the warchief, "C'mon, let's hear it. I'm ready for you. Spit it out, chief."

Pointing to my feet and legs, Kootenae Appe makes a deft running motion with his fingers off in the direction of the Madison. In halting Crow, the chief asks, "You, *napikwan*... run fast?"

Run fast? So that's the way it's going to be. I know what he's getting at and what he wants me to say. I know their cat and mouse game and how they intend to play. I'm to be the fox to their hounds. Primitive sport to appease savage appetites. Hmmph! Funny way to look at it, all right. Play the game, but die like a man. Hah! Man, my ass, a hunted animal is more like it. Chickenshit odds, but it's the choice I've been praying for all along.

Yeah, I can run fast. But, I'm not about to tell you. Let's see how you like being played the fool. I stare back at Kootenae Appe with a dumb, bug-eyed look on my face. Timidly, I shake my head as if I don't understand.

Again, the chief make his fingers run, "You... run fast, *Napikwan?*" He's damned near shouting at me now.

Taking my time, I reply, "Slow... like turtle." And I make the sign of that creeping, crawling, slow and deliberate shell-bound carapaced creature.

He just doesn't seem to get it, and this time it's my turn for frustration to wear thin. "See if you can understand this, you dumb injun."

I drop down to my knees and tear away a patch of grass to reveal the bare sod below. I smooth a spot in the ground, my trigger finger goes to doodling, drawing a scrawny looking turtle right there in the dirt for the old chief to see. Somewhat pleased, I shrug my shoulders proud of the effort. It's the best I can do, and besides drawing and doodling were never my stronger suits.

Kootenae Appe gets it, all right. Finally he understands. Satisfaction spreads over his face as he breaks out into a grin as wide as the Missouri. Turning towards his waiting minions, he cries out in unadulterated glee,

"Spoo-pii... spoo-pii!"

Upon hearing their chief's response the whole throng breaks out in an uncontrollable burst of laughter, picking up the chant. *"Spoo-pii, spoo-pii, spoo-pii!"* They can hardly contain themselves at the thought of such an easy, defenseless prey.

Finally, we have our answer. A run for life or a run for death, it all boils down to whose medicine is strongest today. Huh! Well, I'll be. But, fuck 'em, this thing isn't over yet. They've had a golden chance to finish me off and be done with it. I would've sworn that after what they did to Johnny they would've done to me without a second thought. There is a God in Heaven, after all. Careful, boy, don't tip your hand. Keep the sniveling façade; shake and tremble, let those big blue eyes pop out of your head in mock, wide-eyed horror. Pour it on, twitch and jerk. I cover my face with my hands in a vain attempt to shut out the whole cruel world.

My act is pretty good. They're eating it up. Look at 'em laughing and giggling, slapping their knees and pointing to me the pathetically timid *napikwan* cowering before them. My deception is so almost complete that it's all I can do to contain my own sarcastic wit from truly exposing fraud.

Yeah, *spoo-pii* I am you filthy heathen swine. Just let me get my legs a runnin' and I'll show you the fastest turtle you've ever seen. "Keep it up, John. Keep it up. Make 'em think they've hog-tied a real worm."

But, I'm not fooling myself. I'm scared right down to the tender soles of my bare feet. And I know it. Silently, I pray to God Almighty to give me just one chance. I swear a sacred oath right then and there, if He can see it my way I'll be shed of these mountains and the West forever.

"Lord, hear my prayer. Give thy servant, John, one more chance and I'll be shed of this land for good."

I don't know whether He hears me or not, but anticipating salvation my heart steadily beats faster. I can feel adrenaline gather and surge through my limbs. I fairly tingle with freshly renewed life and spirit. The dull aches, the sharp pains, the suffering, bruised, damaged ribs are still with me. They're not about to vanish. I take several, deep, reviving breaths, suck-up my discomfort, and resolve to command the pain to go away.

The chief, ignoring my prayer, again turns to his anxious battalions and repeats the well-received news. Once again they whoop and cheer over the *spoo-pii's* turtleian response.

I stand with my head bent forward, hopelessly alone. My pulse races and my heart beats and pounds like a gigantic human drum… boom, boom, boom. I try to quell the angst, conserve my energy and my nerve. I whisper, musing quietly out loud to bolster my spirits, "like the Christians and the lions in ol' Coliseum days." Again, I want to laugh, but, God, I know I can't. It doesn't matter. He who laughs last… Nothing else matters now, except getting away, gaining freedom, go like the wind; go with every ounce of strength I have within me.

Kootenae Appe grabs me tightly by my arm and spins me around.

"Come, *Napikwan*," he tersely commands.

We walk out onto the grassy plains away from the tall cottonwoods that border the river. I hear no movement to follow. Casually, I glance back over my shoulder. Good, they're still waiting. No one's making a move. What a break, they're giving me a head start, but how much of one I'll have to wait and see.

Sharp pains suddenly lace and prick the tender pads of my bare feet and I wince in pain. Damn, what in the hell's that? I look earthward towards the cause of my discomfort and instantly recognize the sharp spines of the prickly pear. Those stickers are as sharp as needles and a thousand times more numerous than the quills on a porcupine's back. Another stab of pain and another and another as the stickers again and again lace my hide, penetrating deep into my unprotected soles. Gingerly, I hop about forced to pick and choose every step. The nettlesome cacti are everywhere, dotting the plains abundant as grass. "How in the hell am I gonna run in this briar patch? Quit feelin' sorry for yourself, God dang it. Now's not the time to go soft."

Kootenae Appe sees my dilemma, and for some odd reason feels compelled to help. The ol' rogue pointing to the prickly pear grunts a brilliantly insightful, "*Ugh!* No good."

I look into his narrow-set black eyes, nodding appreciation and with all the sarcasm I can muster, "Well, no shit, chief. Damn kind of you to point it out. Here you're 'bout ready to have your people shred me to Kingdom come and all of a sudden-like, you're worried 'bout me stubbin' my toes. Don't think I'm not grateful. I just don't think much of y'all's hospitality."

Spit flies out of my mouth. I'm boiling and seething, damn near hissing like my Ma's favorite ol' teakettle. I stare him down, spewing a most comtemptuous, "And fuck you, too, you red-hided injun son of a bitch."

I'm beyond anger. I'm downright livid at the death of my good friend Johnny Potts, at the torture, the humiliation, the shame, the beating and the inhuman situation I now found myself in. Immeasurable anger and grief have merged, giving vent to outright determination. Determination into resolve as I steel myself anew for the run ahead.

Out on the short-grass plains, we come to a halt. I look back to the cottonwoods. The old man is not giving me more than three or four hundred yards' lead. Mighty game of 'em, I muse, mighty game. I nod my head. This is as good as its going to get. That's all right. It'll do. I immediately take in my position one last time. I look east and north. All other directions are not worth a moment's consideration. The Jefferson still meanders on my left flank, now over a few hundred yards away. Uh huh! Maybe that's what they expect me to do. I can probably beat them there. But, so what? Where do I go from there? I glance to my right to the south where rests high bluffs rising a couple hundred feet above the valley floor with nothing but open rolling grassy prairies beyond, hardly a good candidate for freedom.

With my arm still solidly in his grip, Kootenae Appe urges me to run. Again, he grunts in his Algonkian dialect encouraging me anew to flee for my life.

The ranks of Piegans still waiting back by the riverbank are suddenly alive with the prospect of the chase. No longer able to contain pent-up ferocity for revenge, their anxiety level reaches a fever's pitch. War whoops explode, slicing through the air, galvanizing the Piegans into one mighty host of avenging spirits.

"Ah-eeee-ah, ah-eeee-ah," scream their untamed chorus.

I hear their cries. I turn my head to see hundreds of the red devils tearing off their fringed hunting shirts and buckskin leggings, stripping down to the near-nakedness of their loincloths, ready for the hunt to begin. Yeah, stripped down naked, all right, but armed and moccasin-shod. Numbers apparently are not enough to pad their deck. No, they like it stacked. They laugh and joke amongst themselves, their glee is sensed and heard. From where I stand, it's easy to discern their evil determination. No thought of any chance is given to me. For me to be their equal is beyond the imagination or the comprehension of their arrogant minds. Even worse, for me to be their better, impossible. Their pride and vanity would never allow it. No, to them that wait so eagerly for the race to begin, this is deadly sport. A contest of friendly rivalry between the families, bands and individual heroes of their nation, with one lone, unarmed man, to play and toy with. They're the hares, I the turtle. Suddenly, the timid naked white man whom they once held in such awe is now the haplessly slow turtle, the *spoo-pii*. Smiles beam across every expectant face as they each ready to win the day. What could be easier or more pre-ordained?

I take this energized scene all in. Good, no ponies, they'll all be on foot. Johnny boy, your prospects are looking up. Suddenly, the door is open; my way grows clearer, my chances to live, to flee, brighter and brighter. There's hope, after all. It's an inward, sly smile that grows as I look ahead across the plains to the Madison. My focus narrows on the intended path ahead, shutting all else from view. I clench my teeth. I can feel the muscles in my jaws forging together like white-hot steel. Mind, body and spirit unite in determination. I gird up my loins in preparation. My legs ready to go as I shake them repeatedly to get the blood flowing. Blackfeet arrogance has infused my confidence with Olympian strength. They will soon find out just how slow the lowly *spoo-pii* really is.

I ignore the raucous melee roaring away behind my back by the forest's edge and look eastward towards the snowcapped Mountains of the Wolf and its pass to freedom. The way to the Madison lies unobstructed, not a single warrior is visible on the entire plains. Get ready, John. No tricks, no dodges or ruses, just get as fast as your legs can carry you. Make a straight beeline east to the Madison. Put time and distance between you. Watch it though, both may be your friend or your foe. Gauge your strength. Use your head. It's up to you now. Deliverance is at hand. Somewhere ahead beyond the plains lies salvation. I stretch my limbs one more time; rotating my shoulders and arms, loosely shaking both legs as Kootenae Appe steps back and watches my exercise. I gather all of my mental and emotional reserves. I prepare to ignite the fuse to start the race of my life, a race I will not lose. Fear and hatred, hatred and fear, the two are equally driving me. Suddenly, I curse aloud the Piegan Nation with every vile expletive I know. Adrenaline surges through my naked body, rushing with the speed and the force of a midsummer thunderclap. I'm ready. God Almighty, I'm ready.

Kootenae Appe knows it, too. He has sensed a change in my attitude. He stands back as if astonished, unprepared for this totally unexpected transformation in the timid *spoo-pii* he thought he knew.

He should've known better. He should've known the caliber of man I was from our very first encounter. Now, he's underestimated me for the last time and by a long shot. Tough shit! As far as I'm concerned, it's a horse on him: his dice, his game, his roll and his loss. He won't get another chance to roll if I have anything to say about it.

"*Napikwan*," he urges. "*Kyi! Kyi!* Go, go away," his voice cracks. That confident air of minutes before has suddenly left him. He's no longer quite so sure.

I don't even bother to glance his way, but swear from parched, cracked lips. "My name's Colter, injun. Don't forget it."

I'm off, with the winds from the West blowing at my back, chewing up the plain's grassy sod, swift stride after swift stride, like an antelope possessed. Ignoring the pain from my bleeding and swollen pricked feet, I run like I've never run before, pushing myself, faster and faster, pumping my arms, lifting my legs. Life now flows through my veins as pent-up emotions of hate and fear release in an unrestrained quest for freedom. I need not look back. A resounding Blackfeet huzzah rips through the air, hurled aloft by a cacophonous human whirlwind alerting me to all I need to know. The pursuit is on in earnest. My first step was the tacit signal that sends the Piegans chasing after me. That they are quick and up to the run, I've no doubts. I know all too well what they're capable of. For they're born to the wilderness. This is their sport.

This is a race they're meant to win. They'll hurl themselves after me with all the grim determination of a rabid wolf pack of lobos hell-bent on a kill.

    Hundreds of near naked armed warriors waste not another second's time and bolt from the cottonwoods like skittery Thoroughbreds exploding from the starting line. Charging headlong out onto the plains, colliding into one another blindly in haste, racing recklessly at full speed regardless of their own stamina and strength, each warrior drives himself to be the first to reach the *napikwan* and bring him down. The competition amongst the varied bands is absolutely fierce. They all have something to prove for this day will live on in the songs and paeans of exultation of their people for many winters to come. One mile flies swiftly by. The pace continues unabated. Sweat flows. Soon another mile passes. Cheers and exhortations are fading by now. War whoops and bravado cease all together, replaced by the steady pounding of a multitude of clad feet and the ragged heave of heavy breaths as each runner digs deep into his own well of endurance. One by one, long sinewy limbs tighten. Lungs burn with every gasp, while hundreds of hearts beat at a much faster, more unsustainable rate. Soon they will pound out of control. The bunched mass of warriors that had lined the riverbank has become strung out in a long, undisciplined column of mostly weary stragglers.

    The tenacious ones, the surviving kin, the *ni-kso-ko-wa* and the veterans of that earlier spring battle push each other forward, strengthened by their hatred, their rapacious hunger for revenge, each one's example compelling all others to greater output, greater effort. They will not stop. They will not falter. The chase will only end with the *napikwan's* death and bloodletting. But, who will bring him down? Whose lodge pole will the *spoo-pii's* scalp dangle from tonight? Which warrior will have the honor of parading the *napikwan's* impaled head about the village in triumph? These are the great, soon to be answered questions. And this is the great competition. Never will a prize be pursued more ardently.

    Yet, as the race wears on and one, two, three miles of grassy, prickly-pear infested plains are soon covered, they can't believe what they're now seeing. The *spoo-pii* is not slowing down at all. If anything his pace has picked up or at least has settled down to a comfortable, seemingly sustainable gait. He shows no sign of weakening. The fun, the victory is not forthcoming as easily as they expected it to. What deviltry, what evil medicine is this to deny them so? Could the *napikwan* have fooled them? His pace seems more like that of a *ponokamita* than a *spoo-pii*. Is his medicine once again stronger than theirs? No, it can not be so. He will tire, soon. He must.

    As Kootenae Appe watches from the edge of the plains he suspects as much. He knew the very instant the *napikwan* fled that he had been hoodwinked by a clever trickster. He watches in horror as the *spoo-pii* speeds across the plains as if on winged feet, like an *ah-wa-kas*, a prairie runner, the antelope, the windeater, faster then all of the speediest of his young warriors. But, he's not quite so sure of who or what he has freed. This can be no ordinary white man, with such swift powerful strides, not when he races across the prairie at near break-neck speed. The *napikwan's* fleeting escape laughs in his face, scorning his mock-generosity, belittling his honor and ultimately his nation's *namachkani*. His whole nation's reputation is now in serious jeopardy if this escape is allowed to go on. He asks himself, from where does this strange white-man derive such powerful medicine? What propels him to such a killing pace? And what has he, the warchief of his people, allowed to happen? He looks to the ground afraid to answer his own question.

How far have I run? How close are they? Are they gaining? I've got to know. Got to look back. No! Don't! You can't. Don't be a fool. Keep going. Keep going. Run. Run. Run.

Doubt hounds my heels, snapping at every step along the way. Fear propels me, my will to survive battling encroaching fatigue with every laboring gasp. Desperately, I think of more pleasant times to keep my mind off of the torture of the run. I recall those distant days of my youth, when, as a young sprout, I ran through the fields and woods of Stuarts Draft to nearby Tinkling Springs. I flew like wing-footed Hermes, exhilarated by the sheer freedom that my swift feet and strong heart and lungs had given me. I had been a runner of renown from my earliest days. Prided myself in my speed, my stamina. I ran for fun. I ran for the love of it. I relished competition, the thrill of pushing myself to the limit and beyond, defying all others to win the day. Try as I might, those sweet memories of yesteryear soon give way to the here and now as the fading cries of my pursuers jog me back to the race of my life.

How long has the chase gone on I can't begin to say. By now tunnel vision has set in, taking a near-blinding hold. Mile after mile at full steam has finally taken my measure. My breaths are shallow now, coming fast and furious in agonizing gasps. My sides ache, wracked with pain. The staccato pumping of my racing heart and pounding eardrums revive that awful thud that had crashed into my skull just hours before. Each stride of leaden legs and flailing arms bring searing pain anew, flashing throughout my body in the most telling of ways. My throat and lungs burn, smoldering as if on fire. Desperately, I want water, even spit or saliva will do. Yet, I have nothing with which to swallow. Capillaries in the interior of my nasal passages rebel at the strain and burst in a torrent of blood, streaming, no, gushing out of my nostrils in an unending flow, splattering my face, my chest and shoulders red and sticky with the precious fluid of my life.

Inevitably it begins to happen. I knew it would. I've put it out of my mind for as long as I can. It's time to pay the piper. I can only hope that my efforts have gained greater ground than has theirs. For I'm slowing down, weakness and exhaustion have set in and are here to stay. Fight as I might, as dearly as I want to, I have nothing left to give; every ounce of my reserve has been used up. The run becomes a stumbling, drunken stupor of a walk. Soon even that effort is too great an exertion to bear and I come to an abrupt, dead stop. Exhaustion bends me over like a wizened stalk of corn; my hands rest heavily on my knees to support a great heaving, sagging weight. My breaths continue unabated in horrid gasps, wheezing and coughing uncontrollably. Phlegm, blood, and sweat pour out of me. I try to come about. I fight to regain my strength, my vitality before it's too late.

In delirium I curse, "You've gone out too fast." On the very edge of unconsciousness, I exhort myself to renew my vigor, my fight and my resolve. "Come on John. Fight, fight," I command myself, screaming intermittently between ragged wheezes. "You're a better man than this. Save yourself. Don't give up now. Think of what they did to Johnny. C'mon!"

Looking back through the fog of fatigue, across the plains from whence I came, I can see that the huge Blackfeet wolfpack has dwindled down to one. The last three or four stalwart warriors have pushed each other onward, beyond the limits of their endurance, until only one, a magnificent young brave in the prime of his aboriginal youth keeps up the chase. He has the look in his eyes of a man not to be denied. He takes great pride in his physical prowess and vaunted warrior manhood. Numerous feathers in his long raven hair belie great deeds as a Blackfeet warrior. The breadth of his shoulders, the strength that they imbue and his obvious great stamina are readily apparent even at a distance. But what really strikes home is his indomitable resolve, a will that keeps him going all the way across the plains, even after all others have fallen behind, until he has me almost within his reach. As he draws nearer, the features of his face become clearer, more distinct and soon curiously recognizable. It is the malice in his eyes, a look so utterly and completely filled with hatred that finally triggers the memory of that fateful day all over again. Whoa! Who do we have here? I know the face. I know this young warrior. Yes! Yes! Where have I seen him before? I look, straining, 'til I finally answer my own question. Good God Almighty… Running Wolf! Instantly, my heart plummets. Suddenly, I know, just like I had sensed deep down those many months ago on the pishkun plains, that it has to be this way.

Ah hah! Looking ahead, through his own clouded and exhausted vision, Running Wolf watches the *napikwan* struggle. The white *spoo-pii*, the devil with the big medicine fire-stick is close to losing them all, just one mile shy of the swift flowing Straight and its many twisted channels and wooded islands. With each closing step he senses his prey's fatigue and his anticipation grows. All the hate that has gathered within him, from the first day he layed eyes on the strange white newcomer those months before now come to bear fully and finally. But, with the prize in reach he becomes oblivious to his own flagging reserves. His hasty youthfulness, his overwhelming desire to be the first to strike blood rashly disregards his body's warning signs. All he knows is that the white man has stopped. The curse of the *napikwan* is about to be lifted with his scalp, once and for all. And he in his righteous fervor is the Piegan warrior deigned by *Api-stoh-toh-ki*, the Great Spirit to avenge his people.

He can barely contain himself. All glory and honor is his to take; standing bent-over in front of him, helpless, exhausted. Obediently, the trophy waits to be vanquished by him and him alone. Let the word be passed to the Siksika and the Blood and the Gros Ventre du Plaines. Let the drums speak around his people's campfires, let the great victory celebration begin, the scalp dance is near at hand. *Maa-koyou-mah'-kaa* soon dons a new mantle to be celebrated throughout his nation as a *mo-twin-ik*... a chief of his people. He will take a new name, as is his right, to be now and forever called *Maa-koyou*... the Wolf, befitting the noble stature of his deeds.

"*Spoo-pii*," he gloats, screaming ever so carelessly during the last few strides of his approach, "you are mine."

I remain all but defenseless, as I watch Running Wolf's charge. I hear his screams. I swear he's gloating. It's almost too easy for him as he rears back his stone-headed spear, grasping the shaft firmly with both hands and lunges forward at full tilt to drive his weapon home.

I have no hope of escaping this young warrior. Instinctively, I felt his presence upon my back long before I heard the sounds of his moccasins skimming across the grassy plains as the winds from the West collided with his magnificent body. I make no overt move to defend myself or to foolishly counsel any further flight. I'm surprisingly calm, patiently watching his final charge as he rapidly closes the span that separates us. Exhausted still, I take several last reviving breaths and prepare myself for the onslaught.

Ten paces, five paces away, Running Wolf's final war cry heralds the *spoo-pii's* intended demise. His arm stretches even further rearward, twisting his hips near-fully to the rear-right to maximize full thrust. His spear's forward motion now comes home in a calculated lunge to run his prey through.

At the last possible second I straighten up and turn obliquely away from the path of Running Wolf's oncoming charge.

"What? No!" he screams from the deepest darkest depths of mortal fear.

Too late, were Running Wolf's final thoughts as he stumbles forward, tripping over his own tangled feet, his body tumbling end over end. He can't stop his spear's downward plunge as the chipped stone-blade buries itself in the hard ground below. The shaft snaps mid-handle throwing the hapless youth head over heels in an uncontrollable somersault, slamming him rudely to the ground below. He goes down way too hard. That and his last bit of exertion takes everything out of him.

He lies sprawled, momentarily without wind or power, defenseless before me. My reaction is not as instantaneous as I wish it to be. My own condition still very much spent and fatigued. But, fear and survival and adrenaline have a way of drawing out of a man more strength than imaginable. I grab the broken shaft and with a mighty tug tear its heavy stone head free from the ground's embrace.

The shift in pursuit has now changed dramatically; the pursuer becomes the prey. With an unforgettable look of terror in his eyes, Running Wolf holds up both his hands pleading with me, imploring alternately in Crow and Piegan, to spare his life.

How ironic, the little red prick begs for mercy, yet would have shown me none. I have no time to waste on unwarranted sympathy. Down I drive the heavy stone blade as savagely as he had tried to do to me. Plunging ever so deeply into his heaving chest cavity and beyond, the force of my thrust imbeds the broken lance once more into the hard plains' sod below.

His death cry is short and final as he flops convulsively in an unfitting throe. Running Wolf never envisioned this, his own tragic end, not in his wildest dreams, or imagined that this would be his final act's curtain. He had only dreamt of glory and honor, vanquishing the *spoo-pii* and taking his scalp. And he had certainly felt no remorse for my friend whose butchered remains lay strewn so ignominiously back on that pebbled beach by the Jefferson. As for the *spoo-pii*, his intended victim, he would've dispatched me with no more thought given than squashing a bug or pinching a pesky mosquito between his fingers. His kind always feels that way about hapless others. It's always the other guy who's meant to suffer and die.

"Comeuppance day, eh, Runnin' Wolf? How do you like it now? Betcha never thought you and the rest of your heathens would see the day."

I stand over him with clenched fists and fire in my eyes, my body, my whole being trembling and shaking right down to the marrow. I'm scowling, glaring at his still quivering remains with outright contempt, yet to come down from the angst of battle and my own narrow brush with death.

I'm still not done spitting venom. "Rather you than me, injun. And that's for my friend, Johnny Potts and the golden rule… do unto others, you heathen son of a bitch…"

CHAPTER SEVEN

It was a hard-bitten eulogy I'd given that young injun as I freed the lance from a still convulsing body. I should flee towards the Madison right now, but I can't. Something within me won't let go, my emotions are running rampant, clouding my judgment. I look down upon the cold countenance of this once, proud young warrior, somewhat sadly remiss that all his trials and labors in the Three Forks had come to this. I never had anything personal against Running Wolf. I never went looking for a fight or for a scalp. That's not my way. I didn't want this. I would have avoided confrontation, Lord knows, I tried. They chose to come after Johnny and me, to kill us as dead as I did him.

I stand there for several moments more, my whole body and being still trembling from the confrontation. I linger way too long for comfort, yet I don't even seem to care. Johnny's last few minutes of life flashed before my mind's eye. I just couldn't shed the shame. I remembered his defiance… and his recklessness. The memory of his audacity drew a hint of a smile to my face. It was such a likeable part of him. But, then my mind chose to bring back the dire darkness from earlier in the day. Grim pictures of his lifeless body riddled with arrows and lead and the way those savages tore his remains apart made me seethe and shudder with anger and revulsion. Their savagery was inhuman and uncalled for as far as I was concerned. They had nothing to fear from us, yet they had done him wrong. My hatred and loathing of the Blackfeet had returned with a vengeance, filling my contempt anew. I looked down again at the still warm cadaver of Running Wolf, this time with utter contempt.

"Injun, you got what you deserved," I spat with all the venom my loathing could muster. I held Running Wolf's weapon in my hand ready to dash him again and again. Right then I wanted to tear his heart right out of his chest, beat his face into an unrecognizable pulp. Unwittingly, I was becoming just like them. My rage, unassuaged, kept flowing in torrents, completely ignoring the imminent peril approaching from across the "prickly pear plains." And that rage was getting the best of me, foolishly delaying any hope of escape. Thank God, I pulled myself back. Jesus, John, what in the hell are you doing? Get a hold of yourself, man.

"*Ahhheeeeeee!*" A savage scream ripped through the air, jolting me back to the race.

I looked to the west towards my nearest pursuers. From a distance, Running Wolf's death had been witnessed by several of his most steadfast companions. They were closing in on me, the last relay leg of wolves to have shared in Running Wolf's final surge. I knew they had to be kin or close friends, trusted members of his warrior clan. There was just something about his band, their youth and swagger, the way they strutted so fearlessly on the pishkun plains that long ago day, baring their naked asses, daring my aim. Yes, that was it, their brashness, the devil may care way that they carried themselves on the field of battle or anywhere else for that matter. They were like the Spartans of old, feared by the strong and weak alike and raised from the cradle to a lifetime of warriorhood servitude. And this particular pack were all right out of Running Wolf's Piegan mold; tall and lithe and strong of bodily physique, emboldened by conceit, insolent beyond any measure I had ever known. The closest to me, a big ugly brute, I instantly recognized as having stood side by side with Running Wolf on the field of battle just months before. His hue and cry were instantly joined by an eruption of cacophonous blasts, waxing and waning from rueful lamentation to outright bloody vengeance. Running Wolf's slaying had suddenly revitalized and renewed their vigor, obliterating in an instant their own great bodily fatigue. Their chase resumed in earnest, but with a new leader emerging to avenge their great loss.

The *napikwan* had killed again. How could this be? Unarmed and naked, beaten and exhausted, alone amidst a host of Blackfoot elite, the lowly white *spoo-pii* had slain their strongest and swiftest, their greatest warrior. At this very moment he was on the verge of freedom. His escape would be a mockery of their whole nation. The word was passed quickly rearward through the long snaking column of exhausted runners until the very last one at the very end of the chain stopped and turned and raced back towards Kootenae Appe near the banks of the Jefferson, on the edge of the plains.

The death report was given, coming intermittently spaced between ragged gasps for air. *Napikwan* had killed again. *Maa-koyou-mah'-kaa* was dead. *Spoo-pii* was fleeing now unimpeded towards the river Straight.

War chief, *Kootenae Appe* was stunned in disbelief, visibly shaken right down to the very marrow of his heathen soul... but not for long. Black, irrepressible fury gathered in his eyes, the furrows in his weather-worn face grew deeper yet. Anger, loathing, determination burst forth from the aging war leader like a human storm, raining down his commands upon the shocked legions of dispirited followers.

"To your *ponokamitas*," he raged, "ride to the river and cut off the *napikwan*. Ring him in. Find the *spoo-pii*. Bring me his scalp and his unbeating heart." No longer the stoic paragon of Piegan virtue, he screamed like a chieftain possessed as if held tightly in the grasp of some ancient ancestoral spirits, guiding the path of holy Piegan vendetta and retribution.

"Hurry... hurry," he exhorted his minions. "The *napikwan* must not get away."

No longer would the game be fair. No longer could he allow the white *spoo-pii* a chance of freedom. He must be found. He must be stopped. He must be killed and made an example for all to see.

Those who had stayed back with *Kootenae Appe*, under the cool, shaded, broad spreading limbs of the cottonwood groves, the ones who had not raced across the plains in playful pursuit, gathered the reins of the runners' ponies and charged across the open plains. The River Straight would soon be reached. The game would soon be over. The chase was now more than ever down to lethal business. Rawhide quirts whipped and beat the painted hides of their lathered ponies, driving their spirited buffalo runners to reach the wide wet lands of the three rivers confluence and hem in the hated white man, cutting off all avenues of escape.

The respite had actually done me good. My strength, my vitality, my confidence returned with every fresh breath. I had gained a second wind and now it was as if I hadn't run, but a leisurely mile. Hell, I even had a weapon now to defend myself. But, whom was I fooling? I knew that my situation was infinitely more dangerous than minutes before… if that could be at all possible. There would be no more running the gauntlet for me, no more fair play for the hated white man. My flight had exhausted Piegan patience.

The cottonwoods and willows loomed to the east less then a mile away. I could smell the cool waters, picture in my mind the many twisted channels and thickly wooded islands of the Madison fork as it neared its marriage to the Jefferson and Gallatin. I had to reach the river, beat the Piegan to the punch. I had to find a riparian haven, a place to hide, to throw the injuns off my trail. Time was not on my side. My pursuers would be right behind me. I would need every skill and instinct I possessed. And then I would need… some more luck.

I took one last long look at those who came on. My lead was cut back to only a few hundred yards and they were coming on fast. The fight with Running Wolf had eaten away at the span that separated the turtle, the *spoo-pii* from the rest of the wolves. It would be close, but I'd make it. Yes, confidence had returned to me by the bucket full. The time for panic had come and gone. My race to the river would not be as chaotic as before, but controlled, tempered by resolve and good old fashioned backwoods' sense. It was time to start praying and using my brains.

Away I went. Refreshed and armed, I resumed my run with a measured gait. Urgency was in my every stride, forcing my every breath. My path was clear and straight as my pace steadily ate up the prickly sod to the Madison beyond. My constitution was still running strong. Shortly, I was outdistancing my pursuers, slowly but surely pulling ahead. Their cries began to fade. Again the span between Pahkee and *spoo-pii* widened, buying precious time. Several more minutes ticked away, the pace continued, the cottonwoods shielding the river looming larger and larger the closer I got.

The woods... I must reach the woods, lose myself in the shadows of the forest, cloak my direction, confuse the Blackfeet, keep them guessing, gain time 'til I could find a hiding place, a refuge. Land a goshen, any damn spot to hole up and throw 'em off my scent would do. I wasn't about to fool myself again. My luck and physical reserves couldn't last forever. Yet, I must hold on. This wasn't a boyhood game... this was life and death. The Blackfeet weren't demigods. They weren't better than me. They were human, just like me. Sooner or later they'd give-up. Or would they?

Suddenly, I had made it, diving headlong into the densely forested copse that bordered the river. Instantly, I vanished from Pahkee view, swallowed by the thick groves of cottonwood and willow. The sylvan floor chafed and lacerated painfully at my swollen and bloody feet. Branches and twigs and underbrush ripped away at me, tearing my exposed flesh. I plowed through ignoring the pain. All I could see was escape and survival.

"Go, go, go," I exhorted myself, darting, weaving and crashing my way through the tangled maze.

My breaths were heavy again, my lungs burning anew. Suddenly my foot caught an upturned root. I tripped, stumbling forward towards the edge of the river, until it was too late to stop. Over the bank I went in a tumbling freefall, plunging headlong into the icy cold of the Madison below. The impact, the frigid shock of those mountain-borne waters instantly jarred my whole exhausted system, chilling me to the bone. I panicked, not... it was all so refreshing.

"Get up," I commanded. I picked myself up off the river's slippery stone and muddy bed, immediately scanning the river and its banks, searching frantically for a place to hide or a way to go. The river raced on uninterrupted. The current's tug was unbelievably strong. It's hold on me powerful, magnetic. The longer I tarried the deeper its cold, icy waters dug into my hide. I began to shiver and shake. I made for the shallows nearer to the bank, caught my breath and looked about. The river confused me; I was befuddled as to where to go or what to do. Answers were not forthcoming. I searched again. My mind, my eyes raced and darted hither and yon for clues and answers, but none were there to be found.

"Steady, John. Think. Something has got to be here."

I reached down and cupped handfuls of cool water, splashing my face over and over to rinse away the sweat and the sticky film left by Johnny's blood. My throat was dry and parched, my lips swollen and cracked. And now, standing in all that water, my thirst was incredible. I fought to resist the urge to drink the river dry. It was no use. My craving was too great. I took my gulps in long, heavy swigs, the cold waters soon wrenched my guts, wracking, twisting my insides. I stood up, bared the pain and moved on out towards the middle of the river, catching the current once again.

"You've got no more time to waste. Go. Go." A hundred thoughts, a thousand or more assailed me without respite. My precious head start had been whittled away. The Blackfeet were coming for sure. They would soon be here; pouring through the woods, spilling over the banks and quickly spreading out over the whole expanse of the Madison's wetlands, right down to the Forks themselves in a massive manhunt. They would be as relentless as the tide. I never doubted their tenacity or their persistence for an instant. But, they weren't going to catch me, at least alive. I wouldn't let them do to me what they had done to Johnny. They had their chance and now I had mine. I still had that spear, I'd use it if I had to. But, something would break. Providence had not let me get this far without a chance to make it. I had to keep going, find my way. Safety lay at Manuel's Fort, two hundred weary, critter and heathen-infested miles away. Yes, the odds against me were still too great, my chances seemed far too slim. The distance, the elements, the savages all aligned against me. I gritted my teeth anew. I became if anything more determined then ever. Hang on, John. Hang on.

I continued to drift downriver treading water, looking about, searching. Both banks raced by me. The sun was now high, perched atop a cloudless sky of blue ether. I swam with heavy sodden limbs, following the flow, half under my own steam, half-borne by the river's irresistible might. Desperately my mind and eyes raced back and forth scanning the wooded shorelines. Sign… give me sign, I prayed. And then it appeared like a beacon of hope, an answer to my prayers… an island amidst an angry sea. Suddenly, salvation lay right before me. I knew it was my sanctuary the instant it came into view. Oh lordy, was I ready for it.

Maybe, it was the result of a snag or a deadfall; a pyre of jammed boughs and branches jutting out into the river, piled high one atop the other.

"Could it be?" I asked, almost unbelievingly.

Yes. It looked like an old, abandoned beaver house, standing taller than a full-grown man, rising straight above the swirling, roiling surface of the river. Yes, there it was, an old stick and bough and mud lodging, worn by time and neglect and abandonment or so I hoped. I didn't care what it was, for time I knew was not on my side, and this ol' house would have to do.

Re-energized, I veered obliquely with powerful strokes and kicks, pulling myself across the grain of the torrent by sheer force of will. I made it across, winded and near spent. I grasped a thick, protruding branch and hung on for dear life. Catching my breath, I turned and once more looked upriver from whence I came. Amidst a forced sigh, I took my breaths and looked about one last time. Nothing stirred. I still had a chance. The Blackfeet had yet to cross my trail or penetrate the river's edge.

"Thank you, Lord," I silently prayed for giving me another chance.

I looked down into the torrent of seething, boiling waters rushing on by. I gathered my nerve, steeling myself, taking several long, deep breaths and descended into the depths below. Hand over hand, I guided myself, branch by branch, limb by limb. I hung on desperately fighting the current's irresistible pull, searching for an entrance I knew must surely be there. Voila! I found it, right where nature intended it to be. Water-strained sunlight soon faded as I slithered through a dark, tunneling hole. The opening was tight, barely enough room for my naked frame to squeeze through. But, I made it, right at the very end of the last of my air. I emerged into a darkened chamber, expelling a giant whoosh of stale, pent-up air. I cleared my eyes, regained my breaths and looked about me. The interior of the lair, upon first look appeared abandoned, deserted. Good, I thought. I was more than grateful right then and there. I didn't need another fight on my hands… man or beast. I was just too damn spent to care.

It was dark inside, though sunlight filtered dimly in from above through a complex web of tangled boughs and twigs. I took a moment to adjust my vision to the chamber's light and then pulled myself out of the water onto a small muddy ledge just large enough to accommodate my bulk.

My luck continued. If only it would keep up, let me stay here awhile without attracting attention, rest up and gain some time. I needed time to figure out what to do. I needed the Piegan to think I had gotten away. I hunkered-down, spent and cold, silently shivering in the dankness of this my sunken sanctuary. I rubbed my arms, my chest and legs briskly, desperately trying to bring back some measure of needed warmth. I looked down at the crudely chipped stone-blade and broken wooden shaft my hand was still clutching, the Pahkee spear that nearly ran me through. A brief wave of revulsion came over me, anew. I shuddered at the memory of how close I came to my life's own end. I sat back, relieved… it was over for now. It seemed like a lifetime ago, and yet the confrontation had only been mere minutes before. I sighed deeply and relaxed my mind, calmness was returning, slowly letting my breathing recover and return me to a more normal state. And there I sat in grim repose waiting for the Piegan wolves to come. It had all happened so fast. I couldn't have been more than five minutes ahead of my closest pursuers. I was right again. I didn't wait for long.

That first wave, Running Wolf's zealot band, had breached the woods close behind on my naked tail. My caroming, trampled path through the brush and woods had left a heavily scarred trail. My collision with the riverbank was a scene any Indian child could read. They wasted no time. From there, their search commenced rapidly up and down both sides of the river sweeping in all directions through the groves and thickets, islands and cricks, even on to the rolling plains beyond.

Arriving at the river's edge, Kootenae Appe's horsemen raced northward paralleling the Madison's western shores for a considerable distance. Wheeling right, Pahkee dragoons curled in a wide arc eastward, fanning out in a classical flanking movement to hem me in. A picket line of Indian cavalry several miles long spread out to contain the turtle, the illusive *spoo-pii*. To keep him confined like the rat he was, all the while, closing their pincers ever so tightly. Until, once again, *spoo-pii* was theirs.

Dismounting, hundreds of warriors spread out on a line just a scant few yards apart, a bronzed phalanx of Piegan infantry stealthily picking their way forward through trees and thickets right up to the river's edge. Hundreds of dark, keen eyes peered into every conceivable place a man could hide or be. Every patch of ground, every bush, every thicket was searched. Nothing escaped their purview. But the white man's sign had been lost where he had entered the running waters of the Straight. The *spoo-pii* was yet to be found. It was as if he was a ghostly spirit vanishing with the wind. But, they kept moving, searching, covering more ground than they thought possible for a naked man to gain. And the more ground they covered, the more unsettled they became. Oh, that *spoo-pii* was quick and cunning. Quicker then they would've dared believe. But, he'd had been caught before. His medicine was not invincible. And yet, each time he'd gotten away. Keep searching, passed the word. He must be found.

I lay cramped and still, much too cold, periodically shifting positions, stretching stiffened joints and wearied limbs, searching for what little comfort I could find. Every sense of my being was alert and on edge, straining to catch the slightest of hints, a wisp of movement or unnatural, manmade sound. I had had it with Blackfeet deception; I wasn't about to fall to any more of their devious tricks. But, was I safe here inside this old beaver lair? Would they come looking? My God, what would I do? The uncertainty was starting to play on my mind. I wanted to leave, but I knew I had to stay. I forced myself to wait and listen. I heard nothing. I knew I wouldn't. They were too good at what they did to be caught by most any white men. Yes, I heard nothing, but I did feel something. Better yet, it was that itch, that sudden unexplainable sixth sense I got when skulking injuns were about. I held my breath, straining to catch whatever it was. And then… it was a sudden, gentle, tiptoeing-like movement, as if a soft deerskin moccasin was testing the stability of my thatched and boughed roof directly above my head.

Oh, my God. They've found me. I became still, very still. I could actually visualize what was happening above as if I was looking through that injun's own eyes. It was an eerie, almost surreal view of what I now perceived to be my fate. I began to question my choice; fearful I'd made a fatal mistake. Shut up, you fool. He doesn't know, yet.

Again a moccasin pressed down gingerly as if not quite sure, then, obviously adding more weight, both feet tested the interlocked branches over my head in a very purposeful way. The roof sagged ever so slightly, almost imperceptibly, except to me. Small particles of dust began to trickle down, shaken loose from above.

I could smell him. I could sense the brave's presence as he stood almost directly over my head. The beaver house, the very structure itself was more than just a little disturbed. A few more thin beams of light penetrated from above. I watched them alighting on my lower limbs, exposing my pale white skin. Panic nearly set in as I pressed myself tightly, as tightly as I could, against the darkest corner of my cell.

It happened again, this time a springing motion from above, stronger, more forceful, as if he was jumping up and down.

What's he doin'? If the idiot keeps this up, he'll find me for sure. And then came a lull. The wait was almost too much to bear. Shortwith, the same, jarring movement repeated itself. But, what was he doing? It was as if the ceiling, its matted roof was being pulled upward and apart with every renewed exertion.

My God, the son of a bitch is tryin' to pull the roof off, branch by branch. I shook my head in near disbelief. Why didn't the idiot enter like I did? It was a hell of a lot easier. Maybe he didn't think of it. Maybe he was scared of the dark. All I could do was wait and listen. If my predicament had not been so dire, it would have been downright comical.

The bastard persisted. The shafts of light grew larger and brighter with each new pulling movement from above. I looked down in horror at my broken spear. It was lying in the middle of the muddy shelf's floor, a beam of light reflecting off its dark obsidian blade. For an instant I was frozen in fear, afraid to move, afraid not to. Slowly my hand moved down to my side. There's still time, I cautioned myself. My hand fumbled on the wooden shaft at first try. I tried again stretching my fingers outward until they firmly pressed the butt end of the broken shaft...

Got it.

Slowly, I dragged the weapon back across the muddy ledge until it was out of the light and firmly in my grasp. I exhaled quietly and went back to sitting still.

But, the injun was getting too close. I had to be ready. Fearing eventual discovery, I quickly prepared myself to reenter the water. I would rather take my chances with the swirling waters of the Madison River… than be caught like a snared critter in this submerged trap of wood and mud.

The movement overhead suddenly ceased.

I hesitated and listened. I could distinctly hear Piegan voices. Several of them appeared to be ridiculing the warrior on the roof. This I surmised by the chuckles and sounds of laughter coming from the shore.

Unknowingly they had saved my bacon one more time. The *spoo-pii* was still in the race. I detected no more movement from above save for departing footsteps leaving the roof of the house. I waited for several long minutes, trusting them naught. And then, for the first time since I entered my lair, I breathed freely.

Silence returned, save for the eternal commotion of the churning waters of the Madison rushing on by. I stretched my sore, aching legs out as best I could and laid the back of my head against the house's coarse inner walls.

"Patience," I told myself, "sit and wait this thing out."

As the afternoon wore on I continued to lay in silence. I stared at the construction of my little sanctuary admiring the critter skill, the handiwork that made this submarine den home.

"Clever little beasts," I thought.

All this work with just two little hands and four big yellow teeth. Teeth, as sharp as ma's favorite pair of scissors and a helluva lot more powerful. I guessed my room was probably only one of many compartments connected by a maze of hidden passageways I was unable to detect. How many former occupants had called this place home? I could only surmise. How ironic can this be? I came here to trap and wound up being saved by the very creatures I swore to kill.

My day had been long, longer and harder than any time I had ever known. My physical and emotional exertions had left me spent, empty. I was exhausted. No catnap or snooze would do. It was time to pay the piper. I didn't fight the sleep that now weighed heavily on my eyelids, slowly and inexorably nodding me away. My last conscious thoughts came as a command… "Don't snore too loudly."

Resistance finally surrendered to fatigue. I slept heavily, unaware of the hours passing away. Desperation, fear and the run of my life had driven me to a state of weariness and depletion, sapping the wellspring of my physical and emotional reserves.

I dreamt while under control of a deep, sound sleep. I saw myself walking through fog, dressed and clad once again in my old buckskins. Yep, that's me for sure! I was wearing my favorite fringed hunting shirt, toting my 'ol' Kentuck' at the ready. I was moving at a steady gait, quiet as a church mouse.

Why, I must be out huntin'. Where am I? I wondered. I've been to this place before.

Yes, I had. I was on a hillside looking down upon a torrent of white water, cascading through a series of four or five boiling rapids, cataracts.

I know this place. I must be near the falls, the Great Falls of the Missouri. Lord have mercy, what in the hell am I doin' here? It's been at least three years since the Corps camped there. If this doesn't beat all, I thought.

I descended the hill to the grassy plains below, just above the river where it bends towards the northeast. I was hunting fresh meat… deer, buffalo, whatever critter showed its hairy-face first. The men were so hungry they'd eat a shoe.

I was hunting alone. I loved hunting alone. I loved the solitude of the woods and the mountains and the prairies. I often wondered if one day, after the Expedition's return, if I'd ever come back.

Up ahead I could see a herd of mangy buff grazing.

They're pretty strung out, I thought.

Easy pickin's, with not a care in the world. Hundreds of 'em, I marveled, damn, there's hundreds of 'em. Boys, there'll be meat on the table tonight.

I loved the vastness of the West, its open plains teeming with game. The rivers stocked with beaver and fish. I loved the high rugged mountain beauty of the Rockies. More so than any other member of the Corps, even more than the half Shawnee Drouillard, I felt I was born to live in the West.

The breezes were shifting, changing directions from whence they came. Instinctively, I reacted. My approach from downwind was slow, furtive, cautious. I never took chances. No need to spook or rile the critters if I didn't have to.

"I'm just part of this here scenery and I'm takin' my time," I whispered softly.

I found me a fat one. I took aim, resting my sights squarely behind the right front quarter of a young buffalo cow placidly grazing. I'd done this before, more times than I could remember.

The men were mighty hungry. Fresh buffalo meat would be welcome, very welcome. I could see their savoring reaction to big juicy slabs of buffalo hump and tasty succulent tongue hot and dripping right from the spit. Hmmmm! Man, oh man, I could smell it now.

I was feeling real good right about then. Doing what I did best. Cocky smart, sure of my aim, my shooting, after all this was how I earned my keep, and I was pretty darn good at it.

I pulled back, cocking my Kentucky's heavy hammer. Took several breaths to calm my nerves, holding my aim steady and true. My trigger squeeze was as smooth as butter. That long rifle discharged its lead in a cloud of smoke as the black powder ignited in a fiery load.

The cow never knew what hit her. The ball slammed into her sides wreaking internal havoc as it came to a sudden deadening stop deep within her insides. She stood there for several minutes teetering, not knowing what made her feel this way nor what to do. Blood poured from her mouth and nostrils and from the tremendous hole blown in her side. Her knees buckled and sagged and finally gave way. She lay in a heap, bawling her last painful cries as her life slipped away.

I crept up to my kill cautiously, not knowing if the animal was dead or still alive. Experience teaches a man to be wary at moments such as this, to take your time and never to rush in. More than one time an unsuspecting hunter had been gored or crushed or killed by a critter he thought dead. I waited and watched. With a final withered gasp, the cow uttered her last breath and expired.

I felt relieved. Death is never pretty, especially that of a splendid beast. Silently, I thanked her with a brief prayer for giving her life so others may live. The men would now have their meat. I stood with my unloaded rifle, priming myself for the butchering chore ahead.

It occurred to me, I couldn't say just when or for how long, that someone or something was watching. I could sense movement. I could almost divine the aura of a presence. Whatever it was, was on all fours, stealthily approaching from down-wind.

I didn't like the suspense and suddenly wheeled about with my rifle ready to fire.

"Holy shit! A big white... a grizz." I couldn't believe my eyes. "Will ya look at the size of him."

That giant brown bear was maybe sixty or seventy yards away when I first saw him and he was closing in, slicker than snot. I froze where I stood, my moccasins anchored to the ground like the roots of a tree. I didn't budge. Instinct and experience fighting between themselves, to stay still, to run like hell. I was having a devil of a time making up my mind.

"Christ, he's huge."

Six hundred pounds of magnificent "ursus horribilis" had been on my trail, stalking me, the hunter. What a turn around. Hah! I didn't like it, not one bit.

Maybe my shot attracted the critter, like a strange noise will sometimes do. Bears are curious animals, smarter than I had been prepared to give 'em credit for. It was a big mistake on my part. In those few short seconds, it became quite apparent that goldurn bear had been following me all along, silent as a panther, watching my whole hunting scene and me none the wiser.

It was not such a comforting feeling realizing how easy a stalk I had been.

I glanced back for a moment at that dead buff' cow, realizing the bear and me both claimed her. There was a real contest of wills developing here for ownership of that there piece of meat. The question being 'who was going to blink first?'

Well, it was my kill and I wasn't about to give her up. Without a further invite, I shouldered my weapon and took aim at where I thought lay the bear's big, beating heart and squeezed the trigger ever so smoothly.

Nothing happened. Powder did not ignite. I was as surprised as I could be.

"Good God, I didn't reload," I screamed.

My nerve instantly turned to shit. It was as if the bear knew I messed-up, but good. And then I made my second mistake. I looked at the big brute, right square in his eyes.

He glared, right back. By staring, I was unknowingly challenging him. And that was more than he could stand. The big bear crept no more. No sir, those ears of his reared back and his pan-wide mug began a scowling, revealing a set of massive upper canines I'd rather forget. And then he came at me, low and fast, hurdling across the prairie like he was shot from a cannon.

The plain was open and broad, the nearest treeline hundreds of yards away. No rock, no bush, no nothing to climb. That 'grizz' monster came at me with his mouth agape and fury in his eyes.

I turned and fled down the sloped plains as fast as my feet would carry me. I ran, ran like I had never run before. He was gaining. I could hear his grunts. I could hear the heavy pads of his paws pounding the ground, closing in on me with every stride. They say that grizzly bears are fast, that they can outrun a horse. Well, I know something about being fast, and I am here to tell you that I'm no competition for a horse.

The distance to the river had been closer than I realized. I leaped from its low banks on a dead run and entered the river a running and splashing. Out I waded, my piece, my powderhorn held high over my head. I kept going as fast as I could until the water lapped at my chest.

Something wasn't right. I heard no further movement from behind. There was no splashing of water. That bear should have been by rights atop of me, but he hadn't even entered the river.

"Strange," I thought, "they ain't a feared of water."

I stopped and turned to see the big bruin at the edge of the river standing on its hind legs to its full height and glory. Oh, he was threatening, all right, big and mean and powerful. But he wasn't making a move, he wasn't coming in after me, he seemed content to stand and stare. No, the beast had no intention of following me and I didn't know for the life of me why. Damnedest thing I ever saw.

I considered reloading. But no way did I have time to reload my piece and fire, especially when I was chest deep in the 'big muddy'.

Disgustingly, I looked at my empty weapon and muttered, "you're about as useless as teats on a bull buff."

There, we both stood, man and the big bear, neither of us making a move. He had me by the short hairs and all I could do was tread water and hope for the best.

"Well, bar, what are you waitin' for?" I yelled. "Why are you standin' there over of me? A feared to go for little a swim?" I chuckled.

Suddenly, the bear vanished; along with the river, the blue sky and that grassy slope I'd just run down in an all-fire hurry. I couldn't even hear the roar of the Great Falls, anymore. The whole scene just disappeared.

"What the hell?" I cussed in confusion.

I went to reload my rifle, but it wasn't there. All I felt was my naked, cold skin, and a dank, muddy ledge.

"That's funny," I thought, "why all of a sudden is it dark?"

I was awake again, realizing instantly that the buffalo cow I shot, the bear that chased me and the cold, wet river was all a dream. And yet, the feeling of the presence of an ominous being standing over me remained. But, it wasn't that of the vanished bear that was worrying me. That bear had taken off three years before and hundreds of miles down river from the Forks from where I now lay.

I looked up. Someone or something was standing atop my beaver house's roof once again. The ceiling sagged once more, ever so slightly. It did it once again, this time testing the matted surface with a little more weight, a little more confidence. Grains of dust and debris fell from the tangled bough and twig roof, landing in my hair and eyes and face.

That fool injun is back. Did he hear me? God, had I snored or talked in my sleep? Did I give myself away? The tension, the suspense was excruciatingly long.

Again I waited in silence, listening to my every breath, the every pounding, pulsating beat of my heart, the unceasing ringing in my ears. I wet my lips and breathed softly. Closing my eyes, I tried to wish him away. How long has he been there? I wondered. Damn you. I cursed at myself for giving in, weakening to sleepless exhaustion.

Is sleep preferable to life, I demanded to know? I knew what was going in that injun's mind. The curiosity was damn near killing him. His pals had made him quit the first time, but he had to have his question answered. And he was the only one who guessed it right. I prayed for his friends to return. Hoped their taunts would chase him down from the roof once again and leave me be. He wouldn't be able to take their bullshit any more than he did before, unless he was as stubborn as I was. And I was betting he wasn't.

But, I was wrong. That Blackfoot warrior was as stubborn as a mule. The young brave just kept pulling boughs and limbs and twigs off of the top of the roof and chucking 'em into the river. If he only knew how true his suspicions were and who waited inside just below. Instincts should never be ignored or disregarded. I had found that out with my dead friend Johnny far too late.

The Indian suddenly stopped and stood for several minutes. Maybe he was tired, not used to working with all that wood. Indian men never did cotton to doing work, preferring to let their squaws handle the chores, while they hunted and fished and played warrior.

The wait was unbearable, grinding my nerves raw. My temper, my patience was growing short. Like him I was losing patience. I dearly wanted to vent my rage. The fear and hatred, the humiliation had all piled-up inside me, until I became a giant emotional volcano, fixing to boil, to steam, to erupt into one great explosion, directed at this one lone, curious red-son of a bitch.

Yet, I did nothing. I bided my time and held my breath until I could hold it no longer. But, as suddenly as he appeared he was gone once again. Just walked away without a second thought. Probably in the end, I thought, that poor bastard couldn't take his buddies' shit. I understood it, knew how important to some folk how much other peoples' opinions could be, though it was never that important to me. That's why it's sometime better for a man to go it alone.

I continued to listen. I knew they wouldn't give up. They'd be putting their heads together, rethinking, wracking their brains for my whereabouts. I sat quietly. Their frustration made me smile even chuckle inside. Though I dare not get carried too far away. The evening's shadows grew longer. The sunlight slowly faded from the beaver house's roof. Twilight had set in and with it a slight measure of comfort came with the darkness. This is what I'd been waiting, praying for. The longest day of my life, I hoped, was coming to an end.

The Blackfeet wouldn't lurk around this eerie place so close to the sacred battlefield of the "pishkun plains." Not in the dead of the night, not with all their taboos about life in the hereafter and certainly not with the spirits of the night skulking about. Even the dastard *'spoo-pii'* couldn't make them abandon their ancient, most deep-seated fears.

"Times a wastin'," I said, mumbling to myself as I grabbed my snapped-handled spear and looked about one last time at my little sanctuary. It was pitch black, only the odors and dankness of its confines were present to remember it by.

I took several long, deep breaths filling my lungs with air. I slid off that little, cramped, muddy ledge, entered the cold, dark waters of the Madison and left behind forever that house of mud and twigs that saved my life.

I broke the surface of the river's churning waters with barely a ripple or a splash and found myself being carried downstream like a piece of lone driftwood, floating aimlessly with the current as it carried me safely away.

One hundred yards, two hundred yards, got to put distance between us. I watched the wooded banks silently pass by. There was no movement and little sound save for the trees and willows fluttering in the nighttime breeze and the ever present slap and rush of the river.

Well, John boy, you got to take a chance sometime, I thought, entering the shallows away from the mainstream. Slowly, purposefully I crawled on all fours until I reached the eroding walls of the river's bank. Motionlessly, I waited, peering into the darkness of the tree line before me.

"Nothin' there," I whispered to myself, reassuringly. "Go for it, John."

I slithered like a snake up over the banks… half arose to a crouch and moved out quickly, running bent over 'til I was completely enveloped by the woods. Again, I waited, testing the quietude of the surrounding forest, listening to every sound, to every nocturnal movement, real or imagined. Fear and doubt chafed at the raw edges of my nerves. The darkness, the gloom, the spirits of the night were testing me, but unlike my superstitious foes, they couldn't hurt this *napikwan*.

I felt my wet, dripping nakedness for the first time since the race began. Shivering in the cool night air, unprotected from the elements, a persistent grumbling in my belly told me what I already knew. I was famished from my exertions. I was hungry, I was naked and I was barefoot with a broken injun spear my only comfort, my only defense.

Potts had been dead for less than a day. But that day had been an eternity. And time was not on my side. Winter would be soon setting in. It came when it wanted to. Fall in these western mountains is always a beautiful, spectacular time of year, a time that should be enjoyed. But it could also be so fickle, of short-lasting duration, quickly replaced by the frigid grasp of winter. And I was in no condition to be caught by its embrace.

I had to move out, light a shuck before I was caught in the open, so completely unprotected. I'd been mighty lucky, if you could call this lucky. I still had to avoid the Blackfeet and the Gros Ventre, live off the land, cross two hundred miles of unfriendly territory and all the while beat oncoming cold weather back to Manuel's Fort. A tall order in the best of times and circumstance. But, at least I was alive. I still had my wits about me.

"Damn, don't this beat all," I whispered, shaking my head and finding I had a little to chuckle about still left in me.

I was keeping my head, my humor. I knew I would need it. It would take every ounce of strength I had in mind, spirit and body to see me through. What was that old Greek expression I had heard many years before as a young sprout? "Know thyself."

Well, I always thought I did, though it'd been sometime since I had taken stock of myself. Funny, how a man tends to judge others: sizing 'em up, wondering if they'd cut the mustard, all the while taking for granted and overlooking his own weaknesses. But, if I was going to make it back to Manuel's Fort, I'd really have the opportunity to find out just how much I really did know myself. I'd been in tough scrapes before, relying on my own instincts and mettle and the good sense my Pa and Ma and the Good Lord had given me… that and experience had been my great teachers, though this by far was the worst shape and scrape I'd ever been in.

I took one last look back at the Forks country. And then, I was off, heading east towards the Gap. Eight, ten good hours of nighttime travel was left for me to reach and cross the valley of the Gallatin and, hopefully, climb the steep, rocky crags south of the pass and then on to freedom… and all done completely undetected. It was a tall order. I had a lot of land to cover and little time to do it. Could I make it before sunrise? Did I have enough time, enough strength in my condition? Would my swollen, still bleeding feet, lanced by half a-hundred sharp needles of the prickly pear, hold up to the walk and the climb? Or would I be humbled, lamed, easy prey for the wolves and bears and other disagreeable critters that roam the land.

And the Pahkees, where were they? What were they up to? Surely, they had gone on ahead. But, would they be waiting for me? Would they lay in wait in ambush by the narrow pass through the mountains, as I knew they would? Would they think that I, the clever spoo-pii, would dare scale the impassable peaks that loomed high above the pass. I hoped not, otherwise this ol' coon would be fresh out of options.

There were far too many questions I asked myself as I fled the relative safety of the wooded wetlands of the Madison fork. I stayed low, desperately trying to be discreet, moving like a quiet breeze on a moon-less night. I pulled myself up those very same sandstone cliffs that bordered the ancient pishkun and pushed on beyond, never stopping, never resting. I kept to the low spots; traveling through the swales, the ravines, the cuts and dips, using every form of concealment the rolling prairie land and the dark of night had to offer. I shunned the crests, the sagebrush and rock-covered knolls. I became a creature of the night, silent and stealthy. I stayed clear of the Gallatin, at least for awhile, knowing the Piegans would be lurking about, haunting the river's course, watching the game paths and that same east/westbound trail that Johnny and me had taken to the Forks. That way would be well covered, they'd see to that. They too would spread out over the land like shadow-less spirits. They would never give up, Kootenae Appe would see to that. The hunt, the chase was still on, nothing had been decided, yet.

The heat of the day was long gone, sucked away by the setting sun. The night's air had cooled, dipping down to a bone-numbing chill. My every step was painful, hard gained as I fought off the cold and my suffering feet. My head still throbbed, my empty gut clamored for food. That last breakfast of boiled beaver tail, delicious as it was, had run its course. The calories from that wonderfully tasty meat and fat were about all used up. I was thirsty, forever thirsty. My complaints were numerous, my discomfort beyond description. Yet, I sucked it up. I kept going, benumbed by the pain, the fear, the desperation of it all, but determined to survive, to go on and live to tell my story.

Somehow, I increased my stride, my arms swinging freely, back and forth like a green buck-private on parade. My cadence, my pace continued unabated as I ate up the two dozen or more miles of ground that lay between the Forks and the Gallatin hole. The way I chose to go was not at random or unintended, I knew exactly where I was going. No, I was cutting across country; saving time, miles, avoiding the familiar trails, the obvious routes, heading to where the river I knew would make a long slow turn, cutting south along the valley floor. The cottonwoods that bordered the river's banks stretched for miles, offering concealment, anonymity and protection.

Dark, silent mountains loomed before me, towering over the valley. I stopped for the first time since I quit the Madison. I could see the vicinity of the gap in the mountains. I could see the tall, jagged granite ridges guarding the pass on its southern flanks. It all seemed so daunting, much higher, more rugged and forbidding than I remembered. For the first time since leaving my beaverhouse lair I began to have doubts. I got that queer itch all over again. That itch was like a sixth sense in me, like an allergic reaction whenever the red-man or danger was about. It wasn't like busting out in hives or fits of sneezing and watery eyes, but more like an unfathomable sense of dread, sinking me to the very depths of fear, of apprehension; shaking my nerves, jitterin' my mind. I could never quite put my finger on the how or the why. It came and went, and thank God it did.

They had to be waiting for me by the pass, sure as shooting. It made good Indian sense. Rather then scouring the whole countryside in near total darkness, looking for one lone, naked white-man, the Blackfeet would just naturally set their trap in the only place they thought I would possibly go. And that gap, that pass was awfully narrow, so narrow even a rabbit couldn't have snuck through.

"Stick it in your craw, injuns. This ol' coon ain't about to oblige."

No, the doubt didn't linger long. I knew I was making the only choice I could. They expected me to walk right into their ambush. After all, how else could I get out of here and where else could I go? It was a good thing I had that long walk, 'cause it gave me plenty of time to think it over. And that's exactly what I did.

We'll see about that, I thought to myself.

My path started to veer towards the southeast. A cold wind stayed with me, that and a few gray owls and nighthawks keeping me company as I reached and forded the Gallatin. And then I turned obliquely and headed near-due east towards the foothills and the gap.

The closer I neared, the more confident I became, embuing me with renewed determination, blessing my exhausted frame with a second wind. They'd never expect me to attempt such a climb in my condition. No, the 'napikwan' was far too weak, too stupid and too scared. Hell, they should have known better. Hadn't I already done what they never thought I could do? Hadn't I already proved that I was more than a match for even Running Wolf and his entire warrior-band?

They had opened a door twice before and unknowingly were doing it again. Ol' Kootenae Appe had realized it as soon as his boys came back from the Madison panicking like squaws. The pride of Piegan warriorhood had returned empty-handed, faltering in their duty. Their vaunted prowess exposed by a single naked white trapper. My escape surely played on that old Piegan's mind and spirit from then on for the rest of his days. His anger was not to be assuaged while the *'spoo-pii'* roamed the land, free and clear, a blot forever on his sacred *'namachkani.'* But, certainly, he remembered the 'gap' through which I had come, my mountainous pass to freedom. The old man had but one choice. He quickly sent his most trusted warriors to seal the gap, to bar my escape, to hunt me down, once and forever. I could feel his frustration, his disappointment and shame. I could imagine his last pleading commands to his most faithful. "Find the *napikwan*. Hunt down the *spoo-pii*. Do not let him get away... not a third time." How pathetic, how remiss this once proud warchief must now feel and be.

And those he sent, who would they be? I thought of Running Wolf and his hunting band. They were the wildest, the proudest and by far the fiercest that day by the pishkun plains: magnificent fighters, undaunted by Salish numerical superiority, daring to challenge the *napikwan's* devilish aim, his deadly fire-stick. And who, really, save Running Wolf, challenged the swift *spoo-pii* in the deadly footrace? And his minions, his trusted friends, his band of red brethern, were they not the first to raise the hue and cry of the magnificent one's death? Yes, they had suffered the most, grieved the loudest, longest. They would be the chosen ones.

It mattered little to me at the time. What was one group of vengeful savages as opposed to another? I was in no position to choose, wishfully or otherwise. I'd have to contend with whomever they sent. So I kept on, moving east, as swiftly as my feet and flagging strength would allow. Quietly, like the spirits of the night that so troubled the very savages I feared I glided across the short grass landscape, my footsteps gingerly picking my way in the darkness of the night. Rain began to fall… a light-drizzle to add to the night's cool air. My dried tongue lapped up the wetness and moistened cracked, parched lips. The refreshing droplets splashing my face tasted good, invigorating.

But, my hunger was growing, unassuaged. I had to eat, to forage for food, to be able to keep warm, to keep moving. I had to survive and now, as I faced this tall, forbidding range before me, I steeled myself anew. For what lay ahead, I had no misbeliefs, no delusions. Once again, like the Biblical Abraham of old, I was being tested, like I'd never been tested before.

I've always tended to be a careful man, especially when it came to the care of my kit and belongings. Out here in this unforgiving wilderness, life is coarse and raw, far from the warmth and familiar comforts of civilization. Survival depends on so many tools easily taken for granted. The Indians had learned it the hard way many eons before and are masters of using nature to their advantage in spite of extreme adversity. And now, I had to call on that very same skill to save my own hide. Bare-bottom, bare-chest naked, unarmed and unshod, I faced the elements in which 'til this day I was never afraid to face before. I still had my wits and my nerve. But, for how long they would keep I didn't know. I just prayed they'd hold out long enough to reach Manuel's Fort.

Finally, I made it to the base of the mountains with several hours of darkness to spare. The foothills were low, densely wooded, easy to walk. Soon, I found myself tackling a steep, well-forested but granite-bound ridge. The rain had slickened the rocky ground slimier than snot, turning my climb into a most frustrating ordeal. Muddy soil and damp, wet undergrowth played havoc with my footing, slowing me down to a near crawl. I slipped and stumbled, cussed and cursed. Nothing stopped me. I pushed on; kept climbing, kept watching my footing, caught myself again and again, muted my accursed swearing, all the while, fearful I was becoming way too loud, far too noisy. As I neared the top, within reach of a rocky ledge, a loose rock shifted under my weight and sent me tumbling over backwards in an uncontrollable fall. Down I went, arms a-flailing, legs a-kicking, 'til I came to an abrupt, painfully painful crashing halt.

It was an old, twisted, gnarly pine, growing out of solid rock that broke my fall. I lay there, bruised and dazed, too tired to rise, too sore, too stiff to move. The fall tore patches of skin and hide off my elbows and knees and left me reeling. I was breathing hard, gasping for relief. My lungs were raspy, filling with fluid. I shivered and shook and felt the cold of the night-air penetrating my bones, sapping my reserves. My misery mounted. I sighed deeply, moaning at the pain the fall had wrought. For once I didn't care if anyone heard me. My head throbbed, my arms, my ribs, my legs ached as if on fire. I lay crumpled in a pile for the longest spell, lost in a fog of delusion and fatigue and shattered nerves. I could barely think, my mind was numb, the will to go on abandoning me like a dirty, yellow coward. My moans echoed across the side of that ridge like a church bell toll.

   That fit of despair didn't last much longer. I was by no means beaten or through. I just needed a breather, a moment to catch my breath and get my nerve back. Johnny's death, my run and subsequent ordeal had gone on way too long. And I still had a long way to go. I knew I wasn't out of the woods, yet. Those Piegan wouldn't give up so easily. They were still looking for me, probably skulking all around the gap, waiting to pounce on the 'spoo-pii' and this time not let that wily, naked white-man get away. The death of their hero, Maa-koyou-mah'-kaa would fester in the Blackfoot Nation's craw for an awful long time. They would never swallow letting me get the best of them. By now that ol' Kootenae Appe was probably the laughing stock of his people. He'd get his revenge, if it were the last thing he'd do. That was enough for me. I couldn't dawdle on the side of this mountain feeling sorry for myself. No, that was never my way. Otherwise, I should've stayed back on the other side of the Mississippi and never ventured west. I was ready to tackle the trail to Manuel's once again. The fog clouding my mind eventually began to clear. The pain wasn't going away, but it was bearable. I could handle it. I had no choice. So, I took in my bearings, emotional and otherwise. Gathering myself anew, I picked my tired, battered, naked carcass up off the ground and took one last look around. The night sky was still dark, the way ahead still wet and slippery and steep. I moved out, taking my time, determined more than ever to see this thing through.

   The morning sun was just poking its head above the tall Absarokas when I hauled myself over the top of a jagged granite crest, high above the gap. That old body of mine was all done in. I just laid right down, curled up like a wee bairn, succumbing that very moment to total and complete exhaustion. I slept that whole long day, oblivious to all about me. I slept the sleep of a man completely worn down to the nubs. I could have slept forever. Such was the way I was. But, something inside me told me to get going, to rise above the exhaustion and pain. So, I arose as the sun disappeared over the western horizon and looked to the East. I took-in my bearings. The way ahead, the gap, the pass below and the way I had come were all quiet, even peaceful. Nothing stirred below to reveal the Piegan manhunt for me surely still underway.

   I took hold of Running Wolf's broken lance and left my aerie without so much as a glance back. I had to make distance, as much and as fast as humanly possible. I traveled all that night through the dense fir and pine forests that bordered the southern side of the pass through the mountains of the Wolf. The going was slow; the footing wore hard, chafing my already too tender feet. But, I was gaining confidence. I sensed that I had given myself a chance. And while I made my way, stumbling through the darkness, buck-naked and increasingly colder, I mentally plotted my course back to Manuel's Fort and salvation. I knew there was no other way. I had to become nocturnal, a creature of the dark hours, mortified of being caught in broad daylight by the Piegans or the Bloods or their Gros Ventre allies. I must avoid the wild critters on the prowl: the bears, the wolves, and panthers that roamed the mountains and foothills and soon the lands that paralleled the Yellowstone River valley. I even shunned being found by the friendly Crow or the lowly Sheep Eaters. I trusted no red-man right then. Such was the fear and uncertainty that gripped me with a powerful angst. My nakedness made me ashamed, humiliated and in so becoming I gradually grew to think myself helpless, indefensible. It was as near a complete breakdown that a fighting man could imagine. I was afraid to be seen or hunted by man or beast alike. My pride, my dignity and honor was fast becoming distant memory… an illusion from a rapidly fading past of another life, another man, another place and time. I became as base as a man could become: right down to the most savage, primordial level shared by the rest of the animal world... kill or be killed.

So by day I hid, whenever, wherever I could, to lay low, to catch a few hours of fitful, nervous sleep, to snatch a moment's rest, to survey the land, the river country and distant mountains. I watched for sign of movement and the presence of my fellow man, I smelled, I listened, I divined, relying on every sense and fiber of my being and instinct. I blotted from my mind my painful feet, my nakedness, my agony and despair.

It was strange almost eerie walking in the dead of that first dark night in an unknown, unfamiliar forest with nothing more than my own beating heart and deep, heavy breaths accompanying me. I walked for sometime in near dread: my fear, my angst close to getting the better of me. But that night proved uneventful and soon passed on to the second and then to the third. Several times during the early and evening daytime hours I had observed off in the distance small families of wapiti and whitetail drinking and grazing down by the river. But they were just too far away and I dared not risk exposing myself. Besides, the effort would have been wasted, futile. I was in no condition to stalk the lamest or oldest of them, unless I got extremely lucky. And my luck had just about been used up. I knew that. And each proceeding day became a tug of war between grubbing for food, catching rest and avoiding the hostiles. I proceeded on, following the Yellowstone, using the lay of the land that paralleled the river to conceal my presence. I made good time, my strength and purpose held. Though little by little, slowly but surely, the toll was adding up, taking my measure step by painful step and increasingly it began to manifest itself in the cruelest of ways.

I was always tired, sleepy, bone weary, eternally hungry, forever looking for food… any food. Continued deprivation of rest and nourishment and a sense of 'well being' had all merged together to challenge me like I had never been challenged before. I was ravenous. *Aux aliments du pays…* yes, to live off the food of the land became my unending search and quest, my golden grail. But those depths, those basest of human indignities to which I was finding myself compelled to yield were rapidly becoming a mockery to the man I was but days before. It was as if some invisible being, some black force of nature or insidious evil spirit from a dark netherworld was tormenting me, laughing at my patheticness. Nothing now was beneath me. Survival drove me. I chewed the bark of the cottonwood, ate roots and berries where I could find them and like the very creatures I had so often hunted, shoved blades of dried prairie grass in my mouth, forcing myself to salivate and chew and swallow. I turned over dead, rotting trees like a hungry bear in an unending search, wolfing down grubs and ants and worms by the handful. I forced myself to swallow gobs of squishy moths, more than I care to remember. I wretched and puked, revulsed by what I forced myself to eat. But, I didn't stop. I kept going. What little I found drove me to find more. But, the pickings were meager; food of all description was scarce. It was if every critter in the land had beaten me to it. Autumn had arrived weeks before. Winter would soon be on the way. Then nothing would be left. And I hurried with a sense of urgency, of desperation. I knew all too well what winter was like in these parts and what it would quickly do to a man so unprepared.

This wasn't my first brush with hunger, by a long shot. No, we had all tightened our belts many times on the Expedition. Subsisting on Mandan corn throughout the winter of 04/05 was bad enough. A man could get used to it, though, if he had to. But crossing the Bitterroots in '05 proved to be more of a chore then we were prepared for. It took the Corps one helluva lot longer than we thought it would and by the time we reached the Camas Prairie we were all starving. I gorged myself on camas roots just as hungrily, as greedily as the next man… and just as equally I puked my guts up, wretching for days. It wasn't a pleasant experience, starvation never is. We had all had our share of *Chim-na-pum* 'salmon cuisine' 'til we got sick of smelling and eating and looking at it. That big Columbia River had nothing else to offer. And that long, wet winter we spent at ol' Fort Clatsop by the western ocean… well, they were all mighty lean times. And this past winter had been no picnic either. I knew it wouldn't be and I had prepared for it. But my subsistance was meager. And trekking five hundred miles in snow and ice on jerked meat left me with very little muscle on my frame to show for all I had been through. Yeah, I've known tough times, but this ordeal was bound to prove something else entirely.

After three or four nights of steady travel I suddenly sniffed an unmistakable campfire aroma wafting in on a northern breeze several hours after sunset. I near froze in my tracks. I could feel my eyes nigh on bulging out of their sockets. Smoke! Meat! Food! My mind careened to and fro with the possibilities. I smelled, but I had yet to see any visible evidence of flame and ember and fire. I didn't have to. I knew it was there. But, wait! Campfire also meant people, and which kind: friend or foe, white or red? Unthinkingly, I eagerly started to head in the direction from whence came the smoke. My gait picked up noticeably, embued with the promise of sustenance. Then, off in the distance the yip of dogs, many dogs. I stopped and waited and listened. Dogs scared me right then, though they kept to their unfettered chorus, seemingly intent on another direction, something or someone else holding their attention. And then the sounds of laughter permeated the air. And with the mirth came human voices in guttural discourse… Algonquin to be sure. I strained to hear the words, though their dialect was quite clear. But they were just too far away and there words too faint to recognize. And I knew so little of the Gros Ventre tongue. Yet, I was certain. They had to be the Atsina, the accursed allies of the Blackfeet. I wavered, indecisively: not knowing whether to stay put or quietly steal-away. My pulse, my heart raced incessantly. I shivered in the autumn night cool. Long minutes passed. Their talk continued unabated. Their voices were filled with confidence as if nothing on this dark moonless night could possibly worry or threaten them. They were the lords of the plains and prairies, masters of ambush, brutal, unyielding paladins of frontier warfare. And yet, they just had no idea.

Finally I came to my senses. Dogs! Camp dogs! My God, what was I doing? What was I thinking? None of Lisa's trappers had dogs, at least no one that I could think of. Hell, a dog was meat in the pot at the first sign of hunger, man's best friend or not. And what white-men in their right minds would be so overtly brazen in Blackfeet country. And Gros Ventre, John what are you thinking of? Get a hold of yourself man. Are you so eager to die? The realization of just how close I was to being found out was at last sinking into my thick skull. I looked about, cautiously sniffing the air and listened one final time before commencing to 'backtrack my trail,' reversing course towards the Yellowstone. The wind continued to blow in my favor. Their dogs hadn't discovered me. The Atsina never knew how close they had come to capturing the *spoo-pii*. Someone or something was watching over me. Again I had been almighty lucky. And it was intensely sobering even in my addled condition. But, I still had a lot of ground to cover. I wasn't out of the deep woods yet. And this fresh brush with the savages had served to scare me anew, revitalizing what little strength and stamina I still had within me. It was as if I had caught a second... no, a third emotional-wind. And it propelled me with a suddenly renewed burst of energy and determination as I quickly made my way back to the river and followed its twisting course east as fast as my swollen, protesting feet would allow. I moved all through the night, not stopping 'til the sun had risen well-up to its morning heights, distancing myself from what would have been certain discovery and sure death.

It was to have been the last spirited charge of my ordeal: the physical, mental and emotional effort had drained my final reserves. The tragedy, the chase, the fear and hatred, the lack of food and rest, withering strength and pummeled feet, my nakedness in the face of nature's unrelenting elements and the oncoming of winter cold all conspired against me, leaving me with nothing left to give. Somewhere along that long, sad trail I lost count of the hours, the days, the miles. Time, distance passed inexorably without meaning. Yet, somehow I pushed on, plodding heavily with swollen, bloody feet of stone and pain, one foot in front of the other in an agonizingly slow pace, all the while realizing my poor brain was feeling the pinch, my sanity slowly slipping away. My trusted, vaunted instincts, the hallmark of John Colter's wilderness savvy, had given way: when and where my beleaguered mind won't say. I had unconsciously abandoned the cause of nighttime travel, throwing all caution to the wind. No longer did I seem to care, no longer did my life and my sacred-freedom even matter. My only thoughts, my only memories haunting me, morosely, of the last few horrible moments of Johnny and ol' Toby's lives. My heart, my soul cried in despair. Guilt wracked me. Why was I being punished this way?

My stomach had long ago quit growling... even it had given up. My feet, my poor feet, they, too, became inured. My only weapon, that broken Piegan lance had become too heavy to carry. I dropped it, just left it behind somewhere on the trail without as much as a thought. By then body and spirit were frazzled and frayed beyond control. I was near out of my mind, drifting in and out of a starkly bare-awareness clouding my every waking moment: a mere shadow of the man I once was but scant days before. Delirium had set in, when or where I could not say. I had lost all sense of purpose and direction, of who and what and where I was.

Until, for some unexplainable, ungodly reason... I had made it. Somehow, the Yellowstone, La Roche Jaune, the *As-to-pah-oan-zhah* magically steered me on the right path. Unaccountable days drifting into weeks, wandering in a fog of mental, emotional and physical strain, unseen by my fellow man... white, red or otherwise. How, I made it, I'll never know, but, somehow, I did.

Somehow, I had found the Big Horn and Manuel's Fort. I had reached the end of my trail, alone in front of the trapper's post's gate, standing as quietly and as unassuming as the gently swaying cottonwood giants nearby.

They tell me that I was a sight to behold, more dead then alive. A still living, still breathing statue of flesh and blood, locked in a lifeless, stony gaze. How long I was standing there, I couldn't say. But, I stood there mesmerized by memories and despair, ordeal and exhaustion, oblivious even to my own fatigue, starvation, to all else, save for the dimmest of thoughts barely lighting the remotest corners of my mind. Yet from deep within this near-hypnotic state, I found the strength to at least sob aloud inside… "I made it. Good God Almighty, I made it."

But, no one heard my muted, albeit inward cries. Those men in the fort might as well have been on the moon. Oh, to be so close, yet so far. I pleaded for recognition: to be noticed, to be heard. Won't someone please hear my cries and help me?

Finally, a nodding, dozing, half-asleep, grizzly bear of a trapper on sentry duty awoke to see me standing in front of the post in plain view. At first look he couldn't believe his eyes. I must have appeared to him like an odd tree, human-like, a quaky aspen, feet and legs rooted in the soil, as natural as natural can be. He rubbed his eyes, clearing away the grit and haze of sleep. What in tarnation was that thing standing there in front of the fort, an apparition to be sure: half-human, half-critter from some unsettling, nightmarish dream? He was startled, unsure, not quite wanting to believe what he was seeing. His trigger finger trembled nervously… he could have shot me right where I stood. That trapper, in fact all trappers, can be an awfully superstitious lot. The wilderness, after all, is full of mysterious, unexplainable things. Had I not myself just months before visited such a place of unimaginable powers and goin's-on? And hadn't I so equally so been unwilling to confide in what I had seen to my fellow trappers just those few months before? And the savages, for sure they can never be trusted. They were a tricky lot, capable of any number of subterfuges… steal you blind, lift your scalp and from time to time wipe out a whole fort full of white folk. It'd been done before, surely it will happen again.

But, that trapper sentry never did squeeze the trigger. He thought better of it, no matter what kind of creature or nightmare it was standing outside the walls. But, he did sound the alarm. And the Fort came alive with activity. The ramparts quickly filled up with more armed, bearded white men appearing with equally itchy trigger fingers to boot. And they too gawked and stared. Literally, dozens of pairs of beady eyes strained and stared at me in disbelief, all equally dumbfounded, all equally without explanation.

No one recognized me. No one moved to come to my aid. Not that I could blame them, because what they saw, they could hardly be expected to believe or understand. I was as thin as a fence rail, gaunt, emaciated beyond recognition. My hair was caked in mud, matted in an unruly mess. My beard was long and scraggly. My limbs were atrophied, my feet swollen, bruised and bloody and my stomach bloated, distended from want of food. I was buck-naked, dirt filthy, dazed and confused, standing before them in a completely addled state, oblivious of all around me. I said nothing. I uttered no words, no communication. I looked at no one. In fact it seemed I barely even breathed. I just continued to stare at those honed palisaded walls with a blank, faraway look in my eyes.

It was for all intents and purposes a standoff and it remained that way for seemingly the longest of time. No one inside the fort was making a move. They just continued to gawk unabashedly, occasionally murmuring amongst themselves still in disbelief, amazed by what or who it was that stood before them and not one of them willing to recognize that I was… one of them. It took my friend, Pete Wiser to set those boys straight.

"By God, ya bunch of damn fools. Take a good look, it's me, Colter. It's John Colter." It took every ounce of strength I had left just to get those words out.

"What?" came an incredulous response from one of the trappers on the ramparts not believing what he had just heard, and then he asked, "Who'd ya say it were?"

"Goddamn it, it's John Colter. C'mon," barked Wiser, "hurry up. Get out thar and give me a hand before der man keels over. Look at him, will ya… he's about done fer."

With that Pete and the boys rushed out to grab me. Good thing they did, because by the time he reached me, my poor legs had had enough. My knees buckled and gave way. I crumpled to the ground, a sad pile of a man. I lay there in my nakedness, quivering, shaking. I began muttering, rambling on… one incoherent thought after another. Nothing I said could have made sense.

Wiser was frantic, worried out of his head. I had never known the man to be so rattled. The look in his eyes, his face, I'll never forget. "My God, man, yer skin and bones. John, what happened to ya? And where's Potts? Damn it, where's Johnny Potts?" Pete by now was yelling at the top of his voice, shaking me over and over.

I heard Pete's pleas. Johnny Potts, my friend, Johnny Potts… oh, what the dirty bastards did to him. I started to cry, uncontrollably. Where the tears managed to come from I'll never know. I was as dry as a bone. Finally, I looked up at Pete, dear ol' Pete. Somehow, I managed to sit up. I grabbed my worried friend, gripping the soft, worn leather fringes of his hunting shirt tightly as if holding on for dear-life. Tears continued to roll down my cheeks. I was beset by an uncontrollable spasm of coughing and hacking… choking on my own phlegm. It took many moments for me to regain myself. And then I let it all out, the agony, the horror of it all, in one giant pent-up rush of emotional fury. From where the strength came, I truly do not know. I screamed, screamed for all to hear.

"They riddled him, Pete. The dirty, fuggin', red sonsofbitches riddled Johnny dead."

CHAPTER EIGHT

"They did dat to Johnny?" Poor Pete was incredulous. He sat inside Manuel's Fort, his elbows on his knees, his face in his hands. Distraught beyond measure, he had lost his best friend. And then he began to weep softly, staying that way, quietly, that whole long afternoon until his eyes had gone dry from the prolonged effort.

"Why didn't he listen to me? I warned him. Damn his hide, I told him not to go."

"I know you did. I know you did. I'm so sorry, Pete." And I was, I really was. I've kicked myself a thousand times since. I was more than contrite. It was deeper than that. Try as I might, the pangs of guilt ate away at me. I blamed myself for Johnny's death even though by rights I shouldn't have. Potts was a grown man, nigh on every bit experienced in the wilderness and savy to injun ways as any man in Lisa's brigades. And he was a veteran of the Corps, maybe my longest friend. And what's more he demanded to go along to the Forks. He kept at it, wearing down even my own powerful resolve, pushing 'til I felt compelled to oblige. He was relentless, bound and determined. Oh, I could have said no. It wouldn't have mattered. He would have followed me anyway. And I knew it. So, I relented against my better judgment. I partnered up with the man when I swore I would never partner up with any man again. Rode west with him, trapped, hunted and lived side by side with him by the banks of the Jefferson. We had become like brothers. He had shared his feelings. He had trusted me, looked up to me, though, he just never seemed to listen to me. And he wasn't up to tangling with the Blackfoot and the kind of trouble they brought. He hadn't bargained on his own demise. I don't think Johnny would ever have. He only saw the trail of life ahead his way. And now he was gone. And I was forced to live with it.

I was beginning to feel that the white man and the Three Forks country were not meant to be… except for me that is. I could take care of myself if unencumbered. I could sneak back into that valley, especially in the dead of winter and do my business, and no red-hided injun would ever be the wiser. Hell, I had just eluded their whole goddang nation, traveling two hundred miles without as much as a stitch of clothes on my back or a rifle over my shoulder. Yep! That's what I was going to do. I was going back… alone. And soon, as soon as I could. It was my way… it had always been my way.

As the days and weeks passed it was as if I willed my strength and vigor to return. Pete had pulled a-half a hundred needles of the prickly pear from my damaged feet and soaked 'em in salts daily, until those poor dawgs of mine finally began to come around. The aching, pulsating throb in my head eventually went away. My busted ribs healed. I shaved my beard, trimmed my hair. And I ate and I ate and I ate. My appetite was voracious. I put meat away like a pack of hungry wolves. I began to look like my old self once again. Autumn had finally run its course. Winter was everywhere. Time was passing on. And, still, I couldn't shake the Madison and the Jefferson, my nightmare at Three Forks or the memory of the pishkun plains. I was obsessed; I couldn't let it go, too much had happened in too little of a time.

I grew-up listening to my Pa tell of the adventures of George Rogers Clark and his rangers, the big knives, and the battles and Indian raids and the red-mans' depravations along the frontier. I was forever shocked by those horrific reports of wanton brutality, their wolf-like tenacity, the outright barbaric treatment the red-man dealt the white… not that my own people were without guilt. There were far too many tales of revenge by all concerned not to cause eternal enmity on both sides. I never wanted to believe it, not in my wildest dreams. How could any man, civilized or savage, do such inhumane things to their fellow human beings was always beyond comprehension.

The white-eyes were as guilty as the red. Some men never seem to respect the ways, the feelings, the lives and property and territory of others. And the Three Forks was Piegan, a place the Blackfeet people bitterly contested. We were the invaders of the wilderness, the trespassers uninvited, there to take what we wanted. Pushing west, the white-man never looked at it the same way the Indian did. To the whites, the red-man was irrelevant, without rights. He was like an animal, to be considered as less than a man. Indian land, its riches, its critters were there for the whites to use as they saw fit.

Yet, the beaver was there, waiting to be taken. And so was my kit, all my precious traps sitting on the bottom of the Jeff, beckoning me to return. And just maybe those Blackfeet never did find our campsite and cache. There was a fortune in cached plews waiting to be dug up and cashed in. I had a lot to think about, all of which were driving me beyond any desire I'd ever known.

Pete sensed my turmoil, watching over me daily while I was on the mend. He knew I was brooding, seething, constantly catching me staring to the west or cleaning my newly acquired shootin' iron again and again till I near rubbed the metal away. He knew my heart was troubled, felt the white hot grief and anger a blazing through my head and soul. And he struggled to mind his own business, but Potts had been his best friend. And me, I was a close second.

"Colter, why in the hell are ya still here? What's keepin' ya? And why do ya keep starin' back to der West, to dem damn Forks? Let it lie man, let it lie. Johnnys gone, ain't nothin' bringin' him back. Dat place is no good for you, for me, for no white man. Let it lie."

Pete was probing, fleshing me out. I could see the worry in his face, I knew he had been reading my mind, my heart and it had bothered him greatly, 'til he could no longer hold it in. "Dis place, dis beaver business is just not cuttin' it for me anymore. I'm fixin' to go back home. I wished ya'd throw in with me, before it's too late."

There just was no putting him off or blowin' smoke up ol' Pete Wiser's ass. He'd been around me too many years not to notice when a fool notion was a cooking up in his friend's brain. So he tried once again to talk some sense, to save a friend's hide. And like Johnny Potts, I wasn't listening.

I took a long deep breath, exhaled slowly and sighed. "Thanks, Pete for carin'. I owe you an awful lot. Your offer is hard to refuse. To tell the truth, I've thought of returnin' to the East most every day I've been here."

"Well, what's stoppin' ya? Ya certainly spent enough time out here for any half-a-dozen men. So what in der hell is the point? You think ya got somethin' to prove? 'Cause if ya do, it sure ain't worth it, not by a long shot."

"I don't rightly know. I guess maybe it's because I'm broke." I paused, knowing it was only partly true. I stammered, completely befuddled, unsure myself at the moment of the real reason.

"So am I," he said. "So's everybody here, 'ceptin' Lisa. He's into every man here, even includin' Johnny. Dat's why der kid went with ya to der Forks. He couldn't stand to be beholdin' to der Spaniard. He could've never gone home owin' Lisa like he did. He knew dat Lisa and der law would've found him no matter where he went. Poor Johnny was obsessed to git Lisa's debt off his back and settle-up… cum hell or high water. And dat's why he took a chance a-going with ya to dat infernal place."

"I know. I know," I sighed. He was right, I knew; yet, Pete saying it didn't make it any more palatable. Then, like a fool who could not let it go, I added rather forlornly, "I guess I'm just too stubborn for my own good."

"Stubborn! Stubborn! Yeah, ya damn fool, ya don't have to add stupid to it, do ya?"

The skin on Pete's face was drawn as taut as an injun's drum, bulging eyes bursting in their sockets livid, burning red hot with indignation. He leapt to his feet, clenching his fists, knuckles stark white and cocked ready to swing and hammer away at God knows who or what; the whole ordeal, the loss of Johnny, now venting full steam.

"Dis shit has got to come to an end." Pete, his voice a veritable storm of fire and fury, screamed, "I've had it with dis beaver business and dose goddanged bourgeois and their 'hi-falutin' airs.' Fuck Lisa and fuck der Missouri Fur Company. Stay if ya please, I'm headin' home… with or without ya."

I was near speechless. Until now, Pete had been a man who kept his cards close to his chest. His had always been the calm voice of reason, of logic. Venting was for other, less confident, less capable men. Yet, since my return his fuse had shortened dramatically, barely able to contain the festering resentment building up within him. Unnoticed by me he had hung on, holding off leaving while I healed. And now he was letting it all go. But, he wasn't any more pissed-off than I was. His just showed sooner… mine was taking a little longer to erupt. Anger, resentment was pouring through my heart and soul like a bitterly evil cancerous-bile. It had been coming for sometime. How long I could keep it up before I too exploded, I couldn't say… but it was coming as sure as the morning sun. The Blackfeet had gone too far, way too far, mocking Potts' life and memory with their cruel, senseless revilement. They had made their point, but butchering and humiliating Johnny and me the way they did was beyond reproach. Somehow, some way…

Revenge, what could I do? They were way-too strong, and now, after the *spoo-pü's* escape, way too wary. I was just one man. But, I vowed to get the final word, I was returning to the Forks to retrieve my traps and if possible, our cache of skins if it was the last thing I'd do. I figured it was the least I could do for Johnny and his kin. Somehow, in the dead of winter, amidst the snow and the ice, I'd find those cached plews. I'd cash 'em in and send Johnny's take back home. And I desperately wanted my traps back. I was a beaver trapping man and those traps belonged to me. And that wasn't the only thing I wanted. I wanted my self-respect back. Once I did, I could leave this place. Then the Blackfeet could suck hind-teat… whether they ever found out or not. I'd have the last word. So help me, God. I had to gain solace, some sense of satisfaction. I had to go back.

Pete subsequently calmed down, but his mind was set and undeterred. I knew there was absolutely no changing it. He, too, looked in my face and could see the determination ingrained deeply like Cap'n William Clark's name etched in the sandstone of Pompey's Pillar. He knew the guilt I felt, the self-inflicted burden that just would not let go. Yes, Pete Wiser knew me all too well.

"Hmmph, yer a-goin' back, aren't ya? Knew ya would. Ya haven't changed a lick since der first day I met ya." Pete stood, shaking his head, the saddest, most disconsolate of looks registering on his face. He knew he was too late. Too much water had gone under the Colter-bridge for me to turn tail and skedaddle east.

"Minds made up, Pete. You already know that, though. I ain't into quittin', never have been. It just ain't in me, and I'm too old to start now. I stayed out here to trap beaver, to make my fortune, to go home with somethin' to show for all the years spent here. Outside of that one winter-spell with Handcock and Dickson, I've been stopped from doin' what I set out to accomplish every dang time I tried the Three Forks. I ain't givin' up 'til I lick this bad streak.

And I certainly ain't giving in to those savages, not after what they did to Potts. Wouldn't be right. No sir! Johnny's take is still out there. So's mine. I aim to get it all back, hell or high water. Blackfeet or no Blackfeet."

Pete looked at me with nary an expression. Hell, we both stared at each other the exact same way, mute, as if there was nothing left to say, just feel. It was a moment of great friendship and reluctant parting.

Finally, Pete broke silence. "Yer a helluva man, Colter. The Cap'n's always said so. Dat's why dey let ya leave der Corps back at der Knife. Drouillard had der savvy, but he was still needed. I doubt if even he was ready to do what you planned to do."

"Thanks, Pete. Thanks for everything."

Pete grabbed and shook my hand. Our eyes met one final time. We had shared much over the last five years. The pain, the loss of our friend had been too great for him to contemplate a moment longer. The man just did not want to go through it anymore… the worrying, the not knowing. He could not stand the thought of me risking my hide again in the Headwaters country and losing another friend to the savages. So we said our goodbyes. He turned abruptly and walked away without as much as a look back. It was the last time I ever saw or heard of Pete Wiser.

I slipped out of Manuel's quietly one moonless December night loaded for bear and hell bent on making the Forks. Pete's last words weighed heavily on my mind. Winter set in early that year battering the mountainous country of the Northwest mercilessly. The months that followed grew increasingly colder, snowing for weeks at a time: monstrous drifts blanketed the land deep white, from the highest peaks to the river valleys. La Roche Jaune nearly froze over, grinding to an icy halt. Bitter arctic winds blew in from the north, pummeling the valley of the Yellowstone, blasting life to a frigid standstill. Little moved save for the hardiest and hungriest of beasts. It was not the time of year or the kind of weather a man should be traipsing around in. But, I was no ordinary man right then, not in my frame of mind. I thought little of personal discomfort even on the darkest, loneliest of nights. Exposure to the raw side of winter was hardly new to me. I wore plenty of warm clothing: my moccasins were made from the thick hide of the buffalo hump, with spares in my pack; and a heavy buffalo robe to keep away the coldest of nights. I was covered from head to toe in fur. Even the rawest of inclement weather worried me not. I wore invisible blinders, a man possessed, proceeding on, determined in a sort of queer, paralyzing way. I was stubborn. I was foolish, though it never even crossed my mind. Potts' death had traumatized me, driving me to gain some measure of revenge or satisfaction. How, I ever thought I could recover my traps from the depths of the Jefferson, that frozen stream, or find caches of beaver plews hidden under deep snow, never penetrated my thick skull. I was obviously deluding myself, lying to the one person I needed to be truthful with.

Physically, I was strong again. My vigor, my stamina had recovered. I returned like I knew I would, passing through the mountains of the Wolf, retracing my steps, until I entered the broad valley of the Gallatin River below. I stopped to get my bearings, to suck it all in. It was a near cloudless day; the glare of the sun intense by early afternoon, its brilliance reflecting off an entirely white landscape. I shielded my eyes, surveying the ice and snow-laden land; the mountains of the Wolf and its narrow pass behind me, the high, rugged mountains to the south and the aimlessly rolling, undulating prairie grassland to the west… towards the Three Forks country. Not a hint of the red man or his campfire smoke was to be seen. Nothing moved, 'til I chanced to see a lone *cayac*, a young buffalo bull nosing aside deep snow and frozen ground to get to a few meager blades of dead grass. He was hungry, mighty hungry. So hungry he failed to notice my cautious approach from downwind.

And he was alone… all alone on the Gallatin prairie, one single solitary beast. He was a godsend right then. The trek through the pass had left me with a powerful appetite once again. And my pack was down to my last few strips of jerked meat. Fresh buffalo meat would suit me well for what I had planned. I could take the time, butcher this beast and lay away enough meat to take care of the rest of my journey. Yeah, this situation suits me just fine.

As I continued to look about I could see no more buffaloes browsing or any other critters for that matter. Even the sky seemed devoid of creatures of flight, except for an occasional 'redtail' on patrol. The pickings on the plains must have been pretty thin right then. Crows were usually hanging around when there was chance of fresh kill to be had, yet I saw nary a one. It was strange, quite strange. But the prairie can be deceiving; the land forever marred by dry coulees and such. It was easy to err when there was nary a sign. It was also all too easy for a critter, any critter, man or beast to use the wind's direction, the dips and folds of the land, shade, wallows and rocky outcroppings, the outright calmness of the day to mask any presence of deceit or treachery. I had made that mistake before. But, still there was just nothing to see and I brought my attention to bear once again on that night's supper.

The old bulls probably banished him from the herd, chased him away from their harem while they were 'in heat.' Poor guy, I thought, he must've been awfully horny. I could relate. But, those old bulls didn't give a dang to be sure and they could make life mighty miserable for a youngster… just when he was starting to feel his oats. Can't help you, fella. I'm too hungry, myself. And with a little luck you're going to be my dinner.

All the while that big beast foraged I was able to move in closer, well within my rifle's range. The wind was still steadily blowing in my face from the west. The young bull continued to scratch the frozen prairie surface, oblivious to any nearby peril. In fact he had made so much noise nosing aside the snow, breaking up ice and whatnot and munching on that gramma that he failed to hear my own approaching snow-crunching footsteps. But, I had been quiet, deliberately taking my time. I was in no rush. And he was the only meal around.

I slowly knelt down on one knee. I again surveyed all that I could see… satisfying myself that we were still alone. One shot would probably have to do. I took careful aim. One, two last breaths and then… I squeezed off my shot, the ignition of black powder popped and echoed throughout the valley soon disappearing off into the void. The cayac, the young bull was struck nigh on instantly and jolted, responding as if receiving a shove from some powerful unexplainable force… desperately trying to regain his balance and equilibrium. He staggered for several feet, teetering on unsure legs, wobbly as if in a drunken stupor, not once realizing what had just hit him. And then his knees buckled, no longer able to support the load. He collapsed, falling to the frozen ground. A 'fifteen hundred-pound heap of brown fur' lay sprawled in its death throes. The beast bawled for several long minutes as convulsion and then death finally settled in.

As he breathed his last breaths I quickly reloaded. I wasn't about to make that mistake a second time. Once again I looked about. Though satisfied, I lingered another few minutes just to be sure. I was taking no chances. A wounded buffalo was still a dangerous animal. Then I arose and walked straight to the buff. My lead ball had found its mark, exploding his massive heart, creating a vast internal mayhem that he surely could not survive. But he had been tough, no instant death for him. It had taken several long, painful minutes for the young buff bull to finally expire. What a magnificent creature I had thought while I waited and watched. The beast finally stopped breathing. His heart beat its last beat. He was gone. And just as quickly I went to work.

But, once again I had that strange, unexplainable feeling creeping up the back of my neck. And it told me that I was not alone. I looked up, simultaneously grabbing my shooting iron just in time to see one, two, three, a half a dozen or more wolves circling and steadily moving in closer, contesting my kill. And they were big 'uns… buffalo-wolves we called 'em. The larger males packing as much weight as I carried on my own frame. And one in particular, the biggest of the bunch, a dark gray, steely-colored like the most menacing of storm clouds, seemed to be hanging back, but running the show. Him and his kind roamed and stalked the outer edges of the buff herds, preying on the weak, the young, the old, the injured. And now they were about ready to fight me for mine.

It wasn't the first time I had had a brush with hungry lobos. In those days wolves were everywhere to be found. Up north, when beaver was scarce the Brits occasionally swapped with the Canadian Plains tribes for wolf pelts, paying them in liquor, 'fire-water.' On many a lonely night their long, solitary howls might be the only music a man would hear in a thousand miles. I'd shot more than my share over the years, even tasted their flesh from time to time. Though I preferred it not. And the thought of eating so noble an adversary somehow dishonored all I stood for. But I wasn't about to let this pack of mangy curs take off with my dinner. Thank, God, though, I had reloaded my weapon. At least I'd get one shot off before I was forced to withdraw my tomahawk from my belt and commence to swinging-away at the bolder ones.

I stood defiantly, straddled atop my dead 'cayac,' daring that big dark gray to draw first blood with me. But he hung back, licking his chops, a million years of hunting and instinct silently going about its business. He was the boss of this outfit, the big chief of his pack. He wasn't about to get his paws wet; not when he had the others there to initiate the killing work. The rest of his pack knew the pecking order and closed right in, until one hefty brute got testy and issued his challenge. His eyes and rabid wolfish stare were mesmerizing, intense as any encounter I had ever known. He started to snarl, revealing a nasty set of dripping canines. I winced for one brief instant. That wolf's toothy glare was enough to make any man feel a little unsteady. And then he came on with a rush, charging straight at me. No hesitation, no fancy, tricky maneuvering. In that split instant I decided to save my lead. The wolf leaped at my throat. I flipped my rifle, grabbing and holding the barrel like a club and then… I swung, cracking the big lobo right on top of his skull. He went down like he was felled by an axe. The crash of my rifle's butt on his noggin was explosive, rocking the air like the clap of thunder. Down he went, howling in pain. He quickly scurried away, his tail between his legs, yelping and yipping.

That was enough for the rest of 'em… their 'big gray chief' included, as they trotted away to what was for them a safe distance. But, they never took their eyes off of me… or the dead buff. They knew I couldn't eat that whole carcass. Sooner or later I would have to share. They'd soon get their nerve back and come around for another go at me. Wolves were awfully smart critters, not easily discouraged. And they could be mighty ornery; tough enough to drive the biggest of grizzlies away from their own kills.

As for me, well, I had had enough. I knew when I had won, just like I also knew it was time to skedaddle. I laid my rifle down and took out my skinning knife, never for instant forgetting the pack. I had neither the time nor the inclination to stay around, not with these hungry wolves hanging nearby and between the lot of us making enough commotion for every Indian from the Yellowstone to the Jefferson to hear. The back strap was what I wanted. And I bent down and removed both strips of tenderloin, carving them out from either side of that young bull's spine, all the while glancing nervously at the pack. I was too easily distracted by those hungry critters. They were losing patience. I could see it, edging ever closer, tightening the circle, the distance between us. Jesus, I thought, what a time it'd be for the Piegans to show up. And then I became really worried.

I finished my butchering chore after but a few quick cuts. It hadn't taken me long, though I wasn't walking away with nearly as much meat as I wanted and needed. But, sometimes a man has got to know when it's time to leave. I backed off aways from the carcass, eyeing those hungry wolves all along, watching their moves, divining their intentions. And they, well, once I was clear of the 'cayac' they couldn't have cared less about me. The big male, the chief of the pack was the first to move in and taste the flesh of victory. It was the tacit signal the rest of the pack had waited for. I didn't wait around to watch them gorge themselves, and lit a hasty shuck towards the river, distancing myself from the pack as fast as my ol' feet could carry me. As I hurried away I listened for the sounds of paw pads, crunching snow on my backtrail, but there were none to be heard, not one critter followed... they just let me go. That pack of wolves was more interested in a tastier meal than a human-man had to offer and were soon muzzle-deep into their feeding, the echoes of rapacious feasting disquieting what was otherwise a quiet winter day in the Gallatin valley.

The afternoon waned 'til dusk. The sun finally disappearing over the horizon. Twilight arrived. Ol' man moon never chose to come out that night, leaving the sky pitch black save for a million flickering stars. I had known many such nights and they were lonely nights. And with little in the way of breezes blowing, it would be quiet, awfully quiet. But, that was all right by me. I needed such a night. I needed to rest up, make myself a good warm meal, to take my bearings and plan my next day. I was weary, spent by too many days of hard travel on a frozen trail. So I picked my spot carefully, making camp close to the river, cozying up among the cottonwoods, out of any threatening winds, kindling a cooking fire of dry aspen sprigs, small and discreet. The smokeless 'quakie' blaze and the light it gave soon proved comforting; it's warmth consoling my chilled bones.

This time, unlike the last, I was shod, clothed and well armed. I was clad to withstand the coldest of winter nights. I was on equal terms with the red-man. This time, I was not fleeing for my life, but returning to rightfully claim what was mine. This time the *spoo-pii* was a man to be reckoned with.

I kept my rifle by my side, handily within reach, taking no chances. A brace of pistols, primed and loaded were stashed in my belt ready to go. My tomahawk, my knife hung on me like they were part of my hide. I was alert; wary, relying on my senses, my instincts, determined not to be had.

"It ain't much," I said softly, looking out into the bleak void of a high country winter night, all the while, rubbing vigorously, warming my chilled fingers and hands, appreciating the blaze, its red hot embers and the solace it brought.

"Beats the hell out of the last time I was here," I mumbled aloud, almost glad to hear my own voice.

I rechecked my possibles, keeping it all within easy reach. I mentally recalculated my next day's march to the valley of the Three Forks. I kept seeing, focusing on the bend of the Jefferson, the shallow waters where I had sunk my traps. Step by step, I went over the trail, retracing every foot of the way. I'd be careful, cautious, taking advantage of every bit of cover the land had to offer. I had to, in all that whiteness one bad move would be visible from miles around. I'd use every trick, every instinct I ever knew. I wouldn't attract attention, not if I could help it.

The Piegan surely wouldn't be lurking about the Forks dead in the middle of winter, not a chance. It just didn't make sense. They won't be expecting the '*spoo-pii*' to return, at least not so soon. They'd be tucked away quietly in their winter quarters miles to the north, not about to leave their warm lodges and warmer squaws to freeze their asses off looking for the likes of me.

I was confident, almost smug. It felt good to be back on my feet again. I was glad to be shed of Manuel's Fort. The stockade's odorous confines had cramped my style long enough; no room to stretch your arms and legs, no clean air to breathe. Twenty to thirty stinking, unwashed trappers biding the winter away, all within the confines of a stuffy room, was enough to repel any man to face the cold bite and stark clarity of a frozen, wintry world.

"Better off out here, even in the dead of winter. The air smells fresh. Everything is clean, healthy-like. To hell with Manuel's... this is where I belong."

I found myself drawn to my little campfire, mesmerized by the dancing flames, by the sharp tunes of its crackling embers, lost in thought as I settled in for a quiet meal and a calm night. I poked and prodded hot, glowing coals with a thin, sharpened willow twig, stoking the embers, releasing the pent-up energy and heat to burn further anew. The aroma of sizzling backstraps waxed succulently to the senses, tantalizing my taste buds, teasing my hunger. I had waited for several days for a treat such as this and nothing on God's green earth could put off feasting one minute longer than necessary.

Not for instant, did it occur to me that buff meat roasting on a spit in the dead of the night would carry well beyond the bounds of caution. No, there wasn't an Indian within a hundred miles. The red-man was way too sensible for that. Only a fool like me would be out here in the dead of winter, putting up with bitter winds and biting cold and wolves and such just to find a half-dozen metal traps in a frozen river that just may not be there any longer to be found.

But, indeed there was, someone or something was out there in the dark on the prowl. I could make out the distinct sound of snow-covered twigs and branches being trampled underfoot, even though the culprit was doing everything possible to avoid such detection. Try as they or it might, soft, carefully placed footsteps or hooves could not avoid nor muffle the crisp crunch of crusted snow nor the thin, brittle, icy mantle beneath. My eyes instantly darted away from the blinding light of my fire. I reached and grabbed my rifle, drawing it to my side. I sat still and listened, craning every sense. And then I smelled the roasting meat just inches away from me. Every critter within miles must have been drawn to it. But what kind of critter was I now hearing?

"Damn," I swore under my breath, "don't this beat all, just when I'm fixin' to eat my dinner."

I kept looking off into the darkness, away from the bright, dancing flames, gradually adjusting my eyes to the dark of the night. Slowly, ever so slowly, I edged back away from the firelight distancing myself from the flickering flames as much as I could without attracting undue attention. Easy does it, Johnnyboy, watch it, no sudden, jerky moves, got to keep this play-acting going, let 'em think they've got you where they want you. I started to hum and mouth a few lines of "Yankee Doodle." Soon I was belting it out. My mouth, my lips were going dry with the effort. Desperately, I wanted to reach down and grab a handful of snow to wet my whistle. But, I declined. Patience, patience, just a little while longer… whatever's out there is mighty interested in you, boy. Humph! Knowing my luck I wasn't betting on it having four legs. I remained near motionless, listening intently, while my left arm casually dropped down to the leather sling of my powderhorn lying on the ground at my side. My right hand grabbed the long thin neck between the butt and hammer of my rifle, securing a firm hold. I was like a cat, every muscle and sinew in my body taut, ready to spring. My pulse was picking up. I couldn't prevent it no matter how hard I tried to remain calm, assured. My jaws tightened, my teeth ground like a gristmill, everything within me waxed unrestrained. My eyes were pin-pointedly keen like a little nighthawk on the prowl, espying the night for any and all signs of life. Seemingly, long moments of silence followed, nothing stirred, not even a wind to ruffle the cottonwoods.

I relaxed, momentarily easing my guard, maybe, 'twas nothin', just some hungry varmint licking its chops over the smell of roasting meat. Maybe… maybe not, you know better than that. Everything within me seemed to say, not now, after all that's happened to you out here. Would you rather die? Is that it, some kind of suicide to repent for your sins? C'mon, man… come to your senses, pronto. Yeah, you're right, what the hell, dinner can wait a while longer.

Then I heard it again. This time the movements were unmistakable and several steps closer than a moment before. Who or what was inching nearer and nearer. What's more it wasn't alone. I was certain of it, taking all my instincts to ferret-out the conspiracy. Carefully-guarded-steps picked their way through crusted snow, delicately, patiently biding time with caution, followed closely by those of another tagging right behind, using his mate's tracks, all the while both moving in coordinated tandem drawing nearer and nearer. The questioned begged… men or beasts? The smell of roasting meat was a magnet no hungry meat eater could resist, nothing else could account for what I was hearing, except for the type of critter who was interested in more than just feeding on meat. Suddenly, I knew… these were the two-legged kind. Everything told me as much. Yes, that was it. Coincidental or not, I'd blundered into another trap. Holy shit! Anxiety, adrenaline, fear raced throughout me. It was Johnny Potts and the Jefferson all over again. What have I done? What have I done? Calm down, you fool, get a hold of yourself. You ain't a goner, yet. Think. Think…

Sometimes, situations don't even allow the luxury of time to let a man think things out. Sometimes you just have to act. For right then an ominous sound split the night … the metallic clink of the cocking of the heavy hammer of a trade musket, a sound I knew all too well. I needed no further introduction.

The animal within me sprung like a tightly wound coil of steel as I leaped over the fire, clearing hot flames just as a musket discharged its load, shattering the cold, calm of the night. I landed running as another musket report followed tail on the heels of the first. A lead ball caromed by me, zinging off into the night. I cringed as its telltale whistling trail compelled my arms, my legs to full speed and exertion. Both shots missed me completely, but not my cooking fire. The first errant ball had struck my fire's red-hot coals dead on, scattering embers, buffalo meat and all, singeing my backside and legs in midair ere I hit the ground. I never looked back.

"Christ, don't they ever give up?" I was dumbfounded, anew, running full bore, all the while my mind raced, wondering how all this came to be. How did they know? Did they follow me? Were they waiting all along? Damn it, damn it, I've got to know. I kept moving, running, making my way through snow and ice and darkness. Listening, straining the senses for pursuit on my trail or deceit lying ahead, waiting to spring yet another clever trap. The questions, the doubt needed answering. Figuring these redskins out just might save my life. C'mon. Think. Think. Maybe Wiser was right. Maybe Blackfeet or Gros Ventre spies had scouted the Fort. Hell, they may have dogged my trail all the way to here for all I knew. Maybe they heard my shot killing that *cayac*. Maybe they found his carcass. Saw my tracks. Hell, maybe those wolves told them all about me for all I knew. I could just about believe anything anymore. Nothing was making sense the way I was seeing it. And instinct had failed to warn me. No, that wasn't exactly right, maybe it had tried and I hadn't listened. Had I been too confident, too set in my ways? Had I been blinded, blinded by own stubborness and obsession? This was a hell of a time to start worrying about it. Yet, I was beginning to see the answer. And I should have known it all along. For once, I should have heeded my friend's advice. For once I should have listened to someone else for that ol' itch of mine had failed to warn me, until just moments ago. How could it, the way I'd been I wouldn't have listened anyway?

But, I was listening now. I moved quickly, darting through the thick cottonwood groves and thickets that flanked the Gallatin's banks. I ignored the deep tracks in the snow that I was leaving behind. There was nothing I could do about them anyway. Besides, my pursuers would be no faster then I was. Again, I was wary, conscious of how the red-man thought. Did they just happen on me, or was this part of a fiendish plan? How many muskets fired? There were two reports, no more than that I was certain. Were they possibly waiting ahead to waylay me again? I had to know. I took the chance. I slowed down to listen. Not one sound of pursuit was to be heard. Why? What's holding them back? My mind raced for answers. Maybe, they wouldn't come right away. Not with the *"spoo-pii"* armed once again with a fire-stick and a brace of belt pistols. They were Piegans, I was certain of it. No other tribe would have the *"cajones"* or the reason. And for sure they knew enough to respect what I could do with a long-rifle. They'd remember how fast I reloaded that long-rifle again and again, pumping red-hot lead into exposed Piegan bellies. No, they wouldn't have forgotten the "pishkun plains" and the napikwan's "big medicine" firestick. They wouldn't come chasing me with empty weapons. No, I was quite sure they'd reload those cheap fusees of theirs before they'd think twice of tangling with me again. And if they knew all that, then who were they: a chance hunting party or sworn avengers? Which were they? I didn't know and not-knowing I liked it not.

Whoa, Johnboy! This is way too confusing. And then a most ironic thought left me shaking my head. What if the sneaky bastards were using Potts' '03 issue or even my old long-rifle. Now, wouldn't that be something?

It'd be just my luck to be shot by my own weapon. Damn, if that didn't make me mad. And atop of that, the bloody bastards will have my dinner to boot. Damn, that makes me doubly mad… a second time. This was all happening too fast, way too fast. Got to get a handle on it. Slow down, you fool. Slow down and think this thing out… if you can. I tried. I couldn't. It was beyond my ability. For once I was compelled to ask for help… for a second time.

"Lord of Mercy," I found myself praying, "I swear on my momma's grave I'll never come back. Just get me outta here."

"*Ak-o-tash-iks.* Hurry, he gets away." But, before the Piegan warrior could give chase, he felt a strong, overpowering grip take hold of his arm, refusing to let go. He struggled not, knowing better than to resist, for Many Horses was much too strong and lately, so unpredictable. His friend, his fellow Buffalo Bull had not been the same since *Maa-koyou-mah'-kaa's* death. He'd become obsessed with this *napikwan*. His grief had gone unassuaged, stalking the white man's fort by the Waters of the Wind for these many moons, long after their people had headed north to sit out the winter. And while they'd waited, bitter cold and hunger had worn them down, whittling away bodily strength, chafing at their patience and resolve. Yet, they both had kept at it, sworn to avenge *Maa-koyou-mah'-kaa*. Even so, the *napikwan* had slipped away entirely unnoticed amidst a blinding blizzard on some strange, unexplainable quest, oddly enough heading right back towards where the rivers come together. Why, what was there for him in their sacred *Ahkoto waktai sakum* that he would risk capture and death once again? This white man was making a habit of confusing them. Maybe he wasn't hisself, either, though his magic still seemed to be as strong as ever. Only chance and a longing for their people's warm lodges had found them here to find his cooking fire. Certainly it was meant to be, though they had little or no time to plan their action. It had all happened so fast. Just as before, *spoo-pii* had been devilishly quick, their well aimed shots missing their mark, spraying embers awry, while he was off like an *ah-wa-kas*. But, why does Many Horses fail to give chase? He couldn't understand his friend's hesitation. What holds him back?

Ak-o-tash-iks stood motionlessly, listening intently, now, barely able to detect the faint, fleeting footsteps of the fleeing *napikwan,* till he heard them no more. He was certain it had been *spoo-pii*, the quick, elusive one. Who else would dare, but this strange white man? This time, though, the clever trickster was not naked or unarmed, but dangerous, formidable, as potent now as he had been that day on the pishkun plains, gut-shooting Piegan warriors seemingly at will. He remembered all too well the death that spewed from this *napikwan's* fire-stick, the dying wails and lamentations of his fellow warriors and friends. Their unavenged spirits haunting his mind and soul till this very day, demanding retribution, to be set free from the limbo of the pishkun plains and released to the happy hunting grounds to join their ancestors.

Yet, *spoo-pii* was indeed dangerous. It was wise and prudent to respect such prowess. Just look at how his friend *Maa-koyou-mah'-kaa*, as great a warrior as he was, had been so easily deceived, disarmed and dispatched. A scene *Ak-o-tash-iks* would never forget. He was not afraid of death, but courage and leadership didn't justify needless or hasty foolishness. No, cunning and patience would one day prevail, they were hallmarks of his people's warriorhood. Yes, he had missed an opportunity. But, he'd have another chance; their trails were bound to cross again. He was certain of it. This *spoo-pii* just couldn't stay away, something kept bringing him back. Better to wait for time and circumstance would eventually be on his side. Indeed, he would have another chance.

His thoughts suddenly drifted to Wind in Her Hair, the little sister, not so little anymore. Her beauty and strength were just as haunting as the spirits of the pishkun plains. Her heart, though, would never be his as long as her brother's murder went unavenged. For now, he would have to wait… wait for a more opportune time. Meanwhile, Wind in Her Hair need not know of this encounter.

Finally he spoke. "Keep tongue quiet, brother, no chase now. *Spoo-pii* come back soon. You see."

PART THREE

"Danger had for him a kind of fascination... Nature had formed him... for hardy indurance of fatigue, privations and perils... His veracity was never questioned among us, and his character was that of a true American backwoodsman."

General Thomas James... "Three Years Among the Indians and Mexicans (1846)"

CHAPTER NINE

I made my way back to Manuel's Fort empty-handed and a changed man. The change was readily apparent even to a stubborn, mule-headed backwoodsman like me. There was no doubt in my mind that the year 1808 had aged me more than I could say. My winter trek, the encounters with the Blackfeet, the escapes and subsequent ordeals that followed had taken the spring out of my legs and sapped my vitality in more ways than a wily old tomcat has lives. I couldn't argue with what was staring me in the face and reminding me in the most nightmarish of ways every sleepless night since.

Yet, it was more than the obvious physical change that I was seeing and feeling. There was something intangible missing, something that had defined John Colter's whole life, from my earliest days in the woods of Staunton to going it alone in the wilds of the Rocky Mountains.

I knew what that something was. It was audacity, it was boldness, that "don't give a damn" streak that marked every move I ever made. I left it back yonder, alongside the Gallatin that last cold wintry night. That and the realization that I failed in what I set out to do everytime I went to the Forks. What was it with that place, to lose a friend everytime I went there? What were the 'fates' trying to tell me? Was it me... was I being too damned ornery, stubborn to listen, to see and realize?

Hell, who was I kidding? I left it with Johnny that fateful day by the Jefferson and on the 'prickly pear plains.' It just took one more slap in the face, one more 'kiss your ass good-bye' kind of scrape for me to finally admit that maybe my run and my luck was just about used up.

I no longer thought of going it alone, of trapping the Forks in solitude and contentment. Beaver and the money it brought didn't seem to matter to me like it once did. It had cost Johnny Potts his life and came close to taking mine, twice again. I looked at the Piegan with an even greater respect and fear. And the Three Forks, their *Ahkoto waktai Sakum*, well, that was a place for me to avoid from here-on out, even with an army of trappers to watch my backside.

Pete Wiser had returned to civilization just like he said he would. I knew I would miss him with his 'get under your skin wit,' his brotherly-like friendship, his clear, 'right on the head' way of seeing things the way they truly were.

Lisa had headed-on back downriver, to prepare for another expedition, or so they told me. When and where-to I couldn't say. Didn't concern me as long as it wasn't out here and didn't include me. Maybe, the Spaniard was finally coming to his senses, like I had come to mine.

My fascination with this here country had become tarnished, my reasons for staying sounding a bit stale and it was growing increasingly harder in my mind to defend it anymore.

My traps and furs I conceded were lost forever. And nothing on God's green Earth could get me to go back and risk my own hide, not for man or wealth, nor anything at all. A man has got to know when to move on, when to count his losses and if need be to never look back. Even so, I continued to struggle; to fight within myself. In the back of all I stood for I still disdained quitting. My heart, my mind was not completely convinced.

Yet, the world we live in is growing smaller by the day. The wilderness, its vastness in distance and time used to harbor and keep safe its secrets from the historical record and the inquiring minds of an ever-encroaching civilization. All that was changing thanks to men like Meriwether Lewis and William Clark and a certain young Alexander Henry up Canada way, daily keeping logs and journals for future Western posterity. But, for the steadfastness of that same Alexander Henry and his journal entries, I might have been none the wiser, ever. And when I finally did find out some years later it was like pouring salt on my wounds. For the saga of Potts and our caches of skins was to linger on, trailing far to the north, just a few short months away in time, one day solving a mystery.

At the time of Johnny's death, no one at Manuel's Fort, nor even further down the 'big muddy' in St. Louis, realized how deeply into the upper Missouri country the influence of the Canadian fur companies on the Piegan and their kin and allies had spread. It all came to a head in the winter of '09, a few hundred miles to the north, at the Brit's Fort Vermilion, on the North Saskatchewan river at its juncture with the Vermilion, deep within the country of the Bloods and the Siksika.

And it was all due to that Alexander Henry Jr. following in his daddy's footsteps. By then young Henry was directing the Canadian-led trapping and trading operation for the Northwest Company. That outfit had for years given the better known Hudson's Bay Company stiff competition and now, they in turn were starting to feel the impact of Lisa's company operating out of St. Louis, pushing north into Yellowstone country.

The Northwest leadership had been an unusual blend of French Canadians, Scots, English and two Americans, Alexander Henry Sr. and Peter Pond. Efficient and ruthless, this alliance of powerful Montreal merchants with their wilderness traders attacked the Northwest trade with energy and a typical Scottish flair for shrewd business. They were a rugged, independent lot, hell-bent on making the beaver business mighty difficult for their main rivals, the Hudson's Bay Company. They had to be contentious, because the Hudson's Bay Company was as equally tenacious and unscrupulous, with a long history of monopolizing the fur trade and refusing to let others compete. They had cut a wide swath, eighty years long, running their operations with an iron hand, defrauding their Indian customers as a matter of course and ruthlessly meting out floggings to their employees and servants alike.

But, they had done little in that time to push for expansion, to develop virgin, untrapped territory. Up till then their profits had been great while they held hegemony, but they were now, also feeling the heat of competition from their new rivals.

Into this vacuum, the highly charged Northwest Company stressing a constant urgency for fresh new beaver country, new exploration, and new trading posts, invaded the sanctity of our very own Louisiana Purchase, thereby setting the course for future encounters.

On the first leg of our expedition the Corps experienced this rivalry first hand at the Mandan villages, when the tribe first greeted us expecting to be lavished with gifts. They had been accustomed to preferential treatment from Canadians vying for their beaver trade.

Our presence on the upper Missouri was soon met with enmity as the northern trading companies took every opportunity to denounce us with the tribes of the Northwest and that meant, predominantly, the powerful Piegans and their northern cousins the Bloods and the Siksika of the Blackfeet nation.

In reporting to President Jefferson the rich beaver potential of the Yellowstone River country, the Captains in their letters and journals wrote:

"The river will afford a lucrative fur trade & will hold in check the Northwest Company on the upper Missouri which we believe it is their intention to monopolize if in their power."

We recognized the tremendous fur value of the upper Missouri and at the same time feared the Northwest Company's possible domination. Little more than three years later, our suspicions would be justified ... verified in Alexander Henry's own journal and own hand.

"Mr. Henry. Mr. Henry, sir." Ian McCloud, assistant to Alexander Henry Jr., burst excitedly into the post's counting room. This was the remote Fort Vermilion and its dimly lit business office had a low, roughly hewn log ceiling with barely enough space for a man of average height to stand erect without risking bumping his noggin. It had its own peculiar stench to it, an odor that was dank, musty, reeking of stacks of tanned animal hides, the dirt and dust of the Canadian plains and that of sweaty, unwashed men, trappers and visiting savages alike.

Early morning found the Fort's compliment more animated than usual and no one more so then the short, ruddy faced Scotsman McCloud who was barely able to control his excitement.

"Come quickly, sir. Come quickly." His tone was more of an urgent demand than a request. "Your lordship will want to see this."

McCloud directed his urgency to a rather tall, stern looking man standing behind a thick well-worn plank that served as the office's business counter.

"Yes, Ian. I heard you quite well the first time. Calm down, man. I'm busy, as you can see. Pray tell dear man, what on earth could possibly be so earthshaking in this God forsaken wilderness as to get you so excited on such a bloody fine day?"

Alexander Henry Jr., outwardly was unruffled, taking to his Company duties in the stern tradition of his forbears and wearing an ever permanent stiff upper lip as befits his mold.

Henry took a last sip of warm, pungent tea, courtesy of the British East India Company, and set his now empty cup down on the thick plank counter next to a stack of new skins he had just finished inventorying. The steaming liquid had tasted good, refreshing, and he always started his day with several strong cups. Tea was his only vice in the wilderness, one he was unwilling to give up.

"We have some new arrivals, Mr. Henry," said McCloud. There was a noticeably nervous edge to his voice. He spoke fast, sometimes stuttering, and as he went on his voice was alternately full of wonder and worry.

"They must've come in during the night. Quiet as ghosts, they are. No one heard them come, not even our dogs barked. And you know how obnoxious they are here. The savages just appeared this morning as if they've been here all along. Amazing. I am certain it is the Piegans, and there are quite literally thousands of them camped across the river by the Vermilion."

The little Scotsman was visibly shaken. His thick, callused hands and short stubby fingers trembled ever so slightly, revealing a palsy that had struck the ruddy-faced, redhead prematurely in life. Although he would never admit it, it was his coming to this wilderness and dealing with the unpredictable nature of its savages that began an eternal twitching, this infernal malaise.

"Hmmmph!" Henry smirked somewhat disdainfully. "The Slaves... thousands of 'em? Pshaw! Come, come, my good man, let us not take leave of our senses. Stick to what you know and have seen."

Henry quietly stared off into the distance rubbing his chin and twisting the curled ends of his thick, handsome, mustachios. He was a vain man, proud of his family's heritage and his station in the Company's life. Yet, he walked in the rather large shadow of his father, Alexander, Sr. His father's tracks had set a wide trail he doubted he could ever match. But, inferiority was never the Younger's weakness, not that he had any. It was just that the Vermilion was so remote, so far away from anything approximating civilization. He was beginning to worry if he could ever fit right back in the refined circles of dignified Quebec or Montreal or London or much less return alive with his own hair. Indians always seemed to unsettle his future. Yet, he always managed to keep himself steady despite the lingering fear. Still, he could not afford to dismiss Ian's report outright.

"Tell me, my dear Ian, with what, worthless items do you think these bloody savages have come to bother us with? You know we aren't trading for wolf skins."

There was a decidedly contemptuous tone in his voice, one he knew he'd better rein in before it got him into trouble. Henry over time had formed a distinct dislike for the southern Blackfeet, the clans he called the Slaves. But, Alexander Henry, Jr., was an astute, discerning man and a keen observer of the wild Indians of the Northwestern Plains. He knew how to deal with them. Trade and survival depended on cool, calculating decisions and a head for warding off trouble before it ever got to you.

"I don't rightly know, Mr. Henry. But, some of the *frogs* have been over to their village early this mornin' talkin' to 'em."

"Yes, yes?" responded Henry impatiently.

The tall, lean Henry abruptly turned his back to the diminutive Scot and began methodically sorting and stacking a pile of furs. Suddenly he jerked his head back towards the befreckled, redheaded McCloud, the look in his eyes impatient, demanding.

"Come, come man, out with it. What do they report? Must I wait all day?"

"Aye, aye. No, Sir! I mean right away, Sir," stammered the clerk nervously. Composing himself, "Well, for one, Mr. Henry, they say they have some prime beaver skins to trade... tanned and packed, neat and tidy like. Mr. Henry, Sir."

"Beaver skins, neat and tidy, the Slaves? Come, come, dear man, surely they embellish. The *frogs* are never what you might call understated in their approximations. One must take everything they say with a certain grain of salt, eh, Ian."

"Uh, yes, Sir. But, they seem so insistent."

Smug and convinced, yet, Henry was not so incredulous enough to forego further inquiry. He placed a bound stack of beaver skins on the floor, and then, straightening up, shook his head rather quizzically.

"Neat and tidy, you say. How odd and totally out of character. Now that's an unusual twist for these savages. All the more puzzling."

And then, almost as an afterthought, he added, "I wonder what poor, hapless devils they buggered to acquire such a catch, eh, McCloud?"

McCloud hurried around the counter, picked up a stack of skins and added it to the growing row of pelts along the walls of the counting room.

Henry ignored the little Scot's obsequiousness. The American born, Canadian fur post commander stood in the doorway, hands on his hips akimbo, staring across the North Saskatchewan River towards the rising plumes of campfire smoke by the Vermilion. The reported plews of skins in the Indian village wore heavily on his mind. He knew he must keep abreast of the happenings below the border. Business demanded it.

"All right Ian, I've been appraised. Go to their village and see what you can find out." And then he added with a smile, "And tell the Slaves as always we'll be happy to do business with them."

"Aye, Aye, Mr. Henry," McCloud instantly acknowledged and reached up to a peg on the wall and grabbed his soft red woolen tam and prepared to depart.

Henry's disdain for the Piegan was readily apparent to all at the Fort. As far as he was concerned, their trade was worthless to the Company. Their manners, their crudeness was abhorrent to this sophisticated scion of trading wealth and power. Beaver they rarely bothered with, unless they could waylay some unwary, hapless victims to commit their thievery and depredations on. He could see no end to their lust for blood or craving for liquor, the 'white men's water', as they called it.

Like all of the trading post officers for both the Northwest and Hudson Bay Companies, he was required to keep detailed journals. And he did so, diligently, making many cogent observations about the new arrivals and entered them duly into his log: This day was no different:

"That power for all evil, 'spirituous liquor,' now seems to dominate them, and has taken such hold on them that they are no longer the quiet people they were. They appear fully as addicted to liquor as the Crees, though, unlike the latter, they will not purchase it. They cannot be made to comprehend that anything of value should be paid for what they term 'water'."

Alexander Henry suddenly had second thoughts.

"Ian, hold up. Wait a minute. These furs you say they have." He was still staring across the river, his face blank, but his mind in deep thought. "These Slaves have my curiosity aroused. I'm coming with you. Have my horse saddled, I want to go with you to the Vermilion and see for myself their village and those skins first-hand."

He turned from the doorway and looked McCloud straight in the eye, "Have the engages make ready. And tell them to do it with a smile."

Then, he jabbed the Scotsman several times gently with his extended right index finger in the smaller man's chest, cautioning, "We must be careful, these savages are not to be trusted."

"Aye, aye sir. I won't....I mean, I will, right away." The clerk donned his favorite woolen tam and was out the door on the double quick.

As Henry watched his clerk disappear, he again turned to stare across the North Saskatchewan. He was a student of the Northwest plains and eastern woodland tribes, knowing well that contact with the white man's smallpox over the last three decades had decimated the Indians of the Northwest, especially the southern Blackfeet who called themselves Piegans. It would be interesting to see if they had indeed rebounded from the plague like all the unsubstantiated reports had told. Until then he would remain dubious and unconvinced.

"Hold up, men," Henry commanded, raising his hand.

The spare but wiry post commander reined in his mount abruptly, coming to a hard stop atop a small grassy knoll. He stretched forward in the saddle to gaze down upon the spreading plains below. And what he saw he was unprepared to acknowledge. They were there all right, in all their primitive glory. The rumors, the reports were all true. The evidence presented so clearly, so blatantly and in such alarming numbers. Hundreds of tanned and painted buffalo-hide lodges as numerous as the trees in the forest littered the plains in a broad circular defensive pattern. Never had he seen such a congestion of Indian dwellings in one place at one time. It was a virtual city, a savage's metropolis of the first rate. People were milling about by the hundreds. Nearby on the plains their horse herd, thousands of their precious ponokamitas, grazed on short grass. There was an air of excitement, of energy radiating throughout the whole Piegan town with absolutely no sense of concern or caution. Why worry, with such amassed strength they had little to fear from any of their traditional enemies.

For once Henry was more than a little disturbed. He didn't like surprises, especially of this magnitude. The Slaves as he called them always gave cause to worry. They were just so volatile, always capable of the unexpected. And in such numbers…

McCloud and the Frenchmen waited patiently astride their mounts, eyeing warily the huge village below. Several *engages* glanced back and forth at each other nervously. There was more than one raised eyebrow; a wariness and angst apparently shared by all. They were not fools. Sure, the *frogs* lived among the red man, married their squaws, bore their half-breeds. But, these Piegans were notoriously unreliable and way too often proved just as treacherous to friend as well as foe.

The Scot's hands had already commenced to tremble. He wanted to say something profound to impress his master, but the words never left his lips. He was just too scared at the moment.

Alexander Henry began poking the air with a stiff trigger finger. Seemingly, every animal hide covered lodge below the target of his concentration and mathematics. He counted away, all the while mumbling consecutive numbers to himself. "One, two, three... Seventy-six, seventy-seven... One-hundred-eighty-two... Two-hundred-ninety four..."

Henry kept counting, his voice faltering, the growing numbers sounding harsh, raspy... yet, he groaned on. He was tiring of the long count, little expecting or imagining in his wildest nightmares to behold such numbers as the primitive domiciles lying before him now confirmed. But, these savages, like the buffalo on the plains, were always surprising him with their vitality for procreation and survival. His lips, his tongue, his mouth became parched from the exercise, until, finally, he finished. Taking out his hard-bound leather jacketed journal, as was his practice, he entered:

"This peculiar Piegan village has a total of 350 lodges, maybe 700 warriors, maybe more..."

And then he looked down at the village once again.

"Disgusting wretches, absolutely disgusting. Polygamists, the filthy heathen are all polygamists." Henry was unable to hide his disdain or temper his voice.

"They never cease to amaze. Evidently, their squaws are as fertile as their horses and their warriors ride them with equal abandon." Henry gloated, smug enough with his own brand of wit to permit a rare unconcealed chuckle.

It was endemic, the *frogs* agreeing instantly with their master's observations, making no attempt to hide their pleasure or mutual sarcasm. Several of their little ponies, agitated by all the new and strange scents wafting up from the plains, sniffed the air and craned their long necks and furry ears forward, straining to recognize the multitude of ponies that grazed below. They too laughed, or rather whinnied rather loudly, all the while pawing the ground nervously with their unshod hooves.

Henry ignored them. He cared not what they thought as long as they did his bidding and didn't endanger the Company's operations.

"Jesus Christ, will you look at that." Henry shook his head, wondering aloud in almost complete disbelief. "Great day, it appears they've doubled their population since last here. My, the buggers have been busy... copulating like they drink, with utter abandon. Sodomites, filthy fornicators."

Irritated, he kicked his mount in the ribs with a heavily booted heel.

"Let's go," he ordered, and turning in the saddle, issued one last terse command, "And watch yourselves."

With Henry in the lead, they rode down from the knoll, directly onto the short grass plains and headed straight towards the village at a deliberate gait. Their arrival and approach did not go unnoticed. There was little chance of that ever happening. Their presence was expected long before they ever left the security of Fort Vermilion. Surprise was never intended. Only a bold front would do. A front that spoke of confidence, of steely nerves commanding respect.

Hundreds of villagers welcomed them with dimpled faces and beaming smiles. Clenched fists punched the air in a show of Blackfoot bravado. A hundred or more discordant voices shrieked and howled to announce the white man's arrival. And with the clamor, a wild, unrestrained cacophony rent the air, reverberating from one end of the village to the other. The din swelled, growing to a deafening pitch, louder and louder. A cold chill swept down their spines, unnerving the white men. Yet, they rode on, deeper and deeper into a massive labrinth of conical lodges.

Waves of mounted warriors leapt forward, racing back and forth on their spirited mounts, performing acrobatic feats of daring-do. Riding blindly backwards on their ponies' bare backs; perilously dismounting, remounting again, over and over again, one side, then the other, at full gallop, deftly holding on to a handful of thin scraggly strands of mane or tail, all the while whooping and howling in sheer naked delight.

Henry marveled at this display of raw equestrian skill. Never had he witnessed such unequaled horsemanship. For once the haughty scion of the Northwest Company was impressed, a singularly rare event. Through it all, he continued to sit astride his own mount, his face a blank, unemotional, noncommittal, never for a moment letting down his guard nor admitting the outright pleasure the moment was providing.

It mattered not to the Piegan. Young and old alike, the buxom and the fair, the wrinkled and the weathered, laughed and cheered. Hundreds of dirty faced, bronzed-skin, naked youths, aspiring warriors to be, ran amuck throughout the village exhorting their older brothers, the warriors of the Nation, on and on and on. The Piegan were in a grand mood. The long, cold winter was over. Spring had come. The warmth of summer and the buffalo, the sacred 'enee', hunt would soon arrive.

Henry kept riding right on through the surging throng, led now by several 'gray hairs' towards the middle of the village. Outwardly calm, reserved, Alexander Henry stared straight ahead as if oblivious to the whole tawdry scene. But, he didn't miss a thing, at least not the things that mattered. His mind made mental notes, noting the odd assortment of their fire weapons, the strength of the warrior bands, the relative sobriety of their warriors. He suspected that his last observation would not last long past the setting sun. Their intent was heavily on his mind. And these beaver skins they came to inspect, from whom did they acquire this supposedly splendid catch of fur. That's what really interested Alexander Henry.

Ian McCloud was flabbergasted by the primitively painted lodges, not for a second realizing their meaning or significance. To the simple Scotsman the display was ostentatious, the height of ignorance and banality, something only children might do. He noted the black pigmented outlines, the red and yellow painted images of their sacred *enee*, and the grizzly, the wapiti and the deer, and the birds of the sky gracefully dressing many of the buffalo skin lodges. And there were more designs that he realized possible; tipis with banded red bottoms and falling stars and others with painted tops, black like the night sky, with unpainted discs like frozen moons or distant stars. He puzzled at these; wondering their purpose, their meaning, and in the end failed to recognize the obvious, the constellation of the Great Bear, Ursa Major and that of the Pleiades. Alas, if only he had, he may have found a new respect for these primitive savages.

Henry, too, mentally noted each detail for later entry into his journal. He despised these people, yet, he was nevertheless fascinated by them and their culture. The more he learned the more he realized how complex these Slaves truly were. It was becoming difficult for him to be objective. His arrogance, his biases too well entrenched for him to acknowledge anyone save for the elite of his own race.

The white men came to a halt in front of two large tipis. Each lodge was larger than all the rest of the village. Each had painted on its front a formidable looking figure of a buffalo... one red, the other yellow, their horns a vivid, glossy black. What appeared to Henry to be the representation of beaver or otters adorned the far sides of both lodges, with butterflies fluttering near the tops.

Henry's men gawked in silence. For once they all were rendered speechless. No one moved. Alex Henry, quite taken with the display, studied each design with an astute, almost scientific, inquiring mind. Right off Henry recognized that both lodges held some kind of powerful medicine to the Blackfeet. Even an Eastern tenderfoot could have seen if right off. He marveled at their artistry, wondered their obviously sacred meaning, vowing to find out at a later time for his own curiosity.

"Quite a spectacle, huh, Ian? All symbolic, I suppose, and all very primitive. There's more to these savages then meets the eye. But, interesting, don't you think?"

"Yes, sirrr, Mrrr. Henry... very much so, I must say," McCloud stammered in agreement.

McCloud's hands were shaking violently, almost beyond his control. He tried to steady himself, but it was an impossible task. There was just no place on earth that he would rather not be.

An *engage* mumbled to the clerk, pointing to two dark stacks lying on the grassy sod between the two lodges. Instantly, the Scotsman recognized the beaver skins in question.

"Mr. Henry." Ian's voice suddenly regained a measure of calmness.

"There's the skins, sir." The clerk dismounted and walked over and immediately began inspecting them.

"I see them," Henry replied coolly, eyeing several smiling Piegan warriors as they held up tanned skins for him to see. One warrior in particular caught his attention. What a big bastard, he thought to himself... and look at that hideous scar on his face. Good God, what a brute! He shuddered inwardly at the sheer ferocity radiating from this giant savage. Smile or no smile a sudden distinct wariness gripped him and would not let go. For once Henry's cool aplomb lay disturbed. Still, he had work to do. He must not show fear.

An *engage* dismounted and took a skin from one of the Piegans. The brave made hand gestures, encouraging the others to come forth and inspect the skins for themselves.

The Frenchman cooed and caressed the thick soft fur of the beaver as if it was alive. "*Bon, bon!*" he murmured. "*Tres bon!*"

"Aye," agreed McCloud. "They're fine furs indeed. Look at these skins, Mr. Henry. They're all thick and lush, expertly stretched and tanned, real craftsmanship. No savage treated these skins, I'm willing to wager."

"And look," McCloud said as he went delicately over every inch of the pelt's skin with his fingers, "they were not shot, if you notice, like the Slaves and the Bloods always do. No sir, these beavers were caught in metal traps just like we use."

A sudden look of consternation appeared on his face. He paused as if inexplicably arriving upon a most disturbing revelation. "Foul, odious play here," he blurted out of a sudden. "By God I swear these pelts are stolen, the whole bloomin' lot of 'em. They must be. No injun out here could do this kind of work. No, sir. Delaware or Iroquois can do it, but there are none of their kind this far to the West, at least not that I know of. The dirty buggers have stolen these from white men."

Henry alighted from his horse, walked over to his clerk's side, and began inspecting the goods himself.

"Careful, Ian. Steady, man!" he said softly. "We are not here to take sides nor preach to the heathens. We are here to trade and... live to enjoy it. Did the *engages* say from where the *Slaves* got them?"

"Yes sir." McCloud's voice suddenly quieted to a low whisper. "Some place I've never heard of. A place they call... "*Ahkoto waktai Sakum.*"

One of the gray-hairs, an older warrior, who led them through the village, suddenly jerked his head at the Scotsman mention of the Piegan phrase. The old brave smiled and grunted, puffing out his chest proudly.

"Ugh! *Ahkoto waktai Sakum.*" He nodded his head, and said in a rough, broken English, "*Menneee-cum-too-geth-err.*"

Again the warrior grunted, smiled and pointed proudly to the two piles of beaverskin. "Good skin... you give 'em much white man's water for trade."

"*Ahkoto waktai Sakum*," Henry thought to himself as he smiled back and nodded back to the older warrior.

He had heard of the place. The Slaves often boasted of it. The place was their favorite hunting ground to the south.

And then he turned to McCloud, "If I know these heathens, they guard the place well. So, it looks like the Americans have finally ventured into the Headwaters country to trap, after all. They're getting close, much too close. It will bode well for us to keep our ears to the ground.

"What else have you found out?" he demanded.

McCloud looked up to Henry, glancing around nervously to make sure no one else was listening. His hands trembled anew, his brow became furrowed, wagon-rut deep. He talked as if he held a black, forbidding secret, daring not to speak too loudly.

"Well, sir," the Scot whispered cautiously, "they aren't talking much, but, somehow, somewhere, they got hold of some liquor and their tongues have begun to wag. They get mighty loose when they're liquored up... braggin', struttin' round like bloomin' peacocks. Actually, quite predictable you might say in that regard.

"Here it is, I know there were at least two trappers, Yanks for sure. It could be no one else that far from the Missouri. We know there's a post on the Yellowstone and the Big Horn. Word has been traveling about Americans being there for some months now.

"A couple of years back these Piegans ran into four Yanks down on what they are now callin' the Marias. There was a set to, some kind of disagreement that went sour. The Slaves got the worst of it, losin' two of their best braves to the Yanks' guns. They got away unscathed, much to these heathens dismay. And you know, sir, that these savages will never forget a reproach like that. No, sir!

"I think they kilt one of 'em down there in that *Ahkoto* place. Least as much as I can figure. But they ain't a talkin' about the other one, like they're afraid or ashamed or both. But, the word's been slippin' out slowly. Our *frogs* keep hearin' about someone or somethin' they call the *spoo-pii*. The *frogs* don't know what it means, but they say this here *spoo-pii* feller has become bad medicine to the Slaves.

"Have you ever heard that word before, Mr. Henry? *Spoo-pii*? Sounds awfully close to spooky, if you ask me."

"No, can't say that I have. Why? What does it have to do with me?" Henry was looking up, his mouth somewhat agape a quizzical look on his face begging for an answer.

"Well, sir," McCloud again glanced about to make sure Henry was the only one within hearing distance.

"Want to know the truth of it? I think the other yank is this *spoo-pii* fella. He got away and they just won't admit it. There's also talk that their best fighter bein' kilt some months back. His name was *Maa-koyou-mah'-kaa*, or some such. It means Runnin' Wolf, and his people are still all het up about it. They claimed he was murdered. I think thar's a connection here. What's more I think that big ugly bastard with the scar had something to do with it. Least ways that's what I've come up with. I'll keep my ears to the ground for sure. Still I donna think all the liquor in the world will pry much more out of 'em. That's my readin' of the situation.

"No sir, it took some kind of a man to outdo these wily red skins and he'll stick in their craw a mighty long time. And what's more, this *spoo-pii* got away at least twice."

"Twice, you say? What do you mean?"

"One of the *Slaves* let the cat out of the bag. That white trapper came back in the dead of winter, near as I can tell. They were waitin' for him, a couple of kin that is of that Running Wolf. That scarface must of been one of 'em fer sure. But, that *spoo-pii* fella was too quick for 'em… got away a second time as clean as a whistle, slick as you please. Imagine that! Not once, but twice. I'd say that's the last we'll hear of that feller. It ain't settin' well with the savages, though. Those injuns won't let it rest until someone pays for it. Gives me the shakes just thinkin' bout it."

Henry was silent. There was much to contemplate. Business was business, but still the depradations did not sit well with him.

Ian the clerk dropped the subject and went about his accounting business. "Anyways, Mr. Henry, there's a small fortune in furs here. Those Yanks must've worked mighty hard gettin' these skins in such fine shape. Poor devils, glad it wasn't me."

"Yes, Ian, poor devils is right. I think our American friends will think twice before venturing back to the *Ahkoto waktai Sakum*," Henry responded ever so cooly with a cold air of detachment. So, one got away, he thought, what a lucky son of a bitch. If he's smart, he'll think again about trappin' the Three Forks country…. if he's smart. These Americans are always full of surprises. I wonder what kind of man he is?"

And then, feeling the luxurious beaver-skin in his hands, he commented, "You're right, Ian, these pelts are magnificent. Great care tanned these hides. Better than I've seen for a long time."

"Yes, sir," McCloud agreed. "Real craftsmanship I must say."

Alexander Henry turned and faced to the south, towards the land of the

Three Forks, and again thought to himself. That man, our American friend that got away... quite a man, yes, quite a man indeed to have outsmarted these cunning *Snakes*. He had better quit, while he's ahead.

Henry gave a shrug of his shoulders and thought no more of the incident. But, he knew the upper Missouri would bear watching for the intrepid Americans. The Northwest Company depended on the Blackfeet to keep the country clean of any unwanted competition and could little afford to be fainthearted. He would encourage them to stay vigilant, even if it meant more of the same skullduggery. More of the same... he shuddered at the thought.

A platoon of *Piegan* waited patiently while Henry and his clerk inspected their booty. Nary moving a muscle, not uttering a grunt of their Algonquian tongue, they stared intently the whole while at the white leader, never for an instant taking their eyes off him.

Henry did not miss the penetrating heat of their stares the entire time he was there. He expected it and likewise knew what was expected of him. He was in no rush. He was cool, and casually so, examining every pelt, one by one, taking his time.

Finally, satisfied, he turned to the *Piegans* and smiled. Then, turning to his clerk...

"Break out a barrel of liquor and let 'em whoop it up. And when they've had their fill, tell them we shall talk trade... and be quick about it. I don't want them skulking about any longer than they have to."

"Aye, aye," stuttered McCloud.

When Henry returned to the safety and comfort of Fort Vermilion, he entered into his journal:

"The trade with the Slaves is of very little consequence to us. They kill scarcely any good furs; a beaver of their own hunt is seldom found among them; their principal trade is wolves, of which of late years we take none, while our Hudson Bay neighbours continue to pay well for them. At present our neighbours trade with about two thirds of the Black Feet and I would willingly give up the whole of them. It is true, we got some beaver from them; but this was the spoils of war, they having fallen upon a party of Americans on the Missourie, stripped them of everything, and brought off a quantity of skins."

The spoils of war apparently were a good enough alibi for young Henry and his unscrupulous Company. He discreetly omitted the rumored consequences suffered by Johnny and me. It's not that he didn't care nor held life so cheap, but, it was the nature of his business and beaver skins were the economy of the Northwest. Johnny's life and that of numerous others to come meant nothing to him. Years of lonely isolation in wilderness trading posts had inured him to the savage excesses and murderous orgies of the Northwest Plains Indians, especially the three bands that collectively made up the Blackfoot nation he so scornfully referred to as the Slaves. Alexander Henry profoundly held them in contempt, but, nevertheless, he eagerly accepted their spoils of war. This scene was bound to be repeated many times in the young life of Alexander Henry, until his early demise by drowning in the swift waters of the North Saskatchewan River at Fort George, Alberta 1814.

CHAPTER TEN

Fleeing the Forks with my tail between my legs was nothing new to John Colter, a bad habit I couldn't seem to break. I had the route just about memorized by then, the Yellowstone trail to Manuel's Fort was as familiar as the back of my hand. But, this winter's flight had a different ring to my way of thinking, one that bespoke of futility and resignation. I was hearing a familiar voice, that ol' itch had returned, accompanying me the whole way back, and it waxed relentlessly, pestering me with doubt, questioning over and over… aren't you tired of this, yet? Don't you think you've bitten off more than you can chew? What more is it going take for you to see the light? C'mon, Johnboy, wake up before you wind up like Johnny P and ol' Toby.

Bullheaded-stubborness was an old Colter clan trait. It was our Scotch-Irish blood, passed down from generation to generation. And it made absolutely no difference whether you were from Dundee or Donegal, the ol' sod or the Shenandoah Valley of Virginia. Wherever we went, it followed us. My ma, Ellen, could attest to that Colter obstinacy, it was as inborn in my family-line as were blue eyes and sandy blond hair. She always said that one day it'd catch up to us… that one of us would have the devil to pay.

The time had come to do some serious thinking, to turn over a new leaf if need be. From the start I knew the stakes. I could accept my losses; my traps and kit, the skins Johnny and me cached. Even my ol' trusty shootin' iron, though I must admit its loss was like losing an arm or a good friend. It didn't set well that some loudmouthed Piegan warrior was toting my weapon and calling it his own, jacking his jaws throughout the Northwest, of how he snatched the big medicine gun, the *spoo-pii's* fire-stick, right from the hands of the hated *napikwan*. Well, there's many more beaver from where those skins came from. And they were still there waiting to be taken… a crick, a stream and a watershed at a time. My credit was good with the Spaniard. My kit could be replaced. And now I carried a Pennsylvania "long" near as good as the rifle I lost. But, it wasn't the lost of my possessions that was bothering me, grating on my nerves, rubbing my resolve and my mettle raw. My fortunes have been up and down more times than a possum shinning a tree. That's the nature of a trapper's life, it's to be expected from time to time. I held no false promises, no self-delusions. I clearly understood myself… the trail of life I chose to follow and the pot of gold at the end of the rainbow I sought to gain. I knew the risk and they were many; there never were any guarantees, I accepted that, along with the privations, the loneliness and the extremes. I had been down that path many times before. But, I had always been resilient. Just give me one good season of trapping, of knocking 'em dead, without them damned Blackfeet always butting in and I'd be on my way back to civilization for good.

But, how many times had I promised myself "just one more time?" And how many times had I come back empty-handed with a sad tale to tell? Was it failure that was finally getting to me? Lord knows I was raised to see a job through despite the obstacles. No, it was something else. And that "something else" had been growing on me ever since the "pishkun plains." Toby and all those fine young Flatheads slaughtered in the prime of their lives. For what, just to feed their people? Then losing Johnny on the Jefferson and the set-to that followed with Kootenae Appe and Running Wolf. For what, just to trap a few measly beaverskins? And to top it off, neither of my two friends had even a simple, decent burial. No graves to be interred within, no markers nor cairns, not even a kind word in remembrance, their lifeless remains left for the varmints, the scavengers to pick clean. And that didn't set well with me, their memory meant more to me than that.

The Piegan of course didn't see it my way at all. We were the enemy, plain and simple. And they clearly understood themselves… enemies were not to be tolerated, but to be dealt with in the harshest of ways. And they backed it up with a tenacity that I had come to fear and respect. There was just no room in the Piegan's sacred *Ahkoto waktai Sakum* for the white man or any of their red neighbors, at least for the foreseeable future.

By the time I returned to Manuel's stockade Pete Wiser was gone, headed east for good. Johnny Potts had been his best friend, his constant companion since leaving the Corps, his pard in the beavering business on the Yellowstone. Johnny's death had hit Pete hard. And then I added fuel to the fire, charging recklessly back to the Forks hellbent on a futile crusade in the dead of winter. Lord knows I blamed myself for Johnny's death. Guilt was slowly consuming me from within, blindly churning an erratic, confused resolve towards irreparable damage. Pete knew it, too, trying his damnedest to dissuade me from certain self-destruction. He warned me repeatedly of the folly of returning, pleading with me not to go. I never listened, spurning advice, shunning the one man who truly cared. So, I left… and he did to. He had had enough. Pete didn't stick around for another day just to get a second dose of bad news. I rued his loss, paying for it in spades, for his absence left me without a true friend.

Lisa had returned to St. Louis to plan his next venture. The Big Horn and Yellowstone were near trapped-out for the time being, the Spaniard's outfit had seen to that. And after the Potts' affair, no one talked of going to the Forks, at least no person of sound mind or of any consequence. Manuel's Fort was almost deserted, manned by a skeleton crew to protect the Company's interest. Game was scarce. The food stocks were low. The place and its men began to have an unhealthy pallor, rotting with malaise from within. The business of the stockade, trapping and trading had ground to a halt. Nobody in his right-mind wanted to be there... including me.

It didn't take much to convince this ol' cuss. I knew I had to leave and not dawdle one day longer. I had to put time and distance between me and the Yellowstone country. I had to get my bearings back, figure out what it was I wanted to do and how far I was willing to go for it. I still wanted to trap beaver, to make my fortune. But, going it alone had cost me dearly. I had enjoyed a brief peaceful sojourn, idly trapping the Yellowstone, 'til Manuel's mission ran me headlong into the Blackfeet Nation and turned the headwaters of the Missouri blood red. Those halcyon days were gone now forever. The white man was in for a rough ride. The question was… did I still want to be a part of it? I didn't know any longer. Maybe I'd find out back in civilization. So I left, glad to be shut of Manuel's Fort, barely staying a fortnight to rest from my latest flight. Stowing in a dugout what little I still owned, I shoved-off early one cold, misty morning, catching the current without even so much as a look-back or a wave good-bye. I was alone once again riding atop La Roche Jaune towards the "big muddy" and points south beyond. But, this time I wasn't stopping at the Platte for man or promise or any wild, hare-brained scheme… no sweet talkin' this fella, no pie in the sky. I just kept paddling, oblivious to day and month, never much giving thought to where I was going or what I was going to do when I got there. It was Handcock and Dickson all over again, though this time I hadn't one tanned skin to show for all my efforts.

I had aged badly. Aches and pains and stiffness accumulated in my joints and every limb from the constant deprivation, the elements and Blackfeet abuse. I no longer felt the same strength and vitality in my arms, legs, heart and lungs. My youth, the friendships I made and my time with the Corps of Discovery were fading memories, seemingly confined to some other lifetime not entirely my own. I had changed from those carefree, uninhibited days, becoming more calculated, more cynical. I was now less inclined towards that reckless and foolhardy dash that had so dominated my life until ol' Toby was so brutally dispatched before my very eyes. The last essence of my youth was dashed that day forever by a stone-headed war club.

That damned Three Forks country would come and go almost at will… I just couldn't get it out of my mind. What was it about that valley? What kept drawing me back? Where was the reward, the fortune gained? Certainly, it wasn't the ugly, purple scar that coursed my leg or the thousand miles of bad trail permanently etched in my heart and my soul.

For now I was out of there, putting trappin' the Forks to rest. I began to think of change, of settling down to a life of domesticated rut and family routine. I could see the benefits, though I was not quite ready to think of myself as a townsman or a farmer, even though I knew that as a veteran of the Corps, Congress had rewarded me with a tract of land and monetary compensation. Yet, it would be a good start, something to build on… if that was what I truly wanted. And that's the rub, I still was unconvinced. It wasn't that I was ungrateful for what my country had granted me nor was the thought of hearth and home and kith and kin displeasing to my palate. I could like such things as much as any man. It was…

Nahhh!

It just wasn't for me… at least for now. I knew I had one more go left in me, one more chance to set the Colter chapter straight, before I lay down my rifle, my traps and wandering ways for good. There was still a fire flickering in my belly. And it was one, burning, defiant, stubborn son of a bitch. It had always been a persistent, unyielding flame, one that had been there since that young sprig of a wild boy with his trusty squirrel-shooter ran like the wind through the woods and fields near Tinkling Springs. And listened wide-eyed on many a dark night to his uncle and his pa's fireside tales of fighting men and fame and glory. Yes, it had been nearly doused these past few months by the sober waters of reality and the Blackfeet Nation. I had taken some heavy, punishing hits. My nerve and confidence had buckled my spirit's knees, sending me reeling back to the settlements, disorganized, confused, unsteady on my mind's feet. But a few months away from the Yellowstone had granted this ol' curly wolf a second wind. The old fire was still there, still strong, still resolute, noticeably tempered, though, by the passing of time and the ordeals of 1808.

Eventually I had reached the outlying settlements on the Missouri above St. Louie, renewed some old acquaintanceships, got my fill of liquid spirits and idle talk, bummed around, checked out some bottomland around Labadie township, thought again and again about trying on the yoke of farming for size. I struggled to convince myself, though the feel of it all just wasn't quite right. Maybe I was trying too hard to force myself into a fit I wasn't ready to wear. What to do? Where to go from here? I just couldn't seem to find my way. As luck would have it, the way found me first…

Word traveled fast on the Missouri and when it was the Spaniard doing the calling it moved as fast as the current would take it. Lisa wanted to see me, pronto, by the river they called the Knife. Months of indecision, of wrestling with uncertainty vanished as soon as I got the call. I thought about it all of about a half a dozen seconds, enough of a time to grab my kit, my powder horn and shoulder my long rifle, boarding the first flat boat I could find heading up river.

The Knife, I knew it well. She was a little stream just north of the villages of the Mandans and the Hidatsas. The Knife and Manuel Lisa and his big doin's were the talk of the River. The Spaniard was at it again, building himself another Fort, on a grander scale than he had ever done before. He was forming a new brigade of engages and rough and tumble trappers. Signing 'em on, fixing to invade the Northwest and the upper Missouri country once again, this time at the head of the biggest concern since the Corps of Discovery. Missouri Fur was amassing all its resources, all the armed men and trappers it could muster and sign. And they came from everywhere; experienced trappers from Illinois, rawboned backwoodsmen of Kentuck, Tennessee and ol' Virginnie. Military men, veterans of the injun wars from many a far-flung frontier outpost. Voyageurs, engages; the hardy French Canucks, legends of the river trapping West. And with these hardened veterans of the American frontier, came a dash or two of "tenderfoots" as green as summer grass. A youngster from Philadelphia out to prove his manhood, a preacher from Connecticut looking to find his God in the Rocky Mountains and a blacksmith from near Boone's Lick to test his own mettle. And there were more, many more. Some came for riches, for fortune, for adventure. And others... for a lark, to get away from the confining restrictions of eastern society, or a life of tedious boredom strapped to a trade, and for those with higher yearnings... to make their marks in life. They hailed from every corner of America, from wherever the sounds of adventure could reach and be heard.

"Ahhh, Jean Colter. At last, you are here, mon ami... And to think Chouteau questioned your coming at all. Tsk. Tsk. I worried not. I told Pierre, that there was nothin' to be concerned with when it came to Jean Colter."

He hadn't changed much since I had last seen him by the Big Horn, except for maybe a little extra weight gained around the middle. The "good life" in St. Louie could do that to any man. His face was cleared up; the beating from the half-breed Edward Rose was now a distant memory. He obviously had regained his old self, smug, cocky, arrogant, once again commanding respect on the River.

"*Bon!* We've much to talk about and so little time in which to do it in. Ah, but isn't that always the way it is between us?"

There was an edge to his voice. I caught it right off. Impatient by my backwoods' standards, his mind was ever on the move, never far from the horizon of his next scheme. Always cooking up, thinking, planning. He had a natural disdain for those men whose imaginations couldn't keep up... and that included just about everybody that came down the pike. Made most folks downright uneasy just to be in his vicinity. He could wait though, as far as I was concerned. After all I just came a thousand miles. Hadn't even caught my breath or taken the time to do my business. Besides, there was just too much activity going on around us not to take notice.

And building was what was going on, mostly being done by the Spaniard's handy French engages. He seemed to have an army of them armed with axe and adze. Honed palisade log walls were up and set in place, ringing the post in a wide protected enclosure. Cabins, storerooms, blacksmith shop, mess kitchen, accounting office were all in the middle of or near completion. Corrals were already in place with nervous little Indian ponies prancing about, kicking up dust and ruckus. The landing down by the river was stacked high with supplies, trade goods and food stocks of every kind. Everywhere I looked the place was humming, a regular human hive of activity with the Spaniard as an unlikely queen bee. Manuel's new fort, his whole enterprise had a feeling of importance, of permanency, unlike the undermanned, ramshackle outpost up in Yellowstone country. The rumors, the river-gossip of his "big doin's" was certainly right on the mark.

"I came as soon as I got your word."

"Quite impressive, eh, Jean Colter?" Lisa was proud of his new fort, looking around, pointing to the goings-on, the work being done, the construction, the mass of supplies, and all the while his vanity was fishing for compliments. Tha man had an ego as wide as the wide Missouri itself.

"For way up here... it sure is. But, I'm just as curious 'bout what you've got up your sleeve for me. There's no beaver 'round here, not by a long shot. And from the looks of it, you aren't ready yet to go anywheres. So, if you don't mind my askin'... why did you need me here in such an all fire hurry?"

I must have sounded a little belligerent. And in truth I was. I meant to keep our talk down to business, directing my gaze squarely into the little Spaniard's black eyes and not a wavering an inch. I still remembered our last meeting up North. He had been less than impressed with my report, even when I was sportin' a fresh musket-ball hole in my leg. I didn't like the way I was dismissed or treated that day, even though I knew it was coming. Nevertheless, I had risked my hide for him and expected better. I had respected Lisa and what he was trying to accomplish with good reason. But I also demanded his... then and now. It's the only way you could deal with a man like him... straight to the point, cut right through the bullshit. Every man knows where he stands and what's expected of him.

The smile on his face disappeared. I was pushing him just a mite too far for comfort. He had forgotten what it felt like, spending all those months back in St. Louis living high on the hog, surrounded by a bunch of sycophantic toadys doing his bidding. He had forgotten how disagreeable us backwoods types could be... especially when we got our dander up. You see, the likes of John Colter were never potential investors, partners as it were. Men like me were not public magistrates or influential government officials like Captain Clark was back in St. Louis. We were the common folk: the penniless, the homespun legions of the American frontier, politically powerless, yet, champing at the bit, challenging the wilderness, the beaver trade itself, taking on the great commercial establishments, the elite of river society without as much as a "by your leave." His kind never cottoned to uppity folks like myself; they didn't answer to people like me. I was nothing in their eyes, just another rube… a simple backwoodsman to do their bidding. But, Lisa held back, capping that notorious temper of his, all the while enduring a patience he seldom displayed. He was squirming, uncomfortably so… and I must confess I enjoyed seeing it.

"*Oui*… but of course." He faced me for several long moments, never changing his expression, curiously assessing me in a way that he'd never done before.

"I know of your *nouveau de malheur*… recent misfortunes with your friend Potts. *Tragique*… tragic! So soon after being wounded by the hands of the Blackfeet."

And then he probed, testing to see how far I would let him go. "Maybe… you were a little hasty going back there with your friend? Eh?"

"Mebbe," I replied, testily, "though it seemed a good idea at the time."

"Still *audace*… bold, and recalcitrant, eh, Jean Colter?"

I looked at him directly, returning stare for stare. What could I say? Yeah, I went back. And yeah, I was here, wasn't I?

"*Oui*! I think that you are still the same man. Maybe… a little wiser, a little warier. I detect *'le petit amertume'*… a little bitterness in your voice, perfectly acceptable in your case. A little is *bon*… good."

There were seemingly long seconds of silence between us. He sensed that the Potts' affair was one with me best left alone. But, he'd found out what he had wanted to… that Mssr. Jean Colter was still his man.

"I will not beat around the bush… as they say. I have sent for you for one reason and one reason only."

"I kinda figured you did," I said, half funnin' with him, a smile coming over my face. "But, go on, Manuel. Forgive my interruptin'… as us Americans say, I'm all ears."

For a moment I sensed his reproach, barely controlling his fury, as if his indomitable will was trying to sear a burning hole right through my brains. I could feel raw heat pouring off of the man. The same kind of internal combustion that backed off more than one burly river rogue who thought he could tangle with this Spanish wildcat. But, I wasn't about to back off.

"*Bon!*" he replied nodding his head, a wry little smile finally busting out on his face. "All right, Mssr. Enough! I think you already know what I have in mind."

"I think I do," I replied. And I did. Lord a mercy, I did. I could see it coming. What else could it have been? "But, I might as well hear it from you, just the same. I've had enough uncertainty in my life of late."

"*Bon!* Then I shall get to the point. It should be no mystery to you as to why. *Le Trois Fourches*... the Three Forks will be like the Company's very own Louisiana Purchase, to be explored and exploited. But of course, you talked so magnificently about it, painting the most intriguing of landscapes. The wealth to be had, the beaver in its streams, the wild game and beasts... and all so plentiful. And yes, you've even warned about the red devils infesting the land like the scourge that they are.

"I listened, Mssr. Believe me, I heard it all, every detail. Even when you thought I hadn't. *Oui*, even the wildest figments of your imagination, your nightmarish ramblin's in the dead of the night. Mssr. Wiser reported your nightly stirrings to me, to be sure. He too was convinced of your veracity, though he dare not tell any of the others. I noted your wounded leg. The fears you evinced. The fate and the valour of the Flatheads you so nobly described. Even the savagery of the Blackfeet did not go unnoticed by me.

"Yes, I believed you, but with reservation, until, that is, the Crow, themselves confirmed it. Even Rose admits that you are 'big medicine' with the Absaroka. And maybe, 'big medicine' to the Blackfeet, too, if they would dare admit it. Eh? I think they dare not.

"So, Jean Colter, where do we go from here?"

I guess I must've looked rather dumbfounded. I said nothing in reply, simply nodding for Manuel to go on.

"*Voila, mon ami*," he chuckled, "it is no mystery. It is simple. We proceed to trap your Garden of Eden for all that it is worth. That is why I sent for you. You are the only man who knows the place... and its savages, the only man who knows the trail to the '*trois fourches*' and has returned to tell about it. Not even Drouillard can say that. And I never could trust Rose."

"Drouillard was there in '05, same as me, same as the rest of the Corps. Why not him?" I asked.

"That's quite true. He was there, by way of the Missouri. And that is a mighty long way to trek. A way I am not prepared to travel or waste the time to do so. Besides, he wants to trap now. He shows no interest in what I offer you."

He looked at me without batting an eye. His forehead was like a field of furrowed ruts. Color seemed to have drained right out of him, leaving his face a gray, ashen pallor. That rare, unexpected smile so recently expressed, vanished. In the parlance, he was not messing around. He was also not expecting me to refuse.

"We intend to establish a post come spring. And you, Jean Colter you will guide us there."

He wasn't asking, he was ordering, as if he was God Almighty, himself, descending down from on high to command the simple homespun mortals. And all I could think of was… "Whew, boy, marching orders, without even the courtesy of asking." The little greaser sure is a brimming barrel of gall and a bucketful of grit. But, he was slick, I'll give him that. He knew I'd have a tough time turning him down. He knew what I was made of since that very day I signed on with him at the Platte. He would've bet his precious little Ramon on it.

My head dipped ever so slightly, exasperated. I made no pretense of concealing the bad taste foaming in my mouth. Lisa knew well enough what had happened to Johnny and me and even ol' Toby. He had seen the hole in my leg from my first Piegan encounter. He knew my fear of the Blackfeet, their tenacity and brutality… their outright unreasonableness. He also knew I had more than my fair share of guts. I knew deep down, that he never questioned my veracity, trusting my instincts, my judgment from the first. After all, wasn't that why he sent for me?

I found myself shaking my head, mostly in disgust, partially in bewilderment. What's the use I mumbled to myself, the man's mind was made up long before. He wore blinders, only seeing what he wanted to see… hard times were for everyone else, not Manuel Lisa. All right, I told myself, I'm game, if he's game. I'll give him my best shot and if he doesn't buy into it, well, whatever happens will be on his head…. Not mine.

"Just let me get this straight," I said. "After all I've told you… about the Salish, those poor Flathead injuns… and then, Johnny Potts, yer still fixin' to go there? And what about me, you think I was on some kind of a church social? Are you prepared to send all those men to their deaths? Think about it, Manuel. Think about it long and hard."

I laid it on strong and thick. I figured I owed it to myself and every man 'jack of one 'em' who signed on. Otherwise, I might not have been able to live with myself.

"The Blackfeet are just too strong," I went on. "And if there ain't enough Piegans to waylay the lot of us, they'll call down their kin from Canada to give 'em a hand; the Bloods, the Siksika and their polecat Atsina friends, the Gros Ventre of the Prairie. There's no end to them or the nightmare they bring. They're all too full of hate and most of it is for us. Make no mistake about it. I don't care how many men you send there, they'll eat ya alive. They'll never be enough firepower to handle them injuns. Not with what all I've seen.

"And you want me to… to take them there, to lead the way?" I shook my head, sneering for all I was worth. There! I said my piece, clearing my conscience for any future debacle or disgrace.

"*Exactamente!* Well put. But of course, that is precisely what I want you to do. And you will do it, my friend. Yes, scouting ahead for a small army of well-armed, well-supplied, experienced trappers and engages. Including your friend Drouillard... and Miguel Immell, the *soldado*. You have said yourself that Drouillard is the best man on the frontier. Did he not lead the way to the great Pacific and back?

"They are the best men on the frontier, chosen well. *Le creme de la creme* of established St. Louis society is behind us, backing this venture with their money, their reputations and authority. We have formed a new partnership, including your own William Clark and the late Captain Lewis' younger brother, Reuben. The Chouteaus, Pierre Menard and Andrew Henry, we are all partners, the most influential men on the River.

"I shall not be accompanying you, though. I, we that is, have decided that Colonel Menard will be in charge. Major Henry will defer to the Colonel. It is agreed. To be sure, you will find them both equally agreeable to the task.

"As you can see, there is no possibility, no room for failure. There is only a fortune to be made from your '*trois fourches*'... if all that you've told me is true."

Oh, we're playing that game, I thought. There's no end to the shenanigans the little shit is ready to pull. But, I listened and he went on.

"And you... Mssr. Jean Colter, maybe you think you are not up to it, eh? A little too risky, eh, after what you have been through? Maybe, you would rather see Senor Drouillard be the man the Company relies upon, eh? After all, this will be the greatest commercial enterprise ever dared in the West. And not for men unsure of themselves, their stomachs or their hair."

"I smell a rather cheap insult, Manuel," I replied with more than a little cussiveness. My blood was heating up. And that's exactly the response he intended.

"Then you should trust your *nez*... nose, *mon ami*."

What a slick bastard he was. The greaser knew I set store by my word. Any man worth his salts did. My reputation was really the only thing I had. He had me by the balls as sure as if he had reached out and squeezed the begeezous out of 'em.

Hell, everyone knew that George and me just naturally rubbed each other the wrong way. We had words a time or two. Learned to give each other plenty of room, often as not like two old bulls staring each other down.. It'd been a shaky truce over the years, one that so far hadn't come to blows. I'm glad we didn't, cause George was quite a man to be sure... and I didn't need the grief.

"I did say George was the best. None better on this or any frontier as far as I am concerned... next to me that is. And that's a fact, you can bet yer poke on it.

"I can get your outfit there. You know I can. So lets cut to the bone and drop that cute little game your playing. I'm not convinced that trappin' the Forks country is such a good idea anymore. You could be sending' these boys into a hornet's nest... maybe even to their graves. I could be wrong, but I don't think so. I just pray this outfit of yours has a little more savvy than that bunch you led to the Big Horn... like your half-breed, trouble makin' friend, Ed Rose.

"As for Menard and Henry... they'd better be up to it. I doubt if either of 'em, fine gents that they may be, have ever experienced the kinda grief the Blackfeet bring."

I hesitated for awhile longer, letting it all sink in. But, I had already made up my mind and he knew it. So the deal was cut.

"Don't worry, Manuel, I'm willin' to give it another go... as long as there's no misunderstandin' between you and me and Menard and Henry about my role in this here affair. I'll do it. I'll take 'em there, but, let's get this straight... right here and now. You can count me in as long as you agree... I ain't responsible for what happens once we get there."

I said my piece, laid down my conditions, all the while ruminating on the prospects of what I had agreed to. Well, why not, I told myself. It just might offer me the one chance I'd get to pull in a mess of prime skins and head-on back east for good. Besides, I'd convinced myself ever since leaving Manuel's last, that I owed it to Johnny to send something home of worth to his kin. It was the least I could do.

So this was it, my last go at the Forks, come hell or high water. I had sworn an oath before to leave and never return. I had broken that vow, time and again. But, now I quietly renewed that oath to my Creator... a vow I meant to keep.

The Spaniard stood as tall as he could stretch, chest inflated, as proud as proud could be. He knew he'd won. He smiled and nodded. His head began bobbing up and down like an apple on a string.

"Ahh, this is *tres bon*. '*Mon carcajou*'... you are like the wolverine and le curly wolf both wrapped into one. You have the *cajones*, Jean Colter, *le grand cajones*. Few men here grow them. Droulliard for sure has them, but his thinking is too limited, *pour certainement* not grandiose, not bold... *audace*, like yourself. When you have something to do... you do it *sans excuse*. I like that. And like me, you will succeed. Maybe that is why men such as us have our way."

Lisa paused for a moment staring at me, probably awaiting my response. I just listened and let him continue.

"*Bon!* By your silence we are agreed. What could be simpler? You shall lead the way; guide the Command to the headwaters of the Missouri. I will instruct them to rely on your judgment. Help them out when need be. They will need your experience, your instincts. Pierre will listen. He is a man of intelligence. His ego will not get in the way.

"Major Henry's the stubborn one. He is also *mangeur de lard*... green to the ways of our trade. But, *certainement*, with a little seasoning he will listen to reason, grow in the ways of the wilderness..

"That is it, my friend. That is all. Get Messrs. Menard and Henry to le '*Trois Fourches*' and then you can do whatever pleases you. Trap, hunt, leave... whatever you wish."

The company departed Manuel's on the Big Horn in March of '10 and trailed west, following the Yellowstone. Armed men, trappers, three dozen strong, mounted on tough, wiry little Crow ponies and pulling a string of pack-ponies weighted down 'til their backs and bellies sagged to the ground from the burden of their heavy loads.

It took a whole slew of implements to carve out a trapper's post in the wilderness, especially in a land as remote and as dangerous as where we intended to go. Men had to have a place to operate out of, to get out of the weather, to keep dry and warm, protected from the elements and the critters, both two footed and four. Cabins had to be built with rooms to handle supplies and foodstuffs and such. Fresh meat had to be hunted, water had to be hauled. The Company's business must be conducted in a proper place, written records of transactions had to be kept and that meant ink, quills, log books, journals of the trade. Kegs of gunpowder had to be stored safe and dry, easy to get to, easy to defend. And the accouterments of the trade: lightweight, durable steel spring-jawed beaver traps. The Company was going to the Forks to trap beaver. Little thought was given to trading with any of the tribes now; the battle of the "pishkun plains" and the death of Johnny Potts had put all thoughts of trade to rest. Staying alive in the Three Forks allowed no time for shenanigans; get in, do your business and get out.

A trapper's post in injun country in every essence of the word was a fort, an armed stockade, built to reflect the size of its command and the danger in which it inheritantly faced. A perimeter would have to be laid out, fields of fire cleared. Trees fell and trimmed and dragged to the site no matter how far the distance. Logs honed, set into trenches deep and stout, raised high side by side, snugly fit and injun-tight. Ramparts to watch from, ladders to reach them. Men couldn't be expected to do these things with their bare-hands... adz, axes and shovels and a host of tools were needed to do the trick.

Corrals for livestock had to be built. Firewood had to be cut. Game had to be shot. The stock had to forage. A lean-to for the Company blacksmith had to be erected, complete with anvil, forge and bellows and a myriad of tools of the trade: tongs and pinchers, files, punches, callipers, hammers, chisels, oil stones, leather apron, taps and dies and on and on and on. Weapons and traps had to be repaired. Leather-goods mended. Those axes and adze and tomahawks would have to be honed on a near-daily basis and knives in particular to skin both game for fresh meat and beaver for their precious hides. Plenty of heavy thick clothing had to be packed away; buffalo robes, spare moccasins, canvas tents and warm woolen blankets to keep away the chill on cold nights. Lead and powder and flint enough to outfit a small army.

The *frogs*, the voyageurs of the western waterways preferred their thick woolen capotes and soft woolen caps. The backwoodsmen were sheaved in buckskin and fur from head to toe... deerskin leggins and breechcloth, fringed hunting shirts and heavy winter coats of thick buffalo fur. Some still wore homespun, some linsey-woolsey. The Colonel and the Major still preferred their store-bought clothes, but they wouldn't last long. They'd soon switch to animal hide. A few men, tenderfoots from the East to be sure, wore clumsy, uncomfortable leather boots, unfit for walking, though most soon preferred the red-man's moccasins... comfortable, light weight, easy to replace. A man or two, like big Mike Immell still sported his Army tunic, proud of his service to his country. It was an odd mix of garb and men, civilized and not so civilized, a company destined to become a buckskin brigade.

Every man toted his own possibles for the trek was long and arduous and the longer it went on the heavier the burden became. The white-man naturally tended to carry much too much to satisfy his comfort. The red-man had learned to travel light and fast, wasting as little precious energy as he had to. Experience taught a man what was important to his kit and what wasn't, something every tenderfoot was sure to learn. And then two hundred saddle-weary miles on horseback, traveling through a land of constant internecine warring, marauding savages. Two weeks of enduring a lingering winter yet to be subdued... in a land, in a time of year replete with unforseen obstacles and surprises waiting around the next bend of the river or just over the next rise... and all on empty stomachs.

I've known such times as the bone-chilling kind of misery a northern cold-snap can bring. Freezing the land, the rivers and streams, trees and rocks... the very ground you walk upon, the air you breathe. Numbing man and beast alike and slowing life to less than a snail's crawl. And for those unlucky enough to get caught out in the open, exposed and unprepared, well, it could get to be a mighty nasty proposition.

In this country the month of March tends to be the nastiest time of all... maybe bad weather's last hurrah. Winds whipping down from the bleak Canadian plains are stronger and colder, as bitter as anything the Arctic can hurl our way. Gales blow furiously without respite like wintry hurricanes, driving snowfall onward and upward to treacherous heights, piling the fine white powder higher and higher or deeper and deeper, becoming mountains of drifts... or seas of white peril and frozen precipitation.

This was a land, a time, a season not meant for the timid or the weak. And traveling, when you don't have to, is simply a bad idea. An unending nightmare of frustration and angst, struggle and exhaustion, draining your strength, fraying your nerves, challenging your resolve, your will. One unexpected pitfall leading to another. Here a tragedy fortuitously averted, there an ordeal overcome, survived. And then, without warning...

Now most Indian nations of the Northwest plains and mountains would be still holed-up in their buffalo skin lodges, warmed by fire and hearth and family, waiting it out, secure in their mountain valleys far from the lands of their enemies. They had learned time after time the dangers of carelessness and the virtue of patience. And if they had put in an ample stock of pemmican and jerked-meat there was no good reason to justify leaving the safety of their lodges or comfort of their women.

But, like the weather you never could tell about Indians. Just when you thought you had them figured out...

It was on our second day out from Manuel's, where the valley of the Yellowstone lay every bit a dismal land; bleak, somber, still locked in the grip of an icy winter. There was not a sign, not a track of man or his beasts to be found or seen. Indeed, life had slowed down. Save for the inexorable current of the not-quite frozen La Roche Jaune and the crinkling of thin, brittle layers of ice and snow crushed beneath our ponies hooves and the constant friction of worn saddles, rubbing equally worn buckskin duds, leggings and near frozen human rumps.

The monotonous rhythm and drone on a horse's back reigned mile after mile, hour after hour. The men became listless, careless. Their limbs grew heavy, their backs stiff. They were saddle sore and saddle weary. They would have been better off walking on their own power, remaining alert and alive, than sitting on a horse waiting to be picked off by an unseen enemy.

Yes, the unfamiliarity of the saddle was a painful throne to many a sore and tender seat. And the cold had a way of subduing even the best of men. Ours were no exception. I had only to look over my shoulder to see how easily the savages could have waylaid the whole column or pick us off one at a time, at a place of their choosing. And we had only just begun our trek. Thank God the red-man had more sense than the white.

A crisp, light breeze was in our faces, blowing gently in from the west.

The sky was clear, the sun bright and warm. It was a good day to travel, to make tracks. I was scouting ahead within rifle shot of the company, riding with one of Drouillard's Shawnee scouts, a taciturn, wiry little redskin named Pla-co-ta. He was like a shadow, a puff of air... barely noticeable, as natural a part of the land as a tree, a rock or piece of ground... and deadly quiet, even for an Indian. No wasted movements or gestures came from this man, seldom did he utter a word save for an occasional grunt or ugh to get my attention or make a point.

That was all right by me, I was used to being alone. It's better that way, better for a man to keep his hair. Besides, I was kind of getting used to him being there. All seemed the way it should be, except...

We could barely make it out when it first caught our attention. A slight trace of smoke, billowing skyward, barely discernible, right in our path and paralleling the river ahead.

"What in the hell!" I was more than a little startled.

I reined in and pulled up to get a better look. The Shawnee did likewise. Something wasn't right. The two of us knew it right off. A steady plume of black smoke kept rising, now starkly outlined against the clear blue sky.

Black smoke meant trouble. Unconsciously I took a tighter grip on my weapon. Everything, every place became suspect. My eyes wandered from weathered pine to ravine to rise, anywhere and everywhere a war party could hide or lurk and skulk.

But, Indians wouldn't be that obvious. And no Company trappers from Manuel's were this far out, at least anyone we knew of. And no savvy man in his right mind would kindle such a blatant fire. Every savage within a hundred miles would soon know it. And nature hadn't anything to do with it, not this time of year. No, whatever was burning had already happened.

Pla-co-ta grunted, "Naw good!"

His right index finger made a sweeping gesture from left to right across the front of his naked throat. He, too, was unsettled. He tilted his head backwards, nose to the sky inhaling deeply, sniffing the airborne scents from up yonder like a red-hide, human bloodhound.

The smell, the aroma grew stronger, and somehow, curiously familiar. And then it hit us with an unmistakable reek... a reek of death, repugnant to the senses filling both our nostrils, watering our eyes, coating our tongues. We looked at each other knowingly. Our faces were blank, devoid of expression. Yet intuitively we read each other's mind like it was our own. Our instincts were communicating in a way that our other senses could never do. We didn't have to see or touch or feel or hear to know it was there. Death assuredly lay just ahead. As sure as there was a bright sun in the morning sky.

My pony's body went taut, every sinew and joint tensed, rigid like forged steel. I felt his anxiety grow steadily beneath me. His nostrils flared, his ears flickered and craned, straining to hear, to detect. Deep from within his massive chest cavity, came low, raspy, cautious cords, as if issuing a warning of what lay beyond. The odious smell of burning flesh wafting our way agitated the critter to the point of bolt and run.

"Whoa, whoa." I gently rubbed his neck, talking softly, reassuringly, calming the anxious beast down.

Burning flesh, I thought. It never has that same tempting quality as roasting meat. The intent is not the same. And this smell was certainly not meat on a spit.

I turned and signaled back to Menard and Andy Henry who continued to approach albeit warily. They too had seen the black smoke arising. The whole column saw it. And now the fetid scents were beginning to reach them. A murmur of discontent and concern rumbled from front rank to rear. Every man was alerted, knee jerking each one right out of their mounted stupor like they were shot from their guns.

Pla-co-ta and me kicked our mounts in the slats and sped off towards a grassy knoll separating us from the smoke beyond. Up and over we climbed at a gallop, putting the heels to our speeding ponies and soon, we vanished from view of the pursuing column.

We drew closer, slowing our lathered ponies to a walk, each of us warily scanning the river banks, the cottonwoods and willows, the ground that swept away from the Yellowstone to the sandstone heights above. The air hung eerily still. I could hear and feel my heart pound and beat incessantly. I barely breathed. I was more alert, on life's thin edge than I had been in a long, long time. Instinctual feelings of fear, of wariness long forgotten suddenly were alive and pulsating. I looked. I smelled. I listened. I read the signs of the scene and the land spread out before me. Nothing moved, save for the smoldering remains of a crude Indian lodge of thin branches covered by a few mangy, worn skins now reduced to ashes and smoke.

Lying on the ground lifeless near the dying conflagration was a young squaw, stripped naked. Nearby lay a little injun boy, obviously the squaw's own. Their skulls were split horridly open like squashed summer-melons, rent by the cruel, telltale blows of primitive stone-headed war clubs or trade tomahawks. The contents of their shattered heads had spilled out and streamed to the ground below, forming unsightly pools of blood and brain and splintered bone, congealing in the chill of slush and ice and frozen air.

I was instantly nauseated. The young woman and her offspring's death throes were far too ghastly to behold. A spasm of revulsion gripped me. I had seen the horrors wrought by the red-man before. I was as hardened as any man on the frontier, inured to the callousness, the savagery. As hard, as cold as my experiences had made me, I never, ever got used to it. Thank God, I never would.

Suddenly, it was as if Johnny was lying before me riddled and mangled and maimed by the banks of the Jefferson. The memory reverberated in my head and heart to the tune of a thousand thundering war drums. I began sweating profusely, though a chilled wind blowing from across the river and whipping up white capped waves had penetrated my thick buffalo hide coat right to my bones. I was so benumbed at the senselessness of these two murders that I hadn't even noticed the rest of the company gallop up.

Soon the whole outfit dismounted and gawked at the spectacle, bewildered by the slaughter and gore. Every eye was drawn to the victims' blackened and charred feet, the putrid piles of their burning flesh.

It was a scene of torture and degradation. Of savage humor and delight... insidious, humiliating, revolting to all human sensibility and dignity. Yet, it was a familiar scene to the red-man in their land. One repeated more often than not. And one drummed into every Indian child. Survival for them was unlike anything the white man's civilization knew.

And many of the men turned away from it... disgusted, revulsed.

"For what, Godly reason," I cried aloud, "could anyone do this to a lone woman and a defenseless boy.

"Damn the murderin' bastards. Damn them. Damn them. Damn them," I screamed over and over.

I was consumed by anger and hatred and loathing. Hatred unabated, festering deep within me. The *spoo-pii* still lived. The *spoo-pii* still remembered. The *spoo-pii* still hated.

I barely heard the muffled sounds of someone weeping softly. Nearby, stood a young trapper, green to the wilderness and green to the trapper-life. Tears were streaming unchecked down his cheeks. His emotional dam obviously had burst. No longer could he control its inevitable flow. His name was Thomas James and for the short time I knew him he would become my friend.

He stood wavering and teetering on unsteady legs. An ashen, sickening look seemed to sweep over him. He abruptly felt the upsurge coming and reacted instantly, clamping both hands over his mouth as if trying to hold back some bilious tide forthcoming. His rifle fell to the ground with a noisy clatter. His actions, though, were all too late. Nothing would have helped him nor stemmed the inevitable tide. The boy puked his guts out, splattering his shirt, his leggings and moccasins with half his insides. He wretched again and again.

Others looked, then respectfully turned away. No one needed to add to his misery or his shame. His friends, Cheek and Dougherty and Weir and

Brown all hesitated, none of them knowing what to do or say. They stood quietly nearby.

I waited until he was through, walked over and placed my arm around his shoulders.

"You'd better get a good look, Tom. Even if it makes you sick again and again. Life is cheaper than dog shit out here, especially for lonely squaws and their brats."

I put it to him about as coldly as I could, no sweetening it up. No buttering-up with honey and jam the bloody reality of the frontier. No sparing the innocent or naive, not if I wanted young James to keep his hair and his nerve.

"Who, why?" he said looking up at me almost pleadingly. His eyes were still moist with salty dew. But, anger seemed to be rising steadily and taking hold. It was a natural reaction by a civilized man to the barbarity of injun ways.

I knew it all too well... from far too many a bloody occasion. It was for survival, out of ignorance and fear. The Northwest frontier bred such wanton mayhem.

And now James' blood began to boil. Revulsion, shame, pity had temporarily run its course. Slowly, invariably replaced by waves of disgust and wrath and maybe, just maybe retribution. He, who never had known such hate before, would soon despise with all his might those who had committed these foul, foul crimes.

I looked around studying the ground, the signs of struggle and escape, reading what could be read. The squaw and her kid had not been alone. There were at least two others here before tragedy struck. But, they'd made a hasty retreat. Alerted, I surmised, just in 'the nick of time'. Just skedaddled as fast as their ponies could carry 'em.

One set of prints were much heavier, deeper... obviously that of a man. A man I didn't think too much of. Yeah, he had been quick, all right. Probably just use to thinking of his own precious skin. It was a helluva way to live.

"Son of a bitch," I mumbled to myself.

There was more there to read in the dirt. The attack had to have been a complete surprise, catching 'em all off guard. I could imagine the terror, the squaws' screaming, the panic and fright in the little boy as he peed uncontrollably, right in his loincloth. What a shame... a little kid.

It was all too easy to picture. I shuddered at the thought, my imagination jerking me spasmodically like a fish dangling and fighting on a line.

The men were milling about, mulling over the slaughter. Everyone was affected... talking it up amongst theirselves: angry, uncertain, apprehensive and all plain, downright scared.

I knew what was going through their minds. Sensed the fear, the trepidation growing among them like a runaway plague, the tightness in their bellies, wrenching their insides, the dryness in their throats and mouths. I continued to watch, mentally calculating what I thought each man's worth, instinctively sizing up every trapper's mettle in a fight.

It was a most natural thing to do. Life had taught me that way, ever since I threw my rifle over my shoulder and headed west. I was neither proud of it nor ashamed of it.

A good half of them probably had never seen murder before, at least not 'plains Indian' style. Several were veterans of the frontier U. S. Army... experienced, capable men like big Mike Immell, lately discharged. Francois Valle was a handy man in a fight with knife, tomahawk or flintlock. Some had the look, the feel of fighting men. Most of the others I couldn't tell a lick about. I suspected that neither Menard nor Henry did either. But, I betcha they were thinking about it now.

Drouillard and his two Shawnee stood off to the side, unaffected, accepting the scene with a detached air. Hell, the Shawnee might've done it themselves, before... maybe even to white women. Many young blond tow-headed youngsters were raised in Shawnee villages brought-up as one of their own. And their people had been on the warpath for sixty years or more against mine. It had been a bitter history of conflict between the Shawnee and the white-man. And now we were riding side by side, frontier life was full of ironies.

Death was not new to them. A squaw, a defenseless kid... it was all part of the way life for most red-men living in the wilderness. There was no civilized law. No right, no wrong... just kill. Or be killed. They accepted the brutality, the finality as a natural part of the landscape and moved on.

I watched George for a moment. He was a half-breed himself. His face and that of his two companions, Pla-co-ta and Luthecaw, were unrevealing, masks of mystery like the Sphinx in ol' Egypt in Biblical times. What went on in their minds, I couldn't say. At least I knew Drouillard would stand his ground. I was certain of it. And his two Shawnee... they'd stick by George.

Menard and Henry were quietly conferring. They, too, showed no emotion. But they were concerned, nevertheless. Each of their faces was a little graver than the day before. Building a post, giving out orders, countin' and tallyin' freshly tanned and bundled skins... these were what the Company's business was supposed to be all about. But, murder always has a way of unsettling the natural rhythm of things.

I knew them both to be capable, confident men. I supposed the two of them were as equal as any in St. Louis to command Lisa's brigades. They watched closely and learned, not missing a trick, assessing each and every man in their command. Making mental notes between them to stow away 'til the time of need came. They were just like me... wanting to know whom they could count on. And who they could not. I understood completely. In fact, I decided then and there that those two men would probably do. I'd have done the same thing... and I did.

Pla-co-ta approached and talked softly. He gestured towards two sets of pony tracks leading away from the encampment. And then he pointed out a whole, jangled mess of unshod hooves, obviously hot in pursuit... a war party, no doubt. The assault, the massacre had been unexpected, swift and so brutally final. It was plain to see. If a man wasn't blind he could read it in a heartbeat.

I turned to James and pointed to the rival sets of tracks.

"Looks like the dead squaw had a husband or a man. He must've heard 'em comin', grabbed his other squaw and hightailed it outta here like his ass was on fire, the gutless coward.

"The murderin' savages are the Gros Ventre of the Prairie, the Atsina from up yonder on the northern plains. I here tell from the Mandans that they're tradin' with the English up north in Canada country. The Brits liquor 'em up. Send 'em down south to do what vile skullduggery they can... along with their allies the Blackfeet. They're formidable, all right. And they hate the American 'white eyes.' As far as I am concerned, they're the worst murderin' injuns of 'em all. But make no mistake, they're all trouble... 'big trouble.'

"The squaw and her boy are what most of the tribes out here call the 'sheepeaters'... distant kin to the Snakes... the Shoshone. They're just shy, simple, poor injuns. No threat to anyone, least of all these murderin' Gros Ventre. All the butcherin' tribes prey on 'em. Kill the men, most of the women, except the young and pretty ones. They do with them as they please. They usually take the youngins, raise 'em as their own, and make the girl child their slaves. Like Hidatsa raiders did little Sacagawea. She told us all about it... and it wasn't pretty. Life for squaws can be a mighty rough proposition. No fancy, highfalutin' balls or church socials to be pampered and wooed. I don't envy 'em.

"And that's the truth of it, Tom... life is a hard-go out here. You'd better get used to it... and mighty quick."

I ended rather coolly... hoping the lesson would sink in. In fact I made sure all those tenderfoots heard me.

Some, though, were ready to fight, tempers flared... agitated by one very loquacious man. James Cheek was always just a short-breath away from letting loose against some perceived insult or inequity or reproach. He was a tall, rangy, rawboned Tennessean. Quick to temper, to fight... fists, knives, whatever. There was no backup in the man. In fact the word was not even in his lexicon.

"I'm fer goin' after 'em. Teach the bastards a lesson. That's what I say. Every red-hide 'jack one of 'em.' Butcher 'em just like they did that little kid. Light 'em on fire and see how they like their piggies and red dicks aburnin'." Cheek didn't hold back any emotions. He was fired up and meant every last word of it.

Pla-co-ta looked at me with alarm and spoke softly.

"What'd that injun say?" barked Cheek, now a little paranoid since he'd gone and put his foot in his mouth.

"He says that there was too many Gros Ventre to go traipsin' after. Way over a hundred, to be sure," I said.

"I don't give a god-damn," said Cheek, obviously not ready to listen to reason. All he could see was retribution and Gros Ventre scalps hangin' on the barrel end of his rifle or belt.

"I feel the same way, Jimmy. But, I'm afraid we're too late to do this here girl and boy any good. And goin' off and gittin' ourselves shot up or scalped and killed ain't goin' do anybody any good." It was Jack Dougherty, James' best friend.

Where Cheek lacked subtlety, Dougherty did not. He was almost too thoughtful for one so young, holding his cards close to his chest and his temper in check. He always watched and listened, biting his tongue when need be and never wasting words unless they needed to be said. Though now friends, Jack proved to be a good counter to the volatile Cheek.

"We won't be the ones bein' scalped or kilt," Cheek fired back, turning up the volume.

And he wasn't alone. Many of the men gathered around the boisterous Cheek, and they liked what they heard. Few could argue the justice of Cheek's ways. There was a rumbling amongst them, a steady rise of anger swelling throughout the whole command.

Maybe, it was because of the cold or the monotony of horseback or the strangeness of the land and the perverseness of its inhabitants and their cultures. Every man here who had lived on the frontier had grown up listening to numerous tales of Indian degradation and cruelty. That unending fear was a fact of life for those who dared risk being in a land that the red-man roamed.

Some had lost kin and loved ones. Several were veterans of recent Indian scrapes, fighting the savages in other parts of the country. And sometimes men just had to bitch or go looking for trouble. Whatever their reasons, an awful lot of them were ready to pursue the Gros Ventre and fight alongside James Cheek, come hell or highwater... at least they were with their mouths.

Menard and Henry watched and listened, neither of them saying a word.

Both wanting to see how it played out... to a point.

Drouillard and his Shawnee were the same way, even though they had long before made up their minds about the fighting heart of most white-men.

Valle, Immell... they weren't so sure. I was with them.

There was tension here. It was a good thing, I thought. Well-needed to keep every man alert and on his toes. As long as everyone remembered just whom the enemy was.

And then Dougherty once again broke the ice, God bless him.

"As best as I can remember it, Jimmy... we've come all this way to trap beaver. And I hope... to get rich, not to be injun fighters or crusaders. As for scalpin' and killin', there'll be plenty of opportunity for that at the Forks. If what Colter here says is likely. And he should know judgin' by the way he reads their sign.

"I think we'd best remember this like John says and make darn sure it doesn't happen to us."

No one said a thing. Men were shaking their heads, agreeing to a man, all coming to their senses. Cheek sensed it, too, and cooled down. No doubt, one day he would have his turn.

The uproar died a natural death. They all cared, they all sought backwoods' justice in the inimitable way of the frontier. Yet, their concern, their anger did little to assuage the dead that lay before us. Sometimes, you have to leave the dead where they lie and move on. And this was just another one of those times.

"All right, men. You've all said your peace. Times a wastin'." Andy Henry had seen and heard enough and decided it was time to move on. "Let's move out."

The grumbling died down. Men began to return to their mounts. The column reformed and for the most part they put the massacre behind them. But, I had no doubts that this scene would stay in every man's memory. And well it did. We had a long way to go and many surprises still lay ahead. It was good they would remember. They would learn and grow and become tougher, more resilient.

Yet, Tom and I lingered for a few moments longer

"But... but the boy?" James had settled down, though he still couldn't resolve the brutality of the Gros Ventres.

Maybe he was feeling a kinship with the young Indian boy, him being so young himself. I don't know, but his feelings were persistent and he just didn't want to let it go.

"Why him? Why not take him alive? I don't understand these injuns at all. It's all so stupid, so utterly unnecessary," James said, shaking his head still in disbelief.

"Yeah..." I said. "The boy. Must not have had the time for him. Who can say... when it comes to injuns?" I spat on the ground in disgust.

"Get a good look," I ordered rather forcefully. "Burn it into your memory and soul. Burn it, boy... burn it. I had a friend wind-up like this once and I don't particularly want to see it happen again."

It was a rude baptism for young Tom as well as for most of the rest of outfit. I could see the makings of a few good men emerging out of the smoke and fire. Tom James, Jack Doughery... they would do. Even Cheek, for all his posturing was a standup man. One way or another they would all measure-up... or meet their Maker.

Death had served a purpose. There was no more sleeping in the saddle from that day forward. Nobody wanted to wind-up like the squaw and her little kid. The memory of their savage deaths and the stench of their burning flesh lingered with the command from that day forward. The Command had found a new, healthy fear for the murdering Gros Ventre and the ways of this strange, wild land. The lesson of the lowly "sheepeaters" would not soon be forgotten.

And well it didn't, for each day, battered by bitter, icy Northern winds and faced constantly with a starkly white, bleak, wintry landscape wore away at the column, sapping each man and their half-starved ponies' strength and vitality, defying their resolve to keep moving, to push on. Exhaustion, hunger and numbing cold wrought fear and desperation, dominating every man's attention. And nothing lying on the horizon before us offered any sign of spring or life or relief.

We proceeded on, each day the same, one day leading to another and then another, always cold, always tired. Man and horse alike were becoming equally listless, lethargic. Nightime brought little relief. Aching-limbs, joints, saddle-worn bodies hampered sleep, restlessness ruled. Growling stomachs constantly reminding the men just how hungry they were.

At the first crack of the new dawn's light we found ourselves in a world of pure, white hell. Snow and ice covered the land like water an ocean, hemming us in on all sides; on the ground we trod, the hills, and distant mountains... everywhere the eye could see. Even La Roche Jaune seemed to wear its frozen mantle begrudgingly.

Yet, the dark, foreboding clouds that dogged our trail since the dead squaw's camp had disappeared, swept along with the passing of night, completely and utterly. From sunup to sundown not a puff or a wisp of their presence was to be seen. The sky was blue, beautifully blue... big and vast. Even the wind had died down 'til hardly a breeze was to be felt. The air was crisp, even agreeable.

It was as if calm had returned. And with the calm, hope, succor. We had reached the midway point of our destination. It hadn't been so bad, after all. Hell, we can make it. A new attitude, a new resolve permeated our ranks. The men, their horses shook the cold and the snow of the winter out of their bones and off their woolen coats and shaggy hides and stepped out a little livelier than the day before.

The morning sun grew bright, gloriously bright, dazzling all with its brilliance as it radiated off the snow-shrouded land as unwelcome as a virulent plague. Its glare was unavoidable. It couldn't be helped. The whole company couldn't walk blindfolded, not with injuns about. It crept up upon the unsuspecting, the exhausted... veterans and tenderfoots alike, all the while lulling them in warmth and comfort. The sun's powerful rays ricocheted from every conceivable landbound direction, careening, glistening off of all that white, sending glaring-hot needles of pain and anguish, pummeling unprotected eyes as cruelly as any Gros Ventre warclub. No man was immune to its blinding embrace. Sooner or later, without a respite, some were going to pay.

Robbie Brown knew there was something building up within him. He had been feeling it coming-on all morning long, but he had been too tired to care. Hell, most of the men were rubbing their eyes, weren't they, complaining as usual? Somebody was always complaining. Besides, there wasn't a part of his body that wasn't hurting. But, this was different. All of a sudden the pain had grown too intense, far too intense. And then it struck, boiling hot, burning, scalding his eyes, right in their sockets.

Brown burst out screaming, instantly dropping his reins. His horse startled and reared, throwing his rider to the ground. The landing was soft, the snow plenty deep. Never realizing that he had been thrown, Robbie's mind was on a different, more immediate problem. He was rolling in the white powder of winter, scooping handfuls of cold snow, massaging the frigid moisture in his eyes, his face...gobs of it, alternately praying aloud, begging for relief. His screams were unabated, the echo of his lament, eerily disturbing the dead of this winter day.

I raced back, dreading the worst. The whole column came at a gallop, closing in upon the destitute Brown, crowding around him in a protective huddle. The men's faces were troubled, confused. One of our own had gone down. Was he wounded, was he riddled by arrows? No shots had been heard. Had the savages snuck in, undetected and did their dirty work? Was it a repeat of the burning squaw and her little boy?

What would happen next? Nobody had said it, but many wondered it. All looked about... searching, divining, ready to jerk their rifles' triggers at the first sign of deceit or red-hided treachery.

Brown sat in the snow, a pathetic looking sight, cupping his hands over his eyes, covering them as if trying to shut out the sun and the light refracted madness of a land of glowing snow. There was no blood, no sign of injury or of foul play. Yet, Brown wailed and ranted on.

"My eyes, my eyes. I can't see. My eyeballs... are melting."

Tears were streaming down his cheeks, hot and steaming.

"My eyes are on fire. James can your hear me? Tom, Tom... for God sakes, anybody, help me.

"I can't see. I can't see. My eyes are killin' me.

"I'm blind... I tell you I'm blind."

"Robbie, Robbie. I'm here. I'm here. What happened? What can I do?"

James was standing over his tortured friend. Poor Tom was as confused as the rest of us.

"My eyes are burnin' up. I can't... see." Brown's voice was pitiful. "Help me, Tom. Help me."

James was frantic, unsure of what was tormenting his friend, much less how to help. Hell, everyone stood about the weeping Brown, dumbfounded, no one knowing what to do or think.

Tears continued to stream down Brown's face. He squinted and winced, the pain so intense I thought his face would burst like a squashed melon.

I knew right off the malady, the curse young Robbie was now enduring. Damn, I cursed myself silently. It's my own fault. These tenderfoots don't know. I could have avoided this. No. No. I can't be everywhere. They're all men, volunteers to a man. They're all suppose to know what they were getting themselves into. Lisa never said anything about babysitting. I'm not getting paid for this.

Going it alone had been easy. I knew what to expect and what survival expected of me. Saddled with forty or more men was a whole new experience. It was not the same as it was with the Corps. Our boys were special. Born to and wilderness bred. We were well trained, disciplined, able to cope and improvise. Nothing daunted us. Our two leaders, Lewis and Clark, were the best there was. I should have thought better on the trail that lay ahead, but I had been in too much of a hurry, back there on the Knife.

Snap out of it, I told myself. And then I took my finger out of that proverbial place. I've got to help this kid.

"Cover him up, Tommy. Cover his face and head... Boys, give Tom a hand. Hold Brown down if you have to.

"C'mon on, Tom, get a move on. Wrap his head, his eyes... with something soft. Be quick about it. The light is killing the poor boy."

James quickly shielded Brown's face and eyes, covering his entire head with his own woolen blanket.

The blanket did the trick. Brown's howling soon diminished, the darkness bringing a small measure of relief. His moans seemed less intense. He continued to weep, still unable to control the flow of hot tears as painful as they were. The fear of the unknown, the unexpected, bedeviled him, yet. James' woolen blanket was doing little to assuage the unknown, the uncertainty of his immediate future. Sudden, excruciating blindness had left him all alone, even amidst the whole command standing by his side.

His friends were there, though, talking to him, comforting him, bolstering his spirits, wanting desperately to lighten his load. Concern was written on their faces. They feared for him. This was all so new, so daunting to many of the men. The unknown is never easy to take or understand. Uncertainty can wear a man down just as suredly as exhaustion.

Some of the men, the Shawnee for example, appeared almost disinterested. Others were just plain curious, looking to and fro to one another, askance, scratching their heads, glad it wasn't them.

Menard and Henry arrived and pushed their way through the crowd.

"You men," cried Henry. "Take your weapons and get back with the horses... and keep a sharp eye. You're causing enough racket for every injun in a hundred miles to hear."

And then he added sharply. "Or maybe you want to wind-up like that burnt squaw and her boy."

He turned and focused on Brown. Henry was incredulous. "What's the matter with him? Is he sick or what? We don't have time for this, you know."

"Snow blindness," I said. "Pretty bad business."

"*Jesu Christe!*" swore Menard.

"Can't you shut him up? He'll drive all of us crazy," said Henry.

I looked at the Major, not at all satisfied with his response. Henry was a hard man, used to getting his way. He had little tolerance for delays, no matter what the cause.

Colonel Menard was more empathetic. He was not the same 'cut of a man' as his partner. "Is it really that bad?"

"It is... as bad as it gets. And we'd better get used to it. This boy's up to his ears in pain. Better hope no one else comes down with it... or we'll all be in a heap of trouble."

Menard looked around at his men. Their faces were all the same; worn out, exhausted and more than a little worried. The ponies weren't doing any better. Forage had been meager, the snow too deep to plod through without effort and the trail, the trek, so far, a lot tougher and longer than he was led to believe. It didn't take the Colonel long to size up his command's fitness or morale.

"Colter's right. We must take it easier, Andrew. We've pushed too hard, entirely too hard. The men, the horses are worn out. We can't afford to lose anyone, just to gain a day or two."

Menard put his hand on Henry's shoulder. They were both feeling the strain of command.

"I'm as tuckered-out as everyone else. It's just… that I want to get this damn walk over with and get to where we're agoin' and the sooner the better. A lot of important men have too much money tied up in this venture for us to be sittin' here, whining over a little discomfort." Henry began to rub his own eyes. A thin, teary stream ran down his cheek.

"We all do, my friend. We all do. My eyes have been burning for two days. I… I just didn't want to say anything. I'm afraid I'm not as strong as I would like to be," he said. "This place, the cold, all that glare… has addled my mind."

"Hell's bells, your doin' right fine, Colonel. You both are. Everyman is," I spoke up. "We just gotta be a little more careful. We still got to get to and over the Pass. And it ain't goin' to get any easier."

"Merci, merci. You are of course, right. But, so is Major Henry. We shall be more careful, but for now, we shall move on, before I, too, lie down and die in this white shit. I am sick of this damned snow, sick of it."

Henry and Menard were finding out that the trail was no picnic. They were both good men, more than capable-enough to lead a company of trappers to the Three Forks. Menard, though, had left a family back in St. Louis and he was missing them dearly. He knew his duty to the Company and to his partners. He would carry out that duty to the best of his ability. But, he had his limits, and he was no fool. As for Andrew Henry, well, the Major was made of sterner stuff. Hard-headed, stubborn as a mule, come hell or highwater he was going to stick it out and the Blackfeet, the Gros Ventre and the 'elements' be-damned.

As for poor Tom James, he was nigh on beside himself worrying, nursemaiding his friend. He was learning the hard way, for nothing in his past had prepared him for this. He was finding out that trapping with a company of men in the wilderness was more than just setting traps and tanning hides, much more.

The torment and the pain, the uncertainty and helplessness of being blind, however temporary, in a strange and dangerous land made his friend Robbie Brown desperate, suicidal. Several times throughout the course of the rest of the day and well into that night, Brown pleaded with his friends "shoot me, shoot me." His moans and sobs, beseeching relief could be heard from one end of the column to the other, until sleep and exhaustion gave us all a rest.

That night I thought of the men of the command. As unlikely a group as I had ever known, so illy prepared for the wilderness and it seemed what we were facing was getting worse by the day. They were a confused mess of patchwork clothing, faded homespun and worn, tanned deerskins begging for replacement. Fringed hunting coats and heavy woolen capotes. Coonskin hats and French Canadian knitted caps. Shredded moccasins and worn-out leather boots. They were motley... ragtag, quilted together into the strangest concoction and assortment of men ever to tramp the frontier.

They all wore the same haggard countenance... a drawn look, skin pasty-white, of leaden fatigue, worn to a frazzle and all just barely hanging on. They had encountered death and a winter no man in his right mind should be caught dead in. Travel was hard going; the days long, exhausting, sleepless nights, bodies bone-weary. Shelter, warmth... there was none, save-for your partner lying next to you in the cold of the night. The rations were meager... unfit for the kind of winter journey we were undertaking. Game, fresh meat... we hadn't seen any for days. But, there were always our horses. And sleep... a good night's sleep was even scarcer to come by than finding a good meal. And we hadn't even had a 'run in' with any Indians, to speak of.

Yet, somehow I sensed that our two leaders and their men were growing in strength with each new day. Pulling together. Learning the hard way. But, learning, becoming more savvy. The trail, the hardship, the fear of the Indians was making them that way. Somehow, Menard and Henry and Immell and Drouillard and Valle and, yes, the likes of young Thomas James and his pal Jack Dougherty were keeping them all together. I would get to know a few of them better in the coming days. And of those who I did... I liked what I saw. I liked their sand.

But, we still had a ways to travel, with too many things that could go wrong along the trail. Even when we got there, it would be just the beginning. And that was what was worrying me. Beaver and trapping seemed like the last thing on my mind right about then. Would I even get a chance to set my traps? And the Blackfeet, the Blackfeet, the Blackfeet, I wondered if they would be there... waiting for the *'spoo-pii'* to return just one more time. The thought lingered in the back of my mind. It just wouldn't go away.

There was a certain, comforting feel, one of familiarity, of security as long as we paralleled the Yellowstone and had that great stream in our sights. The river was always there, our watery guide accompanying us along the way, our constant companion, an old friend you could reach out and touch and see and even listen to. Until it chose to turn abruptly and leave us, heading south towards the mountains of its birth.

The whole column stopped and stared, transfixed by a towering wall...

granite massifs, many miles long, hovering thousands of feet above the river as she faded in the distance, and guarding its valley like great snowcapped sentinels. The very tops of those lofty peaks were hidden, high in the clouds, out of sight of us mortal men, but not from the imagination of those too wide-eyed to even catch their breaths.

The men could only guess at their dizzying heights. They were mesmerized, as spellbound as a church-full of howling Bible thumpers at a fire and brimstone prayer, revival meeting. Few men in the 'command' save for Drouillard and several veteran trappers out of Manuel's Fort had ever seen the like. The Blue Ridge, the Alleghenies, the Smokies of their experience were mere hills, bumps in the road on the way West. The Rockies, the Shining Mountains were near mythical, the blather and lies of the wild Indians to those who had never ventured west of the settlements. Yet for years, persistent word of year-around snowcapped, forbidding ranges had traveled all the way to St. Louis, to the shores of the Atlantic, passed on by voyageurs and trappers and traders for decades. The Indian Nations of the upper Missouri… the Hidatsa, the Mandans, and the Arikara spoke of them with awe. It took the Corps of Discovery to finally remove the mystery and declare these Western ranges bonafide.

It was good that the men were respectful of things bigger than they, the West had a way of doing that to easterners and city folk and those who thought they'd seen it all… Where I come from, the woods, the wide rivers, all of nature, by gum, was beheld that way.

"God is up thar, lookin' down upon us this very moment." The tone was solemn, deep… a tenor's voice for sure. Fervently reverent as only a god-fearing man could be.

"Gentlemen," he said. "I think a prayer is a appropriate."

I turned upon hearing Pelton's voice. The boys called him the 'Preacher.' He was from New England, a Connecticut Yankee, I believe. And he was a different sort, a loner of decidedly spiritual bent. He stared and prayed intently for the longest of time. He was a big, rotund looking individual, often the butt of many a joke. His clothes, his manners, even the way he spoke American were obviously not of the Western frontier. But, this time no one disagreed with what he was feeling or saying.

There proved to be little time to dwell on the river's passing, not with a half dozen hours or more of daylight to burn and a ways still to go. We left the Yellowstone and immediately began for the first time to climb since leaving Manuel's Fort.

And climb we did, the steep, rolling foothills of the Wolf Mountains, mile upon mile, ankle deep in fresh white powder, ascending higher and higher, the snow becoming deeper and deeper. There was nothing gradual to it, nor was the trail marked or the ground friendly. The land, the snow blanketing it, hid many a treacherous pitfall.

The horses struggled and stumbled. They were feeling the pinch, gaunt, weak from lack of forage and constant exertion They labored under their heavy loads, every step becoming an effort of will and determination and bodily endurance.

Men swore and cussed, grunted and groaned and gasped for air. Their hearts pounded. Their lungs burned. Their legs grew weary and wooden. Their stomachs growled. Cold vapors misted with each breath of every man and beast alike as the midday mark hovered well below freezing. Progress was painfully slow... agonizing to watch, worse to realize. Soon the chatter, the eternal griping died down. Talk was a waste of energy... and no one had any to spare. Just keep moving, one foot in front of the other. Keep your eyes ahead, but not too far. Otherwise, if you kept searching for an end to this unending trail, it just might sap your will to go on.

The distance to the 'Headwaters' country was not that far, two, three days of brisk walking... most anytime. And certainly it was not too great when measured by the many miles we had already come. And the little left to do once we cleared the gap in the mountains. How well I knew the way. What was it, my fourth time out? How relatively easy a jaunt it had been before.

But, this trek was different, somehow harder, more challenging. I sensed that the end of our journey would only be the beginning of our troubles. Winter was still with us. It would exact its toll in pounds and flesh and grate a few minds and souls in the process. I prayed they'd be up to the challenge. That no man would be left behind or abandoned to a frozen fate.

It was easy when I just had myself to worry about. I could handle that. Been that way my whole life. But, this was different. I began to see Menard and Henry and the men they led in a new light. This responsibility that Lisa had given me was more difficult than I imagined. Maybe I was meant to be a loner, not a leader. Maybe Drouillard was the better man. Responsibility for others can be a heavy burden. And my shoulders were feeling the weight with each passing mile.

Everyone struggled. Everyone... strong and weak alike. No one was spared. Every man and every horse carried their load each miserable step of the way. The column pushed on... a long, thin, straggling thread strung out for a half a mile or more. Ankle deep, knee deep, damn near waist deep, mired in a sea of unending snow. Horse and man straining for all they were worth.

The weather began to take a decidedly bad turn for the worse, the sky darkened, ominously gray, then grayer, then steel gray and coal black, the two equally intermixed, shielding heaven from earth. The sun had abandoned the heavens and dark shadows soon ruled the land. Not a shaft of light crept through. Wave after wave of tumbling clouds rolled in, one atop the other, dwarfing even the largest of mountains. Day became confused with night. The afternoon quickly disappeared as if gobbled up by the hungry storm. When nighttime finally succeeded the day, no one could rightly say, darkness and the spirits of the night reigned supreme and more than a few men's minds fell prey to their worst bedtime fears.

Snow began to spit and sputter innocently at first. It didn't fool me. The storm hadn't gotten up early enough to do that. I knew what was coming. The question was... how bad and how long was it going to last?

The winds began to whip-up from out of the north, steadily increasing in velocity and strength, like the distant rumbling of an approaching horde of stampeding buffalo...louder and louder, then closer and closer, chaos and confusion ruling supreme. And then it arrived in full force, pounding us with all its howling fury.

The spitting and sputtering snowfall had passed on... far too insipid an assault for what this storm had in store for us. It hadn't stopped, though. No, it was just warming up... flexing its muscles. And down it came, heavy at first, then heavier and still, heavier yet. And on and on, inexorably on... until, absolutely nothing tangible could be seen. Visibility was the length of your horse's neck away. And even that was fleeting. The sky, the clouds, the very slopes we climbed... they all had disappeared from view. There really was no view by then. Just tempest and rage and gale... an unending tumult of falling, dancing, flying, flailing, blinding sheets of snow; blowing and snowing, raging amok. Nature was out of control... and in charge.

And it was cold. So cold, so chilling... penetrating the thickest of fur coats and winter clothing, numbing skin and flesh and bones right to the marrow's core. There was no escape. No place to hide, no shelter to seek. Not a tree, not a rock, nor a hill or sage covered knoll or mound of dirt to hunker behind. Just bare-mountain slopes wallowing in wet, white powder, growing deeper by the minute.

We were caught in the open; men and beasts alike, the colonel, the major, the redoubtable Drouillard and his trail-wise Shawnee, the veterans, the tenderfoots... everyone. Nature spared no one, neither the strong... no matter how lofty their name, nor the weak, the unprepared. Grown men, experienced wilderness men, stumbled and groped in the darkness, crying and cursing, pleading for help; frustrated, bewildered, terrified... utterly at the storm's mercy. Confusion, alarm and fear raced through the ranks, stringing out the entire column in disarray; completely and succinctly. Nothing they did made any sense. Indecision, chaos was near pandemic... every man and beast for himself. No recourse or options were there to be found. The entire Command was in trouble, and that was the whole truth of it. We were stopped dead in our tracks, where darkness and the blizzard had found us. Many men partnered-up in twos and threes… others found themselves entirely alone to anxiously weather-out the long night away. Some tried unloading their horses. Many forgot them completely. Some tried pitching tents… nigh on all futile. Still others covered themselves with blankets or canvas or whatever they could find or grab to ward off the cold and the mounting snow. Sensible men, when they could, huddled together sharing each's bodily warmth. Strong, independent, proud men relying on one another as they had never done before.

It was a long, shivering, sleepless night. A night many worried would never end, a night of uncertainty and fear. Men scattered blindly about, cold, hungry, cheerless, without protection, with little warmth. I dreaded what the morrow might possibly bring. I prayed for the storm to lift, to give respite. I prayed that every man would last the night, to be accounted for come dawn's first light. Responsibility weighed heavily on my mind. Familiar faces came and went, parading through my mind's eye, through the darkest, dimmest hours of that miserable night. I began counting their heads, taking roll and jotting them down, trying to remember their names, where they were from, what they last wore, the rifles they toted, the ponies they led. The effort was wearing me down, the need for sleep wearing me out, sapping my spirit. I tried to put it to rest, but I couldn't seem to stop. My head bobbed. My eyes opened and shut, winked and closed, stuck in a monotonous cadence I could not seem to break. The harder I tried to sleep, the more I seemed to fight it. What the devil was wrong with me? Why can't I fall asleep? I've never had this problem before.

Sitting up, I thought I heard the unmistakable sounds of conversation, spirited at that. Had to be. I was sure of it. Somewhere nearby, men were talking, occasionally breaking out in spurts of song. In fact their singing had every appearance of being hearty, even lusty. I listened intently. Whoever they are, they aren't showing any sign of quitting. God, I groused, are these fools goin' to keep this up all night long?

"Shit!" I swore aloud. "That does it."

I arose, shaking off a heavy dusting of fresh, wet snow covering me from head to toe. I took my bearings, locking in on their voices and then set off, wading through deep powder. I knew I was hearing what I was hearing. Tired as I was, my mind was still sound. But, who in their right minds would find the strength, the energy or even the desire to do anything other than sleep the night away. Well for me, I didn't have far to go, for I could barely see my hands in front of my face. The snow wasn't letting up. The night had actually grown darker. It was madness. I had no business out and about. But, I had to find out. Thank God, the closer I neared, the louder and clearer the resonance became, until, I was almost atop of them.

I could vaguely make-out the shape of a canvas tent, fully covered by snow. Whoever set it up had managed to overcome the dark of the night, in the midst of an angry maelstrom. I had to marvel at such perseverance and dogged tenacity... that and the spirited singing and mirth their voices embued. Despite my fatigue, my curiosity was aroused; these were the kind of men I could ride the river with. The kind of men a man could depend on when times got rough and hairy. As I neared, the singing suddenly ceased, replaced by a lone voice waxing poetic. I hesitated, listening, waiting. I knew the voice, I was sure of it. It was Tom James' friend, Jack Dougherty, speaking like a Gael. But, whose immortal words was he reciting? Forsooth, I recognized a most pleasing passage. Who else, I thought, but the Scot, Robert Burns, could so soothe a lonely heart? I knew that man's works all to well; my whole family did, likewise, on many a candlelit night quoting him directly. His words were music to our Celtic ears.

Dougherty completed his refrain shortly...

> "O saw ye bonnie Lesley
> As she gaed o'er the border?
> She's gane, like Alexander,
> To spread her conquests farther.
> To see her is to love her,
> And love but her for ever,
> For Nature made her what she is,
> And ne'er made anither!"

Silence overwhelmed the confines of Dougherty's tent, gayety and revelry abruptly turning inward towards reflection with the conclusion of the Scot's brief verse. I sensed intuitively that Jack was thinking of someone very special. I suspected they all were. The poet's words had struck deep, sentimental chords of the kindest, softest of memories; the rosy-skinned, fair-haired sweethearts they had all left behind.

I felt like clapping, cheering. It had been years since I had heard spoken such doggerel and rhyme, such fine, wonderful words and in a lilt that pleased my own Gaelic senses. I had to pinch myself to believe it true. A thousand desperate miles from civilization, a half a continent and an ocean away from the country and the man who once penned those sweet memorable lines. Certainly this impromptu recital could not come from the lips of a crude, illiterate backwoodsman. For sure, culture abounded in the simplest of frontier families and homes. The Scotch/Irish never abandoned their love of literature and music and the arts, no matter how far they ventured from the "old sod." My own upbringing had proven that to me on many a night listening to my father and mother solemnly quoting chapter and verse and iambic pentameter. No, we brought our love of our poets with us, as Jack Dougherty was now so amply proving.

"Jesus, Jack, that sure wuz somethin'," Tom James broke the silence, obviously in awe of his good friend. "Where'd ya learn that?"

"Pa was a preacher," replied Jack, "but a poet at heart."

"C'mon, Jack, ya made that up, didn't ya?" asked the voice of the recently snow-blinded Robbie Brown, a voice dubious and incredulous.

"Did I make that up?" groused Dougherty, indignantly. "Why, you ignorant son…"

I piped right in without introduction. "Tis 'Bonnie Leslie,' my lad, from the mind and pen of the lately departed Robert Burns, Esq. And for shame on you, Robbie Brown, for not recognizing a countryman such as he from your own ancestral homeland."

I pulled the tent flap back, spraying them all with wet, moist snow and admitting a violent gust of still bitterly cold wind. And they inside responded accordingly.

"Hey, close the flap, close the flap," all three voices screamed, united in unison.

"Is that you, Colter?" an angry voice demanded from within.

"Colter?" asked another. "Fer cryin' out loud, man, your're lettin' the blizzard in fer sure. Will ya get on in here and close that flap before we all freeze to death?"

"Comin', comin'," I said. "Hold your horses."

It was just as dark inside as it was on the out. But, there was plenty of body heat to go around. And my unexpected arrival had caused a momentary lull in the festivities. I could sense they all were wondering just what in the hell I was doing, wandering around blindly on such a gloomy night.

"Couldn't sleep," I offered, beating them to the punch. "You boys' debauchery was keepin' me up. Curiosity was gettin' the better of me."

"Oh!" said Tom James. "Sorry! It kinda wuz spontaneous, what with this storm and all howlin' about us. I ain't never heard such a ruckus."

"Yeah, I'll second that. We couldn't sleep a wink, either," added Brown. "Lord knows, we're tired enough to."

"Sounds reasonable," I said. "But, y'all really need to get some shut-eye. Tomorrow promises to be pretty darn rough."

There was a moment's silence. And then Dougherty chanced to speak his mind…

"Colter, I can't rightly figure you out."

"How so?" I asked.

"Well, here's a man such as yourself, who went west with Lewis and Clark, didn't go home when he had the chance to like the rest of those boys, but chooses to stay out here with only the injuns, the varmints and the wind to listen to. And then in the middle of this awful stormy night recognizes the words of the poet amidst a god-awful howlin' blizzard. Now very few folks outside the Tidewater are interested in readin' anythin' more than the next day's weather and that don't come from any book. Hell, where I come from you have to look far and wide to find a man who can cite more than his a, b, c's and count higher than the fingers on his hands and the toes on his feet. What I'm sayin' is… you don't make much sense to my way of thinkin'."

"Oh," I said, answering his query directly. "Learnin' was my Ma's doin', she loved poetry, she loved readin'. I listened to her dang near every night of my life. She made sure that I learned how to read and write almost before I could walk. We had a lot of books on the shelf back home. Pa was more interested in history, especially the ancient kind, the Greeks, the Romans and a little Will Shakespeare and Chaucer to boot. Me too, still am for that matter. Pa used to say that those were the folks that paved our Western ways, the people mainly responsible for our laws, our government, our ways of seein' things and lookin' at ourselves. As far as the "a, b, c's" and book-learnin' on the frontier, you're wrong. You've just proved otherwise, recitin' Burns like a born-scholar, yourself, Jack.

"And as for me being a member of the Corps and bein' able to write and all, I suspect that Pat Gass, Whitehall and Sergeant Ordway and both the Captains keepin' their journals, was ample record enough. I knew our daily doin's were in good hands with those men. Besides, I was too busy hunting for game and scoutin' ahead and doin' the things expected of me.

"I happen to like listenin' to the wind, out here it's music to my ears. And just as certainly, I like poetry, too, it's like your spirit, your heart bein' free to say whatever it wants and feels. Kind of like me bein' out here by my lonesome, free to do whatever I want, when I want, where I want.

"I hope that clears your mind up about me."

"Huh! Well, I'll be," replied Dougherty. "Yep, that'll do it, all right."

"Likewise…" said James, "only I didn't realize that you were such a right fart smeller."

I laughed. Soon they all followed suit, smirking aloud, chuckling, taking the better part of a couple of minutes to finally die down, till quiet in the tent resumed. The next sound, a grumble I should say, seemed to erupt from within each one of them. It was getting to be a familiar complaint, one inflicted on the entire Command… a deep growling from within, from empty bellies demanding to be fed.

"That's a pretty hollow sound, boys," I said, tapping on James' stomach like testing an unripe watermelon. "How's the vittles holdin' out?"

"Whewww! Not good! We're down to the last of our jerked meat, barely a half a handful between us," said James, adding...

"It won't stretch longer than tomorrow. I'm sure glad you had all of us lay on a big supply of that elk back on the Big Horn… otherwise we'd be all be suckin' on leather by now."

"Tighten your belts, if you wear 'em. We still have another day or two to go before we have a chance to shoot any fresh meat. You can bet that nothin' will be out in this storm. And game's scarce anyway in these here mountains. The valley on the otherside will fare better."

"Colter," sounded a slightly belligerent Jack Dougherty. "I sure don't think much of this walk you've been taking us on. You tryin' to scare us or tire us out or somethin'?"

"You're about half right, Jack," I said. "Got to make things interestin', don't ya think? Wouldn't want to bore you boys to death before we reach the Forks."

Our breaths were causing a considerable amount of condensation inside that cramped tent. "Say… are y'all gonna be warm enough?"

"Yeah," replied Jack. "Thar's enough fur between us in this tent to do the trick. I suspect that the rest of the boys will be warm enough, all right. We were pretty much prepared for this winter shit and all."

There was a pause. I could tell that they were itching to say or ask something.

"What else is on your minds?" I asked to no one in particular, though, I suspected that either James or Dougherty would have the "sand" to ask.

"Awright, if ya wanna know? Your name seems to be thrown around quite a bit back yonder down the River. It seems like every fella from the Knife to St. Louis has somethin' to say about John Colter… good and bad. Most folks think you're kind of a hermit or a leper or some-such injun-luvin' pariah. Others ain't so kindly."

Jack didn't beat around the bush. He only told me what I already knew; my sojourn below the Platte seemed to draw a heap a lot of skeptical stares once people heard my name.

"You don't say," I replied. "I've heard it all before. People talk, they can say, they can believe what they want. Makes little difference to me. I can't do anything about it, anyways, so why even bother is the way I look at it. The question right now is… what are you boys a thinkin'?"

"Whoa!" cautioned James, half a rising, 'til the ceiling of the tent set him reeling back down. "We make up our own minds. We overheard Lisa months ago telling Menard and Henry to listen to what you had to say. He made no bones about how he felt, includin' your veracity. He told those two that you knew what you were a doin', said you were the man who could get us to the Three Forks. He said… to trust your instincts. That surprised us, all right, what with all the things we had heard 'bout you before. People talk shit behind yer back, you know that." Tom James was blowing no smoke up my ass. Of that I was sure.

"Yeah! *Cajones grande*," added Dougherty, "That's what the greaser-man said you had… Major balls."

We all erupted in laughter, our guffaws echoing far off into the night, no doubt even disturbing grizzlies still sound asleep in the winter dens. It took several minutes before we all calmed down enough to permit Dougherty to go on…

"No lyin', we all heard it, that's what he said. And so far, from what I've seen, the Spaniard has got you pegged just about right. I like the way you handle yourself. You don't get flustered or riled like Major Henry does. And it takes Menard too dang long to make up his mind about anythin'. Besides, everythin' you've said so far has pretty much been right on the barrel head."

"Yep!" agreed James. "That's the way we see it, all right."

I smiled. "Major Henry will do. A mite headstrong… but give him a little time for the rough edges to smooth out… if he lives long enough." I chuckled for a moment or two before adding. "He's findin' out that he can't always have his way. Sometimes you've got to drift with the current; you can't always fight it. And you always got to be looking ahead; there are just too many submerged boulders to upset your canoe. He'll find out, give him time.

"Now the Colonel is more to my liking. He's learnin' everyday. I've watched 'em both closely. Pierre's a mite cautious. He's got a lot to see to, a lot of responsibility no one else has. But, he isn't too proud to ask when he just doesn't know. It ain't always so easy out here, as y'all have found out, especially when you have a company of men to worry about. But, I suspect those two will grow together. And they'd better… where we're goin'."

"Ain't always so easy out here?" laughed Jack. And the others commenced to laugh right along with him. "Hell," he added, "we can't hardly wait 'til things start gittin' difficult. Yeah, we're sick of lollygaggin' around."

"Ya think we'll clear the pass tomorrow?" Brown asked.

"Uh huh!" I replied. "I suspect we will."

"How about the Forks?"

"Two days," I said, shrugging my shoulders, "more or less."

"About time!" snapped Dougherty, slapping his knee.

"Tell me, Colter," said Tom James. He had stopped laughing. Something less humorous was on his mind. His voice faltered, he swallowed hard. I could almost visualize welling-tears and a sagging heart as he commenced to ask his question… "That dead injun woman and her little kid…"

"Get them out of your mind," I snapped at him, abruptly, "and get to sleep. That's the way those savages are, boy. Skullduggery and butchery is what they know best. There's nothin' noble about a tomahawk splittin' a skull or separatin' a bloody scalp from a still livin', breathin' human bein'. They think nothin' 'bout killin' and settin' afire helpless women and kids... or for that matter young white trappers, such as yerself. You had better learn to walk right on past unpleasantness and keep on a goin'. Otherwise, you'd best git on back home and pick up the plow and... never look back.

"Now get some sleep. We've got a long, hard walk ahead of us tomorrow. And nobody falls behind."

They had suddenly gone quiet as I stood up and left their tent. I was sorry I had to do that to young James; he had had a soft spot in his heart for the murdered squaw and her little kid. Hell, we all had. But, that kind of sentiment was sheer folly out here. He needed to hear the cold, hard truth and start growing some thick skin... they all did. And I meant what I had said. I liked those boys. I wasn't about to let them wind-up like another young man I once knew. I shouldered enough grief for a lifetime without accumulating any more.

I stood outside their tent, momentarily lost in thought. Evilness was fixing to reenter my mind, just when I thought I had it licked.

"Oh, hell," I muttered, shrugging it off, "don't get yourself into that same old shit, John, not now, not while you're so close and so many are dependin' on you."

I returned to my own snowcovered bedroll, my curiosity well satisfied by then. Their spunk and spirit had raised me up... I liked that feeling, it was one I hadn't felt in many a moon. And finally, oh finally, exhaustion had set in completely. I need not fight it any longer... gladly and willingly succumbing. My eyes closed for the last time that long night. I drifted away, sleeping the sleep of a man who desperately needed to.

My father had warned years before, "Son, don't go countin' your chickens before they've hatched." Now, there was an age-old axiom that had stood the test of time, passed down from every father to every son since the dawn of man's own time. Assuredly, ignored, subsequently regretted. T'was a right of passage to manhood; a young man has to prove himself in his own way on his own terms in his own time. Young men always seem driven to learn life's lessons the hard way. Eventually most of us learn that dad was right. I had... to be sure. You see, pa's was simple, sage-advise from a man who had earned every right to know. The folks of Stuarts Draft thought so; they knew that he was a righteous man, a veteran of the Continental Army, of Valley Forge, shivering right alongside General Washington himself and fighting' ol'

King George's redcoats from the tidewater to the Hudson to Boston Bay. He had paid his dues, did his duty. All the patriots did back in those days when a man was required to take a stand, to do more than just talk. Now those boys took their lumps in many a hard fought campaign. Got shoved all over the Eastern seaboard, 'til they refused be shoved anymore. They stood their ground, throwing off the colonial yoke, declaring sovereign independence, and a new nation and backing it up with their blood and their sacred honor. Perseverance and sacrifice paid off, their turn came, cornering Lord Cornwallis at Yorktown and giving it back to him in spades. Pa was never far from my mind or my heart. His words still ring in my ears.

The next day we had cleared the pass by late afternoon. The way to the Forks lay before us unobstructed. Life right then couldn't have been more promising. I pointed Menard and Henry and the column towards the Gallatin, all they had to do was walk due west towards the sun. They couldn't have missed it if they wanted to. The Gallatin flowed from the southern mountains, pouring onto the valley floor near midcenter, cutting it in two. Halfway across she made an abrupt turn to the west and headed on the final leg of its journey to the Three Forks. What could have been simpler? Even a blind man could have found it. Just use your nose or stumble into its icy cold waters and you'd find the river for sure.

But, finding the river wasn't the problem; keeping the company together was. We had scattered like autumn leaves. And that wasn't the half of it. Nature was to have its say in the most despicable of ways. It was the suns glare… that unrelenting glare. We'd been enmeshed in it throughout the day on our trek through the pass, ignoring the consequences without a thought or a care. Hell, we hadn't the time; the trail had to be blazed. We couldn't afford to spend another night like the night before. We were just too hungry, too tired and that pass was too exposed to wind and cold. Besides, snow blinding wasn't going to strike the same outfit twice. We were way too smart for that. But, like the proverbial unhatched egg, we counted our chickens too soon. I should have known. I should have paid more attention to the warning signs. Now I was about to learn another hard lesson.

In the waning hours of daylight Robbie Brown's old nemesis had struck anew. Nature was getting a last, insidious laugh. The accursed affliction was without mercy, indiscriminately attacking grizzled-veterans and tenderfoots alike. Even Drouillard and his Shawnees… and knowing them, who would have thought it possible? Yes, the real nightmare had begun… randomly striking in its own time, at its own pace, 'til it had overwhelmed every last man in the "command." Blindness triumphed, inflicting its agony without bias… indiscriminately besetting tender eyes and worried minds alike. No man escaped the misery, the uncertainty and the fear. And the symptoms were all the same... eyeballs rebelling from prolonged glare, orbs frying in their sockets like hen house eggs sizzling on a red-hot skillet. Hot, boiling tears welling like molten liquid, bubbling over, streamin' down cheek and chin.

Adding insult to misery the night air gave every indication of being as cold as hell. Confusion, exhaustion and empty bellies didn't help either. Every man's personal constitution, his strength and resistance were at the end of a very short rope. Some were to fare better than others; some were able to move about, at least for a little while. Some would retain the dimmest of vision, though fraught with difficulty and strain. Some would handle the pain tolerably well, while others screamed in agony. All recalled Brown's recent torment on the Yellowstone trail. But, Brown had weathered it; the torment wouldn't last, God willing, if we kept our heads. And thank the Lord, for many did. The word was passed from man to man, "Hold on boys, we're in this together, steady now, wait it out."

The sun had finally set. Nightfall came on eerily silent, merging a strange alliance of guarded relief and sheer anxiety. It was a tentative, unsure truce at best. The boys dealt with it in their own ways, settling in as best as they could. Some slept, fitfully, others not at all. Several emerged as true leaders, helping their mates, calming them down, soothing their fears. Words of encouragement passed hour after uncountable hour, counseling patience and resolve, advising one another to keep tender eyes and wind burnt faces covered. Protect yourself from the light. Settle down, boys; get as comfortable as you can. Keep your movement to a minimum. Don't stray. Don't worry. Yes, it hurts, but not for long.

That all seemed to help. Yet, no words, no matter how reassuring, could soothe the pain, no compassion, no matter how sincere, could heal or ease the torment of those that suffered the most. Their moans and wails, their delirious fits raged relentlessly throughout the long night.

Pain and fear erased all thoughts of hunger and starvation. But, I knew better. The blindness would go away in time, but empty bellies would not be so easily convinced. Why worry about things beyond your control, I asked myself? There'll be plenty of time to worry about food when the time comes. But, I wasn't so sure. I was use to going without. I had a good grip on myself. I knew how much I could take and what I had to do. But, I was just one of thirty-six. It was the other thirty-five that were now in question. Starving men do funny things when at the end of their ropes.

I didn't escape the pain or the withering effects. My tears, too, boiled over and ran down my cheeks as hotly as everyone else's. My pain was just as excruciating. And my belly was just as empty as any man's. So why do I sound so calm? Pure and simple, I'd been in threatening fixes more often then not.

You've read my life of late. I'd been in worst scrapes. Experience had taught me to weigh things out, take it as it comes, improvise and overcome.

My pony was in the same straits. I knew he was nearby, exhausted, starving, literally wobbling on his last legs. The toil, the hunger had left him gaunt, emaciated... just hide and ribs and little else. I could hear him feebly pawing away at the snow and ice covered ground... sniffing, searching for the thinest blade of dried out grass. The poor beast was in bad shape, all our ponies were. Wolves and coyotes and buzzards and crows wouldn't differentiate between man and beast for long in the shape we were in. Sooner or later someone amongst us would have to make a move. And I had no doubt who would be the first. I took a tight, comforting grip on the long, smooth neck of my rifle. My tomahawk, pistol and knife were all stuck in my belt within ready reach. I forced myself to relax, ignoring the pain and the discomfort. I shut out the fear, all the possibilites that could worsen our plight. I'd lick this blindness and do it dang soon. This dilemma was sure giving me plenty of time to think. And think I did.

"Just get them there," Manuel had told me. That was all I had to do. It had seemed so easy a task. Of course his words were spoken a thousand miles back yonder in the safety of his fort by the Knife. And little did he foresee the trouble that could lie ahead. Why should he, it didn't affect him? But, the last person I wanted to fool was myself. The whole command was in a bad way, and what's more, ripe for slaughter if found out by the wrong injuns. I shuddered to think of the mayhem, the degradation and humiliation if the Blackfeet or Gros Ventres got wind of our dilemma. They'd butcher every "man jack one of us." Take our rifles, our lead and powder. The frontier would recoil in blood and sacrifice for decades to come. They'd be riding high for untold years. Nobody would be safe. God, I hope not. Not them, not those butchers... I prayed silently. Not after all I've been through. Not after escaping their clutches twice before. Not after swearing to God I'd never put myself in this "hell-place" again... not for beaver or riches, not for my pride, not for anything.

How I hated stupidity, looking with contempt and scorn upon the careless, the disrespectful, those who repeated their mistakes as regularly as the sun arose in the East and set in the West, those who never seemed to learn. And now, I may have become the worst offender of all. What the hell am I doing here? Come on Colter, I chided myself. Wake up, you dumb son of a bitch. Wake up! Wake up, I screamed inwardly at myself.

It was soul-searching time once again, a powerful lot of questions needed to be answered. What more convincing did I need? How many times did I need to get hit on the head? Was this the way I wanted to live my life... and end it? Was this all I wanted out of it? To wind up like Johnny... with my bones scattered and picked clean and spread out over the prairie in ignominy, without a grave or a cairn of stones or a simple marker nor a single soul to remember my name, without a loved one to mourn my loss? What kind of a fool had I let myself become? I was awfully hard on myself that night, the questions coming at me fast and furiously, the answers holding back, just beyond an arms reach.

I drifted in and out of slumber as if never fully committed to its course. One long, torturous, spasmodic affair... jerking awake, dozing off, repeating the process the length and breadth of the night. I was like a hooked fish dangling on the end of a line, toyed with, played with, punished by the cruelest of anglers. Never quite releasing me, never quite pulling me in all the way. The longer I slept the more tired I became. I no longer worried about the others. I couldn't. Yes, their fates were beyond my control.

The wind blew softly all night long. The cold stayed with us, the ground we laid upon remained hard and frozen. It had every bit the sound and feel of a graveyard melody. Men shivered uncontrollably, rustling fitfully as they tried to find a semblance of comfort and relief. Ambient sounds of tortured men waxed and waned throughout the night. Occasionally a conversation arose here and there. The talk was idle, the diversion decidedly needed. There had always been others in the column to rely on, to lend a hand or comfort a worried soul during the worst of it. Brown had James and Dougherty to look after him on the trail just days before. Others had partnered up, becoming friends, sharing the trail and their grub. But, this night's travail was altogether different. This night no man moved to help another, each suffering the same. Each man's empty belly growled and grumbled, pleading for relief. And each man dealt with the loneliness and the fear in his own individual way. It had come right down to it in the end...every man for hisself.

Sporadic conversation faded. Even the muted prayers of those few who beseeched their Maker eventually died out, except maybe in the quietude of their dreams. Snores and screams ripped side by side through the night-air unabated. The strange, alien cacophony surely bewildering many a wild critter that night.

Dawn eventually came. The first light tormented all eyes anew. The pain, the burning eyes, the hot tears intensified. The moaning, the crying increased, bringing more misery, more punishment. When would it stop? When would we have paid enough? Please, go away. We need to hunt. We desperately have to eat.

Fog was there with the dawn, an eerie shroud of cold, gloomy mist hovering over the valley. I felt its cool moisture as I lay huddled like an infant upon the frozen ground. Others seemed to be stirring. I could hear men moving about. At least I thought I had. I called out several times, but got no response. Their silence was strangely unsettling. I decided to wait a little longer, to sit quietly and listen to what the morning would eventually bring.

Minutes seemingly hours passed by. Patience was rewarded. I heard the unmistakable sounds of padded feet, moccasins?

"Uh oh!" I mumbled. That's not right. I don't like the sound of this.

I had to look. My curiosity was great. I chanced lifting the deerskin cover I had placed over my eyes the night before. The morning light at first was disagreeable. I squinted with discomfort. At first try I could barely see. My eyes watered, smarting from pain... enough at least to let me know I was not yet out of the woods. Everything before me was blurry, distorted. I remained calm, deliberate. Be patient, I cautioned myself. Then I heard it again, the shuffling of feet. That's it! I knew it wasn't my imagination. I could still trust my ears and my instincts. I began sniffing the air in hopes of catching a scent. The glare hadn't burned that out of me. I took a breath and relaxed. Then, I tried again, harder. Who was it or what was it that was making all these soft, crunching sounds, stepping so gingerly about me? I listened even more intently. Men, I was sure of it. They were definitely not some four-legged critters unless some strange new type of animal had decided to change its ways. No, these were sounds made by animal skin moccasins tiptoeing about, surreptiously, but in no other way comparable to the delicate step of a whitetail or mulee. I'd swear on it. I'd lived in the open far too long to be fooled by man or beast so easily. Whoever it was now, close enough for me to reach out and touch.

Sniff, sniff! There it is. I caught an unmistakeable whiff. God Almighty, redhide injuns, I near jerked to my feet with the realization. Had to be, I confirmed. The bastards had found us. I tensed, expecting at any moment to hear and feel the thud of a war club smashing into my skull. Everything in my being was suddenly alive. The fear, the hate, the angst had all returned, racing through me like bolts of lightning. It had all come back so suddenly, so entirely. I might as well have emerged from that dark, dank beaver house on the Madison that fateful day so long ago and let the Blackfeet do what they intended to do... for all the good my escapes had done.

I continued to sit rock-solid still, without flinching or moving a muscle or batting an eye, awaiting, expecting the worst. I was in another impossible predicament; unable to fight, unable to run... to scared to do anything, but sit and pray. And pray, I did. The others, oh God, the others, did they know? Were they prepared? Got to warn them. But, how can I? Shut up! Sit still, you fool.

Nothing happened. I felt not a single warrior's touch; no redskin's heated breath blowing upon my face. What are they up? Why are they waiting? It was like a cruel game of hide 'n seek and only half the participants got to play. I thought of my companions, wondering if they were experiencing what I was going through. They had to. There were too many savvy backwoodsman amongst us not to. Holy shit, what a fix! Hang on, boys. Not a whisper, not a fart, keep still, keep your mouths shut. The boys evidently were doing real good. Even the moaning had suddenly and inexplicably ceased all together. It was most strange, neither red man nor white having the balls to make the first move.

Yet, the footsteps were still there, gingerly stepping about as if walking on eggs. And there were so many of them… a hunting band, a war party or both. The suspense was killing me. I had to look. I could resist it no longer. If I was going to die, then, I wanted to know who was going to take my scalp. I chanced a peek, daring to confront the elusive ones, skulking about in our midst. I slowly, carefully opened my eyes. The fog was still there, though not nearly as bad as moments before. Maybe adrenaline and fear had combined to even the odds, to give me a fighting chance.

At once I heard and saw more footsteps and the phantoms to which they belonged. I recognized them right off… "Sheep Eaters." Great Jehovah and George Rogers Clark! They're god-danged Sheep Eaters, the same bunch of low life that abandoned the murdered squaw and her little boy back on the Yellowstone. Gutless bastards, what the hell do they want with us? What are they up to?

I was fuming mad, realizing that very moment that our very lives hung in the balance of the most cowardly of all the West's injuns. Now ain't that something, I seethed? Yet, I continued to watch and wait, doing nothing to upset a most delicate, dangerous situation. They were in amongst us, all right, going from man to man. They weren't much to look at, gaunt frames, miserably underfed. Their animal-hide clothing were worn thin, ragged… hardly enough to keep a man warm or cover his privates. They were a shameless lot, altogether, lower than the basest of savages. Even their weapons were wonting… not a metal knife or metal headed tomahawk between them. Tip toeing about, looking into each of our faces, peering into our eyes, checking our rifles, our gear, our clothing. Appraising our horses. Coveting everything we owned. Curious, shy… they snuck-about like timid, two footed deer. They had us totally at their mercy, yet they cowered in front of helpless, blinded men. I could only wonder at such people. How did they possibly survive all these eons with the like of the Blackfeet and Gros Ventre running amuck?

Don't count your chickens, Johnboy. They're still injuns and injuns are capable of every kind of deceit known to man. I sensed that one curious Sheep Eater had grown some balls, edging closer to my firing piece and to me. No doubt the poor fool was smitten with my rifle. Lord knows that that shootin' iron was mighty tempting to any injun, especially from this one's miserable tribe. I felt for him right then, what an urge, what temptation.

Could he possibly dare? I didn't know and that was the dilemma. Hell, it was probably the closest any of his band had ever come to a fire-stick... much less possessing one he could call his own. And right now, three dozen fine lookin' long-rifles were ready to be plucked as easy as you please.

He didn't realize it, but I was staring him down, right as he crouched over in front of me, so close, barely an arm-length away. He was still a blur. His face, everything about him remained indistinct to my clouded vision. But, I could see him well enough to know what he was up to.

I watched near horrified as he reached out with his right arm, his hand coming within a hair's breath away from touching the cold barrel of my rifle. I remained deadly still. I didn't move, quiver or blink. I just sat there as if oblivious to all about me, looking straight ahead, more dead than alive. But, I was ready, lord of mercy, I was ready. Grab my gun injun and you'll be making tracks to the happy huntin' grounds before you can get off your next breath.

The silent standoff stayed that way for several long moments. In the end he just didn't have the balls. That Sheep Eater dearly wanted my shootin' iron. Wanted it probably more than anything he had ever wanted before. But, his outreached hand didn't budge a hair beyond where it came to rest. And then, he had thought better of it, withdrawing his hand and arm, then standing back. I could hear his breathing now, where I couldn't hear it before. His breaths were coming hard and fast. I waited to hear him pissing in his breechclout next, but that never came to pass. He was like all the rest of his kind; too timid, too scared to make a move. Everything in his makeup, his band's National character had avoided what could have been a disaster for us.

I wasn't the only man to know of their presence that day. James had, too. And so did Dougherty and Drouillard and Pla-co-ta and Luthecaw, Immell and Valle... all the seasoned men. Our two Shawnee were apparently quite a curiosity to their red-skinned brethren, for the Sheep Eaters dwelled over them for the longest of time. People of their color, partnerin' up with the white men, what would the Great Spirit think of next? In the end it was all too much for such feeble, ignorant-thinking minds. The white man possessed great medicine... best they leave him alone. As suddenly, as quietly as they had appeared, they vanished like ghosts in the night.

Another day, this of tedium would come and go, passing inexorably by without incident. Somehow, we had grown surprisingly inured to our discomfort, yet the peril of our plight, our utter helplessness was still there. What else could we do? Gradually, however, the accursed blindness was losing its grip. Molten tears no longer boiled over nor streamed down wind-chafed cheeks. And fried retinas and burning orbs, ablaze for days with pain steadily subsided to a more tolerable level. No longer did pitiful cries, jolting bursts of agony and torture puncture the air so chillingly. Even the monotonous drone of many a moan had faded to the merest of whimpers, and soon, with the passing of night the wind whistling over the prairie was all that could be heard.

Morning came, the sun arose, and the day grew bright and warm, commencing a long, anxious wait. Anticipation seemed to grow with the day, hope and fear, side by side, teetering back and forth… the wait, the suspense gnawing away at men's minds, fraying an all too delicate balance. I knew all too well what was going through their heads; sensing intuitively their silent prayers. Several hours passed quietly as we waited the uncertainty out. Gradually, fear subsided and hope grew. For the first time in three days not a single cry of pain or groan of discomfort was to be heard. One by one, they stirred, coming out of their malaise. Could it be, I asked, was it finally over? Yes, yes, I thought so.

They were rousing themselves as if awakening from long deep-sleeps; cautiously stretching stiffened limbs, gently rubbing sensitive reddened eyes, clearing away the mist and the fog of the glare imposed darkness and then, as if not quite sure what to expect, slowly rising to test wooden legs and wobbly nerves. Names were called out, friends searching for friends. Here and there an occasional laugh, a chortle or two, a knowing sigh of relief. There was spirited talk, now, conversations punctuating the air where only yesterday there was misery and despair. Roll was called … present and accounted for, Major, Sir. Orders were barked. Hunters were sent out. Men moved about, checking powder and rifles, attending to their gear. Ponies were fetched and tethered. Wood and kindling gathered. Fires were built. They came together again, shaking off the cold, warming themselves and looking to one another in the most appreciative of ways. What could they say? Ordeal and deliverance had said it all.

The column formed, pointing to the West, every limb and every instinct of man and beast alike fired up, raring to go. We were alive with excitement, like primed thoroughbreds, barely restrained at the starting line, waiting for the shot to be heard to begin the final leg to the finish line… the valley of the Three Forks. Nothing could hold us back now; horse and rider were ready to charge forward with every ounce of speed and dash their bodies and hearts could muster.

Menard and Henry realized it… and they liked what they saw. They appreciated fully just how close disaster had come. They knew with pride how valiantly the men pulled together in time of need. And they thought all the more of them for it, sensing intuitively this very moment a great revival of energy and determination, demanding to be spent.

They had learned just like every man had learned. Learned how to dig down deep into the well springs of their endurance, their strength and courage. Despite all that had happened, they remained solidly at the helm, growing with the command. If anything, they became ever more resolute. They could claim the men's trust and wear the mantle of their leadership with confidence. And they would need to for our next stop had a growing reputation of being a last stop for many a man.

She was shaping up, this Missouri Fur Company, proving itself to be tough, resilient. Now with a little luck, I might get to set my traps after all.

Menard turned in his saddle, looking back over the length of the column one last time. He remained expressionless. Who knows what was going on in his head or what he was looking for, maybe he had to look and pinch himself one last time to believe it true. Every eye was on him. Every man seemingly holding his breath, awaiting the slight Company officer's command.

The Colonel was an interesting man. He was also a curious man. They were all curious men. You had to be, along with a good measure of being a little "touched in the head" to try this business on for size. Pierre Menard's sign was hard to read. He was an educated, dignified man, more at home with societal St. Louis then sharing the travails of the trail with a company such as ours of simple French engages from St. Genevieve and St. Charles and rough-hewn Kentucky backwoodsmen. The colonel was a man who largely kept his thoughts to himself, sharing his intimacy with only one other in the "command." And to that man he now turned.

Andy Henry needed no further prompting, he was bursting at the seams, ready to go.

"All right, Colter," Henry coughed in a raspy voice worn ragged by the ravages of winter rigor, "lead the way, man, and be quick about it. Take us to your damned Three Forks."

Henry turned toward the rest of the men quietly gathered. Anticipation and silence loomed over the company awaiting the expected word to be given. The Major liked what he sensed; a rare smile forming across a once impenetrable face, now burned red and chafed raw by wind and sun and cold and fear and exhaustion.

"All right, you bunch of lazy backwood's bummers and river frogs… move out. We camp tonight 'tween the Madison and Jefferson."

The response was immediate and unrestrained, filled with a spirit and a vitality that had not been felt the whole long trip. To a man, the company cheered; roaring their approval, huzzahs and clenched fists punching the air. Three dozen worn out faces fairly beamed with enthusiasm. New life had been breathed into the trapper command. Even their ponies sensed their exhilaration, stepping out with a light, lively pace as if forgetting all the hard, frozen miles they'd just come.

I moved out, never once looking back. The Three Forks beckoned with faint echoes of conflicts-past, borne by the western breezes, calling my name, heralding my return. I shuddered; realizing full well I was doing what I swore I wouldn't. Deep down in the wellspring of my being trouble stirred within me revolting at the images conceived in my mind's eye; haunting recollections of that familiar river valley and its dark and bloody ground; ghastly scenes of death and carnage inviolate. I recalled the loneliness and sheer uncertainty of my beaver-house lair, my race for life across the briared prickly pear plains and the little Snake warrior whose lifeless body I once held in my arms. It was as if all my fears had come rushing back the moment I pointed for the Forks. That ol' itch, the hackles were stirring once again, rising up to sound the alarm. Unconsciously, I gripped the smooth neck of my shooter a little tighter and took a deep breath.

And with all the irony I could muster, I muttered, "Well, here you go again… one more time into the valley of the shadows…"

CHAPTER ELEVEN

"I suppose I should pile a cairn of stones to honor Johnny," I said solemnly to no one in particular. My voice faltered, the words struggling to come out. It was tough on me coming back and dredging up Johnny Potts and ol' Toby with all the painful memories. And I swore I wouldn't. But here I was... only this time I wasn't alone.

The place where Johnny was so brutally murdered hadn't changed; not the bend in the river, nor the forest and its trees that covered each of its banks with those majestic cottonwoods swaying in the afternoon breezes... and that damn little pebbled beach. All of it was burned into my brain and soul... my hell on earth. Yet, barely a year and a half had elapsed. Out here, though, that could be a lifetime.

I stared at this now, tranquil, riparian scene over and over with my mind's own fine-toothed comb. Searching... searching for something deep down I really did not want to find. The oddity never struck me... that actually finding what I was looking for would only make my misery even greater. For these few moments, this strange twist had a stranglehold grip on me. I continued to look, possessed by whatever it is that inexplicably propels man's curiosity back to relive events of such personal painful, anguish.

What little sign of our struggle had vanished in time leaving not a single clue to show that foul murder had indeed taken place here by the river's bank. No bleached bones, no skull, not a shred or thread of clothing. Nothing that Johnny or I carried or owned. It was as if nature had gobbled up all the incriminating evidence of the Blackfeet's evil doings... or it really never took place after all.

I knew better. Life had gone on and wiped this slate clean. Varmints had dragged Johnny's parts away to feast and gnaw on. And the Pahkees... the stinkin', murdering Piegans had lifted Potts' head and carried it to their lodges. To those savages' ways of thinking, Johnny's skull was a trophy of war and honor and glory to parade around their tribal village, to sing about in praise by the campfire for many a night to come. It was a picture I need not see. What difference did it make, he was gone anyway. The river had done the rest.

I bent down and picked up a fist-sized stone worn smooth and round by the constant eddying flow of the Jefferson. Straightening up, I found myself immersed in deep thought. Johnny's last moments were so vividly horrifying, so real. It still sent a shudder through me. It always would. The goose bumps came on, that nervous twitch in the back of my neck returned. And the aftermath, the chase across the plains, my beaver house, the way to Manuel's

Fort... what an unending nightmare.

I was putting myself through it all again. Turmoil still raged inside and the more I recalled that fateful day the harder I fingered and rubbed that stone's bare surface.

My traps were obviously gone. Carried away by the current last year when the river was heavy with spring bloat or maybe just stolen by the thieving Blackfeet. For what purpose I couldn't say. Maybe, they were just another trophy to them. They were big into such things.

I knew it wouldn't be easy. No, not with my luck. But, that didn't stop me from wading in and groping about the river bottom, searching for cold steel. It was a waste of time... I knew it would be. But, I had to give it a try.

Yes, the traps were gone, vanished without a trace. But, the memories were still there. They hadn't left. And as long as I'm around they'll haunt this place to my last day. Johnny, that hard old chief, Kootenae Appe, and that rabid Running Wolf and all his kind could not be swept away by the river so easily.

I looked skyward to the darkening clouds gathering from the West. A storm was fast approaching, the smell of rain was in the air. I crossed my fingers, praying that the 'old man above' was not watching or listening. He'd look down upon me and say, "John Colter, what are you doing here again? Haven't you had enough? I gave you your last chance. You promised me."

"We'd like to help you build it, John. If... you'd let us," said Tom James with a slight stutter in his voice awakening me from my stupor.

James was standing quietly up on the riverbank, his hat in his hand. Nearby stood Dougherty and Cheek, Weir and Brown and several others that rode with me across the 'prickly pear' plains between the Madison and Jefferson. I had momentarily forgotten they were there. And they had quietly understood, realizing the grief that this place... this hallowed place of my recent past had brought back to me.

"We'd be honored, John," added Jack.

"Aye," said James Cheek proudly. "That we would. That we would."

Cheek's reverence was heartfelt. I sensed that this place and the story I had to tell hit the tall Tennessean hard. In fact they all were.

Especially after yesterday...

We had followed the Gallatin to the valley of the Forks without incident. But, as we drew closer I felt a powerful tug pulling on me. And I knew just where it was coming from. I gathered up James and his boys breaking away from the column and rode to the south out onto the pishkun plains.

It was just as I remembered it; flat, short grass country, lying between sandstone cliffs in the east and gradually sloping away to touch the Madison in the west. Not much to look at, unless you were a buffalo or an antelope or a whitetail. Yet, as we drew nearer, the peacefulness of the plains began to take on another look, altogether. A look that soon gripped the easy going countenances of my companions like a death mask, draining the blood from each of their faces. And they reeled in terror at what they began to see and realize.

For what unfolded on the short grass plains was plainly evident... the grotesque human remains of tribal conflict, of primitive warfare and martial strife. An Indian battlefield strewn with the bare, bleached bones and skulls of hundreds of hapless individuals left prostrated sprawled forever in their death throes. It was a ghastly scene of savage butchery; of bone and skull cleaved by the merciless blows of tomahawks and heavy stone-headed war clubs. Bones of limbs hacked and severed, lying about and picked clean... adrift forever from their bodily frames.

Arrows dotted the field like a forest of feathery little trees. Crow, Flathead and Pahkee by the hundreds could be seen still embedded in the ground piercing the skeletal remains of its long-gone deceased victims... as if the wooden shafts had sprouted from its sharpened stone roots deep within the soil and had become a natural vegetation of the land.

The stench of death had long ago evaporated with the disintegration of its victims' last putrid remains. Yet, what remained was more than enough to fire the imagination of any man. The mayhem, the carnage lying silently before us told all needed to be said.

And now, just one day removed, standing in a peaceful cottonwood grove by the Jefferson fork another field of battle, another tale of woe, another black day in my life was unfolding.

"I never quite believed those stories about you. Figured they were just so much hot air," said James. "There's so much bullshit floatin' around the settlements, that it's hard to tell truth from fancy. You never know who to believe, who's pullin' your leg."

The kid was earnest, easy to read. I liked that in him.

"And now?" I replied.

"Now... all I want to ask is why the hell you ever stayed? And for heaven's sake, why did you come back?"

Every man there was looking at me, silently asking the same question.

"I keep askin' myself that very same question, Tom. I don't know, but maybe one day I will. I think for now its best for me to let it lie and move on. Anyway, this here trip is the last time for me."

"I hope so, John," said James.

"Aye," seconded Dougherty, equally sincere.

"The place is haunted. I can feel it in my bones," blurted-out James Cheek for once daunted. "And yesterday, all that death lookin' at us. Ya know what? I think yer crazy, Colter. I think we're all crazy... fer comin' out here. I'm beginnin' to feel like... like maybe we're all livin' on borrowed time."

Cheek was distraught, seemingly aging right in front of us. It was as if everything he went through, endured and saw these past few days had joined together, to conspire against him, to wear away his nerve. And he was right, the place was haunted... or at least deadly enough to cut off the legs of any man's sanity, right from under him. I felt for him... it wasn't easy, this place, this life. And he and his friends had really never understood what they were getting themselves into from the start.

"Oh, hell, what's the use," I said looking down at that river-stone I was grinding in my hand.

And I chucked it, far out into the swirling, roiling waters of the Jefferson. It disappeared with a splash.

"I think we're well enough along to send some of the men out," said Andy Henry. "Split the command and let's get to it, I say."

"Oui, it is time." The Colonel nodded in agreement albeit somewhat solemnly. "We need wait no longer."

Both men were anxious to begin, but maybe for different reasons. Henry was ambitious, eager to amass his fortune and to build his name and reputation. Alas, his partner was of a different stamp... and maybe not quite cut out for this kind of life. Pierre Menard was a tad homesick, missing the woman and the life he loved. And more than ready to pack it in and head on home with the first of our spring plews.

The company had been at the Forks less then three days and already the walls were well on the way to completion. By the time Menard's engages finished their work 'the Fort' would become roughly 300 feet square. And it was shaping up to be a regular cottonwood castle of the Rockies, ringed by a double stockade of honed-logs, deeply embedded in three feet of firm river-valley soil on a narrow tongue of land between the Madison and Jefferson. Ramparts were raised and set on the inner walls to watch and to fight from and a strong, sturdy gate was placed midway on the eastern wall. The Major had located the site himself, setting the trapper-post half a-mile from each of the rivers, creating excellent fields of fire. The Major knew his military business.

The accommodations, though, would never amount to much. Company officers being the only ones living comfortably, if you could ever call it that. The Fort had a certain feel to it though, like every frontier and wilderness outpost, trading, military and otherwise with few of the niceties of hearth and home. Forever dank, drafty and odorous: reeking with unwashed, ill kept and ill-tempered men. Men who'd go years without ever seeing a bar of soap, much less using one for the desired purpose. And bathing? The river water was much too cold in the spring. And washing clothes, buckskin? That was squaw work. Besides, when you had to wade through rivers and cricks, setting and pulling your traps, that was plenty washing enough. Sleeping quarters for most would be where you found yourself and your bedroll a-lying. There'd be no neat and tidy kitchen such as back home at your ma's. No Sunday go to meeting, unless you were bored enough to listen to the sanctimonious preacher Josiah Pelton. And the fare would most often be the same: meat, animal flesh cooked, boiled, roasted, jerked… if there was any to be had. You could always skin a rattlesnake, a porcupine or any number of wild furry critters. And a beaver in one of your traps always meant a nicely broiled or boiled slab of freshly skinned tail to be cooked up or even smoked like bacon, if you hadn't already gotten sick of having the same old thing 'three squares' a-day. Or maybe a fish fry of cutthroat trout from the nearby channels of the Madison and the Jefferson would suit you like it did me. In season you could always gather a hatful of deliciously fruity currants; red, yellow, black and purple or climb up a steep cliff and gather you a mess of the pineish tasting red and golden 'mountain' currants. Summertime always brought red and blackberries, chokecherries and Boin roche, wild onion bulbs and wild grape. Nature's larder was full of wonderful treats, if you knew how and where to find them.

Life here tends to be too often too little or too much, seldom in between. In times of plenty it wasn't so bad after all. Then winter comes on, seemingly in a rush and you find out what you're made of. Now the red-man had figured it out eons ago. And that is why places like the Forks with all its wild game became so critical to all the tribes of the plains and Northwest. Successful summer buffalo hunts meant survival. And survival meant putting up great stores of jerked meat: buffalo, elk, deer meat pounded fine, mixed with an equal proportion of the fat of the marrow, add some dried serviceberries and chokecherries to sweeten the taste and you have… pemmican, the winter fare of all the buffalo hunting tribes. The white-man and in particular those of us who chose to make a living trapping the West soon caught on. Those at Manuel's Fort on the 'Big Horn' had found out. They had learned the wisdom of being prepared; laying in a goodly store of pemmican and in so doing survived three bitter winters. And the men of the 'Fort' at Three Forks would learn too, or fail. But this fort, this remotest of all outposts would be home, nevertheless, a place to get out of the wind and the rain, to find solace, security from the Blackfeet and the Atsina. A place to bring your plews: to talk, to palaver and trade and renew acquaintances. A place to come back to when you had no other place to go. And as long as the company trapped beaver in Three Forks, the 'Fort' would be there.

And while the engages, Menard's 'frogs' kept plenty busy erecting our home, our hunters had been busy, too, scouring the valley: elk, buffalo, whitetail and mule deer, an occasional moose wandering through the wetlands of the Forks browsing on river greens, does and cows in the middle of calving season. There were hungry black bear and brown, if you had the nerve, but fresh meat aplenty at least in those first few halcyon days. Though, I suspected at that rate our hunters were going it wouldn't be long before they would shoo all the game out of the valley. Graylings and cuttroat were in abundance in the three rivers and nearby cricks, along with honkers and mallard ducks and sandhill cranes pecking away for bugs and such. There was plenty of grazing for our pony herds out on the 'prickly pear' plains and the grassy bluffs to the south. Water was abundant, but had to be lugged all the way from the Madison to the Fort and no man wanted that unenviable task. Digging trenches and felling trees, hauling logs all the way to the site and building a post took powerful appetites and thirsts. And while all these necessary chores were underway other work needed to be done.

"James and the 'mick', Dougherty, Brown and Weir are fixin' to go down the Missouri a-ways tomorrow and try their luck… good spunk on their part, I say. Now I don't like puttin' all our eggs in one basket. We need to spread out some. Cover more territory." The Major had gathered together his trappers. It was time to get down to business.

Turning to me he asked, "Colter, you must have some bright ideas as to where we should send the rest of the boys."

I knew exactly where to send them. Rode right by it myself accompanied by Toby and the Flatheads two years before. It was a helluva spot to set trap lines… streams loaded with beaver sign and an abundance of game nearby to boot. And plenty of thick woods… the cottonwood groves that lined the river would offer good cover, firewood and plenty of fresh water. It didn't get any better.

"Down the Jeff' a-ways. Mebbe a day's ride," I said. "I know a good stretch where we should have plenty of luck. Enough to keep your whole outfit busy for weeks. And we can work our way back here to the valley in no time at all."

And I did know just such a place. I was smitten the first time I laid my eyes on it. But, the Pahkees made sure I never got the chance to try it on for size. She was a small valley at the foot of the northern slopes of the Tobacco Roots. Thick in cottonwood stands and lazy with little meandering streams and channels, teeming with beaver, unmolested and ready to step right into our traps. The Jefferson would be a good, promising start.

"You wouldn't want to be a-goin' along, would you?" Henry piped in, needling me. "You've already done yer job."

"I would," I replied, smiling. "Wouldn't miss it for the world. Yeah... I'm more than ready to try my luck for a change."

And I was. I liked the way things were coming together here. The men had spirit, they were eager to set their traps. The Fort was shaping up, even looking formidable. Menard and Henry both beamed with confidence. And fresh meat in my belly was giving me my edge back again. We'd all been on the trail too long and I was itchin' to bust out like every other soul in the outfit. And the thought of all that beaver waiting to be taken...

"Who are you figurin' on sendin' out?"

"Glad you asked," said Henry. "The Colonel and I were just discussing that very thing. We'll split the rest of the command in two. Half to stay here with me and Pierre and finish up the cabins and walls and keep puttin' in a goodly supply of meat. I'll keep some of our sharper-eyed boys to do the huntin'. We'll lay in as much meat as we can."

"Smart," I said, nodding my head.

"Good," responded Henry. "All right! Drouillard and his Shawnee will go along with you, to make sure you don't get lost. And 'big' Mike Immell and Francois Valle will lead the rest of the men. I'll leave it up to the four of you to see eye to eye and run the show."

"Sounds reasonable," I said, adding "and the sooner we get a-goin', the better I'll like it."

"Bon, tres bon." Menard stepped in, rubbing his hands together. "At last, we get down to business."

Just two years earlier I traveled this same road, searching for the Shoshone and the Flatheads to bring back to Manuel's Fort. And now, we had brought Manuel's to the Forks.

It had been a bold, brazen idea. Not unlike what the Brits up north in Alberta and Saskatchewan had been doing for years. Just march right in, slick as you please, and set up shop right in the middle of all the Indian nations of the Northwest, the mountains and the plains. What difference did it make that you had chosen to trespass in the very heart of bitterly contested hunting grounds, where conflict and battle was waged as regularly as the coming of spring grass. The red-man respected courage, maybe above all things. And the Northwest and Hudson's Bay companies had shown plenty of that. Maybe they had the right idea.

And here I was, back in that accursed *Ahkoto waktai Sakum*, just as bold and just as brazen. Back once again, but not as a solitary rider, alone in a land where I didn't belong. No, this time I was leading eighteen armed men, and making no bones about our presence nor doing a whole lot to hide it.

I still preferred my old way, going alone and making as little to do as possible. It didn't seem to bother anyone else, though, until Drouillard pulled up alongside me and spoke his mind.

"Your Blackfeet are more than likely mighty interested in us right about now," he'd said.

"You know somethin' I don't?" I glanced back at George suddenly alarmed and looking about.

That old itch was getting my hackles up. And he had me looking around, wondering. George was one sharp-eyed man on the trail, full of Indian savvy... more so than any man I'd ever known. I always respected that in him. He had proven it time after time again from St. Louis to the Pacific coast... and back. Add Luthecaw and Pla-co-ta to the mix and you really had something to hang your hat on.

"No. Just a hunch," he'd said. "We're stirrin' up way too much attention. I don't like it."

"Yup! That makes two of us," I said.

We rode on in silence for quite a spell. It was probably the closest time we'd spent together since our days in the Corps. And even back then we had little to say to each other. There always seemed to me to be a natural competition existing between the two of us. I hadn't liked him pushing his weight around. And he never could stand my upstart attitude. At times I just naturally galled the hell out of him. The friction was always there, rubbing, chafing away at the two of us... a confrontation that never quite came to be.

Maybe we were both more alike than we wished to admit. He had always been a loner... like me, preferring the company of few men. He avoided the settlements, unless it was to trade skins or stock up. And just like me, George would much rather have preferred looking up at a nighttime sky full of stars than the ceiling of any man's house or cabin.

He was born a breed... his pa a French Canadian voyageur, his ma a Shawnee squaw. And though equally accepted in both worlds he shunned the white man's civilization. His two injun companions were more suited to the way he liked things to be.

Yet, despite our differences, we each admired and respected the same two men more than all others. They were both Virginians and they both had the profoundest impact on our lives, Meriwether Lewis and William Clark, our captains.

Lewis, especially, had brought Drouillard from the anonymity of the frontier to the lips of every frontier man. And George had never forgotten him. I felt the same way, for Cap'n Lewis had signed me on for the adventure of my life. The memory of these two men elicited the deepest of our emotions and admiration.

I think we were both drawn together because of it. Neither one of us was prone to talking to others about the Corps, unless it was to those who had been one of us. And the longer time went on, the fewer the opportunities arose.

"It's never been the same for me, since the Corps disbanded," George suddenly broke silence, looking straight in my eyes, as if he had been reading my mind.

"Capitaine Lewis was a *une grand homme*, a great man. I always knew he was a-mite touched in the head. But, the man could lead. Nothin' would have stopped him, nothin'. And now…"

His last thoughts and words faded off, never to be consumated or revealed. George Drouillard's emotional veneer, that steadfast carapace of thick skin, wavered for the briefest of moments. It was as close as he could come to confiding in any man and I think it'd been a long time coming.

I didn't say a word. I didn't have to… we both felt the same way. It was as simple as that.

And then from out of the blue…

"Potts was a good kid," said Drouillard.

His voice was sincere. He didn't have to add another word. But, he did, staring me down with a hard, piercing gaze.

"Colter," he said, grim-faced, "you got more gravel in your gizzard than any half-dozen men I've ever known. And what's more you ain't afeared to stand by your word."

That was it. That was all he had to say. His eyes went back to watching the trail, once again lost in his half-injun, half-whiteman's world of thinking.

"Thanks," I said.

And I meant it. It seemed so odd thanking him. I didn't have to do it. But, I knew it was his way of paying tribute to Johnny and to me. In his mind, in both our minds we had all been… like a family. The Expedition, our captains, the men, Janey and lil Pomp… had all been special. It had been a special time in all our lives, never to be repeated. And I think Drouillard regretted it, longing for those days and the company we kept. And maybe he had nothing left to look forward to.

George's somber mood left me with an uneasy feeling. The man was as tough as they come, as capable as a Daniel Boone or a George Rogers Clark. Nothing ever seemed to shake his confidence. And at times it was annoying. I had always found him a little too smug, a little too cocksure to suit my taste.

And yet, there was just too much to admire, no matter how hard I resisted. He took whatever life threw his way without breaking stride. Frailty was for other, lesser men. There was such raw strength in him that I had never known in another man. But, just now I thought I detected a hint of the castle walls crumbling. Like I had become, maybe George was not quite so sure of himself anymore.

"Jim Cheek. You and Hull and Ayers will stay behind and set up camp," commanded the deep voice of big Mike Immell. "Don't worry, don't worry. Y'all will get yer chance. Everybody gets their turn doin' the duty... includin' yours truly."

"Fine with me," answered the gruff Tennessean. "Just make sure y'all bring back plenty of fresh meat. Ya hear? I'm hungry enough to eat a bar's behind, a crow's foot and the insides of Pelton's stinkin' boots."

Everybody had a good laugh on the Preacher. And we needed it, too. In fact we were all more than a little ready to bust a gut. Especially after what the company had endured since leaving the Yellowstone. It hadn't let up even upon reaching the Forks. If anything it had grown worse. There was an understated tension the whole ride out. Something about being in Blackfeet country tended to make a man a little warier and a little more uncomfortable.

And now the pressure seemed to be off. We had arrived without a hitch, without a single sign of a hostile Indian ... Blackfeet or otherwise. And the valley was like everything I remembered it to be. All that was left for us to do was make camp and set our trap lines. The rest would fall into place.

I couldn't help but notice the lonely look on young Billy Bryant's face as we stood there in the clearing, pairing up. He was fresh from the sheltered life of Philadelphia and East Coast society. He'd been drawn out here like many a young man... to the promise of adventure, the fulfillment of manhood. I suppose it all sounded so exciting, so thrilling; the wild Indians of the Plains, the buffalo and the grizzly, the Rockies, frontiersmen the likes of Dan'l Boone and even Drouillard himself. Indeed, right now, people in the East were already singing George's praises, though little did these folks know of the grim reality that awaited the Billy Bryants of our country as they challenged the wilderness, daring to fulfill their dreams.

And now, after all was said and done, he was not so sure he'd made the right decision to head-out West. For him, who had everything, save his father's respect, Bryant had signed on for this great adventure as a lark to prove himself worthy in his old man's eyes. He had never admitted it, and wouldn't... but, I knew it as sure as I did the rifle in my hand.

"Billy, everybody seems to have picked their mates. How about you and me partnerin' up?" I made the offer. I knew he wouldn't turn me down.

Both Valle and Immell looked over, each smiling. I guess they too had worried about the boy.

"Why," stuttered Bryant, "Why, I'd be honored, John."

You could tell it took a load right off of his shoulders. He perked right up, almost took to strutting.

"*Bon*, then it is *au revoir et bon travail*," shouted Francois, giving me a thumbs-up.

"Then we're ready," said Immell, nodding his head.

And then Mike addressed the rest of the trappers.

"Boys, listen up. Let's not forget to keep yer wits about ya. Need I remind ya of that squaw and her boy?

"And spread out for christsakes... this valley is big enough for all of us without steppin' on each other's toes and traps.

"Good huntin' and good trappin'."

The men split up in two's and three's and began to go their separate ways. I had waited for all of them to clear out and then I walked over to Cheek to say my good-byes. I couldn't forget the way he'd been just the other day in the clearing where Johnny had died.

"Guess I don't have to tell you to keep your eyes open," I said.

"Nope, ya don't. We'll be fine," said Cheek confidently, patting the butt ends of a brace of worn looking pistols stuck in his belt. His face was blank, expressionless... not a hint to warrant any worry on my part.

"Besides, I got my good buddies Hull, here, and ol' Ayers to keep me company."

Hull looked up and just shook his head kinda good naturely-like.

And then the Tennessean turned and looked at young Bryant. "Keep yer powder dry, Billy," he said.

"I will, Jim."

"See y'all then... and, hey, don't fergit to fetch us dinner."

"Be back 'bout sundown," were my last words to Cheek.

Billy and I moved out, threading our way slowly through thick stands of cottonwoods, riding away from the campsite in a somewhat southeasterly direction. In no time we had come upon a small, clear running stream entering the river and we backtracked it, working our way up towards the foothills of the Tobacco Roots. It was a quiet time... a time to listen and watch and smell, to pay heed to your horse, to trust his senses and instincts.

I hadn't said a word since bidding Cheek and the others farewell. And that had been less than an hour before. But, Billy hadn't shut his mouth for one second. He constantly peppered me, asking a hundred questions... and never waiting more than a second for a reply, he made more noise than any chattering pair of magpies. And the more he talked the more aggravating he became. He was like an itch I couldn't scratch and I had just about enough. Billy Bryant was either very curious or very scared... or both.

"Billy," I began to say.

Then suddenly both our horses' heads turned, their ears perking right up, straining in the direction of Cheek's campsite.

I heard it, too. It was faint, carried by the wind on the tops of the trees. Then we both heard it... again and again.

"What was that?" Bryant blurted out Their was panic in his voice.

"Shots," I said. "C'mon."

We turned and raced back from whence we came. The solace of the riparian woods, the quietude of its cottonwood forest evaporated forthwith, replaced by the rapid clippity-clop of galloping thunder of our racing mounts' unshod hooves pounding on the forest floor. We quickly ate up the distance and as we did the reports of gunshots became louder and louder.

You didn't have to hit me over the head with a war club to tell me what was going on. No, it wasn't any of our boys shooting a mess of deer or bagging an elk. And Billy and his yapper... for once he was all ears and mouth shut.

"Whoaaaaa!" I said, reining in just before the two of us almost burst right into a wide-open clearing not far from our campsite.

"Back-up, Billy," I whispered softly. "Back into the woods apiece and be real still."

We pulled our ponies into the shaded darkness of the cottonwood forest and firmly secured their leads to a tree. Those two animals of ours were smart to the ways of man, all right... sensing our anxiety, our fear just like we had theirs. They stood quietly, panting... sucking in air. Buckets of sweat pouring out of them from their exertions. And then... low, deep-warning rumbles suddenly emerged from each. Their ears instantly directed towards the clearing... straining to hear.

In the distance horses could be heard running at full speed. Shots continued to ring out.

"C'mon," I said to Bryant.

We crawled on our bellies right up to the edge of the grassy clearing. We stayed low, watching, waiting. And then...

"Look!" Billy whispered in alarm, pointing, wide-eyed.

"I see," I said. "Shhhhh! Don't move."

"But, it's our men, it's our men," he said, becoming more agitated by the moment.

"Shut up," I ordered, "and be still."

In the distance we could make out three fleeing horsemen, hell-bent on flight. They were flailing away, quirting their mounts, whipping their rears sore and tender. And all the while they kept looking back over their shoulders like they were being chased by a whirlwind.

"I think that's Valle," said Billy, pointing to the last rider. "I'd know his horse anywhere."

I nodded. "You're right, it's him, all right, and two of his 'frogs'."

"Look! Look behind 'em," Billy nearly sprang to his feet, the excitement was more than the kid could handle.

"Shit!" I swore. "Get down, and, be still." I reached up and grabbed him by his hunting shirt, yanking him to the ground. I held him there 'til he quit squirming and quieted down.

"Get a hold of yourself," I ordered the boy.

The thunder in the clearing suddenly became louder, more alive. Hot on Valle's tail were a dozen or more long-haired, screaming Indians. Their shrieks, their wild, unrestrained war cries split the air in an 'all too familiar' chorus, instantly recalling my mind to the days of the 'pishkun' and the 'prickly pear plains.'

"Oh, God!" was all I managed to utter.

"What are we gonna do?" whispered Billy, sensing the dread in my two, simple words.

I could feel him trembling right next to me. The look in his face, in his eyes… bulging, wrought with fear. For an instant I flashed on another youth, another day… sitting in a dugout. I could have cried right then and there.

I arose to one knee, chancing a look in the direction of Cheek's campsite. Several last shots were now ringing out. Their reports were instantly recognizable to a backwoodsman's ears… a long rifle, then a pistol shot, and then another one. I knew they were ours, not the weaker pop of a short-barreled trade musket.

I couldn't see either Cheek or Ayers or Hull. They were just too far away and hidden by the trees and the rolling lay of the land. No, I couldn't see who was doing the firing. I didn't have to. It could only have been one man out of that bunch. Of that I was certain. Sure as shootin'… it was the last stand of that big, raw-boned Tennessean, James Cheek dishing it out and making those red heathens pay.

Several of our horses were running about, confused, frightened. And then they scattered with hooves and tails flying. The prairie was suddenly alive with naked warriors… screaming, shrieking. The whole of our campsite area was literally crawling with them.

We could wait no longer. They'd be headed our way in no time, branching out, searching the woods, the river. Cutting off all avenues of escape. I knew how they worked. They'd be fast, methodical, efficient. And they would want every last one of us.

Billy looked up at me. He was scared shitless. If ever there was a babe in the woods, in a land where he didn't belong, it was he, it was right now and it was right here.

"Are they… the Blackfeet, the Piegans, your Pahkees?" Bryant asked, his voice continuing to falter.

"Mebbe," I said. "Anyway, heathen Blackfeet of some kind… Blood, Siksika or even Gros Ventre. It don't make much difference right now."

"We gotta help 'em, Cheek… don't we?" he pleaded, unsure of what to do or say.

"Too late, Billy. We gotta get the hell outta here. Pronto! There's way too many of 'em for us to handle. Sorry, I wish there were another way. Let's go."

We lit out of there, more like worms than men, inching backwards on our bellies 'til we were safe in the timbered darkness. We mounted up without another word and began to work our way through the cottonwood and wetlands' maze towards the distant slopes of the mountains.

We had a ways to go to be free and clear. The river's cottonwood forest was several miles wide, ranging across the valley from the prairie to the foothills and twice as long from east to west shielding the wandering path of the Jefferson in dense woods. We kept on moving, in single file, as quickly and as quietly as we could. And as we fled we listened…riding on the edge of our saddles with an ear permanently cocked and attuned to the rear. The brush of bare skin or tanned leather or a horse's hide crashing through the woods in hurried pursuit… never came. Yet, we couldn't slow down or risk a rest. There was still a chance those savages didn't know who or where we were. But, I wasn't kidding myself. Whether on our tail or skulking ahead, they'd be laying for us, for all of us… somewhere along the trail.

We finally reached the foothills and started to climb, avoiding the open, using the shadows, working our way up steep, rocky ravines, threading our way through forests of pine and cedar. And all the while distancing ourselves from the sure-suicide of returning by the Three Forks trail.

I wasn't about to get suckered-in again by the Blackfeet… not now, not ever again. I prepared to wait 'em out, to out injun 'em at their own game… a game they lived and loved to play. Didn't matter to me. They could wait forever as far as I was concerned. I'd wait that much longer. Do what I had to do.

It came right down to a question of will and discipline… and a lot of luck. And I was betting mine was greater then theirs. We just had to make up our minds to take our time. Listen to our instincts and trust those of our ponies as much as ours. Travel by night. Rest by day. Cinch up our belts. And hope and pray.

Billy had become mighty quiet on the trail. He had liked Cheek… and Francois and 'big Mike' as well. And he had never before seen a man die… not the Blackfeet way, not in his whole short, sheltered life.

"Do you think any of the others got away?" he asked, hoping I'd supply the answer he wanted to hear.

"I don't know, Billy. I don't know. With any luck most of the boys would have been warned off in time, just like we were. Valle and the other two had strong mounts and a good head start. Maybe they'll make it... with a little luck. Francois has a good head on his shoulders and he's a good shot.

"The others, those left at the campsite, I'm afraid, didn't have a coon's chance in hell."

I was reluctant to say it, the kid seemed to put a lot of stock in James Cheek. But, I knew I had no other choice. There was just no doubt in my mind and I didn't want to leave Billy with a hope that just wasn't there. And then I added...

"I think Jimmy Cheek and Hull and Ayers just might have saved all our bacon. Bought us time. And probably, from the sounds of it, took enough of those red devils to make 'em think twice about comin' after the rest of us.

"But, I don't know. I just don't know."

We both mulled it over. A lot was going through the kid's mind. Probably torn between losing his friends and saving his own scalp. I had no such illusions... it was every man for himself. That's the truth of it, the way it had to be.

"Listen, Billy. Get it through your head. There aren't any others. Not right now there isn't... and won't be 'til were safely tucked away in the Fort. It's just you and me agin the Blackfeet. So forget 'em ... and do it right now.

"Until we reach the Fort, our scalps and our lives are what we're looking out for. Do I make myself clear?"

He nodded. He didn't say a word, he didn't have to, for he had that sad, hound dog look all about him. The not knowing was tough on Billy and it showed in his eyes as the tears rolled down his cheeks.

I was resigned to the outcome from the start, be what it may. I had learned the hard way like he was learning now. What concerned me most was just how badly those savages wanted to get at the rest of us. And could they? Were they strong enough to handle more than a couple of armed men? Could they go up against the whole command hunkered down and protected by the high walls of a Fort? Or maybe would they resort to starving us out? I wasn't so sure. It was still way too early in the year for any injuns to be this far south... at least in any strength. The summer hunt was still months away. And we couldn't expect any help from the friendly tribes. The Flatheads and the Snakes wouldn't be back, at least in the foreseeable future. The fight on the pishkun plains had seen to that. And as far as I knew, Indians never wintered in the Forks or anywhere close by, at least not since the advent of the horse and the gun. It was just too risky for all tribes concerned.

And, now, this bloody business on the Jefferson. Those injuns had no right being there, not the way I saw it. And they sure weren't being very neighborly, ruining our operation 'afore we had a chance to set a single trap. I guess they just had forgotten to consult me and the Colonel and the Major. It made me laugh, but it sure wasn't funny.

The Jeff' had looked so peaceful. And just when I was sure I hadn't, I had grown careless. And I swore I wouldn't. I thought we'd be all right working the river this early in the year. Get in and get out... quickly and quietly. I had let Manuel and Menard and Henry convince me that building a strong Fort and showing our strength, our 'firepower' would be more than enough to keep any hostiles at bay.

I tried to tell him otherwise. But, Lisa never did listen... not when it came to those injuns. And now two of his partners were left with little choice.

We took a circuitous route on our return to the Forks... working our way slowly up through the ravines and draws and shallow crick beds that flowed down through the foothills, all the while penetrating higher and deeper into the mountains of the Tobacco Roots. We constantly stopped, checking our back trail, scanning the way ahead with jaundiced eyes, waiting patiently in the saddle for long draughts at a time. We took no chances. We made life harder on ourselves and our ponies than seemed necessary. We cinched our belts. We did without food. We talked low and soft and with our hands. And we found out a great deal about each other.

And Billy was learning fast... how to keep his hair. We'd been both lucky he had gotten the chance, luckier then Cheek and Hull and Ayers. And he knew it, too, tucking away the events of recent days, adding them to the growing list of his experiences. And it was changing the boy; making him hard, savvy, forcing the easy life of Philly to stay behind.

Talk between us of those left behind ceased altogether. Young Bryant became like my right arm, another pair of eyes and ears, another nose to sift through all the scents wafting over the land... natural and manmade.

We descended the foothills, riding clear of the high country and headed east. We found ourselves crossing the prairie land bluffs that ranged to the south of the *Akhoto waktai Sakum*, the same way that Toby and his Tushepaw friends had come just two years before.

It was a dry, dimpled land... short grass country of rolling hills and gentle valleys of scrubby pines and pungent sage. And it was less than half a day's ride, an anxious, wary, half a day away.

We arrived at last, towards the end of the third day, walking our worn out mounts to the very edge of those raised bluffs that overlooked the valley of the Forks. From where we stood we could easily scan the whole valley and its three rivers coming together.

Akhoto waktai Sakum... I remembered the old Piegan warchief's words, ringing in my ears. Yeah... that ol' Kootenae Appe wanted my hide in the worst of ways. Especially, after I had made a fool of him and slipped right through his whole nation's fingers... that son of a bitch.

I looked yonder towards the western-end of the valley and the meandering Jeff', where they murdered Johnny and sent me running. I recalled vividly, my barefoot path across the treacherous 'prickly pear' plains, envisioning the hundreds of naked Blackfeet, hot after my bare ass. I remembered the din of their hideous screams growing ever nearer. I remembered the fear, the hate that propelled me, the jolts of sharp pain pricking my feet, lacing their tender pads stride after painful stride 'til I thought I could flee no more.

I remembered all too well the exact, infamous spot... where the rabid Running Wolf finally caught up to the lowly *spoo-pii*, where we embraced each other in mortal combat. Where I had waited, bent-over, helplessly and hopelessly spent from exhaustion, a defenseless prey, all too easy, too ready to be dispatched by that magnificent Piegan warrior's naked stone-headed spear.

I dwelled for one, long, final moment on the last glimpses of his fleeting life. Once again, I could hear his contemptuous screams as he closed in, recalling ever so clearly his disdain, the fierceness in his eyes, the way he charged me so confidently with his raised spear poised to run me through.

And then the tide of circumstance had suddenly altered both our fates. And ohhhh, how the fearless young warrior had changed. His eyes, his face gone askance... begging for his life when he would have granted me naught. But, my forgiveness was not meant to be. Not for him and not for his whole damned nation. And then...

"Fuck you," I bellowed loudly, scorning his memory and the Piegan race with every ounce of hate and revilement pent-up within me since that vile, evil day.

I was for the moment beside myself, squeezing my rifle's thin neck so hard I might have shattered the wooden stock right in my hands.

"John," Billy whispered. "What's wrong with you? We've made it... ain't no use gettin' upset, now."

I stopped... and let out a long whoosh of stale air, releasing the accumulated emotions of two long years of suffering nightmare.

I chanced to look down to the swift running Madison, to that very same worn-out old beaver house... my sanctuary. It was still there... right where it was when I left it last in the dark of that unforgettable night. Silently beckoning to me once again, I was drawn to it. It was all too familiar, just as I had remembered it. And it disturbed me in more ways than I could say. Yet, life had gone on, though the picture before me remained unchanged.

And then, I came out of my little stupor... just like I had emerged out of that beaver house lair so many moons ago.

"Sorry, Billy. Bad memories, I guess."

I turned to look down upon that narrow finger of land between where the Jefferson and the Madison finally came together and... there she is, the Fort... maybe a half mile back towards the prickly pear plains.

We both breathed an unrestrained sigh of relief; smiles breaking out over both our faces, spreading like the rosy fingers of dawn.

"Thanks, John," The kid said. "Thanks for savin' my life."

"Pleasure!"

The command had been in the valley less than a week's time... and our stockade was already enclosed. But, where was everybody? Nothing moved outside the walls; no horses, no men, nothing. And not a single sentry could be seen walking behind the ramparts.

By then the sun had set and shadows embraced the land. The Fort loomed dark on the plains. It had an uncertain quietness to it, not at all like the rollicking trapper quarters one comes to expect on the frontier. And it left us both wary.

"Be careful and keep your eyes open. You'd better hold your thanks, we ain't out of this yet," I said to Billy.

"What if..." he started to ask.

"Then ride like hell. And don't stop 'til you reach the Bighorn."

And he nodded, chuckling nervously. We both were feeling the tension as we descended the short way down the slopes from the bluffs to the valley floor below. We approached on foot, cautiously, leading our horses by the reins. And as we neared, we looked and we listened. Only the winds whistling over the 'prickly pear' plains could be heard, their eerie tune a cold, lonely melody.

The breeze abruptly shifted to our backsides, whispering gently from the southwest, carrying our scent straight towards the Fort. Nothing was going our way. Even the wind was against us.

Damn it, I swore under my breath.

We reached the gate unchallenged. The absence of sound and movement from within the stockade was now deafening. But, the gate was obviously closed tight and latched from the inside. Someone had to be in there. What the hell's wrong with them. Come on, they can't all be dead or flown the coop, not after all this work.

I was getting a 'mite' irritated and more than ready to light a fast shuck out of here. I had had enough of the suspense.

Whoa... I cautioned myself, coming to a dead stop and grabbing Billy by the arm. I pointed my finger to my lips and he got the message right off.

We had both heard a shuffle of hooves and nervous rumblings coming from within. Somebody inside was doin' a piss poor job of keepin' the critters settled down. I could hear the sounds of those ponies on the other side of the Fort's walls and they were more than a little agitated, all right.

That was enough for me.

"Ho, the Fort," I called out from the darkness of the night.

No one answered… only my echo ricocheting off the Fort's log walls was to be heard. There was an ominous, eerie feel to the post that night, a haunting, abandoned, almost deserted feel. And it was worrisome, not making much sense to either one of us. By now, though, we were both too hungry and too tired to care.

A hammer cocked, closely followed by several more. Someone cleared a dry throat. And then came a gravelly voice from the ramparts.

"Goddam! Who's out thar hailin' the Fort? Answer up, pronto. Who ya be, beaver man or red-hided niggah? State yer intentions… and do it fast."

We both recognized his voice. And that man who owned it was a mite too touchy right then. I could sense his suspicion, feel the tension on his index finger squeezing away ever so tighter, slowly pulling back the trigger; 'til one false move by either one of us and a load of lead would be coming our way.

"Bullshit!" Billy cursed, loud and clear. "Hey, ya goddam idjit, yerself… it's me, Billy Bryant… and John Colter, back from the Jefferson and runnin' low on patience. Now, open up."

You would have thought the kid had rung a bell. Their response was immediate, hairy faces began to pop up from behind those honed logs and men were talking.

"That is you, ain't it, Billee?" came another, familiar voice from within the Fort.

"Oh, c'mon, JT. Quit foolin' around and let us in," Billy was exasperated.

"Open up, boys. They're white men, awright." It was the voice of our blacksmith, the powerful John T. Thrush. A voice that sounded a-mite relieved.

There was suddenly movement inside where there had been none just moments before. The Fort's complement stirred, shouting to one another. The whole place came alive. We could hear many footsteps approaching the gate. Several indistinct silhouettes peered down upon us from atop the ramparts. Rifles were now clearly visible, pointing outward from between the tops of sharpened, honed logs. They gave every appearance of a fort under siege. And yet there were no besiegers, save in the terrified minds of those beleaguered souls inside.

The Fort's thick log gate creaked and trembled with the jarring movement of a heavy, timbered crossbar being slid free from its catch. The gate, like the men inside, opened up, cautiously. It was near as dark on the inside as it was on the out.

Out raced several armed trappers fanning out in front of the opened entrance with their rifles held at port arms, ready to shoulder and fire. Even in the darkened gloom of this moonless night their anxiety was apparent.

"Get a move on... and be quick about it," came the command from within.

"Don't need to tell us twice," I said. "C'mon, Billy."

It had all happened so fast. Billy and I hustled into the compound on the double quick, our escort of edgy riflemen close on our tails behind us. The Fort's heavy wooden gate was slammed shut and barred.

There was a brief moment of silence as we adjusted our eyes to the dimly lit interior of the trapper compound. The stockade was like every other establishment of its kind on the American frontier... ramshackle, dirty and dusty, with low, flat-ceiling log shacks that passed for cabins and living quarters. A small blacksmith's lean-to was set against the west wall. A forge and small anvil resting atop a leveled stump of an ancient cottonwood tree was plainly visible inside. Nervous ponies were penned up inside a makeshift pole corral with barely enough room for them to kick up their heels and snort and fart.

The stench was apparent from the start. It reeked of horse shit and filth, of musky, sweat-stained clothes and leather-goods and unwashed men. No doubt smelling all the worse when you accounted for the many successive days of accumulated, unabated fear building up within each and every one of them. And fear exudes its own distinct odor... cold, clammy, and repulsively profuse.

There was a definite siege mentality predominating. You could see it in the men's eyes and their faces. The way they held their 'firing pieces' nervously at the ready. Their fear, their expectation of attack had been growing steadily, daily since Valle's return. And with no word from the rest of our party, there was mounting fear that we had all been wiped out. And then Billy and me came walking in as if returning from the dead.

The hushed standoff lasted less time then it took a thirsty man to 'swallow a mouthful of water.' And they moved right in, pushing and shoving each other to be the first to reach us, to touch and pinch our flesh, to make sure we were real and not some cruel, hellish, red-skinned trick of an apparition. They wouldn't even allow themselves to trust their own eyes and ears, darn near suffocating the two of us in disbelief.

Yet, disbelief eventually succumbed to belief. And it soon became the hand shaking, backslapping kind of bug-eyed joy that can only from friends, who've stood in death's doorway and lived to tell of it.

The questions followed, a barrage of doubt and concern for their friends and for themselves, swarming over us like angry hornets... whap, whap. How close had we been? Were we seen or pursued? What did we see? Who got caught? Who could have escaped? Might they still be alive, hiding out, trying to get back to the Fort? Should we mount a rescue or stay put and wait and see?

And where in tarnation were the Blackfeet? What were they up to, what would they do next?

It was easy to see the confusion, the fear prevailing over the entire 'command.' They were scared to a man. And they were angry, bitterly so. They feared for the missing, the unaccounted for. They worried about their own hides. They were ready to light a shuck, to run for Manuel's Fort as fast as their feet would take them. Yet, they were ready to fight, to shed blood and seek righteous vengeance. It was in their blood, it was the way of the frontier. And no one, but no one had a handle on what to do next.

"That's enough," said the Colonel, stepping in between the men and Billy and me.

The clamor died down, the push of trappers backing up a step to give their leader room.

He took my hand and squeezed it hard.

"Thank God, you're alive," he said. "We thought for sure... the worst."

"Billy Bryant's ma would've never forgiven me if I didn't bring her little, baby boy home in one piece," I said kinda a sheepish-like.

And I was sporting a rare smile, doing my damnedest to keep up the good front. From what I was seeing of the men and their officers they plum needed a little cheer.

Menard was a worried man, a little too worried. He had aged considerably since leaving Manuel's Fort. And it showed. His hair had become grayer. His face looked gaunt, haggard. His belt was cinched a might too tight around a frame that was already way too spare. The wilderness was harder on some than on others... and on the Colonel it really showed.

"Sacre bleu," the Colonel gasped, shaking his head. "We've heard from no one else since Francois returned the day before last."

"Jesu Criste, mon ami. I thought you... lost your hair for sure," Valle, looking as if he was seeing a ghost, stepped forward and hugged me.

"Not yet," I chuckled, sticking my index finger up in the air. "Wind's not right."

"I should have known. I should have known... you ol' rascal," he said smiling.

"But, the others... what of the others? The savages were everywhere. There were so many. Surely..."

The look on poor Francois' face was grave. He was a proud man, a 'fighting man'. A man who otherwise would have unselfishly given his life for others. But, the Blackfeet attack had been unexpected and quick, their numbers overwhelming. He really had no other choice. We all knew it. We all would have done the same thing. Nevertheless, his pain, his self-imposed guilt was a heavy burden.

I put my hand on his shoulder. I had nothing to add. Time would take care of that.

What was it about this place, I wondered, that could humble the strongest of men.

"Yes, the others?" demanded Andy Henry, impatiently. "What of the others? Did you see any of the others? I refuse to believe these savages kilt every last one of our men.

"And how'd you two get in here unscathed? Your Blackfeet have had us and the valley buttoned up as tight as the preacher's wife for at least two days."

The look on his face said he wasn't a fooling. And Andy Henry always said what he meant, straight and direct.

"Whoaaaaaaaaa," I said. "Slow down, Major. There aren't any hostiles, not on our trail and not anywhere near the approaches to the Fort. In fact, I betcha their ain't an injun now within miles of here."

"John's right," Billy piped in. "We sat up back of here on the bluffs for a couple of hours just to be sure... and the valley's clear, too... just like he says."

The Major looked dumbfounded. In fact, every last one of them had the same, disbelieving look. With Valle's 'hell for leather' escape and return, the boys naturally thought a siege would follow. And they reacted accordingly. They were convinced of their own imminent peril, no one daring to venture out of the compound to see for sure.

Andy Henry was feeling a 'might' foolish right about then. They all were.

As for me, I had more immediate concerns. "Well, while y'all are all thinkin' about it... I'd be obliged if somebody would fetch us somethin' to eat? Billy and I are famished."

The looks, the stares, the questions came to a halt and for the first time since entering the stockade there was silence. The whole 'complement' began to look at one other in bewilderment, shaking their heads, red-faced, eyeing the ground and feeling about as ridiculously absurd as a bunch of men could be.

It was easy to understand the confusion and hesitation running amok since Valle's 'close shave and escape. Cheek and Hull and Ayers faced certain death. And now, a dozen or more of their men unaccounted for amidst a swarm of savages, miles from the relative safety of the Fort.

This 'not knowing' the fate of the rest of the party had left them all adrift, like so many canoes without paddles. Their hopes, their dreams of beaver and quick fortune had suddenly been dashed. The grim specter of that mutilated, charred squaw and her murdered little boy lying back yonder by the Yellowstone loomed large in their own possibilities. They had deteriorated into a pathetic lot, cowering like so many sheep behind their palisade walls, awaiting the Blackfeet wolves to move in and finish them off.

Yet, with Billy and me safely back the picture still had not become any clearer. There were thirteen trappers to be accounted for. Cheek, Hull, Ayers... Valle had given them no chance, not after what he had seen. Still, Francois had not actually seen them die. And the two of us had no idea what had happened to any of the others. All we could do was hope.

And hope was there, waiting for the midnight hour to strike. Roundabout then Drouillard and the Shawnee snuck right up to the stockade walls, completely undetected and none the worse for wear.

They, too, had taken their time, once they had spotted Billy and me 'high-tailing it' for the mountains. I never knew they were there, not for an instant the whole time. George and his Shawnee were awfully good, like shadows... now you see them, now you don't. They had closed-in right behind us, dogging our tracks, making little or no dust, all the while watching our backtrail every step of the way. It was just like George to be 'one-up' on me and every man there knew it.

We weren't the only ones to have troubles. James and Dougherty, Weir and Brown had theirs down on the Missouri two days of paddling away. But, they'd been lucky where their good friend Cheek had not.

They floated the big river in a pair of cottonwood dugouts, setting their traps that first day on some small, unnamed crick, bagging an even half a dozen critters before deciding to move on further down the river.

The second day out, the two got careless. Dougherty and Brown struck a submerged rock smack-dab in the middle of the muddy river, capsizing their canoe and sending them both swimming for their lives.

Gone was their whole shebang... their rifles, powder and lead, traps, even their own personal 'possibilities' lost to the murky depths below. 'Up a crick' was the only way to describe where the boys suddenly found themselves. Dripping wet, madder than mud hens and only two rifles between the four of them and half as much powder and lead, they began to think that life couldn't get any worse. Lord knows that's a depressing way to be. Just when you think that things can't possibly get any darker, you let your guard down and the next thing you know you've lost your hair and maybe your life.

The boys were having none of that, the trail from Manuel's Fort had taught them better. If anything, they'd become quite resilient, quick to size-up a situation and that once done, even quicker to take decisive action. They were no longer 'babes in the woods' in a strange, hard land. They had learned well, adapting to the wilderness as if they had been born to it. After one misfortune, it was time to make their own luck, to keep their heads and wits about them. Above all to watch for Indian sign, while they took the time to figure out their next move.

Time, though, was not on their side. But, luck was. They had pulled their lone remaining dugout into a small tributary, quickly moving up stream a short distance and concealed themselves amidst a copse of cottonwoods. They unloaded their gear, laying out what needed to be dried. They didn't dally, they worked quickly, all the while keeping a constant watch. It wasn't long before their alertness paid off. From the north, across the flats, came six mounted hostiles racing 'pell mell' towards the 'big muddy'. They had to have been seen. They had to have stood out on that big river, bigger than life. But, had the Indians seen them move up that little creek?

Six mounted Blackfeet coming on strong and only two rifles between them to hold off the hostiles… the boys quickly concurred that a hasty retreat was in order. With no time to spare, they lit out on foot on the double-quick, right up the stream's bed, the bordering woods covering their presence and their flight.

They made tracks, moved fast, all the while looking back over their shoulders, watching their backtrail. They didn't stop. They never slowed down. It was a desperate situation. One they should've never escaped. But, the Indians apparently never did follow them. At least the boys never felt their presence on their trail. When nightfall came they chanced leaving the relative safety of the stream's woods, moving out across the open prairie in the direction of the Fort.

When James and his boys finally made it back to the Fort and told their story, I realized that the Blackfeet were not in the Headwaters country in any kind of strength, at least not enough to challenge the stockade. That sure wasn't much of a guarantee. Undoubtedly, they now knew of our Fort and presence. Word would be passed north, alerting all their people. The Blackfeet wouldn't let our intrusion stand. We were an insult to their National pride… a threat to their hunting grounds, their reputation amongst all the Indian Nations, to all they stood for. They'd respond, soon, testing our strength, probing the walls, ambushing our men. It was just a matter of time.

The pot inside the stockade continued to boil. The not knowing worked on men's minds and nerves. And there was friction. Half were for abandoning the Fort and returning to the Manuel's, and half for going on, for riding to Cheek's campsite enmasse and settling the issue once and for all. Some men talked angrily of revenge, an eye for eye, to even the score, while others spoke with uncertainty, with fear, running the whole gamut of emotions and doubt and death and revenge.

As for me, who had yet to count a single, tanned skin to my credit, it was beginning to feel all too familiar. My patience was wearing thin. I wasn't going to go on this way much longer. Something had to break. I wasn't going to sit here forever. And, then...

"Ho, the Fort." The words were loud and unmistakable, bursting through the cracks and crevasses of the log palisade as if shot from a human cannon of a voice... a cannon of a barrel of a chest.

The voice was instantly recognizeable. It was Mike Immell's... big Mike Immell, back from the dead in the middle of the night. And he was mighty pissed off, pounding away with his massive fists on the Fort's gate with 'sledge hammer' like blows.

"Big Mike," I called out to Immell as he, with four of his men, entered the compound. "You're sure a sight for sore eyes. Thought you were a goner for sure. Did you have a run-in with any of those injuns?"

"Had to pass on 'em this time, John," said the big man and then he added rather sternly, "We need to talk, now."

He was a shaken man. Desperation and fatigue was written on his face, on all of their faces. They were hungry. They hadn't eaten or slept in days. And they had seen something, something horrible…that, and three or four days of dodging the Blackfeet had left all of them in pretty bad shape.

Upon seeing Billy and me and Valle and Drouillard, Mike did an immediate tally, counting those of us who had made it back alive. He nodded to the Colonel and the Major. And then to the rest of the men, he seemed to be looking at each and every one of them, straight in the eye.

A black, foul mood appeared upon his face... one that portended a thunderous fury. His powerful hands were balled-up into fists, their knuckles going white, as if livid with rage, ready to rain relentless blows, pummeling those who had dared caused his wrath.

His face became somber for the briefest of moments. He was gathering himself, struggling to put together the words, the thoughts he wanted to say. And then they came...

"Listen up." His voice was deep, demanding undivided attention. The muscle in his jaws tightened everso hard, grinding his teeth. His eyes flashed.

His whole body and being were taut, as if literally ready to explode.

No one moved, except to crowd closer.

"Some of our boys… aren't coming back."

He let his words sink in for a moment. "I found a couple of 'em… and what I have to say ain't pretty. I've seen what the savages did to 'em, at least to Jimmy Cheek. They had another one of our boys tied to a tree. I didn't rightly recognize who he was."

"What'd they do to Jimmy?" one of the men asked.

There was an eerie silence that followed. Every man there knew Jimmy Cheeks and his loss wasn't sitting well. Cheek was one of them, well liked and respected. What's more, James Cheek was a tough piece of meat, a man who could more than handle his own, the very spirit of indomitableness, even among the brashest, toughest of frontiersmen.

"They butchered Jimmy. Gutted him like a god dang hog."

Stark, shattering were Immell's words. There was a momentary pause, then a deep, loud murmur painful to hear echoed off the walls. Immell's response hit the men hard, knocking the wind out of many a pentup emotion. And then the shock of it all took hold. Suddenly, furiously, anger erupted. Discussion, debate about what to do was decided without even so much as a vote or a poll coming to a swift decision after Immell's next revelation.

"Hear me. Their campsite wasn't far from ours. And they're in no hurry to skedaddle. In fact, they acted like they had nothing to fear. They're ripe for the pickin'… the whole lot of 'em."

"Where are the heathen?" demanded the Major.

"I'll tell you where… just as soon as y'all mount up, the whole damn lot of ya and go teach them murdering red-skins a lesson they won't never forget."

Instantly, there was a thunderclap of support. No one held back. The quiet of this dark night and the somberness of the Fort fairly exploded in reproach. Mike had unleashed the tempest. Tore away the lid covering their suppressed emotions and fear. Until, there was no fear, just lust for vengeance… the call for an unrequited blood feud directed solely at the murdering Indians who attacked our men.

Menard put a hand on Mike's broad shoulders.

"I must know, before we leave," said the Colonel, calmly. "Tell me what you saw… I must know what we're up against."

Immell paused and replied in a whisper barely able to hold his voice from cracking. "Aye, aye!" He began to shake and tremble, overcome with anguish and the sorrow he now felt, burying his head in his arms, he held back with all his might the tears welling in his eyes. Plain to see the big man was heartbroken, yet he steeled himself, refusing to cry.

The command quieted down, gathering around, waiting patiently. Immell was a well thought of man, respected by all.

In due time, Mike looked at each one of us, his friends. Composing hisself, he spoke with sorrow, each memory, each detail etched in his mind and soul, almost too painful to relate.

"Damn that awful place… I wish I could wipe it from my mind. But, I can't. No matter how hard I try. I had no idea of what had happened to the rest of the boys. I had been in such an all-fire hurry to set my traps, I just forgot about everyone else. Never even gave injuns a thought. It was beautiful there, so peaceful, not a sign of trouble. We were free and clear. At least I thought we were. Now, well…

"I suppose I was lucky, very lucky. I must have been too far away to hear the ruckus, 'cause I had no clue. I was tired and hungry… lookin' forward to some of Jimmy Cheek's cookin'. He had a way with vittles."

Mike had a misty, faraway look in his eyes, stopping momentarily. And then he went on.

"When I got back to the campsite it was dark. I couldn't see a dang thing. No one was around or making any noise. Then it occurred to me that all our tents and possibles, even the horses seemed to be missin'. I wasn't too concerned. Moved camp to a better site, I reckoned. Had to be, sounded reasonable. Except, to my way of thinkin', word should have been left behind, a note on a tree or one of the boys to wait behind and pass on the word. Bunch of no accounts… it would have been the decent thing to do.

"And then I heard a commotion a ways off. The noise was coming from back in the woods, maybe on the far side of the river. I listened for a spell and heard it again. It sounded like splashing water. They're takin' a bath, I chuckled, that big bunch of stinkin' hogs are frolickin' like river nymphs. And the way we all stunk, it was fine by me.

"So I started in that direction. Made my way through the woods and the willow brakes right up to the banks to where I thought the noise was coming from. But, there was no one there. They had all gone. Trappers and water and taking baths don't rightly mix. So I thought nothing of it. I forded the Jefferson, crossing over to the other side. Once there I took a minute to catch my breath and my bearin's. I didn't exactly know where the hell the boys were. Hell, as long as they knew where they were, I chuckled.

"Good thing I waited, otherwise, I'd been a goner for sure. It took a minute or two for my eyes to adjust. It was dark, I could barely see through the trees, finding a clearing just beyond the woods. What the hell, there was an injun village in that clearin'. Worse, yet. Someone was walkin' directly towards me. Jesus Christ, I swore.

"I shrunk back into the trees, never takin' my eyes off that injun. I put my rifle down and pulled out my knife. It'd be a lot quieter then shootin' my gun. And then I realized the injun was a squaw… a good lookin' young thing carryin' a kettle… a big, ol' brass kettle.

"Hold on, I thought. That kettle is lookin' mighty familiar. Why, that's my kettle… goddamn it. I'd know the son of a bitch anywheres… What 'n the hell is a squaw doin' with it? She passed right by me and headed down to the water's edge. That dumb bitch never knew I was there. I could've reached right out and slit her throat… easy as ya please. I should've. But, I didn't know what had happened to the rest of the men. So, I kept still, 'til she finished her chores and walked on back from to where she come from.

"I kept waiting, watching. It was kind of quiet, not a lot goin' on. I could make out at least thirty lodges, mebbe more. I don't know. But, they didn't seem to be very worried and that had me worried. The wind was in my face. And thank God it was, cause their dogs would've smelt me for sure. I tried countin' as many warriors as I could. The light wasn't all that bad, they had several campfires a blazin' and from what I could see not a soul standing guard.

"Huh! I thought, pretty dang cocky, they are. And then my eyes stopped dead in their tracks. Thar was a naked man, hog-tied to a big ol' cottonwood. He was naked, all right, and white as snow and in a world of hurt. I knew it had to be one of our boys. I looked hard to see who it was. Try as I might, I just couldn't tell.

"Sorry, boys. That's all I could do."

Big Mike stopped and bowed his head and sighed. And then he looked up, straight at me, locking his eyes with mine. "It made me think of you and Potts…"

And then he went on. "Whoever he was, he was all cut up… and from what I could tell, sliced from head to toe, more dead than alive. Once, I thought, I saw him move, but I weren't certain. It was just too hard to say. The poor bastard hung there like a side of raw meat ready to be butchered. I decided right then I'd best get back here as fast as I could."

"We've heard enough," yelled one of the men.

That started an immediate uproar. The men were up, walking towards their horses. The Colonel, the Major, no one could hold them back.

"Hold on, hold on," Mike yelled, raising his hands to calm everybody down. "Don't go off half-cocked. That's not the end of it. I'm with you… and the sooner the better. But, there's somethin' else y'all ought to know… it's about Jimmy."

I knew there was more to this story, especially with four more men yet to be accounted for. He knew what happened to Cheek, but as of yet hadn't said a thing. It was coming…

"I hurried back across the river," Mike went on, "and made my way back through the woods to ol' Cheek's campsite. By then it was blacker than hell. I had to get an idea just what in the hell went on. So I took my time and felt around.

"The place had a feel like a graveyard. I could feel that something wasn't right. And with those injuns close by, my knees were a knockin'. But, I'm a big, dumb son of a bitch… too dumb to know any better. So, I started to whisperin', callin' out low and steady-like… hopin' I'd hear from any of our boys foolish enough to be still hangin' around.

"I heard nothin', 'cept for my own heart poundin' away. And it was as loud as church bells. I kept groping. I could barely see my hands in front of my face. And then my foot struck somethin' lyin' on the ground. Whatever it was hooked my moccasin and almost sent me ass-over-tea-kettle. I froze for a second. That tumble and whatnot had scared the crap outta me. But, wait, whatever the hell I tripped over felt soft. Soft and fleshy, more like a body in repose than a mound of dirt. Couldn't be anythin' else.

"I started to reach down and touch it. And it took all the gumption I had, 'cause I'm not much for midnight surprises. But, I reached down, anyway and touched it. I knew what it was right off. It was a wet, clammy mess of gourd-pulp and ooze, right where a man's scalp should be."

"Good God, Michael," exploded Preacher Pelton.

"Good God isn't exactly right, not if He's the God of white men. 'Cause I knew it wasn' no injun a lyin' there. No, that man had to be one of us… for sure. Had to be.

"I rolled him over for a good look. I didn't want to, but I had to."

Immell suddenly stopped and looked away. The pain was written on his face. The memory, the realization was hitting him hard. His face seemed to squash right up like a dried prune, distorting the features we had all come to know so well.

We pressed forward. The wait, the silent anticipation grew deafening. There wasn't a wet lip or tongue or throat in the group. Just three dozen beating, throbbing, pounding hearts building-up to a drum roll.

"It was Jimmy Cheek," Mike said. "And he was layin' there… stone cold dead in a pool of his own guts and blood. And the top of his head, his scalp… was missin'."

Immell shook mightily like an aspen in a gale. Tears rolled anew. He was powerless to prevent this liquid remorse from streaming unchecked. His emotional dam had finally given way to rivers of salt and sorrow. He was overwhelmed, lost in it all, oblivious to all his friends and fellow trappers standing there beside him.

And then… the muscles in his arms, his biceps and forearms tensed like steel cords. His ham-sized hands clenched, violently, as if he prepared to crush and squeeze the life right out of every one of the murdering assassins.

His eyes flashed like lightning bolts streaking across the night sky. He filled his huge chest cavity with massive quantities of fresh air, and then, from deep within the bowels of his soul and being he bellowed for all the world to hear…

"Kill 'em. Kill every last one of 'em. Ya hear? Who's with me?" His roar caromed and echoed throughout the entire command, shooting off into the vast void of of an empty night. His power, his anger, his bloodcurdling ferocity intimidated even some of the most grizzled of our men. And several stepped away from the giant to a safe distance, not entirely sure themselves… of what the man was capable of next.

Even our ponies cowered and kicked and reared in fright. Clouds of dirt and horse shit hovered about the corral and the inside of the Fort enveloping the entire stockade in a dense fog of dust and crud.

Mike was spent by the effort; the anger in his voice receding. He became almost… sentimental, gentle… "These boys found me sometime later on the trail. Glad they did. I was in bad shape, ready to do somethin' stupid. But they took good care of ol' Mike. Thanks, boys."

There was silence. Everybody was still staring at Immell.

"I liked that Cheek," he said suddenly. And then he looked at me once again, long and hard, locking both our eyes… just like he had minutes before upon recalling the name of John Potts.

"John Colter," he said to me.

"Yeah, Mike," I answered.

"I guess I owe you an apology."

"How so, Mike?" I asked. And I honestly didn't know what on earth he was talking about.

"Been hearin' about that injun crap you had in the Forks with Potts, goin' on more than a year and a half now. Talk of it has made it all the way down to St. Louie. Some people are making like you're bigger than Dan'l Boone or mebbe some kinda medieval knight of King Arthur's court… or the like.

"I thought it was just some more backwood's bullshit… you know, trapper hot-air. Tall tales to make yourself shine. The stories that some people along the river are tellin' about you aren't worth repeatin'. The Spaniard liked to cut you to the quick… as long as you weren't around to hear him. Some of the other high 'n mighty types of his kind did too. But, I'm not noticin' a one of 'em here, now. They don't have the sand. Funny thing about it, I sensed all along that Lisa believed you. He just didn't have the balls to admit it. But, Will Clark sure did. He's a standup man. When he heard about you and Potts on the Jefferson, he set everybody straight… 'John Colter doesn't lie.'

"Cap'n Clark's word cuts a wide swath on the frontier. Nobody would think otherwise. Personally, I thought you were full of shit. That and all those tall tales of traipsin' about in a land of hellfire and brimstone and whatnot… Pshaw, what a crock! I weren't fooled none. No, sir! Made my mind up, you had to be the biggest liar I'd ever heard of. Now, well… I found out better. It's time for me to eat crow."

Immell turned and looked to each of his fellow trappers. There was a moment of silence and then… "Y'all pay attention to what I got to say. Big Mike Immell is here to tell ya he's sorry he ever doubted the word of John Colter and asks his forgiveness."

I looked at Mike, staring quietly back at the big man. I almost didn't know what to say. But, he'd only said what the others didn't have the balls to say. In fact most men avoided me as if I was a pariah, a man to be shunned. I knew all along the questions, the doubts. I knew men snickered behind my back, laughed at my name all up and down the Missouri. I had seen their snide looks before, the way they avoided my eyes and my conversation, felt the quiet scorn and ridicule for two whole years since word of Johnny's passing reached downriver. I learned to live with it, but it never made it any easier. So, I stayed mostly to myself, even when surrounded by a whole company of trappers. It'd gotten to be quite a lonely life. And I was sick of it, 'til Mike Immell's words set me free. And then I saw Valle and some of the other boys nodding, agreeing with him. In fact the whole dang outfit was starin' at me in a way that said as much.

I walked over to Mike and put my arm around his broad shoulders. The man seemed to melt. "Thanks, Mike, comin' from you it makes my heart glad. Sorry you had to find out the hard way."

And then I turned to Menard and Henry. They'd both been waiting patiently, listening to Immell's tale. Something must be done; the decision was up to them.

Menard spoke first. "Well, gentleman, we've been found out and set upon. Soon, I trust, the whole Blackfeet Nation will know. The question is what can we do about it?"

Menard looked to Henry his partner in command. You could see their minds a working, fleshing out our dilemma, weighing calculated response or what lack thereof would bring. Silence reigned. Men barely breathed, while anticipation arose like the morning sun. The two officers stared at one another; both equally grim faced, equally determined, until, finally, the Colonel broke his silence, nodding to his friend and partner. His unspoken mind needed no interpretation, his tacit signal was quite clear to all… Blackfeet reproach could not go unanswered. And Henry knew it; in fact revenge was on his mind from the start. He only awaited the word. As was their habit, each man had thought as one; divining the other's mind and heart and will, not a word had to pass between them.

"By God, we'll strike while the iron is hot. Smite them hoof and nail." While the Colonel was calm and deliberate, the Major was not. Henry bellowed like a wounded bull, his voice roaring across the Fort's earthen floor like black thunder incarnate. And then he unleashed a torrent of commands to his waiting men. "Meat for a week… powder and lead, and plenty of it. Times awastin'. Don't weigh yourselves down needlessly, we've got to move light and fast. We're goin' huntin', boys… scalp huntin'."

Henry turned to Mike and me. "Will that suit ya?" He managed a twisted, almost curdling smile, the first sign of any emotion he'd allowed himself to form in many a day. "Let's get these red sons of bitches 'afore it's too late."

We rode hard, straight to Cheek's campsite… to bury our dead and punish the offenders. There we found our friend Jimmy prostrated, locked forever in a hideous throe of death. Five days had passed, rigor mortis, then the inevitable decay of flesh had set in. The stench of death persisted, utterly repulsive to the senses overwhelming even the hardest of our men.

The stalwart Cheek, uncompromising to the bitter end, had been gut shot, his innards spilled out onto the ground, leaving a putrid pile of vomitable mass. The scavengers of the land: the crows, the magpies, coyotes and beetles and maggots had all been busily consuming his remains.

It was to his friends a most disgraceful end for a man who had been so full of life. He was barely recognizable, even to us who had known him well. Black powder burns scorched his once ruggedly chiseled face. Like Johnny Potts, Cheek's powerful frame had been mutilated, his limbs dismembered, senselessly strewn about the forest floor. And the top of his once proud head a bloody patch… scalped, just like Immell had so horribly described.

"Get a good look," commanded the Major in a stern, cold voice, "and remember the way they did ol' Cheek… when it's our turn to do the killin'."

By now, though, the command was near immune to such depredations. Even so, when it's your friend lying before you it's always hard to take. And yet, no one shied away. Every man burned the death scene into his mind and heart. The vendetta, the blood feud commenced.

But, Jimmy's was not the only struggle to soil this bloody and darkened ground. As we spread out and began our search the smell of more rotting human flesh hung about us like an odious mist.

"Lookee here!" cried Dougherty. "Lookee here."

Jack was standing over what appeared to be a hastily thrown together pile of dirt and brush and twigs and small branches. He bent down and uncovered another body, an Indian warrior's body.

"Here's one injun we won't have to worry about, no more," Jack spat contemptuously on the redskin's remains. He placed one of his moccasins underneath the rotting cadaver, lifted and rolled it over onto its back. He bent down, taking a closer look... "Yeah... will ya look at this. Two balls in his head. And from the looks of 'em, they're pistol shots. Heh, heh, heh... nice shootin', Jimmy."

"Yer right, Jack," said Mike Immell, examining the savage's perforated gourd.

"They're both small enuff to be pistol-ball holes... and Jimmy carried a brace of 'em. God bless him," he shouted and laughed.

And then a look came over his face, a funny, yet, vile look. Big Mike whipped his knife from his own belt and commenced to lift the dead Indian's scalp, deftly tearing away a large black patch of raven colored hair and skin and flesh, yanking it free with a quick, wrenching snap. And then he stood erect, holding the savage's scalp triumphantly high overhead for all to see.

"Voila!" shouted Francois Valle, pumping his arms, reaching to the sky. "We'll fly this red heathen's scalp from atop the Fort and see how these savages like it for a change."

"Like the Good Book says," bellowed Preacher Pelton, adding, "Do unto others…"

"Aye, an eye for eye," responded Immell.

The men instantly roared their approval. By now we were determined to match butchery with butchery... depravation with depravation, the only way the savages would understand. And we had to do it now, to strike while their trail was still warm, before they got too far away, too close to the womb of their heartland.

"Amen to the Golden Rule, I say," piped in Henry. "One scalp in the memory of the Tennessean... and many more to follow."

But, I knew he was speaking too fast. This was only the beginning. We were yet to find them, much less gain revenge. And in our exuberance we were making entirely too much noise. If we wanted to catch the Blackfeet, then we'd have to out injun them, be sneakier, more quiet, more savage. It was a tall order for most white men.

"Doesn't make any sense," I said, looking about.

"What's that? How so?" The Major shot me a quick look.

"Leavin' this'n behind. Ain't like injuns to do that, not when they don't have to."

"Maybe they're closer then we thought," said Henry, turning abruptly. "Spread out boys. We're still missin' four men. And watch yerselves. There's red-hided niggers about."

It didn't take long. Ayers was the next to be found, floating face down nearby in the shallows of the Jefferson, stripped naked, dumped unceremoniously. Bloated beyond recognition, hacked and maimed and disemboweled, he too deprived of his hair and his privates. It was another, sickening scene. One we were all getting entirely too used to.

"Not again," said Billy Bryant, the first to reach Ayers.

And the kid was visibly shaken, fighting back the tears.

"Get a hold of yourself, Billy," I said, putting my arm around his shoulders. "Now's not the time for cryin', but for gettin' even."

He stiffened up. His response was determined, defiant... "Yer damn right it is."

Several of the men carried Ayers back to the clearing to join his friend-in-death, Cheeks. We continued to search the surrounding cottonwoods, right up to the river's bend, for the rest of the missing men. Try as we might, we couldn't find any sign of Hull, Rucker or Fleehart. The three had just disappeared without a trace. It wasn't too awfully hard to imagine their fate.

We all pitched-in and buried our murdered friends, leaving a cairn of smooth river-rock to mark their final resting placel. When we were through with our funeral orations, and the Preacher had said his piece, the whole lot of us followed Immell through the woods to the far side of the Jefferson.

We went looking for the savages' village. But, they were long gone. I knew they would be. Why else would they leave that warrior in Cheeks' clearing. They had spent several days hunting the rest of us down. They might have even seen Immell and his men reach the Fort. Maybe they didn't like the idea of attacking the napikwans' Fort with armed men behind the walls. Maybe they didn't like the odds. Whatever the reason, they were now gone. Packed and fled, leaving little trace that they had been there at all, just a few loose lodge poles strewn about and some camp debris. But the ground had been left in the wake of a maelstrom... torn-up by the unshod hooves of hundred ponies in a mighty hurry to get away.

"This is the tree where they tied him down," Immell declared, his hands gingerly touching the coarse black bark. His face, his eyes strained to find the grim clues he knew to be there.

"Look, here's blood... and hair," he yelled, pointing a hard finger to the evidence as if to verify all he had witnessed days before.

And then the big man raced across the clearing. He was excited, animated, pointing once again to a circle of stones maybe twenty or so feet in diameter.

"Those rocks are where that red bitch's lodge was. She carried my kettle inside, right here. I can still see her wigglin' her little ass."

The tree was what drew our attention. Indeed, faint splotches of blood remained... grim testimony, caked and turning rusty brown. A small swatch of bloodstained hair still clung to the rough cottonwood bark.

The ground at the base of the trunk was heavily disturbed, a mute reminder of its prisoner's last vain struggles. Writhing in agony and mortal fear, with his very life fading away, the white trapper's heels had dug deeply into the sod.

It was not difficult to imagine his dread, the terror he felt as he awaited an uncertain end. The Blackfeet would make a long, cruel game of the rest of his life. Strip his flesh right off of his bones. Disembowel him and let him watch while his guts, his intestines dangled to the ground. They would stretch out the torture, take it as far as humanly possible to withstand and then some. And when and only when they tired and wished to play no more...

Once, Blackfeet cruelty had almost been my fate. I remembered my own fears all too well. I shuddered to think of Hull and Fleehart and Rucker. They had simply vanished, swallowed up by the vastness of the wilderness. Never again would we hear them laugh or cry or swear nor see their familiar faces, lest they came amidst some haunting, midnight dream. We would never know, never find out their tragic end. The whereabouts of their remains would be forever a mystery. Again, the Jefferson refused to give up its grim secrets.

There was now little doubt, even by the most skeptical of our party. And whether or not the Blackfeet or the Gros Ventre knew of the hated Napikwan's return to their sacred *Ahkoto waktai Sakum* and plotted ambush all along or this subsequent battle was simply and tragically a coincidence, mattered not.

We had been discovered, at least on the Jefferson and farther down the Missouri towards the Great Falls. Men were dead as a result. The Fort would be next. The Blackfeet band was beating a hasty retreat to the north and soon their whole nation would know. We had to act. And act, fast. Run 'em down, don't let 'em get away, catch up to 'em... and kill them all, every last one of 'em. Make an example, before they made one of us. Or trapping in the Three Forks would be forever a nightmare.

Inwardly, doubt nagged at me. I didn't really think we had a chance in hell to catch these murderers. We were too late... the Indians fled their campsite in way too much of a hurry. Too many days had passed. Now with the mood the Company was in, we were all in too much of a hurry. And we would be riding right smack dab into the middle of Blackfeet country. It didn't bode well. But, for me to say something, anything right then would have run head-on into thirty angry men, a veritable human hornet's nest. The boys wanted blood and rightly so. They wanted to commit a vengeance as horrendous as the massacre of their departed friends. Lord knows I did too. I couldn't help it, yet at the same time I knew it would ultimately be futile. All my experience, my instincts told me so. And yet, I had to go. I had to see it through. I had to be a voice of reason, of calm if we went too far. It was as much my duty as anything had been in my whole life. There was just no holding the command back.

"Mount up... and keep your eyes open," ordered the Colonel. There was an determination and urgency in his voice. He was waving and pointing to the men, his were eyes flashing, bursting with energy, his every movement was concise and animated beyond anything I had ever observed before in the man. There was absolutely no doubt now as to his qualifications to command.

"Drouillard, you and your Shawnee take the lead and find us those dirty sons of bitches."

"Chasin' the wind," said George with a sort of queer look, shaking his head, for once tacitly agreeing with me.

"Major Henry, tell Immell and Valle to take to the flanks and send out videttes... and be sure somebody watches our backsides."

"Colter, you stay by me... I need your head." Menard was issuing commands as fast as he could spit them out. No more 'slow to think or decide,' he was well beyond that. The loss of his men had spurred in him a deep, unabiding anger. More than any man in the command he wanted to run-down and punish the responsibles.

We were off. The chase was finally on. Adrenaline pumped through our veins like water bursting a ruptured dam. And with pursuit, a crack of thunder... human thunder to rent the air as thirty-odd armed trappers announced their own war cry of vengeance.

"Remember Cheek... and Ayers and Hull and Fleehart and Rucker," was emblazoned on every man's mind and soul and tongue.

We had a lot of ground to cover. Too much lost time to make up. But, we were not to be denied. Nothing, we thought, could stop us now. The Indians had headed north in a hurry. And in their haste they made no attempt to hide their trail. Hell, they'd left tracks a blind man could have followed. Maybe they were running scared. Maybe, just maybe, they had something else up their sleeves. Indians never did anything without a plan. Their whole lives were spent at odds against their neighbors. They were masters of guile and deceit.

George and me had been around long enough to know all that... Luthecaw and Pla-co-ta, likewise. They knew it and I knew it and we reacted accordingly. Now, we were the hunters... and it was up to us to keep it that way. That thought stayed in the back of my mind, never far away from every instinct I owned.

They had taken their buffalo hide lodges, all their personal belongings...

everything they owned. Little was left behind, save a few thin lodge poles, and thirty or so rings of heavy, river stones that once held down the edges of their tipis... that, and some bad memories clinging to the bark of a lone cottonwood tree.

The unbroken ruts of their travois, weighted down heavily by hundred of pounds of sewn, tanned, painted buffalo skins, left deep, unmistakable impressions in the soil. And mingled, side by side, hundreds and hundreds of unshod tracks.

We rode fast, driving our mounts, pushing them to a killing pace. We traveled light, carrying only our rifles, powder and lead, skinning knives and trade-tomahawks and enough jerked meat to last each man a week. The land soon settled down. The terrain flattened. We kept at it, in a northernly direction, away from the foothills of the Tobacco Roots, away from the fading Jefferson, bypassing Three Forks altogether.

We were soon paralleling the Missouri, closing in on them. Their tracks, the ruts seemed fresher, newer. We were emboldened, pushing ourselves, our mounts harder and harder.

The path they chose was in rich country, buffalo grass country, flanked by tree-covered, snow-capped mountains and high craggy, granite ridges... eternal heights, vigilant, brooding, forever gazing down upon on the perpetual wanderings of the 'Big Muddy' since that mighty river first peed upon the land.

It was land that should've been feeding herds of grazing critters. But something had disturbed the beasts, interrupted their peaceful existence and sent 'em packing to the hills. Something had spooked them. That something or those somebodies who may have been spooked themselves. It showed in an unabated pace, in the clouds of still settling dust they left behind in their wake. It showed on their trail... as one by one, we came upon our own traps littering the ground, discarded in panic.

"Leave 'em be," ordered the Major. "They'll slow us down fer sure."

"Sorry, Major. But, I ain't leavin' 'em," said Immell. "These traps are all that I own.

"I told you the bastards were too lazy to tote 'em, too much work. They took 'em just to spite us, anyway," the big man added in disgust.

Mike got off his horse, reached down and picked up one of the traps. It had been lying in a pile of pony dung and it was encrusted with shit, right in the middle of the trail. He shook off the dirt, the dust and the pony droppings that clung to the teeth of the trap and held it up for us to see.

"Look at this, will ya," he said sarcastically, a scowl suddenly appearing on his face. "Crapped on my trap. Dumb savages."

"Yeah, they probably thought you'd get a kick out of it," I chuckled.

"Look, here's another," said Immell pointing to a second trap lying on the trail, nearby.

"Pack those traps on the spare ponies," ordered Henry, riding up. "We're wastin' way too much time."

Traps weren't the only valuable found abandoned on their trail. No sir, those Indians were riding hard, driving our stolen ponies into the ground to save their own prized herd, their buffalo runners, their precious ponokamitas. The Blackfeet were, smart, indeed, making good time at the expense of our own captured horses. And it was having the desired affect.

Several times, we ran across our poor critters… gaunt, lathered, and just plain worn out. Most were barely able to stand. Fog-eyed, tongues slaked, crying from thirst, all were ribs and skin and bones and not much else. Just shadows of the game little animals that had carried us all the way from Manuel's Fort.

"What a shame," bemoaned Menard.

"Let 'em be," I told the Colonel.

"But, but…" Menard started to say.

"You said you wanted to use my head. Well, here it is… those ponies are all in. They won't be able to keep up. They'll just slow us down. We'll pick 'em up on the way back."

We proceeded on, driving hard once again. When nightfall arrived, the cavalcade came to a stop and made a hasty, dry camp. We hunkered down. Tired, worn out men, sucking on stringy, leathery strips of jerked meat and washing it down with muddy brown water. The chase was taking its toll. The horses and the men were feeling the affects of hard riding and those uncomfortable Crow saddles it was our misfortune to own. Legs and backs were stiff and aching, exhausted from the constant strain of too many hours in the saddle. And many a tender rear end was rubbed raw, bleeding, agonizingly tender and painful to the touch.

We huddled together, sharing our bodily warmth. We made no fires to give us away. We had to stay tough. To take the elements as they came. And do so without regret.

Somewhere along the line, I got a sneaking suspicion the Indians knew our every move. And when I peered out into the darkness of the night and quietly listened to the nocturnal sounds of birds and beasts, wind and water, I felt that strange itch of mine once again creeping down my neck.

The men were restless, sleeping fitfully. It'd been a hard grind, a week of hell and little else. They were all on edge, even our taciturn Shawnee. And nothing ever seemed to shake them before. It was a strangely silent encampment. Bravado was out the door. Conversations were few and those that did were muted to grunts and nods and fearful stares, out into the nighttime gloom. Imagination played havoc on some, and once again like the days of the Pass the men were drawn together.

Rain began to fall steadily as springtime in the mountains struck with force, cold as ice, mucking the trail in mud and wearying both horse and rider and human resolve. Punishing pursuit had now slowed to a foot slogging walk. Spirit and determination was under attack, ebbing with each struggling mile. No longer did cries of Blackfeet blood and taking scalps leave their lips. Resolve was dwindling, slowly but surely. I sensed it. Surely, Menard and Henry did too.

It was an unfamiliar, strange, rugged land, chipping away at the men's minds, wearing them down. The Blackfeet were a mystery, elusive, playing on their imaginations and fears. No one had to say it. No one did. But it was there, nevertheless, written on every man's face.

Game had disappeared all along the trail. Our ponies were withering under the strain. For two long days, we stayed on the heathens' trail, gaining ground steadily… anticipation, anxiety rising every bit as steadily. Their tracks, their travois ruts were too easy to follow. Deliberately, taunting us. Daring us. Their lack of fear defied all sense and logic. It was as if they wanted it that way… inviting us to close in and catch them.

Yet, we kept on, oblivious to the dangers ahead, further and further north, paralleling the Missouri, until we had reached deep within the Blackfeet realm. It became clear, abundantly clear. This is what the Blackfeet wanted… the whole time. Keep pulling us along, farther and farther to the north and farther and farther away from our Fort. String us out in the open, tire our mounts to a walk. Watch us grow hungry, disenchanted.

They played a game of cat and mouse. We followed their carrot. And they had done a masterful job. Because by then, their trail had splintered into many trails, each with smaller and smaller groups veering off in a half dozen different directions. It was all meant to be most confusing. We were suddenly at a loss as to what to do or where to follow. For them it had been child's play. And the more we realized it the more exasperated we became.

Finally, we came upon Drouillard and his Shawnee stopped on the trail. For once George seemed stumped. He'd been out-injuned and it was vexing the arrogant half-breed to no end.

They had dismounted, studying the confusing tracks with great interest and deliberation. And they were arguing, hot and heavy, the first disagreement we'd ever seen between them. Old George was beginning to boil; I could see it coming. He'd been outsmarted the whole time… and he didn't like it at all.

My old riding companion, Pla-co-ta, pointed first to the northwest and then to the north and then, again to several other directions. He was shaking his head. This was all very confusing to the little Shawnee scout.

George looked up and nodded. No, he tacitly said. And then he went back to reading the ground. A stubborn streak seemed to have completely overcome the man.

"Bahhh!" grunted the taciturn Pla-co-ta, shaking his head in disgust.

"Seems to me, ol' Pla-co-ta here… and you ain't seein' eye to eye," I said to Drouillard.

"What's that injun have to say?" barked Henry, his bark having a decided bite to it. "Don't your Shawnee ever talk to the rest of us white men… or is it all they can do is grunt? I swear I ain't never seen the like."

The Major's sarcasm bit George a mite-too-hard. We were all on edge and it was beginning to show. Fatigue hit Menard and Henry and most of the newcomers a lot harder than it did Drouillard and me and his Shawnee. In fact it hadn't touched us at all. We'd been at it too long. So long, it'd become our way of life. But, this new development, with its obvious frustration was more than either George or the rest of the men could handle. George's stare would've frozen a panther. And when he began to answer the Major I saw a fight a brewing.

But, wily ol' Placota stepped right in and began spouting some pretty good American lingo. Now, that Placota was a spare built Indian as Indians tend to go, lean with a hawk-shaped nose and keen, black eyes, intense eyes that never seemed to miss a trick.

"Pla-co-ta say… Pahkee split up like the rivers by the Fort. No say which way we go."

The Shawnee then bent down to the ground and with his fingers pointed to the various separate trails of unshod ponies heading off in many different directions.

"Colter, you know these injuns better than anyone. What do you make of it?" asked Menard. "Is this a trick or somethin'? Are they gonna double back on our trail or what?"

"I know 'em better than anyone? Well, I know I don't like 'em. I know they're smarter than we are. And they got us up a crick. And what's more… I'd say there's a mess of 'em right now watchin' us and there's not a damn thing we can do about it. That's what I make of it, Colonel. The question, now, is what are we going to do?"

I walked over to Pla-co-ta and we talked for several minutes. He knew what I knew. And that was all there was to it. We had chased a ghost… or a band of ghosts, with no hope of catching any of them. Surprise was never on our side and without it, a big, loud bunch of trappers had little chance to catch these wiliest of Indians.

"Well?" The Colonel's tone was short, indignant and restless. He was fidgeting in his saddle as uncomfortably as a mangy ol' hound full of fleas.

Henry was no different. Drouillard was ready to cuss and swear and do 'God knows what' and the whole danged outfit itching to give up the chase and call it quits.

I couldn't blame them. We had to give it a try, who knows, we might have gotten lucky.

"Relax, Colonel," I said. "Ain't none of us likin' this a bit."

"Yes, you're right. Accept my apology," Menard said with a heavy sigh. "This whole affair has become too long and too tedious. Far more than I expected."

"All right," I said looking him right in the eye, "here it is, at least the best that me and Pla-co-ta can figure it out. I think this chase has run its course. Sorry to say it, but that's the way I see it. They're splittin' up, all right. The main group still seems to be headin' north. I'd say towards the Marias or thereabouts. But, maybe, that's just another trick to sucker us in. George, here, knows the area well, 'cause four years ago he and Cap'n Lewis and the Field boys had a scrape with this band's very same people. I reckon, they've been spoilin' for a fight ever since. Now, we're close to obligin' em. Who knows, mebbe they planned it this way all along?"

Drouillard suddenly spoke up. "Colter's dead on. These Blackfeets are smart. We didn't stand a chance of catchin' 'em from the start. But, y'all wouldn't have it any other way."

George had no argument from me. He was right. And as much as we all dearly wanted to avenge Cheek and the boys it would have to wait for another day.

"Colonel," I said. "These injuns always have a plan. You can bet on it. What doesn't make sense to the white man's way of thinkin' is the injun way of doin' things."

"If that is so, then what do we do next?" Pierre Menard wore a puzzled look on his face, a look that said that exasperation had set in.

Nothing was working out right. The Shawnee weren't getting any closer to the Blackfeet. In fact, the whole shooting match was getting farther and farther away from the safety of the Fort and deeper and deeper into Blackfeet land. And the men, the ponies were worn out. Our food was almost gone. Someone would have to do the huntin' pretty soon or we'd be in worse shape. This was not the time or the place to be wandering off. The Colonel and the Major had much to ponder.

I went on, "You just can't always figure these savages out. Sure, they want us to split up and foller 'em. And then, up the trail a ways they'll split agin, then agin and then what? Are we gonna keep splittin' up 'til we're all strung out in little groups agin, just like we was on the Jeff'?

"Hope not. I don't know this country well enough to go traipsin' around, lookin' to get shot up and scalped. We'd all be lost, surer then shit and all the while gettin' closer and closer to their whole dang nation. And that's about the clearest picture I can paint."

"Yes, you've painted quite well," the Colonel said.

His mind was still waxing and waning, all too indecisively. And Henry knew it right off. "George," said the Colonel.

Drouillard turned and faced Menard.

The Colonel then looked to Andy Henry and then back to Drouillard and over to Immell and Valle. They all waited impassively… each prepared to do whatever the little Frenchman commanded.

It began to rain, turning instantly into a squall. Would it pass or would it be a typical Rocky Mountain spring downpour, washing the trail away and leaving it cold forever. The confusion we now faced becoming infinitely more puzzling.

Then Pla-co-ta whispered in my ear. Luthecaw behind him mumbled… his head bobbing up and down in agreement.

"What did he say?" asked the Colonel, still undecided.

"Yeah, tell him to speak up so's we can all hear," Henry fumed.

"I'll let him tell you, himself," I said and nodded to the little Shawnee scout.

"Pla-co-ta say… the Blackfeet are like ghosts."

"Ghosts, my ass," Henry blurted out in frustration. "You Shawnee don't want to admit you've been out injunned."

"Maybe so," I said. "Nevertheless, the trails gone cold, and I'm plumb outta ideas."

"Hmmmph!" grunted Henry. "If that don't beat all." Henry would've followed the Blackfeet to hell. And that's probably where we all would have ended up if he had his way.

The rain had cleared Menard's head and helped him make up his mind. "It's time, Andrew." And he said it with reluctance. "We've done all we can do here."

"I can't believe what I'm hearin'," Henry answered.

Big Mike Immell stepped forward. The pain, the frustration was all there in his voice and he seemed to speak for the rest of the men. He had plenty of Indian fighting experience with the U. S. Infantry. And the man certainly knew his frontier history.

"Colter's right, we've been playin' injun checkers and we've been checked. We'd be luckier than a preacher in a whore house if we could catch up with any of these wily sons of bitches. Oh, I'm not a sayin' it can't be done. Cap'n Clark's older brother, Gen'rl George Rogers Clark proved that at Vincennes when he and his Virginians captured that British bastard Hamilton, the one they called the "hair buyer" and all his injun allies back durin' the Revolution."

Upon hearing the legendary name of George Rogers Clark, the old Shawnee Pla-co-ta let out with a loud grunt and uttered his people's name for the Revolutionary War hero and his feared rangers. "*Gitchi Mokoman. Gitchi Mokoman.*"

"That's right, Pla-co-ta. *Gitchi Mokoman.*" Immell nodded to the little red man.

And then he turned back to Henry. "He oughta know the name of George Rogers Clark, his kin fought him way back yonder and when. As far as us avengin' Cheek and the boys and wipin' out these here injuns from the land, I want at 'em more than any man here. But, as sure as the nose on my face, today, right now... we're just too late. They plain outfoxed us. Instead of standin' here, fightin' between ourselves, I suggest we get on back to Fort, while we can and bide our time. They'll come back soon enough... and bring their whole damned nation to boot."

I had to smile. I knew I liked the big man all along, and now even more so.

"You're right. All of you are right," nodded Menard and turned to Henry. "I've heard and seen enough, Andrew. Turn around and head back to the Fort while we can."

Henry nodded, he too finally seeing the light. "You heard the Colonel, boys. Mount up. We're heading out. Colter, take the lead with Bryant. George, you and your Shawnee can watch our backsides. Now, let's move."

We had penetrated far too deeply into Blackfeet country and all along it had been a wild goose chase. The closer we came to catching them the farther away in reality we were from avenging our friend from Tennessee. It was a dismal ride back to the Forks to our dreary little post. The mood was morose, the men sullen with few having anything to say. But, there was a powerful lot going on between their ears. And what lay ahead was on every man's mind. And the two most worried were Menard and Henry.

I was no different than the others. Except, I had been through it before... many times before. Like I've said before, it was getting to be a bad habit. Not even George had come close to going through what I had. Nor lost the friends that I had lost. In fact, compared to me, he was used to things going his way... just like Lisa.

Young Billy Bryant rode alongside me the entire way back. He had become like an itch I couldn't scratch, latching on to me since Cheek's death as if holding on for dear life, becoming sullen, even morose, closing right up to everyone, including me, 'til now.

"I've been watchin' every man in the Company," he suddenly said, breaking several days of silence.

"Uh huh, what's the point?" I retorted.

"They're scared, every last one of 'em, includin' me... all except for Drouillard and you."

"George and me are just used to it, that's all," I replied.

"Uh huh!" Billy responded, mimicking me.

"Look Billy, I guess I've gotten my own fair share of scare in my time. Including a little bit right now. There's nothin' wrong with bein' scared when you got a right to be. Only a fool would think otherwise."

"Are ya gonna stay?" Billy was staring at me, waiting for my response.

I returned his gaze and held it steadily for long seconds, ruminating on my response. I wasn't real sure right then myself. The massacre by the Jefferson was weighing as heavily on my mind as it was on his. "We'll see. Maybe things will change."

"Yeah," he said rather unconvincingly, "maybe they will... and maybe they won't. I tell you, I don't know rightly how much more of this I can stand. It's not anythin' like I pictured it to be."

"It almost never is," I said, turning my gaze away from him.

"I know you're not likin' this anymore than I am. And you've been at it a helluva lot longer than the rest of us. I swear none of 'em has a lick of sense here. You take the Colonel, he don't want to be out here. He's as homesick as the rest of us. He's always writin' letters to his wife... like he can get the post-rider to deliver 'em anyday... what a laugh.

"And Andy Henry, I don't rightly know what to make of him. I think he'll get people killed if we don't watch out. I mean just what in the hell are we here for anyway? Nobody is trappin' any beaver, it don't look like we ever will. I didn't sign on to fight or chase injuns either. The army can do that. Hell, after what I've seen those injuns do I don't want any part of 'em. And you, I bet yer sick of 'em."

He paused, still looking at me squarely in the eyes. "What're ya gonna do, John, and how much longer of this shit are ya goin' to put up with? I mean to say... do we have to wait 'til half the outfit has been scalped or kilt? I sure hope not, cause none of this is worth it."

I stared right back at young Bryant. He had the whole shebang pegged about right, including Menard and Henry I suspect. And what's more he wasn't afraid to say it.

"I ain't made up my mind just yet."

"Well, will ya let me know when ya do?"

CHAPTER TWELVE

In those days the great "white bear" ruled the game trails of the Forks. One grizzly in particular, ol' Ephraim, a big brute as far as Rocky Mountain bruins go, was the orneriest, most aggressive critter of them all. On this day, he was in no mood to share his meal.

He had come upon a small family of elk cows refreshed from a cool draught of that good tasting river water. The cows were moving back up the trail now away from the Madison... the very same well-worn trail to the river they and their kind had used for ages. Elk by nature are wary, instinctual critters, but the breezes this day were not right, at least they did not have the decency to carry ol' Ephraim's scent their way.

One cow, heavy with unborn calf was a mite too slow, uncharacteristically careless for one in such a delicate stage of imminent motherhood. The burden in her womb was kicking up an awful ruckus, all the while fixing to drop, making mama elk's day most uncomfortable. Quietly, she struggled, lagging behind, completely unaware of a pair of greedy, narrow set eyes devouring her every step.

The silvertipped grizz was quiet and patient for such a big, ponderous beast, biding time for the exact right moment to suit his purpose. Suddenly, he burst from concealment, covering the few yards separating him from the cow in lightning fast time. God knows he was quick. So fast had he sprung his deadly trap, that the expectant elk cow barely had the time to turn her head, much less flee to save her and her unborn's lives.

It mattered not. For her reaction was way too late, and the bear's presence so totally unexpected. The blow from his powerful right forepaw was instantly telling, leaving no doubt. He was just too strong, too overpowering. The telltale crack of vertebra snapping with a resounding pop had left her completely helpless, paralyzed into submission. Shock set in, and with it the horror, the realization that while her heart still beat and she still breathed... she and her unborn calf were about to be consumed alive.

Ol' Ephraim was too hungry to spare her a few last moments in peace. He never considered the sanctity of motherhood. Fact was, that human of a thought never entered his one-tracked-mind. Powerful canines and jaws ripped into the elk cow's flanks, tearing away whole mouthfuls of flesh.

Yet, today, just as the breezes had not been right, something else about this Madison game trail was, also, not quite right. As Ephraim commenced to gorge he, too, failed to notice another pair of dark orbs, eyeing him discreetly from a short distance away. It would not have mattered to his "surliness"... since there had not been a single ursine competitor in the whole headwaters-country to mount a serious challenge to his reign in half-a-dozen summers.

Luthecaw was trailwise, and a man who had learned to pick his fights and his prey. Today what appeared in his sights did not particularly suit his brand of good judgment. Ol' Ephraim looked like a large dose of bad medicine, one to avoid, if possible. The grizz was immense and obviously too hungry for one hunter to tangle with, at least under normal times. But, today was not anywhere near normal times. Not with Luthecaw's belly growling the way it was and as empty as a sack full of air.

There were many empty sacks of air that day. Every man-jack-one-of us feeling the pinch, and tightening our belts one more time was finding favor with no one. Ribs were beginning to show, hunger was wearing us down. Nerves were fraying all the way around. The Gros Ventre incident had Menard buffaloed to the point that he locked-up the Fort tighter than a drum, manning the palisades in shifts from dawn to dusk to dawn and then some.

We were in a tight spot and all knew it. Between injun treachery and game suddenly gone scarce near the Fort: the whole company was desperate. And desperation demanded that some take the risks or we would all slowly suffer the consequences. Injuns or no injuns, we could wait no longer. It came down between saving our scalps or slow starvation... and our bellies won the toss.

Luthecaw remained downwind from ol' Ephraim. Seeing enough, he began to pull back, and, yet, strangely, he found himself making no headway. Something very powerful held him there. Maybe, it was his fear miring him in place. Maybe it was an unconscious drooling, licking-away at his chops, and craving fresh meat, sustenance. Hard to say for at that moment Luthecaw was not exactly himself. Every sense in his being told him to move away, to let the bear be. Try as he might, he couldn't. That elk, freshly killed, was beckoning, tantalizing his senses, daring him to fetch her up... skin and spit, roast and feast upon. He could smell the fresh, sticky blood, literally taste its flesh and with all that juicy fat bear meat waiting to be savored was just too tempting for this hungry Shawnee to let go.

Nervously, he looked down upon his long-rifle; his sole defense and meat-getter. For once he saw and felt, sweat moisten the palms of his hands. He had never known such a wont of cool or calm. Shawnee were raised to be steady, stoic, without fear. Until this very moment, he had known no other way.

He was an excellent shot; at least that is what he had always told hisself. Now, possibly, with his life riding on such doubt, he was not so sure. There was a vast difference between killing an elk or a defenseless deer to facing-down seven hundred pounds of brutish nightmare. One shot, one well-placed lead ball would have to do. Could he do it? Would it do it? It was a hell of a risk for a man to take when he need not take one.

Luthecaw wet his lips for the umpteenth time. Again, he thought of lean elk steaks and deliciously greasy bear roasting meat. Hot savory juices dripping on the embers, sizzling, crackling, all conspiring to bedevil the senses. He swore he could almost smell the smoke and aroma wafting from the fort's cooking fires. He closed his eyes for the briefest of moments and then…

The Shawnee took careful aim, sighting down the long barrel. The beast was too close, too big and too easy a target. Luthecaw knew he couldn't miss. Then he squeezed, ever so carefully.

The stillness of the narrow game trail suddenly exploded with the thunderclap of blackpowder ignited, instantly enveloping the riparian path in a dark gray cloud and the noxious reek of burnt gunpowder.

When the air finally began to clear… Luthecaw couldn't believe his eyes. He knew he had hit him… smack dab in the giant's heart. There was no doubt in his mind. By rights that lead ball should've kilt that grizz right then and there and blown the bear's backsides to smithereens.

He was still standing. What's more, ol' Ephraim was mighty upset. All Luthecaw's musket ball had served to do was to infuriate the hell out of the giant bear, temporarily putting off his dinner… until he dealt with this strange, two-legged intruder in the only way he knew how.

The report from Luthecaw's lone shot came from deep within the red willow thickets, soon followed by a distinct, rumbling roar, one all too familiar to my memory. And then he screamed… and Shawnee warriors don't scream, unless…

"Grizz!" I swore.

I was not the only one to hear the ruckus. We all heard it, all five of us converging in a rush on the narrow clearing nigh on simultaneously. Just as simultaneously, we all froze in our tracks. By now the men were inured to death and the dangers that waited just outside the perimeter of our fort, expecting the worst, yet totally unprepared for what our eyes now beheld. That bear was a giant, all right. Big and bad, as immense a beast as I have ever seen. Yet, the sight of the bear and poor Luthecaw was almost comical if not so dire. The grizz stood there in all his eminence, holding the injun by the nape of his neck in his powerful jaws, shaking him like a rag doll. All the while poor Luthecaw dangled helplessly, his moccasins not even coming close to touching the ground.

Ol' Ephraim glared away, his narrow, squinty, beady yellow eyes, flickering back and forth, alternately, eyeing the five of us, anger, fear and hatred boiling within.

No one was making a move. It was a standoff with one scared, helpless injun's life on the line. Poor Luthecaw! That big brown bear had him firmly in his jaws, canines digging deeply into his thick woolen capote. And luckily for him, his capote had bunched up about the back of his neck in thick folds, temporarily saving his hide from a fate every bit as bad as momma elk's had been but moments before.

"What are we gonna do?" Tom James, speaking out the side of his mouth, wore a look on his face every bit as worrisome as Luthecaw's.

"Just keep a bead on that bear's skull," I said, adding. "What do you think, George?"

I could see Drouillard out of the corner of my eye. His expression was as blank as ever. George held his aim steady. I knew he was calculating the odds, waiting for the bear to give him a good shot.

"Keep 'em in yer sights'… bar won't stand thar long," he said rather coolly, not for an instant taking his eye off the bear or his friend.

Luthecaw, gasping for breath, was anything but cool. "Shoot, shoot," he implored. Near-panicked, his voice was losing strength.

The bear shook his massive head, immediately silencing our Indian friend. Looking back and forth, eying, alternately, the five of us and his avenues of escape, the beast left no doubt he was fixing to bolt… taking the Shawnee with him. The time to act was running out.

"Keep your mouth shut, Lu," George ordered, his tone steady, unchanging as ever. Little cracked his veneer, even his friend's dire plight.

"Call it, George," I said.

Sweat trickled even amidst the coolness of the shaded willow brakes. In unison, as if on silent command, we all took aim. The wait, the pressure, the effort challenged our patience and our strength. The bear continued to eye each one of us warily. His eyes darting back and forth ranging from man to man. He seemed to counter our every move, almost human-like, as if able to read our minds, divine our intent. Finally…

The bear was fidgeting. "Watch 'em, he's gonna make his move," warned James.

"Lu," said George calmly. "Play possum."

The Shawnee went limp, sagging lifelessly in the bear's jaws.

Suddenly, the bear stood still. The whole trail was still. Nothing stirred… except almost imperceptibly one man's trigger finger.

"I'm shootin' first," said George under his breath. "Pick yer spots, 'n fire away." His rifle leapt, blowing a hole in the side of the beast's thick neck, severing the jugular as neat as slicing taut twine with a honed blade. The bear jerked, I squeezed, sending my shot right into his massive skull, exploding his left eye socket and penetrating right into his dazed, confused, addled brain. His jaws went slack, releasing his hapless victim to drop to the ground below.

Instantly, the others squeezed off their shots to wreak their own swath of leaden havoc.

"Reload!" I shouted. Five shots never seemed to be enough to douse a grizzly's lights.

The bear swayed like aspens in a storm, wavering on unsteady legs, all the while reeling in pain and shock, confusion and disbelief. What was keeping him up I could not say. Finally, his massive underpinnings gave way, the giant crumpling to the ground. He lay there in a heap, his last few breaths laboring to an almost imperceptable puff, his life fading away before our waiting eyes.

We eyed the dying beast with a healthy amount of respect. As long as he still breathed and his heart still beat, we would give him his due from a safe distance.

"Get 'em off me. Get 'em off me. He's crushin'…" A hoarse, muffled scream, barely audible seemed to emanate from deep within the bear's bowels.

Luthecaw, we forgot poor Luthecaw. Yet, our friend was not deep within, but underneath, pinned by a great weight, imploring our help. We rushed forward and with a heave-ho rolled the great dead weight off, freeing our friend from certain suffocation.

Luthecaw, jackrabbited to his feet as if shot from a cannon. Gasping for air, his flattened face an odd collage of ground-in dirt and fur, sweat and blood. He was besides himself, touching and feeling, pinching every part of his squashed frame.

"Sacre moste, l'est crazee monte. Damn that bear, he dang near mashed me to death."

More grizzly encounters followed as hunters ranged the headwaters in search of fresh meat but even the great bear's presence soon wore thin. By mid May we were hungry again. Something or someone had driven the game out of the valley, I was certain of it. Even the buffalo herds from beyond the *pishkun* had vanished… at least from our valley view below.

Remember the lesson of the skunk, the two-legged kind? When relying on proven instincts, one does not necessarily have to see, smell or hear… to sense an offending presence. I was getting that old itch again… as troublesome as mange on a cur dog. The more I scratched, the more it bothered me. There was no injun sign to put my finger on yet I knew we were not alone. Trouble was how to explain it to the likes of Menard and Henry, pragmatic, sensible men who needed to see, smell or hear to believe. Yet, the wilderness and the red man never seem to cater to the white man's ways. Warriors do not stand in ranks like fields of wheat awaiting harvest. Deceit and treachery, guile and a well-laid ambush were more to their liking. I had little choice, time could well be running out… give it to them, straight up and hope they listen.

It was late in the day, the sun gradually disappearing behind the western mountains, and darkness fell. Near the center of the stockade, a crackling-hot fire blazed away, drawing-in lonely men to its warmth and light, and friendly talk. Yet, there was little conversation this particular evening, only quietude, as men milled about idly, others sat nearby with faraway looks, absentmindedly feeding wood chips to the flames, all the while lost in their own thoughts.

"At least the fires gettin' fed," a grizzled trapper remarked with more than a little acrimony. His voice was low as if only meant for him to hear; yet, few missed his remarks or intent.

The mood remained somber, the men hungry and listless, few if any paying any mind to George Drouillard and his two constant companions, Luthecaw and Pla-co-ta, as they entered the gate and quietly headed towards the corral.

I saw them entering the Fort, wondering, briefly, where they had been and what they had been up to. Certainly, they were not shouldering any freshly killed game. Maybe they had found what I had found. Hmmph! Good, the Colonel will have to listen to Drouillard. I could use a little backing up, I thought as I turned to Pierre Menard.

"Colonel," I said aloud for I wanted everyone to hear, "we got company the way I read it. Felt 'em around for days."

"What?" demanded a startled, ever-defiant Andrew Henry, butting in before Menard had a chance to chew on what I said.

I kept looking to Menard, ignoring the belligerent Major. "Injuns. Blackfeet of some kind, I reckon probably Piegans if I had to bet on it. They seem to roost here more than any other tribe."

"Felt 'em? Felt 'em? What kinda bullshit are you feedin' us? How come the Shawnee ain't felt 'em … or Drouillard?"

I knew Henry would not get it, especially coming from me. We never did hit it off. Mattered not as far as I was concerned, I was not hired to please him, just to get it right.

"C'mon, Colter. You'll have to do better than that. We need more than just a little mystic scaredy talk. Or er yee just gettin' maybe a might too edgy to handle the job?"

Henry was playing to the company, cocksure of himself. Play your game all you want I told myself, but I am not buying into it, with lives at stake. I took a deep breath before proceeding and then looked him straight in the eye…

"Maybe, I am. Maybe, I ain't. Believe what you want, Major. Makes no difference to me. Personally, I don't give a goddamn what you think. Lisa pays my freight, not you. You want to go get yourself killed, go ahead. Hope no one else pays the price for your foolishness. As for the Blackfeet, I'm tellin' you straight. Game's gone, driven out of the valley days ago. Someone's doin' it. That's good enough for me."

"Aw, bullshit. It means nuthin', I tell you."

Menard raised his hand. The stockade was suddenly quiet as if waiting to see whose side the Colonel would take. I was not so sure right then.

"Gentlemen, please. This is getting us nowhere. I agree; we must be prudent, and listen to Mssr. Colter's considerable counsel. We do not want to lose another man.

"John, I trust your judgment. But, how can you be so sure?"

How can I be so sure? Will you listen to the two of them; they can't even find their own britches without a compass and a sextant. All right, here I go, pissing-in-the-wind again for the umpteenth time. "I…"

"Save yer breath, Colter." A terse Drouillard interrupted as he strode forward from the back of the crowd to stand between the two company officers. "Squaw talk. Yer all actin' like a bunch of 'sheep herdin'' squaws… scared of yer own shadows."

He spat on the ground with all the scorn he could muster. He was not finished.

"To hell with the Blackfeet, I say. While y'all been frettin' yer yaps, we've been settin' our traps, right up the Jeff' fork less than an hour's walk away…

"Show 'em!" he barked, turning to his two Shawnee companions.

Pla-co-ta and Luthecaw stepped forward, a pile of freshly scraped beaver pelts cradled in their arms. George then added his *piece de resistance*, emptying the contents of a painted Crow *parfleche*, a half-dozen or more, plump beaver tails falling to the ground.

"Hungry, boys? There's more of that where they come from, a lot more."

Now that caused a stir. Andrew Henry suddenly was wearing a wide smirk, nodding approval. Even Menard was pleased, forgetting our sober conversation of just a moment before. The men were on their feet, gawking in near disbelief, looking back and forth to one another, their eyes greedily devouring Drouillard's catch.

As for the doubting Henry, he was spreading his feathers like a peacock. "Felt 'em? Hah! This is feelin' 'em," roared the Major, slapping his thigh.

"What about them injuns Colter smelt?" asked a confused Billy Bryant in all earnest.

"Yeah, what about 'em?" piped in James, a stern look on his face.

"What injuns? There ain't no injuns. Otherwise, I would have been the one smellin' 'em," George fired back at Bryant and James, the look on his face, the tone of his voice full of contempt.

The boys were more than a little taken aback. They had heard fewer than a dozen words out of Drouillard since leaving Manuel's Fort. Most of the men gave him plenty of distance... his reputation and fame, his sullen, surly disposition commanding respect if not outright awe. George was a man who spoke sparingly; even so, it did little to mask his disdain for nearly all things white. The breed in him was coming out, the half Shawnee nearly always preferring the Indian way of things. He moved about the red man and the wilderness easier than any man that I had ever seen... breed, white, red or otherwise. Maybe, in circumspect, a might too easy for his own good.

"Fuck these Blackfeet... I'm too much an injun to be caught by any injun... Piegan, redhided skunk or otherwise."

Drouillard grabbed several skins from Pla-co-ta and held them up for all to see.

"You came to trap beaver, not waste time hunkered down behind log walls shittin' your britches," George replied rather drolly. "Stay if you want or tag along. Makes no difference to me. We're headin' out come mornin'... with you or without you."

"Well, you heard the man, get crackin'," roared a delighted Andrew Henry.

Drouillard certainly was convincing... to some. He had saved Menard and Henry from making a difficult decision, when time had just about run out. Right then, I felt like all but the forgotten man, a pariah. Outside of Billy and Tom, no one wanted to hear what I had to say. Not after fresh meat and prime pelts were layed out before them.

I had said my piece, told them straight from the way I saw it. What else could I do? Just tag along, set my traps and see how the venture played out.

By first light, George and the Shawnee had cleared the gate, already heading west for the Jefferson fork. I watched them for a half a mile as they crossed the "prickly pear" plains between the Fort and the river treeline, until they entered the woods, disappearing in the forest shade. Lingering unconvinced, I listened far longer than I needed to. Yet, there was only silence. Humph! I blew a sigh of relief, shaking my head. Damn that George. Listen to yourself. Let it go, you and him have been at it since Wood Island. Admit it, you resent being shownup in front of the company, especially that son of bitch Henry. Do not begrudge the man his due, Cap'n Meriwether always set store by the "sign talker." You know it. Yeah, I know it.

There was something in the way he carried himself that morning, sitting atop that little injun pony, not a care in the world, master of the wilderness and all its denizens. There was quite a different feel in the Fort that morning,

George had seen to that. Men were smiling for the first time in weeks, a little roasted beavertail the night before whetting their appetites for more. Daybreak did not disappoint; it had all the makings for a fine day of trapping. The sun peeked over the eastern mountains, bright and warm, revealing clear blue skies, a hint of a breeze from out of the west gently blowing our way.

We lit out a short while later, soon reaching the woods and entering a shaded world of cottonwoods and willow, alder and birch. There is something reassuring about a warm spring day, a gentle morning wind swaying the tops of the forest giants, an undulating rhythm, almost entrancing, settling a man right down, putting his mind at ease.

We were not entirely alone. Chick-a-dees and cedar-waxwings flitted about busy as beavers in their own right. Redwing-blackbirds and bluebirds, gold finches and swallows; the river woods were suddenly alive with flying, darting creatures. A pair of long-legged sandhill cranes pecked away out on the plains, nearby. An occasional silent red-tail hawk or osprey eying us discreetly from above. Magpies and crows as curious about our doings as I was about theirs. I watched them all, especially their movements.

"Pay attention, boys," I called out. "Watch the woods. No need bein' stupid about this."

I moved forward, taking the point. Hanging right behind me was Billy Bryant, all ears and eyes and nose, developing an "itch" of his own. Inwardly, I smiled. The kid had come a long way since Cheek's campsite.

"Nice day," said Mike Immell joining me.

"Yep," I said, smiling. "Certainly is."

"George sure had a lot to say last night."

"Yep, he did," I said, turning to face him. "Ya got somethin' stuck in your craw?" Instantly, I regretted my tone.

"Yeah, I do," he said matter of factly. "That Drouillard's either the luckiest man in the world… or hell-bent on gettin' kilt."

I shrugged. "Mebbe." And then I asked, "If so, Mike, why'd ya come along?"

He waited for a moment, taking his time.

"Like I said, that was an interestin' lil talk last night. Nobody wantin' to believe you and all. Most folks never like to face up to trouble or the truth. And I'd say Major Henry, especially. I know his kind, as pig-headed as they come. He's gonna git somebody kilt one of these days. His type never sees the storm a comin'. Just bull right in, and the hell with everybody else. Stupid, just plain stupid! That George, though, he must have nine lives. Question is… how many has he already used up? I believed ya last night, even if them other fools didn't. You're right, in fact you've been right from the very start. Them injuns are here, all right. I can feel 'em, just like you said. The difference is…

this time I'm waitin' fer 'em. When they come, they're gonna pay."

"Way to be," I nodded. "Keep yer eyes open."

"Yep. Will do," Mike replied as he walked off to join his good friend Francois Valle.

It's strange, I thought, how some men can think so much alike... while others never seem to get it right. Maybe I wasn't a pariah after all.

A few minutes later Billy finally broke his silence. "You like him, don't ya?"

"Mike? Yep, sure do. He's a good man."

"Good. If anything happens to you... I'm stickin' by him," Billy said.

"Billy Bryant, I do believe you're growin' up," I chuckled. The kid was learning, indeed.

We proceeded at a good, arm-swinging, leg-stretching clip, lengthening our strides, the walk, the woods, the fresh air away from the confines of our fort, adding buoyancy to our step, lifting our spirits, and our prospects. We followed George and the Shawnees as their trail threaded their way through the cottonwoods that bordered the river.

The morning was passing quickly. Change, though, was in the air. You could feel it coming on, apparently it was in a hurry. The warmth of the early morning sun suddenly took a decided drop. Bad weather surged forward led by strong winds; tree crashing winds the vanguard of an imposing array of natural forces, blowing in from the west, barely impeded. The sun had all but disappeared, the sky increasingly grayer, masses of roiling clouds sweeping forward, darker, blacker. Angry winds now howled from seemingly every corner of the compass, drowning out all other ambient sounds. The ruckus and din grew louder, stronger, unabated, until the full fury of the storm unleashed its sodden load directly upon us.

Men swore. Others remained as stoic as the stoney mountains of the Tobacco Roots. Yet, no one looked back to the comfort of the Fort. No one said, "quit." One determined thought pervaded our ranks... George was still ahead of us. The storm wouldn't stop that man. And after taking his guff and challenge, nobody was about to turn tail in the face of a little discomfort.

All that was about to change.

"What the hell..." Suddenly, I was confronted with a most gruesome sight, one all too familiar in years past, stopping me dead in my tracks. "God, no," was all I could manage to say.

The two Shawnee... Pla-co-ta, my scouting companion and Luthecaw, so recently saved from the massive jaws of grizzly death... lay prostrated on the forest floor, their bodies pincushioned, riddled with arrows. The woods lay strangely quiet, the roar of the storm but minutes before all but forgotten. What unnatural devilry was this, nature and man conspiring murder.

I raised my arm, signaling Billy behind me and alerting the others. Billy had already stopped, simultaneously seeing the two Shawnee. Quickly, I took to one knee, bringing my rifle to bear, while I scanned the woods. Biding my time, I resisted the urge to run to our two fallen companions.

"Watch it, Billy. Keep yer eyes peeled."

Immell and Valle were suddenly by my side. Tom James, Dougherty and Brown came up fast. Others followed closely behind, rifles at the ready, wary eyes scanning the woods, every man's heart pounding at a furious pace. We held our collective breaths, watched and waited.

"Steady, boys, I'm goin' in."

Reaching their bodies, I knelt on one knee and touched each corpse, instantly verifying what I already knew. I had seen death too often in this valley to hope for anything else. They were both gone, by the looks of their many telling wounds probably never knowing what hit them. Not even Luthecaw's heavy woolen capote could have saved him this time. And Placo-ta... I refused to believe that any man alive could have injunned-up on my little Shawnee friend and done him this way. Yet, I had to, his death mask was staring me in the face. A wave of coldness raced down my spine, realization warning that we were up against a decidedly crafty bunch.

The attackers had been quick, quiet, deadly, each Shawnee's torso peppered with stone-headed arrows like human porcupines... like Johnny. Yet, something was missing; a tangible something that should have been missing was not. Neither Shawnee was mutilated; they both still had their scalp... and their dignity. Yet, that is where the scene began to stink. No self-respecting Blackfeet would leave such a valuable trophy behind. Enemy scalps were badges of honor, proof of their vaunted *namachkani*. Unless...

I looked about, searching the clearing, finding little sign other than a profusion of moccasins tracks heading west. Then I remembered Drouillard. How in the hell could I forget George? Come on, John, think, stow the cobwebs. Where is George? Wait, he was on horseback. Maybe he had separated from the two, gone on ahead to scout things out. Shit, that is it, they were expecting three and only found two.

Instantly, I was up and off. My heart pounded, pleading. Not George! Not George! You red devils ain't gettin' him, not now, not this time. Go! Go! Go! I exhorted myself. Thick forest giants appeared in my path, blocking my way, branches, twigs, brush ripped away at me, scratching my face, pulling, clinging, yanking on my hunting shirt, grabbing at my long rifle. Nothing could stop me. I was oblivious to it all. It was Colter's run all over again...

I didn't have far to run. Bursting upon yet another forest clearing, not altogether far from where Johnny got his, I found George... and his horse. The great scout, the great Drouillard lay riddled with arrows... and worse

His executioners had exacted from him just like they had from poor Johnny Potts, every bit as cruelly, as barbarously, as savagely and inhumanely as they could.

Tears began to well as I gathered-up his strewn remains and placed them side by side as reverently as I could. I knelt down beside what was once a proud, honored man, taking a few quiet moments in repose. My mind was awash in a hundred, in a thousand vivid memories of Drouillard and Johnny Potts, of ol' Toby and Pete Wiser, of the Captains, Sacajawea, lil Pomp and all the men. All our trials, the hard days, the bitter days, the good days… days best forgotten and days well remembered, all coming down to this. God giveth and God taketh. I reached over and snapped midshaft one of the arrows piercing George's chest. I stared at it for the longest of moments, hatred welling within me anew.

I did not notice the others hurried approach, until I felt a hand upon my shoulder. It was Immell's massive paw. "Come on, John," he said softly.

"George put up a helluva fight," I said, near-choking. Standing, I looked about, surveying the scene of Drouillard's last stand. "Got at least three of 'em, judging by these blood trails. They're runnin' fast, awright. Mock-er-sinn tracks goin' every which way. He scared the shit out of 'em, by God. George scared the livin' shit outta 'em."

"Look at this, willya," Big Mike was pointing to a single moccasin track, all the while placing his own substantial boot entirely inside the imprint. "This'n's a big buck, fer sure. I've never seen the like, six-six, if an inch."

I stared along with the others at that same moccasin track for a moment mesmerized by its sheer size and imprint. Humph! I thought to myself, something mighty peculiar about that track. What is it? For the life of me, though, I could not put my finger on it.

"Filthy murderers."

I glanced over to see a red-eyed Billy Bryant staring at the remains. Tears rolled, unchecked, down a face gone pale white. The grip on his rifle so firm you could almost hear its wooden stock groaning under the pressure. His whole being trembled, yet his youthful voice was completely under control. "They got to pay for this."

"Aye," seconded Immell; his attention still glued to the large, imposing moccasin track. "This one's mine. Do y'all hear me, the big un's mine?" Immell roared. "The filthy beggars won't get away with this, not a second time, by God."

Tired, scared, hungry men had reached their limit. George's mutilation was the last straw and Billy's words became the rallying cry… they got to pay for this. I looked at each and every one of them nothing on God's green earth could restrain them now.

"Enough talk! We're goin' after 'em," I barked in no mood for further delay. "Sing out if you see anything… and keep your eyes peeled for tricks."

My mind lay on a single, determined track… it was reckoning time. I took off running, the rest of the boys right on my tail, picking up the scent, following the blood trails, the hurried flight. No hesitation, no fear, caution bedamned… a pack of white, two-legged wolves on the chase, thirsting for blood… Piegan blood. This was it, I told myself, my last chance, my only chance… our only chance. Toby's, Johnny's and George's. Vengeance was mine, sayeth the Lord, an eye for an eye. Do unto others afore they do to you.

"They ain't tryin' to hide their trail," I yelled back over my shoulder, knowing the injuns were now running for their lives. "They're makin' for the river. C'mon, faster," I exhorted.

"Were with ya, John," Immell yelled. "Keep on 'em."

Here… a half a moccasin print, there, another drop of blood. A snapped twig, a swatch of matted hair, a bloodstained leaf. Limp bodies dragged along, leaving a trail on the forest floor even a baby could follow. They were slowing, they must be. Hate drove me. I could almost see the painted red devils up ahead through the cottonwoods, smell their foul unclean bodies fetid in sweat and sticky blood. Their worthless savage lives oozing away with each avenging swing of my tomahawk as I hacked and hacked and hacked.

Until, bursting upon the Jefferson, their individual tracks disappeared among the slippery stones of the swift running river, gone without a trace. I scanned the far banks, as far as I could see. Up and down the river the men looked, searching, praying… swearing in futility. The white-hot zeal of pursuit and retribution was going to go unfulfilled. Soon even the most ardent was resigned to it. We were just too slow, too late, no matter how hard we tried, no matter how much we wanted otherwise. They had too much of a lead, too well thought out an ambush.

"Damn this river," I swore, realizing where I now stood. "How much can a man take?" I was screaming aloud, the irony almost too much to bear. This was the very shore where Johnny had met his fate that sad, sad day. This is the place where the *spoo-pi* was born, where Kootenae Appe swore eternal revenge upon the wily *napikwan*. My head bent forward, staring down at the gravelly beach. I could almost hear the rippling waters of the Jefferson laughing. They are mocking me, I thought, just as they mocked Johnny.

Big Mike came up alongside me. I could hear his heavy breathing, even over the din of my thoughts.

"I make about eight of 'em unscathed, judgin' by their tracks. No more than a dozen of 'em were in on the ambush, countin' the wounded they carried away. They must've known how close we were, cuz they sure didn't waste any time lightin' a shuck."

"Yep, that's about the way I see it," I said, staring off to the far side of the Jefferson.

"Funny thing," Mike went on. "I can't shake the feelin' that these injuns were waitin' for George and his Shawnee all along. Probably watched 'em the last couple of days when they wuz closer to the Fort. Waited fer them today to git far enough out so's we couldn't mount a rescue in time. George messed 'em up, though. They didn't count on the man's sand.

"One more thing, they're a different pack of savages then those Gros Ventres we chased."

I turned to Mike, holding up the snapped arrow I had taken from George's body.

"Your right, they're not, they're Piegan. I've seen enough of 'em to know, thousands of em' to be sure. Get a good look... the shaft is sarvis berry, the sinew wrappin', the markin's under the featherin'... these painted stripes, are Piegan enough to suit me."

"Well, what do ya think?" Mike asked somewhat nervously.

"What do I think? I think word travels fast. I think these here Piegans were the first to hear about us being in the Forks and got down here real fast-like. There's somethin' about this here band, but I just can't put my finger on it right yet. They won't go far, though. They'll wait for the rest of their people to get the word and come arunnin'. Then we'll be in trouble, big trouble. It's only a matter of time... that's what I think."

"Damn!" was all that big Mike could say.

"C'mon," I said, "let's gather up George's and the Shawnees' remains and head back towards the Fort. We'll bury 'em on the way. And then we'll sit down tonight and think this thing out."

"Preacher, do ya want to say a couple of words?" I asked the portly Pelton, as I stepped back from the freshly covered-over gravesite.

We found George and his Shawnee a quiet, peaceful clearing by the river where they could lie together for the rest of eternity. Alas, Drouillard didn't get his cairn, just like Johnny hadn't got his. Not with injuns about, ready to defile their remains the moment we turned our backs. At least we could honor them with some decent words and a moment of respect.

"Almighty Father, look down upon these men, your servants ..." the preacher began.

As Pelton droned on in his own inimitable way, I quietly paid my own homage, eulogizing in my mind George and Luthecaw and Pla-co-ta, and the two dear friends that I had been unable to ... two years before. Maybe one day someone will carve their names in stone.

It was a somber walk back to the Fort. Yet, somehow we were not alone in our grief. The constant swirling winds that forever crisscross this valley seemed to allow a brief respite. The swaying, undulating grasses of the "prickly pear" plains lay perfectly still as if painted on a broad canvas. Even the boiling, turbulent river seemed somehow mute, placid as if in some small measure nature itself was respecting our loss.

Yet, there was no apparent change on the face of the land. The passing of men meant nothing to other living creatures. The birds still chirped, wild flowers bloomed, game would return ... and life in the valley went on. And the twisting, swirling, churning river could never really be quieted. I was not oblivious to it at all. On the contrary the foul deeds wrought here in this valley by the cruelty of the red man was part and parcel of life in the wilderness... and death, too. For life here was an eternal struggle. Only death brought real peace.

The silence inside the Fort that night could be heard and felt in every man's heart and mind and soul. While many struggled with the wont of what next to do or say or where to go, I held no such uncertainty. I vacillated not. I had made my vow a long time before. And now it was time to keep it. Because, at last, God Almighty at last, I had conquered my ownself, my overpowering will to succeed, to acknowledge at least one success before I left this country forever and headed east to civilization and a new life. I had defeated the curse of the Three Forks at least enough to satisfy my own mind. The battle of the *Ahkoto waktai sakum*, the many-come-together, had denied me bringing in the friendly western tribes and some sense of accomplishment. The Shoshones, Flatheads and Nez Perce would never trade at Manuel's Fort. The slaying of so many proud Salish warriors and one old Snake man so dear to my memory was a loss I would never overcome. The valley had mocked me and Johnny and our attempts to reap its bounty in beaver that we had dared so much and worked so hard for, taking my partner's pitiful remains to its womb as an unearthly compost and driving me away a near-whipped, beaten man. It had denied me in my most insane desire to re-acquire my precious traps and cached skins and any semblance of self-respect. I had fled, demoralized, unable to chart my own life's trail. But I came back. I challenged that curse one more time. This time I won, at least to my satisfaction. I led Henry and Menard and their men to the valley of the headwaters of the Missouri. That is all I hired on to do. It seemed so simple, yet knowing the land and its inhabitants, nigh on impossible. Now, I could live with that. I could even reconcile the deaths of George Drouillard and his Shawnee and Cheek and Ayers and Hull and Fleehart and Rucker, and those unfortunates yet to fall. They were Menard, Henry and the Company's curse. They would have to live with that.

This time this place was not going to turn into another Colter's run. I wasn't running away at all, I was going home on my own terms. John Colter's mind was irrevocably made up... finally and irretrievably. It only awaited the words to leave my lips and the morrow to see it come to pass.

The whole command was there that night, gathered around inside the confines of our stockade, sitting alone or in groups of twos and threes, all brooding, all awaiting for what... I couldn't say. Though I shared their despair I no longer shared their uncertainty. I had been through it too many times before not to sense, to commiserate the depths from which they felt. It had every bit the feel of a dank, dark prison, of men awaiting the chopping block or the hangman's noose. And these were brave men... determined, tough, hardened men. But, of all they had sought to accomplish only tragedy hadn't eluded them.

"What're ya gonna do, John?"

I heard Billy's familiar voice, whispering softly in my ear.

I looked over at the kid. He sat quietly waiting, returning my stare directly. He was ready to go, and yet, he was just as equally prepared to stay. He was leaving it up to me. And that me said that I wasn't about to lose this kid like I did Johnny Potts.

Billy had seasoned these past few weeks like a fine oaken plank and in so doing became a great deal wiser, stronger, more savvy to the follies of the wilderness and his fellow man. We had just seen it in him by the banks of the Jefferson. The boy from Philadelphia had found himself, realizing at last that he had only himself to prove a thing to. And he had done that. The trapper's life was not for him. It had been a hell of an adventure; one that he now prepared to put behind him.

I arose and stood before our two leaders, Menard and Henry, and the rest of the men. I suppose I had a lot to say. I mean, I'd just spent the better part of the last seven years of my life in the West. I'd done more than most men ever even contemplated, seen more things than I cared to remember, lived through more tragedy than any man should ever have to endure.

And my name ... my name was known from the Tobacco Roots to Monticello. Some of my peers looked up to me. Rightly or wrongly ... some thought I was crazy, a man to be avoided, even ridiculed from afar. Some thought I was the biggest liar in the West. And some like Captain William Clark and even Manuel Lisa knew better. When I had something to say, they had listened.

Regardless of how history chooses to see me, I am once and forever a man of my word. Whether rich or penniless, scared stiff or atop of the world, in the end my word is all that is really sacred to me. I set store by it. I lived my life by it. And I will go to my grave content that I had stood by it.

"Oh, hell," I announced, dispensing any attempt at formality, "come mornin' time, I'm leavin'. And anybody that wants to go along is welcome to come."

The Fort's whole complement looked at me like they couldn't believe their ears. Many mouths were agape, yet no one uttered a word. The Colonel was stunned. He started to stand up, wanting to say something, anything. And Andy Henry desperately wanted to object, as was his way.

"Save your breath, Pierre. A deal's a deal. I've done what Manuel hired me to do. I led y'all here like I said I would. Now it's your turn in the barrel. My mind's made up. Long ago I swore to Almighty God… if he'd give me just one more chance… I'd leave this place for good. Well, it's time to go. I'm keepin' my bargain with ol' Jehovah, once and for all time."

"I'm goin' with John," Billy stood up and spoke. There wasn't an ounce of hesitation in his voice. He'd never been clearer or more determined in all of his young life.

Even big Mike nodded approvingly, smiling at the kid. He too had realized how much Billy had grown in these few short weeks. Mike Immell was a man I was going to miss. In fact there were a lot of men here I was going to miss.

"Count me in," said the blacksmith John T. Thrush. "It's the first sensible thing I've heard since leavin' St. Louie."

It was a long, quiet night, that last night in the Fort. Few slept, talk rambling on into the wee hours of the morning. Billy and J. T. packed their belongings and said their goodbyes. Some of the men commiserated of their homes and families, James and Dougherty in particular. No one, though, cared to mention the Blackfeet… we had already done enough of that. Besides, they weren't going anywhere. Even Menard and Henry were reconciled to that dire fact.

As we were preparing to leave Pierre Menard caught up with me, grabbing my arm and pulling me off to the side away from any prying ears.

"John," he spoke in a near whisper. He was obviously troubled. "I have personal letters for my wife, Nell. I would be much obliged if you would see that she gets them. She will be worried. I, I don't know if I will ever…"

He stopped mid-sentence, unable to finish his thought. The future as he chose to see it was apparently all too painful and gloomy.

"I understand, Colonel," I said. "Don't fret, I'll see to it myself." And then I added, hoping to reassure the man, "Buck up, Pierre, y'all will be home in no time."

"Merci, my friend, merci! Au revoir." He hurried off, the desperation, the strain in his face, his voice was plainly evident. The burden of command, the specter of failure, of death was more than he had bargained for. And how he must have missed the comfort of his home, his loving wife. Only his manly pride and a strong sense of duty kept him from calling the venture a failure and throwing-in with us right then and there.

Tom James, Jack Dougherty, Weir and Robbie Brown were all waiting for us at the gate. Immell and Valle were standing off to the side, each with a pleasant smile and a friendly nod.

Dougherty stepped up. "Colter, boys… we want y'all to know we all think yer doin' the right thing."

"Thanks, Jack," said Billy. "Y'all can come, too. Nothin's holdin' ya here."

"Hell, Billy," piped in Brown, "we won't be far behind ya if this here gloom keeps up. Pretty soon the injuns will own all our traps and ponies and be bangin' on the gates, demandin' them too."

We all had a good chuckle. Not one of us wanted to part company, at least not this way, not after all we had been through together.

"John, ya got any plans? I mean, where are ya goin' to go? What are ya goin' to do when you get back home?" asked Tom, quite sincerely. "I sure am goin' to miss ya."

Tom had left a good taste in my mouth from the first day we met and nothing in between had changed my mind. He was a stand up sort of fella, straightforward, the kind of man to ride the river and the Dalles with. I, too, hated parting with his kind. As far as I was concerned my adventurous days were close to an end and his were only beginning. Who knows, maybe one day the two of us would sit on a porch, share a jug and wile away many an afternoon in tall tales and remembrances. I would like that.

I smiled … for once I was leaving the Forks without my tail between my legs. I wasn't ashamed to admit it. It was a good feeling.

"St. Louie…" I said, almost shouting to the sky. "Gonna look up Cap'n Clark and make my final report. I hear tell thars a good piece of bottomland and a sackful of government gold waitin' for me to collect back yonder in civilization. And God willing, a good lookin' flaxen-haired young gal to settle me down and make a farmer outta me. Maybe even give me a mess of brats to raise and take care of me when I can no longer fend for myself."

And then I added, "Hell, Tommy, maybe one of these days I'll form my own outfit and be right back trappin' the Yellowstone in company with Colter and Sons. Now that's a wild thought, ain't it?" I chuckled aloud, everyone did.

We shook hands, all the way around. There were smiles on most faces and they were genuine, yet forced. A gloomy pall had descended over the entire command and no one was shaking it. We three were trying to by leaving, but our success was by no means a sure bet. It was risky at best going it nearly alone. I held no delusions, knowing the Blackfeet as I did. And all those we were leaving behind, well… their future boded more of the same I suspected. But we were all determined to make the best of our send off and farewells. We had become closer, like brothers, the ordeals, the hard scrabble existence and the tragedy of those we had lost had seen to that. Desperate situations have a way of bringing men together, allowing them to find their truer selves. And for once, trapping beaver, making fortunes didn't have the same ring to it as it had just weeks before. Life was what was really important and true friendship a close second.

"Mind yer hair, boys," said Mike Immell stepping forward and extending a big mitt, "and listen to that ol' curly wolf, Colter."

"Never you mind about my hair, big Mike," said Billy, clasping both hands tightly atop his head. "Ain't no red-hided injun touchin' these golden locks."

"Au revoir, John Colter," Valle smiled and saluted. "Adieu, mon compagnon, mon ami."

"See ya, boys," I said, giving big Mike and the rest of the boys an easy salute.

"See ya," said Tom and Jack, each long-faced and forlorn, watching us depart.

"C'mon, boys, let's vamoose, before the sun catches our sorry asses leavin' the valley."

That was all there was to it. We lit out from the Fort, forded the Madison for the last time and headed east for the pass and the Yellowstone. The smell of springtime was in the air, a good, clean, fresh smell, one that sang of new life and rebirth.

Funny thing, though, as we were leaving the Forks I began to get that ol' itch again, those danged hackles bristling just below the surface of my neck. Now, what is this, I asked, some kind of danged trick messing with my mind? Come on, John, you are worse than an old lady. If it is convincing you need, don't bother. You're getting out of here and that's all there is to it. No need scaring the boys, they have enough to worry about without you piling on some more. Keep it to yourself. Hellfire and brimstone, they wouldn't understand, anyway.

Blackfeet country had a way of doing that to me. Trust your instincts and your rifle and little else. Remember? Yeah, I do. Well, then, prove it. Put your poke where your mouth is. Don't talk it, do it. Just because you are quitting the Forks is not the time to change habits in the middle of the stream. You know dang well which habits I am talking about, the ones that have kept your scalp on their head. So, get to it. Keep your wits about you. Watch, listen, sniff for sign; an awful lot can happen between here and Manuel's Fort.

There was something else happening to me. Something new to my emotional repertoire. I was concerned. I was always concerned. But, I was also doing a slow boil. I knew not what lay ahead on the trail. Yet, every fiber of my being was coming together, merging, as if preparing for one final set-to with my injun friends, seeing who would have the last laugh, the last word. I had to catch myself, loosen up; otherwise, the tension I was exuding would be a dead give-away. And I didn't want to unduly alarm Bryant or Thrush or alert any other watching eyes.

And my pards … those two never walked easy on the land, not since leaving Manuel's Fort on the Big Horn. So far what they had seen and done had been plenty troublesome to both my traveling companions. Thrush was salty, all right. He'd spent his whole life on the frontier. Death was not new to him, but fighting apparently was. I had watched him like I had watched every man in the company. There wasn't much to go by, but I suspected that he was game, that he would do. I could sense by the way he carried himself that when the fight was brought on he would be a man to stand with. He was a powerfully built man, a blacksmith by trade. And he held his long-rifle like knew how to use it.

Billy was another story entirely. Wet behind the ears and as green to the frontier as the first blades of spring grass, he had had his fill of the Menard/Henry Expedition and Blackfeet and Gros Ventre brutality. Young Billy had all the advantages of growing up in the East, the City of Brotherly Love, Philadelphia to be exact. Except that out here that kind of upbringing was no advantage at all. He was a-might soft to begin with, but the rigors of poling the Missouri and the Yellowstone and the ordeal from Manuel's to the Forks had gone a long way towards hardening him up, phyically and mentally. Seeing death, though, for the first time had rattled the kid enough for him to know that he didn't like it one dang bit. But he was learning fast; picking up the things that might save a fella's life, and just when he needed it the most… in the nick of time.

We walked all that day, retracing our steps to the pass in the Mountains of the Wolf, oft times checking our backsides, scanning the lay of the land ahead with a wary eye. The red man, though, never revealed himself, not that I expected him to. Still, one could hope.

Maybe they missed us; it was pretty near dark when we snuck out of the Fort and skedaddled across the Madison. We'd been quiet, careful, treading like fawns across an open field.. Nothing stirred then; even injuns are averse to shucking a warm blanket on a cold, frosty morning. Maybe our luck would hold after all. Uh huh, just keep thinking that way. Too many maybes, I shook my head, too many to risk our scalps on. Good, you're thinkin' smart, just remember the last time you failed to listen to those little warnin' hairs on the back of your neck. Uh huh!

My mind wandered, though, memories and questions whipping up, battering me like early evening winds from out of the west. What time of the year was it getting to be … late April, early May? Just two years since I came out of the mountains and met up with ol' Toby and Three Eagle to share a meal of chokecherry cakes and revel in the expectation of a good hunt. A lot of murky water has passed under my bridge since that dark day. Good men had died. Dreams squashed like bugs under a heavy boot. Everything hoped and planned for naught. So, what had I learned about this place? The Salish had come to the Forks, peacefully, while we are leaving it behind. They weren't looking for trouble. Neither are we. Yet, trouble sure seemed to find us, no matter how we wished otherwise.. That's what I had learned.

Damn it, I swore, catching myself, shaking off the malaise, the fear, the doubt. It ain't healthy to walk around in a perpetual state of gloom. It clouds your mind, distracts your senses, and unsteadies those very same legs you need to anchor yourself to the ground.

"C'mon, boys, shake a leg, daylight's passin' us by. And keep your eyes peeled."

"Hell, John," cracked Billy, "I can't go any faster. And we ain't had hardly a moments rest since leavin' the Fort."

Thrush burst out laughing… "I thought I was the only one getting' a crick in my neck and worn out dawgs."

We all had a good chuckle. Young Billy and J T had both broken the ice jam of nerves we were all feeling.

I had come to know Billy Bryant well enough by my own reckoning. Still, J T Thrush was somewhat of a stranger to me. And that might not do for the trail ahead. I struck up a conversation to see what wound his clock, where he stood once the set to got going. For the most part, he had been a quiet, reserved man from the first day to the last. He was like many a backwoodsman I had known, calmly taking it all in, saying little, listening, watching, slowly making up his own mind. Sooner or later when he felt he had something to say… he'd let you know. He was a friendly sort, though, always ready with a smile or an agreeable nod, pulling his weight as much as any man in the Company. And what's more he'd shown good sense leaving when he did.

"J T, I heard tell that you were from ol' Limestone… Maysville on the Ohio," I said rather casually as we walked along.

"Born and raised just a hoot 'n holler away," he responded proudly, his head bobbing up and down, a wide-smile quickly spreading across an even wider cherubic mug. The thought of home appeared to strike a pleasing chord with J T.

"How about that? Been there, myself, back in '03. Went there to join the Expedition. Signed on with Meriwether Lewis, himself, right down there on the wide Ohio itself."

It was getting to be an old memory by now, made old by the miles and the wear and tear. Yet, the thought of that day, that wonderfully exciting day, in my mind was as clear now as the cool, clean waters of the Madison.

J T was looking at me, nodding his head. "Big doin's, huh?"

"Yeah, I'll say it was. I still remember that day like it was yesterday… ol' Meriwether himself comin' from up river, standin' tall on that fine new keelboat's bow, lookin' like General Washington himself, regal and dignified, decked out in a tight-fittin', fine lookin' blue military tunic… brass buttons a shinin', chest all puffed-out proud-like. Everybody was taken right away by that man. It gave me goose bumps just to be there awatchin', especially with those soldier boys of his standin' at attention, rifles at port arms, drums a rollin'… real pomp and ceremony. It was somethin' to see, all right. And the crowd a-waitin' at the landin,' burstin' with pride, patriotism. Seems like half of Kentucky came to see us off. I ain't never seen so many folks at one time in one place. Flags a-wavin', band a-playing, strikin' up the ol' tunes, like Yankeee Doodle and such. Young gals dressed in their best, lookin' mighty fine, flirtin', smilin', doin' the things that drive a man to restlessness. Kids cheerin', runnin'wild. Jugs of shine passed around freely everywhere you looked, like a regular 4th of July."

I stopped in my mental tracks right there that very moment, reliving in my mind that long ago day and the swelling pride that we, the men of the Corps all had felt. And we never forgot it that whole long trip. "Made me feel proud, real proud."

"Hell, yeah, ya should've been proud," Thrush said matter of fact, looking at me straight on. "All of Kentuck was behind ya, includin' me and my kin."

"Huh! You wuz there?"

"Yep! Damn straight I wuz thar. Me, my pa, my brothers, all our menfolk kin, hellfire, half the goldang state was a-waitin' and a-watchin'. Hell, ya know yerself how fast word travels down the river. I tell ya people wuz awaitin' Lewis' arrival like the ol' gospel lovin' Hebrews themselves, awaitin' fer Moses to come down from the mountaintop."

I guess I must have looked to J T like I didn't believe a word he had to say. But, it wasn't so much his words as it was the fire behind them. Thrush was suddenly embued with spirit, with passion and his abrupt change had taken me by surprise. He had never for one moment since the day I met him let on, holding it all within, 'til now.

"Ya don't know, do ya?" Thrush said, shaking his head at me. "Don't ya realize how much what y'all were a-doin' meant to the rest of us? Don't ya know the whole dang east coast was pressin' up agin Kentuck, Tennessee and the Ohio Valley, waitin' to bust out west? Hellfire, I'm here to tell ya that yer the very reason I'm here today. I watched you leave Maysville… bound for glory on that thar keelboat, wishin' all along I was a-goin' right along with ya. It ain't no secret… you expedition boys were what's what on the frontier."

"I'll be darned. I never reckoned we caused such a fuss."

"Wait'll you get back home," he said. "St. Louis is hoppin', people are movin' in, buyin' up bottomland. Civilization is on the move, settlements are springin' up along the Missouri like wildfire. You'll have plenty of opportunity to get some fer yerself, if that's what you want. Your Captain Clark is now Brigadier General Clark, the United States injun agent in St. Louie and a big government man. The talk is that your name carries a lot of weight with him. I reckon you'll do pretty dang good by him.

"I'm glad I've had the chance to tell ya. This beaver business, this here wilderness country ain't like I thought it'd be, not fer me anyway. I'm glad we're headin' home while I still got my hair and my nerve."

Yeah, keeping our hair… ain't over yet, sonny, not by a long shot. As far as heading back home, I really had not given it much thought, though, I was looking forward to meeting up with "big red" Billy Clark. Pardon the impropriety, General William Clark, that is. I always liked the redhead, we all did. How could we not help it? He was one of us, if you know what I mean. He was a man who knew his roots, where he came from, never arrogant or high and mighty. The men were as comfortable around him as he was around us… and it showed, every dang day.

We moved on, the valley of the Gallatin looming ever closer. Towards late afternoon the winds picked up from out of the west. Storm clouds were blowing in, an already gray overcast sky darkening, blotting out what little sunlight remained, till day became night long before its scheduled arrival. Temperatures dropped, steadily, portending a chilly night and a slow, wet, soggy march. We kept at it, quickening our pace, soon fording the Gallatin and emerging out onto the valley floor. Ahead lay the foothills, the mountains and the pass and between where we stood and where we had to go there was no cover to shield us once downpour arrived. The winds increased, coming on stronger and stronger, until the din howled like a million lobo wolves drowning out all other ambient sounds. The cacaphony was almost too great to bear. We cupped our hands, yelling to hear each other even when only arms lengths apart. Rain now pelted our backsides, permeating our buckskins, soaking right through our skin, until our very innards seemed to slosh in a watery misery.

"Push on. Keep goin'," I told the boys. "I don't want to get caught out in the open… not here in the valley or in the pass." There was urgency in my voice, soberness beyond question or doubt.

"Suits me fine," said J T Thrush. "I'd just as soon not spend another minute in this place. Storm or no storm."

"Fine by me. I ain't tired at all," said Billy. "Nuthin' wrong with a little fallin' water, helps to keep us awake."

"Now yer talkin', that's the spirit, Billyboy."

It continued to pour, raining the rest of the afternoon and on throughout that evening and into the depths of the night. It never let up, growing violently in intensity at times, an angry mountain storm hurling its displeasure. Lightning streaked through the nightsky, jabbing the earth in a hundred places like a bare-knuckled puncher picking his spots, choice, tender spots, punishing indiscriminately with telling, painful blows. The land cried out for mercy. Yet, there was no respite this night. Thunder clapped. Wind, rain, hail all joined the crescendo, beating the earth mercilessly. Rivers of water and mud cascaded dangerously down the slopes that flanked the gap. Our footing, our every step became a nightmare of slipping, sliding and sloshing. We were soaking wet, pure wringing, sopping misery from head to toe: our moccasins, hunting shirts, leggin's, packs, possibles and rifles. That, we could endure. Our gunpowder, though, was another story and it had my concern.

"Yer powder horns, keep your powder dry," I yelled, straining to be heard above the storm. Pointing to their weapons, again I yelled. "Do you hear me? Keep your goddang powder dry."

They both nodded, bobbing their heads like corks riding swells, on a roiling, unfriendly sea. The looks they gave, the grim frowns on both their faces wore the worry and desperation of uncertainty, and… discomfort beyond anything they had ever known. Their bodies shook and trembled from the wet and the chill. They desperately wanted this nightmare over. Their minds wandered dreaming of home, of warm fireplaces and friendly people and maybe even their ma's homecooking and a dry, warm bed.

The pass, the very land we trod, was soaked through like a giant terrestrial sponge, a slick, sodden, damp mass of mud and ooze, sucking on our moccasins every step of the way. Yet, we kept on, plodding our way throughout the long night, right into the wee hours of morningtime. Finally, the rain stopped. The storm subsided above as it moved on, passing us by to spew and foment further eastward. The winds died to barely a faint puff. Dawn arose to greet us just as we topped-out atop the pass. We stopped, quietly viewing what lay before us. It was as if our ordeal throughout the night had beaten all talk out of us. Yet, none of us needed to express in words our relief. The trail ahead was a familiar one, wandering through a narrow, rolling valley of high-moutain grasses, with stands of "quakie'" aspen and crick-lined willows. To our left on the north flowed a small meandering creek, shrouded by dense thickets of red willow covering both banks. Several small mountain valleys dropped down from the north and northwest, revealing the possibility of another route, maybe several routes, paralleling our trail… more passes through the mountains of the Wolf, I surmised.

On our right to the south, arose mountains thick with forests of pine and fir, uninterrupted. A long jagged line of granite cordillera stretched far to the south and southwest beyond sight.

The hard-driving storm had washed away much of what was left of the winter snow pack in the pass. Weeks before this very same trail was covered by a broad field of ice and snow and deep treacherous drifts, that challenged our mettle and stamina, our will to go on. And now the signs of spring were clearly evident everywhere. Off in the distance a curious family of mule deer spotted our appearance, watched us for awhile and then suddenly scampered off, only to stop a "stone's throw" away and resume their browsing.

Satisfied, we made for the little stream in the willows to lighten our loads and catch a deserved rest. Thrush and Bryant were moving slow. I could see that they were plumb tuckered out, their heads hangdog heavy. A couple of tired, sodden, sad looking stories.

Now me, I wasn't much better. So I hung back a-ways, watching them, all the while taking in the Wolf Mountains and the trail ahead. The morning and the land looked quite innocent and I waited until I was satisfied there was nothing else caution could accomplish. I followed the boys' trail right down to the willows and soon we were all drying out in the solitude of a small clearing by the banks of that unnamed stream.

"I'd sure like to get a fire goin' and maybe cook somethin' up," Billy said, looking for approval. "My gut's been growlin' a powerful lot ever since we left the Fort. Hell, it's been a full day without vittles of any kind.'"

"Uh huh!" I mumbled, not bothering to look his way. "Light a fire, huh? Kinda wet, don't you think?"

Thrush stood off a-way, shaking his head and smiling.

"Sure, Billy. Why don't you gather up some dry kindlin' and get it a goin.' I'm sure J T and me could stomach some of your cookin'. That is… if you can find any dry kindlin' in this sodden mess."

Thrush continued smiling, and me… I had to hide mine. The kid was fun to josh and now seemed as good a time as any to let off a little steam.

"Why, I meant. I mean… I was thinkin' you could do the…" Billy started to protest.

I don't know how or why, but I suddenly did know. There was a faint breeze blowing in from the northwest, just enough to carry a scent. It was coming from across the willow bound stream, from the direction of those several small mountain valleys that had earlier caught my attention. I smelt something both unpleasant to my senses and my memory. The odor was unmistakeable. Thrush and Bryant didn't catch it. How could they? They never had the experiences that I had had. Nonetheless, they caught my abrupt change and froze in place.

I quickly brought my right index finger to my lips, signaling silence. Billy's eyes were widening with each renewed breath. Thrush was behind me a few feet away. His movement was deliberate, controlled. I glanced to see him bend down slowly and pick up his rifle. I nodded to Billy... who followed suit, grasping firmly the thin neck of his long-rifle, the act, the weapon now in his hands, seemingly settling his nerves.

Good, I thought, sit tight, Johnboy, and let's see how this thing plays out. It was now quiet in the clearing, deadly so. A sobering pall hung over us: as if man, the clearing and all of nature were holding their collective breaths.

And then... I caught the bare whiff of a scent again. Yes, yes, I was more than certain. Getting stronger, too, but, how many? There I was not so certain. Yet, there was just no doubt in my mind. That pebbled beach on the banks of the Jefferson had ingrained Blackfeet stench in my nasal memory forever.

Surprisingly, I was relaxed, almost calm. Yet, every bit as taut as a primed steel trap, ready to snap and spring, tear and eviscerate. The hairs on the back of my neck were as rigid as the tines of a metal rake, standing straight and tall, ready to pile up all in my swath. For one last remindful time, Toby and Johnny flashed through my mind's eye. Yes, I was ready, as if fate had preordained this very moment, at this place, and had chosen me as its executor to execute its will.

I snapped to in time, shamefully reminding myself that I was not alone. Billy and J T's welfare was something else again. They were now my responsibility. Their safety and lives depended upon me using the good sense the Lord gave me. I reached behind me to the small of my back and grasped the smooth wooden handle of my tomahawk, gently moving it up and down several times for easy withdrawal from my belt. My skinning knife rested comfortably in its deerskin sheath within easy reach.

Billy stared hard, watching my every move. The boy seemed to be holding his breath. I nodded, ever so slightly, hoping to reassure him. His eyes darted from me to the willows and back, desperately wanting to reply, desperately wanting the tension, the drama to come to an immediate end. Thrush was now completely out of my view. I had to count on him doing the right thing, holding his own, protecting our backsides. I sensed he knew. Everything about him convinced me he would stand tall.

There was little warning, the last-second swish and twang and twack of thin red-willow limbs being hurriedly brushed aside by charging, screaming half-naked bodies. On they cam, converging upon the three of us in a wild, chaotic charge. Four, six, eight long, raven-haired, painted nightmares... I lost count. The first, the nearest headed straight at Billy. The boy's feet were stuck to the ground mired in mud and dread, a gurgled gasp of surprise erupting from the bone-dry reaches of his throat..

This was my fight, my battle. Thrush and Bryant could do the cleaning up. Toby and Johnny were not to be cheated. I wanted every one of the red sons of bitches to feel the *spoo-pii's* cold steel and lead-shot one last time. I stepped right in front of the kid and faced the charging redskin. He wavered- not, a fierce *Piegan* war cry left his lips, howling with froth and spit and venom, splitting the serenity of the red willow clearing and the mountain- pass' morning air. I leveled my weapon from my hip, holding steady a moment longer and then, fired a hot ball of lead right into the savage's exposed belly.

The igniting black powder's discharge was deafening, a man-sized cloud of black smoke instantly enshrouding its victim in gunpowder fog. As quickly as it had appeared from the end of my barrel the smoke cleared, swept clean by the valley breezes. That little lead ball had blazed a mighty trail into that warrior's guts, blowing his gizzards and backsides to smithereens and his spirit to the happy hunting grounds. Hurled backward by the force of the blast and slammed to the ground in the rudest of ways, his death song was altogether brief, his last feeble chants fading away, dying with him.

Instantly, I turned. Others came at me now. I was the offender, the real object of their hatred. As adroitly as I had that long ago day by the icy Gallatin, straddling my dead *cayac*, defending my dinner against a pack of hungry wolves, I turned my unloaded rifle into a war club. The second attacker, veering his course from Billy to me, miscalculated my intentions, his tomahawk arcing harmlessly over my shoulder. I ducked his blow and with a vicious butt stroke of an uppercut brought the full weight of my swing to bear, striking him cleanly on his exposed chin. The jaw-crunching impact was overwhelming, overpowering daylight with darkness. He never knew what hit him. Down he went as lifeless as a sack of spuds. Time was not mine to waste. Rearing back the butt of my rifle to shoulder level I drove my weapon downward, brutally hard, shattering his skull as easily as if it was a ripened gourd of summer squash... brains, blood, gore splattering indiscriminately.

"Eat that, injun."

I was beside myself. Blackfeet blood, the battle, the fear and excitement it generated drove me like a demonic warrior possessed. All traces of decency vanishing like the wind with the first blows struck. This wilderness mayhem was not a scene for the meek or the weak-hearted. Lord knows I've had my fair share, spilt blood had become for me every bit as natural as corn ripening in the hot sun.

Another rifle discharged and then another, renting the air with sharp crisp cracks of black powder thunder. Billy had fired point blank in haste, his shot missing dead center, instead grazing his attacker's ribs. His young adversary had only flinched at the flesh-searing pain, never wavering in his charge. No, his adrenaline, his ancient bloodlust pumped natural opiates to every corner of his mind and body, numbing the senses, inuring him to mortal pain. He was on the kid in an instant, knocking him to the ground. The two became locked in the fight of their lives, grappling, struggling, rolling over and over, catch as catch can, pummeling each other without respite. Knives slashing, stabbing, thus far both youngsters had missed their marks. Mud and grass, sweat and blood, a tumult of man, red and white, savage and civilized too close to call.

Soon Billy was barely hanging on; no match for the wilderness-bred warrior now pinning him to the willow clearing's dank floor. I leaped atop his tormentor, grabbing and yanking on his long black mane, snapping his neck and head rudely back. I deftly retrieved my tomahawk from my belt and in one fell swoop I brought that vicious weapon down on his head, mashing skin and flesh, cracking and splintering skull and bone. An ugly thud, contact of metal versus bone, ringing a chord of unmistakable notes, resonating throughout the willow copse like a wilderness death knell... stunning, stopping all combatants, momentarily.

I yanked the young warrior off Billy, deftly casting his now lifeless body aside.

"Get up, Billy. Get up now, we've got a fight on our hands."

I didn't yell, I was calm as stone as I looked down to young Bryant. And he looked up at me askance, near petrified at the closeness of his call, unable to utter a word nor even to nod or thank. I could see the tears welling in his eyes. He tried to stop, to brush them away. But he was coming around, stirring from the fog of battle. He jackrabbited to his feet, instantly grabbing his unloaded rifle. He glanced down at his dispatched foe, near-saddened by the bloody pulp that was once a proud, handsome young warrior in the prime of early manhood, knowing right then that for the grace of God that dead brave could have easily been him.

"Reload," I ordered. "You ain't got the time for regrets."

The struggle went on. It was a confused scene in the little clearing: heavy brush, weedy undergrowth, willows as thick as fleas on a hound's rear-end and flaccid Indian bodies bloodied and maimed, starting to pile up like stacks of human cordwood.

    Billy grabbed his powder horn, his soft deerskin pouch of smooth, round lead balls and began reloading. His hands, his fingers amazingly calm, steady, as he measured and poured the precious powder, then rammed a little ball home. In an instant he cocked and brought his charged weapon to the ready, quickly surveying the scene for a fresh target, no longer the reluctant eastern tenderfoot, but a young warrior who had come of age.

    "Atta boy," I said before turning my attention to the scuffle behind me under way and the man no longer guarding my back.

    The heat of battle left little time for a bad case of the jitters. The shooting had stopped, but not the sounds of heavy panting, cursing, screaming and the pounding away at human flesh.

    J T had not missed his mark. He couldn't have. Not with two warriors breathing down on top of him just as he jerked off his one shot. And it was a good one, blowing a hole right smack dab in the middle of a heaving human chest. His shot had fired from so close that the red man's upper torso turned from sun bronzed to black powder soot to blood red.

    Unthinkingly, Thrush stood as if mesmerized, riveted by death and fear and his own racing adrenaline. This was all so amazing to him, exhilarating beyond anything he had ever known. And it was all happening so lightning fast. So fast, he never saw the second brave coming. And then he felt a terrific glancing, numbing blow on the side of his own thick head, nearly tearing his ear off. Down he went and as he fell he fought to stay conscious; to keep from passing out as a strange, eerily black world seemed to envelop him as completely as a moonless night. Bright, glittering stars twinkled in the darkness of his mind's eye as the sounds of a fierce struggle still raging about him grew dim, fading to a near-deathly silence.

    He fought the sleep that meant death for sure. Panic, fear and will to live made him do so. He was a strong, powerful man, son and grandson of frontier blacksmiths from Maysville on the Ohio and Boones Lick. A son of early Kentucky, born to and wilderness bred, raised from the cradle to manhood to a life of lifting, grasping, hoisting, twisting iron and forging heavy metal. His great strength now rallied to his cause. Instantly, he came to, shaking off the fog that clouded his mind. His will to survive ignoring the pain, the desperate situation. The feeling of a great weight pinning his body to the ground spurred him to action. It had been that second charging warrior that downed J T with a vicious blow from a heavy stone-headed war club. The Blackfeet nightmare pounced on top of Thrush, taking his wind, swinging away once again with his war club. From deep within some primordial well of courage, some ancient forgotten stone-age instinct, J T battled back; his thick, powerful arms able to block and ward off every telling blow, thus far.

He wavered, though, teetering back and forth, gravely weakened by that first crippling blow. Blood was spewing out of the side of his head where lay a torn, gashed, dangling ear, spraying the ocher-painted nightmare slashing away at him. The sight of the white-man's blood drove the savage to further frenzy. And all J T could see were the crazed whites of the red man's eyes and a perfect set of gnawing, gnashing, gritted teeth, frothing with spit and hate and unrestrained fury.

Indeed our fight in the red willow clearing was happening too fast. For no sooner had I turned from Billy's defense, the instant after hearing the sound of a second rifle report, I looked to see my rotund friend struggling for his life. The big, powerfully constructed *Piegan* brave atop him was winning the scrape, hell bent on committing murder.

"No you don't!" Gravel and grit spewing my every word, I roared from across the clearing as I rushed forward to end the fray, my own tomahawk dripping with blood and gore and matted hair, unsatiated, eager for more.

That Blackfeet brave stopped right on the brink of triumph, turning instantly towards the sound of my voice. Glaring directly at me, his face, the venom in his eyes filled with loathing and unexplainably… recognition…

"*Ahhheee*," he screamed, "*Spoo-pii!*" His resounding cry split the air again and again. "*Spoo-pii! Spoo-pii!*"

"*Spoo-pii?* What in the hell," I cursed, momentarily puzzled. Then in an instant it dawned on my thick skull. It's me they wanted all along. That's why they're here now, they're looking for me, the turtle, the *spoo-pii?* Now, I knew. It was me they waited for by the Jefferson. And got Drouillard and his Shawnee instead. There was no other explanation.

Holy shit! I was shocked right down to the very soles of my moccasins, though I never should have been. Somehow, someway the other day by the banks of the Jefferson, by George's lifeless body, by those big moccasin tracks etched so clearly and deeply in the sandy soil of that riverside trail, I should have put together the whole dang thing.

Vengeance boiled within me. They shouldn't have done that to my friend, George. Suddenly stopping, I glared right back into that big son of a bitch's dark cruel eyes, instinctively spreading my feet wide apart, digging in, taking up the challenge. Instantly, I saw the hideous scar blazing across the whole rightside of his cheek, spanning the bridge of his nose. His visage was nightmarish, the embodiment of the worst of frontier fears of depravity and outright horror. The way he scowled, so full of arrogance and hate, was at this very moment somehow vaguely familiar. Then it all clicked. He was right out of *Running Wolf's* mold, all right. And what's more, he knew my voice instantly. He should have, he had been searching for me ever since he lost sight of my naked backsides fleeing from *Running Wolf's* demise towards the

Madison and freedom that long ago day.

My voice, as weak, as timid as it had been back on the gravelly banks of the Jefferson, had never been forgotten. Committed to memory, he still recognized it to this very day, even amidst the din and strife and confusion of battle. And upon seeing my face, my form, instant verification…the *spoo-pii*, the *napikwan* with the feared fire-stick of the *pishkun* plains, the slayer of his best friend, his blood brother, *Running Wolf*. After all this time, what tenacity, what dogged perseverance, what outright hatred, the realization was chilling. Yet, one way or another, it would soon be finished, as if preordained by the Creator, himself. Yes, only a blood vendetta could have prompted *Running Wolf's* loyal band to wait for my return that cold winter night by the Gallatin River so many moons ago. Were some of these the same warriors who lay in wait for me that night? Was this scar-faced demon there too? It was a question, I need not ask. Of course, he had been there, leading the ambush. He was the bronzed giant who stood by *Running Wolf* on the *pishkun* plains. In just a fraction of a second it had all become so abundantly clear. I was the sharp thorn deep in his nation's pride; the bitter barb that could only be retracted and reconciled by my death and humiliation. Of course it fell to this scarred demon to avenge his friend and his Nation's honor. Fate would not have it any other way.

Completely abandoning his scrape with Thrush, he leapt to his feet to challenge the *spoo-pii*. Two years of pent-up fury propelled him like a cannon ball straight across the clearing. Rearing his war club back for maximum delivery, on he charged, all the while hissing, screaming, venting retribution unrequited.

Those still standing watched in rapt attention, stalling their own pending struggles. It was as if an ancient, climactic clash awaited, Homeric in scope… Hector versus Achilles… a fight to the death by the chosen champions of their race.

That kind of fight was for history books and fairy tales. I was having none of it, no sir, no fancy-Dan duel for me. No being rode rough-shod over anymore. They had had far too many goes at my expense, costing me dear friends in the process. No, I had had enough of his kind and their unequal ways. I was not inclined to fight it out, blow for blow, while there was still half-a-war-party standing by and the odds still in their favor. I wanted this set-to ended right now.

The giant closed in, swinging for all he was worth. His energy was boundless, his determination without peer. His mind and body equally impervious to pain and fear his reason for existence coming down to this point in time and place and being.

I deftly stepped inside his warclub's long looping arc, swiftly driving my own tomahawk's heavy blade squarely into his forehead, splitting his skull like a dry log with a tremendously resounding crack. He waivered but a second, soon crumpling to the ground, the darkness of eternal sleep coming over his eyes, ending his vendetta and his life that very moment

The report of crushed skull was unmistakable, reverberating throughout that red willow clearing like a church bell's grim funeral peel, as starkly crisp as the ominous claps of thunder and lightning the night before. The battle in the clearing stopped on that sharp ringing note. No further war cries were to be heard, no death song wails or heathen dirges to be sung, for death had come instantaneously to my *Piegan* avenger and had taken the fight right out of the rest of his disheartened band. *Running Wolf* was forever to be unavenged. The *spoo-pii* remained unconquered, to live and fight another day.

I stood straddled over the now-twitching body of that dead scar-faced warrior, my legs spread apart, left arm akimbo, tomahawk firmly grasped in my right hand and dangling ominously by my side, fully prepared for the next brush with death and the next... if I must. I glanced down one last time. The doggedness of his quest had been chilling, his hatred and resolve to finish me off beyond any obsession I could ever possibly fathom. And yet, I hadn't even known his name. I shook my head at the inanity of it all. With his death, though, I sensed that this madness might be over. Maybe I could finally go home in peace.

I looked about the clearing. The fighting had ceased, indeed. The remaining *Piegans* had lost their leader, their resolve and their nerve, the few survivors fleeing as quickly as they appeared, beating a hasty retreat back through the red willows. *Namachkani* had failed them again. With their swift departure, silence returned, save for heavy panting, gasping for air and the rapidly pumping, pulsating, beating hearts of three white trappers, gradually regaining their composure.

We watched, listened and waited. Sweat poured from J T's brow, blood from his horrid wound. He retrieved a dry, homespun shirt from his pack and pressed it firmly against the side of his head, stemming the flow from his dangling, mangled ear. Billy, still very much stunned, still trembling, yet holding his loaded rifle fully prepared to let it speak.

Five bloodied *Piegan* bodies littered the clearing. The sounds of their comrades crashing, tearing, fleeing through the tangled willow-brakes drifted back to us on the northern breezes. And finally, a trio of quick remounts, the distinct slap of leather quirts whipping, striking the bare flesh of their sacred *ponokamita's* rumps. Startled ponies snorting protests, unshod hooves galloping away from the willows, pell-mell. And as I suspected, heading to the northwest, to another pass through the mountains of the Wolf.

"John," said Billy breaking the silence moments later.

"Shhhh!" I whispered softly, again pointing a stiff index finger to my lips. We continued to wait quietly, until the sounds of pounding hooves eventually died away. Then and only then did we breathe a collective sigh of relief.

I looked at Thrush standing by with a growing smile steadily spreading over his face, nodding his head, as if pleased by what he was no longer hearing.

"I count about eight ponies by the sound of it, no more than that. We whipped 'em... No, that ain't exactly right. You whipped 'em, John. You whipped 'em real gooood."

"Eight's about right," I agreed. "I'm pretty sure they were that same band that waylaid George by the Jefferson. I've been half expectin' 'em to dog our trail."

I paused for a moment, looking down towards the ground. And then I said, almost contritely. "This thing here was personal. It was all about gettin' me."

They both looked at me quizzically.

"Ohh!' I said, finally explaining. "Kinda like settlin' an ol' score. It goes way back to that *Running Wolf* fella and the white man they called the *spoo-pii*. Me bein' that *spoo-pii* fella, that is."

"Huh! Well, I'll be," J T stood shaking his head. "So that tale was true all along." He looked down at the big *Piegan*, as if pondering the abruptness of the fight for his life and his own luck. "Say, will ya look at that big ugly son of a bitch. He had me dead to rights and let me go. Just forgot killin' me at the sound of yer voice. Boy, he sure must've wanted you... awfully bad."

And then he looked to me askingly. "Have you ever seen a scar like that?"

Without bothering to look, I shrugged and replied. "Mebbe. Mebbe not. Scar or no scar, he looks familiar, especially the size of him. I bet it was his mock-er-sinn track Big Mike found the other day by George's body. Come to think of it, I may have seen him standin' by *Running Wolf* that day on the *pishkun* plains. I think they were friends. He's big enough to fit the bill. But, hell, they all could've been there. There's just no tellin'."

I found myself shaking my own head as I looked down one more time at that dead injun. I was a little numb, myself, the aftershock of the fight finally coming-to-light. My own thoughts became distracted, wandering off to God knows where. A moment or two passed and then I heard myself rather sarcastically say to no one in particular, "I never did get his name... but he sure knew mine."

"Colter, I'm beholdin' to ya fer savin' my hide. I wuz a goner fer sure." J T was staring at me, the look on his face leaving no doubt the veracity of his every word.

"As for those that lit a shuck, no wonder... you should've seen the look in their eyes when you split scar-face's ugly melon. I swear to God, the fight, and whatever else has been pushin' 'em on, went out of them right then. These scalps, by rights, are all yours."

Thrush, temporarily forgetting his own pain, stood looking down at the dead, surveying the dark treasure trove of Blackfeet scalps waiting to be lifted, all the while remembering just how close his own scrape had been.

I looked at him, pausing a moment to consider his sense of frontier propriety.

"Naw!" I said. "I wouldn't want any more of this'n's kin lookin' for me. Ya kill one and their whole nation is on your trail. They all have too long a memory... and too much hate. I thank you, nevertheless, for the consideration"

"In that case," said Thrush. "I'll leave 'em be for the varmints to take care of. Anyway, I never did like the practice... unchristian-like, if ya know what I mean."

"Hey," broke in Billy, sounding somewhat irritated. "Listen to you, will ya. You sound like you were half expectin' 'em to show up."

I raised my eyebrows, a broad, mischievous smile appearing on my face. I was beginning to lighten up a bit. "You never know... do ya?"

Billy, ashen-faced, glared at me. His head shook. His lips trembled. His eyes were full to the brim with fury and indignation. Unconsciously, he clenched his fists into tight balls, all the while his body quivering like an aspen in a mountain storm. Then, staring at the carnage in the clearing, he shook his head again, half-unbelieving what his eyes were seeing and his ears were telling him.

Then he spoke. "Those three that got away, I saw the look in their eyes when you halved that big 'uns gourd. They didn't want any part of you, no sir, not today, not tomorrow ... ever. They couldn't get out of here fast enough. I knew right then that you could've killed all of 'em if you wanted to. Nothin' could've stopped you. Those redskins didn't stand a coon's chance in hell."

Billy paused for a moment and then added with an almost accusatory tone, "That's all right by me, though I'd swear you half-enjoyed it, maybe even wished for it."

He couldn't quite make up his mind whether he was angry or grateful or both. One way or the other, it was plain to see that the fight had taken its toll out of Billy. I had to set him straight.

"You think so, huh?" I said, looking at the youngster with a stern, hard stare, the smile on my face disappearing without a trace. There was a sarcastic coldness in the way I answered the kid. Yet, he was near right. I wasn't gloating, mind you, but I wasn't ashamed of what I had done either. I could've killed all of them, just like he said. And just as certainly I was fully prepared to die trying. It wasn't that I enjoyed it, but that I had it to do. I didn't expect him to understand. But he trusted me, stood by and looked up to me. I felt compelled to ease his mind.

"Look, Billy, we got a ways to go and we don't need any ill feelin's cloudin' our trail. So let me clear it up right now. This fight has been a long time a comin', not that I've been lookin' for it, mind ya, or goin' out of my way to find it. No, it's the last thing I wanted, 'til the other day by the Jeff. I've pushed my luck way too many times. We all have at one time or another: Toby and the Flatheads; Johnny and me; Cheek, Ayers and Fleehart: George and the rest of the boys in the Company. And the Blackfeet… they've been pushin' for it ever since Lewis and Drouillard and the Field brothers met up with 'em on the Marias in '06. Hell, I was just the first white man to come along that they could sink their teeth and blades into. More to the point, after I kept gettin' away from 'em they just could not let me go. I guess I became sorta their national embarrassment, if you want. Y'all saw that in that big injun's eyes and heard it in his voice. That was no accident or coincidence. I need no further evidence.

"There had to be a reckonin' of sorts. I should've known that I couldn't get away from this infernal place without some kind of final accountin'. Maybe I wanted it to come down to this. I don't rightly know. Be what it may, call it recompense if you want, revenge, squaring the deal for murdered friends. Toby, Johnny, George… may they now rest in peace. I had a powerful lot of hate growin' inside me. Enmity I just as soon not carry home. I did what I needed to do, cleared the slate, now I might have a chance to be free of it. This, boys, is the last straw for me, the last huzzah. Somebody else can take my place if they have the sand. Thank you Lord, I've had enough, I'm headin' home."

"Holy Shit!" said a somber Billy Bryant and then he let out all his frustrations, all the pent-up emotion he had been holding back since his friend James Cheek was murdered.

"I heard people talk in the settlements about you bein' touched in the head and all. They say you shun white-folks and white-ways, that you'd rather be a loner, out in the wilderness livin' like an injun or a wild animal. People say a lot of shit about you, that you're a yarn spinner, a liar, that none of that shit at the Forks… with the Flatheads and Johnny Potts and your run, ever happened. I didn't know at first what to think, none of the boys did. We all tiptoed quietly around you. But, James and Dougherty came to think right much of you. Tom said you were the best man he ever knew: that you always spoke the truth. And, then I got to know you these last few weeks. Big Mike Immell told me to stick by you, he knew what kinda man you were. Hell, they all came to know. I told Mike that he needn't worry, that I, too, saw what you were made of. Even Major Henry told me I was in good hands. Can you believe that, Andrew Henry, who gave you nothin' but shit?

"It got to where I thought I knew ya, but, this... this fight, I don't rightly know now what to think. Hell, it weren't no fight a'tall. You were like the avengin' hand of God Almighty, like Samson slaughterin' the Philistines, with a razor-sharp tomahawk instead of a jawbone of an ass. And another thing, you certainly didn't need the two of us agin any amount of injuns. J T and me might as well've been sittin' down by the crick, cleanin' our toes, pickin' our noses and watchin' the show for all the good we done. Hell, we just got in your way."

He stopped talking for a moment, looking forlornly to the ground. He began weeping, softly. "I didn't come out here for this. I tell you, I'm sick of this place. I'm sick of these murderin' savages and their murderin' ways. I've had enough. I wanna go home and never see this wilderness again."

Billy turned abruptly and walked away. He was still incredulous, still shaking, tears still steadily flowing down his cheeks. The fight, the closeness to death had struck him all too hard.

Thrush stood by silently letting Billy's rant run its due course.

"How's your head?" I asked him.

"Stopped bleedin', I think. But, dang, my ears are ringin' like church bells. Oh hell, my head feels like shit. But, I'll be fine once we get shed of this place and as far away from these stinkin' Blackfeet as we can. And it won't be soon enough for me." J T ran his tongue, licking dried lips and managed a weak unconvincing smile.

"Don't worry about the kid," he added a moment later, "he meant no disrespect. He'll be awright, once we get outta here."

I nodded. "I know he will. As for your head, I'll sew up that ear of yourn later on. Best we make ready and head for the Yellowstone while we have daylight on our side, put some miles between us, before our *Piegan* friends change their minds and come a lookin' in force.

"Go on, get your gear together and keep an eye on Billy, will ya? We'll be outta here shortly."

"Gotcha!" he nodded.

Thrush went about securing his shirt firmly around his head, covering his torn ear and bloody scalp. He moved quickly and reloaded his rifle, checked his remaining powder and lead, and in no time had gathered his and Billy's belongings. Shortly, a somber Billy Bryant quietly returned to the clearing, seemingly ready to leave. Neither man had another word to say. They stood by, each with his hat in his hand, waiting for me to give the word.

I lingered, unable to part without taking one final, albeit long look to the west, to that infernal, unconquerable valley that had challenged me so, paying my last respects to both an old friend and an old foe, alike. A myriad of thoughts and memories good and bad came on fast and hard, just like the Blackfoot attack barely minutes old. My earliest recollection, how long ago was it, Johnboy? What will it be, some five years come mid-July since the Corps laid eyes on the Three Forks for the first time? Lot of miles since then, lots of tough miles. A lifetime ago, five years filled with tragedy and death. Yet, with it all, one constant vision of pride remains clearly in my mind... Cap'n Lewis, himself, as fine a figure of a man ever to walk on God's green earth.

I can still see him, erect and purposeful, scaling the sandstone bluff overlooking the rivers convergence on that warm midsummer July day. So eager to take his readings; longitude and latitude, surveying the valley, the rivers, the distant mountains, making his celestial observations, methodically jotting them down as was his practice. I remember the pride I had felt while watching him. I wasn't alone, though, hell, we all felt that way. The significance of the Forks, what we were accomplishing never did escape any of us... even little Janey, the little *Snake* injun gal, she knew too.

Often we would look over their shoulders, those keeping a log, to see them put in writing what we were all experiencing. The written word has a powerful *namachkani*. In the Corps case, those journals gave more credence, more meaning, verifying and sanctifying the importance to us of what we signed on to do and what it meant to the future of the Republic. The written word gave us strength, motivating us to proceed on undaunted in our quest, no matter what we came to face. I saw it in ol' Meriwether's eyes that long ago day and never forgot the simple, straightforward words he penned:

"believing this to be an essential point in the geography of this western part of the Continent I determined to remain at all events untill I obtained the necessary data for fixing its latitude Longitude &. ... Saturday July 27th 1805."

The bad memories, the nightmares have haunted me long enough. I can handle them now. Besides, this is not the time to relive them; they will be around to contend with for the rest of my days. No, I'd much rather remember the *many-come-together* country and the red-man whose paths I've crossed the way I first saw them... wild and free. Any other way would not do.

"You've had one helluva run Johnboy. Let's just leave it at that," I said aloud.

"Amen, brother!" J T muttered quietly under his breath, nodding his head.

I turned and faced my two companions. They are looking at me with the most muted of stares, as silent as the dead injuns themselves lying prostrate before us. They hide it well, yet they are still shakened, nervously a time or two touching their scalps, no doubt counting their blessings. Deep down in my guts I am smiling; been there myself a time or two. Nothing to be ashamed of; a little fear is healthy, helps keep a man on his toes.

The little mountain stream flowed through the willows unabated. The morning sun had risen a little higher, the day growing a little warmer. The wind came up on cue, blowing in from the north.

I glanced about the clearing, mentally collecting my kit, and then commenced to gather up my possibles. The kid still concerned me, though. We still had to worry about the long reach of the Blackfeet Nation and their allies. We still had to watch our trail between here and Manuels for roving bands of *Gros Ventres* bucks on the prod for scalps and plunder. No, we weren't out of trouble, by a long shot.

"You boys like it here or somethin'? Maybe you want to stick 'round for another helpin' of *Piegan* scalp stew."

"What?" choked Billy, incredulously, scratching his head, all the while not realizing when his leg was being pulled. "No, I don't. And I don't like your tone, either. What gives ye the right to toss your weight around like you wuz Andrew Henry or somethin'? I thought we were done with that."

Billy is dang near yelling now, clenching his fists he puts one foot forward in an unmistakable stance, fight is written all over his face. Damn, the boy is ready to scratch and claw right now. I like that. He reminds me of another defiant youth. There is a difference, though… Billy gets a second chance today, while Johnny Potts never got his. Yes, Billy Bryant is going home alive if I have any say in the matter.

I caught Thrush smiling out of the side of my eye, barely able to contain hisself. Good, I need all the help I can get. Unnoticed by Billy, I winked at J T. He nods ever so slightly. The charade is on.

"Ready to fight me, are ya? I thought you were sick of fightin'?"

"No, I ain't ready for no dang fight. I am sick of it. I just want outta here and be left alone."

"Well, then," I barked back rather disdainfully, "what're you waitin' for, boy? Grab your rifle. Let's get outta here 'afore them *Piegans* come back with a whole dang war party and slit our gizzards from top to bottom. Now get the lead out of your pouch and start movin'."

I turn away, desperately trying to restrain a mischievous little smile forming on my face.

"Whaddiya… Dang yer hide, Colter, you're actin' mighty peculiar," Billy flares-up in a fluster, spit and snot flying every-which-way.

Thrush chuckles, unable to stop, he is soon rolling on the ground, pain forgotten, torn ear and all, blood a flyin', dust a kickin'. That does it, I can't contain myself a moment longer. The willow clearing peels aloud, echoing our laughter from one side to the other, all at flustered Billy's expense.

You couldn't blame Billy, what with all the goings-on since leaving Manuels. There was more than enough carnage to go around for even the most experienced injun fighter to handle. And Philadelphia never prepared him for this. The youngster stands before us in all perplexity, yet to calculate just what it is his two conspiring partners are up to. We can see his dander mounting, coming together, growing darker and darker like gathering thunderheads, fixing to clap and burst and rain upon us at the slightest of provocations. Then dawn at last breaks over our young dunderheaded friend. He smells two scheming rats at the height of their intrigue. Game's up. Light glows upon his countenance where darkness and confusion reigned but a moment before. A smile slowly spreads across his face. His eyes no longer filled with suspicion and doubt and anger, but now all seeing, all knowing, wise beyond his young years. Hands on hips, shaking his head, indignation turns to sarcasm. "Why you two hee-hawin' jackass sonsofabitches, y'all can kiss my ever-lovin' ass."

Fit-to-be-tied, J T stifles a robust snort and strains to muffle a bellyful of mirth bulging inside him begging to bust out and be set free. His head, his torn ear pounds and throbs, yet somehow he manages the pain. Billy Bryant is his best friend and right then and there, he is mighty proud of the kid.

J T stops laughing. A big smile, wide and warm forms on his round cherubic face. Eyes sparkling as fresh as this very spring morn, he pats Billy on the back warmly. Soon he's hugging and squeezing. "Buhhhhhh! That's the spirit, Billyboy. Now you're talkin'."

Inwardly I am smiling. Good, the kid is going to do just fine. It hasn't been easy on him or Thrush for that matter, injun warfare 'tis not for the faint of heart, but they're both shaking it off, the fear, the closeness to death's door, the killing, the savagery of it all. They've both learned the hard way, toughening-up in time to keep their scalps, to see the sun rise another day. As for Billy Bryant, I'm no longer concerned. He can handle come-what-may all the way back home to the City of Brotherly Love.

There's nothing left for me to do or say, save…

"Times a wastin', boys, let's go home."

Calm has returned to the red willow clearing. The early morning chill has finally worn away, giving rise to a warm, sunny day. The air smells clean and fresh, of pungent sage and the aromatic delight of pine and cedar still moist with dew. The trail ahead is wide-open, nothing warns of pursuit from behind or deception ahead. It is good to be alive, to be going home. Time to make tracks, head east with the Yellowstone as our guide.

THE END

EPILOGUE

John Colter left the Rocky Mountains never to return. Tradition has it that he and his companions made their way to Manuel's Fort on the Big Horn. From there the legendary mountain man, in a dugout canoe, paddled down the Missouri and arrived in St. Louis, sometime in late May of 1810, covering almost 3,000 miles in approximately thirty days.

The ill-fated Menard/Henry Expedition to the Three Forks region of southwestern Montana would soon split up. The short-lived trapper's fort would be abandoned just a few months after its construction, never to be used again. Sixty-six years later, one Lt. James H. Bradley, who would be killed at the Battle of the Big Hole with the Nez Perce a year later on August 9, 1877, would enter into his journal on March 26, 1876:

"Within sight of our camp the mighty Missouri takes its rise... Both from this circumstance and from the history connected with it, the locality is one of the most interesting in Montana it being that the first fur-trading establishment on the Upper Missouri stood. In 1870 the outlines of the fort were still intact from which it appears that it was a double stockade of logs set three feet deep, enclosing an area of about 300 feet square, situated upon the tongue of land (at that point half a mile wide) between the Jefferson and Madison rivers about two miles above their confluence, upon the south bank of a channel now called Jefferson Slough. Since then the stream has made such inroads upon the land that only a small portion of the fort-the southwest angle-remains."

Lt. Bradley had one further distinction in American history. With his U. S. Army Indian scouts, he would be the first cavalry officer to arrive on the scene of the Battle of the Little Big Horn and find the remains of General George Armstrong Custer and his entire command.

Today, nothing remains of the fort's site. All evidence of its existence has vanished save for the fort's blacksmith's anvil, and it can be viewed today in the little corner stone-building at 202 Main St. that houses the Headwaters Heritage Museum in present day Three Forks, Montana.

The Tinkling Springs Presbyterian Church, Fishersville, Virginia, is still going strong, with uninterrupted service since 1740. The Church and the Tinkling Spring Presbyterian Fellowship Hall are both listed on the Virginia Landmarks Register and the National Register of Historic Places. And the nearby community of Stuarts Draft still claims John Colter as one of its own with a state historical marker commemorating his life located on Rte. 608 at the intersection of Rte. 340.

History reveals that Colter conferred with Captain William Clark in St. Louis later that year after his return and retraced his movements to "Colter's Hell," Jackson Hole and the Grand Tetons and the vicinity of present day Yellowstone Park. Clark subsequently would pen on his map... *Colter's Route of 1807* in the Biddle-Allen 1814 edition of *Lewis, Meriwether, and Clark, William. History of the Expedition, 1804-5-6*, thus inscribing Colter's fantastic winter trek of discovery of 1807/1808.

Decades later, with the arrival of new trapping operations, Colter's discoveries would be verified and enshrine him forever as the first white man to set eyes on the mysteries and wonders of the future Yellowstone National Park.

Much of John Colter's life and whereabouts during certain time frames of his stay in the Rocky Mountains remains a mystery. But, what is known is that upon his return to civilization he would marry, taking a wife who has been listed variously as one: Sarah, Sally or Lucy. They had a son named Hiram. After clearing and settling certain accounts and receiving his remuneration from a grateful Congress of the United States, he made his home in Franklin County, Missouri, and settled down to a peaceful life of farming near Boeuf Island in Labadie Township just west of St. Louis, Missouri.

John Bradbury, a forty-three-year-old English naturalist and author of *Travels in the Interior of America in the Years 1809, 1810, and 1811*, accompanied the Wilson Price Hunt Expedition up the Missouri River in March of 1811. At the encouragement of William Clark, Bradbury visited Colter. On March 18th of that year, Bradbury in his interview with Colter wrote of the death of John Potts and the legendary mountain man's encounter and escape from the Blackfeet at the Three Forks. Colter, during the interview, accompanied Bradbury for some miles on foot and as they talked Bradbury would later remember...

"He (Colter) seemed to have a great inclination to accompany the expedition (Wilson Price Hunt's); but having lately married, he reluctantly took leave of us."

The lure of the West was still in his blood. The following year, when numerous Indian tribes allied to the British cause began their depredations of the outlying settlements of Western Missouri at the start of the War of 1812, John Colter again answered his country's call and enlisted on March 3, 1812, in the U. S. Volunteer Mounted Rangers. Led by company commander Captain Nathan Boone, son of the celebrated Daniel, Colter would serve for the last two months of his life.

Irony defies reason. John Colter, a man of superb wilderness skills and physical hardiness, a frontier athlete of Olympic proportions, who survived all the tests and ordeals that nature and the red man threw his way, was struck down in the prime of his life by jaundice just two short years upon his return to civilized life. The rolls of Nathan Boone's Mounted Rangers list the discharge from duty of his renowned scout on May 6, 1812. Just two months into active service John Colter died the following day on May 7, 1812.

Whether from illness or battle wounds suffered, his untimely and seemingly premature death would remain a mystery for us to contemplate for all time. "Old Glory" would not hang at half-mast nor would the church bells across the land peel and mourn his loss. His name would be absent from all the history books save for the entries in Lewis and Clark's journals and those of Gass, Ordway and Whitehouse and the immortal praise of Washington Irving. Historians and authors throughout the intervening years would keep his flame aglow. And Colter, of course, upon the return of the Corps of Discovery, would be one of just a few men singled out for special praise to the Congress of the United States by President Thomas Jefferson, the author of the Expedition.

Perhaps the most distinguished testament to John Colter's character and worth would come four years after his death from one who knew him well. Fellow-patriot and frontier warrior Nathan Boone, son of the "Prince of the Prairies," Daniel Boone, who, by all accounts was the hallmark of manhood on the early western frontier, on May 3, 1816, fathered a young son whom he named John Colter Boone.

THE COLTER STONE

With little written documentation and virtually no physical evidence to substantiate the remarkable journeys of John Colter, a most interesting discovery occurred in 1931 on the western slopes/basin of the Grand Tetons. Approximately five and one half miles from Tetonia, Wyoming, William Beard, a local farmer, and his son were clearing their land of lodgepole pine and aspen that lay between the north and south forks of Leigh Creek when their plow struck and pulled out of the ground a rather curious stone shaped like a human head.

Burton Harris in his *John Colter, His Years in the Rocky Mountains* states, "On one side of the stone, rough irregular letters spell out the name John Colter, and the year 1808 has been scratched on the other. There is an outcrop of lava near where the stone was found of similar composition to the Colter Stone. The stone itself is a slab of rhyolite lava, 13 inches high, 8 inches wide at the broadest part near the top and 4 inches thick. One edge has been crudely shaped into the form of a man's face in such a way as to suggest that the carver had merely emphasized an already strong facial resemblance by chipping off a few pieces of rock…"

According to Harris, the Beards had no knowledge of John Colter and only kept the rock as a curiosity. In 1933, two years after the find, the Beards swapped the stone with their neighbor, Aubrey Lyon, for a used pair of riding boots. We have Mr. Lyon to thank for posterity, for sometime later he donated the Colter Stone to the museum of the Grand Tetons National Park. Burton further relates, "The authenticity of the Colter Stone was established only after exhaustive investigation and tests by National Park officials."

At the time of this writing the Colter Stone, which is owned by the National Park Service, Grand Tetons National Park, is currently on loan and display at the Teton Valley Historical Museum, Driggs, Idaho.

For further information regarding the Colter Stone contact:
Ms. Kay Fullmer
The Teton Valley Historical Museum
137 N. Highway 33
Driggs, Idaho 83422
208-354-6000
tvmuseum@tetontel.com